A KNOT OF PLOTS

A KNOT OF PLOTS

THE SIMULACRUM · BOOK 3

Egathentale

Podium

Cover design by Podium Publishing

ISBN: 978-1-0394-1120-3

Published in 2023 by Podium Publishing, ULC

www.podiumaudio.com

A KNOT
OF PLOTS

CHAPTER 1

PART 1

I had to admit, the nightscape of the town of Timaeus certainly had its charm. The public park, in particular, was especially scenic due to the combination of moonlight and the evenly placed streetlights illuminating the meandering walkways under the autumn leaves, with the cobbling giving them that extra layer of old-world class. I would even go as far as to call the environment romantic in a quiet, introspective sense of the word, so I immediately made a mental note about taking Judy and Elly out for a stroll here once things had calmed down a tad bit.

The park also felt distinctly different from the last time I'd been here, which I believe was around the time I had my first proper meeting with Snowy. If I had to pinpoint exactly why, I'd say it was probably because now there were other people around the area. All of them were placeholders, naturally, but they were of the partially developed, more animated variety, and their mere presence made strolling through the park feel more natural. It also helped that the simulation or whatever apparently didn't get far enough to present things like homeless, drunk, or otherwise shady people on the benches, which had naturally forestalled any and all awkward situations involving them.

I'm going to be honest here: this line of thought made me feel a little depressed. Not because I really wanted to see homeless people around, but because the slow and steady development of the placeholders around the city was prime research material, but I simply didn't have the time and energy to do work on it because I had way too many things on my plate already.

Let's just put the fact that I lived in a dazzlingly artificial world running on fiction tropes aside for a moment, and just focus on the more tangible threats and complications surrounding me. First and foremost, I still had to make sure my unwitting harem protagonist friend was up to speed and able to deal with all the supernatural shenanigans the world was throwing at me in the form of the various secretive magical folks in general and a freaking mad scientist using *sentai* tactics in particular. On top of that, there were tiny little shape-shifting monsters scurrying around the city, the big boss arch-mage of the island was probably responsible for both those and the flamboyant mad scientist harassing us, and on top of that, I was more or less forced to accompany a crazy Japanese huntress and her even crazier sentient sword on hunting trips around the more scenic parts of Timaeus.

Any one of these would've been an absolute headache by itself, but when combined, they ate up all my attention and forced me to put my long-term goal of understanding the world and its mechanics on indefinite hold, which was something even my usually adamant assistant/girlfriend agreed with.

Speaking of Judy, I pulled the scarf she insisted I wear a bit tighter around my neck, and glanced around while waiting for the return of my wayward companion for the evening. She disappeared about five minutes ago, not long after saying something about how she needed to investigate a thing, and even with the extra layers and the scarf, I was getting just a little bit chilly and... Oh, who am I kidding? I was still a little feverish to begin with, so standing around in the open like this made me feel like my family jewels were about to freeze off. My dear girlfriend even forced me to wear a thicker coat *over* my usual coat, and yet I still felt cold. Nice scenery or not, I would've much rather stayed at home and under about four blankets at the moment.

Unfortunately, that would've required me to have a say in the matter, which I obviously didn't have. Judy wasn't particularly happy about it, but it was either this, or risking a certain infuriating huntress invading my house again.

Speak of the devil, just as I looked around one more time, I finally found Rinne in the distance. She was walking towards me at a brisk pace, and as I took a closer look, I couldn't decide whether I should laugh or cry. I kept internally debating the issue until she got within earshot, and by that point, both the laugh and the cry party came to a compromise in the form of a tired sigh.

"You know, I can't decide what I find weirder: the fact that you would want to drink frozen slush in this weather, or that you've actually found someone selling them at this time of the day."

The aggravating huntress, clad in her usual purple pantsuit and carrying her wrapped-up sword on her back, gave me an odd look as if what I'd just said made no sense whatsoever, and then she took a large gulp out of her slushy before replying with, "Your comment is incomprehensible. When else would you consume cold beverages? It's for—"

"Tempering the body and spirit, yes, yes, I've heard already." I cut her off and pocketed my gloved hands.

Rinne took note of my action, and after another bite, she began to honest-to-goodness lecture me.

"It's because your body lacks tempering that you suffer from feverous conditions. Your yang must be out of balance. You must temper your constitution and…" She didn't finish her sentence; instead her words slowly trailed off into silence before she abruptly nodded to herself and added, "Onikiri wonders if you're currently attempting to mimic weakness to exploit our generosity in an attempt to deceive us into handing our tempering material over to you." The moment after she said that, the frustrating huntress pulled back the hand holding the paper cup while simultaneously covering it up with the other. "We must inform you that, regardless of your response, our answer is no."

"I don't want your slushy," I told her with my inner Judy once again bubbling to the surface.

The slightly-less-creepy-but-still-pretty-annoying huntress narrowed her eyes at my comment, and after no doubt listening to whatever her considerably more infuriating sword was spouting, she stated, "Onikiri wonders just how wide in girth your cranium must be for you to deny yourself even the chance to receive our tempering material."

I immediately rolled my eyes in exasperation and responded by telling her, "Tell your stupid sword to make up her mind."

"Onikiri says—"

"I don't care." I nipped the argument in the bud and sharply pointed down the walkway. "How about we just get on with today's patrol already?"

My unwelcome companion spaced out for a moment, but at last she gave me a nod, yet not before telling me, "Onikiri requests that you consume excrement."

"Tell her that I don't listen to oversized kitchen utensils with delusions of grandeur," I responded while pocketing my hands again and began walking.

Rinne was rooted to the spot for a moment, but then she hurriedly followed after me while expressing, "We do not exactly understand what Onikiri is trying to make us tell you, but instead we want you to acknowledge that we are not required to convey your messages, as Onikiri is perfectly capable of understanding you."

"I know. I just refuse to talk to her on principle," I told her offhandedly as we continued our leisurely lap around the park.

"Onikiri wants you to know that you are a useless person, you are out of rhythm, and that you are really mean."

"Says the sword that would make sailors blush with her constant swearing. Speaking of which, ask her if one of her ancestors was a cutlass."

"Onikiri says that your jokes are not as witty as you think they are."

"… Ouch. That is the closest your sword has come to actually hurting my feelings."

"Onikiri says Onikiri is glad to hear that."

I shrugged my shoulders in a defiant display of indifference, and for a short while we continued our patrol in silence, save for the occasional slurping sounds my erratic companion made while she was steadily devouring her slush. That said, while I certainly didn't want her frozen treat, it didn't mean I couldn't use a drink, so when we reached a familiar corner of the park I gestured for her to follow after me.

"Did you find our prey?"

I tried to ignore the way her eyes sparkled at the mere mention of the possibility and shook my head.

"No, I just remembered that there's a vending machine around here somewhere, and I want a warm drink."

"Irresponsible consumption of yang energy like this only exacerbates your weakened condition."

"... Sometimes I really can't put my finger on your vocabulary," I mumbled so low she probably couldn't hear it. I ignored her continued nagging, and we quickly found a familiar coffee machine. I offered to buy her something as well, as basic courtesy dictated, but she naturally refused, so a disinterested grunt later I pressed one of the buttons, and very soon I had a fresh, warm cup of hot cocoa in my hands.

So, there we were: a young woman in a fairly thin pantsuit drinking a frozen slush with a straw right next to a tall, handsome, fit, intelligent, and criminally humble young man dressed as if he was on an expedition to the South Pole, with a warm cup in his hands. We must've looked quite a pair.

I wasn't really in favor of just standing around in silence, though, so after some consideration, I decided to broach a subject that'd been on my mind for a while.

"Hey, Rinne?" The unpredictable swordswoman jolted in surprise and took a step away from me while grabbing onto her weapon with her free hand, so I had to amend my words with a pretty damn confused, "What?"

"We've already warned you against using our name so informally!"

"... Okay, then what should I be calling you other than your name?" I inquired with the utmost seriousness.

"We've told you: our name is Onikiri no Tsukaite Rinne. Our name is written as *gallant* and *mountain*!" She explained it as if what she said was entirely self-evident, although I had absolutely no idea what she was blabbering about.

"Soooo... What you are trying to say is that I should call you Mountain Girl?"

Mountain Girl responded to my query by giving me one of her typical "Am I having an aneurysm, or is this guy really this stupid?" looks and stated, "We don't understand the question."

"It's not that hard though. You said I cannot call you by your name, you said your name means mountain, so I'm calling you Mountain Girl. Simple."

"We're not sure we like that."

"Too bad, I'm using it," I stated on the spot, and just to accentuate it, I also flashed the third iteration of my roguish smirk, which itself was a branch of my roguish smile line of expressions. It must've worked, because Rinne stopped squeezing the handle of Onikiri, and she was actually looking at me quite attentively. As such, I immediately moved on by saying, "Anyways, there's one thing I've wanted to ask you for a while now: Where did you learn about the Chimera on the island?"

She became visibly crestfallen the moment she heard my question, making me wonder just what exactly she was expecting me to ask her. Probably something silly, like if she wanted to hunt leprechauns together. Nevertheless, after pointedly taking another large gulp out of the cup, she unreservedly told me, "Our clan received the news from a nameless source."

"So it was an anonymous tip, huh?" I wondered without even trying to hide my suspicion. "And how about after you arrived here? Were you contacted by Amadeus?" Seeing her uncomprehending expression, I clarified by saying, "I mean the head of the Magi on the island."

"Are you talking about the daimyo? For if you were, then no. If he were to call upon us, we would pay our respects, but our clan is not beholden to his authority."

"Really? So you've never even met him?" She shook her head. "Then where did you learn about me?" This time she was just looking at me funny, so I stifled a groan and explained to her, "You obviously knew who I was the first time we met. Who told you about me?"

"Your image and the description of your deeds arrived from the same source as the news about the creature of the underworld prowling the streets of this once-peaceful city."

"I think it's still pretty peaceful, but that's beside the point," I rebuked her before falling silent for a while. Truth be told, I actually expected that Lord Grandpa might've been careless enough to make direct contact with her, but in retrospect, I might've overestimated his folly a little bit. After all, if he really was behind it all, and he intended to hoist Rinne upon me for some reason or another, even a true idiot would make sure not to show his face like that. But then again...

"Hey, Mountain Girl?" Curiously enough, she actually responded to my call. "You said you got a picture of me?"

"Yes," she confirmed, and before I could even ask her to do it, she used her free hand to reach into the breast pocket of her suit and extracted a folded-up piece of paper.

"A moment."

After saying so, I quickly drank the last of my drink and threw the empty Styrofoam cup into a conveniently placed nearby trash bin before returning to her and taking the photo. I fully unfolded it, and after some squinting in the dim light, I had to conclude that it was indeed a mug shot of yours truly. As a matter of fact, it wasn't just any mug shot, but one I was really familiar with.

"Can I keep this? I mean, it's not like you need it to recognize me anymore, and I think I could find a use for it."

Rinne shrugged her right shoulder only, which I figured must've meant agreement, so I returned her gesture with a thankful nod and pocketed my first piece of evidence.

Since I'd finished my hot cocoa, it was about time we moved on, and when I did so, she quickly finished up the last of her drink and obediently fell in line next to me. For the next ten or so minutes, we continued our round around the park without much else to talk about, right until her head suddenly snapped to our left near one of the crossroads where the paved paths met.

"Is there a problem?"

Instead of just giving me a straight answer, she gestured for me to quiet down before she walked a few steps forward, only to come to a sudden halt less than two seconds later. Once she did so, my fickle companion dramatically looked around, kind of like one of those phony genius detectives when they were assembling the clues or reconstructing the crime scene in their heads in those late-afternoon crime dramas. It didn't last long, though, as in the end she merely pointed at a small clearing not too far away from the paved path.

"One of the vile denizens of the underworld has been here. Recently."

I glanced around, but I saw nothing out of the ordinary that would indicate something like that, so I reflexively asked, "What makes you think that?"

"We can detect the remnants of the traces of the lingering presence of the tracks left behind them," she clarified in a way that didn't clarify anything at all.

"So you can 'detect' Abyssals?" I fished for a slightly clearer answer, with air quotes implied.

"If you're referring to the denizens of the underworld, then yes," she confirmed with a confident nod. "It is due to our years of experience, and it's why no reviled spawn of darkness can escape our sight."

"Uh-huh," I grunted, and if skepticism was a power source, the amount condensed into those two syllables could probably power human civilization until the sun burned out. "Does it work on the actual Abyssals, as well?" Instead of answering me, Rinne just tilted her head to the side in the mirror image of a confused pug, so I clarified for her, "I mean the ones that normally look human."

"Ah!" My annoying companion's eyes sparkled with recognition as she straightened her neck and stated, "You are referring to the oni!"

"*Oni*, huh? I wonder if the way nobody seems to stick to the same damn terminology is some kind of secret in-joke among the supernatural folks..." My stray comment only earned me a "Just what the heck is this idiot babbling about?" kind of stare, so I exhaled hard and amended, "Never mind. More importantly, can you detect the oni, as well?"

"With the utmost certainty," she told me while proudly puffing out her chest for some inexplicable reason. "We can smell the foul stench of their ilk from a nautical mile away."

"That's very impressive," I responded with my nearly perfected poker face. "Just for the record, have you smelled any of them recently?"

"No. Their deviousness is only matched by their rarity on the surface, so we would most certainly track them down the moment we found one."

"In that case, you might want to have your nose checked." She obviously couldn't understand my words, which wasn't surprising considering I only whispered them under my breath, but I decided to move things along anyway by gesturing towards the general direction of the trail she'd discovered. "Does that mean we can track them?"

"No, it's too old." Rinne circled around the spot like a trained but slightly-less-endearing bloodhound, and then she immediately declared. "This is a land they frequently frequented. We shall lay and ambush and ensnare our prey!"

"... Now?"

"Yes." She nodded two times in a row for some reason and pointed at a strip of shrubbery nearby. "We will lie in wait over there."

"Wait, was that one of your royal plurals, or did you mean both of us?" I inquired, and she more or less answered it by walking away from my side. "What about me?"

That one earned me another "Is this guy actually denser than a white dwarf?" kind of frown as she very slowly explained, "You will stay here. You are the bait." She must've realized that I was not particularly happy with the arrangement, to put it mildly, so she added, "You've already agreed, so stand right there."

I glanced down, then back at her, and with my incredulity barely restrained I asked, "You seriously want me to simply stand here, in the open, and just twiddle my thumbs just in case a mini Chimera shows up?"

"Precisely."

"..." I looked the glorified supernatural pest control in the eye for a good five seconds, and since she seemed entirely serious, I simply threw my hands into the air and told her, "I'm going home."

"What? Why?"

She sounded exceedingly alarmed by my declaration, but I'd already cast the die, so I pressed on.

"Because it's cold, it's late, and because your plan is stupid."

"No, it's not," she vehemently stated as she walked back to me. "It's hunting discipline at its most basic."

"I don't care. I'm not going to just stand around in the cold just on the off chance that a—" I countered, but then I noticed something moving in the corner of my vision, and after focusing on it for a moment, I hastily added in a whisper, "Listen, I think there is something in the bush you were just going to hide behind."

"Are you certain?" she asked for clarification without bothering to tone her voice down, and I nodded in the affirmative.

I wanted to tell her to act natural so as not to startle whatever was in the bush, since I wanted to take a closer look, but by the time I could've said anything, she was already wearing her slasher grin as she turned but leaped back, the purple cloth around Onikiri unfurling and trailing behind her mid-flight like a comet's tail.

What followed was something that could best be described as history's first successful hybrid of a human and a chaffcutter in action. The whole ordeal lasted for less than ten seconds, leaving me no space to intervene, so I could only take a better look at the end result of her carnage after she stopped whacking the greenery. I was a little afraid of what I might see, but once I finally took a closer look, I immediately let out a breath of relief.

"Another successful hunt," Rinne declared with her slasher smile still prominently plastered on her face as she turned towards me. "Once again, the crimson lifeblood of—"

She only got so far in her tired old diatribe before I'd had enough, so I furled my middle finger, raised my hand, and swiftly delivered the mother of all forehead flicks to her unsuspecting noggin. Now, I admit that it connected really well, and that she was probably really surprised by it, but her comical reaction of flailing around, recoiling back, and then nearly slipping on the wet ground was still entirely uncalled for.

"Why did you hit Rinne!?" she exclaimed with the indignation of a boiling cauldron full of angry ferrets, and for a moment I couldn't decide what was more surprising: her over-the-top reaction, or the fact that she'd just referred to herself in the third person. My momentary bewilderment was just that though, as I quickly mirrored her scowl.

"Because you're an idiot! I told you there was *something* in the bush! It could've been someone's pet for all we knew, and yet you immediately flew off the handle! Look at what you've done!" Saying so, I pointed at the aftermath of her rampage, which manifested in the form of the entire clearing being covered in broken twigs and branches of various thickness, shredded leaves, and random splashes of blood.

Speaking of which, even though she was always going on and on about bathing in the blood of her prey, she'd somehow managed to cover almost every surface in blotches of blood in a five-meter radius, yet by some small miracle her own suit remained entirely spotless. How did she even do that?

However, let's put that small tangent aside for the moment and focus on the scene, because in the middle of all of that, there was the mutilated body of a deformed creature that seemed to be a curious crossbreed between a chicken, a crocodile, and a sloth.

"That," I emphasized as I trained my finger upon the carcass, "Could've been a squirrel, or a dog, or a stray cat."

"It could?!" she exclaimed, for some reason considerably more mortified by the possibility than I expected.

"Yes. This time it wasn't, because..." My words trailed off into silence as I glanced back at the remains, only to discover that almost half of it was already gone in a way that looked like it was melting into the ground. I gave the sight a slightly disturbed "Huh" and then continued, "Well, it was whatever *that* used to be. But what about next time? It could be an innocent bystander!"

"Like a cat? Are there really cats around here?"

Her fixation with possible feline casualties was odd, but not the oddest thing I'd seen from her by a long shot, so I decided not to dwell on it, and instead I told her, "Sure. The park is right next to a residential area. I'm sure some people keep cats there, and they could be out adventuring in the park even as we speak."

"No one told us there would be cats..." Her comment seemed almost remorseful, which I took as a great opportunity to press on and try to avert any future collateral damage, be they people, pets, or just shrubbery.

"And another thing—!" I began, only for my impassioned words to come to a screeching halt the moment I felt a distinct buzz in my coat pocket. "Give me a moment," I requested with one finger raised while I simultaneously used my other hand to unbutton my outer coat and fish out my phone.

I unlocked the screen, and after checking the caller ID, I immediately used my Far Sight to glance at Snowy. I found her in the entryway of our house, still dressed in her favourite uniform and with her phone raised to her ear. At a quick glance, there didn't seem to be anything dangerous going on, so I let out a relieved breath that sneakily got itself pent up in my chest, and I picked up the phone.

"Hi, sis. Is there a problem?"

"Problem?" Snowy repeated after me a tad uncertainly, after which she let out a somewhat uncertain sound. "Nm. I'm not sure if it's trouble or not, but we have a visitor."

"At this hour?" The question slipped out of my mouth, but on second thought I had to admit that it wasn't actually that late, just the sun started to set fairly early, so I quickly amended myself and asked a considerably more important thing. "Who is it?"

"I don't know him. He's tall, and he..."

"You don't need to describe him; it's enough if you just take a step or two towards the door."

"Oh, right. Sorry."

I wanted to tell her she didn't need to apologize, but in the meantime she moved into position, so I decided to do that later, and instead I focused on the unexpected visitor by reentering Far Sight and changing my vantage point so that I could see the other side of the door.

Right there, I found a young man, somewhere in the vicinity of his early twenties, covered in about as many layers as I was at the moment. He was indeed fairly tall, and even though it wasn't readily apparent at first glance, he was sharply dressed, and he even had a pretty neat black leather briefcase and an admittedly pretty stylish hat. What were these things called again? Flatcaps, I think? I wasn't an aficionado of men's fashion, but what he was wearing looked distinctly cappy, and it was flat enough, so let's go with that.

Anyhow, he didn't appear particularly dangerous, but if I have learned anything, it was that looks were more often than not deceiving around these parts.

"What did he want?" came my next obvious question as my perception snapped back to my actual location.

"He was looking for you. He also mentioned something about, um…" Snowy inserted an awkward pause into the conversation right here, then after a second or two she added, in a very low voice bordering on a whisper, "… Celestial… business…?"

This, ladies and gentlemen, was yet another one of those *dun-dun-duuuun!* moments. As if my life needed more.

"Ooooookay then. I suppose I better get home ASAP and see what he wants from me. I'll be there in a jiffy."

"Okay," Snowy uttered in the verbal equivalent of a relieved sigh and put down the phone, no doubt expecting that I would show up behind her in a matter of seconds. Unfortunately, before I could do that, I had to excuse myself from the currently ongoing hunt, except when I directed my attention back to my greenery-ravaging companion, I found her completely spaced out.

"Hey? Mountain Girl? Hello?" She didn't react, so I was just about to poke her in the shoulder to get her attention when she abruptly shivered and she looked me in the eye.

"We have to go now. We've already tracked down today's prey, and so we must go and make sure that no innocents would suffer in the process of our relentless pursuit for the rivers of blood spilled by our abominable prey."

It took me a second to unpack her sentence, but then I presented her with a skeptical frown and asked, "When you say *innocents*, you are talking about cats, aren't you?"

"We shall pursue the thrill of the chase another day, Hunter of Dunning!" she declared without bothering to answer (or deny) my question, and then she suddenly leaped away like an oversized grasshopper and disappeared into the park before I could even say, "Who's a Hunter of Dunning?"

At the end of the day, I simply shrugged, accompanied by an exasperated "Oh well." I mean, I wanted to part ways with her anyway, so her leaving like that was not a bad thing, just somewhat sudden. Kind of like her interest in cats. Speaking of which, I made a quick mental note about looking into that, as my tingling trope senses told me her reaction to the mere mention of them was simply too blatant and conspicuous for it *not* to be important in one way or the other. From the top of my head, I guessed she could either be one of those gap moe types who would immediately melt into a puddle of bliss the moment they're in the proximity of cute animals at best, or she could have been raised by a group of samurai ninja cats at worst… Oh, how I wish I was joking with the second option.

Anyhow, I'd decided I wasted enough time pondering Rinne's feline connections, so I quickly got back to the walkway and headed for the closest public restroom. Technically I could've Phased back home from right where I stood, but I figured it was better to be safe than sorry and do so from a location where no one else would be able to accidentally see me do so.

That was a sensible idea. Too bad I never got around to it.

I only took about ten or so steps from the clearing when all of a sudden the whole world flashed in reversed colours before settling down into an ominous, purple hue that permeated absolutely everything, with some red, circuit-board-looking patterns on top for good measure.

"Lovely," I muttered under my breath in sheer, industrial-strength exasperation. The moment this happened, I immediately had a hunch, so I used Far Sight and checked on the most likely culprit behind my current predicament, and when I did so, a throat-shattering groan escaped my mouth even against my best efforts to stifle it.

"Kihihi!" came the auditory confirmation of the fact I was already well aware of, and so I turned around very slowly and deliberately in order to show off just how brassed off I was with this whole bag of shite. I shouldn't have bothered, as the target of the gesture didn't even notice, and he continued his introduction with, "We meet at last, Leonard Dunning! I am Dr. Robatto, and unfortunately for you, you are already in the palm of my hand! Kihihihihi!"

I gave the blithering idiot standing in the middle of the crossroads a look I hoped adequately expressed just how little of a damn I gave about his theatrics, but my attempt once again fell on deaf ears.

Lab Coat Guy and his personal android were, as I already mentioned, currently standing smack-dab in the middle of the road, with a small group of about twenty or so ineffectual robots behind them. They were both naturally wearing their supervillain (or in this case, *sentai* villain) outfits, and Lab Coat Guy was trying (and failing) to menacingly cross his arms in front of his chest, made somewhat difficult due to the over-sized, angular shoulder pad thing he was wearing getting in the way. The trigger-happy android, on the other hand, was entirely relaxed and didn't even seem to pay much attention to what was going on.

Anyhow, after a long moment of pause for effect, I pointedly cleared my throat and told him, "I believe this is against the rules of engagement."

I couldn't really see it because of the nontransparent face mask he was wearing, but I could swear our self-styled budget villain sent a panicked glance at his companion, but since she didn't do or say anything, he clumsily changed his posture so that he was now standing arms akimbo and declared, "There are no rules in war!" in an unusually high-pitched voice.

"This is not a war," I responded dourly. "Also, I'd appreciate it if you dropped the theatrics and just told me what you want, because the number of shits I can give at this point is steadily approaching zero."

This time Lab Coat Guy outright froze up for a moment before whispering, "Galatea, I think he's not intimidated by our ambush."

"An astute observation as always, Master," she responded while sounding entirely disinterested.

"What should we do?" He continued to whisper so loud he might as well not even bother. "Should we bring out the big guns?"

"Whatever Master thinks best."

"Okay then, do as we practiced." Once he said that, Lab Coat guy turned back to me and, after finally noticing how impatient I was, he let out another forced cough before he declared, "You're already in my palm!"

"Yes, you said that already."

"Yes, but... It doesn't matter! Now look upon my masterworks, and tremble!"

After saying so, he clapped twice, at which point two of the robots in the back brought forth a large metallic sphere. It was about a meter in diameter, and while it was hard to tell in the unnatural lighting conditions, it looked like it was made of brass or copper and its surface was covered in deeply etched geometric shapes and diagrams. The robotic minions inelegantly swayed and staggered to the front under the weight of the sphere and then dropped the ball, both figuratively and literally, as one of them slipped and the round object fell down. It rolled away and stopped roughly at the halfway point between me and their group.

"Err..." Lab Coat Guy was obviously and reasonably flustered by the development, but he somehow gathered his wits enough to continue his act. "Kihihi! Exactly as planned! Now, Galatea!" He paused yet again, probably for dramatic effect, and pointed his finger at the ball exactly the same way as a fictional attorney would. "Activate the Biomechanical Gigant!"

"Yes, Master." The android continued her display of utter indifference as she also pointed at the ball and said, "On."

For once there was no awkward pause or anything of the like, as the moment she said the word, the sphere unfurled into several slices of various sizes. From within the gaps gushed forth a viscous violet liquid (or at least that's how it appeared in the purple ambient light), and as the pieces of the sphere kept turning and transforming into other shapes, the insides began to form into six thick limbs right in front of my eyes. The whole process only took a few seconds, and soon I was standing face-to-face with a vaguely humanoid *something*.

It didn't have a head, but instead it possessed an odd-looking glowing triangle where the base of its neck was supposed to be (if it had one, which it didn't, either). It was standing on two short digitigrade legs on the bottom and had no less than four arms, each ending in three-fingered hands tipped with bits of the original sphere in place of claws. Speaking of the sphere, its parts spread out on the body of the creature and formed a kind of outer shell or armour on its chest, abdomen, groin, and upper arms.

However, it didn't end there, as the moment the *thing* in front of me finished transforming, Lab Coat Guy exclaimed again.

"And now, Galatea! Make it grow!"

"Understood." After she gave her reply, the android raised her hands to the odd headdress she was wearing and pointed the stubby unicorn horn on it at the Biomechanical Gigant and chanted, "Magical crown, make my monster grow," with a tone so wooden she made the Amazon Rainforest look like a master thespian in comparison.

But back to the events at hand: once she spoke her line, the horn on her forehead lit up with a bright red light, and it shot out a visible beam of something at the creature. It honest-to-goodness flashed for a moment, like a video game sprite, and then all of a sudden it... well, grew. As expected, really.

Anyhow, in the matter of a few seconds, the originally-about-two-meters-tall Gigant began to live up to its name, and it steadily swelled to a size of almost five or six meters, then its growth spurt slowed down and it finally settled at around nine or so meters. In other words, I was now standing just a short distance away from a three-stories-tall behemoth of a monster that was constantly making a sound like a roaring furnace.

I looked it over one more time, from head to toe, and once I was sure I didn't actually feel any threat from it, I jerked my head towards Lab Coat Guy to get his attention. Once I had it, I said, "You know, with all the stupid outfits and the useless robots, it was kind of hard to take you seriously, but credit where credit's due. That"—I pointed a casual finger gun in the direction of the creature, and continued—"*That* is actually freaking impressive."

"Kihihihi! Scared, are you!?"

"Not really," I told him honestly. "If anything, I'm just curious why you found it necessary to bring this massive thing into the open."

"So that you know there's no escape!" he declared. "You cannot leave this sealed Restricted Space until I allow you to leave, and you're all alone against my army of Sprockets and my Biomechanical Gigant! So why don't you just sit tight and listen to what I have to say?"

For a moment I couldn't decide if he was serious or just pulling my leg, but he sounded sincere enough, so after I stifled the incredibly powerful urge to just face-palm myself into oblivion, I took a deep breath and very slowly and carefully elucidated, "Pal, I'm sorry to burst your bubble, but I've been waiting for you to say your piece since you appeared. In fact, I would bloody well appreciate it you got on with it already."

"Oh... I mean, I will! Kihihi!"

"I'm listening," I urged him to get started already while trying to ignore the imposing-yet-totally-motionless creature looming over us. In the meantime, Lab Coat Guy inelegantly crossed his arms again in preparation of his no-doubt-very-riveting explanation.

"Kihihi! My ever-present agents tell me you're at odds with the Lord Amadeus Endymonion," he stated expectantly.

"To put it mildly," I replied to keep things rolling, and he let out yet another grating laugh in response.

"Kihihi! So I've heard! Listen to me, my friend!" I wanted to point out we were so far from being friends our association didn't even share the same postal code, but I deemed it better to just stay quiet and wait for him to finally get to the point. "You and I, we're not so different! I also want that pesky old man gone!

"Do you now?"

"Yes!" he cried out in a voice so hammy it could fill an entire butcher's market. "Our goals align, so tell me, why don't we join forces?"

For a while I could only blink in incomprehension at the idiot in front of me while hoping my own expression wasn't too dumb, but at last, I closed my eyes, exhaled to calm my nerves, and then once I looked at him again I asked, without even bothering to pretend I was taking this conversation seriously anymore, "Excuse me, but weren't you supposed to at least try to butter me up a little before you came out with the 'Join me!' speech?"

"Why bother with the formalities?" he replied with a voice that, for the first time, made me believe he wasn't reading from a script. "Not to mention, you don't have a choice! You're trapped in here, with no chance to escape and no way to oppose me!"

"So first it was 'Join me!' and now it's 'You can't escape me!' What's next? 'I'm your father'?"

"Errr..." Stumped, Lab Coat Guy turned to his companion again and whispered, "Galatea, I think he is still not intimidated."

It was at this point that I couldn't take it anymore, as I let out an exasperated noise and threw my hands into the air.

"Okay, that's it. I'm out," I declared with a scornful frown. "I figured I'd be nice and hear you out, but if you're not taking this seriously, then I have nothing to say. I have places to be, and I'm already late because of you."

"But... I just told you that you cannot leave..." the flustered Lab Coat Guy muttered, and I rolled my eyes in a mixture of fake nonchalance and a genuine sense of exhaustion as I decided to put my primary exit strategy into action.

"You're one of the Research Society guys, right?" I asked, but didn't let him answer and immediately followed it up with, "You know a lot about both science and magic, right?"

"Erm... Yes, I'd say I do?" he replied just a tad uncertainly.

"Good. Then here's a quick question: how much do you know about illusions?"

"A little," he told me, this time with palpable uncertainty. "Why?"

"For you see," I began as I forced a friendly smile onto my face. "I'm not actually here."

And with that, I Phased home, with my only regret being that I was unable to see his reaction. Unfortunately, as I said, I had places to be, and I figured I'd already made my guest wait long enough.

PART 2

How could I best describe the sense of tension enveloping my living room at the moment? *Palpable* sounded about right, but I felt it just wasn't quite meaty enough. *Oppressive*, on the other hand, was just a little too strong. It was, if I may dare to be poetic for a moment, like the kind of tension emanated by a single bunny dropped into a pen filled with a whole brood of hungry snakes.

Speaking of which, our bunny for the night awkwardly glanced around for what felt like the hundredth time in the past two minutes. The young man was sitting on the sofa across the coffee table, and his fidgety, nervous body language told me he was well out of his comfort zone. He was indeed tall, about the same height as I was, with a fair complexion, bright blue eyes, a prominent chin, and maybe most importantly, a head of short blond hair that seemed to be strategically tousled to the precise point where it could be still considered attractive. In other words, just by looks alone, I could immediately categorize him as a side character, or a unique placeholder at the very least.

Narrative classification aside, he introduced himself as Michael Khurshid when I let him into the house, but he hasn't said anything else since we sat down. I likened him to a bunny before, and even on a second look, he was giving off the same harmless impression. He was also still tense as a bowstring, probably because it was only the two of us in an unfamiliar room. Snowy was in the kitchen at the moment, and based on the few words we'd exchanged when I arrived, she was probably preparing drinks and snacks for the guest. Very maid-y, as usual.

Anyhow, I was just thinking about how to get the conversation rolling with my fretful visitor when he unexpectedly broke the ice and spoke up first.

"So... aren't you going to take those off?"

He was weakly gesticulating towards my direction, so I looked down and belatedly realized that, even though I took off my outer coat and cap in the entryway, I still had the lighter coat and my gloves on.

I considered my options for a moment, but since I was still chilled to the bone after my little hunting trip, I ultimately answered, "No, I'm fine."

"Oh... Okay, just checking."

After that curt answer my guest fell silent once again. I wondered just what his game was. He said he came here on Celestial business, yet he didn't seem to be about to get down to it anytime soon. At last, after waiting a couple of seconds to see if he would add anything else, I lightly cleared my throat and decided to ease the atmosphere with some small talk.

"You seem to be on edge. Is there a problem?"

My tactfully spoken question surprised him for a moment, but after a moment of tongue-tied silence he sharply shook his head.

"No, it's not really a problem; it's just that I didn't sleep much last night."

"Insomnia?"

"No, I just have a lot of papers to turn in before the end of the semester," he told me with his words accentuated by a somewhat-strained smile.

"I guess that means you're attending university," I ventured a guess, resulting in a small nod of confirmation. "Is it here in Timaeus?"

"No, no," he repeated twice, most likely for emphasis. "I live and study at the University of Hermocrates in Locri. I study pharmaceutics."

"Locri is on the other end of the island, isn't it?" If my memory served right, it was the second-largest city on the island behind Timaeus and the seat of one of the six administrative regions.

"Yes," he confirmed with a nod and just the barest hint of an amicable smile.

I was just about to continue the conversation along this thread by flexing my extensive geographical knowledge a bit more, but my plans were quickly torpedoed by Snowy entering the room with not one but two trays in her hands.

"I'm sorry to interrupt," she apologized while placing the platters onto the table. "I've brought biscuits and crackers. I forgot to ask what our guest would like to have, so I made tea, coffee, and lemonade."

"Thanks, Snowy. You're a treasure," I told her with the newest iteration of my brotherly smile, and she gave me a demure one in return.

"Ah... Um... Thank you?" our visitor mumbled a little absentmindedly, his gaze sweeping over the table before landing and ultimately staying on my sister as if being glued there.

I expected that she'd stay around, but instead she did a perfect curtsy and left the room with measured steps, followed by the eyes of our guest all the way to the exit, and he still kept looking in the direction of the kitchen door even after she was long gone.

"Is there something bothering you?"

My calm and very diplomatic question, which certainly wasn't tinted by a smidgen of hostility over the fact that he was just openly ogling my sister, earned me a panicked look, and he hastily waved his palms in dismissal.

"N-no! I just found it... unusual that you'd have a maid, that's all." In the following few seconds I may or may not have drilled holes into his forehead with my eyes, and so he awkwardly added, "She is also really cute."

"We can agree on that."

"So... is she your...?" My expression must've looked a little confused, because he then made an odd gesture with his hand and clarified, "I mean, is she working here full time or...?"

"She's my sister."

"Oh? Oooooooh..." The man's already fair expression completely blanched, only to immediately turn beet red as he hastily excused himself by saying, "I'm sorry, I didn't know that. I just... didn't expect that... Why is she wearing a maid uniform?"

"Do you have a problem with how my sister chooses to dress at home?"

My unfailingly polite words made him shudder for some reason, and he hastily denied my suggestion.

"No! Not at all! It looks great on her! It really brings out her... um... personality?"

"... Was that supposed to be a joke?"

"No, sorry. I'm going to shut up now before I put my foot in my mouth again."

I sent a skeptical stare my guest's way, but he stayed true to his words and remained as silent as a herring, so I let out an ever-so-slightly-exasperated sigh and decided to just get things over with.

"You know, I was under the impression you came here to discuss 'business.'" To my shock and horror, I found myself making air quotes with my fingers, which I immediately stopped with extreme prejudice. Goddammit, Sebastian; one day I'll get you for infecting me with them! That said, I let my hands down and finished my previous sentence with, "We can hardly have any discussion if you refuse to talk."

"I know, I'm just..." After realizing that he was talking in a high-pitched voice, my guest cleared his throat and started again, this time more firmly, "I was told by my contact that you are quite something. I just never expected that you would be so... um..."

"Young?" I attempted to help him out, but he immediately shook his head.

"What? No, I knew you were in the second year of high school, so I wasn't surprised about that. The word I'm looking for is more along the lines of... err... *intimidating*, I think?"

"Intimidating," I repeated after him with a gallon of added incredulity on top, but he only nodded with the utmost sincerity. That still left me less-than-totally convinced, so I quickly made a decision and called out to the only other person in the house. "Snowy?"

"Yes?" my sister responded immediately as she stuck her head through the doorway. "Did I miss something?"

"No, you didn't. Please come over here for a moment. I want to ask a question."

I could practically see the illusory question marks circling around her head, but after only a second of hesitation she fully entered the living room and pattered over to my side.

"Can I help?"

"Yes, actually. Just a quick question: do I look intimidating?"

Snowy was obviously surprised by my blunt inquiry, but to her credit, she didn't dwell long on it, and instead she looked me over from head to toe. Then she did the same from toe to head. *Then* she leaned closer and observed me like I was a piece of postmodern art in a prestigious gallery. At the end of the day, she stood tall again, looked me in the eye, and simply told me, straight and simple, "You're not more intimidating than usual."

"Well, that's good to h—" My eyes involuntarily narrowed at the same time I swallowed back the second half of my sentence, and instead I commented, "That could be understood in more ways than one. Am I *usually* intimidating?"

"Uh... Not really," Snowy replied while shaking her head so hard her twin tails flailed around like, well, flails. As in, the medieval weapons.

Anyhow, she stopped doing so just as abruptly as she began, and after leaning closer and observing my face from various angles one more time, she authoritatively stated, "On second thought, I think you might be a little more intense than usual."

"Really? How so?"

"You are frowning a lot," she clarified on the spot.

"Is that supposed to be surprising?" I huffed a little. My rhetorical question seemed to pique her interest, so I exhaled hard and explained, "You know, I'm fairly certain you'd be just as grouchy too if you had to spend two hours hunting outdoors in this weather, and with Rinne to boot."

"Oh? Were you hunting Chimeras again?" Our guest's playful voice and wide grin told us he was obviously trying to ease the mood, but when neither of us laughed along, his smile slowly withered as his jovial expression first turned into one of confusion, following which it swiftly morphed into disbelieving horror as he whispered, "Oh sweet Deus, you actually were..."

"Yeah." I confirmed what sounded like his worst nightmare, and he nervously glanced around the room, as if he thought a surprise Chimera would burst through my walls at any moment, kind of like an off-brand Kool-Aid Man, except maybe slightly less creepy.

"Is there... really another Chimera? Here, on Critias?" my hapless visitor asked in a voice that told me he wasn't even sure he wanted to know the answer.

"In Timaeus, even!" My happy-go-lucky answer clearly didn't appeal to him, and since I was obviously way too good-natured to find his nervous squirming amazingly amusing, I immediately flashed him my friendliest smile and added, "In fact, there are about a dozen of them out there."

"Leo!" My sister's sudden rebuke made me jump in surprise. I turned to her and wordlessly communicated the question "What?" via my eyebrows alone. Snowy gave me an uncharacteristically stern look, and after sending a quick glance at our guest, she leaned really close to me in a conspiratorial huddle, and she even cupped her hand as she whispered almost directly into my ear. "Don't be mean. Chimeras are really scary."

"Are they?"

"Well... maybe not for a brave Chimera slayer like you."

I didn't think my honest question deserved a snappy response like that, so I turned my head and sent a wry glance at her... only to realize that, somehow, she was actually 101 percent genuine, and before I knew it, my face slackened into a blank, stupefied stare.

"W-what is it? Is there something on my face?"

Her words quickly shook me out of my momentary stupor, and I subsequently quickly shook the last of said daze out of my head and whispered, "No, there's absolutely nothing wrong. Nothing at all. That said... you mentioned Chimeras are supposed to be really scary, right?"

"That's right," she affirmed with a serious look in her eyes.

"How scary?"

"Uh..." She thought for a long moment, all the while unconsciously making a noise, kind of like how an old PC would buzz when it was under a heavy load, and at last she explained to me, "Just the other day, Angie told me that Celestials would scare their misbehaving children with stories about Chimeras, so... what is the thing young children are most afraid of in the mundane world?"

"... Dentists?" I blurted out without any thinking, and for some unfathomable reason my sister gave me a slow nod as if my answer was really profound.

"I see. Then, imagine that Chimeras are like... um... like *super-dentists* to Celestials."

So, if I understood her words right, I was the supernatural equivalent of a super-dentist slayer.

Oh my god, I mustn't let Judy hear about this! Ever! She'd call me *that* for the rest of our lives, and worse yet, she'd think it's cute and affectionate!

"Leo, you are looking weird," Snowy noted with a puzzled expression. "Is something wrong?"

I immediately dismissed her with the surefire combination of a firm shake of my head and my absolute best innocent smile.

"Nonsense. I'm fine. You're fine. Everything's fine."

"If you say so," she granted me, though obviously not without any reservations, and then she sternly warned me, "So don't be mean, and don't make fun of others' fears."

"O-kay," I promised, my enthusiasm only very slightly lacking, but it seemed to be satisfactory for her, and she stood straight with a satisfied enough expression. A shallow sigh later I turned towards my increasingly befuddled guest, and after donning the closest approximation to an apologetic smile my tired face could muster, I told him, "I'm sorry that we ignored you, but my sister just told me that I shouldn't tease you."

"So... does that mean that there aren't *really* any Chimeras in Timaeus?" he asked, his voice almost comically hopeful.

"Nah, they are out there."

"Leo!" my dear sister called out to me again, but this time I faced her head-on.

"But it's true! There are a bunch of Chimeras out there." I inserted a short pause for effect into the conversation here, and then I shortly added, "The only thing I forgot to mention was that they are about *this* big."

Saying so, I indicated the rough size of the mini Chimeras I'd seen so far with my hands, and the man in front of me gave me a blank look in return.

"They are only *that* small?"

"Not all of them, only the ones running around the town right now. My expert on supernatural stuff that goes bump in the night tells me they are pieces of the standard big, nasty version that are sent out to scavenge food for it." He was still looking at me as if I was an aluminum Christmas tree, so I promptly elaborated on the topic by telling him, "My 'expert,'" I emphasized hard, accompanied by the judicious use of air quotes (Insert another melodramatic joke about how Sebastian's influence is ruining my ability to communicate like a sane person here.), "Is a Japanese monster hunter ninja with a talking sword."

"Ah!" My guest suddenly pointed at me, his previously tense and frightful face all but shining with excitement for some (no doubt thoroughly unreasonable and baffling) reason. "That's why I'm here!"

"... Would you care to elaborate?" I requested while doing my best to stay unfazed by his sudden outburst.

"Oh, my apologies. You're right. I completely forgot my manners." After saying so, my suddenly strangely enthusiastic guest cleared his throat and told me, "So, as I've mentioned, I'm here about Celestial business."

"Yes. I'm still curiously awaiting your explanation about what that actually means."

"Right, I'm on it." He flashed me a confident smile and began by stating, "As you might imagine, the recent events that took place on this island couldn't evade the attention of the Celestial Intelligence Division."

That comment made me raise a brow right away. Simply put, the Celestial Intelligence Division was, in practical terms, the military arm of the Celestial Intelligence Network. To illustrate the difference between the two, the CIN was an umbrella term for all the assets, field agents, and bureaucrats organizing intelligence from around the world, while the CID were the people whose job was to analyze, double-check, and act on said intelligence. For example, Angie was technically part of the network, even though she was barely qualified to be called a sleeper agent, while Admin (aka, me) was part of CID. At least on paper.

"So you are a member of this organization?" I asked a tad warily. The last thing I needed right now was supernatural James Bond types snooping around my neighbourhood.

"Me? Oh, no, no," he denied while waving his hands, much to my hidden relief. "I'm but a simple field agent, nothing as lofty as being an actual CID operative. However, we're naturally interested in the recent events that took place on the island in general... and a Japanese swordswoman in particular."

"So you're here because...?"

"Simply put, my contact told me you are an information broker, so I figured I would offer you a fair trade."

"So, in short, you want to buy information from me about the monster huntress on the island."

"Correct."

I took a deep breath and thought long and hard about the prospect. Considering my access to the Celestial Hub, I sincerely doubted that this guy could provide me with anything I didn't already know. Hell, based on what I knew about the modus operandi of the Celestial Intelligence Network, I was probably a hundred times more informed than he was. However, that didn't necessarily mean he had nothing to offer, so with that in mind, I assumed my patented evil mastermind pose and opened the negotiations by first attempting to determine this guy's net worth.

"Before we start, I'd like to know exactly what makes you qualified to negotiate this deal," I stated as dryly and straightforwardly as any lawyer.

"I understand." The smile accompanying that statement looked like it came out of a con artist's handbook on how to appear as trustworthy as possible. Subtle. "You see, while I might be just a run-of-the-mill field agent at the moment, my father is actually a chief officer in the Seraphic Safeguard."

His assertion made me raise a brow right away. To put that into context, the Seraphic Safeguard was a branch of the Celestial military. Contrary to their name, they weren't actually guards, but a sort of supernatural special operations division. Whenever something or someone was threatening Celestial interests (or even just the supernatural masquerade in general), they would be sent in to fix the situation by any means necessary, ranging from armed raids to kidnappings and assassinations. In short, they were the military enforcers of the higher echelons of the Celestial hierarchy. Also, their name could be abbreviated to SS. *Very subtle.*

More importantly, if my memory served right, being a chief officer in the Celestial army, which naturally included these guys as well, was a hereditary position with no small amount of prestige and wealth included.

In other words, if this guy's words are to be believed, he was the equivalent of a son of a noble house. His looks certainly matched the part...

"That means you do have some connections after all," I stated while doing my best to maintain a neutral expression.

"Trust me, I do," he responded with a considerably more genuine grin. "I don't want to brag or anything, but I'm also on very good terms with the man responsible for all our incoming intelligence reports."

"Really?" My brow rose even further as a sneaking suspicion reared its ugly head in the back of my mind.

"Yes. Why, he recently entrusted me with organizing a part of our intelligence reports, and just the other day I even received his written thanks and his acknowledgment of my hard work! He's a great guy, and while he's technically not my superior, we are kind of like friends, I think, so since I was already on the island, I decided to help him."

"I see," I muttered with my suspicion becoming more definitive by the word. "Sorry for the off-topic question, but I have to ask: how did you find me again?"

"Oh, that?" He was only surprised by my sudden question for a moment, after which he showed me yet another variation of his smiles, this time a modest one. "Confidentiality is important, but I think I can say that I just happened to know a guy who happened to know a gal who gave me your address and told me that..."

It was about that point that I completely tuned out of the conversation as recognition settled in, and it took all my willpower to keep my nonchalant façade from crumbling. I mean, who the hell would've thought that *this guy* would show up on my doorstep, about as oblivious as a deaf man accidentally dialing a phone sex line, and on top of that, trying to get information from me so that he could give it to me?

Nonetheless, this obviously changed the entire context of this conversation, so I let the last vestige of tension trapped in my chest out in the guise of a slightly amused sigh. It didn't escape my guest's notice, and so he immediately stopped the recounting of his philosophy about how giving away more information about his contact would violate the unspoken laws of something or the other.

"So, in a nutshell, you want me to give you information about the huntress so that you can hand it over to this other person who's not really your superior but he also kind of is," I summed up his whole motivation for coming here in one sentence, and after a long moment of thinking, he nodded in the affirmative.

"Yes. And in exchange, I'd give you nonclassified intelligence," he stated as he suggestively patted the side of his briefcase.

"I don't need it." My blunt refusal shocked him way more than I expected (or was reasonable), so I hastily explained myself. "I currently don't need Celestial information. However, I have something else in mind."

"Such as?" he questioned me after a comically loud gulp.

"Artifacts," I declared without beating around the bush.

"What... kind of artifacts?"

"Anything will do," I replied with a small shrug.

"Leo?" I faced my sister after being called by name, and she sternly warned me, "If you play around with enchantments and get sick again, Judy and Elly are going to be really mad."

"I know, I know. I'm going to be careful. Everything in moderation and all that."

"Excuse me? What was that about playing with enchantments?" our guest wedged himself into the conversation with a truly bemused expression, and after stifling a chuckle at his expense, I faced him again.

"Don't worry about it. It's a long story. Anyhow, what do you think about my offer? A small collection of random artifacts of any kind or quality in exchange for the information you want."

"Well, it's... I mean, I can gather some, for sure, but I don't have any artifacts on me at the moment."

"Then I suppose you better collect some by the next time we meet."

"Yes, but I kind of wanted to have something to show for my work by tomorrow, sooo..."

I gave the downcast Celestial agent a skeptical look, but at the end of the day I shook my head, exhaled a theatrical sigh, and told him, "You know what? Let me give you a few morsels, free of charge. Consider it a gesture of goodwill."

"... Are you serious?"

"I sure am."

If my reply didn't convince him, it appeared my winning smile did, as he immediately reached into his briefcase and retrieved one of those small notepads you would see old-timey journalists use to take notes. He also found a pen, and after testing it first, he immediately focused all his rapt attention on me.

"So, our monster huntress," I began, and he faithfully put every word I uttered to paper like a seasoned scribe. "Her name is Rinne. She is about one-sixty-five tall, fairly lithe. She has short black hair with a red streak, and she has a penchant for wearing purple suits and leather gloves. She also always has a sword on her back, which may or may not talk. Also, she is decently manageable under normal circumstances, but when she hears about hunting monsters, she gets her switch flipped and her tirades are... well, they kind of remind me of a pizza cutter."

"Pizza... cutter?"

Both my guest and my sister were giving me odd looks, so I explained, "All edge, no point whatsoever."

"Ah, I get it now!" Snowy suddenly beamed at me, while the local Celestial field agent only gave me an even odder look.

I decided to ignore him, and I continued to share some of the tidbits I had learned about Rinne, including information I knew from the source the guy sitting in front of me provided me with. I figured it would help give the rest of my statements more weight and authenticity.

"... and apparently she can smell Abyssals, but don't quote me on that. Aaaaand that's about it," I closed my dissemination of mostly useless minutia, and my guest gave me a look that said he wanted more. "Sorry, but that's all I'm giving away for free."

"I understand." He put away his notes with a visible show of reluctance and then told me, "I can't promise anything concrete at the moment, since I'm supposed to be undercover, but if you give me a few days, I should be able to call in some favors and gather a few artifacts for you."

"I'm glad to hear that."

What followed was several seconds of me trying to tell him "You're done with your business, so go away" with my body language, but he apparently wasn't fluent in eyebrow wriggling, as he only looked at me funny. A second later he checked his fancy wristwatch, which almost made me think he got the memo after all, but alas, I thought too soon.

"Sooo... here's the thing: my next train back to Locri is going to leave in about one and a half hours."

"That's late," I added to move the point along, and he gave me a nod in return.

"Yes, and it's the last train for the day. Originally I wouldn't mind staying at the train station for a while... but then there is the issue of the dozen or so Chimeras out there..."

"They are not that big a deal, though. They are comparatively tiny."

"That just makes it worse!" he suddenly burst out. "I mean, think about it; you can see a big monster from far away, but what about a small one? There could be one hiding in a trash can, or under a bench, just waiting for you to come close and jump at you."

"That sounds a little far-fetched for me, but fine, I'm listening. What's your angle?"

He fell silent for a few seconds, and at last he sheepishly asked, "Can I stay around for a while longer?"

At first I couldn't really tell if he was serious, but he looked sincere enough, so I resigned myself and told him, "Might as well."

"Thanks! I'm in your debt, Mr. Dunning."

"Oh, please." I rolled my eyes and firmly told him, "Being called *mister* by someone older than me makes my skin crawl. Just Leonard will suffice."

"Are you sure?" I nodded, and he immediately beamed at me and exclaimed, "All right! In that case, you can also call me Mike!"

I had to wonder if wearing one's emotions on one's sleeve was a Celestial thing, but it didn't stop me from shrugging my shoulders and saying, "Sure."

He looked remarkably pleased about my response for some reason, but I couldn't muster the will to care, especially since after he left, I was planning on using Far Sight to check on Lab Coat Guy and his reaction. I figured that even if I couldn't observe him extensively, I should at least glance at him now that there was a lull in the conversation. Needless to say, I briefly closed my eyes and I did just that.

It was a quick Far Glance, but based on what I saw, they were still in the purple-with-red-highlights zone in the park, with Lab Coat Guy pacing up and down while rattling on about my disappearance, while his android companion was in the process of trying to stuff the normal-sized Biomechanical Gigant back into its shell. It kind of reminded me of someone trying to stuff a travel bag already past its capacity with an entire set of duvets. There wasn't anything immediately relevant to my interests in their conversation, so I quickly left the scene.

On second thought, if I was already using Far Sight, I figured I might as well do a full roll call. As such... nothing on Josh... nothing on Elly... nothing on Judy... nothing on...

When I laid my eyes on the next member of the posse, I involuntarily paused for a while, and after a brief moment of deliberation, I opened my eyes and addressed my sister.

"Hey, Snowy? Could you please make a cup of that terrible minty-appley-peary infusion tea thing?"

She looked at me funny for a moment, but then the proverbial light bulb over her head lit up at once and she responded by asking, "Isn't that Amelia's favourite?"

"Yes."

"Okay then."

With those two words, she immediately turned on her heels and entered the kitchen with light steps. Well, at least one of us was having fun. Unfortunately, the night was far from over, and I was already tired.

Sometimes I wished I could sleep. Or barring that, an evening without any surprise visitors would be fine, too.

Thinking so, I directed my attention back to the person sitting in front of me, and I found him curiously observing the collection of cards, tokens, and other related items sitting on the cabinet by the corner.

"Hey, Leonard? Do you play poker?" Mike asked with an almost childish light of curiosity in his eyes.

I glanced at the cards, allowed an irritated sigh to escape my lips, and then I told him, "No. I'm not allowed to anymore..."

CHAPTER 2

PART 1

"... and then...!" Mike's voice reached a crescendo, only to come to a sudden halt as he barely managed to stifle a chortling laugh. He raised his hand into the air, asking me to wait for a moment, and after a few measured breaths he yelled out, "And then he said, 'You fool! That's dihydrogen monoxide!'"

There was a long beat for effect, and then my merry guest burst into frenetic laughter that saw him almost falling off my couch. I also laughed, though mine was considerably less over-the-top. I mean, his story was funny, but it wasn't exactly a knee-slapper. Maybe it was one of those you-had-to-be-there kind of jokes?

Anyhow, once he finally collected himself, Mike softly cleared his throat and stated, "And that's how I passed the entrance exam."

"Very educational," I responded with a profound nod, which earned me a satisfied grin in return. I had a feeling he was about to get started on another anecdote, but time was just about up, so I raised a hand to stop the conversation. "Hold on for a moment, please."

He was looking at me attentively; I figured he probably thought it was my turn to share a story. I wasn't about to do that, though, and instead I turned towards the kitchen and called out, "Snowy? How's the fake tea coming along?"

"It's just about done," came the chirping reply from the inside.

"Great." Saying so, I rose to my feet while simultaneously gesturing for my guest to remain seated.

A brief, muscle-pain-induced groan later I headed over to the front door. I stood in attention, waited for the right moment, and then I threw it open and welcomed my new guest with an enormous grin and an unnecessarily chipper, "Hi, class rep! What a surprise!"

Ammy stayed stock still for a while, but then she slowly unballed the fist she raised in preparation for knocking and used the same hand to adjust her glasses instead.

"It obviously wasn't," she emphatically stated, and after a momentary pause, she asked, "This wasn't the first time you did this. Did you put trackers on us?"

"What? Me?" I showed her a suitably wounded expression before I looked just past her right shoulder and said, "I have to say, only a complete asshole would put surveillance on someone without their knowledge."

I accentuated my words with a small wink. Ammy was reasonably confused by my actions, and she even glanced over her shoulder.

"... Who were you talking to?"

"Don't worry about it; it's just a bit of hypocritical humour on my end." Saying so, I extended my hand in a gentlemanly gesture to welcome her in, a motion which may or may not have been accompanied by my phantom limb cutting through a tiny little floating eyeball that may or may not have been gently floating behind her.

The class rep was still looking at me like she thought I was weird, but she followed my lead all the same, only to come to a sudden halt the moment she noticed the unfamiliar boots and coat in the entryway. In the end, I had to push her a little so that I could close the door.

"Do you have guests?"

"Just a single guy, and he should be leaving soon. He has a train to catch."

My second guest glanced back and forth between me and Mike's boots before ultimately settling on me.

"How soon? I have something very important to discuss."

"I figured you would." She looked like she was in the process of reading something into my stray comment, so I hastily clarified, "I mean, you showed up at my house this late and by your lonesome, so it's pretty obvious something must've happened."

"I see."

After that verbal equivalent of a shrug we both fell silent, yet Amelia still looked like she really, really wanted to tell me something. I couldn't bear to watch, so I decided to give her a way out.

"How about you give me the footnotes version while you take off your coat?"

She seemed doubtful of the idea at first, but then after mulling it over for a while she nodded anyway and told me, "Very well. In short, I've caught Grandfather red-handed."

"You have?"

She nodded in the affirmative while she took off her outerwear and explained, "I wanted to know whether he really had anything to do with the attacks, so when I saw him secretly discussing things with Pascal, I hid around the corner and overheard their conversation about contacting Dr. Robatto."

"That's... unexpected," I muttered under my breath. I wasn't talking about the fact that he would use Armband Guy to contact our resident mad scientist; I already knew that he was their little messenger. No, the surprising part was that the old man would be this sloppy. "When did this happen?"

"Right after I got home from visiting you in the afternoon. I came here so late because I waited until Grandfather returned to the School before I left."

I was curious about what exactly she overheard, and I had my doubts already, but it was too early to draw any conclusions, so I told Ammy, "That's indeed worth a discussion. Come on in."

I gestured for her to follow after me, and we entered the living room at once.

"Um... Hello?" My already-present guest greeted Ammy with an awkward smile and an equally clumsy wave of his hand.

I wanted to get ahead of any unnecessary pauses, so I stepped forward and introduced the two of them to each other.

"Ammy, this is Michael. He is here to do business with me."

"What... kind of business?" she interjected, and to my surprise, she wasn't only forgetting to do her menacing thing with the glasses, but she sounded downright bashful compared to her usual tone with me. Actually, was it just my imagination, or was she really hiding behind me, too?

Anyhow, it was rude to keep her waiting, so I told her, "It's nothing important. I'll explain later. But back to the original topic: Michael, this is my classmate Amelia."

"Nice to meet you?"

For some reason, the guy's greeting came out as a question. Odd.

"I'm equally pleased to make your acquaintance."

And now the class rep was getting super-polite and reserved. I mean, the latter part wasn't that surprising, as she used to be pretty awkward when I first met her, but I didn't expect her to revert to her introverted self out of the blue.

"The pleasure is mine."

Aaaaand now the usually hapless Celestial agent was trying to give her a charming smile. What is this? I don't even...

Anyway, I rubbed my face for a moment to get my thoughts in order and ultimately addressed the guy on my couch.

"Ammy is here to discuss something personal. What did you say, when does your train leave the station?"

"It's..." he started, only to stop, glance at his wristwatch, and then finish with, "It's still a little more than three-quarters of an hour."

"I see. And how long would it take for you to get to the train station?"

"With a taxi? About fifteen minutes, twenty at worst…. Why? Do you… want me to leave early?"

That was kind of the *thing* I was getting at, but before I could state it in no uncertain terms, Ammy suddenly wedged herself into the conversation.

"I don't want to inconvenience you two. I'll wait."

Oh well, there went my plan to get rid of Mike early. I mean, I didn't hate the guy or anything, but being constantly mindful of my comments and even word choices, lest he would somehow draw a connection between Admin and me, was mentally exhausting, and I was tired enough already, thank you very much. But alas, the class rep already sealed off my opportunity to send him home, so I had to work with what I had.

"If you say so." I shrugged my shoulders in an open display of disinterest and gestured towards the couch. "Please take a seat."

Ammy glanced between me and the empty spot I was pointing at, and after a brief moment of hesitation, she nodded and warily walked over to sit down. Normally this would've been the point where I also took a seat and maybe engaged in some of my patented brand of small talk, but I had something else in mind at the moment, so I called out to the kitchen again.

"Snowy! Ammy is here!"

"I'm coming!" my dear sister responded in a fairly upbeat voice, and a blink of an eye later she also entered the living room with a small, round tray in hand. On top of it stood one of our spare cups filled to the brim with that unholy brew that the class rep for some ungodly reason preferred over proper tea. But then again, it was her choice, even if she was objectively wrong, so I wasn't going to judge her absolute heresy too harshly.

I watched as Snowy placed the beverage onto the table, next to the already-present drinks and snacks, and then she instantly assumed her attentive maid posture. The class rep looked at the hot drink on the table as if it was a white raven covered in black wool, but before she could ask any more uncomfortable questions about how I knew she was coming over ahead of time, I pointedly cleared my throat to get everyone's attention.

"Please excuse me, but I have to take my cold medicine. I will be back in a couple of minutes. Snowy, please see to it that our guests have all their needs met."

"Understood!"

I couldn't help but smile in the face of her unusually enthusiastic reply. Was she really so happy about her maid role-play, or did she think I was depending on her? Whichever was the reason behind her good mood, it made the cold cockles of my heart tremble with just a tinge of warmth.

Anatomically inaccurate analogies aside, I directed a polite smile towards my guests, after which I quickly turned on my heels and headed up the stairs with unhurried, measured steps. It was only when I reached the first floor and entered my room that I let out a pent-up breath and hastily sat down on the corner of my bed.

To be honest, I was just a teensy bit rattled by the class rep's declaration of catching Lord Grandpa red-handed. As far as my understanding of the current events was concerned, practically every single thing messing with our peaceful days tied back to him in one way or another. More importantly, if not for my out-of-context ability to observe people from afar, we should've had no reason to suspect, let alone know for a fact, that he was behind both the *sentai* attacks and Rinne's involvement. The only thing I couldn't tie to him yet was the appearance of the mini Chimeras (and the alleged big Chimera), but with his track record, I was pretty sure he also had a hand in that, as well.

In metanarrative terms, all of this made me consider him as our current antagonist. Furthermore, since he was a the-man-behind-the-man type, I took it for granted that until Lab Coat Guy got caught, he would stay in the back, and only swoop in to reveal his involvement and the nitty-gritty details of his motivations at the very last second. Because of this, I was under the impression I still had a lot of time to prepare for his sudden but inevitable betrayal, but if he really slipped up in front of Amelia, then things might've been moving along faster than I expected.

Therefore, using what little time I had at the moment, I figured it was imperative that I quickly checked on the two most important players in this tempest of excrement. I closed my eyes, and a quick Far Sight leap later I was already observing Lab Coat Guy... in an elevator. A familiar elevator, if I might add.

Let me paint a picture for a moment: Lab Coat Guy was standing right in the middle of the metal box, still clad in his baffling outfit (including the exceedingly unwieldy shoulder guard), and he was fidgeting like crazy. This time he didn't have his souped-up welder's mask over his face, and while at a cursory glance it looked like he was calm, his smaller gestures told me he was either on the brink of a mental meltdown or he really, really needed to use the toilet.

His hypothetical biological needs aside, he wasn't the only person in the elevator; the android woman and, surprisingly enough, the school nurse were standing right behind him, and they looked considerably calmer than the guy in the front.

"Master?" the funkily dressed android spoke up, drawing everyone's attention to her, only to stay silent right until Lab Coat Guy began to gesture exaggeratedly for her to continue, at which point she declared, "My analysis is complete. The results are negative."

"Are you sure?"

"Yes," she reaffirmed with a small nod, which made Lab Coat Guy start fidgeting again. It thankfully didn't stop her from elaborating, so that I would at least know what they were talking about. "After reanalyzing my sensory data regarding both his biometric and manametric readings, I concluded that none of them show any sign of tampering."

"Damn." Lab Coat Guy did that thing where it looked like he was biting onto the fingernail of his left thumb while he cursed under his breath. "No one told me he was an expert illusionist!"

"Correction: an expert illusionist wouldn't have been able to fool my sensors."

"Then a master illusionist! I don't care about semantics right now!"

"Calm down, Friedrich," Peabody chided his maybe-nephew while theatrically wiping his forehead with a handkerchief.

"I'm perfectly calm!" he exclaimed while stomping his feet, a picture-perfect image of a composed and unruffled person if I've ever seen one.

"I'm detecting elevated heart rate," the androidess interjected while scrutinizing the man in front of her. "Conclusion: Master is not perfectly calm."

"Thank you, Galatea, but I already noticed," the old nurse stated with an unexpectedly deadpan voice.

"I tell you, I'm—!"

Without any prior warning, the fembot let out an odd beeping noise, and the glassy parts of her built-in earphones or what have you on her head also flashed with a green light, prompting Lab Coat Guy to abruptly close his mouth with an audible clatter of teeth.

"Master, I have something to report. After reviewing my auxiliary sensor data, I believe I have detected a minute disturbance in the fabric of space-time upon the target's departure. It could indicate long-range tele-portation instead of the use of perception-altering magic."

"... Galatea..." The panda-eyed mad scientist much less said than groaned her name while simultaneously rubbing his forehead. "Did you see any building-sized magic arrays on his back?"

"Parsing memory... Negative. No record indicating such structure was detected by my sensors."

"Then how exactly do you think he teleported away!?"

It was at this very moment that the whole elevator shuddered as the cabin came to a halt, and the automatic doors opened in the company of a stereotypical little *ping* noise, revealing a stoic Pascal, better known as Armband Guy in certain circles, on the other side.

"Who teleported?"

There was an uncertain glance shared between Lab Coat Guy and the old nurse following the straight-laced question coming from the bespectacled connoisseur of upper-arm fashion (seriously, the guy was wearing his student council band even now), and at the end of the day, it was Peabody who let out an embarrassed noise as he stepped forth to answer.

"Oh-ho-ho... Don't mind us, my nephew and his aide were only discussing hypotheticals."

Armband Guy gave the man a sidelong glance but didn't comment. Instead, he turned on his heel and wordlessly gestured for the three to follow after him. I'm not going to lie, if I had lungs at the moment, I would've probably let out a content little chuckle, as I apparently choose to use Far Sight at just the right time to catch a rare opportunity.

Anyhow, after about a minute of following my targets down the corridors of the underground School facility, I found myself inside a familiar study.

The arch-mage's place, which looked exactly the same as the time when we visited it in person (except for the different doors, of course), was still completely silent even though there were five people inside. Well, four people and an android, to be exact, but let's not get bogged down by semantics.

Lord Endymonion, anachronistically dressed (including the silly panama hat) and inexplicably infuriating as always, was sitting behind his desk and was in the process of reading through the contents of a thin manila folder, the kind you would see in a spy drama with *Top Secret* stamped on it in bold, red letters. On said desk, there were stacks of various documents, a few magical trinkets, and an open liquor bottle with an already-half-filled glass in tow. Or maybe it was half empty. I was never any good with these philosophical litmus tests.

While I observed that, Pascal closed the doors, and I'm not going to lie: the eclectic group of a student in uniform, a mad-scientist type wearing oversized shoulder pads, a portly old man, and a fembot in a skin-tight suit matched the overall aesthetic of the place about as well as the Dalai Lama wearing a Wehrmacht helmet. Once the group more or less lined up, the owner of the room lazily folded his reading material and placed it onto his desk, his brows already in the process of furrowing into a troubled frown.

"I have to say, I most definitely did not expect to meet you again so soon."

"And we didn't expect that you would withhold vital information from us," Lab Coat Guy quipped back, which made Peabody take a sharp breath and nervously glance around for a moment.

"Not one for small talk, as usual," the arch-mage noted with a troubled smile partially hidden by his beard. "But let us put your lack of etiquette aside for a moment. Would you elaborate on the reason behind your previous statement?"

"I meant—!" The resident mad scientist raised his voice, only to halt when the school nurse let out a strained cough by his side, and after locking eyes for a moment, he also cleared his throat and spoke up again, this time in a decidedly more subdued fashion. "We've engaged Leonard Dunning, as we agreed before."

"Have you now?" the old man responded with a curiously raised brow in tow. "Did he finally reveal some of his depth?"

"He didn't," Lab Coat Guy spat out the words in a huff. "He wasn't even there."

Hearing that, Lord Grandpa slowly straightened his posture in his seat and stated, "I am afraid I have to ask you to further elaborate on that statement."

"He wasn't there," the mad-ish scientist repeated his words once more. "It was an illusion the whole time! Why didn't you tell us he was an expert illusionist?!"

"A master illusionist," the android corrected, but no one seemed to care the least bit.

"I find your statement quite unlikely." The old coot fell silent for a second as he stroked his beard, then asked, "May I ask you if you have any proof of your assertion?"

"Well, he disappeared right in front of my eyes. Not only that, but Galatea was with me as well, and she didn't notice anything until he was gone. He has to be at least an expert to fool her sensors," Lab Coat Guy declared as he pointed at his android companion.

"Can I trust the senses of your creation?"

"Can you trust his senses?" Lab Coat Guy jabbed back, this time while pointing at Armband Guy.

Lord Grandpa fell silent once again, and then he shook his head, seemingly in defeat, and said, "I shall concede the point. However, even if I were to grant you the possibility of the young mister Dunning having access to high-level illusions, I fail to see how it would be more than yet another entry in his impressively diverse lists of capabilities."

"Are you serious?" Lab Coat Guy all but glowered as he glared at the old man on the other side of the desk. "Expert illusionists don't grow on trees! Are you telling me that you, the freaking arch-mage of the island, didn't know he was one!?"

"Friedrich, please..." Peabody muttered under his breath, but his words bounced off their target like a BB pellet off the Popemobile.

"Your accusation hurts me," the old Mage stated with a wounded expression, which only lasted for a moment before he took a carefree sip of the liquor on his desk and stated, "I believe we both swore to perfect transparency in our contract. I staked my name and station as a guarantee upon the signing of it. Why do you take my word so lightly?"

"Are you trying to tell me you really didn't know?" Lab Coat Guy asked back, his tone just a smidgen less combative than before.

"I believe we have already established beyond any reasonable doubt that our young friend is a box of mysteries, to say it mildly. While I personally still find it hard to believe that he could be a practitioner of the arts, it would not be the first time he surprised me." For some reason the old man let out an amused chuckle and added, "For example, did you know that he already established a romantic relationship with the scion of the Dracises? Not only that, but they accepted him with open arms! Most peculiar, I must say!"

For some odd reason, it was the school nurse who let out a surprised noise and said, "O-ho-ho? Doesn't that mean he already allied himself with the Winged Ones?" Seeing that he was suddenly the center of attention, he paused to theatrically wipe his sweaty forehead, after which he added, "To be honest, it's not an unexpected development."

"True, yet potentially troubling nonetheless." After saying his piece, Lord Grandpa fell silent for a few long moments, his fingers quietly yet irritatingly drumming on the wooden top of his desk.

Likely seeing this as an opportunity to interject, Pascal made a small noise to draw his attention before he suggested, "I believe that conclusion might be somewhat hasty."

"You truly think so?" the head of the School spoke with a surprisingly attentive look in his eyes.

"Yes. Based on my assessment, he is the fiercely independent type, the kind who would not subordinate himself so easily."

"Hmm..." the arch-mage mused aloud while theatrically stroking his beard, completely ignoring the other people in the room. "That is true. He also gave me an impression most similar to what you described, especially in the form of his dogged determination to foil my every attempt to keep track of the well-being of his cohorts." For some curious reason, the old man absentmindedly rubbed his left eye as he said that, but then he noticed what he was doing, and subsequently he closed his eyes. "That said, while he is definitely a young man of numerous talents, I would think he should be already aware of the dangers of pioneering a new path. After all, knowing the limits of oneself is also a talent in and of itself."

"O-ho-ho. True, but just because he has other talents, it doesn't mean he has that particular one," Peabody elbowed his way back into the conversation, earning him another thoughtful sound from the old Mage and a disapproving glare from yours truly. Or at least he would've if I had eyes at the moment, but I think everyone gets that by now.

"A perceptive observation, exactly the kind I expected from you, old friend." After saying so, Lord Grandpa reached over to the shot glass on the corner of his desk and took another sip of the brown liquor in it. "It is always prudent to listen to multiple points of view before reaching a conclusion." Saying so, the annoying old man pushed the manila folder on the desk back and forth for a moment while thinking, and at last he inquired, "Speaking of points of view; since you are already here, would you care to discuss what we have learned so far? It is a rare opportunity, after all."

"Only if you swear you won't hold back any information from us," Lab Coat Guy stated without a moment of thinking, earning him yet another disapproving look from his uncle.

"I believe I have already made such an agreement, but very well. If it puts your heart at ease, I once again swear that we shall be transparent in our dealings. That said, Pascal?"

"Yes, sir?"

"For a start, would you care to recount your assessment of the young man in question?"

"Understood," Armband Guy responded as he stepped forth, put his hands behind his back, and continued with a tone reminiscent of a foot soldier giving a report to his superior. "My evaluation of the target is as follows: in our daily interactions over the span of the current school year, Leonard Dunning had shown consistent awareness of my presence, yet avoided direct contact."

"What about that one time?" Lab Coat Guy cut in with a frown. "Didn't you complain about how he suddenly walked up to you the other day and demanded to shake your hand?"

Pascal gave him a flat look and amended, "He avoided direct contact, except for that one time he demanded to shake my hand. I believe it was some sort of power play, but he did not engage in any further discourse and left right away."

"How curious," Lord Grandpa mused, his eyes alight with poorly concealed interest. "Please, continue."

"Yes, sir." After a solid nod and a short-but-intensely-aggravated glance sent at the mad scientist, Armband Guy took a huge breath and continued. "Over the same time period, he made contact with the representatives of each member of the Winged Races on campus while maintaining his cover as a mundane student, including the Celestial sleeper agent even we were unaware of. He also does not seem to discriminate against the denizens of the Abyss. At the same time, he recently clashed with—"

"For the love of Sophia, Pascal... I asked for your assessment, not his entire history," the old man grumbled, and Armband Guy immediately nodded like a good little soldier.

"Understood. To avoid further redundancy, I will now strive to share my conclusions regarding the subject. He shows outstanding awareness, and he either possesses superb intuition, or he truly has access to a source of up-to-date intelligence. He doesn't discriminate based on racial origins, yet at the same time his hostility towards personages with political power shows that he is not willing to work with any of the currently established authorities. As such, I find it reasonable to conclude that he is unlikely to subordinate himself; I believe he is aiming to create his own, separate power base."

"So your independent judgment parallels mine." After saying that, the arch-mage glanced at the rest of the group. "How about yours?"

Lab Coat Guy and Peabody glanced at each other, and after a momentary beat of silence, it was the portly school nurse who stepped forth to speak.

"O-ho-ho. Academically speaking, the young man is not particularly outstanding, yet firmly above average. As for his capabilities, due to our approach, we, unfortunately, weren't able to collect any observations besides the one my nephew already shared with you."

"I see," the arch-mage whispered, followed by a chuckle. "Very well. I believe it is not unreasonable to adopt a patient approach for the time being. Even if the young man truly desires to create his own path, it does not mean that we will not be able to make use of him. As for his capabilities..."

"If I may speak," Armband Guy raised his voice and looked at the resident mad scientist. "I believe last time we talked, I emphasized the need for direct engagement, and I was promised a swift and up-front resolution."

"And we have done so, just as we promised," Lab Coat Guy countered just a smidgen defensively.

"Speaking of which," Lord Grandpa spoke up again, his bushy eyebrows already drawn into a small frown. "How exactly did you attempt to test his capabilities?"

"Well," Lab Coat Guy began a little awkwardly, but he quickly firmed up his voice and stated, "We had enough trouble with the rest of the group, so we tried to make contact with him when he was alone."

"I thought the contract explicitly stated that you cannot engage the targets individually," Armband Guy commented in yet another obvious attempt at heckling.

"Yes, but he's the big Chimera slayer, right? Not to mention, considering we still have no idea about his capabilities, I thought I could cut myself some slack and make sure that we had the advantage without any other variables present. You know? So that we could see how he reacts without the chance of being *slain* in the process."

"Oh? And how did he react?" Lord Grandpa inquired with an amicable expression hiding his intrigued eyes.

"I already told you: He disappeared. Poof. Just like that."

"Is that so? Would that not mean that, were we to consider it a given that you ambushed an illusionary body double, he knew about your actions ahead of time and prepared accordingly?"

"Erm... I suppose it does?" the scientist with the panda eyes nodded, if just a wee bit hesitantly, and the old man's eyes all but sparkled with mirth.

"Truly curious, is it not?"

Honestly, this part of the conversation made me curious, as well. Apparently the ambush was not only an unsanctioned one, but Lab Coat Guy didn't mention a single thing about his offer to me in front of Lord Grandpa. Could it be that he really planned on stabbing the arch-mage in the back? Based on the discussion I currently observed, they didn't seem to be on the best of terms, so it was a possibility. On the other hand, I've never seen anything hinting at any kind of foul play during the previous times I'd used Far Sight on him, not a single mention of rebellion or playing the old man behind his back.

In fact, for a moment I even entertained the thought that they might've been putting up a play in front of me, but I quickly dismissed the idea. Now, I admit I might've been a little too careless with the information I gained through Far Sight, but even if they figured out I had access to inside knowledge, their first guess should've been a leak, not that I could listen in on their conversation while inside the arch-mage's sealed-off study. Either way, I figured I should try to be just a tiny bit more conservative with the way I used the intel I gained like this, just in case.

That said, there was another thing that roused my interest in the discussion so far: the mention of a contract of some sort. Now, I couldn't be sure if it was a written one, or one of those fancy-pants, swear-upon-a-golden-chalice-filled-with-virgin-blood-mixed-with-the-petals-of-blue-roses kinds of contracts (which was actually a *thing*, if the entry about it on the Celestial Hub was to be believed), but just in case it was, it gave me yet another reason to find an opportunity to snoop around in the old man's office.

Regrettably enough, there was a single obstacle in my way: I couldn't tag him yet. I have, after being reminded by Judy, placed a mark on Armband Guy, and if the mad-science team wasn't having this meeting here, I would've probably used his mark to see if I could take a look at the old man. However, while Armband Guy had seemingly free rein over going back and forth in the School facilities, I never found the right opportunity to teleport over without anyone else being present. Or rather, I had that one opportunity, but I didn't take it because I was enchantment sick.

Putting that aside, I made a mental note about the contract and focused my attention back on the scene at hand, just in time to catch Lord Grandpa refilling his glass.

"Putting such matters aside, I believe we still have to discuss the capabilities of the rest of the younglings. I am particularly curious about the discovery regarding young Joshua Bernstein." After he said that, the arch-mage gingerly picked up the folder on the desk and opened it up right in the middle. "It appears this ordinary young man might be in possession of an unexpectedly impressive heritage."

"I have also seen it with my own eyes," the guy with the fancy armband interjected. "It might have been just a glance before the rest of his group hid him from my sight, but I can definitely confirm that he must be the descendant of a strong Abyssal bloodline, possibly even a bastard of one of the lords."

"Kihihi." Lab Coat Guy, for maybe the first time since he entered the room, let out one of his grating chuckles and then stated, "I don't know about bloodlines, but as much as it pains me, Galatea's scans agree with Mister Collect the Information We Want or I'll Break Your Arms here."

Lord Grandpa's eyes narrowed in annoyance, and he glanced over to the alleged arm breaker in question.

"Pascal? Did you really threaten our collaborator with physical violence?"

"Certainly," he responded without a shred of guilt or self-awareness.

"... Well, at the very least you are honest," the arch-mage stated a little dourly after somehow stifling a groan and taking another sip of his drink. "Sometimes I wonder where I have gone wrong in your education. Nevertheless, see to it that you apologize later."

"Why can't he apologize now?" Lab Coat Guy interjected, only to be dismissed with a single, disinterested glance.

"Now, back to the issue of the youth in question," Lord Grandpa mused while absentmindedly leafing back and forth between a few pages. "If your intuition and your scans are correct, it would definitely explain why the Lord of Inanna would be willing to sacrifice what little goodwill I had remaining towards his house. A Winged One of the Abyss with a strong-yet-unknown bloodline would definitely serve as a powerful pawn in his hands... Yet I cannot help but feel that we are missing something."

There was a long pause in the conversation here while Armband Guy and company patiently waited for his... boss, I suppose? Now that I think about it, just how were these two related, anyway? And how were the rest related? Apparently, Peabody was his old friend, and Lab Coat Guy was that guy's nephew, but then... Ugh, these were questions for later, I supposed, as the old man all of a sudden stood up and walked over to the cabinet in the corner.

"Once again, it is made obvious that we must observe them further. Speaking of observations, I believe we were talking about the individual prowess of the group centered around the young mister Bernstein."

I continued to watch for a minute longer, but aside from being able to take a better look at the eclectic contents of the old arch-mage's liquor cabinet, I didn't learn anything new after this point. I mean, if there was one person on this island who knew the ins and outs of the abilities of every single member of our group down to the tiniest details... it was probably Judy, but I was a close second!

Anyhow, since listening to them any further was pointless, I ultimately returned to my room. After taking a moment to collect myself, I had to conclude that, while this Far Sight session raised about as many questions as it answered, it still provided me with yet another solid, indisputable piece of evidence about the collaboration between Lord Grandpa and Lab Coat Guy. Furthermore, based on the content of their discussion, it was hinted that he was trying to find out about our capabilities, and it somehow tied into his trying to make use of us. Or was it just me? Either way, while his methods weren't particularly dangerous, they weren't completely harmless, either, so as far as I was concerned, he was still firmly in the antagonist category.

That said, I checked the time on my phone, and to my shock, I realized that I'd spent a bit more time spying than I thought. I pocketed the phone, jumped to my feet, and immediately headed downstairs, only to stop after I exited my room. I held my breath for a moment to better focus on my hearing and... was that laughter just now? I expected a lot of things after leaving those three alone for a while, but merriment wasn't among the options.

Now granted, it would've taken me zero effort to just use Far Sight to look at what was going on, but I figured I might as well snoop around the proper way every once in a while, so I continued to hold my breath and slowly inched towards the stairs until I could finally overhear the discussion downstairs.

"I can soooo understand!" This exclamation was the first sliver of the conversation I could make out, and as I came closer, I could also hear a soft sound that I could identify as Ammy giggling. "My father always told me, 'Son, you have to be the best amongst the best amongst the best!' I seriously grew sick and tired of that line!"

"I can imagine," the class rep agreed in an unexpectedly friendly voice. "Grandfather once told me that the military and academia are not so different once you get high enough in the hierarchy. His favourite line is a little different though: it's 'Publish or perish.'"

"Uh... right. I admit that sounds a little less overbearing, but *perish* in the military is sliiiightly more literal than in the academic circles, so I think I will stick to my father's line, after all."

Amelia honest-to-goodness giggled in response to that. Was that supposed to be funny?

Anyhow, this whole situation felt really fishy, so I decided to show myself by simply walking down the stairs. The two in the living room fell dead silent the moment I came into view... which begged a certain question right out of the gate.

"Sorry to keep you waiting, I had something to take care of." With the lead-up done, I stopped at the foot of the stairs and exaggeratedly looked around. "Where did Snowy go?"

"She said she had to go to the toilet," Ammy responded with a modest smile, the kind I haven't seen on her face for ages. "Didn't you meet on the way?"

"I can't say I did." I spoke softly as I walked over to their side and pointedly glanced at the clock on the wall. "So, Mike? I'm sorry to interrupt your talk, but weren't you supposed to catch a cab right around now?"

The unlikely Celestial followed my gaze, and he quickly jumped to his feet.

"Oh snap, you're right! My ride should be here at any moment now!"

"Then I suppose I'd better see you out so you won't miss your train."

"I... I suppose you better do?" he mumbled a little awkwardly before catching himself. He was still dragging his feet, though, so I was just about to egg him on a little when he sneaked a glance at the class rep, and after a conspicuously long beat he told her, "It was a pleasure to meet you, Miss Amelia."

"I assure you, the pleasure was mine," she responded with the same demure expression and a choice of words that sounded like it came out of her grandfather's mouth. Things were getting fishier by the moment, I'd say.

It was around this time that I'd had enough of their little interplay, so I simply stood behind Michael and began to forcefully push him out of the room.

"All right, let's get going. I'll be back in a moment."

With that, I successfully removed the guy from my living room, and I patiently watched over him as he put on his coat before I politely opened the front door for him. However, despite my best efforts to expedite his departure, he turned around in the doorway and looked me in the eye.

"Hey, can I bother you for one second longer?"

I honestly wanted to tell him, "No, go away," but by the time the words left my mouth they somehow morphed into, "Feel free to do so."

My answer made the Celestial field agent oddly fidgety for a moment. He glanced behind me, and then he leaned closer for a conspiratorial huddle.

"You see, I couldn't help but wonder if you and Amelia were a..." His words trailed off by the end with an implicit, "You know? Like that?" tagged on in a whisper.

I raised a slightly baffled bow and asked, "... Are you trying to ask me if we are a couple?"

"Um... more or less?"

Mike flashed me the perfect image of a harmless smile, and I couldn't help but groan in return.

"No, we are not," I stated in no uncertain terms. "Why?"

"Oh, nothing, I was just a little curious," he hastily stated while still maintaining his impeccable smile, and at this point I was fairly certain it was much less innocent than it appeared on the surface. The suspicion might've shown on my face, as he abruptly declared, "Never mind. I'm going to get in touch with some old acquaintances and gather as many artifacts as possible, and then... errr... how should I contact you?"

"You don't have to; I'll contact you in time," I responded in my most enigmatic voice.

"Oh. Okay then." He stared me in the eye for a couple of seconds, but when he saw I didn't have anything else to say, he awkwardly added, "Should I... give you my phone number or something?"

"No need," I responded while employing an inscrutable smile of my own. I wasn't kidding, either. I literally had the guy's mobile number in the Hub's contact list, and I imagined acting like I knew everything would help to solidify my image as an information broker.

I figured we were done, so before I forgot it, I peeled off my gloves and offered my hand to the Celestial in the doorway. He quickly mirrored my gesture by taking off his own glove, and he firmly shook my hand.

"I'm looking forward to working with you."

"Erm... Yes, the feeling is mutual," he stated after a momentary stutter.

With that, I now had another mark. Sometimes I wondered if I had a limit to the number of people I could tag like this, and considering how absurdly useful this particular ability of mine had proved to be so far, I sincerely hoped I didn't.

Anyhow, it was just around this time that I noticed a familiar taxi turning the corner onto our street. I pointed at it, and after following my finger, Michael hurriedly said his goodbyes and rushed over to the roadside.

I was a little curious to see if it was the usual cab driver this time, as well, but not curious enough to go out into the cold, so I waved to him and closed the door without further ado. It was only then that I let out a tired sigh, put my gloves back on, and headed back to the living room and to what promised to be a fairly heavy conversation.

PART 2

"I'm back." I announced my return to the living room with those half-hearted words, and I found the class rep exactly where I left her. On a slightly more interesting note, my little maidster came back while I was in the entryway, and now she was happily discussing something with her. Said discussion immediately stopped the moment I set foot within the room, with the tail end I could barely catch being something about how someone was "Really goofy." I guess they must have meant the recently departed Celestial, so I put it out of mind and walked over to their side.

"It's getting a little late, so let's not waste any time," I proposed the moment I stopped, earning me a small nod from Ammy, and she was just about to say something. However, just then I remembered something, so I raised an open palm to stall her before she could get started. "However, there's one last thing before that." Saying so, I turned to Snowy and unsubtly pointed at the clock. "Could you glance over there for a moment?"

She followed my pointing finger and after reading the time she turned back to me and said, "It's still before curfew."

"Yes, but you still have to pack your bag and put away your uniform, don't you?"

"Uh... That's right," she quickly relented in the face of my insistence, and her shoulders drooped in resignation. "I'll clean up the table."

"You don't have to; I'll clean up after Ammy leaves. Just go and prepare for tomorrow. I also want to see you in bed by ten; you're still growing, so proper sleep is very important."

"Understood," my sister said with just a tinge of sulking in her voice, so I immediately stepped closer to her and placed my hand on top of her head as step one in my anti-pouting countermeasures.

"You did well today, so go and rest up. You don't want to show up at school with circles under your eyes, right? What would your fans think?"

"Oww!" She hurriedly escaped from my vigorous head pats and sent me a peeved glance. "I don't want any fans!"

"I've heard you already have some though," I teased her with the appropriately brotherly grin on my face. "I was actually thinking about joining, as well. What do you think, are they going to accept me?"

"Don't you dare," my sister threatened me with her angry puppy look, and I couldn't help but chuckle at her expense.

"But why not? It's my duty as a big brother to promote my cute little sister and simultaneously let the little moths know how much trouble they would be if they tried to get closer to this particular flame."

"Uh... You really don't have to do that though."

"Well, I could be convinced otherwise, but only by good little sisters who keep the curfew. Are you one of them?"

"You are a meanie," Snowy suddenly burst out and turned on her heel. She dashed up to the stairs, only stopping to turn back and stick out her tongue at me, earning her yet another hearty chuckle from me, before she made her way up to the first floor.

I watched her go, and once she was out of sight I let out another soft chuckle and turned to my remaining guest. The moment our eyes met, she immediately asked a question I was pretty sure qualified as being rhetorical.

"She's become a lot more expressive lately, hasn't she?"

"She sure has," I answered as I walked over to my usual spot and took a seat. "I'd personally like to take credit, but it's probably because of everyone's efforts to make her feel accepted."

"You say that now, but just a few seconds ago you were teasing her quite mercilessly," Ammy sent a verbal jab my way, and oh look, the menacing glasses tweakery was back. I was almost missing it. Except not really.

Anyhow, I shrugged my shoulders and responded by saying, "It's every big brother's privilege, nay, *duty*, to tease their little sister."

There was an odd look on the class rep's face, and after a short while she let her glasses-tweaking hand down, and she dryly stated, "You aren't really brother and sister, though."

The moment she uttered that, the corner of my mouth involuntarily twitched twice. Once I got that under control, I took a deep breath and stated, "I say so, and if anyone else tries to dare say otherwise, they are going to be in a world of pain before they know it." I saw my conversational partner twitch in apprehension, so I hastily added, "Present company excluded, of course. For the first offense, at least."

"Very gracious of you," Ammy commented, only to ponder for a moment and add, "But what about when Noire comes back?"

"Oh, trust me, he is going to be in for a rude awakening," I answered with what in retrospect felt like a vicious grin. I quickly wiped it off my face and then loudly cleared my throat for good measure. "Not to mention, he has bigger problems at the moment, being bedridden after some handsome devil poisoned him and all."

"He was poisoned?" Ammy's eyebrows shot up in surprise. "And what was that about handsome devils?"

"Don't concern yourself with that," I dismissed the topic with a shake of my head. "The important bit is that he's incapacitated at the moment, and his faction has bigger problems than to come looking for trouble over here."

"How would you even know that?"

"Information broker," I stated just a tad smugly as I pointed at myself. The class rep didn't really appreciate my answer, as she immediately rolled her eyes.

"Speaking of which, was that why Michael was here?"

Her question made me raise a single curious brow. Not because of the part where she figured out that Mike was here to exchange information (since I told her he was here for business, anyone could put two and two together, let alone her), but because they were already on a first-name basis. Could there actually be some chemistry between those two? Wouldn't that break the harem? Though again, I guess I already kind of did that when I accidentally snatched the princess out of Josh's nefarious clutches, so who knew? Maybe it was open season already.

Not that it was any of my business, so after a suitably long beat of silence, I returned to the conversation at hand by stating, "Yeah, he was looking for info."

"About what?"

"It's confidential," I stated in no uncertain terms. I mean, apparently my information broker cover story ended up making me into one, so I figured it was for the best that I acted the part, at least on the surface, and I was pretty sure info traders who tattled on their clients didn't make it far in the industry. Speaking of which, was this an industry? Did information brokers have a union? I supposed I would look into that later.

In the meantime, Ammy took my rejection fairly well, as she only spent a few seconds adjusting her glasses while glaring at me. Nevertheless, I figured we've dragged things out long enough, especially considering my previous declaration about not dragging things out, so I expertly dodged her scowl and decided to get started with the real discussion.

"So," I opened by assuming my traditional mastermind pose in my seat. "You wanted to discuss something you discovered about your grandfather, didn't you?"

"Yes, I did," she told me with just a hint of huffiness in her voice.

"Then please start at the beginning."

"All right. As I said before, I noticed Grandfather and Pascal were discussing something at home. I think they didn't know I was home yet, since they left the door to the conference room a little ajar."

"You have a conference room?"

That was the question that slipped out of my mouth, though in retrospect there was another one I should've asked. It was naturally about why she was living with her grandfather. I actually observed her enough that the fact that I had never seen her parents became suspicious. I mean, I had yet to meet with Angie's adoptive parents in person, and somehow I never met with Josh's parents, either, but I at least knew they existed through my Far Sight observations of them. As for the class rep, however, she might as well have been living all alone for all I knew. It was just a little bit suspicious, but I didn't have the opportunity to ask this time, either, as the conversation moved along before I could bring it up. Oh well, there's always the next time.

"Yes, we have one for when Grandfather doesn't want to take someone down to the School. It's mostly for meeting with city officials and other mundanes. More importantly, I have overheard him telling Pascal that he should contact Dr. Robatto."

"Oh? Did he actually refer to him by name?"

"No, not directly," Ammy stated, suddenly sounding much less assured than just a second ago. "However, he talked about giving an order to their collaborator, and he mentioned making sure that they would confront you in particular." Suddenly the class rep's brows descended into a frown, and she looked me in the eye before declaring, "That's the main reason why I wanted to talk as soon as possible. You need to be careful."

"Thanks for the warning, I suppose, though it's a little late." Her brows went a full one-eighty and ascended as high as they could in surprise, so I elaborated by saying, "Do you remember that I had plans for this evening?"

"The ones Judy was really angry about? Yes, I remember. Why?"

"Well, they involved going outside, and in the process, I was already caught in an ambush by our resident mad scientist. Oh, and before you ask, yes, I'm fine."

"I wasn't worried about you," she suddenly stated while pointedly looking away.

"I see. So you came over in a hurry to warn me about a possible ambush because you weren't worried," I teased her a little, earning me yet another frown.

"Leo, don't be a jerk. I meant I was sure you could handle yourself."

"I know, I know," I soothed her for a moment before adding, "Though again, if you wanted to warn me ahead of time, you could've just called me on the phone. At least it wouldn't have been a surprise."

"I couldn't," she asserted quite emphatically. "I was afraid Grandfather would notice, and then he would know I overheard them talking."

"Errr... Listen, class rep. I don't want to dishearten you or anything, but I'm fairly sure he knew you overheard, anyway."

"Why do you think that?" she asked in a provocative voice, and I answered, but not before I let out a small sigh.

"To put it bluntly, I've been fighting a surveillance cold war with your grandfather since even before I first met him in person, and not only is your home filled with these creepy floating eyeball things, he also has a habit of putting them on people. Such as you."

"Eyeball thi— Do you mean recorder orbs?" All of a sudden she visibly paled and asked, "Do I have one attached to me?"

"Not anymore, you don't," I responded as I waved my finger in front of me. "I told you how I can disrupt magic, right? I tend to break any of those damn things the moment I see them, on principle."

"So Grandfather knows that I came here. He most likely also knows I overheard them." Ammy fell silent in a moment, her face scrunched up as she thought hard, and then she glanced up at me and asked, "Do you think I was set up?"

"Possibly," I granted her without much ado. I mean, that was the first idea that came to my mind, as well, when she told me why she came over, but hearing it from her mouth made things much easier for me. As such, I donned my mastermind pose once more and added, "Let's assume for a moment that he really set things up for you to overhear him. Can you venture a guess as to why he'd do that?"

"It's obviously because he wanted to leak information," she asserted without much thinking, once again mirroring my thoughts. "It might have also been a test of character, to see if I would tell you about it."

"I wouldn't call it a test of character, per se," I rebuffed her words while once again shaking my head for emphasis. "If I had to guess, he might've thought that there was a traitor in his organization and wanted to see if you were the one."

"You somehow made it sound even worse," she grumbled, but I only grinned at her in response, so she quickly calmed down. "Does that mean that he no longer trusts me?"

"I can hardly comment on that," I admitted freely. "We still don't have enough info on his motivations to say for sure. It might've been a test of loyalty, or just a practical joke."

"Grandfather doesn't do jokes."

"If you say so," I shrugged and moved along. "So, what else have they talked about? In particular, have they mentioned anything specific that could be traced back to that particular conversation?"

"Let me think for a moment," Ammy asked for some breathing space, and I naturally granted it to her. After about half a minute she took a huge breath and began by saying, "As I mentioned, they talked about ambushing you in particular. Aside from that, they talked about administrative issues regarding the School, setting aside a part of the budget for a special grant, and... that's about it." She paused here for a moment, and after noticing that I wasn't exactly riveted by what she said, she added, "If there was one thing that was somewhat peculiar, it was when Grandfather warned Pascal not to threaten their collaborator."

"How is that peculiar?"

Amelia gave me a flat look and emphatically stated, "Pascal is not the type to threaten anyone, so it was something that really surprised me."

"Are you sure he isn't?"

"Of course I am," she huffed quite indignantly at my question. "I've known Pascal since we were little. He is a gentle boy."

"Really now?" I mused under my breath, and after a moment of deliberation, I decided to tell her, "That *gentle boy* just recently told Lab Coat... I mean, *Robatto*, that he was going to break his arms if he would not play along."

"Pascal would never say that!" she denied quite vehemently, so I pushed right back.

"He sure as hell admitted it, and right in front of both your grandpa and Lab Coat Guy."

Ammy looked like she wanted to retort again, only to instead fall silent for a good three seconds before she asked, in a deceptively quiet voice, "Leo?"

"Yes?"

"How would you even know that?"

"It's a trade se—"

"Don't say it's a secret!" she interrupted me with a genuinely angry look on her face. It was surprising, to say the least, so I decided to wisely shut up for the moment. Seeing that I didn't say anything, the class rep let out a pent-up breath and in a low voice she told me, "Leo, you're holding too many secrets."

"Well, it's kind of my thing," I tried to excuse myself with a jokey tone, but she wouldn't have any of it.

"I'm serious. I told you before, and so I tell you again: you are being too secretive with us. Do you really mistrust us that much?"

Seeing how serious she was, I couldn't help but abandon the mastermind pose and instead face her with the same gravitas.

"It's not about trust, really," I explained a little more awkwardly than I originally intended. "There are some things that I just can't talk about."

"Why? Can you actually give me a reason? Or at least a good enough excuse?"

"Well..." I began, only to fall silent right away. I could have given her an excuse, maybe a few little white lies or technical truths, but I had a feeling that it would be just me digging myself even deeper, so after exhaling hard I ultimately told her, "You're right. I am keeping a lot of secrets, but there are a lot of different reasons why I can't just share them with everyone."

"Do you share them with anyone at all?" she pressed on, but I had an answer ready.

"Actually, I do. Judy knows practically all my secrets already."

"What about Eleanor?" she continued her offense, and this time I was actually stumped for a moment.

"She knows... erm... *some* of my secrets?"

"She is your girlfriend, and even that isn't enough to confide in her?"

"I told you, it's complicated," I mumbled as I found myself on the defensive, and she didn't let me catch my breath, either.

"What about Neige? You adopted her, and you're always vehement about how she is your little sister no matter what anyone says. Does that mean she knows all of your secrets?"

"Well... not really. I mean, she knows *different* secrets than Elly, but..."

Seeing how disappointed Ammy looked made me feel just a tiny bit ashamed, so I soon fell silent again. Seeing that I was done, my guest let out a deep sigh and shook her head.

"Leo, you need to understand something," she began by looking me in the eye and talking in a level voice. "Neige trusts you. So do Eleanor, Angie, and Josh. So do I, even though you make it really hard sometimes."

"Thanks, I guess?"

She gave me a small nod in response, though the look in her eyes told me to stay quiet just a while longer.

"You also have to understand something else: trust is a two-way street, and it really looks and feels like you don't trust us at all. You don't tell us anything ahead of time, keep pulling resources and abilities out of thin air, and act like all of that is completely self-evident. I mean, you have a secret underground base full of Fauns, and it might be the most normal thing about you."

"Now, that's just a hyperbole if I've ever heard one," I grumbled, but got dismissed on the spot.

"It's true. And it makes it hard to continue trusting you, especially when you keep all of us in the dark about these things right until they are convenient to be revealed. For example, if I knew you already had an informant in the School, and let's put aside how crazy that is for a moment, I wouldn't have rushed over here to try to warn you about something you already knew about ahead of time."

I wanted to note that I didn't actually know about the ambush ahead of time, but I didn't have a good opportunity to interject, as she immediately continued.

"Things like these might not mean much to you, but by keeping us in the dark, your secrecy has led and will lead to us being worried and afraid for your safety and ours. How are we supposed to work together and watch one another's backs when you can't be bothered to tell us anything ahead of time and prefer to lord over your secrets instead?"

At last, there was a momentary pause in her scolding, so I exhaled sharply through my nose and began my verbal counteroffensive.

"Very well. For the record, I want you to know that I understand your point of view and your arguments. However," I paused for a beat and raised a finger for emphasis before I continued with, "I'm not keeping secrets just for the sake of keeping them. I'm not even keeping them for the sake of some hackneyed reason, like protecting myself or you guys. The truth of the matter is, everything I try to keep from you is because failing to do so would lead to unexpected consequences for the entire world."

"What exactly do you mean by that?"

"I'm talking about reality-warping, existential-crisis-inducing, literal world-shattering shenanigans."

For a moment we were both silent, with the class rep obviously scrutinizing my face to see if I was serious, and once she seemed to be convinced enough she whispered, "That's... considerably more grave than I thought."

"Tell me about it," I grumbled with a huff, then added, "It's also important to note that, even when it comes to the less cataclysmic secrets of mine, I keep them a secret because of tactical reasons."

"Tactical?" she repeated after me, brows once again arched high.

"Yes," I nodded and elaborated by telling her, "Let me give you an example: let's say I had the ability to turn Abyssals into stone by touching their heads."

"You can do that?"

"No, I said this was hypothetical. So let's say I could do that, and there was no way to resist that ability. Let's say Crowey showed up and demanded that I hand Snowy back to him. If I kept my ability a secret until the last second, I could simply petrify him when his guard was down, and then I could put a pointy hat on him, and we would have a brand-new garden gnome. However, what would happen if I didn't keep it a secret?"

"He could come up with countermeasures," she muttered under her breath, but then she continued with a stronger voice, "I understand, but it sounds like a very specific scenario."

"Of course, it was an example to illustrate a point. However, if I wanted to go with something more down-to-earth..." At this point I fell silent for a while as I weighed my options, and after a few long seconds of deliberation, I decided on what to say. "Since you spent so much time dressing me down, I suppose I should show you that I understood what you tried to tell me with actions. Consider this a token of goodwill, if you like." The class rep's ears immediately perked up, and she looked almost comically expectant, so after taking a quick breath I stopped delaying things and simply told her, "I have an ability called Far Sight."

"Far Sight," she repeated after me, a little surprised by the looks of it. "Isn't that a high-level mystic art?"

"It might share the name, but I assure you, it's probably not the same thing. To put it bluntly, I can mark people, and after that point, I can observe them from a bird's-eye view at any time I want."

"... Are you serious?"

"Perfectly."

"What are its limitations?"

"I can only watch one person at a time," I answered honestly, yet she started scowling at me again.

"Leo, I'm serious."

"So am I," I retorted, a little hurt by her lack of trust, especially after she went on and on about it not too long ago.

"Okay, then how much mana does it—?"

"It doesn't," I answered her question before she even finished it.

"What about the maximum range?"

"I have no idea. How far is the Abyss?"

"You can watch people in the Abyss?"

Ammy sounded more incredulous by the second, so I nodded with the sincerest expression I could muster at the moment.

"I use it to keep tabs on Crowey, so yes, I can."

"What about the duration? Can you observe someone for more than a minute?"

"I think my record so far is about two hours." At this point she was staring daggers at me, so I quickly added a supremely puzzled, "What?"

"Leo..." she began as she raised her left hand to her ear, but for a change, it wasn't so that she could adjust her glasses, but to massage her temple. "Are you trying to tell me you have a surveillance ability that doesn't have cost, range, or duration limitations?"

"More or less," I answered truthfully, and she shook her head in denial.

"That makes no sense. Every mystic phenomenon, from the simplest spells to the most complex rituals, have to obey the Rule of Threefold Balance."

"Could you refresh my memory about that?" I requested with a raised hand to get her attention. "What exactly is this rule of balance thing again?"

For a moment she looked at me like she thought I was teasing her, but when I showed her my sincerest puppy eyes, she quickly relented and explained, "It's the principle that states that any mystic phenomenon has three attributes. They are the *cost*, the *duration*, and the *magnitude*. In the case of a surveillance spell, the *cost* usually refers to the mana required to cast or use an already-deployed spell, the duration is the time until the phenomenon loses its coherence and fizzles out, and the magnitude is the maximum distance at which connecting to the spell and observation is still possible. If you want to increase one attribute, you must, without fail, sacrifice one or both of the other attributes in the process."

"Wait, that actually sounds a little familiar," I mused as I tried to recall where I've heard something like this before, and I snapped my finger the moment it came back to me. "Oh, I know! It's the magical version of the Scope Triangle!"

"The what triangle?" Ammy muttered with a deadpan expression, apparently a little confused after I jolted her out of her groove.

"It's a thing in business and project management. The three corners of the triangle are time, cost, and quality. If you want to increase one you have to compromise with the other two. Say you want something done fast, it will either cost more or it will have a shoddier end product, or if you want to have high quality, you either need to give it more time or put in more money. It's pretty similar to what you described."

"Yes, but... why do you even know about something like that?"

"Well... Let's just say that the internet is a vast place, and I have poor impulse control when it comes to following links to random wiki pages."

The class rep's expression said she still didn't understand what I was getting at, but she quickly gave up and announced, "Putting that aside, if what you say is true, then your Far Sight goes against all the known laws of mystic phenomena and should be flat-out impossible."

"I suppose, and yet it's probably still the most harmless out of all my common-sense-wrecking secrets," I responded with a knowing smirk. "It's also why other people wouldn't expect it, hence why it's so important to keep it under the lid."

"I suppose, but..." As she was looking for words, the class rep's expression slowly hardened, and she ultimately asked me, "I've been too surprised by its illogical nature to ask something that I should've in the beginning: Have you used that ability on me?"

"Yes, I have," I told her without an ounce of reservation.

"So you've been spying on me without my knowledge," she stated with just a hint of accusation in her otherwise level voice.

"Calling it *spying* is a bit of an overstatement. I'm not a voyeur; I only check on you guys occasionally, to make sure you are all right."

"*You guys*? So you have marked all of us like that. How exactly is that any better than what Grandfather is doing?"

"For a start, it's because I know for a fact that my intentions are benign, and I can't say the same about him." I could see in her eyes that she was about to object, so I hastily raised my voice and amended, "Much more importantly though, the main difference is that for him, putting a magical bug on someone is a conscious action on which he has to actively spend effort and resources, while for me, it is just *something I do*. It's practically involuntary, and it would probably take more effort to avoid accidentally marking someone I'm in daily contact with than to actually do it, and once it happens, it would be a waste to just ignore it. Not to mention, it has other important uses."

"Such as?"

I sent a frown her way and flatly told her, "I already shared one of my big, magic-theory-shaking secrets with you. Don't be greedy."

"In retrospect, I probably don't even want to know." She relented much easier than I expected. I took that as her way of dropping the topic, so I decided to move on right away by, ironically enough, moving backwards.

"Aaaaanyway, we went on quite a tangent without even concluding how or why your grandpa would try to set you up." Ammy was only looking at me attentively, probably waiting for me to make that conclusion, so after a short while I continued with, "From what you said, it didn't seem like there was any marking information in their discussion that could be used to identify you as a leak. However, considering that you were under surveillance, there is a good chance that he wanted to know how you would react to the new information."

"And I came over as soon as I could to warn you," she spoke in a dispirited voice. "So it might have been a test of character, after all."

"If it was, then you have passed with flying colours by my standards, and let us be honest, those are the only standards that matter." She apparently didn't find my jest amusing, so I let out a shallow sigh and added, "Jokes aside, we should give you a plausible cover, just in case."

"For what?"

"So that if your grandfather asks about what you were doing out this late, you would have an explanation, giving you plausible deniability and hopefully preventing him from completely locking you of the loop."

"I'm listening."

I fell silent for a while as I considered the available options.

"How about this? The time line roughly adds up, so why don't you tell him you came over in a hurry because I contacted you after being ambushed, and as the resident magical expert, I wanted to discuss the Biomechanical Gigant I encountered." I paused for a second as I thought it through again in search of obvious holes, and when nothing came to mind, I nodded to myself and said, "That sounds about right. What do you think?"

"If Grandfather really spied on me, he will know I didn't talk with you on the phone," Ammy objected, but I dismissed her concern with a wave of my hand.

"Unless he literally kept an eye on you for the entire afternoon, he has no way to know we didn't have a few-seconds-long talk during one of his blind spots, and even if he did, he couldn't call you out on it without revealing that he bugged you, which he almost certainly wouldn't do. After that, you just have to take refuge in audacity and stick to your story, and he'll have no choice but to go along with it."

"If you say so," she ultimately granted me the benefit of the doubt, which was honestly good enough for me at the moment. However, just a moment later, she slightly tilted her head to the side and inquired, "Did you actually see one of those giants?"

"From up close."

"Can you... describe it for me? Just in case Grandfather asks about them."

"... If you are curious, just say so. There is no need for excuses between friends."

Ammy gave me a long, silent look, but then the corners of her lips rose ever so slightly and she stated, "You are right. So are you going to tell me about them or not?"

Seeing her unrestrained curiosity on full display made me stifle a chuckle, and just like that, the storm clouds were gone, and we continued our discussion in a considerably more lighthearted atmosphere. If only all my problems could be solved by a single good talk like this...

PART 3

It was a little after midnight that I returned to my room with a damp towel over my head. I still felt a little bit sickly, but the hot shower managed to wash away most of my fatigue, so I was feeling pretty good overall, especially considering the long day I had.

After our brief-yet-in-depth discussion about the big ball-monsters of Lab Coat Guy, I managed to convince Ammy that it was getting a little too late for any further discussions, and since I was against letting a girl (even if she was a Mage with a golem for a bodyguard) wander the night streets alone, I did the usual thing and called a cab for her.

This probably wasn't a surprise anymore, but it was the usual cab guy who showed up to take her home. Not only that, but after sharing a few words with him, it turned out that he was also the one who took Mike to the station, so yeah, apparently this man was the only taxi driver in the entire city. I wasn't even surprised anymore.

Anyhow, once the class rep left, I made sure that my sister was asleep, and then I quickly came to my room and put all the things I'd learned today to electronic paper, and only after that did I take a shower.

As it often happens, the running water also managed to get my thoughts flowing, and so I quickly took a seat in front of my computer to capitalize upon the inspiration while it lasted. I moved my mouse a little to wake the machine from standby mode, but before I could get started, my attention was drawn to the exclamation mark on one of my browser tabs.

At first, I wasn't entirely sure I wanted to know what it was about, but curiosity won the tug of war against caution, and I maximized the Hub's tab and clicked on the highlighted PM box.

"W1NG3D N1NJ4: HEY, ADMIN? ARE YOU ONLINE? (￣▽￣)ノ"
"W1NG3D N1NJ4: HELLO!? (•_•)ノ"

"W1NG3D N1NJ4: IF YOU ARE ONLINE, ANSWER ME BACK! I HAVE A BIG LEAD! HUGE SCOOP! (≧▽≦)ノ"

"W1NG3D N1NJ4: HELLO!? YOUR PROFILE SAYS YOU ARE ONLINE! WHY AREN'T YOU ONLINE WHEN YOU ARE ONLINE!? (̄ ～ ̄ ')"

"W1NG3D N1NJ4: IT MAKES NO SENSE!!! (@_@)"

"W1NG3D N1NJ4: HELLO!? PLEASE ANSWER IF YOU ARE THERE! IT'S WAY LATE OVER HERE AND I SHOULD BE IN BED ALREADY, BUT I REALLY WANT TO TELL YOU WHAT I FOUND! IT'S SUPER HUGE! (✧ω✧)"

I was getting a mild headache from just looking at that message history, and I admit that for a moment I was tempted to just close the window and be on my merry way, but I figured there was no sense in delaying the inevitable. As such, I let out a slight groan under my breath and began to type.

"Admin: I'm here."

"Admin: Also, I have already warned you about spamming, haven't I?"

"W1NG3D N1NJ4: SORRY, BUT THIS IS SUPER-DUPER IMPORTANT!!! (∩‿∩)"

I took a deep breath to brace myself and responded by typing:

"Admin: I'm listening."

There was no answer for a long while, but then all of a sudden my screen was flooded by messages.

"W1NG3D N1NJ4: SO LISTEN! I TOLD YOU I KNEW A GUY WHO KNEW A GAL WHO KNEW A GUY RIGHT!? ＼(∩o∩)人(∩-∩)/"

"W1NG3D N1NJ4: HE IS THIS HARD-CORE INFORMATION BROKER LIVING IN TIMAEUS, SO I WENT TO HIS PLACE AND MADE AN AWESOME DEAL WITH HIM! (•ω<)~☆"

"W1NG3D N1NJ4: BUT WAIT, THERE'S MORE! HE HAD A TOTALLY CUTE LITTLE SISTER WHO WAS DRESSED LIKE A MAID, AND SHE WAS SUPER-CUTE! LIKE, SO CUTE YOU WOULDN'T BELIEVE!! TOO BAD HER BROTHER IS SUPER SCARY! (((〉 〈)))"

"W1NG3D N1NJ4: BUT THEN I MENTIONED MY FATHER AND I MENTIONED YOU AND I WAS TOTALLY SUAVE AND ALL, LIKE A PROPER SECRET AGENT MAN, AND I CONVINCED HIM TO GIVE US SOME INFO ON THAT MONSTER HUNTER GAL YOU WANTED TO KNOW ABOUT! (* ^ ω ^)"

"W1NG3D N1NJ4: I WILL WRITE A PROPER REPORT LATER, BUT HE INDEPENDENTLY CONFIRMED MY OLD SOURCE, SO YOU CAN TOTALLY BELIEVE THAT NOW!"

"W1NG3D N1NJ4: HE ALSO CALLED HER A PIZZA CUTTER, BUT I DID'T REALLY GET THAT... (-_-')· · · "

The torrent of messages stopped at this point, and as he didn't seem to be writing anything, either, I guessed he might have been waiting for me to respond.

"Admin: A pizza cutter?"

"Admin: So all edge and no point?"

"W1NG3D N1NJ4: YES! THAT'S EXACTLY WHAT HE SAID! GREAT MINDS MUST REALLY THINK ALIKE!!! \(★ω★)/"

"W1NG3D N1NJ4:... I STILL DON'T GET IT THOUGH... (-_-')· · · "

"Admin: Never mind that. Do you have anything else to report?"

"W1NG3D N1NJ4: AH, RIGHT, I DO! BELIEVE IT OR NOT, HE DIDN'T ASK FOR MONEY, OR CONFIDENTIAL INFORMATION, BUT ARTIFACTS!!! HE DIDN'T EVEN CARE WHAT KIND!"

"Admin: I see. Can you provide him with any?"

"W1NG3D N1NJ4: ACTUALLY, I WANTED TO ASK YOU IF YOU COULD... YOU KNOW... REQUISITION SOME FOR MY USE? PRETTY PLEASE? (´-ω-`)"

"Admin: I can't. I'm not even on the same continent as you."

"W1NG3D N1NJ4: AW MAAAAAN!!"

"W1NG3D N1NJ4: THAT MEANS I REALLY HAVE TO ASK MY FATHER FOR HELP...。· (>‿‿<)·。"

"W1NG3D N1NJ4: WISH ME LUCK! (((〉〈)))"

"W1NG3D N1NJ4: OH, SPEAKING OF LUCK!!! YOU WON'T BELIEVE IT, BUT I WAS LUCKY ENOUGH TO MEET THE CUTEST GIRL EVER TODAY!!! o(>ω<)o"

"Admin: Was it the sister of the information broker?"

"W1NG3D N1NJ4: NOOOOO!!! SHE WAS CUTE, TOO, BUT I TOLD YOU HER BROTHER IS SCARY! I DON'T WANNA DIE YOUNG!!! (x‿‿x)"

"W1NG3D N1NJ4: THE ONE I MET WAS ALSO VISITING HIM, AND SHE IS CALLED AMELIA, AND SHE IS THIS SUPER-DUPER CUTE GLASSES GIRL! SHE IS HIS CLASSMATE, AND THEY ARE JUST FRIENDS, AND SHE IS HYPER-SUPER-DUPER CUTE!!! (♥ω♥)"

"Admin: Yes, you already told me that she is cute, you don't have to repeat yourself so much."

"Admin: Also, just for the record: is this information broker of yours the rumored Chimera slayer of Critias?"

"W1NG3D N1NJ4: YUP, THAT'S HIM!!"

"Admin: I just read his files the other day. Isn't he in the second year of high school?"

"W1NG3D N1NJ4: YES? SO?"

"Admin: Then correct me if I'm wrong, but if she is his classmate, isn't she about sixteen years old?"

"W1NG3D N1NJ4: I WOULD THINK SO, BUT I STILL DON'T KNOW WHAT YOU ARE GETTING AT... (‾ ～ ‾ ')"

"Admin: How old are you again?"

There was another short pause on the line that lasted for almost half a minute, then...

"W1NG3D N1NJ4: COME ON BOSS MAN! I WILL BE TWENTY IN THREE MONTHS! TECHNICALLY I AM STILL A TEENAGER! (#`д´)"

"W1NG3D N1NJ4: ALSO, IT'S JUST THREE YEARS!! IT'S NOTHING AT ALL!!"

It seemed like this approach didn't really achieve the desired effect, so I decided on a more-circumspect-yet-hopefully-more-effective one.

"Admin: So this girl is part of the Chimera slayer's social circle, right?"

"W1NG3D N1NJ4: I'M PRETTY SURE SHE IS. WHY? (¬_¬)"

"Admin: Give me a second to look up something..."

After typing that, I fiddled with my thumbs for a minute or two while pretending to be browsing the database entries, and after I figured I had him wait long enough, I wrote:

"Admin: I found it."

"Admin: Leonard Dunning's closest circle includes Joshua Bernstein, Judy Sennoma, Eleanor Dracis, Angeline Dionne, and, most importantly, Amelia Rhearn, the granddaughter of Lord Amadeus Endymonion of Critias."

"Admin: What did you say, what was your crush called again?"

There was radio silence for several seconds, and then...

"W1NG3D N1NJ4: BOSS, I THINK I HAVE TO LEAVE NOW AND THINK ABOUT THE MEANING OF LIFE. BYE. (╥ω╥)"

And with that, he disconnected from the server. When he did that, I couldn't help but let out a relieved sigh. I mean, I had nothing against the guy, and he had been pretty helpful on the Hub, but him getting involved with Ammy without knowing about her background sounded like another incident in the making. Not to mention, trying to snatch a love interest out of the harem protagonist's group was pretty much the recipe for landing in the role of an NTR love rival, which was statistically the most hated type of antagonist in fiction, and I wouldn't wish that fate on my worst enemy, let alone poor Ninja. Though on second thought, I *might* wish it on Crowey after all, but he's a special case.

Anyhow, now that I finally got that sorted out, I let out a pent-up breath, limbered up my fingers, and got ready to put to paper those shower insights... except I found that dealing with Mike made me forget practically all of them.

"Well, damn," I whispered under my breath, and after some pondering, I decided to forget about the whole idea and just watch a video podcast where four guys talked about hilarious, dumb, or hilariously dumb product reviews on the internet.

It was pretty much as brainless as entertainment went, but considering I was incapable of sleeping, I figured it was the second-best thing.

CHAPTER 3

PART 1

"Can I join this round?"

In retrospect, my question came out just a bit more sheepishly than I originally intended, but before I could correct my tone, my request was rebuffed with the bluntness of the business end of a war hammer.

"Denied," Judy declared in no uncertain terms, and I couldn't help but groan in disappointment.

"Are you sure we can't let him in?" my second girlfriend edged the first in my favor. "He looks so sad to be left out."

"No," my dear, if at the moment somewhat uncooperative, assistant shook her head as she pointed at me. "This is his punishment. The Chief is a cheater, so he will be excluded and has to sit on the sidelines and watch until he mends his ways."

"But I cannot mend my ways because I didn't cheat!" I objected, though I have to admit, if I was listening to my words, I probably wouldn't have believed myself, either. As such, after a brief moment of consideration I quickly amended, "Or rather, I only cheated a tiny little bit."

"Chief, stop digging yourself any deeper and deal already," Judy urged me on. We locked eyes for a moment, but it was a foregone conclusion that I couldn't win against her like this, so I decided to get back at her at some other opportune moment, and instead I let out a sigh and began shuffling the deck of cards in front of me.

"I do hope we don't have to sit through listening to *that* after every round," a certain annoying butler commented on the side, earning him a hearty chuckle from the head of the household.

"Come on, Grandpa! Let the kids have their fun!"

Sebastian sent an irritated glance in the direction of Abram, and he whispered back in a low, almost threatening voice, "What did I tell you about calling me grandpa in front of guests, lad?"

"Oh please!" the Dracis patriarch dismissed him with a scoff. "We are all one big family, aren't we?"

"Not quite," Lady Emese jabbed at her husband before she took an elegant sip from her fancy crystal champagne glass, and then she used her free hand to point at me first, then at Judy, and finally she said, "While I acknowledge them, these two are not quite part of the family yet."

Now, this might be a bit of a tangent, but I couldn't help but make note of the fact that her glass was filled with Coke of all things, and her side of the table was jam-packed with various soft drinks, snacks, and sweets. There was such a huge mountain of them she was almost buried behind it all, but none of the other family members even batted an eye at the sight, so I figured it was her usual modus operandi. But back to the scene at hand: after being rebuked, Papa Dracis immediately doubled down on his previous claim.

"But they almost are, and it's all just a formality at this point, anyway!" Abram declared in a boisterous voice before he glanced at me in the company of a broad grin, a gesture I have long since learned to associate with him requesting support. Unfortunately for him, I was too busy shuffling the cards at the moment. Not that it stopped him from pointedly calling out to me in the form of, "Isn't that right, son?"

I gave the man a slightly annoyed look in return, but seeing how hard he was trying to maintain his upbeat grin, I ultimately gave up and answered, "It sure is, father-in-law."

The moment I said that, the middle-aged man's expression shone like that of an especially cheeky kindergartener who just got let loose in the vault housing the national candy reserve.

"You see, dear? Leo is already part of the family, and so is Judy! Isn't that right?"

There was a momentary pause in the discussion, as no one seemed to want to answer his rhetorical question, but then thankfully Sebastian intervened by diverting the flow of the conversation with a declaration aimed at me.

"My boy, if you dare to follow the lead of this foolish descendant of mine and attempt to call me something puerile, such as great-grandfather-in-law, in a vain attempt to garner endearment, I promise I will remove you from the premises in an instant, most likely through the windows."

"Oh, don't worry, old man," I answered with the finalized v1.0 of my roguish grin. "I can assure you that I would sooner try to squeeze rock until delicious Russian caravan tea came out of it than to try to endear myself to you!" I scoffed at the mere idea, but since I accidentally reminded myself of something important, I quickly added, "By the way, I enjoyed your tea very much. When can I have another?"

"Everything in moderation, my boy," the incognito dragon told me with an inscrutable and ever-so-slightly-aggravating smirk. "Let's say I invite you for another cup once you find ten more cursed items."

"Oh my, does that mean you scrounged your collection just for me? How nice, I promise I won't break any of th—" I was just about to finish my cordial discussion with the old man when I was stopped in my tracks by something touching my leg. I glanced down and under the table, only to find Judy's left heel repeatedly tapping against my shin.

I sent my girlfriend a questioning glance, and she responded by flatly telling me, "Stop picking a fight with Sebastian."

It was only then that it dawned on me that this was most likely yet another one of her oddly harmless efforts of inflicting slapstick violence upon me. It was inexplicable, but kind of cute, as usual.

"I'm not picking a fight," I denied her baseless accusations and simultaneously sent a glance towards the butler before adding, "We're getting along swimmingly, like a house on fire, aren't we, old man?"

"The proper idiom is getting on like a house on fire, my boy, and as much as I hate to admit, I feel your choice of idioms quite apt in this situation."

"It's the burning part, isn't it?"

"Indeed," the old butler told me with a wistful expression. "It reminds me of the good old times, before we first met and I made a small mistake that haunts me to this day."

"Aw, don't be so sentimental, or I might be tempted to call you gramps just to make you stop."

Sebastian gave me a long, exasperated look and then buried his face into his palm and muttered something along the lines of, "I can't decide if that's better or worse than great-grandfather..."

Before I could respond, Elly let out a decidedly girlish giggle by my side, immediately short-circuiting my thought processes. When I directed my attention to her, she looked genuinely surprised by it for a moment, but then she quickly stated, seemingly to herself, "It's nice to see Leo and Sebastian getting along."

"How does that even remotely look like getting along to you?" my assistant asked with incredulity seeping through her usual deadpan demeanor. "Their words were practically seeping with barely disguised sarcasm."

For the record, they weren't. I mean, I can't speak for Sebastian, but I for one never tried to disguise sarcasm. Not that I had to in this case, as we were having a perfectly friendly conversation (by our standards, at least), so I had no idea what Judy was talking about.

"But... They *do* get along, don't they?" the princess stated just a smidgen less certainly, after which she looked at the butler and asked, "You said you get along, too, right?"

The old lizard appeared to be stumped for a good second, but then he forcefully cleared his throat, and through visible effort, he forced a considerably strained smile onto his face that obviously didn't reach his eyes.

"It is, without a shadow of a doubt, an undeniable fact that our personal relations have definitely improved in the recent past to some degree," Sebastian declared, and after spending a second to untangle his sentence, I tentatively nodded along. I mean, he wasn't wrong, per se...

"Could you please just deal already? We don't have all day," the lady of the house grumbled a little as she tapped her fingers on the table, and after one last shuffle, I graciously obliged.

Now, in case it wasn't entirely obvious yet, our little group was playing good ol' Texas Hold'em poker inside the Dracis mansion's spacious poker room. No, I'm not kidding; they literally had a room just for that. It even had a professional-looking round poker table with a green felt top and everything, and the rest of the room was decorated to invoke the look of a certain famous Las Vegas casino... or at the very least that's what Abram told me, and considering I'd never visited any casinos before, Las Vegasian or otherwise, I decided to take his word for it. If I had to give a quick description, it was uselessly posh, with way more mahogany wall paneling and crimson velvet highlights than good taste dictated.

To make a long story short, playing poker like this was apparently a long-standing family tradition among the members of the Dracis estate, and Elly insisted that being part of a session was pretty much the ultimate seal of approval we could receive from the family. The whole thing felt a little silly to me, to be honest, but I could imagine worse ways to spend a Saturday afternoon.

There was only one small issue with the game, though, namely the fact that I was barred from actually competing by Judy, who completely convinced everyone that I should not be allowed to play, as I was, to paraphrase, "A terrible, compulsive cheater who refuses to let anyone else win even one round." It was a gross overstatement, as the last time we played, I can clearly remember her winning *at least* one.... Or was it a tie?

Either way, because of her lobbying to Lady Emese in particular, I was relegated to the role of permanent bank and dealer. It was a thankless job, but someone had to do it, so I sacrificed myself for the greater good and wore the mantle with pride and honour. Any claims about my being bitter about it are false news spread by disinformation agents, and should not be trusted.

Anyhow, while I mused about this, I finished dealing the cards to everyone present and declared, "The starting bet is twenty. In the last round, the blinds went full circle, so we are starting from my left again."

The moment I said my piece, Elly and her mother put in the small and big blind bets, as if by reflex, and when they did so, everyone took up their hands.

"I call," Papa Dracis exclaimed with the polar opposite of a poker face, and after he threw in two tokens he continued with, "What were we talking about when the last game ended?"

"I fold." Sebastian decisively threw his cards into the corner before facing Abram and telling him, "I believe you were discussing the success of the 'streaming service,' as the boy called it."

At this point it was barely worth a mention, but he naturally used air quotes when he said that. I used my heroic willpower to stop myself from sending a snide remark his way, and instead I acknowledged Judy placing two tokens into the pot.

"You're right, Grandpa! Thanks!" I could see the old butler had something on the tip of his tongue, but before he could say anything, Papa Dracis barreled on, forcing him to settle for a defeated sigh. "As I was saying, the website has only been online for two days, and it already made back two-thirds of the initial investment we made for the server park and the staff! If things continue like this, we are going to make a net profit by the end of the week! It is absolutely amazing!"

"To be honest, I'm considerably more amazed by how you managed to put all my ideas into practice in such a short time."

Abram let out one of his patented hearty chuckles and told me, "Don't sell yourself short, son! Anyone with enough money and connections could do my part!" I wanted to bring up that those two things were pretty damn significant in and of themselves, but at the end of the day, I decided to just take the compliment and let him continue. "Your ideas were the ones that made all of it possible! I could never in a million years come up with things like the subscription model, or the streaming service! Ah, I also raise twenty!" There was a momentary lull in the conversation as everyone matched the bet and I revealed the next card, but then Abram abruptly asked me, "By the way, how did you even think of these ideas?"

My hand paused for a moment and lingered over the newly revealed king of spades, which made Judy unusually excited, so I figured she must've had at least a straight. Putting her literal poker face aside, my alleged father-in-law's question was one that I had already spent a lot of time thinking about.

Really, just where exactly did my knowledge and expectations for modern technology and conveniences come from? From the moment I awakened into this world on the first day of September, whenever I ran into a brick phone, a VHS tape, or a CRT monitor, I immediately and instinctively considered them old and outdated. That meant that, through some currently unexplained means, I was aware of a certain technological level, which wasn't present at the time I regained (or gained, depending on whom you ask) consciousness that morning, and I compared things to it.

Sure, the world, for another entirely unknown reason, quickly developed to meet my expectations, but it still left the original question open: Why did I consider the previous tech level outdated, and why do I consider the current one perfectly fine? Where did that initial value judgment and expectation come from? And why was it that it all plateaued at a certain tech level instead of going any farther towards holographic interfaces and androids, the occasional magitech fembot notwithstanding?

These were but some of the many nagging questions that routinely annoyed the heck out of me, but I could never get to the bottom of them because every single time I would think I could get some breathing room to spend with theory crafting and experimentation, the world always threw a wrench into my plans. In fact, considering how fairly uneventful my past couple of days had been (apart from the periodic *sentai* attacks on Josh and Co. and my evening strolls with Rinne), I had a slowly mounting feeling of apprehension in the pit of my stomach telling me that it was just another calm before the storm; it was only a matter of time before something annoying was about to happen again. Like an alien invasion. Or a tax collector showing up on my doorstep. Or worse yet, an invasion of alien tax collectors. Brrr...

But putting my Cassandran tendencies aside for a moment, I quickly retracted my hand and told Abram, "It wasn't a new idea, just taking an old idea and applying it to a new consumer demand to reach a modern solution."

The Dracis patriarch looked at me funnily for a moment, then he requested, about as sheepishly as I have ever seen him, "Can I use that line at the next shareholder meeting?"

"I don't mind," I replied with a shrug, earning me a toothy grin from our host and an impatient huff from his wife.

"Can we get on with the betting already?"

"Of course, dear." The Dracis patriarch seamlessly moved his smile over to my prospective mother-in-law, only to glance back at the new card on the table and immediately exclaim, "I raise forty!"

"It's not your turn..." I tried to object, only to get completely ignored.

"I call," Judy followed up by throwing her chips onto the pile practically at the same time Abram's landed.

"I fold." Elly decisively discarded her hand, followed by a moment of silence as Lady Emese pondered her next move.

"I call, and raise another forty," she proclaimed at last, followed by the clinking of tokens, and now it was Abram's turn to consider his options.

While we waited for him, I noticed that the lady of the house was subtly eyeing me. Small correction: she didn't actually start just now but had been doing so since we sat down around the table, but it was around this point that my patience began to dip into the red, so I sent her a questioning gaze and followed it up by an actual question.

"Is there a problem?"

"What makes you ask that?" she asked right back and crossed her arms in front of her ample chest while making sure her hand wouldn't be accidentally revealed in the process.

"I couldn't help but notice that you've been more irritable than usual," I told her straight as an arrow, tact be damned.

"Are you trying to tell me I'm usually irritable?" the lady of the house sent another question my way while her husband pushed a small pile of small denomination tokens into the pot.

"More or less."

It was at this point when I received yet another love tap under the table, followed by a borderline pouting scolding by my dearest assistant.

"Chief, stop picking a fight with Emese. Also, I call."

"I'm not picking a fight," I retorted with a small frown. "I'm just telling the truth. Or are you telling me she isn't high-strung?"

Judy seemed like she wanted to respond to my question, but Emese beat her to the punch after one last glance at her cards.

"I fold. Also, I admit that I might be a little more worried than usual," Mama Dracis told us while still looking at me in particular. "For the record, it would help if someone did something about the people routinely assaulting my daughter."

"... Is that why you're staring a hole into my forehead?"

"Yes," Lady Emese huffed. "I'm looking at you because I can distinctly remember you declaring that you had them in the palm of your hand, yet they are still running amok, completely unabated."

"Mom, please stop putting Leo in a corner," the princess sprung to my defense with a pout on her lips. "We all agreed to leave them be for now."

"You have?" she inquired, with her question still aimed at me by the looks of it.

"Yes, we have." My confirmation resulted in the lady of the house lowering her brows into a disapproving scowl, so I quickly elaborated, "We are maintaining the status quo for our own ends. If the ambushers become more trouble than they are worth, I already have the means to shut them down with extreme prejudice."

"Then why haven't you done so already?"

"I already told you," I answered, mildly exasperated. "The ambushers are just a front, and I'm still in the process of collecting evidence on the actual mastermind, so we discussed this with the rest of our friends and agreed to put up with the inconvenience for the time being."

"Easy for you to say when you are not the one who has to fight them."

The Dracis matriarch's verbal jab made me pause for a moment as I wondered how she even knew that, but it didn't take a genius to figure it out, so I sent a slightly miffed glance in the direction of my draconic girlfriend. The moment I did so, she immediately sprung to action in my defense, completely oblivious to the intent behind my gaze.

"Mooom! I told you it can't be helped! Leo's been sick the past couple of days, so he couldn't help us even if he wanted to!"

"You're sick?" came the next question, and it finally managed to unknot the brows on Emese's face.

"Just a little," I confessed. "It's nothing serious. I just overworked myself a bit. I'm still not on top of my game, but I'll live."

"Oh." After that eloquent response, the lady of the household fell silent for a second or five, but then she added, "If you're feeling unwell, should we postpone the..." Her words trailed off into an implicit silence, and I promptly shook my head.

"No need, I'll manage," I reassured her, and this time it was Elly who gave us an odd look.

"What are you two talking about?"

"Don't worry about it, princess, you'll see it soon enough," I told her with a wink and an enigmatic smile, and lo and behold, against all odds, it actually worked, and she let it slide with a fairly neutral "Oh, okay then" whispered under her breath. As such, I turned back to her mother and told her, "So just to return to the previous discussion, while I'd like to ask for your patience, if our silly ambushers are bothering you that much, you're free to intervene."

"Unfortunately, we're not. We've already issued an unofficial complaint, but Endymonion didn't move, nor did he explicitly tell us we can take care of things," she scoffed and then added, in a low voice, "There must be some internal politics involved."

"You're more or less correct, I suppose," I agreed and cut the conversation short as I glanced over to the last two players still holding their cards and asked, "Are you done betting?"

"I think so," Abram replied in an unusually tame voice, and Judy nodded with an affirmative grunt on her end. "Okay, so the current pot is..." My voice trailed off as I quickly calculated the value of the chips in the middle, and my brows involuntarily descended in a small frown as I asked, "Did you two throw in half of your funds during the first round of the game? Again?"

Abram only cleared his throat in what I figured was embarrassment, yet Judy simply nodded again, as if this was the most natural way to play the game.

"Okay then," I shrugged and revealed the last card.

"All in!" Judy declared before I even finished flipping the river card, and she simultaneously pushed in all her tokens.

"I call!" Papa Dracis exclaimed in kind and roughly shoved his pile of chips into the middle. I, for one, spent a second glancing between the two before I exhaled a tired sigh.

"Are you two going to do this in every single game?" They must have thought it was a rhetorical question, as they didn't bother to enlighten me. In the end, I let another groan escape my lungs and easily told them, "Fine. Please reveal your hands."

The words barely even left my mouth when Judy put her cards onto the table and stated, maybe a smidgen smugly, "Straight flush."

"Oh boy," Abram responded as he scratched the base of his neck with his free hand and reluctantly revealed his cards, which were... a pair...

"Did you seriously go all in on *that* hand?"

He answered my incredulous question with an embarrassed shrug and by muttering, "I was sure she was bluffing."

"You two have been doing this for three games in a row!" I complained as I pointedly smacked the deck of cards in my hands against the table a couple of times. "How are we going to play together if you two insist on knocking one of you out of the game in the first round every single time?"

There was no answer to my inquiry, so at the end of the day I stopped hitting the edge of the deck against the tabletop and proposed, "How about we take a break?"

"I believe it is an opportune time," Sebastian agreed with me, as planned, so I turned to my other collaborator.

"What do you say, Dormouse?"

My girlfriend gave me a flat look (or at least one that was flatter than usual), and commented, "I hate it that you decided to do this when I was winning."

"Decided to do what? Take a break?" Elly interjected with tiny, invisible question marks circling over her head, so I sent an eye signal to my other girlfriend, and after some more nudging, she finally rolled her eyes and stood up from the table.

"Don't worry about it; the Chief's just being weird as usual." Saying so, she walked over to the princess's side and began to tug on her blouse. "Let's go out and freshen up a little."

"Erm... okay, we can do that?" After saying that, Elly sent me a questioning look, but instead of saying anything I just gave her my best encouraging smile, and after a few long seconds of hesitation, she ultimately rose from her seat and followed my lovely assistant's lead.

Just before they left the room, Judy turned back for a moment and gave me a look that said, "You owe me one," as if I requested some kind of back-breaking task from her. Anyhow, I acknowledged her, and once I did, she quickly closed the door behind her. With that part of the so-called plan finished, I let out a pent-up breath and turned to the remaining three people in the room.

"All right, with my girlfriends out of the picture, I'd like to officially open the first annual 'What should I gift Elly for her birthday?' brainstorming session."

"Oooooh, so that's what this was all about!" Abram exclaimed as he did that thing where he dramatically dropped his fist into his open palm.

"More or less," I responded with only mildly faked modesty. "I asked Judy ahead of time to distract Elly for a while. Since her birthday is coming up soon, I figured the time was nigh."

"Wait, dear? Did you know about this?" Abram asked his wife, and she nodded without any reservation.

"Yes. Judy told me about how Leonard wanted to discuss something to that effect today."

"What about you, Grandpa?"

He turned to the old-and-at-this-point-fairly-drained butler, and he told him, "Yes. The boy and I already discussed the plans for today ahead of time."

"So I was the only one who didn't know?"

He looked a little confused by his exclusion, so I decided to just straight-up tell him, "No offense, dad-in-law, but we all concluded that you'd probably let it slip if we let you in on the secret."

There was a moment of silence, but instead of continuing the discussion, Abram only let out a chuckle and declared, "Dad-in-law! I like that!"

This announcement was followed by yet another, this time even longer pause, right until Mama Dracis let out a defeated sigh and turned to me again.

"So you wanted to ask us for advice on what to give her?" she asked me with just a hint of curiosity in her voice, and she was apparently quite surprised when I shook my head.

"No, actually, I already have a gift in mind; I just need your cooperation."

"Oh?" The Dracis matriarch did a perfect single-eyebrow raise at me and inquired, "What exactly do you need our help with?"

"I'll tell you in a moment," I responded by flashing a toothy grin at her, after which I began to clean up the poker table by moving the chips and the cards out the way. Abram and Sebastian also helped me a little, and in a couple of seconds we freed up the middle. "Okay, this should be good enough," I noted with a satisfied huff. "Sebastian, please take out the plot device."

"The what?"

"The spear, I meant the spear," I stressed, earning me an exasperated grunt from the old man.

"Why you keep refusing to refer to things by their proper names is a mystery I would very much like to solve one day," he grumbled, but then he reached under the table and retrieved a long object wrapped in a white cloth, possibly a simple bedsheet by the looks of it, and he placed it onto the table.

"Is that the...?" Abram mumbled in an uncharacteristically low voice, but his question became redundant the moment Sebastian unwrapped the thing and revealed the plain and intensely eye-straining Spear of Dragonslayicus, or whatever.

"Long story short," I began as I stood up and slowly rounded the table, "I knew that Elly's birthday was coming up soon-ish, but I couldn't think of a good gift. I mean, what can you give to a girl who has it all? But then, due to a recent discovery, I realized there *was* something after all." By the time I reached the end of my not-at-all-awkward speech (which I may or may not have written up in advance for dramatic effect), I stood in front of the seated Emese. I looked her in the eye, and after taking a deep breath, I softly asked, "Ma'am? May I take a look at your wound?"

PART 2

"It's smaller than I expected," I mused as I looked at the neat white line on the right side of Emese's lower back, just under the kidneys. At the moment she was standing with the help of her husband, and she looked supremely embarrassed, probably because of the way her pants were pulled down a little so that I could take a good look at her scar while I was crouching behind her.

After observing her already-healed wound for a moment, I asked, "Does it still hurt?"

"A little," she told me in a low voice.

"According to the doctors, the injury caused by the spear damaged her pelvis and grazed the sciatic nerve," Sebastian supplied the details, and I hummed as if I had any idea of what he was talking about.

"And you actually threw an armoured guy across a table with an injury like that?" I asked as I gingerly touched the scar, earning me a hiss that sounded more surprised than pained.

"Adrenaline," she told me just a little bit sheepishly, then added, "At the time I didn't even realize how bad it was. I thought it only hurt so much because I was in my draconic form, and it was only after the fight was over that I realized I couldn't move my right leg properly."

"Hmm..." I let out a suitably brooding sound as I considered what she just said. "Does that mean that getting stabbed didn't disrupt your transformation?"

"No, it just hurts," she told me curtly.

"So the curse of the spear doesn't directly prohibit transformation," I stated as I stood up. "Does that mean you could transform if you wanted to right now?"

Mama Dracis hurriedly pulled up her pants to cover her skin, and only then did she tell me, "I tried to do that in the past, but when I do, it hurts a lot. Not just the wound, but my whole body feels like it's on fire, down to my bones. It's a thousand times worse than usual."

"Hold on," I halted her explanation with a raised palm. "Please don't tell me you are in constant pain..."

"Not constant," she told me while gesturing for Sebastian to get her wheelchair, but I once again stopped them by shaking my head, so after sending me an annoyed glance the lady of the house dourly stated, "It *is* nerve damage, and it tends to flare up at the most inopportune of times."

"Then I suppose we best do something about it," I told them with a (hopefully) reassuring smile as I crouched down once more. Abram was just about to make her wife's scar visible again, but I told him, "No need, I can work through the clothes. I just needed to know where exactly the wound was."

After saying that, I took a deep breath and placed my hand on Emese's back. I couldn't see any magical glow around her scar, but that didn't mean there was nothing to be done, so I gently poked the area with my phantom limb, aaaaand... there was no reaction whatsoever. That wasn't a good start.

However, it was too early to throw in the towel, so I took a deep breath and reached deeper, at least metaphysically speaking, which mainly felt like I was swimming in a river of syrup in a completely black space that tasted like iron and dried coconuts, until I reached Emese's core, so to speak. I forced down the slowly rising sensation of nausea by slowly counting to ten, and then I took a closer look at the object I was observing.

The best way to describe it would be to say that it was a giant, multi-layered ball of yarn the size of a family sedan, with each layer composed of thousands upon thousands of small, constantly shifting two-dimensional filaments that simultaneously looped upon themselves and at the same time connected to one another and yet reached into the infinite distance at the same time. In short, it was really trippy.

Now, the last time I attempted to touch the core of something, it resulted in me getting an absolutely terrible headache and a giant cacophony of mugs, so this time I was considerably more cautious in the endeavor.

As such, I steeled my nerves and ever-so-lightly poked said core, and even that was enough to fill my poor brain with a flash flood of weird, organic, and decidedly non-Euclidian information. Maybe it was because I was already a little more familiar with this kind of phenomenon due to my previous exposure to this space that makes no sense, but I managed to keep my calm and cut the connection. For the next couple of subjective minutes, the ever-so-helpful part of my mind that was at least somewhat familiar with these things organized the information I gleaned from the experience, and while I had no proper words for what I'd just learned, it kind of felt like a piece of some enormous mathematical equation, except with colours instead of numbers and angry koalas instead of symbols. I know that doesn't make a lick of sense, but at this point it would probably make less sense if it did.

Anyhow, this didn't really help me with the task at hand, but I'd come too far to turn back now, and since there was thankfully no sign of the infernal headache so far, I decided to keep poking the core in front of me until I could find something useful.

As far as my personal perception of time was concerned, I was doing this for a solid hour before I decided to take a break. In that time, I had managed to conclude that the different layers corresponded to stuff like the body, the unconscious mind, memories, history, relationships, current thoughts, and all kinds of other stuff that was constantly cross-referenced between the layers and ultimately formed a coherent whole which was, in this case, a person.

If I had to make an estimate, I would've said that if I wanted to completely map out all the layers of the core, it would have taken me a solid month or more, though I once again had a nagging feeling that I was doing things in an incredibly inefficient way, and if I was doing this properly, I could do it all in seconds and then freely turn her into a pterodactyl with a monocle and a top hat or something. While I found that image somewhat amusing, another part of me was quite vehement about that being an extremely bad idea and one that I shouldn't even consider as a joke, and it was so oddly reasonable I had to wonder if I had developed a tiny little Judy in my head.

Jokes aside, once I figured out where I should be searching, I started combing the layer responsible for the body of my patient, so to speak, and once I zeroed in on the target, it didn't take long to find the portion I was looking for. Once I digested that, I decided it was time to take a proper break, as my brain was starting to feel like an overstuffed library bookshelf with the catalog missing, so I slowly withdrew my phantom limb, and after going through the whole swimming-in-a-nauseating-syrup-river thing in reverse, I let out a huge, pent-up breath and almost fell on my ass in the process.

Thankfully I managed to regain my balance in the last second, though not before Sebastian could reach out and support me by my shoulder. Insert a grumble about it being unnecessary and his acting thoughtful being creepy, et cetera. Anyhow, once I reoriented myself, I quickly asked, "For the record, how much time has passed?"

Papa Dracis and his hidden ancestor shared a meaningful look between each other and at long last he told me, "If you mean since you put your hand on her back, then about ten seconds."

"Really? That's surprising," I muttered as I shook off the old butler's hand and carefully rose to my feet. This meant that the time dilation was even more pronounced this time than when I was manipulating enchantments. Speaking of which, I gestured for the man behind me and asked, "Sebastian, could you please give me the spear for a moment? I want to cross-reference something."

To his credit, he didn't bother with asking any silly questions, and instead he immediately walked over to the poker table, picked up the spear, and came back to my side. I absentmindedly reached out towards it, only to get my right thumb zapped for my trouble, forcing me to jerk my hand back in the company of a series of stifled curses.

"... with a bloody grapefruit spoon!" I ended my swearing session while shaking my hand until the feeling returned to it, and only then did I notice that both Abram and Emese were looking at me funnily, which was actually fairly understandable. More alarmingly, the old man was giving me a look that said he was actually expecting something like this would happen and he found it really amusing, so I sent him a silent glare in return before I faced the other two and excused myself by saying, "Sorry, but this oversized toothpick really seems to hate me for some reason. Just give me a moment."

After saying so, I reached out once again, this time already prepared for the shock, and I firmly grabbed onto the weapon and took it out of Sebastian's hands, only to then swiftly smack it against the floor a couple of times, startling my hosts in the process. It took a good four whacks to stop the spear from resisting, plus two more, just for good measure, and once it did, I faced Emese again and told her, "Sorry for the intermezzo; let's continue."

"I'm no longer sure this is a good idea," Mama Dracis whispered under her breath as I crouched down again.

"Don't worry, dear. Leonard knows what he is doing... I think...?"

I ignored Abram's anemic efforts of coming to my defense, and instead I once more focused on the task at hand. First, I quickly glanced at the magical innards of the spear in my hand, and once I peeled away all the superfluous bits and pieces surrounding the core enchantment, I spent some time memorizing the curse parts of its effects. It took a considerably longer time and much more effort than I'd originally planned on, as the part of my mind that was inexplicably clued into the workings of my powers (and yet refused to share, the git) kept throwing up red flags at every turn and stopping me from manipulating even the slightest details.

Still, after I felt confident enough, I withdrew from the enchantment and turned to my prospective mother-in-law again, then I warned her, "I'm going to try something. I have no idea whether or not it will hurt, so please bear with it for a moment."

She only gave me a determined nod, her mouth set in a thin line as she no doubt clenched her teeth in preparation for whatever I was about to do. I also took a deep breath to focus my attention and dived right back into her metaphysical representation of extra-dimensional non-Euclidian space or something.

Once I reached her core and found the relevant bit, I began to slowly and meticulously comb through her... well, I wanted to say *data*, but that just didn't feel right. Calling them just *strings* also felt wrong. In the end, I decided on *records*, at least until I found a more apt designation for the phenomenon I was reading at the moment. Maybe I should ask Judy later, I mused as I continued to work, only to stop the moment I found something.

"Jackpot," I... well, I didn't *say* it because I was disembodied at the moment, yet the word that somehow emanated from me seemed to send waves through the very fabric of the geometrically impossible space I currently occupied. It kind of freaked me out for a moment; I was honestly worried I might've broken something. After waiting for some time for the waves to die down, I let out an implied breath of relief and decided not to do that again anytime soon.

Anyhow, back to the thing I found: If I wanted to describe what it was, it was kind of like an imprint the spear's enchantment left on Emese's body. It was not immediately obvious at first glance, but more like how the west coast of Africa and the east coast of South America roughly fit together because they used to be part of the same supercontinent.

Putting my analogies aside, I focused my attention on this imprint, and once I isolated it from the rest of the records, I attempted to interface with it through the supernatural stratum, only to get shouted at by the back of my own brain, as if I was trying to jump into a bonfire or something.

Okay, so the direct approach didn't work. Apparently, just like the spear itself, this wound was a plot device that I wasn't supposed to touch, and the knowledgeable corner of my mind made it quite obvious that trying to do so was a really, really bad idea. Unfortunately, I'd already made a promise. Not to mention, I wasn't exactly well known for following rules, even if they were rules set by me. As such, I attempted to analyze the curse once again, against my own judgment, because I decided so, even though I really didn't want me to do it. Man, I was confusing...

After doing a lot of skirting, nonintrusive probing, and using the other half of the enchantment from the spear as a reference, I managed to put together a rudimentary map of the curse. Or rather, it was more like a diagram? Like one of those wiring ones... or maybe like a circuit board? I could probably spend an hour trying to describe this confusing thing and still couldn't make it sound like it made sense, so let's move on to the meaty part of the discovery: the curse was actually really rudimentary in its execution.

Its goal of disabling the draconic transformation was really obvious even from a single glance, however, for some absolutely baffling reason, it didn't actually inhibit the actual process of the physical changes, but instead it overwhelmed the nervous system with signals to stop the victim from completing the transformation. I had no idea why that was the case, and I even wasted some time checking if maybe it was impossible to do it the obvious way, yet no matter how I looked at it, disabling the physical shape-shifting was in no way more difficult than the option they ultimately went with. Now granted, whoever enchanted this weapon probably didn't have access to the supernatural stratum the way I did, but it was still a pretty circumspect way to achieve the same goal.

Furthermore, the longer I looked into it, the more baffled I was by the imprint. It also inhibited any healing relying on the *essence of the dragon* (there was that oddly specific tag again...), but what was the point of doing so when the victim couldn't transform in the first place? Not only that, it had an entire set of anti-tampering and security measures interwoven into the entire imprint, none of which actually tied into any other parts that would lead to adverse effects upon breaking them. It was as if someone installed a state-of-the-art security system in their house, but didn't link it to any alarms or the police. It was downright nonsensical.

In fact, looking at the curse as a whole, it reminded me of a single term: spaghetti code. It's a programming term for convoluted source codes where, usually due to multiple iterations of the code being built on top of one another, the end product ends up a tangled mess. What I was looking at felt pretty much the same, as if someone took some already-existing enchantments and effects, smashed them together, and once they confirmed that it worked they moved on without trimming off the unneeded parts or checking for errors... And *that* gave me an idea.

Once I had that, I immediately jumped back into the work without any further ado and began to analyze the wiring diagram in front of me. My goal was simple, yet really difficult at the same time: breaking the curse would've been fairly easy, and it wouldn't have caused any side effects due to the disconnected safety seals, yet doing so was something that at this point I knew was a bad idea as firmly as I was sure the sun was rising in the east. However, just like with the spear, my aversion to manipulating it only applied to doing so with my phantom limb, not by other means. What other means did I have at my disposal? To put it bluntly, I was planning on simulating the supernatural equivalent of a system crash by subtly tweaking things in a way so it would look like the curse collapsed on itself due to its terrible coding.

Of course this was infinitely easier said than done, but I absolutely relished the challenge, and the more absorbed I became in the process, the more I felt in sync with the part of me that seemed to have some form of knowledge about these things, and before I knew it, I actually managed to find a couple of strings that looked perfect for the job. I double-checked everything, just to be sure, then triple-checked my double-checks to be extra sure, and only then did I carefully extend my ethereal appendage and slowly, ever so slowly, tied together a few of them, all the while on the lookout for any changes or red flags popping up somewhere.

The whole process felt like it took ages, even with the apparent time dilation, but once I was done and did a quadruple-check, just to be on the safest side, I pretended to exhale a breath of relief and slowly withdrew from the meta space I was in, and I once again nearly fell on my butt in the process.

More alarmingly, when I regained my wits I noticed that I was drenched in sweat and my hands were slightly trembling.

"Well, this doesn't seem good," I muttered as I was subsequently hit by a rush of nausea and nearly fell backwards, my involuntary tumble once again stopped by the intervention of Sebastian.

"What happened? Are you all right?" At the moment Abram seemed to be torn between supporting his wife or coming to my aid, so I raised a hand to halt him and forced a smile on my face to show him I was okay. It apparently didn't work, as he only looked even more concerned, so I quickly cleared my throat, and with the unsolicited-yet-not-entirely-unwelcome help of Sebastian I successfully rose to my feet.

"I think I overdid it a little bit. Don't worry; I should be back to normal in a moment or five." My slightly shaky words still didn't seem to completely persuade them, so I decided to quickly change the topic by turning to Lady Emese and asking, "More importantly, are *you* all right?"

"I'm... fine, I think," she muttered while looking at me like I was a ghost or something, but then she tried to completely turn around, only to let out a low hiss.

"Before you move around any more," I halted her with a raised (if slightly trembling) finger, "First try to transform."

She was confused for a moment, but after some more wordless urging using my patented brand of eyebrow wriggling, she hesitantly took a deep breath while still supported by Abram. That soon changed as her whole body abruptly shuddered, and with a surprised gasp, she took half a step forward, accompanied by a series of ripping sounds as her clothes couldn't handle the physical changes of her transformation, and I swear to god, I nearly got my eye poked out by a button flying off her outfit.

After a short-yet-long second, the previously pale and somewhat-frail-looking lady completely disappeared. In her place stood a tall, fit woman with a full set of horns adorning her head and a long, muscular tail trailing behind her, and as she straightened herself, a pair of large, leathery wings sprouted from her back, completing the draconic look... and nearly knocking down the ceiling lamp in the process.

Mama Dracis let out a surprisingly girlish yelp and pulled her wing back, but in her hurry she managed to whack her husband right in the face with her other one. Then, in a spectacular demonstration of slapstick chain reaction, Papa Dracis fell back and into one of the chairs, which then immediately buckled over backwards, and he landed with a meaty thud.

For lack of anyone else, I sent a deadpan glance at Sebastian, and the old man's expression perfectly mirrored mine. Sometimes the oddest of things could make the strangest bedfellows, I supposed.

In the meantime, Emese regained her balance and finally noticed what happened, and she immediately rushed over to her husband's side, seemingly without any thinking.

"Ah, darling! I'm so sorry, I didn't think I... I..." She came to a stuttering pause as she looked down at her own two legs, and after glancing at the man still lying on the floor, she muttered, "I can... walk?"

"You can walk!" Abram immediately repeated after her as he jumped to his feet and grabbed his wife by the hips. "Are you all right? Does it hurt anywhere?"

"I'm... I'm all right!" she beamed at her confused husband and suddenly hugged him with all her might. "Nothing hurts! Absolutely nothing!"

Then she laughed. It was a burst of pure, clear laughter, like spring water bubbling up from under layers and layers of silt, determined to wash them all away, and it was answered by a series of relieved chuckles from the man hugging her with all his might. Emotions were running high in the room, and I would've been lying if I said I wasn't a little touched, but at the moment I still had to deal with the aftermath of my actions, so I gestured for the butler to take the spear from me. He did so without a word, and once my hands were free, I quickly grabbed hold of one of the chairs in the room and sat down before my legs could've decided they'd supported me for long enough already.

Once I took a seat I immediately took several long, deep breaths, and successfully managed to get both the feeling of vertigo and the trembling under control. While I did that, Sebastian looked over me with considerable interest (and maybe just a hint of concern) in his eyes, and he only spoke up when he deemed I was not going to die on the spot.

"May I ask how you did that?" he asked me while using his head to gesture towards the elated couple, who in the meantime has moved on to kissing each other in relief. I saw no harm in explaining things to him, so I said:

"In short, I've short-circuited the part of the curse that makes the draconic transformation hurt. The rest of it is unfortunately still intact, but I figured being able to walk on her own two legs was the most important part to accomplish first, so I decided to go for that."

"So she is not fully healed?"

"Unfortunately no, but I'd say if she kept transforming back and forth a couple of times every day, it would soon wear the curse down to the point where her injuries should start healing."

"Truly?"

"I suppose. Sadly I have no idea of the timescale, and I'm too exhausted to check, but hopefully she shouldn't need her wheelchair anymore by the time Elly's birthday rolls around."

"Mom?"

I blinked in surprise as a new voice entered the fray, and I glanced over to the source. There, I found the princess frozen in the doorway, her eyes as wide as saucers as she was looking at the scene in front of her. Once the enthusiastic lovebirds realized their daughter was in the room, they quickly untangled themselves, and when that allowed Elly to take a better look at her mother, she let out a shocked gasp and she much less walked than leaped over to her side.

"Mom! You are... What happened!?"

While the two were reunited, in a certain sense of the word, my dearest assistant also made her way into the room and walked over to me. Once she got within earshot, I sent her a rueful glance and told her, "You had one job, Dormouse. One, single, job."

"It couldn't be helped," she answered with just a hint of sulkiness in her voice. "How was I supposed to stop her coming in when you made such a ruckus?" I wanted to tell her that she should've improvised or something, but before I could do so she suddenly leaned closer to me. "Chief, you are pale as a sheet. What happened?"

"The usual," I told her with a disinterested shrug. "More importantly, we should—"

I got exactly that far when my dodging senses suddenly flared up and tried to have me dive out of the way. As it would happen, I wasn't exactly in the right shape to do that, so instead I had to take the full brunt of a blonde comet colliding with my chest in a flying tackle, nearly blowing me off the chair if not for Judy's support. Once the stars finally stopped circling around in my vision, I glanced down, and unsurprisingly, I found the princess giving me an enormous, rib cage–cracking bear hug.

"Thank you, Leo. Thank you..." she whispered to me between sniffles.

I glanced over at her parents, then at Judy at my side, and I ultimately tussled her hair a bit and told her, "Happy birthday in advance, I suppose."

My words only seemed to crack the dam open even wider, as she went from sniffles to outright sobbing and she squeezed my chest even harder. It was actually hurting quite a bit, so I quickly sent a pleading glance at her parents. Regrettably, probably because of their emotional state at the moment, they completely misunderstood my intent, and instead of helping me with my predicament, Lady Emese walked over, lowered herself to one knee by my side, and proceeded to hug the both of us at the same time.

"Thank you. I am forever in your debt," she told me, her expression telling me that she was also just a hairbreadth away from breaking out into sniffles.

"You're... welcome..." I squeezed out the words, and was just about to request that maybe, if possible, she could stop the situation escalating any further, but then all of a sudden we were all trapped in an even bigger hug, as Abram sneaked up behind me (which wasn't a small feat, considering the man's size) and he swept all of us up in his arms, which incidentally also included Judy.

With that, there was only one person in the room I could turn to, as insane as the thought might've sounded, yet when I peeked at him between the arms and heads that composed the ball of bodies that currently encased me, Sebastian only gave me an odd look. Then, after locking gazes with him for several seconds, he let out a sigh, rolled his eyes, and then said, "If you insist..."

Then he walked over and joined the group hug by holding onto Papa and Mama Dracis.

Damn it, old man, that wasn't why I was looking at you!

By this point the emotions in the room had once again reached their boiling point, with both Elly and Emese bawling their eyes out, Abram laughing like madman, and Judy... well, she was mostly just snuggling up to me like a well-fed cat. And then there was I, trapped in the middle of all of this and feeling... well, not too horrible, considering the situation. In fact, in some ways it was surprisingly cozy. It was different than when I cuddled with Judy and Elly, and it felt, for lack of a better word, wholesome.

I could've done with slightly less snot on my shirt, though, but then again, no family is perfect. Mine was at least unique.

PART 3

"... and that's why I literally can't go around patrolling with you today," I explained in a low, neutral voice, just like how you would describe something to a child, and just as expected, Mountain Girl let out a disappointed huff.

"Then how are we to track down and slay the horrid creatures of the—?"

"Please, stop," I pleaded to her with my palms raised. "It's cold out here, I'm having a migraine, and I just want to go home. I promise I'll hunt with you once I feel better, so just let it go this one time, okay?"

I kid you not, she actually puffed up her cheeks like she was a chipmunk. I admit that, if Judy, Elly, or even Snowy was doing the same, I would've probably found it super-adorable, but since it was our resident annoying monster huntress, I could only groan in response.

At last, after spending nearly half a minute staring at me in silence, she let her shoulders slack a little and she told me, "Very well. We shall go and scour the rotten underbelly of the city for the trails and tracks of the vile fiends of the underworld! All alone!" After saying her piece, she dramatically turned on her heel and took a few steps away from me, only to stop, turn back, and declare in a sulky voice, "We are going to unearth the greater fiend, and then we massacre it, and then we drench the streets with its lifeblood, and you're going to miss it, and you're going to be sorry!"

"Um... Good luck?"

"Onikiri wants you to know that you are the worst and a prepubescent penis."

"A prepubescent what now?" I muttered in response to her unusual insult, but instead of answering me, she let out another huff and dashed away, leaving me all alone in the park. For a moment I couldn't decide if I should shake my head or let out a groan, but in the end I decided not to waste my time on either of those options, and instead I quickly made my way over to the closest (and inexplicably clean) public toilet in the park, hid myself in one of the stalls, and quickly Phased back home.

"Welcome back!" I was immediately greeted by Snowy as I appeared in the living room. I still remembered how she would freak out every time I appeared in front of her, but by this point she was totally used to it. Humans (or in this case, Abyssals) are really adaptable creatures, I supposed.

Anyhow, she quickly bounced over to my side and helped me slip out of my coat, and I belatedly realized that this time she wasn't wearing her maid outfit. Instead, she was sporting a pretty stylish ensemble, including a puffy white blouse, a black skirt, stockings, and even some simple jewelry in the form of a bracelet and a thin silver necklace. I was actually a little baffled by that for a moment, but then my poor, overexerted brain finally managed to connect the dots and I remembered that she told me in the morning that she was invited over to Angie's place for a movie night and a sleepover.

I checked the clock, and it was a little before six in the evening, so I told her, "Shouldn't you get going soon?"

"I already called a cab," she answered in an upbeat voice as she left the room with my coat in hand, and when she returned empty-handed she added, "It should be here soon."

"Good," I said with a nod. "You know the rules, right?"

My sister gave me a determined expression and told me, while counting on her fingers, "Be a good guest, be respectful to her parents, don't do anything Judy would be mad about, and... um..."

She seemed to forget the most important part, so I gently patted the top of her head and said, "... and have fun."

"Right, that's the one," she murmured with a smile, and I couldn't help but tousle her hair even harder for a moment.

"Awawa! Don't! You're going to make my hair all ruffled!" I stifled a chuckle and stopped messing with her hair, just in time to hear the horn of a car from the driveway, which immediately perked her up. "My cab is here!"

"Nice timing," I said as a used my now-free hand to rub my chin. "What would've happened if I came home a little later though?"

"I would've waited for you, obviously," Snowy told me with a twinkle in her eyes as she headed to the entryway. I followed after her and watched as she put on her boots and her coat in record time, then, after making sure she got everything, she beamed at me and gave me a small wave. "I'm off!"

"Have fun." I waved back, and five seconds later she was already in the cab.

The moment she left, I let out a groan worthy of the history books as my shoulders involuntarily drooped. I didn't want to make her worry, so I toughed it out in front of her, but I was already feeling worse than the last time I overexerted myself with the enchantments. I didn't know if it was because mucking with the curse and the core and what have you the way I did was just that much more exhausting, or because I hadn't fully recovered from the previous stunt, but either way, at the moment I felt sick and tired like a three-legged workhorse.

Since there was nothing to do in the entryway, I went back into the living room and contemplated the idea of just sitting down on my comfy chair and putting my brain in standby mode. It was a tempting idea, but not a particularly productive one, so I shook it off and forced my legs to carry me up the stairs and into my room.

When I arrived, I immediately fell onto my bed and spread out on my back. It made me feel just a tiny bit better, though even that was a small mercy. Serves me right for trying to do something nice for someone else, huh?

Oh, who am I kidding? No matter how I sliced things, I had to admit that I was a little proud of myself. Maybe not even just a little. I mean, I was sick as a dog because of it at the moment, but I did more or less cure my girlfriend's mother of a debilitating curse. That probably earned me a ton of brownie points, and Emese's attitude became noticeably warmer towards me... maybe even a bit too much to be honest. I couldn't help but wonder, were all Draconians this emotional, or was it just this family in particular?

I didn't dwell on the question for long, as it was obviously a moot one, considering that my sample size of Draconian families was exactly one. Speaking of sample sizes, I forced my body into a sitting position, and after taking a few slow breaths I dragged myself over to my PC.

To be perfectly honest, I really wasn't in the mood to take notes, but I figured doing so was as good as any other method for taking my mind off the fact that I was sick as a politician allergic to dishonesty. As such, I turned on the machine, limbered up my fingers a little, and once the desktop loaded in, I opened up the usual files and browser tabs.

When I paused for a brief moment while I considered where I should start, my attention was grabbed by the public chat room of the Hub flashing with a series of notifications. I'm not going to lie, I was a little apprehensive of joining in, but the more I thought about it, the more tempting the button looked in my eyes. I mean, when it came to these guys, it was about as likely to find something amusing as it was to run into an absolutely brain-numbing discussion, but after the poker party this afternoon, I was still in the mood for a bit of gambling. I ultimately pressed the button, and it opened up a new window with lines upon lines of text already in the logs.

"MoroseMoose: Hello, Admin."

"MoroseMoose: It's been a while."

The <Admin joined the room> notification barely showed up, yet I was immediately greeted by Moose. I reflexively wrote "Good evening," but then I remembered my cover story and quickly corrected myself.

"Admin: Good day, and yes, it's been a while."

"Admin: Where have you been?"

"MoroseMoose: Mostly work. It's been a busy week in the office."

"Admin: I can imagine, though I don't really want to."

"W1NG3D N1NJ4: HEY, IT'S ADMIN! HI!! (￣ ▽ ￣)ノ"

"Admin: Hello. I should have known you'd be online as well."

"W1NG3D N1NJ4: I HAVE A LOT OF FREE TIME BEFORE THE EXAM PERIOD STARTS! (—‿—)"

"W1NG3D N1NJ4: MORE IMPORTANTLY! ADMIIIIIN!!! (☆ω☆)"

I waited for a few seconds, as I was under the impression that he had something else to say, but when there was only radio silence, I decided to respond first.

"Admin: Yes?"

"W1NG3D N1NJ4: I THOUGHT ABOUT THE MEANING OF LIFE, THE UNIVERSE, AND EVERYTHING, AND DECIDED TO BELIEVE IN THE POWER OF LOVE!!!! (≧‿≦) ♡"

"MoroseMoose: ... I think you lost me there. What exactly are you two talking about?"

"Admin: Ninja has a crush, but she has a scary grandfather."

"MoroseMoose: Oh."

"MoroseMoose: I'm still lost, I'm afraid..."

"Admin: Don't worry, it's nothing important."

"W1NG3D N1NJ4: HOW CAN YOU SAY THAT?!?! (: ○ ⌄ ○ :)"

"W1NG3D N1NJ4: I'M SUPER-DUPER SERIOUS, YOU KNOW!?!? (>_<)"

"W1NG3D N1NJ4: I DON'T CARE ABOUT WHAT SOCIETY THINKS, EVEN IF IT'S A FORBIDDEN LOVE!!! I'M LIKE A MODERN-DAY ROMEO!!! ♡\(￣ ▽ ￣)/♡"

"MoroseMoose: You know that the play ended with both Romeo and Juliet dying, right?"

"W1NG3D N1NJ4: ARGH!!!"

"W1NG3D N1NJ4: WHY ARE YOU GUYS SO MEAN?!?! (#`Д´)"

"Admin: We are just teasing you."

"MoroseMoose: That's right. I mean, putting the drama aside, just how forbidden can this love be?"

"Admin: He's crushing on the Critias arch-mage's granddaughter."

"MoroseMoose: Oh."

"MoroseMoose: Well then, it was nice knowing you. I'll make sure to send some flowers for your funeral."

"W1NG3D N1NJ4: *SOB-SOB* o(￣﹏￣)o"

"Admin: How about we put teasing Ninja aside for a moment?"

"Admin: What were you guys chatting about before I logged in?"

"MoroseMoose: Can't you just scroll up and see it for yourself?"

"Admin: TL;DR."

"MoroseMoose: Fair enough."

"MoroseMoose: I was just giving a warning to Ninja."

"Admin: A warning about what?"

"W1NG3D N1NJ4: AAAAAA!!! THAT'S RIGHT!!! THE KNIGHTS ARE COMING!!! (((> <)))"

That gave me a long pause, but then I quickly typed in:

"Admin: Can I get a slightly less dramatic explanation, please?"

"MoroseMoose: I'll do it."

"MoroseMoose: You asked me to keep an eye out for any suspicious movements regarding the oathbreakers."

"MoroseMoose: In the last couple of weeks, there have been a number of attacks on their strongholds in Europe and in the East."

"MoroseMoose: Both sides suffered only minor casualties, yet all of their cells have gone underground."

"MoroseMoose: The last report before they went dark said that they would be moving their forces to Critias for some kind of operation."

"MoroseMoose: Since I knew Ninja lived on the island, I told him to be careful."

"W1NG3D N1NJ4: DON'T WORRY ABOUT ME! THEY MUST BE AFTER THE SCARY DRAGON PEOPLE IN THE CAPITAL!!"

"MoroseMoose: Do you have anyone you're not afraid of?"

"W1NG3D N1NJ4: HEY! SCARY THINGS ARE SCARY!! \\(° □ °1|1)/"

"Admin: That's a little unexpected. Are we sure they are moving in on the Dracis family?"

"MoroseMoose: Can't say for sure, but it's the most conservative assumption we can make based on the little information we have."

"W1NG3D N1NJ4: YEAH!! THOSE GUYS HAVE A HATE BONER THE SIZE OF A QUANTUM LEAP AGAINST THE DRAGON GUYS!!! (¬_¬)"

"MoroseMoose: A quantum leap is actually really tiny."

"W1NG3D N1NJ4: STOP NITPICKING, MOOSE!! YOU ARE MAKING ME LOOK BAD IN FRONT OF THE BOSS MAN!!1! (#`Д´)"

"Admin: Please stop fighting, you two. This could be serious."

"Admin: Critias is already a powder keg. Throwing the oathbreakers into that might lead to an incident that will make Cardhouse look like small potatoes in comparison."

"W1NG3D N1NJ4: GOT IT, BOSS MAN! I WILL BE TOTES SERIOUS NOW!!! (☆ω☆)"

"Admin: In that case, can I rely on you to gather intel on-site?"

"W1NG3D N1NJ4: DO I HAVE TO??? (̄ ᴧ ̄)"

"W1NG3D N1NJ4: NO, WAIT!! I COULD TOTALLY ASK THE INFO BROKER FOR THAT! THIS MIGHT WORK OUT GREAT! (♥ω♥)"

"MoroseMoose: How so?"

"Admin: Ninja probably wants to have an excuse to stay in contact with him."

"Admin: So that he would have more chances to meet with his crush."

"MoroseMoose: ... Is Ninja crushing on the information broker?"

"W1NG3D N1NJ4: NOOO!! STOP TEASING ME!! (` ω ´)"

"MoroseMoose: We will stop when it stops being funny."

"Admin: On a more serious note, I would prefer if you didn't rely on the Chimera slayer too much."

"MoroseMoose: Wait."

"MoroseMoose: The Chimera slayer of Critias is your informant? I thought you were allergic to scary people."

"W1NG3D N1NJ4: HE'S NOT SCARY!!... WELL, MAYBE A LITTLE, BUT HE IS ALSO REALLY COOL, AND HE HAS THESE COOL PIERCING EYES AND HE IS ALSO REALLY COOL!!"

"MoroseMoose: ... Are you sure you are not crushing on him?"

"W1NG3D N1NJ4: MOOOOOOOOOSE!!1!!ONE! (#`Д´)"

"W1NG3D N1NJ4: JUST YOU WAIT! ON THE DAY OF THE NEXT OFFLINE MEETING, I'M TOTALLY GOING TO KICK YOUR ASS!! (#`Д´)"

"W1NG3D N1NJ4: I KNOW KUNG FU AND STUFF!!! (#`Д´)"

"MoroseMoose: If I had boots, I would be quaking in them right now."

I really wanted to ask how (and why) these alleged elite Celestial field agents were having offline meetings, but considering what I'd recently learned about the Knights, I figured this question was be so low on my priority list it should be right next to dinosaur bones.

"Admin: Moose, where can I find the reports about the recent developments involving the oathbreakers?"

"MoroseMoose: I'll send the list over in a PM later."

"Admin: Good man."

"Admin: As for you, Ninja, I want you to keep an ear out and write regular reports."

"Admin: Also, I'm going to send a circular to all the assets on Critias and tell them to forward their reports to you for screening."

"W1NG3D N1NJ4: HOLD ON!!"

"W1NG3D N1NJ4: DOES THAT MEAN THAT I'M PROMOTED TO FIELD SUPERVISOR?!? (*°▽°*)"

"Admin: Informally. Do it well, and I will put in a couple of good words for you and we'll make it official."

"W1NG3D N1NJ4: YAAAAAAY!!! I LOVE YOU, BOSS MAN!!! YOU ARE THE BEST!! \(≧▽≦)/"

"MoroseMoose: So now you are crushing on Admin? How fickle of you."

"W1NG3D N1NJ4: MOOOOOOOOOOOOOOOOOOOOOOOOOOO OOOOOOOOOOOSE!!!!!! ٩(╪◉益◉╪)ﻭ"

It was at this point that I decided to leave the bickering duo to their own devices and instead I minimized the tab and leaned back in my seat. Once I felt suitably collected, I reached out to my phone on the desk and dialed my assistant.

"Hi, Chief. Do you feel any better?"

"Thank you for the question, but my malaise is the least of our problems at the moment."

"Did something happen?"

"Not yet," I stated, after which I shared with her the short version of what I'd just learned from the Hubbites. She listened to my explanation until the end, without a word, and as the finisher I asked her, "What's your opinion?"

"It sounds like foreshadowing."

I let a tired groan escape my lips and reiterated my previous question because apparently I wasn't clear enough the first time.

"I didn't ask in narrative terms, but whether we should warn Abram ahead of time."

"No, you asked for my opinion," she retorted with a huff. "I gave you that."

"... Okay, then let's hear that first, and then I would like to hear your advice on the second question."

"Certainly," she told me a smidgen smugly before she immediately adopted her usual, dry mannerism and expounded, "I believe that your interference with the *sentai* arc caused the narrative to start the next arc early."

"Don't you mean 'our' interference?"

"You were the one who insisted on avoiding the genre shift, you were the one who undermined Robatto, and you were the one who magically hacked the transformation devices," Judy countered in rapid succession, then after a self-satisfied huff she finished with, "As such, I wash my hands of this whole affair."

"You can't really. You are my assistant, so you are liable for any unforeseen consequences caused by our actions as much as I am. It says so in our contract."

"What contract?"

"The one where you agreed to all that. Did you think employment at our company was all sandwiches and no responsibility?"

"I don't like that. Can we change the contract?"

"Sure. Do you have the funds to pay back all the sandwiches you've earned so far, with interest, plus the contract breach penalty and the legal fees?"

"Why would I have to? I've never heard of any of this."

"In that case, my young lady, you should learn to read the fine print at the bottom. Insert villainous laughter here."

"Oh, the humanity. Woe is me. My current level of distress is at least three standard deviations away from normal."

"Insert continued villainous laughter here."

"... On second thought, can I pay you in kisses?"

"What is the current exchange rate on those?"

"I have no idea."

"Then come up to my office tomorrow, and we will discuss the terms."

"Okay." There were several long seconds of silence on the line, and then she told me, in her normal voice, "If you can joke around like this, I guess you must feel a little better."

"Oh, that? Nah, I still feel so deep under the weather I should be inside the Earth's crust. It's just that talking to you and hearing your voice makes me a little happy, and it helps me to ignore it."

Another short bout of radio silence ensued, and then my assistant softly told me, "That was unusually sweet of you. I'll take it."

"You're welcome," I answered as I couldn't help grinning, even though it was pointless to do so on the phone. With that, I considered our tangent over, so I cleared my throat and asked, "Seriously though, what do you think we should do with the info about the Knights?"

"If you ask me, you should—"

It was right at this moment that I suddenly picked up a strange, unfamiliar sound. It was kind of like marching band music or an anthem of some sort.

"Ooookay, this is weird. I have to put the phone down, Dormouse. I'll call you back."

I didn't wait for her answer; instead I quickly cut the call and rose to my unsteady feet in search of the source of the sound. I didn't have to look for long, as I quickly found it in the form of the old brick phone on the shelf at the back of my room. After I'd changed phones and carriers, I held on to the old one and kept it charged, just in case my theoretical parents or the like attempted to contact me. Which was apparently happening just now.

Odd and slightly disconcerting as it was, I still reached out towards the device, undid the simple keylock, and checked the caller ID. Surprise surprise, it belonged to the only unknown number in my old contact list, and the one I'd cheekily renamed to Mystery Number X on the very first day. I had attempted to call it a couple of times in the past, but I always got the stock "The number you are attempting to call is not in service" automated reply, so it more or less completely slipped my mind as of late.

I had a feeling that this call was fairly significant, so I took a deep breath in preparation and then pushed the little green button and raised the phone to my ear.

"Hello?"

There was a momentary buzz on the line, followed by silence, but just as I was about to call out again, there was a soft sound on the other side followed by the voice of a man, as deep as the Mariana Trench and huskier than an entire dogsled team combined.

"The time has come, brother."

He only said that single, insanely foreboding line, and then he immediately cut the line. I blinked in surprise as I slowly pulled the phone away from my face, and then I whispered, with all the eloquence I could muster at the time:

"Well... blimey, that was ominous..."

CHAPTER 4

PART 1

"All right. Preparations are complete," I declared as I dramatically rubbed my palms together. I was currently situated in the living room in the company of Judy, and for a change, I wasn't sitting on my favourite comfy chair but the couch. It was mainly so that she could sit next to me, since the previous arrangement of her sitting on my lap, while really cozy, was not exactly conducive to our current activity. Once I felt suitably prepared, I picked up the brick phone on the table, turned to my girlfriend, and subsequently told her, "Let's begin the operation!"

"I still think this is silly," my dearest assistant threw a bucket of cold water on my enthusiasm right away, and I couldn't help but shake my head in the face of her negativity.

"Come on, Dormouse; don't be like that! The plan is foolproof, and even if it doesn't work, we won't lose anything."

"True, but I think you have overcomplicated it," she told me, and after a momentary pause she added, "A lot," probably for extra emphasis.

"What? It's not overcomplicated," I denied just a touch defensively. "Let's go over it one more time: I pick up the phone, and I will dial Mystery Number X."

"That part is self-evident," she agreed with the usual nod in tow.

"Yeah. So then, once the line connects, I will do this." As I said that, I raised my left hand and extended my index finger, as if I was pointing at the ceiling. "And then, when I do this," I continued as I abruptly bent my finger, "You start shaking your melons. Simple."

Judy's brows imperceptibly sunk for a moment, and after a heavily implied sigh she raised her hands and asked, "I've been meaning to ask, but why do you keep calling these melons?"

Saying so, she shook the two maracas in her hands, making a distinct, sharp sound in the process and earning a confused glance from yours truly.

"I call them that because that's what the packaging says. Look." While I was speaking, I put the phone back onto the table, and then I reached over the armrest of the couch and picked up the discarded hard plastic package on the floor and showed it to her. "It says so right here: *Rumba melon childhood playmates. This will be a gift to give children the best. Clown. At home.*

Hurry up and collect! What is so hard to understand about that? It makes perfect sense to me."

My girlfriend rolled her eyes, snatched the package out of my hands, and after studying it for a second, asked, "Just where did you even find Chinese bootleg toys like...?" Her words trailed off as she took a closer look at the other side of the container, and instead she asked, with almost palpable levels of incredulity (at least by Judy standards), "What does *Unlimited joy makes children more lively and lovely! Infinite pleasure!* even mean, and what does it have to do with a pair of maracas?"

"Do we even really want to know?" I responded while shrugging my shoulders. "As for your previous question, I bought this at the same place where I got my fake mustache and wig during the let's-get-Snowy-an-ID operation."

"You bought this back then?" she uttered in surprise as she finally put the silly, multicoloured package covered in incomprehensible machine-translated garbage aside, and I once again shook my head.

"No, of course not. I got it this morning, not long before you came over."

"Good. I was afraid you wanted to do this so badly you bought these weeks in advance."

"Don't be silly, Dormouse. I didn't expect I'd get an ominous call from MNX yesterday, let alone a week ago. Speaking of which..." I took the package from her, threw it behind me, then I got hold of the phone again and extended my left index finger one more time. "So just to be clear: straight finger, silence, bent finger, artificial radio static noises."

"I got it," she answered, followed up by a quiet "I got it the first four times you told me. I still think it's silly," which I probably wasn't supposed to hear, so I pretended I didn't.

"Great. Let's get started then."

With that said, I took a huge breath, prepared myself, and dialed Mystery Number X. To my relief, the line actually connected, and there was even a ringback tone, so we'd already cleared the first hurdle. I held my breath as I waited for someone to accept the call on the other end, aaaaaand... the call was forwarded to voice mail.

I didn't let that discourage me, so I terminated the line and I immediately dialed the mystery number again. The same thing repeated itself: connection, ringback, voice mail. It was around this time that holding my breath became uncomfortable, so I let it out in the form of a sigh.

"Oh well. As they say, third time's the charm."

After I said that, I immediately dialed again, and one bated breath later... someone actually picked up the phone! I immediately signaled to

Judy with my eyes and made sure that my finger was straight as an arrow, and as much as she complained about it, she dutifully raised her maracas high and stayed alert, her eyes glued to my signaling hand.

"I told you not to call this number unless absolutely necessary," the deep, gravely, and still-completely-unfamiliar voice of a man answered my call with words that were practically dripping with annoyance. I took a deep breath, glanced at my assistant one last time, and then I promptly bent my finger.

"Hello? Are you there? The line is terrible, I can't hear a thing!" I spoke in a strained voice that was just on the verge of shouting, while at the same time Judy provided the background static to complement the illusion.

"What?"

"Did you say something? I can't hear you!"

"I said I'm here!" the impatient voice on the other side yelled into the phone, which signified the fact that he took the bait. It was too early to celebrate though, and so I continued with the information extraction.

"Oh, you're there! Finally! You called me yesterday, but I couldn't hear a word!"

"I called you to tell you it's time!"

"Whine? I'm not whining! I'm asking because the reception is absolutely terrible!"

"No, I said it is TIME!" he shouted so loudly it distorted his voice.

"Time? Did you say time?"

"Yes!"

"You want to know the time?"

"NO!"

"Then why did you say time?"

"I said IT. IS. TIME!"

"Oh... Time for what!?"

"For the operation!"

"What? I couldn't hear that! Are you getting a surgery?"

"No, not that kind of operation! It's the attack on the wyrmbloods!"

"Ooooooh! I get it now!"

"Good! Finally!"

"What? Did you say December!?"

"NO! I said FINALLY! How did you even mishear that?!"

"So the attack isn't in December!?"

"NO! It's as planned!"

"What?! I still can't hear you!? Is it in December or not?!"

"I said IT IS AS PLANNED! THE OPERATION IS ON THE THIRD OF NOVEMBER, AS PLANNED!!"

The man on the other side bellowed so furiously I wouldn't have been surprised if his voice damaged the tiny speakers in the phone. That meant that I was probably drawing this out a little too much, so I decided to wrap things up as soon as possible.

"Ah, I think I got it! You wanted to tell me that the attack on the Dracises is on the third of November, right?"

"Yes! That's exactly what I wanted to tell you!"

"Okay, I got it! Thanks! Also, we should change carriers! The reception on this island is shit!"

"I hear you, brother! I'm hanging up now!"

"Wait, did you say you can't hear me?"

"No, I said I'm HANGING UP THE PHONE NOW!"

"Aaaah! Got it!"

And just like that, the line was cut, and for some reason I couldn't help but imagine the guy on the other side slamming the receiver down so hard he not only broke the telephone but even the table it was sitting on, even though I logically knew he was probably using a mobile phone, as well. Anyhow, I turned to my girlfriend, who was still steadily (if not exactly enthusiastically) shaking her so-called melons, and after straightening my finger I told her, "You can stop now; he hung up."

"Did it work?" she inquired the moment the sound of the maracas died down, and I responded by giving her a huge nod.

"Waaaay better than expected," I told her with a not-at-all-cocky grin as I put the old phone away and leaned back in my seat.

"You can't be serious."

"But I am! He took it hook, line, and sinker."

"So?" I didn't really get what she was asking, so I responded with an inquisitively raised brow, at which point she clarified, "I couldn't hear the other end of the conversation because you made me shake these. What did you learn?"

"I think it should've been pretty obvious from hearing just my end, but if you insist: apparently there's going to be an attack on the Dracis family next week. In fact, since today is the twenty-sixth, it means it will happen the next Monday."

"Did you confirm that it's the Knights?"

"I didn't want it to be too blatant, but considering he called them wyrmbloods and what I learned from the Hub, I would say it's about ninety-nine percent certain." I paused for a moment to breathe there, and then I tentatively added, "That said, I think the fact that we discovered the exact date of an attack is the more important detail we must focus on. We should presume it was the Knights, just to err on the side of caution, and we're going to learn if it was them for sure when the time comes, anyway."

"True," Judy nodded as she scrutinized me, apparently waiting for me to broach a certain topic, but since I wasn't in a hurry to do so, she ultimately let out an impatient grunt and said, "Since you refuse to address the elephant in the room, I'll do it in your stead: Does this mean that you are related to the Knights?"

"Probably," I answered, followed by an ambiguous shrug. "I mean, I can't say for sure due to my amnesia, but the fact that someone calling me brother conveniently contacted me on my old phone just as I learned about how the Knights are coming to Critias is a bit too much to chalk up to coincidence."

"I agree. It would also explain the lack of a Knight in Joshua's harem."

"Please rephrase that."

"In Joshua's circle of acquaintances," Judy did so right away, much to my appreciation.

"Much better, thank you." After saying that, I let out a shallow breath and attempted to get my thoughts in order, resulting in the words, "I think there is more to it than that, though."

"What makes you say that?" Judy inquired, and before I knew it, she already had her phone at the ready.

"Well..." Instead of answering right away, I labouriously roused my aching body off the couch and began my usual routine of walking up and down while thinking, and only then did I say, "For one, while this new revelation tells us that I was probably linked to the Knights, I doubt I was one of them."

"Chief, you're tall, fit, know how to fight with medieval weaponry, and they called you brother," Judy interjected. "All of that makes it fairly obvious you are one."

"True, but at the same time, I have abilities that don't require magical artifacts to work, I can speak Faunish, I engage in Dominance to train, and the only available weapon that belonged to the Knights not only doesn't give me superpowers, it actively rejects me," I countered. "All that points to the fact that I'm probably not a Knight."

"If so, then why did they contact you?"

"If I wanted to give you an educated guess, it could be that before I lost my memory, I was something like an informant or a sleeper agent, not necessarily clued into everything, but called in for support when the situation demands it."

"Kind of like the assets of the Celestial Intelligence Network," Judy noted while typing so furiously I was afraid she would break the screen of her phone.

"Precisely what I was thinking of."

"That would still leave you with a connection to them, though, and wouldn't explain any of the other idiosyncrasies you mentioned before," she pointed out, eliciting a slightly flummoxed "Hrm" from me.

"I can't say much to that. I'm just as lost as you are."

"Noted," she said as she literally committed my words to her notes. "Putting your origins aside for a moment, what do you plan to do about the information about the attack?"

"What to do about that...?" I pondered aloud as my pacing came to a slow halt. "I spent a lot of time thinking about it last night, and I think we don't really have much of a choice in the matter. Unlike the *sentai* wannabes, the Knights mean business. We must warn Elly's family."

"I'm glad we agree on that," Judy approved without looking up from her notes. "What about Robatto?"

"Right, that," I muttered with no small amount of distaste as I resumed my pacing. "Considering the circumstances, we can't let them be any longer. We not only can't be sure of their motives beyond Lord Grandpa's vague plans, even though I've been observing them a lot, but considering they never used those Gigants against the group, nor did Lab Coat Guy or his android participate, we can't even be sure of their true combat potential. In short, they could prove to be a fatal distraction once the Knights also enter the picture, so we should try to sort them out before that."

"In other words, you want to neutralize Robatto before next Monday," Judy posited, and I nodded in agreement.

"Neutralize... that's a very tactful way to put it, but yes, that's the plan. Unfortunately, that means we'll have to confront Lord Grandpa on top of that, which is probably going to be a bit of a pain in the butt considering I still don't have enough demonstrable evidence to pin him down."

"And you want to do all that in the span of a single week?"

"Technically it's eight days, but putting pedantry aside, we don't have much of a choice, do we? I mean, the option of not interfering with the narrative and staying impartial observers has already sailed, so if we are going to meddle, we might as well do it swiftly and decisively."

"Is that your excuse for putting yourself in danger this time?" my dear assistant asked with just a tiiiiiny bit of an edge in her words, so I stopped once again and shook my head.

"Nope. We are going to do things slightly differently this time around."

My comment elicited an interested "Oh?" from my girlfriend, followed by the obvious question of, "Then what are you going to do?"

"I'll have Josh deal with Lab Coat Guy," I told her straightaway.

"How?"

"I... didn't quite work out the details yet, but it should be fairly straight-forward," I elucidated to her while doing my best to project confidence. "It mainly involves getting Josh and Co. to storm Lab Coat's hideout, catch him, and then bring him in front of Lord Grandpa."

"What if he denies his involvement?"

"Oh, I have a separate plan for that," I told her, this time with genuine confidence and just a little bit of mischief.

"Does it involve doing something dangerous?"

"It shouldn't. In theory, at the very least."

"... If you are trying to reassure me, you are doing a terrible job."

"Come on, Dormouse! I'm serious here. I learned my lesson, and I'm only going to make my move when everything is perfectly safe. Trust me."

My girlfriend looked me in the eye for a second, then stated, "That's slightly better. You're learning."

"Thanks, I think?" I muttered in response to her compliment, but then I shook my head and declared, "Anyhow, it's not something I can do while I still feel like ten pounds of wet socks stuffed into a five-pound bag."

"Ew."

"You're welcome for the mental image," I said as a flashed a grin at my girlfriend, and then I added, "But putting that aside, our primary concern should be warning Abram, and doing so in a way that it wouldn't raise suspicion. I mean, we can't be sure that I used to be the only sleeper agent on the island."

"That's right. If they notice that the Dracis family is preparing to defend themselves, they might realize that there was a leak, postpone their plans, and then we would be back to square one."

"Precisely. And that's why I'm going to Phase over there and discuss this in person."

"When?"

"As soon as possible."

After hearing my answer, Judy glanced over at the clock (which was probably done for my benefit, as she could have just as easily checked the time on her phone). It was just a little after ten in the morning, so I wasn't exactly late from anywhere, yet once she confirmed the time, she let out a determined huff and put her phone away.

"Be back by lunchtime."

I observed the unnecessarily resolute glint in my dear assistant's eyes, and after comparing it to the last time I had seen her like that, I quickly drew my conclusion.

"... Do you plan to cook?"

"Yes," she confirmed as she stood up. "You're sick, and sick people need home cooking to recover faster."

"I'm not entirely sure that applies to enchantment-tweaking-induced exhaustion as well, but I'm not going to stop you."

"Don't even try," she told me in no uncertain terms as she headed towards the kitchen.

I didn't even bother to try to stifle my chuckles, and once she was out of the room, I took out my phone. Before anything else, I quickly checked on Abram using Far Sight, and I found him in his mansion, or to be more precise, his study within the mansion. I had little trouble recognizing the room even though I had never been there, considering the place was stacked almost to the ceiling with boxes upon boxes of music records, including actual honest-to-goodness vinyls.

I only spent a few seconds gawking at the sight before I moved on to my actual target and confirmed that there was no one else around. As such, I quickly returned to my body and dialed the number Papa Dracis gave me a while back. After a few short seconds the line connected, and I was greeted by my self-described father-in-law's usual enthusiasm.

"Hello, son! What do I owe the—"

"Hello, Abram," I cut in before he could start babbling. "Can I ask you a little favor?"

"Depends," he answered. "If you ask for my permission to elope with my daughter, I'm afraid I must say no! Everything else is fair game!"

"I just want you to walk over to the door and stay there for five seconds."

"... I can do that!" he declared, and a quick Far Glance told me he did just that. "I'm here! Hello?"

Instead of answering him, I put my phone away, and after waving at Judy in the kitchen to let her know I was leaving, I immediately Phased over to the other side of the study's door. Once I reoriented myself, I took a deep breath and knocked on the door. I could hear shuffling from the other side, though it only lasted for a moment before Abram threw the door open and looked at me as if I was a ghost.

"Erm... Son? Is this a prank?"

"No," I told him, and he let out a breath of relief right away.

"Good! I'm not good with pranks..." His relief only lasted for a moment though, as his brows soon descended into a curious frown. "But if it's not that, then why did you sneak into our house like this?"

"I'll tell you later. First, let's go get Emese and Elly. Sebastian, too,"

I added after a little hesitation. "What I'm about to tell you concerns all of you."

PART 2

After the initial confusion over my unannounced arrival died down a little, we decided to change the scenery, as Abram's office was not only stuffy, but I considered the haphazardly piled up boxes a serious health hazard. After considering the dining room and Sebastian's study first, we ultimately decided on a third option in the form of the trophy room where I met with the family head for the first time.

The first one to heed the summons was, surprisingly enough, the mother of the household, and she made quite an entrance at that. Emese was already (or maybe still) partially transformed (as in, there was a conspicuous lack of wings on her back), and unlike her usual modest and dignified appearance, she was currently wearing a low-cut blouse and a pair of tiny shorts that left little to the imagination and showed off the flat, light-red scales covering her arms, thighs, and the area between her neck and her cleavage. She also wore her hair in a thick, somewhat-loose braid that reached down to the small of her back, and it momentarily made me wonder about how Elly would look with the same hairstyle.

The moment she entered the room she locked her eyes on me, and before I could properly react, she dashed over to my side with a beaming smile and glomped me in an embrace that was simultaneously too hard and unnecessarily squishy.

"Leonard! I didn't know you were coming over!"

"It was kind of the point," I tried to object and worm my way out of her hug, but she just clamped down on me even harder, followed by a mirthful giggle that made me feel just a tad embarrassed.

"Mooom!" my girlfriend suddenly burst into the scene and grabbed hold of her mother's shoulder. "Let go of Leo! You are smothering him!"

"Oh my? Could it be that you are jealous of your own mother?" Emese teased her, yet it wasn't Elly who answered first.

"To be fair, darling, even I'm getting a little bit jealous..." Papa Dracis mumbled behind me, at which point Emese finally let go of me with a breathy "Oh, you!" and she subsequently attached herself to her husband instead.

My unhugged state lasted for only a split second though, as Elly immediately replaced her. Not only that, she more or less hung from my neck with a defiant expression and rubbed her face against mine like a cat desperately trying to mark its owner after he petted the neighbour's kitten.

"It appears everyone is here already," came a stray comment from the last arrival as Sebastian quietly closed the door behind him.

"Right. Let's get started," I addressed everyone with a slightly raised voice as I simultaneously peeled the princess off my neck. "Please sit down."

The Dracis family shared a few curious glances between one another, but at the end of the day they obediently followed my instructions and formed a small cluster on the nearby canapé... except for Sebastian, who defiantly kept standing by them, ramrod straight like a British palace guard.

I didn't take a seat, either, but instead I stood before them, and after taking a deep breath, I decided to stop delaying and began by telling them, "First off, there is something important I want all of you to know. Elly is already aware of this, but I suffer from a case of retrograde amnesia."

"Amnesia?" Sebastian repeated after me while raising a single incredulous brow at my expense.

"Yes. I have absolutely no memory about practically anything before the first of September."

For some reason, the Dracis parents seemed absolutely shocked and mortified by this, yet Sebastian only looked at me funnily.

"I'm sorry to hear that, but was this truly the reason why you asked us to gather on such short notice?"

"No. It's just something that I wanted to make clear before we move on to the actual reason why we are all here." I paused here for a long moment as I considered how I should broach the topic, and at last I decided to employ the blunt approach. "I'm not going to mince my words here: Until last night, I was entirely unaware of my own background. Unfortunately, all evidence points to the fact that I'm related to the Knights of the unnecessarily long name."

Despite my feeble effort to dampen the impact, the atmosphere in the room immediately turned tense like a piano wire.

"You're one of the accursed Knights?" Abram promptly broke the developing silence, his voice more incredulous than anything else.

"Maybe, though I find it a little doubtful," I told him honestly and shrugged my shoulders. "The one thing that is certain is that I was contacted by them yesterday."

"That's... unreal," Lady Emese muttered, and for some odd reason, she seemed to be the one who took the news the hardest. "So... Are you a spy, or an infiltrator, or something?"

"I'll be damned if I know. I had more important things to focus on, so I didn't bother to ask."

"What could be more important than learning your own history, my boy?" Sebastian asked me with an unexpectedly concerned look in his eyes.

"Thank you for asking," I replied with a bit of forced enthusiasm, and then I cleared my throat and explained, "My background also wasn't the main reason why I came over to talk to all of you, just another detail I wanted you to know in order to explain where I got the following information: the Knights are coming to Critias, and they are planning an attack on you."

"When?" Sebastian leveled the question at me right away, and I answered on the spot.

"On the third of next month. I couldn't narrow it down any further without raising suspicion."

"We need to prepare then!" Abram declared without a hint of hesitation, and it was my turn to feel a little odd. I mean, even knowing their respective personalities, considering this incident was related to the Knights, I expected at least a little bit of suspicion.

"Actually, could you not?" That comment earned me an almost comically baffled expression from Papa Dracis, so I hastily clarified, "What I meant to say was please make sure to be subtle, so that they wouldn't know that you are expecting the attack."

"Oh, I get it!" the Dracis patriarch exclaimed with an excited grin. "We are going to ambush them! Give them a good taste of their own medicine!" He paused there, only for as long as it took to give me a thumbs-up, and then he added, "I approve!"

I gave my self-imposed father-in-law a wry look, but since he didn't respond to it, I noted, "To be perfectly honest with you, after telling you about my connection to the Knights, I expected slightly more apprehension than none at all."

"Oh please, son!" Abram scoffed at my comment, and he even emphasized his words with a dismissive wave of the hand. "If you can't trust family, then who can you trust?"

"While I would like to object under normal circumstances," Sebastian cut in after letting out a shallow sigh, "It *is* an undeniable fact that you have already proved your loyalty without a shadow of a doubt. It's to such a degree that I can't help but wonder why you found it necessary to preface this discussion with the reveal of your background." I must have looked either really curious or really confused at this moment because after taking a single glance at my face, the old butler's shoulders drooped in resignation, and he clarified, "What I'm trying to tell you is that, as much as I loathe to admit it, if you came to us by saying that your alleged information network warned you about an incoming attack, I would have believed your words just as readily as I do now."

I stayed silent for a moment as I let Sebastian's comment sink in, then eventually I told him, "I'm not going to lie, I'm flattered by the amount of trust that you place in me, yet I think you're all misunderstanding something."

"How so?" Emese poked the conversation ball to keep it rolling, and so I told them:

"I told you all that mainly to forestall any predictable complications in the future. For example, imagine that the Knights show up, with their shiny armour and swords and all, and everyone is squaring up against one another, and just then... Bam! One of the Knights looks at me, and then yells something like, 'Let's go, brother! Stab them in the back, for great justice!'"

"That... was certainly something they would say," Emese commented, putting me off my original train of thought right away.

"They would? I thought I was lampooning them... Anyhow, let's say I didn't tell you about my background and you heard that. You would probably get surprised, maybe even stunned for a second, and then you actually get stabbed in the back while you are paying attention to me, and let me tell you, fixing you up once was hard enough, so I would prefer if that wouldn't happen."

For some reason Abram found my description of a possible life-and-death battle amusing, as he could barely contain his chuckles. Meanwhile, Sebastian raised his hand to his chin in one of those ever-so-slightly-insufferable sophisticated-intellectual poses and stated, "That is a possible situation that slipped my mind. I shall grant you the point."

"You'd better," I told the old man with a smirk, but even while I was doing that, my attention was being drawn to something else, or rather, the lack of something. While we were having this whole conversation, Elly stayed suspiciously silent, so I sent a questioning glance at her and quickly noticed that she seemed to be straining herself quite a bit. "Is there... a problem?"

Mama Dracis followed the direction of my eyes, and a moment later she giggled out loud and told me, "Oh, you mean her? I'm holding her back right now."

"... I can't decide whether I'm more curious about the how or the why..."

"It's just bloodline suppression. Anyone with a pure enough draconic heritage can do it," Sebastian supplied the answer, which somehow only made me more confused.

"Okay, I bite: Why did you use this suppression thing on her?"

"Because if I didn't, she would've jumped on you the moment you told us about your connection to the Knights, and then we couldn't have had a proper discussion," Mama Dracis explained to me as dryly and straightforwardly as if she was talking about the weather.

"So... can you please stop that? She looks really uncomfortable."

"Are you sure you want that?" she asked, and I immediately nodded.

Without further ado, my girlfriend twitched, and then she practically flew off the canapé (which, incidentally, was also the point when Abram was no longer able to stifle his laughter and he began heartily chuckling at... something), and then she turned on her heel and glared at her mother.

"Mom, you are an idiot! A meanie! A nincompoop!"

Oh, that was her rule of three of silly insults! I haven't heard that in a while... I might've even felt nostalgic, if not for the fact that in the blink of an eye the princess put me in her crosshairs, and she leaped at me with such gusto I was afraid she wanted to tackle me off my feet. My first instinct told me to do that thing where I casually step out of her way at the last moment and watch her fall flat on her face as she missed her lunge, but then a more rational part of me concluded that doing that would've been mean, so instead I decided to dust off my slightly rusty girl-catching reflexes.

Just like that, I managed to slip my hands under her armpits, and by turning a full 360 degrees on my feet, I managed to disperse all the momentum so that in the end I could simply set her down onto the ground in front of me. Hm? That actually sounded a little familiar.

"Hey, princess? Didn't we already do something like this in the—?"

I got that far with my question before Elly grabbed hold of my clothes and began shaking me.

"Leo, you jerk! Why didn't you tell me!?"

"Easy there!" I rebuked her as I hastily unclamped her fingers, and after a brief consideration, I decided to keep holding on to her hands, just in case she wanted to grab onto me again in the future. "If you mean about me being related to the Knights, even I only learned about that yesterday."

"That's no excuse! You should've told me right away!"

"Yes, and that's why I came over to tell all of you about it today," I spoke in a level, soft voice while looking Elly right in the eye, and it didn't take long for her to avert hers.

"Yes, but..." she began to grumble, only to ultimately lean her head against my chest... or so I thought, but instead she headbutted me! It was probably since I was still holding onto her hands, but it was still harsh. She repeated the process a couple more times, and then she burst out, "Argh! This is so weird! Why does everything have to be so complicated!?"

"I don't know about weird," I mused as I tried to position myself to be out of the way of her headbutts. "I mean, isn't everyone and everything around us pretty weird already? This doesn't seem particularly special."

"Maybe... I mean, I get your point, but... Argh!"

Just like that, we were back to head-inflicted-trauma country. Lovely. Not to mention, as if that wasn't enough, I couldn't help but notice the parents of the household sharing a laugh at my expense, and while their harmonious little huddle was cute and all, I was way past the point where I could appreciate it.

"Lady Emese? Can you please teach me that bloodline suppression thing? I could really use it right now..."

"Call me Mom," my previously taciturn alleged mother-in-law demanded, but then she amended her words with an impish smile. "Not to mention, you're doing fine without it."

"If that's what this looks like from there, you should—" I began, only for my words to get cut short by Elly suddenly crying out.

"Ouu! I don't care! Knight or not, I still love you!"

I was almost relieved by that remarkably quick turnaround on her dilemma, but my happiness was short-lived, as she quickly yanked her hands out of mine and proceeded to catch me in a hug that would have made a fully grown Siberian bear skulk away in shame and embarrassment. To be fair, I would've loved to join said theoretical bear, as spending time in the corner in the company of a vicious predator felt vastly preferable to standing in the crossfire of the sickeningly affectionate gazes directed at me.

"Awww. Look, honey! Elly is having a forbidden romance right in front of our eyes," Mama Dracis commented while snuggling up to her husband, careful so that she wouldn't poke his eyes out with the tip of her horns.

"It's nice, isn't it?! Oh, the fire of youth!"

I really wondered what Papa Dracis considered fiery youth, considering the way he was hugging and flirting with his wife was pretty much the dictionary definition of hormone-addled lovebirds, but instead I exclaimed, "Could I humbly ask the peanut gallery to at least pretend that we are having a serious discussion about an impending threat to the lives of everyone in the room?"

"That definitely sounds rich coming from you, my boy, considering your current situation," Sebastian commented with his usual, unflappable voice, after which he quickly added, "However, I do find your choice of words curious. Bearing in mind you said 'everyone in the room,' could it be that you are already considering yourself part of the family after all?"

The look I gave the old man at this point had its exasperatedness levels measured in giga-class-reps (a novel metric I was still developing, patent pending), then I sent a considerably softer and maybe-just-a-teensy-bit-defeated glance at the girl still trying to crush my chest, and at last I said, "It's not like I have much of a choice in the matter at this point, do I?"

"Did you hear that, honey?!" Papa Dracis suddenly exclaimed, followed by a mirthful giggle from his wife.

"I sure did! Leonard is finally willing to be accepted into the family!"

"We must toast to this!"

"I advise against drinking just before lunchtime," the incognito butler intervened, earning him a thoughtful huff from the patriarch.

"You're right, Grandpa! Let's have lunch, and then a toast!" Abram beamed at Sebastian first, then at me, which I considered his own way of asking if that was a good idea.

"I can't stay for lunch. I already have an appointment," I stated without any reservations, but instead of its intended effect, it only made Emese jump to her feet (she really, really enjoyed being able to walk again, I supposed).

"In that case, I'll go and tell the staff to arrange a cold cuts buffet."

"How is that better than..." I began, but then my words got overwhelmed by Abram also rising to his feet with a merry bellow.

"I'm going to the cellar to pick a great vintage for the occasion! See you kids in the dining room!"

And just like that, both parents rushed out of the trophy room, leaving me with the slightly-less-grouchy-than-usual butler and the involuntary lung compressor I affectionately call my girlfriend. After the dust settled, I decided to ask a question that had been on my mind for a while, and I directed it to Sebastian.

"How the hell did these happy-go-lucky people manage to survive being hunted by a whole knighthood of angry dragon hunters for so long?"

"Listen, my boy," Sebastian raised his voice, apparently by reflex, then he fell silent for a long beat before finally admitting, "That... is a question I often asked myself in the past, yet I am no closer to an answer than you are."

PART 3

"Aaaaand I'm back," I announced my arrival and immediately plopped myself into one of the spare chairs in my kitchen.

"Oh." Judy froze up for a moment to process my sudden appearance, but then she casually picked up the ladle at her side and greeted me with a cautious, "Welcome back. How did they take the news?"

"Too well." I much less told than groaned the answer, which earned me a skeptical look from her.

"How can someone take bad news too well?" she asked the obvious question, and all I could provide in place of an answer was raising my hands and shrugging my shoulders.

"I have no idea, but they managed," I clarified as I let my hands down, only to change my mind halfway through and raise one to rub my temple instead. "They didn't care one bit about my connection to the Knights, didn't seem particularly bothered about the coming attack, and then they instead threw a small party to welcome me into the family."

"How did the first two points relate to the third one?"

"I'll be damned if I know," I grumbled in a soft voice before shaking my head. "Anyhow, as odd as their reaction to the news was, telling it to them hopefully got ahead of any future complications. I can only hope that Sebastian's going to keep them alert and safe."

There was a lull in the conversation after I said that, so I used the opportunity to take a deep breath to reorient myself. When I did that, my nose was immediately tickled by the rich scent of whatever Judy was cooking on the stove, and before I knew it, my stomach was already rumbling. It was actually a little surprising, considering that as much as I tried to hold back, I somehow still ended up eating about half a plate of cold cuts at Elly's place, so I didn't feel particularly hungry until now. It must've been the magic of home cooking.

"What are we going to have for lunch?" I asked while I craned my neck to take a better look at the pots, but Judy immediately moved in to block my line of sight.

"It's a surprise," she stated in an unusually firm tone, and since insistently looking her in the eye wasn't effective at getting her to elaborate, I ultimately shook my head and rose to my feet instead.

"Oh well. I suppose I'll be just looking forward to it then."

"No peeking," she warned me while pointing the ladle at me, only for her ears to abruptly get flushed. She quickly put the ladle down and repeated the motion, this time with only her finger, and added, "I'm serious. If you peek, I promise that I'm going to hate you for at least an hour. No, make it an hour and a half."

"Then I better not peek," I placated her with my best attempt at a smile, and after a moment of hesitation I decided to tease her a little by saying, "You know, you looked just like your mother for a moment there."

"Erase that idea from your mind," she commanded me with a frown. "In fact, erase the memory altogether."

"I'm sorry, but that's something no man or god could do," I replied with a slightly easier smirk this time and walked out of the kitchen.

Once I was inside the living room, I stretched my back first, after which I checked the time. It was still a while until lunchtime, so I decided to wash up a little and check the Hub before coming back to see how Judy was doing. However, just as I was about to take the first step towards the upper floor, I froze mid-motion and put my foot down again, and then checked the time once again.

"Hey, Judy?"

"Yes, Chief?"

"Is Snowy home yet?"

There was a moment of odd silence, then my dear assistant asked, "Couldn't you just use Far Sight to find out?"

"Yes, but I'm asking you first," I replied a tad impatiently.

"No, she's not home yet."

Once Judy told me that, I immediately entered into Far Sight and looked for my sister's dot, and once I found it, I let out a relieved sigh.

"Judy?"

"Yes? Is there a problem?" she responded by coming over and poking her head through the doorway.

"Depends. How many portions are you making?"

My girlfriend's visage turned unusually serious for a moment, and then she asked, "Are we going to have guests?"

"Yup," I confirmed without beating around the bush. "Snowy is on her way home, and it seems Josh and Angie tagged along."

When she heard that, my dearest of all assistants let out a shallow groan and mumbled something along the lines of, "I have to check if we have any more penne pasta..." and then she disappeared back into the kitchen. I didn't even attempt to stifle my chuckles at her expense, but once I was done with that, I did a quick roll call on the rest of the gang.

Amelia was, for a change, relaxing and reading a book in her room. Good for her, I thought, and I quickly moved on while trying to pretend that I didn't see that she was perusing a textbook on accounting. I'd just said goodbye to the princess, but I decided to check on her, just to be on the safe side, and she was currently receiving terrible relationship advice from her mother. Okay, so that was another thing I better pretend I didn't see.

Moving on, I glanced at Lab Coat Guy, and I found him in his hidden evil lair, where he was evilly welding what looked like the evil arm of an evil mecha or something. That was at least mildly interesting, but not enough to actually linger at the scene, though I made a quick mental note about the giant arm thing. Maybe it was part of a second-generation biomechanical whatchamacallit? Anyhow, for the moment I was satisfied with knowing that he wasn't out prowling the streets looking for a chance to ambush us.

Speaking of prowlers, I checked on Rinne next, and at the moment she was in the process of devouring an entire grilled duck. My stomach was grumbling a lot already, so I really didn't need to see that. As such, I quickly moved on to the next target: Armband Guy. He was... patrolling the school. On a Sunday. That was just sad.

Last, but not least, I decided to see how Mike was doing, and once my vision stabilized, I found him inside a fairly-puritan-yet-oddly-welcoming apartment, and on closer inspection, I found him in front of his computer playing some kind of hack-and-slash game... with his character looking suspiciously like the class rep. Should I consider that a coincidence or creepy, I wondered, and in the end I realized I didn't care enough, so I just stopped my observation and returned to my home.

I was momentarily tempted to see what Judy was cooking, but I decided that if she was so insistent on my not looking, it might've been an attempt at reverse psychology to make sure I would be looking, and I didn't want to play into her hand. But then again, she knew me well enough to know that I would be thinking that, so maybe it was a reverse reverse psychology, and by not looking I would do exactly what she wanted. But then again... I was too tired to follow this train of thought, so I decided to just ignore it and go and freshen up a little. I reckoned Snowy and Co. should be home in about five minutes or so, and by then I wanted to welcome them in a presentable condition.

Predictably enough, it took me roughly four minutes and fifty-nine seconds to clean up, change my clothes, and dash (read: shuffle like an old man with full-body arthritis) back to the living room. I was almost by the entryway when I noticed the characteristic sound of jingling keys coming from the front, and not a moment later the door opened wide.

"I'm home," Snowy announced in high spirits, and she was followed up by Josh.

"Pardon the intrusion... oh, hi Leo. You look like shit."

I gave my cheeky friend a withering look and told him, "You're lucky I also feel like shit, or I'd kick you out this door with my own feet."

"Nah, you wouldn't. You're too nice for that," came the next comment from Angie as she pushed her childhood friend through the threshold, and once she closed the door behind her, she took a good look at me and stated, "Wow, you really do look sick."

"Don't worry about it; I just overworked myself a little. Again."

The Celestial girl completely disregarded my words and walked over to me without bothering to take her coat off first, and before I could say anything more, she rose to her tippy-toes (even though she really didn't have to; I wasn't *that* tall) and put her palm on my forehead.

"Oh no! You're burning up!"

"No, it's just that your hand is cold," I corrected her.

"Really?" Saying so, she removed her hand and placed it on her own forehead, then after a long moment she walked over to Snowy and did the same thing to my hapless sister, and only then did she declare, "I guess you're right."

In the meantime, Josh peeled himself out of his coat and took a few obvious sniffs from the air.

"What are you cooking?"

"I'm not cooking anything. It's Judy."

"Oh, okay then. So what is *she* cooking?"

"I have no idea," I told him with a small grimace. "It's apparently supposed to be a secret."

"I'll go and help," Snowy proposed on the spot, and she immediately walked away in the direction of the kitchen.

"Hey! Don't leave me out!" the Celestial girl called out after my little sister as she hastily shed her outerwear and then rushed after her, leaving me alone with Josh.

I gestured for him to follow after me, thus we wordlessly entered the living room and both took a seat in our usual spots.

My butt barely even touched the cushions when Josh abruptly cleared his throat to get my attention, and then he asked, "So? What's going on this time?"

"What do you mean?" I answered his question with one of my own, since I had no idea what he was getting at.

"You look like crap, and you said you overworked yourself. That means something must have happened to get you into that state. What is it?"

Well, I had to give credit where credit was due; Josh didn't beat around the bush. After a brief moment of deliberation, I took a deep breath and told him, "Okay, so just to be clear, something did happen, but it is mostly unrelated to my current condition. First, a quick question: Do you remember when we discussed the big players in the supernatural politics?" Josh immediately nodded. "Good. Then I presume you remember the Knights with the pointlessly elaborate name?"

"You mean the Knightly Brotherhood of the Most Heroic Bloodlines?"

"... You seriously remembered their full name?"

Josh honest-to-goodness scoffed at my question as he crossed his arms and stated, "Unlike some of us, I don't have the luxury not to pay full attention to these things."

"That's... um... commendable. Anyhow, the reason I brought up the Knights is that they are coming here to cause some trouble for Elly's family."

"Did you tell them?"

"Of course. Not that they were particularly worried about the prospect, but they definitely know."

"Oh. Good."

I expected him to keep talking, but instead he just fell silent, followed by a drawn-out sigh. That was ever-so-slightly suspicious.

"Time out," I said and raised my hands in the standard T position. "What's eating you? Is there a problem?"

"No, it's just... well, maybe."

He apparently didn't really want to say whatever was on his mind, but since we'd come so far, leaving the topic at that would've been unsatisfying, so I looked him in the eye and prompted him with a firm, "So?"

"You're going to make fun of me if I tell you."

Josh looked unusually timid, so I reassured him by saying, "I promise I won't make fun of you. Just get it off your chest, will you? It will probably make things easier for the both of us."

Just like that, the last of his reservations melted off my friend like snow off a rooftop in an early spring heat wave. He slouched his shoulders and then, at last, he told me, "I'm just sick and tired of it all."

"Of what? Life?"

"Nah. I'm talking about Dr. Robatto," he finally spat it out. "I've had enough with always being on edge whenever I step outside with the others. Like, normally when coming over, we would go through the shopping district to do some window shopping or buy some snacks on the way. You know? Hang out, have fun, that sort of thing? Instead of that, we were just hurrying along while constantly on guard."

"Wait a moment. Are you telling me that it's been just a week, and your nerves are already fraying?"

"Well, excuse me for not having your nerves of reinforced titanium," Josh huffed quite indignantly, and I quickly raised my hands to placate him.

"Sorry, that came out wrong. I didn't mean it like that. I just thought the rush of being able to use your new abilities to whack some inconsequential robots would last a little longer."

"I mean, yeah, it was a rush, but..." he stammered for a moment, then in the end he told me, "It's like... we are high schoolers, man. We're supposed to have fun, hanging out in town and stuff, right? Living in constant fear of an attack is no way to spend one's youth."

There was a long, deafeningly loud silence as I stared at Josh with a mixture of skepticism and bafflement, and at long last, I simply covered my face with my palm and uttered, "I honestly can't decide if that was deep or just needlessly melodramatic."

"Hey! You said you wouldn't make fun of me!"

"I'm not making fun of you. I'm just making an observation," I corrected him while restoring my posture. "So your point is that you don't want to play around with Lab Coat Guy anymore. Well, it's your lucky day then because soon we are going to put an end to his shenanigans."

"Really?" Josh looked almost comically surprised by my words, but he quickly shook it off and inquired, "Does that mean you've collected enough incriminating evidence on Ammy's grandpa?"

"Regrettably, no," I admitted, followed by a shallow sigh. "I'm not planning to let the old coot get away with this, but the Knights are coming in a little more than a week, so I want to prioritize taking Lab Coat Guy and his ambushes out of the picture before that happens. Preferably in the next couple of days."

"That's... soon. So how are you going to do it?"

"That's the best part!" I exclaimed with a toothy grin. "I won't need to do anything because it's your job."

"... You can't be serious."

"And yet I am," I replied, this time much more seriously. "Listen, Josh, I still have the whole creepy Chimera hunter lady business on my hands along with trying to pin this total circus on Lord Grandpa, and now I'll have to do something about the Knights, as well. I can't be at every place at the same time."

"Why do you have to deal with the Knightly Brotherhood of the Most Heroic Bloodlines? Just let Elly's scary butler handle them or something," Josh argued, and I immediately shook my head.

"Can't do. You see, I'm actually related to the Knights. Or at least I was before the... you know?" I hinted while tapping my forehead, and Josh immediately got the memo. Unfortunately, he wasn't the only one.

"You're a Knight?!" came the astonished exclamation from the direction of the kitchen, and when I glanced over, Angie was already skipping towards us. She practically jumped over the couch and landed just beside my startled friend, and the moment she did so, she instantly began to inundate me with questions, such as, "Seriously? Why didn't you tell us? Did you tell Elly? How did she take it? What about her parents? Do you have a cool sword? Can I see it? Pretty please?"

It took me a moment to process the torrent of questions coming my way, so I raised a palm to quiet the overly excited girl.

"In order: Yes, because of certain circumstances, yes, pretty well, they didn't mind, I don't, and so you can't."

Now it was Angie's turn to think hard for a moment while she paired her questions up with my answers. In the meantime, there was more movement from the direction of the kitchen and soon Snowy also joined us.

"Um... Did I hear that right? Are you really one of the Knights?"

Her question was naturally addressed to me, so I gave her my perfected big-brotherly smile and answered, "It's a tiny bit more complicated than that, but for the time being, let's just say that I'm very closely tied to them."

Meanwhile, Angie untangled the answers and suddenly declared, "That's great!"

"Is it?" Josh muttered under his breath, but since he was right next to her, his childhood friend naturally overheard him.

"Of course it is!" she began to explain with her usual gusto. "Think about it: Leo is a Knight, right?"

"He just said that it's more complicated, but yeah, let's go with that," my friend agreed, if a bit tentatively.

"And he is going out with Elly, right?"

"Along with Judy." This time it was Snowy who added to the conversation as she made her way over to their side and sat down next to Angie.

"Yes, but now it's Elly who is important! It's a Knight and a Draconian going out! It's amazing! This could be the first step to end a thousand-year-old conflict!"

"It's not a thousand years old, and to be honest, I doubt it," I told her in a level voice.

"Come on, Leo! With your track record of fighting discrimination, you are going to break through this millennium-old feud in a jiffy!"

"Millennium means a thousand years, too, and I told you that... Bah, forget it. I'm more curious about when I ever fought discrimination."

"Are you serious?" she asked me with her eyes as wide as saucers before she pointed at her face with both of her index fingers. "Look! It's a Celestial! And she can walk in the open without having to fear the Mages! Oh, and look!" Suddenly she threw her arm around the shoulders of my surprised sister and directed her free finger at her. "It's an Abyssal who is completely free to live on the surface without anyone harassing her! And we are besties to boot! Isn't that right?"

"Uh... R-right," Snowy meekly agreed while repeatedly nodding her head, which made Angie giggle with satisfaction.

"It's absolutely crazy! Celestials and Abyssals are never supposed to get along, and yet here we are!" After saying that she sent a stealth glance at the silent guy by her side and she added, "I mean, we are not in perfect agreement about *everything*, but still! Besties!"

"I'm happy to hear that, but that still doesn't mean that just by being in a relationship with the princess I would magically make the Knights and Draconians get along."

"Oh please, don't be so pessimistic. Aim for the stars! Even if you miss, you can still go for a stable orbit!"

"And what exactly is that supposed to mean?" Josh inquired with one of his masterful, incredulous single-eyebrow raises.

"I... don't really know, to be honest. It sounded way cooler in my head," the Celestial girl admitted.

Meanwhile, I used the momentary lull in the conversation to think a little. While Angie's proposal sounded simple and naive, was it actually a bad idea? Even since the possibility of the Knights showing up on my doorstep reared its ugly head, I had considered them a threat and had been thinking of methods to stop and eliminate them, but what if I could reason with them? It couldn't hurt to try. Even if I couldn't ensure a fairy-tale ending where everyone would be living in perfect harmony, maybe I could avoid a fight, or even the whole conflict altogether. It was food for thought, is all I'm saying.

Anyhow, while I was having these thoughts, Snowy suddenly raised her voice and asked Angie, "Did you tell them the thing Judy asked you to tell them?"

The slightly circular question drew everyone's attention, and in a moment the Celestial girl let out a slightly embarrassed "Ooooh!," followed by, "Thanks for reminding me. I totally forgot! Listen, guys, since Judy originally only made enough casserole for three, she had to modify the recipe on the fly to increase the number of portions. Because she wasn't sure how that would turn out, she told me to come over here and sneakily dampen your expectations a little."

"... Is that how you do that? By telling us outright?" Josh asked in the company of another skeptical look, but Angie instantly shook her head.

"Nah. I'm going to do that now." Saying so, she straightened her back, cleared her throat, and solemnly announced, "Judy's custom casserole is nearing completion. Soon, the living shall envy the dead."

There was a very, *very* long beat of silence following her words, but then a certain assistant of mine abruptly called out from the kitchen, her voice soft yet chilling at the same time.

"Angeline, could I ask you to come here for a moment? I'm afraid I can't leave the pan alone, but I need you in arm's reach so that I can strangle you."

Angie let out a hearty chuckle that would have made Abram proud and responded with, "I'm kidding, I'm kidding! I told you it's going to be amazing! You're like ten times better at cooking than I am: it will be fine!"

"That doesn't say much," Josh mumbled on the side. "Ten times zero is still zero."

"Oh, now you did it, mister!" Angie suddenly turned on her childhood friend, and the two began playfully tussling with each other on the couch. Snowy, wisely, chose to leave the vicinity at this time, and she sidled over to my side.

"Is everything going to be okay?"

"With those two? They should run out of steam soon enough."

"No, I mean... with the Knights," my sister clarified with a voice that was walking on eggshells.

"Ah, that... I can't guarantee anything, but you shouldn't worry," I reassured her by patting her back without standing up from my chair. "I know that they dislike Abyssals about as badly as they do Draconians, but even if push comes to shove, I'll make sure to keep you out of the cross fire."

"I didn't mean that," she shook her head. "I'm more worried about you."

"Awww, that's sweet of you," I said with a genuinely delighted smile and I redoubled my back-patting efforts. "Don't worry, I'll be fine. I mean, I don't want Judy to kill me, so I have all the incentive in the world to avoid danger."

"That's true," she muttered in a considerably more relieved voice. In the meantime, the childhood friend duo ran out of steam, just as I'd predicted, and after a few exaggerated heaves, it was Josh who spoke up first.

"Can we go back to the previous discussion for a moment?"

"Sure," I granted him, though I wasn't sure which part he was referring to.

"Can you tell me how I am supposed to deal with Robatto?"

"You are going to deal with him?" Angie interjected, resulting in my shaking my head.

"No, it would be more accurate to say that *you* are going to neutralize him. Plural. As in, the group, minus me and Judy."

"Yes, but how?" Josh pressed on, and after a second of thinking, I shook my head again.

"You know what? How about we hold a big meeting tomorrow in the secret hideout, and we discuss this with everyone? I mean, I'm sick, you are tired and on edge, Angie is going be strangled by Judy... It's best we do this when everyone is in better condition."

"That... makes sense, I suppose," my friend agreed somewhat hesitantly. "So what are we going to do today?"

"I dunno," I responded with shrug. "What were you planning to do when you came over?"

"I mostly wanted to come here to talk to you about Robatto, but we already postponed that, so... I have nothing else."

"Well, we still have Elly's spare poker set. We could..." I proposed, only to get shot down immediately.

"Let's not," Josh said with a completely deadpan expression. "Don't you have anything else?"

"I don't have a gaming console, so that's out of the equation. No board games, either." I counted off the things that we couldn't do, only for Angie to suddenly exclaim:

"Well then, I suppose we have no choice! We *must* continue our *Trucy the Werewolf Huntress* marathon!"

"Must we?" I asked back.

"Definitely," came the enthusiastic confirmation from the Celestial girl. I sent a questioning glance at Josh in turn, and his expression said "Whatever, we might as well," so I turned to Snowy next.

"Is that the show you talked about last night? I'm actually a little curious about it," she spoke while looking at Angie, and our friendly neighbourhood Celestial asset's face immediately lit up like a Christmas tree.

"That's right! Neige wasn't around when we had our last marathon! This is a grievous mistake we must rectify right away!"

"Okay then, that's four out of four so far. Who's going to ask Judy?"

"Not it," Angie immediately raised her hand, then she sheepishly added, "I don't want to be strangled."

"I'll ask," my sister proposed in her stead right away, and she swiftly walked over to the kitchen door.

In the meantime, I leaned back in my comfy chair and exhaled a shallow sigh. Things were bound the get more hectic... or rather, even more hectic than usual, so I figured having one last lazy afternoon during the calm before the storm wouldn't hurt anyone. The fact that Amelia was excluded this time around felt a little off-putting, but then again, if I called her over now and we had one more mouth to feed, Judy would probably strangle me, too. Sorry, class rep, but that's just how the casserole crumbles.

CHAPTER 5

PART 1

"Hold on, I need to sit down for a moment," I muttered between two hoarse breaths, and my ever-so-mindful (if at the moment slightly overbearing) girlfriends grabbed hold of my arms like clockwork. I gave each of them a wry look in turn and tried gently to shake them off, to little apparent success. "I'm not going to collapse. I'm just a little woozy."

They didn't seem to care about what I was saying, as they proceeded to drag me over to the nearest chair in the so-called reception area of our hidden base. It might have sounded grand, but in reality it was just the refurbished room right outside the teleport closet. I naturally continued to grumble all the way there, but took a seat anyway. I mean, what other option did I have?

"Is Leo okay?" Angie inquired while trying to take a better look at my no-doubt-pale face, so I quickly shook my head.

"I was still feeling a little sick from the other day. Transporting you... or rather, *using the teleport circle* with you guys in tow just made it a hundred times worse. That said, I'll live."

Even though I managed to catch my slip of the tongue early, the class rep still sent me a suspicious glance, so I quickly and very naturally averted my eyes and pretended I didn't see her.

In the meantime my nausea slowly abated, and so I let out a self-deprecating sigh. As much as I hated to admit it, my current condition was almost entirely the result of my own carelessness. I was already overworked to being with, and yet, despite Judy's repeated warnings, I was running around like a headless chicken the whole morning.

For a start, I contacted Mike and received the first deposit of magical doodads from him, then I had to visit our family doctor to get a medical certificate for my days of absence (which I successfully received after just a bit of badgering), and once I got home I checked all the artifacts, and then, after all that, I Phased everyone over to the secret base. In retrospect, it was no wonder I felt weaker than homeopathic whiskey.

Anyhow, I already felt marginally better after sitting down for just a moment, so I carefully stood back up and stretched my back under the scrutinizing gazes of my girlfriends. The others, on the other hand, were paying very little attention to me, as they were considerably more interested in the reception room.

"I like what you did to the place," Josh stated with a profound voice as he looked over one of the freshly painted ocher walls and the simple wooden furniture. "Very... errr... minimalist?"

"Yes, yeeeees," Angie agreed while she pretended to twirl a nonexistent mustache, and then she continued in some kind of fake and altogether undecipherable accent, "It certuunly possesss a certuun untaangibl sharm. A stroong presanse of industrial steil, with juuust a daaazs ov mid-censurii modaarn detektaabl in ze kompoziisuun. Trulii marveluuus."

"Um... Yes. What she said," Snowy said between repeated nods, though based on her expression, she had no idea about what she was agreeing with. To be fair, she wasn't alone in that regard.

"Stop fooling around. We are here on serious business," Ammy scolded the trio right away, and their back-and-forth quickly faded into the background noise as I literally moved things along by walking over to the metal door leading to the main hall of the complex.

It had a wheel in the middle, kind of like a ship door on a submarine, and it was also freshly painted in a dark, almost brownish red that made it both fit the colour palette of the room and at the same time stick out like a sore thumb. Putting my inner interior decorator's assessments aside for a moment, I grabbed hold of the wheel, and since the door wasn't actually locked, I could push it open without having to turn it.

It opened up without a sound (the Fauns were very particular about maintenance and lubrication, it seemed), and once the other side came into view, Josh immediately let out an impressed whistle.

"I like that room, too, but I *really* like what you did with *this* place," he told me as he followed after me, and embarrassing as it was, I felt exactly the same way. I mean, I was the one who ferried over all of the raw materials and all the modular furniture with large *Assembly Required* stickers over them during the past couple of days (or rather, nights, but that's beside the point), but even though it wasn't my first time seeing Brang and Co.'s handiwork, I was still amazed by how they managed to turn the very utilitarian interior of the main hall into something so different it was hard to imagine how bare it looked just a couple of days ago.

First and foremost, all the old furniture was removed from the place and placed inside one of the side rooms we designated as the storage area. The new-and-improved chamber was now divided into four areas by functionality, with the walls of each segment painted in a different pastel colour. Oh, and speaking of that: the ceiling was painted sky blue with actual fluffy white clouds, and the cluster of lamps in the middle was serving as the sun. I had no idea why though. Maybe one of the Fauns had an artistic side that suddenly came to the forefront or something?

Anyhow, on my left was the training area, which was roughly half the size of a standard basketball court. The actual sparring arena in the middle was considerably smaller, and it was surrounded by simple, three-step bleachers made of aluminum tube understructures and brightly painted wooden benches.

Farther back, past the open end of the arena, there was a meeting area where tactics, strategies, or recent plot twists in TV serials could be discussed, and it had several rows of seats along with a patently huge dry-erase board. The latter sat on a metal scaffold, and it was about a head taller than I was, and at least twice as wide. Let's just say that Phasing that thing over was an absolute pain in the neck, but I managed to do it, anyway.

The third area was a workshop and armoury rolled into one, where the Fauns kept and maintained their weaponry and armour, as well as their more mundane tools. It had all the wrenches, hammers, saws, and power tools you would see in any self-respecting handyman's garage, and I could even save a few pennies on this part by simply bringing over the unused tools from my own.

Last, but not least, there was the smallest of the four segments, right next to the door through which we'd just arrived. It was a cozy little recreational area, complete with a bar counter, those small round stools that looked hilarious when a Faun tried to balance on them, an honest-to-goodness air hockey table, and even two vintage massage chairs. The last two were impulse purchases, as they were on sale in a bundle, and while the massage chairs didn't prove successful (probably because Brang and his men could barely even sit on them), the hockey table was an instant hit and became part of their hand-eye coordination training. They also kept score and held a mini championship at the end of the day, ostensibly as a way to improve performance through competitive practices. It obviously had nothing to do with enjoying themselves, and I most certainly didn't participate in the past.

I'm not going to lie, I had my reservations about putting all these facilities into a single chamber, even if the available space allowed it, but Brang was very insistent about doing things this way. It had something to do with how the Fauns' mustering area was arranged back in the Abyss. It seemed quite inefficient to my layman's eyes, but in the end I left the minutia in the hands of the professional.

"Woooow! This looks amazing!" Angie expressed her admiration with the kind of childish glee I expected from her, and she immediately homed in on the recreational area with the precision of a bloodhound. "Oh my gosh! You've got a hockey table! That's so cool!"

"Look! They even have a minibar!" Josh added to the commotion. "Our old tree house has nothing on this secret base..."

"We had our comic collection, though," the Celestial girl argued back.

"True, that does level the playing field a little," my friend mused as he browsed through the contents of the tiny fridge.

"How much did this all cost you?" Ammy leveled the question at me, and unexpectedly enough, even she sounded mildly impressed.

"More than I originally set aside for it, but less than you would expect," I told her with a mysterious smirk, but before she could react, our conversation was interrupted by Josh exclaiming from literally inside the minibar.

"Holy hell, you seriously have Crystal Pepsi in this!?"

"Brang likes it," I absentmindedly answered his question, even though it was most likely rhetorical, and just then I noticed a large shape coming our way from the direction of the armoury area. "Speak of the devil..."

"Welcome, tiny heir," Brang greeted Snowy in his usual gravely, yet at the same time affectionate voice the moment we were in earshot. He looked the same as usual except for two slightly anachronistic details: he was wearing a thick leather apron, the kind you would see on a medieval blacksmith, and on his head, there was a pair of XXL-sized transparent protective glasses that looked absolutely hilarious on him. He also saluted to her by placing his fist on his broad chest, and then he turned to the rest of us and did the same. "Welcome, regent. Companions."

"Regent?" Ammy raised a curious brow at my expense, so I gave her a shrug in return.

"It's a long story and not exactly relevant right now," I unsubtly dismissed her and turned my attention to the Faun general instead. "[I hope my greetings find you in good health, general. Mine eyes tell me you and your men did not shy away from labour in the days since I last visited your temporary abode.]"

"[Aye, thine eyes play no tricks on you Blackcloak, albeit thine countenance appears worrisome enough to make this old man's heart fear you might see double.]"

"[Your observation is accurate, as my current disposition is akin to the backside of an ornery horse.]"

"[I wish you a recovery as swift as the unseen knife in the dark.]"

I sent the friendly Faun a skeptical look, but he seemed perfectly serious, so a brief sigh later I replied, "[I shall accept your unusual wishes of positive regard. On more pressing notes, where could your men be at the moment? Were their ears preoccupied when I informed them of the date of our arrival?]"

"[Nay. They just recently completed the facsimile of the firmament above in a haste most unusual, and are thus currently in the process of ridding themselves of paint.]"

"[That's... understandable. Please instruct them to come and join us as soon as possible, for I wish to start discussing matters of the utmost seriousness.]"

"[Aye,]" he grunted with a nod and then turned on his heel and headed in the direction of the barracks... which was just one of the side chambers refurbished and filled with beds.

"I just can't get used to him," Judy grumbled behind me, and when I glanced over my shoulder, she also added, "And I don't like it when you growl at each other, either."

"I told you already, it wasn't growling. The Faun language is actually really complex and expressive, and..." My words trailed off when I noticed that it was only the two of us standing by the entrance, and so I asked, "Where's the princess?"

My dear assistant wordlessly pointed ahead, and when I followed her finger, I found Elly and Angie right next to the air hockey table.

"Oooh? You wish to challenge me?" Elly asked in that high-pitched, faux-haughty, and just-a-tiny-bit-cute voice she occasionally used when she was feeling threatened.

"Yeah!" Angie declared while grabbing hold of one of the strikers. "We still have to settle our score from the other day!"

"Very well! I will show you that you cannot defeat me, no matter the game!"

After proclaiming so, she pointed a challenging finger at the similarly psyched up Celestial girl, a look that was further emphasized by a charming little overconfident smirk, but then her eyes met mine as Judy and I walked closer, and said finger quickly turned into an outstretched palm.

"I accept your challenge... but first I have to talk with Leo!" She didn't even wait for Angie to react; instead she immediately scampered over to our side and whispered, "Leo, quick! Tell me how you are supposed to play this game!"

"You don't know how to play air hockey?" my other girlfriend inquired quite incredulously, and after a brief moment of hesitation, the princess shook her head so hard I was afraid she would lose her balance.

"I've never played this game before," she admitted. "But I can't back down now!"

"Why did she even challenge you in the first place? What is this score you have to settle?" I asked in a low voice, though I had a feeling that Angie could probably hear our every word. I mean, we were only a couple of meters away from her, but it didn't stop the princess from whispering her answer, like it was top secret.

"The other day we had a long game during practice, and she thinks she was winning even though I had her on the ropes for the last set, but then it started to rain, so we had to wrap things up."

It took me a few seconds to wrap my head around what she was talking about, but then the proverbial light bulb finally lit up over my head.

"You are talking about tennis, aren't you?"

"Yes, of course," Elly stated as if it was completely self-evident, and it reminded me of the fact that the two of them were rising tennis stars or something.

I never really paid much attention to the princess's sports career, but now that she'd jogged my memory, I couldn't help but ask, "I've heard you were playing professionally. Something about tournaments and the mainland or something..." I vaguely muttered, hoping that she would bite and fill in the blanks, and my dear draconic girlfriend did just that.

"Ah, that's right. I used to do that when I was in elementary school. Not anymore."

"Why not?" came the unexpected question from Angie, who'd sneaked up on us while we were talking, and she made the princess jump in surprise.

"I'm curious, too," was the next question, which came from the mouth of Ammy. She'd somehow managed to sneak up on us even harder, to the point even I barely noticed her before she spoke up, and Elly straight-up yelped in surprise. Maybe the class rep really was a ninja after all? Like, a super-secret experimental Mage-ninja hybrid? It's sad to admit it, but at this point it wouldn't even surprise me if that was true...

Anyhow, once my draconic girlfriend calmed down a little (and stopped holding on to me like a slightly-less-fluffy koala bear), she sighed aloud and explained, "Mom used to be a professional tennis player before I was born, but then her injury made it impossible for her to do it anymore, so I tried my best to learn how to play well to make her happy." At this point she let out another, even deeper sigh, then added, "Unfortunately it turned out I was only mediocre."

"You call that mediocre?" I asked in surprise, as I could distinctly remember that I was pretty damn impressed by her when I last saw her have a match with Angie. It also made me wonder how playing tennis in tournaments was okay, yet becoming a singer was dangerous, but I had to put the question aside for the moment due to Angie honest-to-goodness stomping her feet by our side.

"Yeah! How dare you!" the Celestial girl huffed, and when she noticed that we were all looking at her with question marks over our heads, she hastily amended, "I mean, she is my rival! If she says she is mediocre, that means it would make *me* mediocre, too! That's just rude!"

"But I am..." Elly's response was not only a little sheepish, but she was fidgeting so adorably I wanted to give her a big hug. Of course I realized it was inappropriate to do so at the moment, and since I was a very mature and rational person, I naturally decided to do it a little later. Anyhow, while I battled my inner demons (read: hormones), she continued to explain herself with, "I only got the silver medal in the European Youth League Championship, and I barely managed to make it to the top five in the internationals."

I was a little skeptical about my girlfriend's words, but no matter how I looked at her, it didn't feel like she was humblebragging, so in the end I straightforwardly told her, "Listen, Elly. I don't want to start an argument, but I feel like I'm obligated to point out that if you call that mediocre, then it would mean that ninety-nine percent of all tennis players would be below average."

"That's statistically impossible," Judy remarked on the side, earning her a slightly frustrated nod in the process.

"Yes, that was my point. Getting second place in a championship is about as far from mediocre as it can get."

"I... don't think you are wrong..." Elly finally agreed with me using a textbook double negative, but before the conversation could get any further, the arrival of Brang and his not-particularly-merry men put an end to that, with my friends staring at them in mild bewilderment. I have to admit, I wasn't entirely immune to it, either.

"Leo?" Josh called out to me as he also walked over.

"Yes?"

"Why are they all blue?"

"Well, they are not *entirely* blue," I objected to his choice of words, but he didn't seem to appreciate it, so after a short while I explained to him, "The Fauns were the ones who painted the ceiling, and they didn't have the time to clean up."

"I was meaning to ask about that..." Ammy cut in while her eyes alternated between the Fauns and the facsimile of the sky over us, and it didn't take long for her brows to furrow in perplexity. "Please wait just a moment. Wouldn't that mean they just finished painting all of this?" she said as she gestured upward.

"Apparently," I agreed.

"So why is it that they are covered in blue paint, yet nothing in this place has even a drop of it on it?"

"That's... actually a very good question. Why don't you ask them about it?"

"Uh... No offense, but I would rather you do it."

"Maybe later," I responded a tad ambivalently as Brang and Co. finally arrived, and they all went through the whole greeting and saluting routine. Once we were done with that, our fairly sizable group moved over to the meeting area, so that we could finally discuss the reason why we gathered here in the first place.

I walked up to the whiteboard and waited until everyone took a seat, and only then did I clear my throat to open the gathering.

"Listen up, everyone! I now open our first grand tactical meeting." I paused for a moment and sent a piercing look at my only male friend. "And for the record, if *any* of you asks something silly, like 'What makes it grand?,' I will personally stuff this black marker up his nose."

"I wasn't going to ask that!" Josh denied everything while vehemently shaking his head, which was, let us be honest, enough evidence of his culpability to make even the most lukewarm judge find him guilty on the spot.

Anyhow, once I got ahead of the heckling and established my position, I took a deep breath and declared, "We are here today to discuss the current situation, upcoming threats, and how to deal with them in an efficient, hassle-free manner. First and foremost," I began as I stepped closer and started to write on the board, "We have Lab Coat Guy and his army of ineffectual-yet-annoying robots."

I paused to see if anyone wanted to add something, but since they stayed silent, I continued by writing up the second issue, in the form of, "Then we still have the issue of the Chimera running amok... or rather, laying low and attracting a monster hunter who is running amok. Same difference, really."

"Did you seriously just tell me that a legendary, magic-immune, dreaded monster of mass destruction is the same thing as an allegedly annoying huntress?" Ammy interrupted while adjusting her glasses, and her comment earned a few stray chuckles from the Fauns on the left.

I gave her a look flatter than an uncapped bottle of Coke left out in the open overnight and responded with, "You try spending a few hours with Mountain Girl every evening, and we'll see whether or not you would agree with me."

"A moment, please," Judy suddenly interrupted with her hand raised. "Did you give her a nickname?"

"Yes. I kind of had to because she refused to let me use her real name," I clarified, yet it only made my assistant's expression more grave as she turned to Elly by her side.

"Did you hear that? We must employ more anti-harem countermeasures before it's too late."

"Oh, ha ha ha," I cut in before she could respond. "Just because I call her by a nickname, it doesn't mean I'm the least bit interested in her. What's next? Are you going to claim that I'm interested in Armband Guy?"

"Are you?"

"... Dormouse. Don't make me go over there and tickle you."

There was a long moment of silence following my threat, and since Judy didn't react, I considered the tangent finished... but then Josh raised his hand.

"Yes? What is it?"

"I just want to know why is it that I get threatened with physical violence before I even say anything, but she only gets a mildly flirty warning?"

I directed an ever-so-slightly-incredulous look at my friend, and I eventually told him, "It's just simple, run-of-the-mill nepotism. Wasn't it abundantly clear?"

"And why are you so smug about it!?"

"Because I can afford to be," I replied before gesturing with my hand to cut the tangent short, this time for good. "So back to the issues at hand, the third of which is the coming of the Knights."

I wrote the word *Knights* onto the whiteboard, as well, then I turned to the group and continued by saying, "A quick recap, so that we are all on the same page: Lab Coat Guy is working for the arch-mage, and he is under orders not to cause too much distress. The Chimera is currently in hiding and sending out these tiny versions of itself to gather food, which I'm reluctantly hunting at the moment. The Knights are coming to the island to cause trouble to Elly's family, and I am related to them. Now, let's discuss how to deal with the first two before the third comes in to muddy up the waters." Our at-the-moment-not-so-little group exchanged timid glances between one another, so a quick sigh later I decided to forcibly move things along. "How about this? Let's start with the one that is the least dangerous, though not necessarily the least annoying at the moment."

After saying so, I turned to Brang and asked him, "Did you find out anything about the whereabouts of the Chimera?"

The old Faun raised a finger to say something, but then he shook his head and stood up instead. He walked over to my side with his usual lopsided gait, and he said, "[May this old man borrow the tool of drawing in thy possession?]"

"Sure," I answered and handed him the black marker. It looked comically small in his hand, yet that impression only lasted for a second before he stepped up to the whiteboard and began to draw a series of lines so straight I probably couldn't even make them with the help of a ruler in hand. After the first couple of lines, he began to add other shapes, and in a matter of minutes, I was startled by the recognition of the city's rough map from a bird's-eye view. I said rough because it lacked any street names or other indicators, but as far as I could judge by eye, it was about as accurate as the large tourist map I had seen in the park a couple of times. I couldn't even imagine how someone could make a map like that from memory, but considering who we were talking about here, I had to conclude that the scout part in Brang's old title wasn't just for show.

Once he was done with the drawing, he drew three impeccably perfect circles onto it. "Nests. Target moves." He paused for a moment while he put the cap onto the marker, and he used it to point at the circle in the upper-left corner. "Here." After saying that, he pointed at the next circle and said, "Then here," and after moving to the third one he repeated, "Then here. In circle. Pattern is predictable, timing is not."

"So if I get this right, you managed to pinpoint the main Chimera's hiding places?" Brang nodded, so I pressed on by asking, "Does this mean you know where it is right now?" He nodded again and pointed at one of the circles.

"Here. Surrounded by tiny sentries. Numerous escape routes. Confronting in nest... difficult. Would lose element of surprise. Would find new nest to hide. Frustrating."

"I see," I muttered as I considered his words. If I could believe them (and why wouldn't I?), it meant that the Chimera was routinely moving around in the city, which either meant that the daily hunts of the tiny Chimeras to draw it out was pointless, or that it already worked and it realized it was being hunted, so it decided to keep moving. Either way, the result was the same, so I proposed, "If assaulting its lair is risky, I guess our best bet is to ambush it while it is moving from one hidey-hole to the next."

The old Faun flashed me a toothy smile and gave me a nod so deep it was almost a small bow.

"My plans exactly."

I disregarded his deferential tone and instead I focused on the map again. I drew mental lines between the three circles and tried to match the actual lines they crossed with the streets from my memory, but I quickly had to give up on the endeavor. It was something I probably couldn't have done well even when I was in top shape, and so it was doubly impossible at the moment. As such, I decided to depend on the person with the most experience in the room and asked, "In your opinion, what are the best spots for ambushing it?"

The moment I asked that, as if waiting for those words, Brang removed the cap from the marker in his hand and drew four small squares that roughly sat on the imaginary lines I drew between the circles before.

Once he was done with that, he pointed at them one at a time and explained, "Should move tonight. Site has cover. A lot. Area is populated, Zone necessary. Second site. Moves in one or two days. Moves on rooftops. Little cover, no worry for collateral damage. Third site. Moves in three or four days. Part of woods in city. Park? Part of park. Lots of cover, Zone is easy to make. Fourth site, same day as third site. Narrow alley. Easy to corner, no cover."

I let out a small "Hm" in place of a more nuanced opinion as I considered the options he'd presented. The first area was in the middle of a residential district, so it was right out of the question, Purple Zone or not. The second option was better, but fighting a Chimera on a rooftop brought back some nasty memories, and I decided it was better not to tempt fate. I mean, I could totally imagine the whole falling-off-the-roof bit happening again just to provide an ironic echo or something.

That left only two options on the table, and after some consideration, I told Brang, "Let's go with the ambush in the park. You said it would move through there in five or six days, right?"

"Estimate. Target is not predictable."

"That's a bit of an issue," I muttered as I rubbed my chin, but I ultimately decided to risk it. "It's a little too close to the arrival of the Knights for my comfort, but we should manage. I will tell the huntress about it, and hopefully I can delegate dealing with it to her. Please keep a lookout on the Chimera and inform me if its behaviour changes."

"Will do," Brang responded with a smaller version of his usual salute. I acknowledged it with a nod and then turned to the rest of the group.

"Okay, that's about it for the Chimera for now. Does anyone have anything they would like to ask or add to the conversation?" I asked to be polite, and unsurprisingly, no one reacted. It was to be expected. I mean, it was my subplot, so to say. In fact, if I had to rank our current problems based on narrative terms, it would be that one side plot that got resolved off-screen because it didn't directly affect any of the main characters. Now, as for the main plot, it was obviously going to be the main topic of our conversation, but before that, I had to discuss one more side plot first.

"Speaking of the Knights, how are the preparations going on your end?" I leveled the question to my draconic girlfriend, and for some reason it took her a few seconds to answer.

"Oh, you mean us? Yes, Dad and Sebastian are already working on an ambush." After she said that, Elly abruptly snapped her fingers and added, "That reminds me; Dad told me to tell you to come over to our mansion later so that he can discuss something with you."

"Again? At this rate, I'm visiting your place every single day."

"You can always move in, and then you won't have to do that ever again," my girlfriend offered in a manner that would have sounded quite self-assured and flirty if not for the fact that her ears were red as a lobster.

"Thanks for the offer, but I decline. Anyhow, I will talk with him after I escort you back home today. But back to the Knights: as of now we don't know much about them, so I want all of you to be on the lookout for any new faces."

I paused as I noticed that Josh had his hand raised over his head as if we were in the classroom, and I motioned for him to speak up.

"Could you be a little more specific?" he requested as he let his hand down.

"Unexpected midterm transfer students, substitute teachers, people with unusually nice hair or fancy clothes, these kinds of things."

"What does hair have to do with the Knights?" came the next question from Ammy, and I was tempted to answer with a suitably dramatic "Everything!" but in the end I decided on a more conservative approach.

"Just trust me, and keep an eye out for new people."

"Does Mike count?" the class rep spoke up again, and her question drew everyone's attention at once.

"Who's Mike?" Josh inquired with an unusually apprehensive expression.

"He is an acquaintance of mine," I answered in Amelia's stead. "And before you ask, no, he is not a Knight."

"Well, of course he's not," Angie declared on the side, and so all the eyes previously glued to Amelia turned to her in an instant, so she hastily added, "I mean, he's, like, my dad's second cousin's stepson, you know?"

"Wait..." The class rep raised her voice with just a tinge of alarm. "If he's related to you, does that make him...?"

"Yes, he is also a Celestial," I clarified, earning me a glare from the local Celestial asset.

"Leo! That was supposed to be a secret!" Angie whined, but frankly speaking, I couldn't care less about her objection.

"Then maybe you shouldn't have let the cat out of the bag first. Also, could we please try to stay on topic for just five damn minutes? Pretty please?" Everyone fell conspicuously silent, which I interpreted as agreement. "Okay, so just to reiterate: if you see anyone with a very distinct appearance, inform me right away. As for what we are going to do about the actual attack, it will depend on Elly's family."

It was at this point that I took a huge breath and decided to stop skirting around the meat of today's meeting, so I pointed at the very first word I wrote onto the board and said, "Last, but not least, we have to discuss what to do with Lab Coat Guy in general and Ammy's grandfather in particular. At this point it is a well-established fact that they are working together as part of some sort of overarching-and-as-of-yet-not-exactly-sensible master plan. We decided to put an end to their interference before the Knights arrive. However, before we discuss that any further, I have one quick request to make. Class rep?" Even though I'd just addressed her, she didn't seem to hear me, so I raised my voice and tried again. "Amelia?"

"Hm?" She flinched as if she'd just awakened from a daze, and she immediately looked me in the eye. "Ah, yes? Can I help?"

"Yes, you can," I answered firmly. "I want you to arrange a meeting between your grandfather and me, as soon as humanly possible."

"I... think I can manage that," she replied a little uncertainly, and I could practically see the unspoken "Why?" in her eyes. I didn't let it manifest, though, as I immediately moved on.

"Good, please do so. Now then, here's the main thing we have to discuss: How do you plan to take care of Lab Coat Guy and his flunkies?" I could see the budding confusion in some eyes in my audience, so I quickly told them, "I have already discussed this with Josh, but to be frank, I'm going to have my hands full with the Chimera and preparing for the Knights, and I am going to need Brang and his men to be on standby for that. This means it falls on your shoulders to deal with our serial ambusher on your own."

"Does that include me, too?" Judy asked with a raised hand, and I immediately shook my head.

"Nope. You are a noncombatant, so you are obviously excluded. That said, this reminds me of something." I swept my eyes over the group and addressed them as one. "After this meeting is over, please hand over your Magiformers for the rest of the day. I recently got access to some communication artifacts, and I plan to integrate some of their functions into the uniforms so that you can communicate with the outside even while in a Purple Zone. Also, I am planning to make Judy into our mission control."

"Chief, stop," my dear assistant spoke up in a comparatively dire tone. "You already look terrible. If you are going mess with enchantments again and get sick, your school attendance record is going to get completely ruined."

"Don't worry, Dormouse, it's not that big a deal."

"The enchantment or the attendance record?" Josh asked a little absent-mindedly, and I answered in the only appropriate way.

"Yes."

My friend immediately rolled his eyes, but I naturally ignored him and continued the previous discussion unabated.

"So back on topic: I can provide you with the location of their base, and I can provide info on their movements, but as far as actually going in and bashing heads together, I'm afraid I can't help with that."

For the record, what I'd just said wasn't entirely true. The truth of the matter was that I could, if I really wanted to, put an end to Lab Coat Guy's shenanigans in many different ways. Just to give an example, if I considered him a serious threat to the lives of my friends, I had all the tools necessary to assassinate him by, say, making an IED using plans from the Celestial Hub, and then Phasing into his bedroom while he slept and putting it under his bed.

It would be a quick and permanent solution, but I had two good reasons why I wanted to avoid such a development at all cost: on one hand, I was afraid that resorting to lethal force would somehow drag everything into a darker, grittier direction, which was a possibility I simply couldn't rule out without first understanding what made the world react to my actions. This was something I have been considering ever since I accidentally poisoned Crowey, and I decided it was better to be a little softhearted now than to be sorry later when it turns out I accidentally changed this into a world where, in the grim darkness of the near future, there is only war and merchandising. I mean, reading about a setting like that might have been a guilty pleasure of mine, but I sure as hell didn't want to live in it.

Let's put grimdark space war games aside for a moment, though, and return to my other reason why I didn't want to blow Lab Coat Guy into smithereens: I simply found the idea of ending someone's life, unless in clear self-defense, an ethically indefensible action, and so I wished to avoid it if at all possible. Not to mention, I also had to wrestle with the notion that the bad guys I would be facing in the future would be, in practical terms, preprogrammed actors designed to serve an antagonistic role, and as Brang's example illustrated, once decoupled from their original role, they could turn out to be perfectly friendly and reasonable people. In short, I found even hurting our antagonists more than necessary to be morally dubious. Except when it came to Crowey, of course, because screw that guy.

However, my aversion to dirtying my hands aside, I had another, narrative-theory-driven reason why I figured I could leave this to Josh and Co. while I focused my attention elsewhere: Josh was the protagonist of this world. Whether or not there was something like an AI director that threw plot at him (and by proximity, us), there was a preplanned story we were unwittingly playing out, and the fact that Josh was in the middle of it all remained a constant. In our previous discussions on the subject, Judy and I had long since concluded that the attacks by Lab Coat Guy and his supposedly hidden connection to Lord Grandpa were the A plot of the current arc of Josh's story.

Why was that important? Simply put, just like how the Chimera seemed to be my side plot designed to keep me busy, either by the ever-elusive Narrative or the not-so-elusive Lord Grandpa, the main plot of the arc was necessarily something that the main characters were supposed to resolve. I also wasn't particularly worried about them, not only because I knew how strong they individually were firsthand, but because as main characters, being the resident battle harem protagonist and his love interests, I was fairly certain they enjoyed at least some measure of plot armour. This was just a theory made on strong inference, but considering that the entire gang managed to weather a battle against one of the Lords of the Abyss with only minor scratches, I had a feeling I was onto something.

Speaking of injuries, though, while they managed to get through multiple battles without shedding a drop of blood, in the same time span I had been injured and fallen ill so many times I almost understood why Judy became such a worrywart. That told me that I was either really unlucky, or that I simply didn't have the same plot armour as them. On the same note, I felt it was safe to guess that side characters possessed no such plot armour, either, so I felt as if I was entirely justified in focusing my attention on Elly's family, as they were the ones in actual tangible danger without any narrative safety lines.

But let's put my ponderings about the nature and possibility of plot armour aside for now, and focus on the discussion. Or rather, the lack thereof.

"Come on, guys, don't look at me like that!" I exclaimed as I swept my eyes over the hesitant bunch in front of me. "You can handle this much on your own, can't you?"

"Maybe, but I would feel safer if you were around," Snowy said in a low voice, and she was immediately supported by Angie.

"Yeah! You are the leader! The idea man! The boss! How can you expect us to just do things without you!"

"Hold on for just a moment!" I stopped her with a raised palm. "Who made me the leader?"

"You just kind of... are?" Angie told me, this time a little less eagerly. "I mean, you are the guy with a secret base and an army of scary Fauns, and you are also the only one of us who seems to know what's going on at all times... so... yeah..."

I awarded her sincere words with a frown that almost made my forehead hurt and responded by telling her, "Well, sorry to disappoint you, but I am definitely not leader material, and thus I won't do any leading."

"You are making linguists cry. Shame on you," Judy cut in with an absentminded voice, probably by reflex.

"Doesn't matter. The important thing is that if you want to get rid of the silly robot ambushes, you have to come up with a plan on your own, and that's my final word on the matter."

"Oh, I see what you are doing!" the Celestial girl pressed on, her enthusiasm completely unabated. "You are doing that mentor thing where you are throwing us into the deep water to teach us how to swim on our own!"

"No, I am *literally* not able to be in two places at once, so I simply want you to do this one thing on your own. If you absolutely *need* someone to lead you, you have Josh right over there."

"Ah, so he is your deputy, then," she stated with a profound nod, and by this point I decided to give up.

"Fine, call it whatever you want. Anyways, Josh, do you have anything to say?"

My hapless friend looked equal parts startled and indignant by the unwanted attention, but he quickly collected himself and told us, "Actually, I had this idea. I don't know if it will work, but..."

"Just say it, and we'll see," I encouraged him a little, if only so that Angie would focus on him instead of me.

"Well, you see, Dr. Robatto is working with Ammy's grandfather, right?" I nodded and urged him to continue with my patented eyebrow wriggling. "So, if I remember right, they kept in contact by using Pascal as a messenger, but Pascal and Robatto didn't seem to like each other at all. I mean, Ammy told me there was something about broken arms or something..."

"That's correct," I confirmed, which seemed to have made Josh slightly more confident.

"So I was thinking: If they don't like each other, couldn't we play them against each other? For example, we could set things up so that Pascal would have to come to our rescue in some form, and then we could have them tire each other out."

"So you want to use Pascal to capture Robatto," Ammy mused as she absentmindedly adjusted her glasses.

"Yes. Since they are already on bad terms, we could indirectly provoke them so that they would focus on each other, and then once they are out of breath, we could capture Robatto, and Pascal wouldn't be able to let him get away like the last time," Josh added.

"And then we could take them both to Lord Endymonion, and then we could force him to confess and explain himself," came the next addendum from the princess. "I could even ask Sebastian to come with us. He cannot fight Robatto for us without breaking the truce with Endymonion, but if Sebastian was with us when we present the two, Ammy's grandpa couldn't dismiss us that easily."

"That... could actually work," Ammy granted it to Josh, and I used the opportunity to get everyone's attention by clapping my hands once.

"That's a decent first plan, and suitably devious to boot. Now you just have to work out the details and try to put it into practice. See, it's not that hard."

"You are right," Angie agreed with a huge nod. "To think that your leadership skills would rub off on Josh so well, you are a great mentor after all!"

"... You know, you are lucky you are too far and I can't be arsed to walk over to you just to flick your forehead." The Celestial girl let out a giggle in response to my grievous threat, and so I exhaled in a long groan and told them, "It seems like this discussion is going nowhere fast at this rate. How about we call it a day for now and I let you guys make your plans on your own time?"

"Sounds great," Angie exclaimed, and she elbowed Josh in the side before she sprang to her feet. "The last one to the hockey table is the spoiled egg!"

"What does that even mean?" my friend grumbled, but got up and followed after her all the same, and before I knew it, the others began to leave, as well. Ammy seemed to be unusually interested in the facilities of the secret base, Snowy took two of the Fauns with her and began preparing refreshments from the minibar, while Judy and Elly quickly walked over to my side and dragged me to sit down with them, claiming that I looked unsteady.

All in all, I couldn't help but sigh in exasperation. They claimed I was the leader of the group, yet at times like this, I felt more like a shepherd trying to herd cats...

PART 2

"Are you sure you won't be staying over for dinner?" my draconic girlfriend asked me with upturned eyes, which, while admittedly pretty cute, was still not enough to change my mind.

"I told you I can't. I still have to meet with Mountain Girl and explain the plan to her. Also, pay attention while walking."

"I don't have to. I'm already holding on to you," Elly declared while she simultaneously squeezed my upper arm even harder. "Not to mention, even if I stumbled, you would catch me, anyway."

"True, but if you keep relying on me like that, then what happens if you stumble when I'm not around?"

"That's easy; it's not a problem if we are never separated," she replied with a bright smile and by cutting off the circulation in my arm even harder. "I just have to make sure you are always around."

That sounded just a wee bit impractical, not to mention stifling, but I chalked it up to her still being in the honeymoon period. Love made people say all sorts of silly things; it was almost as bad as politics in that regard.

Anyhow, we reached the Dracis mansion hand in hand like that, and we made our way inside without the slightest reservation. It was a little funny, to be honest; I couldn't pinpoint exactly when it happened, and yet at some point the grand, opulent interiors became familiar and, dare I say, homey. Not only that, but at one point or another, the previously blank or guarded glances of the stereotypical placeholder maids running the place turned welcoming and even a little respectful at times.

As I mused about how far my integration into the Dracis family progressed without my notice, we reached the large living room slash reception hall of the mansion, and the moment we entered, I was greeted by a familiar belly laugh.

"Hi, son! I didn't expect you would be coming over so soon!" Abram welcomed me with his usual complete lack of an indoor voice.

"Hello, dad-in-law," I greeted the Dracis patriarch in turn, which immediately elicited the reaction I was expecting, namely another bout of hearty chuckles. I ignored the laughing man and turned my attention to the other occupant of the room. "Hello, Emese."

"Why aren't you calling me mom-in-law?" the mother of the household leveled the question at me on the spot, her pout such a mirror image of her daughter's that they couldn't deny the family resemblance even if they tried.

"I'm starting to fear that by healing your injury I might have ruined your character," I muttered under my breath, but she could clearly hear it all the same.

"Don't you worry about my character, young mister!" Emese exclaimed as she somehow managed to pout even harder. "Stop being so formal, or I swear I'll go over there and give you a motherly ass kicking."

"You see, that's exactly what I was talking about..." I grumbled and unsubtly rolled my eyes before I addressed the elephant in the room. "Fine. So, mom-in-law, why are you in your wheelchair again?"

"It is a pivotal detail in our plans," stated a brand-new, if not exactly unexpected, voice entering the fray.

I glanced over my shoulder, just in time to see Sebastian elegantly close the door behind him. Now normally I would have asked why, or even how, someone would close a door *elegantly*, but I didn't want to hold things up, so I chalked it up to yet another weird *thing* Sebastian did and let it slide.

"Hello, old man," I greeted him with an only-50-percent-fake smile. "I see you still have your penchant for dramatic entrances."

"At my age, I believe I can afford a predilection for the dramatic, my boy," he responded with a disturbingly grandfatherly smile. I knew it was to unnerve me, so I refused to give him the satisfaction and contorted my face into an impeccably amicable smile of my own. For some reason that made Elly giggle, so I hastily cleared my throat and moved the conversation along.

"So why did your plan require Emese—?"

"Mom-in-law," she immediately corrected me, so a barely stifled groan later I started again.

"So which part of your plan requires *mom-in-law* to stay in her wheelchair?" I asked, much to her (and for some odd reason, Elly's) apparent delight.

"I will explain in a moment," Abram stated in a somewhat-uncertain voice as he patted himself down. I was tempted to ask what he was doing, but then his face lit up the moment he reached into his back pocket, and he exclaimed, "Ah, here it is!"

I peered over to see what he was so hyped about, but I didn't actually need to, as he quickly made his way over to our side and presented a large envelope to me. I gently peeled the princess off my arm before I accepted it, and a single touch told me that there was something small and rectangular in it. Abram didn't seem to want to tell me what I was holding, as he only kept looking at me with the expectant stare of a kid at a birthday party waiting for the host to finally cut the cake, so I decided to forego any formalities and just open the envelope and get it over with.

Once I peeked inside, I found a simple A4 page folded in half, as well as a shiny golden plastic card. I pretty much recognized it at first glance, but I took it out, anyway.

"It's the new debit card you asked for!" Papa Dracis couldn't help himself and told me the obvious.

"That was quick," I muttered under my breath as I observed the piece of plastic in my hand.

After I discovered my connection to the Knights, I immediately became suspicious about the source of the money in my account. I'd already looked into the account number where my monthly allowance came from, but it quickly turned into a dead end, and while I could have used the Hub to dig further, I kind of forgot about the whole thing because of bigger, more apparent issues I had to deal with.

Either way, in preparation for any future complications, I decided to move my savings over to another account... except I immediately ran into a minor complication in the form of the fact that I was, well, a *minor*, and thus I couldn't open one myself. Also, banks were apparently way less lenient about these things than phone carriers. Who would have thought?

After I told Abram about this, he graciously offered to make me a brand-new account by pulling a few strings at the bank where the Dracises were keeping most of their record company money. I had to admit, I was a little impressed by how fast he operated, and I was just about to thank him when I noticed that he was unsubtly glancing at the envelope in my hand with an expectant look on his face. I put the plastic card aside for a moment and reached inside to recover the piece of paper, the only thing that he could be interested in. Or rather, I figured he was interested in my reaction to it, so I steeled my nerves for a moment before I unfolded the page and read its contents.

"That's... a lot of money," I uttered as I reached the end of what appeared to be a pretty hefty account statement, with at least one more zero at the end than there was supposed to be.

"Congratulations on your first paycheck, son!" Abram exclaimed while patting me on the shoulder, though maybe because of my weakened condition, it felt like he was trying to break my collarbone. Once I successfully squirmed my way out of his painful show of affection, I glanced at the page again and then faced him with what I felt must have been a somewhat-troubled expression on my face.

"So you transferred back all the investment I made in the streaming business, plus consultation fees and dividends?"

"Yes!" he said with a gigantic grin on his face. "You are an investor in this project, and investors are supposed to get their investment back once everything's in the black!"

"Maybe, but I don't think it's supposed to be this direct," I muttered as I took a third look at the account statement.

"Don't look the gift horse in the mouth," my dear girlfriend told me with a genuinely happy smile, so I decided to follow her lead and let it go. The fact that somehow I now had more money than what I'd started out with, even after spending a small fortune on the refurbishing of the secret base, made me feel a little weird, though. Was it really supposed to be this easy to earn money? And why was I secretly feeling a little giddy about it? Oh no! Was the draconic nature of my in-laws rubbing off on me?

Theoretical gold fever aside, I decided to thank Abram once again, and I pocketed the envelope and its contents, and I was just about to lead the conversation back to the topic of the counter-ambush on the Knights when I recalled something else.

"Abram, can I ask for your help with one more issue?" I addressed my host, and he gave me a nod that more or less said, "Why are you even asking such a silly question?" so I threw away my remaining reservations. "I told you I lost my memory, right? Among my old belongings, I found a deposit box key without any notches and only a single number on it. Do you happen to have any associates in the banking sector who could tell me which bank it belongs to?"

"Sure, I can ask around!" he replied with a grin that made him look a little unreliable. "Can you show it to me?"

"Not right now. I don't have it on me. To be honest with you, I totally forgot about it until recently, but considering it's one of my few unidentified belongings, I figure it might have something to do with the Knights."

"Then I will make sure to put my top men on the case!" Papa Dracis declared, this time a little more reliably.

"Thanks, it would help me a lot," I thanked him, and I was entirely serious. I'd already attempted to find where the key belonged to, but internet searches didn't turn up anything useful, and I simply didn't have the time to visit every bank with a deposit service on the island, hoping I would sooner or later stumble upon the right one.

I made a mental note to pocket the key once I got home, and then I finally broached the topic that made me come here in the first place... for the third time.

"So again: wheelchair. Please explain."

The Dracis family shared an odd look at my expense, and at the end of the day it was Sebastian who stepped forth to explain things to me.

"We have decided on a strategy of drawing in the accursed Knights with a false show of weakness," he told me as he casually made his way around us and stood behind Emese in her wheelchair. "As our foes are unaware of the recovery of the matron of the family..."

"Don't call me matron," Emese cut in while sending a glare at the old man over her shoulder. "It makes it sound like I'm old."

"During the last family meeting," the old butler continued without even sparing a glance at the fuming woman, "We agreed upon the following details: the lad and I will head to the port and leave the island on..." He paused while he raised his hands and then added, in the company of the ever-so-annoying air quotes, "'*urgent business.*'"

"... I figure you aren't actually going to leave," I ventured a guess, and Abram immediately confirmed it.

"No, of course we aren't! Well, not for long, anyway! After a day out on the sea, we'll fly back under the radar!" There was a beat of silence, with the man's expression telling me he was expecting me to do or say something, but since I had no idea what he wanted, he hastily clarified, "In other words, we are going to fly very close to the water! You see! Under the radar!"

"Oh, I got it!" Elly exclaimed, and the father-daughter duo let out a series of chuckles. I, on the other hand, finally understood why the princess required comedic coaching from Judy.

"The fact that the two of us left the estate alone will not only tell the accursed Knights that we are unaware of their plans," Sebastian continued with the expression of a long-suffering father embarrassed of the antics of his children... which I supposed wasn't too far from the truth. "By leaving our gates unguarded, we shall lull them in a false sense of security, so that when *Lady* Emese rises from her seat and we strike them from the back, we shall have the advantage of ultimate surprise."

"Isn't that a little risky?" I asked the obvious question, and the old butler promptly shook his head.

"Dealing with the accursed Knights is always a dangerous business, but this is the most effective way to destroy their forces."

"Oh, I get it now. Your goal isn't just to repel them, but to crush them."

"Precisely," Sebastian confirmed with the utmost conviction. "Destroying the enemies attacking us is the most effective way to reduce and ultimately eliminate the risk they would pose in the future."

"That's the family mantra!" Abram commented on the side. "It's served us well to this day, so don't worry, son!"

"It's also a good opportunity for me to stretch my legs a little," Mama Dracis added as she playfully swung her legs, only to let out a pained hiss. "Ouch... I keep forgetting that it still stings when I'm not transformed..."

And that, ladies and gentlemen, was how I discovered from whence Elly got her airhead side... Seriously, the more I learned about this family, the more baffled I felt about how they'd survived for so long. Also, speaking of survival...

"Let's say I understand the gist of your plan. I have just one question: What happens if they bring along a dragon-slaying weapon? I just fixed mom-in-law's legs, so I would prefer if they stayed fixed."

"So do I," Emese remarked while she rubbed the right side of her hips with her hand.

"Don't worry, my boy. The number of weapons forged for the express purpose of ending my kin can be counted on one hand, and practically all of them were lost or destroyed over the centuries."

"Right, that also reminds me of something," I raised my voice and looked the old man in the eye. "I presume you are taking the spear with you, right?"

"No. It would be too conspicuous."

"Wait, what? Now, hold on for a moment!" I raised my voice even higher. "Doesn't that strike you as extremely risky?"

"Not particularly," Sebastian replied flatly. "As far as the accursed Knights are concerned, their spear was destroyed right after the ambush that led to the *lady's* injury."

I wanted to argue back, but my mouth froze halfway open as a sudden realization hit me, and I closed it so hard it made my teeth hurt.

Okay, let's take a step back and look at the big picture here by asking a single question: How would the attack of the Knights play out if I hadn't come to these people right away and told them about it? The pieces on the chessboard are as follows: an ancient dragon, a dragon-slaying plot device, an injured Draconian with a curse that made transforming debilitatingly painful, and a group of dastardly Knights. If I was a hack Narrative or whatever, how would I play this out?

First off, the dragon-slaying spear was a Chekhov's gun in its more elementary form. In short, Chekhov's gun is a trope, or rather a writing technique, that is used a lot in various media, and it is a particular form of setup and payoff. The term comes from the writer Anton Chekhov, and his parable goes something like this: if there is a gun hanging on the wall in the first act of a play, that gun must play a role in the second or third act; otherwise there is no reason why it should be there in the first place. In other words, if a plot-relevant item is introduced and foreshadowed, said item *must* be actually relevant and used later on.

Now, I know this is going to sound like a stretch, but hear me out: we have a DRAGON. SLAYING. SPEAR. That sounds like it was probably supposed to play a role in, oh, I don't know... maybe slaying a dragon? Oh, and look! We have a dragon in disguise right over there! What a koinkidink!

Keeping that in mind, I think it's pretty obvious that the spear chiefly exists to be used on Sebastian. Whether it is to just injure or to outright kill him to up the stakes is something I cannot say for sure, but I was pretty damn sure that the reason why I couldn't tweak the spear with my phantom limb was because doing so would have resulted in it no longer being able to fulfill its narrative purpose.

As for the other plot device I've discovered, namely Emese's curse, it would also fit into this situation. Let's say Sebastian is stabbed and Elly is threatened. Since the curse doesn't stop her from transforming, she would do so in order to chase off the Knights, but it would come at a cost. Being bedridden, comatose, dead... take your pick, the end result is the same: the Knights are established as a huge threat; the Dracis family is in shambles, making it ripe for a dashing hero to come in and save the day. This hero was, naturally, Josh, and then he could go ahead and fulfill the prophecy and what have you while he is at it. The end.

Granted, what I just outlined was a vague theory at best, and it had at least one giant, Abram-shaped hole in it, but I had a feeling I was more or less on the money in regards to the two plot devices. Luckily I had already sabotaged Emese's curse, so that was a problem out of my hair, yet the spear still remained. There was only one question left: What should I do about it?

"Quick question: Can we actually destroy the spear now?" I went with the direct option. "For example, there was that volcano idea I gave you the other day? Let's do it."

"No," Sebastian replied with unusual bluntness.

"Oh, come on, old man! It's a spear designed to kill you! Don't tell me you don't want to get rid of it!"

"No, I don't," he told me, and his words gave me pause for a moment. He quickly realized I was just a smidgen flabbergasted by his answer, so he slowly explained, "Listen, my boy. Do you recall where the spear currently resides?"

"In your study," I answered reflexively, but after I thought about it for a long moment, I could scarcely believe my own conclusion. "Please tell me you are not being obstinate just because it's technically part of your collection..."

"To be more precise, it is a prized trophy, and one I do not wish to part with."

"You've got to be kidding me!" I exclaimed with just a hint of genuine anger. "That's like keeping a loaded gun on your wall for sentimental reasons!"

"I do believe some people do that."

"Yes, and it's reckless, stupid, and weird," I countered, but the old man only scoffed at me, so I turned a hopeful eye to the Dracis patriarch instead. Regrettably, he only kept grinning like a well-fed lion.

"I would appreciate some support, dad-in-law! It's your family's lives at stake here!"

Abram let out a chuckle, meaning my words didn't faze him at all, and told me, "Don't worry too much, son! Grandpa knows what he is doing! If he says it's fine, then it's fine!"

I was straight-up flabbergasted by the man's cavalier attitude, yet since it became obvious he wouldn't help to convince the old man, it meant I had to do it on my own.

"Fine, then we aren't going to throw it into a volcano. Can we at least take it somewhere else? For example, how about we dig a big hole in the backyard and bury it there until the Knights are chased off?"

"You truly worry too much," Sebastian responded, following a sigh. "By the date of the attack, the lad and I shall be back and awaiting their arrival. Even if the accursed Knights knew of the preservation of their weapon, whether it stays locked away in my study or hidden underground makes little difference to dead men."

I glanced around in the room, yet everyone, even my girlfriend, seemed to share this reckless sentiment. At the end of the day, it appeared I had no other choice but to let it go and allow Sebastian to keep the stupid spear. Or at the very least act like it...

"Whatever, suit yourself," I concluded with a suitably frustrated expression on my face, and I moved the conversation forward by asking, "Putting the spear aside, I have another question. Where do you plan to stake out until the Knights come?"

"We were actually wondering if we could stay at your house, son," Abram answered in an unusually low voice.

"You want to stay over at my place?" I reiterated after him, resulting in a huge nod.

"It is reasonably close to our estate, and it is arguably the last place where they would be looking for us."

"I'm not sure it's a good idea," I explained with a frown that was as deep as it was involuntary. "Sure, they won't be looking for you, but they might be looking for me. Considering my connection with them, it's not far-fetched to think that the Knights might show up in front of my doorstep before the attack on the mansion. What exactly do you think would happen if they found you two there?"

"A battle of epic proportions!" Papa Dracis exclaimed with apparent delight, and I'm not ashamed to admit I was pretty startled for a moment.

"The lad is correct," Sebastian added on as he unsubtly cracked his knuckles. "If they were to appear to converse with you, it just means we could deal with them right then and there."

"And wreck my house in the process?"

"Don't be daft, my boy," the old butler rolled his eyes and told me, "It is quite obvious we would erect a Restricted Space before we would commence with the hostilities."

"... Was that supposed to make me feel better about you fighting in my house?" Neither of the men answered my rhetorical question, so I let out a tired sigh and told them, "Fine, I'll think about it."

"Don't think too long. We only have a scant few days to prepare," Sebastian warned me, which sounded rich from the mouth of the dragon who refused to remove the thing designed to kill him from his own study, but I digress.

Anyhow, somewhere along the way Elly attached herself to me again, and seeing that, the old man let out one of his absolutely annoying grandfatherly chuckles. I naturally ignored him, especially since Emese also called out to me.

"Are you staying for dinner today?" she spoke in an expectant voice, and I had to let her down by shaking my head.

"No, I have other plans for the evening."

"Aw. A shame," she muttered under her breath, and before I could tell her a suitable excuse, my attention was grabbed by the old man once again.

"Does that mean you are not interested in the items of my Berlin collection, either?"

"I... would be lying if I said I wasn't, but not at the moment. Studying and modifying enchantments take a lot out of me, and I have already done that today. I have a lot on my plate right now, and I need to recover my strength in case I'm needed, so I'm afraid I can't play around with your toys today."

"Are you still sick?" Emese inquired as she rolled up to me. "Now that you mention it, you do look a little pale."

"I'll just have to restrain myself from messing around with enchantments for a while, and I should be back to normal soon... I think."

"The day of the attack is still a week away; you should rest a lot until then," the lady of the house offered her advice, but I could only shake my head at her kind words.

"I have other things to do in the meantime."

"Such as?" Sebastian inquired, but before I could give him one of my intentionally vague answers, Elly replied in my stead.

"We are going to deal with Robatto."

"Really? About time," Emese muttered under her breath before putting on a determined expression. "Do you need our help?"

"Honey, we've already discussed this," Abram cut in, his voice sounding just a tad exhausted. "Until Amadeus gives us a response, we cannot fight on the island. It won't do us any good to ruin our relationship with him."

"We'll just have to make sure he won't find out," she told us with a wink. "Or do you want Leo to fight alone in that condition?"

"There are... multiple issues with what you just said, so let me come clean..." I interrupted her and quickly explained the current plan, including using Pascal, leaving things to Josh, and some other small details.

After hearing me out, Mama Dracis reluctantly dropped the topic, though she made sure to remind me that if we actually needed help, they would happily provide it. After we concluded that, we spent a couple of minutes discussing other, less crucial topics, and it was around the time when the Dracis parents began to argue whether they want a grandson or a granddaughter first that I figured I would take my leave. But first...

"How about we go to your room for a bit?" I addressed the question to the princess. "It's been a while since we spent some time alone."

"Are we going to cuddle?" my girlfriend asked back with sparkly eyes, and I couldn't help but smile back at her.

"If you want to."

"Then we are going to cuddle!" she declared as she began to drag me out of the room.

I disregarded all the "It's so nice to be young!"s and "They look so cute, don't they, honey?"s behind us and followed after her. Once we were getting close to her room, I reached into my trouser pocket and put my finger on the small, metallic object in it. It was one of the artifacts I'd received from Mike this morning: a bracelet with a simple design holding a deceptively complex communication enchantment. I had it on me because I'd used it as a template when modifying the Magiformers of the group, but since it was the only thing on hand, I had to work with it.

As such, when we stopped in front of Elly's door, I gently poked her face to get her attention and told her, "You know, I'm still a little concerned about the spear."

"Don't worry, Sebastian always knows best," she responded with a line that felt so canned I was worried it was something they kept telling themselves over the generations. It would have certainly explained how the old man could end up so eccentric. However, that was beside the point.

"Maybe, but just for my peace of mind," I said as I pulled my hand out of my pocket and showed her the bracelet, "Can I ask a tiny little favor from you?"

CHAPTER 6

PART 1

"It's been a while," I whispered under my breath and stretched my back under the sunny, if not particularly warm, autumn sky.

"What's been a while?" Judy inquired without looking up from the lunch box she was unpacking at the moment, so I told her:

"Since the last time we had lunch on the school rooftop like this."

"That's true. You've been on sick leave a lot lately." There was just a tiny bit of edge to her words, but I decided to ignore it, and instead I sidled closer to her on the bench.

Even though the weather was just a touch wintry at the moment (which also resulted in the placeholders avoiding the place like the plague, hence why we had the whole place for ourselves), Josh and Co. had already picked the cafeteria in the morning. That meant we could either eat in the classroom or here, and Judy voted on the latter, probably so that we could spend some quality time together for a change. As for why we'd decided to separate ourselves from the rest of the group in the first place, it was so that they could have their strategic discussions about how to capture Lab Coat Guy without my unwitting interference.

I mean, the whole point was to make Josh a bit more independent and protagonist-y, and subconsciously seeking validation from me all the time got in the way of that. Although it pained to me to admit it, I was legitimately guilty when it came to his developing this bad habit in the first place, so I figured I might as well help him course correct.

I mean, Angie had a legitimate point; I'd been acting too much like a leader-type character as of late, so I couldn't blame them for mistaking me for one. Hopefully I would have the time and opportunity to change that impression, or failing that, to become a shadowy mastermind character instead, the kind that stayed in the background and manipulated events in the main characters' favor without taking the lead themselves. Nevertheless, that was a fairly distant goal, and I had much more important things on my mind at the moment. Such as lunch.

"What are we going to have today?"

"Sandwiches," Judy answered as she handed a wrapper-covered packet over to me.

"We are back to our roots, huh?" I muttered as I unwrapped my package and checked the contents between the buns. "Fried chicken. A classic."

"Indeed," my girlfriend nodded and reached behind the lunch box. "You should also have this."

I was just about to take a bite out of my food when I laid my eyes upon the thing in Judy's hand, and I immediately rolled them. My eyes, I mean, not Judy's hands. That would've been just plain weird.

"Are you serious, Dormouse? It's the lunch *break*. How am I supposed to enjoy the tasty sandwiches my lovely girlfriend prepared for me like this?"

"Don't even try to butter me up," my dearest assistant scolded me and placed the open history textbook onto my lap. "You've been missing a lot of lessons lately. If you don't catch up, your grades are going to suffer."

"I know, but can't I catch up *later*?"

"That's something a slacker would say," Judy suddenly declared with a voice more wooden than an entire Viking longship. "Are you a slacker?"

"... Where did that come from?" I asked, mildly bewildered.

"What do you mean?" she responded innocently, but by this point I was proficient enough when it came to reading her to tell that she was embarrassed by her previous words.

"That sounded like something you rehearsed ahead of time," I pressed on, and after a few short seconds of silence she finally gave in.

"It's from a self-help book. For motivation."

I continued to scrutinize her for a moment, but it appeared she was entirely sincere, so I stated, "Okay, I bite. Why did you read a book like that?"

"To motivate you to study, obviously," she answered as if it was entirely self-evident. "Recent studies have shown that school performance and financial success scale linearly, and financial stability is one of the key requirements of a conflict-free and relaxed family life. To ensure our future happiness, I decided it was necessary to motivate you."

"Just for the record, you do know that I'm rich, right?"

"That's not an excuse to slack off," she countered as she unwrapped one of her own sandwiches. "You're going to have to provide for *exactly* two wives, and at least four kids."

"At least?" I asked back absentmindedly between two bites, and she gave me a firm nod in response.

"Yes. I want at least three, and Elly said she wants one for sure."

"I think you two are thinking just a smidgen too far ahead. Also, it's not like I really have to provide for you two. Elly is silly rich, and with your grades, I'm pretty sure you are going to do great."

"You're still going to provide for me," she countered with a huff. "You have to pay for my assistant's fees, and my contract lasts for a lifetime."

"If you insist," I told her with a chuckle.

"I do, so you better start studying."

My chuckles immediately turned into a stifled groan as I rolled my eyes and pleaded, "Come on, Dormouse. Think of the situation. Winter is coming, and soon we won't be able to have lunches together up here. Do you really want me to waste what very well might be my last opportunity to have a rooftop rendezvous with my girlfriend by ignoring her and studying instead?"

"If you put it like that..." she finally relented, and so I quickly picked up the history book and put it aside before she could change her mind.

"There you go. I promise I'll look over the parts I missed later. For now, how about we just relax a little?"

"Fine," she spoke with just a hint of sulkiness in her voice, and for a few short minutes we silently consumed our required dose of calories for the afternoon.

"Chief?"

"Hm?" I turned to Judy, and I admit I was a little surprised by the way she called out to me out of the blue.

"This feels nostalgic," she stated with a vaguely wistful look in her eyes.

"Now that you mention it, it kind of does," I agreed with her after considering it for a moment. "This roof is where we first met."

"Yes," she stated with a nod. "It's also the place where you hired me to become your assistant."

"I believe we are talking about the same event," I muttered a little uncertainly, but then I added, "That said, it really feels like it's been ages since that day."

"A lot of things have happened. Back then, you even thought this was just a school life harem setting." She waited for a beat, probably to see if I would add anything, then she flatly added, "You were wrong."

"I wasn't wrong; I just didn't see the whole picture. Just because Newton didn't know about relativity, it doesn't make Newtonian physics wrong. Just incomplete."

"I'll now graciously skim over the fact that you likened yourself to Sir Isaac Newton, and I won't make fun of you for it."

"Thank you for your small mercies. You are truly kind."

"You're welcome."

"That said," I began as I nimbly unwrapped my next sandwich, "It feels like we've come far, yet at the same time we are still standing by the starting line."

"Mmmm," Judy... agreed, I think? It was hard to tell because her mouth was currently so full she reminded me of a chipmunk, but once she swallowed, she properly agreed by telling me, "True. We have discovered many things, but just as many things are shrouded in mystery."

"Let's hope that once we weather the coming flustercuck with the Knights, we're finally going to have some downtime and can get some research done for a change. For example, I'm itching to experiment with the supernatural stratum through enchantments, but as long as there's uncertain danger afoot that could require my urgent attention, the way it knocks me out for half a week every single time is too much of a liability."

"I don't want to rain on your parade, Chief, but I think the main reason why we are having a hard time with the arrival of the Knights is exactly because of your meddling. With the Narrative, I mean."

This comment made me pause for a moment and give my assistant a wry look, but since she didn't back down, I decided to just outright tell her, "I thought we were over this. Not every single thing that happens to us has to be because of the Narrative jerking everyone's strings. There might be perfectly reasonable explanations for the sudden appearance of the Knights."

"Really? Do you have a sensible Watsonian explanation then?"

"Maybe," I countered with a frown. "Do you have a sensible Doylist one?"

"I do," Judy stated with perfect confidence, but then she continued to chew on her food without actually saying it.

"So?" I prompted her, just a tiny bit impatiently, and after she finished up the last bite she finally turned to me and began to explain herself.

"I believe we've already discussed this, but let's reiterate our theory regarding the main plot so far: by saving Joshua from Noire, you ended the first arc."

"Technically we saved him, and Snowy, too, kinda, but otherwise you're correct."

"In conclusion, the first arc existed to set things up and then expose Joshua to the supernatural elements of the setting in a dramatic fashion. Are we in agreement on that?"

"More or less," I granted her with some minor reservations.

"If that is the case, then the second arc would be about an introductory villain, and the main characters learning how to work together in order to overcome them."

"That would be Lab Coat Guy."

"Precisely," she declared quite firmly for some reason.

"And if that's the main plot, then Mountain Girl and the stray Chimera are just side plots."

"Not only that," my assistant raised her voice while also extending an index finger in front of her, "That side plot has nothing to do with Joshua.

This tells us that the Narrative created it just for you, either as an acknowledgment of your impact on the original plot, or as a way to keep you busy and away from the main plot."

"Uh-huh," I grunted in what could be best described as skeptical agreement. "So in your interpretation of the situation, where do the Knights fit into the arc?"

"They don't," she told me with just the barest hint of smugness permeating her tone. "The Knights were most definitely supposed to be the focus of the next arc. If we follow genre conventions, the first couple of arcs would each focus on a different harem member. However, since you've disrupted the current arc by sabotaging the *sentai* elements and revealing Dr. Robatto's connection to the arch-mage of the island, it upset the natural progression of the plot and led to the next arc bleeding into the current one."

"... You're talking awfully confidently, considering you have little evidence for any of this," I grumbled while reaching for the thermos by the lunch box. "For a start, I'm not entirely sure about your arc hypothesis. It's just as likely that the original scenario had a branching route structure."

"Would that mean that, since the Dracises and the Knights are coming into focus, we are entering Eleanor's route?" After saying so, she thought for a moment and then added, "Also, if we presume we are in a route-based narrative, can we even be sure we are out of the common route yet?"

"I don't know, and I don't dare to guess just yet," I answered as I unscrewed the beverage holder and took a whiff of its contents. "Huh. That's new."

"Sebastian gifted me some of his tea blends when I visited the Dracis library the last time," Judy stated offhandedly, yet she couldn't hide how attentively she was looking at my reaction. "He said you'd like it."

"I very much do," I answered with a smile, and then I poured a portion into my plastic travel cup. "Thanks for the treat."

"You're welcome."

I took a cautious sip from my cup, and even though it couldn't exactly match up to the brew the old man made himself, it was still really, really good.

"So where were we?" I asked after savoring the taste for a moment, and Judy told me right away.

"We were at the part where you poked holes into my theory without providing a reasonable Watsonian alternative."

"Well then, I suppose I'd better do that right away." I flashed her my perfected roguish smile, and once it achieved the desired effect, I moved on by stating, "According to how I view it, while the narrative scaffoldings of a preplanned plot almost certainly exist around us, the current events are best explained by the consequences of our individual actions, and there is no guiding intelligence that constantly tries to maintain said preplanned plot."

"Does that make you a Narrative Deist?" my dear assistant leveled an unexpected question at me, and after a moment of thinking, I answered with a tentative nod.

"I suppose?" I granted her, but then I quickly returned to the main topic by telling her, "So let's take the elements of your arcs into consideration for a second: Lab Coat Guy, while he certainly fits the role of a mostly harmless starting villain, is technically just Lord Grandpa's flunky. On the same note, it turns out that while he covered his tracks a little better with Rinne, he still used my student ID photograph to prime her to look for me, and I'm fairly sure that he is behind the appearance of the Chimera, as well. I've talked with Brang and Snowy about it, and those creatures are really, really dumb. Without someone giving them direct orders, they would even forget to eat and starve to death."

"Really?"

"It was an extreme example, but Snowy said so, so it must be true. She said it's some kind of fail-safe mechanic so that they wouldn't go out of control and start hunting anything that moved. Anyhow, since it's sending out its spawn to forage and keeps moving around the city, it means that someone must've given it the orders to do so."

"And you still think that's Lord Amadeus."

"It's not like we have a huge list of suspects," I gave a firm answer, though I would've been the first to admit my reasoning was based on way more conjecture than I would've preferred. "There are no more Abyssals on the island, the Dracises have nothing to do with it, we would know if the Celestials had a hand in it because of the Hub, it doesn't fit the Knights' MO, and as for Lab Coat Guy, I figure he would've slipped up during the time I was observing him if it was him. Oh, by the way, he's already moving out to ambush Josh after school today. Please remind me to tell them, in case I forget."

"Noted," she replied, and then she filled her own mug with tea. I waited for her to finish, and only then did I continue.

"The point I was trying to get at is that the events of this entire arc you are talking about are the handiwork of Lord Grandpa, no ubiquitous Narrative involvement required. Not only that, but your theory doesn't explain why we almost had a genre shift, which would've made your proposed next arc about the Knights and Elly's family moot because then this wouldn't be a battle harem narrative anymore."

"If so, then how do you explain the sudden appearance of the Knights?"

"Thank you for asking," I said with a not-at-all-cheeky smile. "For a start, remember how I handed over a lot of sensitive intelligence to Sebastian about them? According to Moose, a lot of their bases were hit by what I presume to be other Draconians, which would explain why they would speed up whatever operation they had in mind on the island."

"You said that the man on the phone told you that the attack would proceed as planned," Judy countered. "Wouldn't that mean that the date was fixed well ahead of time?"

"I... suppose, yes..."

"If so, then that means they didn't move any of their plans up."

The two of us locked eyes for a few seconds, but since I couldn't come up with a snappy comeback, I was forced to grudgingly admit, "Fine, my theory doesn't explain everything, either."

"Mine explains this one, though," my girlfriend told me with a triumphant smirk (which, for the uninitiated, probably looked like nothing more than the corner of her lips twitching a little). "Since the day of the attack was information that everyone was unaware of, it was the equivalent of a Schrödinger's plot device. In other words, the Narrative could've retroactively changed the date in order to fit the pace of the plot."

"I find that impossible to refute on account of it being a black box."

"Which also means that it's impossible for me to prove it, as well," she concluded, earning her a nod.

"Almost everything we discuss about the Narrative boils down to this. To be honest though, I'm starting to think that the truth lies somewhere between the two extremes of our interpretations."

"Possibly. It's sad but true that until we learn more about the underlying principles of the world, the best we can do is post hoc rationalizations of events and the occasional prediction based on genre conventions."

"Oh, thanks for reminding me." I snapped my fingers and then pointed at her. "In your opinion, how will Josh's attempt at catching Lab Coat Guy turn out?"

"Depends," Judy answered a little absentmindedly, no doubt because she was too busy unpacking the desserts she'd brought.

"What are those?" I asked while redirecting my finger at the round pastries in her lap.

"Jaffa Cakes. Angeline's recommendation," she answered and handed one over to me, which I graciously accepted.

"Thank you very much. On a separate note, what do you mean by depends?"

"It depends on whether or not Robatto operates on *battle harem* or *sentai* tropes," she explained as she picked a cake for herself and began nibbling on it. "If he stays within the *battle harem* framework, then it's likely that once he's captured, he would turn into a tertiary character, possibly a comic relief one."

"I can kind of see that happening," I answered while sneakily snatching another cake from Judy's lap.

"If he follows *sentai* tropes, it's a little harder to tell."

"I guess. For a start, *sentai* villains are not supposed to be defeated before the end of the season," I mused as I quickly devoured the surprisingly delicious confectionery in my hand.

"Not unless they are a bait-and-switch paving the way for another antagonist, or in rare cases, an eeeeeevil organization of—"

"Bfff!"

Oh my god, I almost choked! What was that completely wooden *eeeeevil* just now?! And why was it so gosh darn adorable?! Dammit, Dormouse, do you want to assassinate me with cuteness!? Because at this rate, it might actually work...

"Chief? Are you all right?"

"Um... Yes, perfectly fine. I just need to drink a little," I mumbled as I reached for my mug and downed the remaining tea in it with a single gulp. "So you were saying something about bait-and-switch antagonists, right?"

My dear assistant was eyeing me through suspiciously squinted eyes, but at last she continued with, "I think that the Knights are supposed to be the antagonists to swoop in and one-up Robatto by posing a more competent threat."

"Is that part of your hypothesis about arcs, or is this a separate one?"

"No, but the two are not entirely incompatible."

"Fair enough. It does feel like you're really pushing the idea that the coming of the Knights is going to completely change the status quo once again."

"Do you think it wouldn't?"

"Well, maybe if it'd happened before I healed Emese..." I mused aloud, and Judy gave me such an intrigued look that I couldn't help but explain to her my previous idea of how things might've gone down if I didn't mess around with Emese's curse, and how it related to the two plot devices I've found so far.

She listened to me attentively, and once I reached the end of my tale, she let out an unsubtle sigh and told me, "Chief, if you keep this up, you might trigger the third arc before we even start the second one."

"What would that be about?" I wondered as I picked out the last cake, broke it in half, and handed the slightly larger piece over to Judy.

"Considering that we already had Noire, Robatto, possibly Lord Endymonion, and the Knights for antagonists, I'd guess it would be the Celestials' turn.

"It's okay, then; we already have a leg the size of Italy up on those guys, so I doubt they would cause too much trouble."

"... I can't decide if I should scold you for jinxing it, or for proactively ruining the third arc, as well."

"How about neither?"

"That's not an option," she stated quite resolutely, but I could see a small glint in the corner of her eye, so I pressed on, anyway.

"Okay, then what can I do to make it an option?"

"Chief, I can't believe you'd try to bribe me," she exclaimed in mock horror. "I want you to know that I'm an upstanding, law-abiding citizen, and I most certainly won't look the other way for any less than ten kisses."

"That was refreshingly direct for an upstanding citizen," I commented, and tried as I might, I failed to stop the corners of my lips from turning up in a smile. "Can I make my payment in installments?"

"Yes, but then I'll have to charge an interest."

"Whoever heard of charging interest on bribes?" I playfully scoffed, and in response, Judy sidled even closer to me on the bench until our tights touched.

"It's not a bribe; it's a direct form of lobbying."

"If you say so," I said under my breath as I leaned in for a kiss, yet our lips barely touched for a second when we were interrupted by the opening of the roof access door.

"Look at the lovebirds getting along!" Josh called out with an irreverent grin, and I couldn't help but jab back at him on the spot.

"Is that jealously I hear in those words?" I inquired with a provocative smirk, which immediately made him pause in his tracks.

"Well, excuse me. Not all of us than be as popular as you are."

My smirk slowly wilted off my face to be replaced by an incredulous grimace, but since he seemed to be perfectly serious, I could only groan and tell him, "You know, Josh, if lack of self-awareness hurt, I'm afraid you'd be screaming twenty-four/seven."

"What's that even supposed to mean?" my friend blurted out with invisible question marks over his head, but ultimately I decided it was more trouble than it was worth to explain myself, so I dismissed the topic with a wave of my hand.

"Never mind. More importantly, what are you doing up here?"

"Ammy said someone should warn you that lunch break is almost over, so I volunteered to come outside, into the cold, and tell you to come in."

"Uh-huh," I responded with a single and not-at-all-convinced eyebrow raised high. "Let me guess; you actually lost a bet or something and had to come. Am I right?"

The only answer I got to my question was a decidedly sheepish, "Lili is surprisingly good at rock-paper-scissors," and to be fair, it was good enough.

I stood up, turned to my slightly miffed girlfriend, and then I told her, "You've heard it, Dormouse. I guess we'd better head back to the classroom before Ammy scolds us."

She only responded with a fairly noncommittal "Mm," but she began to pack the empty lunch box away, so I figured she agreed with me. In the meantime, I noticed that Josh was unsubtly gesturing for me to come closer, so I stood up and did just that.

"Hey, so, since I'm here already and stuff, can I ask a favor?"

"Unless it's something silly, then sure," I responded fairly nonchalantly, yet it seemed to take a huge weight off my friend's shoulders.

"You see, we kinda finalized our plan to take down Robatto, but before we do it, I wanted to run it by you before we give it a go. Are you free after school?"

"Chief." Hearing Judy's call, I turned to her, but she only said, "Be reminded."

It took me a long moment to realize what she was getting at, but then I let out a silent "Oh, right," and turned back to Josh at once.

"I don't think that's going to work. Lab Coat guy is already setting up an ambush for after school."

I could see it in Joshua's eyes that he really wanted to know how I knew about that, but he held back the urge, and instead he asked, "In that case, how about during the next class?"

I momentarily wondered what he meant by that, but then I realized that we were about to have PE, and that I was going to sit on the sidelines because I was still recovering, and once I connected the dots, I immediately agreed with him.

"Sure, let's do that. What's going to be your excuse for sticking to me?"

"I'll think of something while we change," he answered just as Judy finished packing and walked up to us.

"Let's go," she urged us on as she gestured towards the door with her chin, only to pause and look me in the eye. "I'm still going to collect the installments, plus interest."

After saying that she walked past us, leaving Josh visibly flummoxed.

"What was that about?"

"Oh, you know," I responded with a shrug. *Lovebird stuff...*

PART 2

"I must disagree with the assessment of my esteemed colleague," stated a certain annoying placeholder by my side. "The chart says that Mrs. Applebottom's stocks among the male populace show a steady increase regardless of outside factors."

"Humbug!" Mr. Spiky dismissed his bowl-cut-haired... friend? Were they friends? Did I even care?

"As we are all aware, the maximum amount of popularity among the eligible boys within our school is a finite resource," Mr. Bedhair added while completely disregarding the basketball that was heading towards his face. While watching the impact would've been admittedly pretty amusing, my better judgment still made me reach out and pull him out of the way, so that the ball harmlessly bounced off the wall and back into the hands of one of the players. I knew better than to expect thanks, but the way Mr. Bedhair continued to speak without even acknowledging what happened made me just a tad miffed, anyway. "Since that is the case, it logically follows that an increase in the popularity of one of the goddesses would necessarily mean a decrease of overall popularity the other goddesses receive."

"Yes, that makes perfect sense," the fourth amigo, whom I dubbed Mr. Crew Cut, agreed with exactly four measured nods, and I could barely stifle the groan that attempted to escape my throat.

At the moment we were right around the middle of PE class. Once I cleared things up with Mrs. Applebottom, I was told to sit by the sidelines in the indoor gymnasium while the rest of the boys formed three teams and started playing streetball on one side of the court. The girls, unusually enough, were doing the same thing on the other side.

Speaking of which, I'd originally wanted to move over to their side, as both Judy and Elly ended up in the same team, and so I wanted to cheer for my girlfriends. Josh was playing in both the first and second rounds, meaning that for the time being I couldn't talk strategy with him even if I wanted to, yet misfortune struck my plans down before I could even get up from my seat, and it came in the form of the four woodenly enthusiastic bozos surrounding me.

I mean, there's nothing wrong with being wooden, considering they were placeholders and all, but for Pete's sake, they could at least talk about something other than torrents of exposition about terribly inconsequential popularity politics!

"Tell us, Leo. What's your opinion on the matter?"

I was momentarily startled by Mr. Spiky suddenly addressing me, but before I could form a coherent response, I was cut off by Mr. Bowl Cut letting out a melodramatic huff.

"As we are all aware, Leonard is too deeply invested with the five goddesses to provide us with an unbiased opinion." I wanted to ask if it was so, then why they even talked to me in the first place, but then Mr. Bowl Cut faced me directly and began to vomit out yet another torrent of words by telling me, "You're a transfer student who lives alone. As we all know, you're currently dating Eleanor, and you're the brother of Neige. It is well-known that you're also friends with both Angeline and Amelia, and it is no secret that—"

"Argh! Stop, stop!" I burst out as I could no longer hold back my indignation, and I shared my most witheringest glare between the four scarcely animate annoyances. "Do you plan to drive me crazy by reciting exposition at me, or do you guys have something actually useful to say?"

The four of them froze up in a familiar display, which only lasted for a second and a half before they shared an uncertain glance between the four of them. At the end of the day, it was Mr. Bedhair who cleared his throat and, after a short beat, got around to explaining himself.

"I believe this is common knowledge," he began and immediately earned another scowl for his trouble. He paused again, and then he tentatively continued with, "On the other hand, considering Leo's circumstances, it's very understandable that he may have never heard of The Gathering."

There was a short spell of meaningful silence, as if the word itself had some kind of power to it.

"Ah, yes... The Gathering," Mr. Crew Cut echoed him in a slow, ever-so-slightly-overdramatic voice, which was quite an achievement considering these guys were still talking like community theater actors.

"Indeed... The Gathering!" Mr. Spiky followed up with even more gusto, and it was around this point that I'd had enough of them.

"Okay, I got it. It's a thing. Would any of you care to explain what it *actually* is and what it has to do with me?" I pressed on even though I was fairly sure it couldn't be anything good. Or sensible. Or sane...

"The Gathering is a quarterly event dedicated to the five goddesses," Mr. Bedhair enlightened me, and I let out another involuntary groan in response.

"Of course it is..." I whispered under my breath, and the four of them nodded in unison as if it was a statement rather than a plea for mercy.

"Naturally," Mr. Spiky spoke up with mild enthusiasm. "As we're all... I mean, as most of us are aware, it's when the most dedicated followers of the goddesses come together in secret to share their love for their idols. Therefore, it's called the The Gathering."

"So... it's like a tiny underground expo for..." I almost said *stalkers*, but I decided to soften it to, "... *fans*."

"Precisely," Mr. Spiky confirmed with a series of nods.

"It's also the time when the representatives of the statistics and journalism clubs share the quarterly rankings," Mr. Crew Cut added.

"Uh-huh... For the record, how many fans are we talking about?"

"The numbers differ from session to session, but generally speaking, just enough people to fit into the empty social sciences classroom," Mr. Bedhair informed me. "The meetings are held there after school."

"And as we all know, the next meeting is going to be tomorrow!" Mr. Spiky chimed in. "Since we've already said this much, I believe it is time to invite Leonard to The Gathering!"

"Are you out of your mind?" Mr. Bowl Cut cut in, and contrary to his harsh words, his tone was disturbingly mild. "Leo is already in a relationship, and with one of the goddesses to boot! As we're all acutely aware, only single men who wish to adore the goddesses from afar may be permitted entrance to The Gathering!"

"That's correct," Mr. Bedhair doubled down. "The only exception is Joshua Bernstein, who had been banned in advance from all of the The Gatherings due to his monopolization of the goddesses."

"You're correct. I'm ashamed," Mr. Spiky stated in a not-at-all-ashamed tone, though at this point it would've been weirder if any of their stated emotions matched their tones. "I simply hoped that by bringing Leonard along, he could vouch for the authenticity of the displayed artifacts of Neige."

"Oh, that's a highly valid reason, yet the rules are the rules," Mr. Bedhair stated, yet before he could continue, I quickly cut in.

"Did you just say *artifacts*?"

"Yes indeed," Mr. Spiky declared while he puffed out his chest for some inexplicable reason.

"What kind of artifacts are we talking about?" I pressed on as I latched on to the unexpected keyword, and after sharing a glance between one another, it was Mr. Bowl Cut who came forward to give me an answer.

"As everyone here already knows, during the The Gathering, there is the much-anticipated auction, where the admirers of the goddesses can acquire their artifacts, collected by the tireless efforts of the collaboration between the photography club and the groundkeepers. They are all treasures, and we all get a chance to get our hands on one of them. Why, during the last The Gathering, I successfully managed to gain the ownership of a well-timed photo of Mrs. Applebottom showing no less than two square centimeters' worth of panties. They were black."

"A truly mature colour," Mr. Crew Cut agreed with the kind of gravitas one would reserve for inspecting fine art.

"It's the centerpiece of my collection," Mr. Bowl Cut proudly declared, and it was only at this point that my brain finally managed to digest the insanity unfolding in front of me, so I tentatively asked them:

"Just for the record, are all of these artifacts voyeur photos like that?"

"Naturally not," Mr. Bedhair told me just a smidgen smugly. "There are also material artifacts, such as successfully recovered plastic utensils used by the goddesses, used tissues, or various lost articles recovered by the groundkeepers."

"Oh, great..." I groaned under my breath as I closed my eyes and began to massage my temple.

This whole conversation was a little creepy to begin with, then the whole The Gathering thing brought it up a notch to pretty damn creepy, but this? This was straight-up stop!-abort!-creeper-country-ahead! territory. And yet, there was one more thing I had to ask...

"Does that mean that *all* of the 'goddesses' would have 'artifacts' on display during 'The Gathering'?" I inquired with judicious use of air quotes, and for a change, I found their usage entirely justified.

"Naturally," Mr. Bedhair confirmed with the obliviousness of a deer in front of a speeding rocket sled. "If the previous The Gatherings are an indication, we can affirm that the auction will have artifacts from all five of them with an exceedingly small margin of error. Why? Are you interested?"

Fortunately (or unfortunately, depending on how you look at it), it was at this very moment that the sharp sound of a whistle cut our conversation short, and my placeholder companions immediately stood up and walked onto the court without even sparing a single word. It was probably for the best, as I was getting just a wee bit worked up over the sheer amount of what-is-this-I-don't-even I was bombarded with. It wasn't long after that when Josh finally came off the court and made his way over to my side.

"The other guys are getting better," he stated absently as he sat down beside me. "Now I almost have to try even when you're not on the court."

"That's just rude," I responded just as vaguely as I sent one last glare in the direction of the four amigos lining up for the next round of streetball.

Josh followed my line of sight, and once he figured out what I was looking at he said, "I don't want to pry, but what exactly were you talking about with those guys?"

"Tiresome, infuriating, and mostly inconsequential stuff. Don't worry about it."

"Oh, okay. Then I won't," he stated. When he saw that I wasn't reacting, he glanced around to see if there was anyone in earshot, but then he decided to lean closer into a conspiratorial huddle anyway, probably just to be on the safe side. "So... Can I run the plan by you?"

I took a deep breath to get my temper under control, and only then did I give him the green light.

"I already promised, so sure, go ahead."

My friend audibly gulped and looked about as nervous as if he was taking an oral exam, and I was just getting impatient enough to try to prompt him to get on with it.

"So your task was to solve an equation where you plus the girls plus a tactic equals one captured Lab Coat Guy. Now please make your case and show your work."

"You're not making this any easier with that. You know that, right?" my friend inquired with an annoyed frown, but since he no longer looked nervous, I still considered it mission accomplished, so I only showed him a perfectly friendly smile in response. He breathed out a shallow sigh and, at last, began to explain his plan. "Okay, so here's what I've got: the strategy that we came up with consists of three steps, and it will require all of us, save for you and Judy."

"The last part's a given," I murmured under my nose. Judy was a noncombatant, so she couldn't help much, anyway, while I already told them I'd have my attention elsewhere.

"In the first step, Elly, Lili, and I would act as a diversion. The idea is that we make a big show and draw all the Sprockets' attention to us. While this is happening, Angie will scout the Restricted Space for its primary anchor point."

An anchor point, as the name implied, was the place where the Purple Zone was tied onto boring old reality, kind of like the stakes of a giant circus tent. Purple Zones, contrary to what one would expect, couldn't be called down all willy-nilly; small ones, like the one that covered the school during the kidnapping incident, would require at least one anchor, while the large-scale stuff that covered multiple blocks, the kind that Lab Coat Guy and his mechanical cronies were pulling off, would require several. Once it's set up, anyone who knows the location of the anchor can slip in and out of the Purple Zone without having to rely on complicated spells or brute force.

However, if one actually managed to get into direct contact with the anchor, they could do all sorts of zany stuff with it, like changing the size of the area mimicked by the Purple Zone, closing it and forcefully ejecting everyone inside, or...

"Are you planning to lock down the place so that Lab Coat Guy can't escape?"

"Yes, that's the plan," Josh confirmed my educated guess with a nod. "Ammy said that it usually takes a while to gain control over an anchor set up by someone else, but she knows a trick that would give her temporary control."

"Temporary, you say? Are you setting yourself up for a time limit?" I asked, suddenly feeling a little skeptical of this idea.

"More or less," my friend responded a little uncertainly. "Ammy is our expert, and she said that getting control over the anchor the normal way would take too long, and Robatto would realize what we were doing and escape."

"Is there a chance that Lab Coat Guy will realize what you are doing, anyway?"

"Ammy sounded really confident about doing it her way, so I don't think it's likely."

"Plan for it, anyway," I told him, and seeing how reluctant he looked, I let out a sigh and explained myself. "Listen up, Josh. When it comes to these things, unlikely is the same as pretty damn likely. If it's a one in a million chance, then I can guarantee you that it's going to happen for sure. The best way to work around this is to plan for the worst, and in the best-case scenario, you are only going to be pleasantly surprised by how smoothly everything worked out."

"I... will take that to heart."

"Good," I stated as I directed an appreciative smile at him. "So part one was the three of you serving as a diversion; part two was about Angie and Ammy finding the anchor and temporarily locking Lab Coat Guy in his own trap... What's part three?"

"That's the tricky part," Josh admitted a little dryly, but then he took a deep breath and he clarified things by telling me, "The third stage of the plan is to use Pascal to pin Dr. Robatto down long enough for us to regroup and then capture him. The only problem is that we don't know how to draw him out to do that."

"Can't the class rep just ask him to follow her and have her lead him to the ambush point?" I posited, but Josh immediately shook his head.

"That was my first idea, as well, but Ammy says that he doesn't seem to trust her the way he used to. It has something to do with her failing a test or something. I honestly didn't get it."

"It's a long story. Anyhow, that means that using her to draw him in might not work."

"Which, if I follow your advice, means that it definitely won't work," Josh chimed in, and while I could detect a well-concealed jab under his words, I nodded in the affirmative all the same.

"In other words, you need a good reason for him to follow you. A kind of bait, if you will."

"Yes. We couldn't think of one yet, so for the time being, we figured Ammy would give a distress call to him and hope that he would show up in time."

"That's way too vague," I voiced my criticism as I crossed my arms in front of my chest. "So vague I would be normally tempted to say you shouldn't rely on him and go back to the drawing board."

"... I can sense a *but* coming," Josh stated, and he mimicked my posture by crossing his arms, as well.

"And you'd be correct, except now I can't do it anymore because it would be grammatically incorrect."

"When did that ever stop you?"

"A valid question, but kind of irrelevant at the moment," I dismissed him on the spot, and after a deep breath I added, "You're not planning on putting the plan into action today, right?"

"No, of course not. It's nowhere near complete enough, as you graciously pointed out already."

"You're welcome. On a different-yet-related note, Armband Guy is in the student council, right?"

"On the disciplinary committee, but yes, he is," my friend answered a touch apprehensively, obviously uncertain about where I was going with that question.

"Disciplinary committee, you say? That's even better," I mused as I dramatically rubbed my chin. "Would that mean he would be extra touchy about students breaking regulations?"

"I guess..."

"In that case," I further mused as a wide grin settled onto my face, "Do you want to crash a meeting of such students?"

"Depends. Please elaborate," Josh prompted me.

"It's a gathering of fanboys who trade for up-skirt photos of the girls."

"By *the girls*, do you mean *our* girls?" he inquired with a sudden sense of ferocity in his eyes.

"Yep."

"Where do I sign up?"

"The better question is, do you think Armband Guy would like to sign up, too?"

"It's guaranteed," Josh muttered, but then a second of pause later he quickly added, "Or rather, the chances of that are... one in a million!"

For a moment I couldn't decide whether I should let out a groan or applaud him, so in the end I settled on awarding him a high five, and then I spent the rest of the PE lesson hatching a new plan with him which would, with some luck, kill two birds (read: annoyances) with one stone (read: unwitting armband connoisseur).

I had to admit that the info about this whole 'The Gathering' balderdash showing up on my doorstep right now was just a wee bit too convenient, but as they say, when life gives you stalker lemons, you make creepy lemonade.

PART 3

"We've arrived," the class rep solemnly declared as she stopped in front of the familiar basement entrance by the side of the main school building. Classes were already over for a while, and most of the placeholders left the school grounds a while ago, save for the ones having their club meetings, like the sports club members hyping themselves up on the nearby tennis court. They couldn't see the two of us due to the picket fence between the main grounds and the sports field, but I could still hear their chanting all the same.

Anyhow, once we arrived, Ammy turned on her heels and locked eyes with me for a few long, silent seconds, and then she eventually stated, "I think I should go with you, after all."

"No, you shouldn't," I replied in no uncertain terms, which earned me an increasingly-rare-yet-still-somewhat-menacing glasses tweaking from her.

"I'd feel considerably more at ease. I'm too afraid to leave you alone with Grandfather."

"Oh, please. I know he agreed to this meeting a little too readily, but you don't have to worry about me. Even if he tries something underhanded, I have multiple exit strategies up my sleeve."

"No, I'm not worried about you," Ammy denied my words in a clearly exasperated tone. "I'm worried that if none of us are around to keep you on a short leash, you're just going to escalate the situation and make things even more complicated."

I wanted to ask "When did I ever do that?" but she wasn't in the mood for hypocritical humour, so instead I told her, "Don't fret about what-if scenarios; they are only going to give you wrinkles." She didn't seem to appreciate that comment, either, so I quickly added, before she could launch into a lecture, "Not to mention, the others are waiting for you, aren't they?"

"That's true..."

She was still reluctant to leave, but before I could push her just a little bit more, her brows abruptly descended into a frown, and she asked, "Speaking of waiting, you still haven't told me where you and Josh disappeared to after the end of classes. We agreed that we would meet by the lockers, and I had to wait for almost twenty minutes for you!"

"We had something to discuss with the disciplinary committee." I told her a half-truth I'd prepared in advance, yet it only made her narrow her eyes even further.

"Are you two in trouble?"

"No, it's some other guys." My answer still didn't satisfy her, but my lips remained sealed. There were some things that she was better off not knowing about...

We locked eyes for a few long seconds, and once she realized I wasn't going to elaborate, she let out a tiny little sigh and raised a hand to poke me in the chest.

"Fine, I'll go with the others. Don't escalate things with Grandfather."

"I promise I'll make an attempt to try."

That earned me another frown, but at the end of the day she gave up all the same and told me, "You should know the way to the elevator. I arranged a guide for you to take you to Grandfather's office. And once more, for emphasis," she paused as she poked my chest again, this time a little harder, "Don't. Escalate. The. Situation."

"I get it, I get it. Geez."

I gently pushed her finger aside, and after one final huff, she turned on her heels and walked away, though not without sparing me one last glance as she rounded the corner of the school building. I had to wonder, was this the sisterly type thing that the four creepy amigos asserted was her main claim to popularity? Did people like to be pestered like this? Though on second thought, someone being worried for me and trying to look after me was oddly nice, even if the unneeded nature of it all made it just a teensy bit annoying.

Anyhow, putting all that aside, I decided to enter the den of the lion without any further ado. As embarrassing it was to admit it, when we came here as a group, I was mainly just following after the class rep, and I didn't pay much attention to where the elevator door was. Because of that, it took me a few really embarrassing minutes to find it in the basement.

After a short ride down, surrounded by the familiar and slightly unnerving stock elevator music from the last time, the automatic doors opened and revealed a stocky, middle-aged man standing in the middle of the well-lit stony corridor. He was wearing semiformal apparel under a thick, brown leather apron, had a bushy beard with a few white strands here and there, a balding head, and one of those jeweler's eyepieces on his forehead. In other words, he looked exactly like an artificer (specifically the type that I had already seen talking with Ammy through Far Sight), and the moment our eyes met he immediately stepped up to me with a broad smile.

"Leonard Dunning, I presume?"

He offered a stubby hand ending in thick fingers, and I had no reason not to take it.

"Yes, that's me. Pleased to meet you."

"The pleasure is mine," he squeezed my hand, not too hard yet tight enough to show that he could turn his grasp into a vise if so he chose, and then shook it. On a closer listen, he had some kind of accent, but it was refreshingly subtle. Irish? Maybe Scottish? Some kind of Celtic influence, of that I was fairly sure. Anyhow, he let go of my hand and continued with, "The little miss told me you'd be visiting the lord today, so I volunteered myself to be your guide."

That explained a few things. I had no idea why Ammy had arranged a guide for me, considering the arch-mage's office was at the end of the same corridor where the elevator had arrived, but looking at the eager man in front of me, I had a feeling it might not have been her idea, after all.

"I presume you had a reason for that," I mused aloud, and the man, who conspicuously avoided properly introducing himself, nodded in confirmation.

"Certainly! You see, I'm an artificer."

"I've gathered as much, yes."

"What gave it away?" Since he was tugging at his leather apron, I figured it was a rhetorical question, and so I didn't bother answering. After a short while he added, "Not too long ago, the little miss asked us to fabricate a few artifacts for her. I was in charge of the project, and suffice it to say I was quite shocked when she showed me the modifications you made to her device. Since the opportunity presented itself, I decided I would use it to introduce myself and maybe discuss matters of the craft with you. I'm not ashamed to admit that I was quite entranced by your work and was curious about its maker."

"Thank you for the compliment, but could we do that after I talked with Lord Gra— I mean, Endymonion?"

"You're right. Please excuse me; I'm just somewhat excited at the moment." He gestured for me to follow after him, and it didn't take us more than two steps before he continued, anyway. "I must say, the changes you made to the suit stored in the artifact were absolutely marvelous. I naturally couldn't inspect them too closely, due to the security measures you implemented, but even at a cursory glance, it appears you took our prototypes and turned them into some of the most sophisticated enchantments I've seen in my career! The fidelity of the warding array alone was astounding! Is it true that you made it without the aid of any instruments?"

"I didn't have any on hand, so I had to improvise," I responded offhandedly, as at the moment I was preoccupied with memorizing the locations of the magical surveillance balls in the hallways.

"Is that so?" My guide perked up even more than before, and he even leaned closer to me while we walked. "Can you show me how it's done? I was told ever since I was an apprentice that the techniques to directly interact with the inscriptions of a magical array were a lost art! Where did you learn them? Can you teach them to me?"

"Can we discuss this later? I think we are almost at our destination."

"Ah... Please forgive me; I let excitement get the better of me again."

"No problem," I said a little vaguely, and once we arrived at the large double door leading to Lord Grandpa's place, I decided to throw the man a bone and amended, "That said, while my technique is not something I could teach to others, I'm not against exchanging some pointers once things calm down a little."

"In that case, can I ask you to attend the symposium this weekend?"

"Symposium?" I repeated after him, the word accompanied by a curiously raised brow.

"It's a regular conference where us artificers gather to discuss new findings and exchange ideas. We haven't had a guest speaker for two years, and I'm afraid my colleagues would flay me alive if they learned I've kept you all for myself."

"Being a guest speaker might be a bit too much, but as long as you can bring along some interesting artifacts, I can probably open up some time in my schedule."

"Trust me, friend; if there's one thing you won't find wanting, it's the number of odd and exotic artifacts on display."

"In that case, you can count me in," I told the friendly artificer with a smile, then exhaled and pointed at the door in front of us. "Let's discuss the details later; I want to get this over with."

"I understand. Give me a second. I'll knock."

"No need. I'll let myself in," I told him with the smallest of smirks, and I placed my hand on the door... at which point there was a bloodcurdlingly melodramatic "Noooooooo!" on the other side, and before I could even start pushing, the surface of the door lit up with a web of circuitry-like patterns, and it slowly opened up without any effort on my part.

That made me curious. I'm not talking about the bloodcurdling bit, but the light show that followed after it. It was evident that there was some kind of magic involved with the door, so was it a spell laid on top of it, or was the whole thing a single artifact? I was never one to let an opportunity to sate my curiosity go by, so I quickly extended my phantom limb and plunged it into the retreating door wings.

What I found was quite surprising, yet at the same time it perfectly explained something that had been bugging me for a while. I'd been in the old man's office many times, mostly as an incorporeal observer, and it always struck me a little odd that, unlike the rest of the underground School, this place had a conspicuous lack of security. No magical cameras, no fancy mystic laser beams, no nothing. Now I knew why.

Contrary to my expectations, my phantom limb didn't interface with the doors, but the entire room, which was covered by a single, enormous security array. After proverbially leafing through its functions, I found that it was an interlinked system of multiple, layered wards that were a step above Snowy's handiwork, a full anti-surveillance system, a spatial relocation suppressing subsystem (read: anti-teleportation stuff), and a whole bundle of anti-tampering functions rolled into one. It was no wonder the old man freaked out when I broke his door; it was the linchpin of the whole structure.

Speaking of which, I really didn't want history to repeat itself, so after committing as much of the array in front of me to my memory as possible, I quickly retracted my extra appendage. To my silent relief, it seemed like the security system was no worse for wear.

I may have taken just a tad too long, though, as by the time I finished my inspection, the door was already open, and I was face-to-face with a certain grandfatherly-and-yet-still-eminently-punchable old man staring daggers at me. I took a quick breath to calm the rising tide of irritation in the pit of my stomach, and once I exhaled, I let my still-raised palm down and addressed the owner of the room.

"Sorry, I spaced out for a moment."

The arch-mage was still only glaring at me in silence, which I naturally took as an invitation. I directed a grateful nod towards the enthusiastic artificer by my side, after which I promptly entered the room, and not a second later the wings closed shut behind me.

"Good afternoon. It's been a while," I casually greeted the old man and took a few steps towards the large mahogany desk with my hand extended, yet he remained seated without any apparent intent to return the gesture.

"I must say, your unexpected request to meet me was sudden, to say the least," he said in a steady, measured voice, still showing no sign of reciprocating my attempted handshake. I suppose it was to be expected. When was the last time anything went smoothly in my life? Anyhow, while I let my hand down and considered what alternative approaches I could try, he continued by asking me, "Pray tell, could it be that you are looking for assistance?"

"You wish," I responded with a smile that ended up a teensy bit more vicious than I originally intended. After I reined my emotions in, I quickly added, "As a matter of fact, I'm only here to give you an update on the tokens of your appreciation that you dumped on me the last time I was here, and maybe a few questions besides that."

"An update, you say? How unusually courteous of you, and yet a pleasant surprise nonetheless," the old man stated with an inscrutable smile partially hidden under his beard. "What exactly have you found in your endeavors?"

"Many things, most of which don't make you look particularly reliable, or capable, at that," I responded by employing an equally inscrutable smile of my own. I paused here for a long moment to let him stew in his own juice, then I continued while slowly walking up and down in front of his desk. "First and foremost, let's discuss the Chimera running around on your island."

"A Chimera, you say?"

For some reason the old man's eyes lit up with something resembling approval. I didn't like that, so I quickly threw some cold water on him by answering, "Yes, though I think you're focusing on the wrong part. I'm more worried about the fact that you let a literal monster prowl your island without doing anything about it."

"I have sent a renowned Chimera slayer to find it, have I not?"

"That would only make sense if you knew that it was a Chimera from the beginning, and you hid that information from me," I countered, which finally made him stop smirking at me like an idiot. I decided to press on while the iron was still hot, so I told him, "On an unrelated note, you're also letting the idiot with the silly robots run amok, as well, without lifting a finger. Not only that, you even red-taped the Dracises from dealing with them."

"I naturally did. There are rules by which all who live on my island must abide, and I will not make exceptions." After saying so, Lord Grandpa's eyes glittered with a hint of playfulness as he added, "Why does it matter to you? Could it be that you wished to employ the aid of the Winged Ones against the Research Society?"

"It is true that with their help we could've shut them down a while ago, but no. I only brought them up because it almost feels like you're trying to maintain the current chaotic situation by refusing to intervene and by holding any third parties at bay."

"Oh? And what exactly would I gain from doing so?" he asked me, and I couldn't help but notice how he was only asking questions and never giving a straight answer. Not that I minded, as I was still busy trying to figure out how to mark him, so firing blanks back and forth in this verbal duel suited me just fine.

"How should I know? I'm not a mind reader," I responded with a shrug, and I wanted to continue pressing him on Lab Coat Guy, yet before I could he cut me off with another question.

"In that case, what can you tell me about the third lead I provided to you? Did you find out anything about the unknown swordswoman?"

"She likes cats," I blurted out offhandedly and forcibly returned to the previous conversation before the old man could react. "Anyhow, I still don't understand why you haven't taken any action against the Research Society. They are a constant menace that threatens your own granddaughter, as well. Could it be... that you don't consider them as a threat?"

"It would be more accurate to say that after the recent events pertaining to House Inanna breaching the security of the School, we simply can not spare the manpower on a wild goose chase. If only we could locate their headquarters..."

"Oh, I can help you with that," I told him with a toothy grin, and for the first time since I'd entered the room, the old man appeared a little apprehensive.

"Could it be that you have pinpointed the location of their headquarters?"

That made me pause for a moment while I internally debated how I should respond to that, and in the end I decided to go with the safer choice, and after adopting a suitably miffed expression, I answered with, "Well, not yet, but it's only a matter of time."

"In that case, I am afraid there is little I can do about the rogue elements of the Research Society at the moment. With that said, let us return to something we have unfortunately skimmed over: could it be that you have learned something in regard to the unknown swordswoman?"

"Yes, I learned that her sword is really rude," I answered quickly and decisively before I once again grabbed the reins of the conversation back from the old man. "More importantly, based on what you said, wouldn't that mean that if I did find the hidey-hole of the Research Society, then you would actually get off your backside and do something about them?"

"It all depends on how reliable your information proves to be."

After hearing that wishy-washy answer, I couldn't help but scoff at the old man.

"And how am I supposed to prove the reliability of the information? Storm their base, capture them, and then say, 'See, I told you so?'"

"On second thought," Lord Grandpa interrupted me, his brows set so low in a frown they looked like two bushy caterpillars sitting on his eyelids. "I must advise you against such hasty actions. Even if you were to discover the hidden headquarters of these ne'er-do-wells, the Research Society possesses a long and well-documented history of employing mystical and mechanical traps of all shapes and forms. Assaulting their stronghold without the aid of the right experts could prove fatal."

Look at that. It seems like I touched a nerve there. Now, I didn't want to push the old man too hard, lest he warn Lab Coat Guy and muck up Josh's plans, but I figured giving up too readily could be just as suspicious at this point, so I made one last counter.

"And let me guess: Only you have such experts?"

"I could hardly claim so, but it is true that you would be hard-pressed to find any such specialists on this island who do not already belong to my School." I remained silent on purpose for a while, and just like that, he barreled on and proposed, "Just in case you were to somehow discern the location of the stronghold belonging to the Research Society, I would like to advise you not to be reckless and inform me first."

"And then we all go there right away and get rid of them, right?"

"Well, maybe not right away. Such operations require careful planning, and assembling the required experts could take at least a day, if not more."

"But then we all go there and smash them down, *right*?"

The arch-mage let out a shallow sigh and ultimately said, "Yes, we do that."

"Why didn't you say that in the first place?" I muttered aloud, followed by an exaggerated roll of the eyes. "If that's the case, I'll focus on finding their hideout first. In fact, I think I should start right now, so if you don't mind, I would take my leave."

"Is that so? Very well then. I also happen to be a busy man, and I have a meeting to attend soon, so I believe ending this discussion here is entirely reasonable."

"So we're in agreement for once. That's nice."

Saying so, I stepped even closer to the desk and offered my hand once more. At this point it wasn't exactly surprising, but the old man still didn't take it. Not only that, he didn't even move from his seat. Reaching over the desk would have been too forceful, and I couldn't accidentally brush up against him, either, which left me in a pickle as far as my original plan was concerned.

I was hoping that by keeping my arm outstretched, social anxiety would sooner or later make him take my hand, but instead he magnificently ignored me and commented, "It is fine to be enthusiastic, yet you must not lose sight of other matters. Such as the unknown swordswoman."

I had absolutely no idea about why Lord Grandpa was so fixated on Rinne, and I was already getting pretty annoyed by his staunch refusal to allow me to mark him, so after boring a hole into his forehead with my eyes, I let my hand down with a huff and uttered, "Annoying."

"Are you referring to me or her?"

My host was a little baffled by my outburst, but I couldn't say I cared, so I pocketed my hands and simply told him, "Yes," before I turned on my heel and took a step towards the entrance.

That was all I needed to do, as the arch-mage hurriedly tapped his fingertips on his desk, following which the door immediately swung open. He was most likely afraid there would be a repeat of what happened the last time or something; I didn't really care enough to speculate.

Once I was outside, I noticed that the friendly artificer was still around. He quickly stepped up to me and commented, "You finished sooner than I expected."

"It was only a courtesy call," I responded just a smidge dryly, then added, "You didn't need to wait for me. I know the way out."

As it turned out, I didn't even need to say the last bit. Before he could even offer to lead me outside, Lord Grandpa called out to the guy from his office.

"Gowan? May I have a moment of your time?"

"Sure, my lord," the man responded before showing me an apologetic smile, then he whispered, "So about the symposium..."

"I'll attend. Let's iron out the details through Amelia." I tilted my head towards the office and added, "Go ahead, don't make the old man wait too long."

The artificer gave me a tight-lipped smile and followed my advice without much further ado. In the meantime, I quickly walked over to the elevator and pushed the Up button. Luckily I didn't have to wait at all, as the car was still on this floor, so I dashed inside and pushed the button corresponding with the ground floor before I quickly entered into Far Sight. While I was tempted to use my newest mark right away, instead I focused on one of the few dots that still remained in the School building, and I immediately Phased over.

"Oh," my dear assistant let out a small sound when I materialized in front of her desk, but she quickly collected herself. "Hi, Chief. I presume you're finished with your business?"

"Not yet, I'm afraid," I answered and then hurriedly walked over to my own desk. I reached inside, and I retrieved a small bag. It was slightly larger than the one for my gym clothes, and inside there was a baggy, neon green tracksuit, a pair of black gloves, and a stereotypical-yet-effective ski mask. I'd stashed all of these away a while back, and now they were about to serve their purpose.

"Are you planning to infiltrate somewhere?" Judy inquired with a façade of indifference.

"Yes. There might be an opportunity to sneak into Lord Grandpa's office now, and I don't want to miss it."

"Danger level?"

"I just had an opportunity to inspect his security system, so close to zero."

"What are the chances of something going wrong?"

I wanted to respond with a nonchalant "One in a million," but I decided I really shouldn't temp fate, so instead I told her, "Don't worry, I'll be super-careful."

"You know what will happen if there is even a single scratch on you when you return?" she threatened me in the guise of a question, and I couldn't help but smile at her in return. Why was it that, when the class rep was nagging me to be cautious, I found that annoying, but when Judy did it... well, I still found it annoying, but also kind of nice and heartwarming? It was probably those pesky hormones again.

Anyhow, I pulled the tracksuit over my school uniform (there was a reason why it needed to be baggy), and at the same time I also engaged in a bit of multitasking by simultaneously keeping the eye on the situation inside the arch-mage's study through Far Sight.

"... perceptive." I caught the end of whatever the friendly artificer was saying.

"Both of them?" Lord Grandpa asked back just a touch incredulously.

"Yes, my lord. Both the one by the elevator and the one above the entrance to your office."

With that, I had enough context to figure out that they were most likely talking about the surveillance spells in the hallway.

"Are you entirely certain he looked at them?"

"Artificer's eye, sir," the man responded by pointing at his face... which was apparently enough to convince the old man. Maybe it was a code, or possibly an inside joke? Who knows?

"That would certainly explain how he could always find my observer orbs... What about the handshake? Have you noticed anything unusual?"

"I can't say I did, my lord."

"I am afraid that does not preclude the chance that he might have done something all the same." While he said that, Lord Grandpa walked over to his liquor cabinet and grabbed one of the bottles without bothering to get a glass with it. "There had to be a reason why he was so insistent. Maybe some kind of mystic art, or a hidden artifact. Something that requires physical contact to operate?" The old man paused for a moment, but only to take a hard swig from his bottle, then he placed it onto his desk and let out a pent-up breath. "I could not even stand up until he left. Throughout our discussion, I always felt as if he was waiting for me to show an opening. I have yet to feel such a sinister pressure from a man so young."

"With all due respect, sir," the artificer interjected with a voice that was walking on hummingbird eggshells. "In my humble opinion, the young man felt anything but sinister. I could even say he was surprisingly cordial and forthcoming."

The owner of the room gave his guest a once-over, from head to toe, and then muttered something along the lines of, "Could it be that it is a form of mental interference designed to grant the user some influence over the target...?"

"My lord... why are you looking at me like that?"

Before answering, Lord Grandpa took another swig from his bottle before he pointed at the artificer and declared, "Gowan, follow me."

"Yes, my lord... but where?"

"To the isolation chamber," the arch-mage stated as he headed towards the entrance. "We must ascertain whether or not you are under the influence."

"Err... Sir, with all due respect, you're the one who was drinking, not me."

"Not that kind of influence, you..." he began, but then his words trailed into half-spoken murmurs of "...surrounded by..." and "...every day..." and "... good help nowadays..."

I didn't have time to pay closer attention to what he was saying, as I hadn't finished changing yet. I frantically tugged on the zipper on the tracksuit, and once it was up, I hastily pulled the ski mask over my head before I gave a thumbs-up to my still-wary girlfriend.

"Stay safe," she ordered me, and I only nodded as I checked the artificer's location one last time, and once I locked on, I immediately Phased over.

It was a close call. If I was just a second or two late, they would've been out of range. Granted, I could've still Phased over, theoretically, but the last thing I needed during a clandestine infiltration operation into the most secure chamber on the island was an extra dose of vertigo.

Speaking of which, I took account of the situation one more time before moving, just to be sure. Disguise, just in case I would be noticed? Check. Gloves, to hide my fingerprints? Check. An entire treasure trove full of documents and possibly incriminating information all around me? Check, check, and check.

Now there was only one question left to answer: Was this how a fox felt when it was locked inside a chicken coop? In case anyone wondered, yes. The answer was *definitely* yes. Insert happy fox noises here.

CHAPTER 7

PART 1

"Hi, I'm back!" I announced my entrance as usual as I reappeared in the classroom. By this point Judy was so used to my Phasing antics she barely batted an eye at my sudden arrival.

"It took a—" she began, only to abruptly stop her sentence as she looked me over, and then she asked, "Where's the tracksuit?"

"Oh, that?" I glanced down and tugged at the sleeves of my jacket on purpose. "I figured I should get rid of any possible physical evidence ASAP, so I hopped over to the secret base and asked Karukk to dispose of it."

My dear assistant spent several long seconds scrutinizing me, from my shoes to the top of my head. Once she finished with that, she looked me in the eye and asked, with the utmost seriousness, "Are you sure you didn't do it to hide the rips and bloodstains?"

I had to think for a long moment to figure out what she meant by that, but then I awarded her a flat glance and stressed, "I *did not* get into any incidents, so no, there were no bloodstains to hide. I told you I would be super-careful, didn't I?"

"You did," she stated, and then after a long beat, she stood up from her desk, walked over to my side, and then began mechanically patting my shoulder with the words, "Good job. Good job."

"Um... Thanks?" I uttered in mild confusion, at which point she immediately stopped and took a step back.

"On a separate note, it's been exactly thirty-six minutes since you left."

"Yeah, I know. Sorry for making you wait, but I had to make the best of this opportunity."

Judy accepted my apology with a soft grunt, and she simultaneously began to pack away the books on her desk. I watched over her for a while, but she didn't seem to want to ask the obvious question, so I decided to poke her a little.

"Soooo? Aren't you curious about what I found?"

"A little," she admitted with some reservation.

"Then why aren't you asking me about it?"

"Because you're going to tell me anyway," she stated just as she finished packing and locked her bag. Her answer felt just a tad unsatisfying, so after weighing my options, I decided to employ the dreaded disappointed puppy eyes. My girlfriend gave me a skeptical look in return, but at last she relented with a sigh. "Fine, I'll ask. What did you find?"

"Another plot device!" I declared with a grin so wide it made the corners of my mouth hurt a little.

"... Of course you did," she uttered with just a touch of resignation in her voice before she picked up her bag and added, "Tell me about it on the way home."

"Actually, I had something else in mind," I stated after I decided to hold back on elaborating. I walked over to my own desk and slung my bag over my shoulder, then as I returned to her side I told her, "Just to be safe, I think we should Phase over to the secret base. You know, just in case someone would note that we left late and draw some wildly-reaching-yet-annoyingly-accurate connection between that and some things missing from the old man's study."

"Please tell me you didn't actually steal from the arch-mage's office..."

"Technically? No. Do you remember the door beside the old coot's liquor cabinet?" Judy was thrown off the rails for a moment, but then she quickly nodded. In retrospect, I was the silly one to ask. Of course she'd remember; she had a terrifyingly good eidetic memory. Anyhow, I quickly continued with, "That door leads to the archives of the School, so technically it wasn't from the office. I took photos of everything that looked remotely interesting with my phone, but there was one thing that was way too important to just let it gather dust there."

I could practically see the gears turning inside my girlfriend's head, and after a short while she uttered, "You took the plot device."

It wasn't a question, but a statement of fact. What can I say? She knew me too well.

"Yep. I left it at the base, too. Come on, I'll show you." I gestured for her to come closer so that we could Phase out, but she only stared at my feet. I followed her gaze, and after a few long seconds of silence I added, "Don't worry about the indoor shoes. Knowing our luck, we would totally bump into Armband Guy on our way to the lockers."

"True," she finally relented, only to then have her eyes climb up my body and settle on the top of my head instead. "Please lean forward a little. You have balaclava hair."

"What the heck is balaclava hair?" I mumbled under my breath, but it didn't mean I wouldn't comply and let my girlfriend straighten my hairdo.

"There you go," she declared in a satisfied voice as she crossed her arms and observed her handiwork. "Now you won't embarrass me in front of the Fauns."

"I don't think they really care," I responded, just a smidgen self-consciously. That said, being the only embarrassed person in the room was against my core principles, so I used the opportunity to lean even closer and plant a quick peck on my girlfriend's forehead. I flashed a cheeky smile at her and quickly added, "Thanks, Dormouse."

"You... are welcome," Judy answered with a level voice, but the small pause and the fact that the tips of her ears were getting flushed told me that I was successful.

I let out a content little chuckle, and without any further ado, I used my free hand (plus one intangible appendage) to embrace her, and after a brief moment of transitioning through the space filled with audibly colourful tastes and the last digits of irrational numbers, the scenery changed around us without any issues. We stood within the workshop section of the main hall inside the underground base, and I could already hear the grunty-snappy-clangy sounds of the Fauns training nearby.

"[Welcome back, Sir Blackcloak.]" I was immediately greeted by Karukk practically the moment we arrived, and the fact that he also took my sudden appearance in stride was a testament to how often I'd used him as my anchor point when Phasing. He was wearing the same leather apron that Brang wore during our last meeting, and he had an antique-looking knife in one hand and a normal-sized whetstone in the other, both of which looked comically tiny between his huge fingers. He hurriedly put them down onto a nearby workbench and then flashed a friendly smile at us that made Judy twitch in my arms. "[You weren't kidding when you said you'd be back soon.]"

"[Aye,]" I responded with just a smidgen of irritation as I let go of my girfriend (who then proceeded to unsubtly hide behind me), and I added, "[Unless my memory fails me, I can recall with the clarity of crystal water that I requested that you would cease addressing me by my unwanted title, let alone broaden its weight by the needless attachment of honorifics.]"

"[Ah, about that...]" The slightly-more-casual-than-average Faun awkwardly scratched the base of his neck, and after a long moment of silence he sheepishly admitted, "[Since you're the regent, it would be rude to call you without an honorific... sir.]"

I stared at him with all the skepticism I could muster, but even under my ocular assault, he seemed entirely serious, so I ended up exhaling a shallow sigh and said, "[If that is the case, since you have already vested undue authority in my person, could I request you at the very least cease referring to me as the One Cloaked in Black?]"

"[I... think that's a bad idea,]" Karukk mumbled, and then after a moment of hesitation he leaned closer and whispered, "[I wouldn't mind, but the general told us to give you all courtesies, and if I accidentally didn't call you that, he would get really mad at me.]"

"[... Is your general that harsh?]"

"[He is a little... old-fashioned about these things,]" he stated as diplomatically as I had ever heard him speak.

"[Fine then,]" I gave up with a small grumble and made a show out of looking around for a moment. "[Where may I find the items that I recently recovered?]"

"[They should be right where you left them,]" Karukk answered while gesturing towards the recreational area with his head.

"[In that case, we shall head over and leave you to your task.]"

He gave us a deferential nod in response, after which he picked up the whetstone and resumed his tinkering with the dagger. With that, Judy and I walked over to the other end of the hall, and it was only when we'd already passed by the air hockey table that she let go of the back of my jacket.

"Are you still afraid of the Fauns?" I teased her a little, yet to my surprise, she actually nodded.

"A little," she admitted while conspicuously averting her eyes.

"But why? They aren't actually scary."

"Maybe to you, but they didn't chase you around in a dark school building at night," she countered, and for a moment I didn't know what to say.

"Well... um... touché?" Based on the tiny little twitch around her eyes, that wasn't the response she was looking for, so I cleared my throat and continued with, "That said, while I admit they look pretty fearsome, so long as you're with me and Snowy, they would probably sooner take a bullet for you than hurt you in any way."

"You think so?"

"Yep," I answered with a huge nod. "In fact, the worst thing they could ever do to you would be if, once they digest the fact that we're dating, they would start calling you something silly, like consort regent or the like."

"Really?" Judy paused for a moment, and then mused, "I'm personally more partial towards the term queen regent."

"Oh, yes, I can totally see it before my eyes," I replied as I raised my hands into the air as if looking at a painted portrait in a gallery. "And here she is, Queen Regent Dormouse the First. Just rolls off the tongue."

"Says Regent Leonard S. Blackcloak Dunning the Growler," she jabbed back as she reached out and held on to my hand with two fingers. At first I was a little confused about the last part, but then I figured that she was probably trying to pinch me for teasing her too much. It only tickled a little, but as a good boyfriend, I pretended that it was effective and pulled my hand away with a perfectly-natural-and-not-at-all-overacted hiss.

In the meantime we reached the bar, and when we arrived, my dear assistant immediately sent me a skeptical glance.

"Didn't you say you only took your alleged plot device?"

"I did."

"Then what is that stack of papers?" she asked as she gestured towards the hastily piled-up documents on the bar top.

"I technically didn't take those," I explained as I picked up the whole stack and began to organize them. "The archive had an old photocopy machine, and I used it to make copies of a bunch of documents while I searched the place."

"That's slightly more reasonable than expected. Consider yourself praised."

"Thanks, I think?" I responded a little uncertainly, but she didn't pay much attention to my words.

"So? What are these documents about?" Judy inquired as she tried to take a peek at the papers in my hands, so I handed them over to her.

"I don't really know, to be honest. I found the originals in a safe, so I just threw them into the feeder on the top of the machine and started hunting for other interesting things while it did its work."

"In a safe," she repeated after me as she glanced up from skimming the pages. "Please tell me you didn't accidentally find the combination on the first try."

"Nah. Not everything can be as conveniently low-security as the Celestial Hub," I answered with a small smirk as I recalled the memory, but then I lightly shook my head and followed up by saying, "Actually, I take that back; this time the security was even poorer. It wasn't even locked."

"Seriously?"

She looked just about as incredulous as I was when I'd grabbed hold of the safe door and it opened on its own.

"Apparently Lord Grandpa had so much faith in the room's magical defenses he became pretty sloppy with everything else. I'm not even sure there was a lock on the door leading into the archives."

"You're right. That's astronomically sloppy."

"Yep," I concurred, after which we both fell silent for a while as Judy continued to browse the pages in her hands. From the outside it might've looked like she was only skimming the pages, but I knew better.

In the meantime, I walked around her and quickly found the other thing that I'd borrowed during my excursion. It was a tiny, outwardly inconspicuous wooden box, and it was sitting on the bar top, exactly where I left it. It was small enough to fit snugly in one hand, and it was covered in glowing blue patterns forming interlocking circles with various runic symbols in them. According to the Fauns, said circles and symbols were completely invisible to the naked eye, and Karukk even thought it was a simple music box.

"Is that the plot device?" Judy inquired as she glanced up from her reading, and I nodded in the affirmative.

"Yeah, this was also in the safe. Or rather, in a secret compartment within the safe, but same difference."

"Was it also left unlocked?"

"No," I answered just a bit more brightly. "It was a magical lock, so I used my phantom limb to check the enchantment, read the keyword, and then unlocked the compartment using it. Easy peasy."

My dearest assistant rewarded my comment with a flat look, and after setting her bundle of photocopied documents aside she dramatically rubbed her forehead and told me, "Chief, this phantom limb of yours is too much of a cheat. If Joshua didn't already have the position, it would make you the obvious protagonist of this world."

"Don't even joke about that; I have enough problems as is," I chided her, and then I raised the box to eye level and explained, "This box is nothing particularly special. I could probably disable the sealing enchantments on it in a couple of minutes without forcefully breaking them. The interesting thing is what's inside it."

"Then why haven't you opened it yet?"

"Because it has a lock," I responded by pointing at the tiny keyhole on the front of the box. "It looks really cheap, so once the magical protection is removed, I think you could open it with a simple hairpin, but I obviously didn't have any with me at the time."

"Then how do you know what's...?" she started to ask, but then stopped and instead she said, "You stuck your phantom limb through the keyhole and poked the item inside."

"Close enough," I told her between two chuckles, and I couldn't hold myself back from rubbing her clever noggin with my free hand. "I simply slipped it through the box itself, no keyhole required. Intangibility has a lot of neat perks like that."

"I see," Judy responded in an unusually docile voice, and on a second look, she appeared to be in a comfortable daze. Maybe I should pet her more, I considered? I mean, we were both petting Snowy a lot, so I kept forgetting that Judy was also an eligible target for head pats. I decided to rectify this grievous oversight in the future, but for now, we had more important things to worry about, so after one last tousle, I unhanded her and posed a question to her.

"Anyhow, do you remember the non-prophecy of the Magi?"

"The Conduit of the Grimoire of the Last Truth," Judy replied in detail even though a single yes or no would've been enough. She glanced at the box in my hand and asked, "Is that the titular Grimoire inside?"

"Nah, it's not. It's a large pearl or jewel embedded in a hexagonal pedestal covered in jewels, but based on the enchantment and how vitally important it is, they seem to be related."

"So it's one of the Grimoire Keys," my assistant stated as if it was completely obvious.

"Um... yes. Definitely," I told her with a confident nod, but she saw through me right away.

"You have no idea what that is," she declared without even bothering to stick a "Right?" to the end of her sentence to dampen the impact a little.

"I think I've read about something like that on the Hub, but no, I'm afraid not," I admitted straightaway, and she let out a disappointed sigh that hurt my pride a little, so I quickly continued with, "Come on, Dormouse! You know I don't have your photographic memory! Please cut me some slack!"

She apparently did so, as she took a shallow breath and moved on, without dwelling on the issue.

"The Grimoire of the Last Truth is hidden away by the Assembly. To access it, one would need two of the three keys, which are held by the three most senior members of the organization."

"And Lord Grandpa is one of the key keepers." I shook the box in my hand and added, "Or at least he was. This should serve as a pretty nice bargaining chip in the future."

"Maybe," Judy stated, yet I could feel a *but* coming, and lo and behold... "*But* we are talking about one of the only three keys for the most important treasure of the Assembly. Stealing it like this might lead to some dire consequences."

"It's a good thing I was careful about it, then," I noted with a reassuring smile. It didn't work on her, but hey, who can fault me for trying? "Not to mention, what's done is done. I couldn't properly mark the old coot, so I can't take it back even if I wanted to." It was obvious Judy was still far from reassured, so I also added, "On a more optimistic note, I wouldn't worry too much about him discovering it's missing anytime soon. According to the enchantment on it, the hidden compartment of the safe wasn't used in years."

"In that case, let's hope you're right and you didn't accidentally cause another international incident."

"Don't worry, Dormouse. I don't plan on holding on to this for long. I mean, unless Josh suddenly decides to stop setting the flags of my sister and turn his attention to the class rep, the Grimoire of the Last Whatchamacallit is useless to us. Once Josh catches Lab Coat Guy, I plan to use this as our trump card during negotiations to pressure the old man, and after that, I'll exchange it for a favor or something. For example..." I paused for a moment to get my phone out and showed Judy a couple of the pictures I took. "Look how much data there is! And not just boring old ledgers, either; I found an entire section dedicated to magic theory and experimental records! This place is an absolute treasure trove of the kind of info we need the most!"

"Do you want to blackmail the arch-mage into granting you entry to the archives?"

"First off, don't make it sound so immoral. Secondly, I plan on earning us entry, to be precise. Having access to a lot of data about magic should help a ton when it comes to understanding what's magical and what's just run-of-the-mill trope weirdness in this world. It would also cut down on the number of experiments we'd have to run in the future. A lot. I'm also relying on you to do the organizing, as usual."

"Sounds reasonable, but I don't like how you're ditching the boring part of the job onto me again."

That ever-so-slightly-sulky comment made me pause for a moment, and then I hastily told her, "I mean... we both know you're much better at this part than I am, but if you don't want to do it alone, just say the word, and I'll come and help you."

"I'll do that, then." After she said that, she fell silent for a brief while, but then her eyes suddenly lit up and quickly added, "However, I want compensation in advance."

"... I sooooo knew you were going to say that."

"Hush, Chief. Don't ruin the skit," she warned me, but I shook my head.

"Let's skip the skit for now. How about we take a look at the papers I photocopied instead?"

"I already did," Judy told me with the tiniest of pouts.

"Oh? And?"

My still-sulky-yet-very-dedicated girlfriend let out a small huff, but she still picked up the bundle of documents all the same, and after leafing through them, she picked out three pages and showed them to me.

"These are a contract between Lord Endymonion and a certain Friedrich Günther Wissenschaftler. He seems to be a high-ranking member of the Non-causative Science Research Society."

"Eh, that's just Lab Coat Guy's real name," I revealed without much fanfare, much to my dear assistant's shock and complete bafflement, which she was hiding really well behind an exasperated façade that said "How come this is the first time I've ever heard of this?"

"I was under the impression he was called Dr. Robatto," she noted with a mixture of her previous sulkiness and some resignation.

"That's just a fake name for the *sentai* shenanigans, I think. Anyhow, let me take a look at this." She handed over the pages, and just by quickly skimming them, I could tell they fit our observations to a T. There was even a side clause about using Armband Guy as a point of contact to relay messages during the operation, and the rules of when and how Josh could be ambushed were spelled out in black and white. "Look at that! Yet another piece of juicy blackma—*cough*, I mean, *evidence* against the old man... but why does it feel like half of it is missing?"

"Because you only copied one side of the pages," Judy told me and pointed at the numbering on the bottom of the sheets. "It goes from one to three to five."

"Ugh... You're right..." I acknowledged, once again embarrassed by her observation. "In my defense, I was in a bit of a hurry, and I didn't check the photocopier settings. Also, we have the last page with the signatures, so it should still be good enough."

"I agree."

After she said that, there was a few seconds of unusually tense silence in the air, so I forcefully cleared my throat and proposed, "Anyhow, I just checked, and Snowy is home. How about we go back and—"

"Spend some quality couple time together without doing anything risky, tedious, or something that would cause a supernatural political scandal?" Judy cut in before I could finish my sentence, and based on the look she was giving me, she was entirely serious.

"... Yes, that's exactly what I wanted to do," I agreed, just a little overwhelmed, but then I quickly perked up when I remembered something, and I immediately gave my girlfriend a hug. "Not to mention, I believe I do owe you an evening watching the sappiest romantic comedy on the planet..."

And with that, we both disappeared from the secret base, and not even my dearest assistant pinching my forearm could wipe the wicked grin off my face.

PART 2

"This... actually wasn't nearly as bad as I expected," Judy spoke up the moment the credits started rolling. She snuggled a little closer to me under the blanket covering us and added, "I want a refund."

"For what?" I asked while shifting my posture a little to accommodate her. My couch was big, but it was not quite large enough for three people with their legs tucked under them.

"For false advertising," my girlfriend answered with transparently fake indignation. "I was told we would be watching the worst, sappiest romance movie ever made. This obviously wasn't it."

"I don't know. It was bad enough to make Snowy cry," I told her while pointedly rubbing the back of my sniffling, red-eyed mess of a little sister.

"Chief... Romance movies are designed to make you do that."

"Then how come I'm not crying?"

"It's because you're a boy," she answered right away, with a tone that said she was offended because I made her state the obvious.

"In that case, why aren't you crying?"

This time it took her a considerably longer time to answer, and she ultimately settled on, "It's because Judybot doesn't have her crying app installed yet. Beep-boop."

I unsubtly rolled my eyes, but before I could properly respond to her, we were abruptly interrupted by a certain Abyssal girl blowing her nose like a trumpet and then placing the used, crumpled-up tissue onto the steadily growing pile at her side. I decided to use this opportunity to change the direction of the conversation, so I reached for the remote on the table, turned the DVD player off, and on the way back I picked up the empty (and really cheap) jewel case of the movie in question and turned its back to my girlfriend.

"Look! The blurb on the back literally calls this '*Titanic* meets *Dirty Dancing*... IN SPACE!' In all caps! And here! It says it's 'the *Romeo and Juliet* of space operas,' right under the laughably cheap CGI mecha! I thought this would be hilariously bad; how was I supposed to know that there would be a competently-written-and-executed romance plot hiding under all of that C movie schlock?"

"That's not an excuse," Judy huffed, but it was obviously just her staying in character. "I expected a one or two out of ten. This was easily a seven."

"Oh please! That's an exaggeration if I've ever heard one! This was, at most, a weak five."

"You think so? How about you, Neige?"

I silently frowned at her shameless attempt to draw my sister into the fray, yet her answer surprised both of us.

"On a ten-point scale?" she asked back while wiping the corners of her eyes, and after Judy nodded, she declared, "It's a three at most."

"Really?" the question slipped through my lips before I even realized it, and my sister grunted in the affirmative.

"Yes. They had a really great screenplay, and there was a lot of chemistry between the lead actors, but then they just had to ruin it with silly giant robots and incomprehensible space battles! These characters deserved a much better movie!"

"So... You think it's a bad movie?"

"Yes," Snowy delivered the coup de grâce on my assistant without even realizing it. "It's disgraceful."

I sent a triumphant smirk at Judy, which she grudgingly acknowledged, but I didn't rub it in, as I quickly thought of something amusing. I wondered, just how much would it actually cost to get the IP rights of this movie? Considering how cheap the sets, the CGI, and everything else was, I reckoned that it wasn't much. Maybe I could get Abram to pull a few strings for me. I'd been thinking about what to give to my sister for Christmas, and you had to admit, a budget-movie franchise was a pretty novel gift idea.

Oh, but I was joking. Well, half joking. Half serious, at best. Anyhow, I decided this was as good of a note on which to end our chill-out session as any, so I nimbly slipped out from under the blanket and stretched my back.

I was just a bit sore after sitting in place for so long, but otherwise, I was feeling fairly okay. I still wasn't in my top form, but at the very least this confirmed that just looking at enchantments and magical formations didn't worsen my condition.

I turned the lights on and glanced at Judy over my shoulder, then I said, "The quality of the movie notwithstanding, this was surprisingly enjoyable. We should do this more often."

"Agreed," Judy concurred with a nod, then added, "But the next time, I expect a genuinely terrible movie."

"This was terrible," Snowy cut it a little angrily. "So much wasted potential..."

"Yes. And that's why we should watch a movie without any potential to begin with, so that we can make fun of it without any reservations."

"Oh, I get it now!" my sister exclaimed with a beaming smile, and my girlfriend immediately rewarded her with a head pat. How wholesome...

Unfortunately, as much as it hurt my heart to break up this idyllic scene, I'd already made some plans for the late evening. I still waited for Judy to finish, though, and only then did I call out to her.

"It's getting late," I said and gestured towards the clock on the wall. "How about I see you home before it gets dark?"

"You could do that," she responded without any indication of getting out from under the blanket. "Or I could call home, tell Mom that I'm sleeping over at a friend's place, and stay in your room again."

"Not this time, I'm afraid," I responded with a shake of my head. "I already made plans with Brang; we're going to scout the ambush site tonight. I'm also going to have to talk with the exhausting, highly visible ninja and her potty-mouthed sword, so I probably won't be back until late in the night."

"I can wait."

"I repeat: *late in the night.* What do you want to do at that point?"

"There are *lots* of things a young couple could do in a bedroom after dark," my girlfriend answered as she... repeatedly blinked at me? What was that about?

"... Is there a problem?" I asked as I took a step closer to her and leaned forward for a better look. "Did you get something in your eye?"

When she heard the question, she instantly stopped blinking, and after looking me in the eye for a tick or two, she let out a defeated groan.

"No, Chief. I was fluttering my eyelashes at you."

"Ah, so that's what you were doing!" I straightened my back with a small smile, which immediately turned into a frown as I linked that with her previous sentence. "You really should practice being coy a bit more. Also, if I read your innuendo right, don't you think that would be rushing things a little?"

"I don't think so, Chief," Judy responded as she finally got up, as well. "You're the one being too passive."

"I don't think I am. Not to mention, isn't this a topic we should broach when Elly is around, as well?"

"We're way ahead of you," Judy stated with just a hint of smugness as she stood in front of me. "I've already discussed this with Eleanor, and she gave me the green light to go ahead and start dropping unsubtle hints about the topic of reproductive activities."

"Just like that?"

"Just like that," she repeated after me, with a small nod for emphasis.

"How?"

All of a sudden the previous hint of smugness rushed to the forefront, my assistant's lips ever-so-slightly curled upward in a smirk, and then she declared, "I won the right in rock-paper-scissors."

I gave my girlfriend a flat look, and ultimately asked her, "... You know that by saying that, you just made me take you even less seriously, right?"

"You should, anyway. According to my research, physical intimacy is one of the top three most important aspects of a healthy relationship."

"Yes, I'm well aware; I just don't think this is the right time to discuss this. Or place," I added and subtly gestured towards my sister, who was still tucked under the blanket and watched us with a frankly worrying amount of interest.

Judy followed my gaze, and then retorted, "Neige is an Abyssal Seducer. There's no reason to refrain from discussing this topic in front of her; she should have more knowledge of the subject than we do."

"Do you?" I leveled the question at my enraptured little sister, and she instantly blinked in surprise.

"I-I'm well versed in the... um... *theoretical* aspect of s-sexuality..." she stated with just a bit of stammering, earning her a curiously raised brow in the process, but before I could ask what exactly she meant by that, my attention was grabbed by my girlfriend again.

"You see, Chief? There's no reason why we cannot discuss the topic of—"

"Yes, there is, because it's embarrassing, and no, we are *not* going to do it, because I have places to be. Can we do it another time?"

Judy looked quite disapproving of my request, but in the end I won our staring contest, and she relented with an obviously displeased huff.

"Are you leaving, then?" Snowy inquired as she cocked her head to the side, and after a moment of hesitation, Judy responded with a shrug.

"I don't seem to have much of a choice in the matter."

"Then I'll clean up!" my little sister suddenly declared while looking at the empty popcorn bowls and plastic bottles on the table.

"You don't have to, I'll..." "Take care of things once I'm back" is what I wanted to say, but before I could reach the end of the sentence, Snowy had already kicked off her blanket and began to tidy up the place. Judy also turned on her heel and headed to the entrance without a word, so I quickly followed after her and left my delightedly humming sister to her odd hobby.

By the time I caught up with my assistant, she'd already put on her outdoor shoes, so I followed suit and got dressed, as well. I wasn't feeling feverish anymore, but I still put on an extra layer, just to be on the safe side. I had no idea for how long I'd be staying out this time, and the nights were getting really chilly as of late. Or rather, even chillier than before, but I digress.

We got ready to go outside without uttering a single word in the process, and I was getting ready to spend the way to her house in awkward silence, yet my expectations were quickly betrayed when Judy immediately addressed me the moment I closed the door behind us.

"We are no longer within earshot of your sister. Can we continue the previous discussion where we left off?"

"Do we really have to?" I half asked and half pleaded, but she was firm as a mountain. An especially sulky one, with a frown and... is that just a play of the light, or does she actually have dimples? That's surprisingly cute, aaaand I totally lost track of my analogy again. Bummer. It was a good one, too.

Anyhow, since she didn't seem to budge, I was afraid I had no choice but to accept my fate, so I gestured for her to follow after me with only the barest hint of well-concealed trepidation.

"I don't know why you are so hell-bent about this, but fine, let's get this over with."

"I don't like your attitude," she griped, but then a moment later she followed after me and explained, "Eleanor and I are concerned with your lack of initiative. We have been alone with you on a number of occasions, yet you show no signs of trying to move our relationship forward. In a physical sense of the word."

"I don't think I'm keeping any distance," I denied her accusation as I recalled all the times we'd spent together as of late. "Aren't we cuddling enough as is?"

"Yes, but you avoid going any farther than that."

I sent a skeptical glance her way, but she didn't seem to receive it, so I voiced the same sentiment by telling her, "Dormouse, we've only been going out for two weeks. We didn't even do any of the slurpy, mouth-sucky tongue stuff yet. Don't you think that jumping right into pillow wrestling would be rushing things just a wee bit too much?"

"That's the problem." Judy abruptly raised her voice and pointed at my face. "Boys are supposed to be rushing these things. You're too reserved."

"Am I?" I asked, yet even I had to admit it was a rhetorical question at best. "Well, fine. Maybe I *am* a little reserved, but considering how much we have to deal with already, can you blame me? The last thing we need right now is a teen pregnancy subplot to complicate things."

"Contraceptives exist," Judy objected, but I overruled her with a shrug.

"Even so, I don't think it's worth the risk right now."

My girlfriend fell silent for a couple of long seconds, and I almost entertained the vain hope that I convinced her... but then she threw me a curveball right out of left field.

"Chief? How often do you watch porn?"

I was glad I wasn't drinking anything at the moment because otherwise this would've been a perfect example of the clichéd spit take scene.

"... Come again?"

"I asked, how often do you watch porn movies? Or read porn magazines, if that's your thing."

"It's not, and I don't."

"No need to be embarrassed about it. Everybody does it, and I only want to know for scientific reasons."

"Uh-huh. In that case, why don't you tell me first?" I challenged her by throwing the ball back into her court, and while that gave her a short pause (along with turning her ears to such a bright shade of red they were visible even in the evening twilight), she still gave me an answer, much to my surprise.

"About twice a week."

"... Seriously?"

"Um," she grunted as she nodded, then after that, she added in a slightly lower voice, "If we count the times I do it without supporting material, it's closer to four times a week." At this point she paused again to gauge my reaction, and then she further explained, "I do it when I feel pent up or frustrated."

"Isn't that a lot?"

This time she shook her head and told me, "No. According to what I read online, it's well within the range of the statistical average for our age group. So? What about you?"

I had to admit, she'd cornered me quite magnificently. After she'd said all that, there was no way left for me to weasel out of the conversation, so I ultimately had to give up and just say it.

"I don't really do *that*."

"You do it without porn?"

"No, I mean, I don't do it, period."

My dear assistant gave me a look as if she'd just seen a white raven landing on a black sheep.

"Chief, I don't want to be rude, but... How should I ask this tactfully?"

She honest-to-goodness seemed like she was genuinely looking at me for advice, so I hastily told her, "I can't help you because I have no idea what you're trying to say."

"In that case, I think I have no choice but to rely on the tried-and-tested WWJD method," she suddenly declared with a serious expression.

"WWJD?" I echoed after her, and before I knew it, my brows had already set themselves into a curiously raised arch. "Are you talking about one of those wristbands?"

"Don't be silly, Chief. What would my What Would Judybot Do? slogan do on a wristband?"

With that, my brows immediately returned to their resting deadpan position. So much for that.

"I'm about ninety-eight percent sure the *J* is supposed to stand in for Jesus in that acronym," I told her, yet she just shook her head with unusual irreverence.

"But it doesn't, because it stands for Judybot. Speaking of which, beep-boop, I know what to say now," she declared as she raised her hand up and did a twisting motion with her wrist. I had no idea what that was supposed to be, even after she repeated the gesture a couple more times. At last, her shoulders drooped just a tiny bit, and she muttered something along the lines of, "I'm sorry, but it appears Judybot's finger-snapping app crashed."

"... You have an awful lot of missing or broken features, don't you?"

"It can't be helped. Judybot is in early access."

"How original. I've never heard that one before." I paused for a while, mainly just to let her soak in the bucket of industrial-strength sarcasm I'd dumped on her, but then I asked, "What were we talking about before this sidetrack again?"

"About whether or not your lack of interest is due to," at this point, she raised her fingers for air quotes and finished with, "... 'hardware failure.'"

I had no idea how to react to that. In fact, I had no idea how to even interpret her words, and it took me several seconds to link all the stray parts of our conversation together and figure out what she was getting at.

"Aaah... You are alluding to ED, aren't you?" I asked with the kind of mixed enthusiasm you'd get when you'd solved a hard problem, only to wish you didn't.

"Yes, Chief," Judy responded just a tad morosely. "Thanks for wasting all my tact."

"You're welcome," I responded with a forced, upbeat grin as my next move in our emotional chess game. Or was it checkers? It was hard to keep track of what we were doing at this point...

She gave me an odd look, and then said, "If you can grin like that, I suppose you don't have it."

"I can't say I do, no," I answered with a shrug, finally dropping the happy-go-lucky act. "In fact, I'm kind of having the opposite problem as of late, and it's pretty annoying; I just don't have a strong urge to do anything about it, and then it eventually goes away."

And now she looked like the black sheep suddenly turned into an honest politician, with the raven being its campaign advisor when running for the presidency. Did I really say something weird? No, wait... even if I did, I would probably recognize it if it was that weird.

Anyhow, Judy soon jolted me out of my thoughts by asking, "Are you trying to tell me you have no sex drive?"

"I wouldn't go that far, but at the very least I don't consider it a high priority in my life," I answered with the utmost sincerity, yet it only seemed to make her even more worried.

"That's troubling. I have to consult Eleanor, and we have to do something about it posthaste."

"Is it really that big of a deal?" I asked, half jokingly, yet she gave me an honest-to-goodness glare in return.

"Yes, Chief. This is extremely serious."

"Errr... Okay, if you say so... Also, we've arrived."

My comment made Judy freeze up for a moment, and she hastily glanced around, only to visibly deflate when she noticed we were standing right in front of her house.

"Let's continue this conversation tomorrow," she proclaimed, and I could barely stop my exasperation from showing on my face. However, before I could say my goodbyes, she raised her face and even extended her hands in an obvious display of requesting a goodbye kiss.

I, of course, had no reason to decline, so I leaned forward a little and planted a peck on her lips... Or at least that was the plan, except I didn't expect that she would clamp her hands around my head. My initial surprise was then raised a notch by the touch of her warm, wet tongue prying my lips open and entering my mouth. My first instinct was to clamp down, but I was afraid that I would bite her, so I endured the urge and let her clumsily explore the inside of my mouth at her leisure.

The kiss lasted for a good fifteen or so seconds, and once we separated, I actually felt that my face was burning a little. That said, compared to my girlfriend, who was currently gasping and red as a lobster, I think I did fairly well.

Once she caught her breath, Judy gave me an unusually awkward glance, and stated, "You have no cavities. That's good."

"Thanks for the compliment?" I responded a little uncertainly, and then added, "And you tasted like popcorn."

"I see. So how was it? Did that get you excited?"

"Well... I would be lying if I said it didn't," I admitted just a tiny bit more sheepishly than I intended.

"Enough to make you change your mind and make you want me to stay with you for the night?"

"I... wouldn't quite go that far."

My dear assistant clicked her tongue in a mixture of frustration and disappointment, but then she looked me in the eye again and declared, "There's still hope. Also, now that we have done a tongue kiss, you cannot use that as an excuse anymore."

"I wasn't. Also, I'm not sure that fully qualified."

"Then we just have to practice every day until we get it right," she stated with unusual intensity... which she then immediately ruined by doing that blinking thing again.

"Dormouse... I love you, I really do, so don't take this the wrong way, but you're *terrible* at playing coy. Please stop."

She did just that, but only to declare, "I'll have to practice even more."

"If you really want to..." I muttered in resignation, and then I gestured towards the entrance in front of us. "Let's call it a day. You are going to catch a cold by standing around like this."

"Fine," she relented after a short while, but instead of going inside, she first held my hand, stood on her tiptoes, and planted a small peck on my cheek. "Stay safe," she told me with an earnest look as she stepped away, but she only let go of my hand when she was out of arm's reach, and she even sent me a small, demure glance before she disappeared behind the door.

I didn't stand still for long; after waving goodbye I quickly turned around and headed to the closest hidden crook in the area.

I prepared myself for Phasing away, yet as I did so, I couldn't help but touch the spot on my cheek and wonder, "Maybe I was wrong, and she does have a talent for coyness?"

And with those words, and an inexplicable smile on my lips, I promptly disappeared.

PART 3

"[Ah? It is you, Blackcloak.]" The Faun ex-general immediately perked up the moment I arrived. Using his usual spear as a crutch, he rose up from his crouching position with slow, deliberate motions, shedding the orange film of light covering his body in the process. Once he stood straight, he raised a fist to his chest in the customary salute and added, "[Greetings to you.]"

"[I wish a delightful evening upon you as well, general,]" I returned the courtesy with a smile, and the ram-headed muscleman in front of me let out a low, rumbling chuckle in return.

"[Aye. This night was made for hunting.]"

"[In that regard, I defer to your experience,]" I responded as I surveyed the wooded area of the city park around us. "[Will this be the grounds upon which we shall lie in wait?]"

"[Aye. The Chimera shall pass by these woods in two nights' time. Is it thine wish to inspect the slaying grounds?]"

"[Such were the intentions behind my visit, yes,]" I replied. By the looks of it, Brang wanted to get going right away, so I hastily raised a palm to halt him. "[Forestall your equines, general, for before we shall attempt to scour the land in a mundane endeavor, I wish to attempt something that may yield results in a different manner.]"

"[Is that so?]" He set the butt of his spear against the soft ground with a quiet *thunk* sound and gave me an intrigued look.

"[Aye. I wish to employ the Rites of Dominance in an effort to aid our exploration of the land.]"

"[You wish to scout the terrain while we test our mettle in combat?]"

"[Your assumption is within the distance of striking upon the truth. I wish to have one pair of our specters of Dominance locked in battle, thus fulfilling the spirit of the rite, while the rest of our specters shall scour the land and seek to commit its lay to memory in preparation for the day of the covert slaying of the beast.]"

Brang's ears swiveled around for a while, an act I had long since associated with confusion, but at last he raised a hand to his chin and told me, "[Such use of the rite is, to say with soft words, highly unorthodox.]"

"[That it may be, but is it an act that we may pursue?]"

"[I see no true obstacle in our way,]" he granted me in a contemplative tone, then after he rubbed his chin a bit more, he flashed a toothy smile and added, "[At the very least, it shall serve as a novel experience.]"

"[Undoubtedly,]" I responded with a grin of my own.

With that said, we locked eyes for a moment, and the odd, tingling sensation of Dominance quickly followed. As previously agreed, I immediately sent out an orange ghost copy of myself, and Brang did the same. The two phantoms immediately entered into a familiar routine that was very reminiscent of the battle we fought the first time; he had more range and experience, I had more mobility and better reflexes, resulting in a stalemate.

That said, I don't want to brag or anything, but my own specter was doing considerably better this time around. It was probably due to our sparring like this every other day or so, but I'd gotten quite used to Brang's movements. When I had my training spear with me, I could even land a few lucky hits on the guy every once in a while. I didn't have it on me this time, though, so I had my specter focus on dodging instead.

Once the familiar rhythm was established, I sent out four more transparent phantoms, and my opponent followed suit with four of his own. Once they were out, I had them scout on our left, and as if by an unspoken agreement, Brang's copies did the same on our right. I waited for a couple of seconds to see if there were any complications or unintended side effects, but everything seemed to be perfectly normal, so I simply allowed the specters to continue exploring in a slowly expanding circle.

That said, while I admit that getting the map of my surroundings slowly etched into my brain was, using Brang's words, "A novel experience" indeed, it wasn't particularly riveting after a while. As such, I decided to try to strike up a conversation with the Faun. I mean, if I had to stare at him like this for an extended time, anyway, I might as well make the most of it.

"[So, general...]" I casually addressed Brang, yet to my shock, he actually blinked in surprise and nearly broke the connection. The specters wavered for a moment, but once he regained his balance, they also continued on as if nothing happened.

"[I sincerely request that you refrain from surprising me like that in the future, Blackcloak. This heart of mine is no longer young enough to bear it.]"

"[My apologies of the most sincere kind. I only wished to converse while we await the completion of our exploration.]"

The Faun gave me an odd look, then stated, "[It is rare to find an opponent who may employ more than three spirits of the mind. To think you would possess leeway to converse even under the weight of five of them tells volumes of thine willpower.]"

"[I admit I find it unwarranted, yet I must thank you for the compliment all the same. With such things spoken, if talking under the Rite of Dominance strains you so, I'm willing to decrease the numbers of our spectral facsimiles.]"

"[Nay. I may be old, yet I shall not shame myself by backing down from a challenge, even if it's you who propose it.]"

"[Hearing so fills me with feelings of mirth.]"

Brang gave me an appreciative, if somewhat shallow, nod.

"[If so, then may I humbly ask why you addressed me?]"

"[I only wished to engage in conversation of diminutive size.]" That didn't come out right, so I lightly cleared my throat and tried again. "[I meant to convey that I wished to inquire about your well-being, alongside that of your men.]"

"[Thy request strikes me as odd. Have you not seen to our needs in detail? Thine stewardship provides us with food, shelter, and purpose. We can seldom ask for more.]"

"[Not even that second table of indoor sports?]" I teased him a little, and just as I expected his ears immediately turned in two different directions as he hastily told me:

"[Mayhap with the exception of that.]" We both stifled our snickers, lest they would interrupt our oh-so-heated mental battle. "[With such things told, I must confess that thine treatment of my kin and me is remarkably pleasing.]"

"[Is that so?]"

"[You have already earned the loyalty and respect of the young ones.]"

"[How about yours, general?]"

"[Well, you would be hard-pressed to earn something you already possess, wouldn't you agree?]" he responded between chuckles, and I couldn't help but smile along.

After that, we remained silent for a while, at least until Brang addressed me for a change.

"[You inquired about my well-being. May I do the same in turn?]"

"[Certainly, if you deem that courtesy dictates so.]"

"[Aye, albeit I admit I do wonder about thine welfare beyond the realm of courtesy.]"

"[Is that so? What makes you entertain such worries?]"

"[For the sake of explanation, I would call upon thine troubled countenance upon thine arrival.]"

"[Your eyes are sharp as ever, general, for I was troubled, indeed.]"

I intended to leave it at that, yet seeing the expectant look in Brang's eyes, I ultimately decided that I might as well tell him about my problems. I didn't expect him to give me advice, but I figured that getting it off my chest couldn't hurt, and it was as good a topic as any to pass the time while we explored the area. As such, I did just that, and I gave him a footnotes version of the argument I'd had with Judy.

He listened to my words with his full attention, and once I reached the end of my retelling, he gave me a sage nod.

"[I must agree with thine lover's concerns.]"

"[You do?]"

"[Aye. For the family to remain strong and independent, the continuation of thine bloodline is paramount. Only by siring progeny can you ensure that thine legacy shall endure and thy descendants may one day proudly wear thine mantle.]"

"[... I wish you no offense, general, but I hope with sincerity of the most sincere variety that you are aware that I am not a Lord of the Abyss. I possess no title or mantle my children may inherit.]"

"[Hmmm. Thine words ring true. Thine title of regent is one of importance, yet one which is not subject to inheritance.]" At this point he paused as he tilted his head to the left in yet another familiar gesture. "[Yet, if that is the case, then why did thine betrothed wish for a child?]"

"[I must explain, for I believe you are labouring under a misunderstanding. Her wish of intimacy had more relation to the deepening of our interpersonal associations rather than procreation.]"

"[Truly? I must confess, I am not well versed in the intricacies of such matrimonial relations, for my kin engages in no such thing.]"

That actually reminded me of something I'd wanted to ask for a while already, and given the opportunity Brang had just presented, it would have been awfully sloppy of me not to strike while the proverbial iron was hot.

"[Do forgive my curiosity, but this question has plagued my mind for days: Do your kin possess females?]"

My Faun companion once again found my question perplexing, at least based on his ear movement, but he soon answered all the same, with a headshake slow enough to keep our eye contact uninterrupted.

"[Nay, Blackcloak. My kin does not possess thine kin's dimorphism.]"

I decided to put aside the question of how the Faun language was complex enough to use terms like *dimorphism*, yet it was so rigid it made me jump through hoops when trying to describe Snowy's and Crowey's nicknames, and instead I focused on the actual content of this answer.

"[If that is so, then from whence do your neophytes spring forth?]"

Okay, that's it. I wanted to ignore it, but I can't.

First off, I only wanted to ask, 'Where do baby Fauns come from?' How did such an innocent question turn into that!? And what even is a neophyte, anyway!?

In the meantime, Brang was completely unaware of my linguistics-induced existential crisis. He considered my question very seriously, and at last he told me, "[My kin is borne from the Emperor's Well.]"

"[Please do elaborate,]" I prompted him, and he obliged without any objections.

"[My kin was conceived by the power of the Emperor. The first Fauns were all fully grown by the time they first opened their eyes to the world. We do not sire or bear little ones.]"

"[If so, then by what method do you procreate?]" I asked, followed by a relieved sigh; this time I'd managed to use the right terms.

Brang fell silent for a while, and while I couldn't perfectly read his expressions yet, because of the surface emotions exchanged between us during Dominance, I could feel that he was a little conflicted.

"[Upon our demise in our duty, all of the Faun Abyssals are entitled to our final rites. The fallen is taken to the Well of the Emperor, and from the bodies of the dead, a new scion is born, carrying the will of their predecessor.]"

"[Just so?]"

"[Just so.]"

"[... The lights you shed upon my question revealed just as many things unknown to me as they made known. May I request that you enlighten me even further?]" He immediately nodded, so I continued without any further ado. "[You mentioned the Well of the Emperor a number of times. Could you elaborate on its details? Is it one of the famed Wellsprings of Primordial Magicka of the Abyss?]"

"[Thine supposition is correct.]"

"[If so, then which clan of the Abyss does it belong to?]"

"[None. The Well of the Emperor is neutral ground, guarded by the Faun Undivided. It awaits the return of the one true Emperor, for only he may bind the Well to his will.]"

I guessed as much by the name, but I still flashed an appreciative smile at the helpful Faun.

"[I welcome your explanation. I have one more doubt, and I hope you could assuage its incessant itch: If your neophytes are reborn from the flesh of the fallen, then how do you increase your numbers?]"

"[Thine question is astute. In words as straight as a well-made sword: the more venerable the fallen, the greater the number of the scions who emerge from the Well after their final rites.]"

"[I believe I understand,]" I told him and fell silent as I contemplated what I'd just learned.

In short, Fauns were mono-sex, they had no childhood, and when they died, their bodies were recomposed into one or more new Fauns, each one inheriting bits and pieces of the original's memories and/or personality. I reckoned the last part was so that they could cut back on basic training and make them combat ready ASAP, but even without that deduction, it was easy to tell that they were a species artificially created and bred for battle. That wasn't surprising at all.

The thing that actually baffled me a little was that, while they were obviously made and conditioned to be murder machines, they weren't *single-minded* murder machines. They had their quirks, their odd artistic talents, and Brang was a straight-up virtuoso of the air hockey table. Now, I could chalk a lot of this up to the good-old placeholder-development hypothesis, but there still had to be a grain of potential in them to develop in such directions. I wondered, was I mistaken about the Fauns being simple mooks? Did they have some sort of more nuanced narrative reason behind their existence? Or was it just my inadvertent meddling causing bigger waves than I'd ever imagined?

All of those were questions for later, though, as my attention was drawn back to Brang upon his letting out a wistful sigh, followed by a tingle of forlorn emotions being transmitted to me through Dominance.

"[Generals in service of the Houses all receive grand processions upon their fall. I also wished to be laid to rest in such a fashion, yet I'm afraid the chances of such an occurrence are all but vanishing. It is truly a—]"

"[Halt, general!]" I interrupted him with a tinge of panic in my voice. "[I implore, nay, I order thee to cease elevating your banner of demise!"]

The old Faun looked me funny for a moment, and then asked, "[Pardon my ignorance, Blackcloak, but I have yet to learn about this... 'banner of demise' you speak of.]"

It took all my willpower to keep myself from face-palming in frustration. I already had a terrible time when it came to expressing simple idioms in Faunish; just how was I supposed to explain tropes like death flags to him? Nevertheless, I had to give it a try, if only so that he would stop looking so comically confused.

"[A banner of demise is...]" I began, only to stop as I ran a couple of permutations of the explanation under my breath before settling on, "[It is a choice of words which make the shedding of your earthly coil more likely.]"

"[Is that so?]" Brang mused, and it was easy to tell he wasn't completely convinced. Whether that was because of the strangeness of the concept or because my explanation was inadequate, I couldn't say. Either way, I felt obliged to press on.

"[It is so, and so I request that you watch your words. I would be truly troubled if the funeral procession you described ever came to pass.]"

Brang blinked at me in surprise, followed by a strangely jovial chuckle.

"[If you request so, I have little choice but to obey and avoid these banners you speak of in the future.]"

I couldn't help but involuntarily narrow my eyes in response to his words, and even though he sounded completely serious, I couldn't help but feel that he was taking the piss out of me. That said, a promise was a promise, and I was just about to drop the issue when I was jolted by something one of my specters saw.

"[Trouble approaches! General, prepare to disengage!]"

I'd barely even finished my line by the time Brang cut the Rite of Dominance short and he readied his spear.

"[Is it the Chimera?]"

"[Nay, something much worse!]" No sooner had I said that, I confirmed Rinne dashing towards us through the wooded area on our left, her slasher grin all but glowing in the dark. I could've sworn that when I checked her location before I Phased over, she was nowhere near the park, but that was the least of my problems at the moment. "[We shall continue this conversation at a later date! For now, I shall distract her, and you must use the opportunity to hide your presence!]"

"[Understood!]" Brang responded with the kind of gusto you would expect from a military man... ram... person. Let's go with guy.

With that sorted I quickly dashed to the left, allowing my Faun companion to do the same in the other direction, and I called out to the annoying huntress in the only way I could be sure I would get her full attention.

"Rinne! Look out!"

Now, let me make one thing clear: I expected her to look my way, and maybe even bark back at me about calling her by her name again, giving Brang a few precious seconds to activate his invisibility Sigil and slip away. What I didn't expect was that she would twitch, veer to the side, and then run head-first into a tree with such a painfully loud *thunk* that it made me involuntarily shudder. So... would this make her a creepy, annoying, highly visible, and *clumsy* ninja? That's a lot of adjectives...

I really, really wished I could just leave and pretend I didn't see anything, but my inner Good Samaritan vetoed my every attempt to just turn around and flee the scene of the crime, so I resigned myself to my fate and walked over to the young woman cradling her head on the ground.

"Hey, Mountain Girl? Are you all right?"

She froze when she heard my voice again, and she immediately jumped to her (somewhat wobbly) feet.

"Yes, we're the perfect image of fineness!" she declared in a loud voice, but a single look at her teary eyes and the large, red lump on her forehead was enough to tell that she wasn't. "We were hit by a surprise attack, but it would take more than that to deter us from our eternal quest for the eradication of—"

"Yes, yes, you are very edgy as usual," I cut in with a not-at-all-subtle roll of my eyes. "I guess that means you're all right."

My unwanted conversational partner honest-to-goodness puffed out her cheeks in indignation, but before I could tell her that no matter how much she did so, it was waaaaay too late for her to try to reinvent herself as a cutesy moe archetype, her eyes abruptly opened wide, and she glanced around in a hurry.

"Where is the foul creature of the underworld!?"

"I think he ran away in the commotion," I told her while taking a half step to the right, so that I would partially block her line of sight of the already-cloaked Brang. As far as I knew, she couldn't see through Snowy's invisibility Sigil, but it never hurt to be careful. I decided to keep her occupied for a little longer, so I asked her, "What are you doing here, anyway? I thought we agreed that we'd meet near the docks today."

"Yes, we did," she told me while wiping the corners of her eyes with the lapels of her suit. "We were heading there under the deep, ever-permeating darkness of the night when we recognized the unmistakable stench of the despicable creatures of the Abyss."

"So... you're telling me you followed your nose here?"

"Yes, we did," she declared rather proudly, completely ignoring the incredulity in my voice. "Here, we saw you engaging the horrid monstrosity, and we rushed forth to share in the bounty of the bloody carnage that was sure to follow!" After saying that, she touched her forehead and let out a small, pained hiss. "Yet, before we could paint the ground in the garnet of flowing life, we were struck by a cowardly attack by some unseen assailant!"

"No, you hit a tree," I told her in no uncertain terms.

"Nonsense," she rebuked me with one of her sharp looks that seemed to ask whether I was blind or just stupid. "We are Onikiri no Tsukaima Rinne!"

"That doesn't change the fact that you hit a tree," I repeated, this time with added exasperation.

"That's not how Rinne remembers it!" she declared with an actual pout on her lips. It only lasted for a moment, though, as her face slackened, and a few seconds later she gave me an apprehensive squint. "Onikiri says that you're a suspicious person. She said that you must be working with the creature of the underworld and called out to me to allow them to escape! Were you?"

That was surprising. It looks like her sword was pretty *sharp* after all.

That was a terrible pun. I feel ashamed, and I apologize.

Anyhow, I shrugged my shoulders and told her, "No, I just wanted to warn you."

"In that case, it's fine," she declared with so much conviction I felt like I was hit by conversational whiplash. She didn't seem to care (or notice), as she pressed on by telling me, "Let us embark on our journey to find and massacre the creatures of the underworld! The night is young, and carnage awaits us!"

"Yes, yes. Let's go," I spoke in resignation, following which my creepy... well, no, actually. Calling her creepy at this point was kind of inaccurate. Lately having her around started to feel more like I was looking after a chuunibyou cousin over spring break... except that cousin was actually older than me. She wasn't really creepy anymore, just kind of cringey and annoying.

Putting that tangent aside, I sent a covert nod to the still-cloaked Brang observing us from afar, and I followed after Mountain Girl who, for some reason, began to prattle about the number of cats she'd found in the neighbourhood. Oh well, at least it was no longer about bloodbaths and overly flowery monologues about hunting.

Oh, how far my bar for acceptable topics has fallen...

CONTINGENCY PLANS

It was around five in the afternoon when the young scientist, still wearing his multicoloured collar-armour-cum-shoulder-guard over his usual white lab coat, stormed into the common room of the hidden Research Society workshop. It was a small, yet surprisingly cozy room, with a well-lit interior, several comfortable-looking navy-blue beanbag chairs arranged around a simple wooden coffee table, a water cooler in the corner, an honest-to-goodness antique cuckoo clock on the wall, and even a sizable aquarium with a fair number of colourful tropic fish minding their own business inside.

Then the man slammed the door hard, scattering the fish and making the old man reading a book on one of the beanbag chairs nearly jump to his feet in fright. Peabody glanced around in a mild panic, but once he noticed his nephew, he let out a small breath of relief and slowly retook his seat.

"Please, Friedrich... you're going to give me a heart attack one of these days."

Lab Coat Guy completely disregarded his complaints, and instead he walked over and more or less fell into one of the seats with a small puffing sound upon his landing. The school nurse kept eyeing the younger man for a while, but at last he closed his book, put it aside, and then subsequently he addressed his conspicuously silent nephew.

"O-ho-ho. I reckon things didn't go as planned?"

"It's the opposite," Lab Coat Guy answered with a long face, and for a moment the bags under his sunken eyes seemed even darker than usual. "We set the stage, got them cornered, I said my lines, and then there was a fight... Everything went as it should."

"Then what's the problem?" Peabody inquired with understandable incomprehension.

"The *problem*," Lab Coat Guy stressed the word while he simultaneously tried to massage his temples, which was made more difficult than necessary by his bulky upper-chest armour. "The problem is that they're taking everything we do in stride! There was no hesitation or surprise or anything! It's like... those kids are treating this as if it was a game!"

"O-ho-ho? Really?"

"Yes, really!" the younger man burst out in a fit of frustration. "We're supposed to scare them, but they don't care at all! I even brought out one of the Gigants to give them a fright, without making it grow, of course, but do you know what the Abyssal girl said?" He waited for a beat, but since his uncle didn't speak up, he continued by exclaiming, "She said it was cute! CUTE! What is wrong with these kids!?"

"O-ho-ho! Children today are adaptable for sure!"

"This goes way beyond mere adaptability!" Lab Coat Guy countered, fuming, and so Peabody narrowed his eyes and thought about his words for a moment.

"They aren't common children, that's for sure. They met a Chimera and yet lived to tell the tale, didn't they? Surviving such an encounter... I would be more surprised if it didn't steel their nerves."

"Again, this goes waaaaaay beyond that!" Lab Coat Guy denied with a scowl, only to fall silent right afterwards as his brows slowly knit together into a thoughtful frown.

"Uncle? Can I be honest with you for a moment?"

"O-ho-ho. Are you implying you are not honest with me otherwise?"

"Not now, uncle. I'm not in the mood for wordplay," he griped, then after a long sigh he quietly stated, "I think we are being had."

"You mean we are deceived? By the children?"

"No, of course not them!" Lab Coat Guy exploded again. "I'm talking about the arch-mage!" Peabody once again looked upon his nephew with a profound sense of incomprehension, so he let out a tired sigh and explained, "I've felt that this deal was too good to be true from the beginning, but since you vouched for the arch-mage's sincerity, I still signed it in good faith. After all, we were only supposed to scare a few kids! How hard could that be?"

"Oh-ho-ho! Harder than it seems!" the old man declared with a jovial smile, much to his nephew's chagrin.

"Stop messing around. I'm serious! I was suspicious about this deal from the very beginning! The arch-mage gave us the funds and raw materials to keep our research running for years, and he only asks *that* in exchange? Does that make any sense to you?"

"Amadeus is a... smart man. A genius, even," the nurse stated after some hesitation. "This wouldn't be the first time I couldn't follow his thought processes. Like that one time, back in the academy, when we had to—"

"I've heard the story, Uncle," Peabody was interrupted by his huffing conversational partner. "You had to make a focus apparatus for a decoder array, and he made you run a bunch of errands that didn't make sense at the time, but then he assembled a revolutionary new apparatus based on the Horten-Swarz effect. You tell me this same story every time I tell you the arch-mage is up to something fishy!"

"Oh-ho-ho? Fishy, you say? Such as?" the portly nurse asked with a curiously raised brow.

"Do you want me to go by bullet points?" Lab Coat Guy asked back with thinly veiled sarcasm, only to get momentarily stunned when the old man gave him a nod. Seeing that, he threw his hands into the air and exclaimed, "Where should I even begin?! How about the part where he withheld crucial information about the kids? Like how one of the boys was an expert illusionist and the other one was an Abyssal? Or the way he's treating us as lackeys instead of business partners? Or how he's refusing to meet me as of late by citing security concerns? Or how the kids are completely unfazed by the ambushes? No, I'll go even further! I'd bet my doctorate that they're no longer feeling under pressure because they know when I'm going to ambush them ahead of time! Just like today; they almost looked impatient, and the moment I pulled them into the Restricted Space, they immediately jumped at the Sprockets as if they were waiting for me!"

"That sounds unusual indeed. Are you sure?"

"Yes, I'm sure," the man, who apparently had a real doctorate, stated with a metric ton of emphasis. "They had to know that Galatea and I were coming; there's no other way to explain their behaviour."

"Are you implying that Amadeus told them when you were going to ambush them?" the old nurse asked a question that sounded entirely rhetorical.

"That's precisely what I'm implying," Lab Coat Guy stated quite author-itatively. "He *must* have told them. It makes sense, too; why else would he want us to tell him about our plans a full day ahead of time? He put that clause into the contract so that he could use it against us. He's playing both sides!"

"I still don't see why Amadeus would do something like that," the nurse stated with his bushy eyebrows scrunched up so hard they were on the verge of forming a unibrow.

"Me neither, but it's the only thing that makes sense," the man in the lab coat countered as he leaned forward in his seat. "How else can you explain how they knew about our plans? It's just the three of us here, so no one could leak our information from the inside. That means it has to be him."

"O-ho-ho. Aren't you forgetting about Pascal?"

"Please, Uncle," Lab Coat Guy answered in a dismissive voice as he shook his head. "We both know that he's the arch-mage's personal lapdog. Do you think he would do anything the old man didn't personally approve?"

"You might be correct, but that doesn't mean someone we know had to leak information," Peabody pressed on with his counterargument. "Maybe it's a spy who's doing it? Or a third party? For example, how about that one time someone sneaked into the workshop?"

Lab Coat Guy's face instantly twisted in a grimace at the mere mention of the incident, and he really did look like he'd just bitten into the world's sourest lemon.

"Don't worry, Uncle! I learned from the failure! Galatea and I have upgraded our security system to the bleeding edge of mystic engineering! Next time those pesky Celestials will think twice before they would try infiltrating the workshop!"

"O-ho-ho? So it was a Celestial spy after all..."

"Well, err... I'm not entirely sure," Lab Coat Guy admitted as he awkwardly scratched the back of his head. "Galatea's sensor logs are inconclusive, but I don't think there's anyone else who could or would sneak in here." He paused for a moment, but then he forcefully shook his head and sat up straight before declaring. "It doesn't matter! Even if they managed to sneak in once back then, they couldn't possibly leak our later plans! Only the arch-mage knew about those!"

"You really want to believe that Amadeus is plotting against us," Peabody muttered under his breath, followed by a tired sigh.

"It's not about belief! Once you take all the facts and eliminate the impossible, the only answer remaining must be the truth. There can be no leak on the inside, no infiltrator can sneak in anymore, and we have swept the whole workshop for bugs. Unless there's some kind of invisible, intangible, undetectable fairy spying on us, the only remaining solution is that the arch-mage is leaking our plans to the kids."

"Maybe... but why would he do that?"

"How should I know?! Maybe it's some kind of ploy to get rid of us without him dirtying his hands, or maybe it's some kind of convoluted ruse to make the kids indebted to him? Who the hell knows at this point?"

After his latest outburst, the two men fell silent for several long seconds. Then, out of the blue, Lab Coat Guy abruptly let out a lung-shattering groan that made the fish in the aquarium scatter again.

"Argh! I knew I shouldn't have signed that binding contract!" he hissed between clenched teeth and grabbed his head. "I should have known! There's no such thing as a free lunch! Now we are totally and irrevocably screwed!"

"Now, now. Calm down, Friedrich."

"I'm perfectly calm!" Lab Coat Guy exclaimed before he hunched forward and cradled his head in his arms, but then he abruptly looked up and snapped at the nurse. "And why are you so calm, anyway!? We're trapped between a rock and a hard place! If we follow the contract, we're going to get stabbed in the back! If we breach the contract on our side, we'll lose all the resources and give the School an excuse to go after us! We're more screwed than a display board in a hardware store!"

"O-ho-ho! That's a pickle."

Lab Coat Guy was just about to give a no-doubt-very-witty retort in response, but then both of their attention was drawn to the door of the common room as the last member of their oddball trio entered without any fanfare. This time she wasn't wearing her *sentai* villain outfit, but a simple white T-shirt with an obscure anime mascot and the word *Fumoffu!* on the front, blue sweatpants, and a pair of brown bunny slippers. With her outfit and her long, purplish hair down, she would've looked like a sloppy-yet-still-inexplicably-attractive elder sister type, if not for the two glowing earpieces on her head.

"Finally!" the younger man exclaimed with a palpable sense of relief the moment he laid his eyes upon her. "I thought you'd never get here! Quick, help me get out of this thing!"

The android glanced over at the mad scientist frantically tugging at his metal collar-pauldron thing, but instead of following instructions, she casually walked over to the fish tank, and under the scrutinizing eyes of the men, she picked up a small tube of fish food and began to sprinkle it on top of the water.

"Galateaaaaa?" Lab Coat Guy spoke the word through clenched teeth, and while the android turned her head to face him, her hands continued to feed the fish with mechanical motions. "What exactly are you doing?"

"I'm providing nutrition to the fish in the aquarium," she stated without the barest hint of reservation, then after a second-long break she pointed at the clock on the wall and added, "Master ordered me to take care of them, and it's feeding time."

Lab Coat Guy opened and closed his mouth a few times, obviously at a loss for words. In the end, he simply buried his face in his palm, following which his uncle let out an unsubtle belly laugh at his expense.

"O-ho-ho! I see, I see... Your daughter is still going through her rebellious phase."

"She's not my daughter!"

"Master is not my father."

Lab Coat Guy and the fembot denied the old man's words at once, yet it only made him laugh even harder. At last, Peabody rose from his seat and picked up the book he'd previously put aside before stretching his back and turning to the still-seated man.

"O-ho-ho! Don't worry too much, Friedrich. I've known Amadeus for decades. He might be incomprehensible from time to time, but he's never stabbed anyone in the back."

"If you say so..." Lab Coat Guy noncommittally grumbled under his nose, but it seemed to be enough for the nurse, as he stretched his back again, and after flashing a smile at the fembot still feeding the fish, he left the room with leisurely steps.

Once he was out the door, the man on the beanbag chair let out a long sigh before fixing his eyes on the android again.

"Are you finished yet?"

"According to my calculations, I am seventy-eight percent done. Seventy-nine," she responded ever so monotonously.

"Hurry up," he grumbled as he tugged at the armoured collar, but then he closed his eyes for a moment before calling out to her again. "Galatea?"

"Eighty-one percent."

"I'm not asking about that!" Lab Coat Guy snapped, then he glanced at the closed door again before he continued with, "How is the contingency plan progressing?"

For once, the android stopped her feeding motions, and she turned her full attention to the man.

"I'm still analyzing the sensor logs of the security system. So far I have found two vulnerabilities and one possible backdoor access."

"Good. Keep up the good work."

Such compliments might have been fairly rare, as the android appeared genuinely puzzled for a moment. In the end, she simply nodded in the affirmative and returned to her task without a word. In the meantime, the man leaned back into the folds of the chair and let out a small sigh.

"I want to trust Uncle's judgment," he said in an absentminded tone. "However, just in case he is wrong and we have to bail..." All of a sudden, his exhausted expression morphed into a sly, devilish smirk, and he quietly added, "Kihihi... If we have to bail, we are definitely not going to leave empty-handed!"

CHAPTER 8

PART 1

I never thought I'd agree with Josh's old sentiment, but it was true: once exposed to enough strange things, it was the simple days of mundane, everyday life that would start feeling uncanny instead. Take this day for example.

It was already after school, with most of the placeholder classmates well on their way home, yet absolutely nothing unusual happened till now. No sudden info dumps by random creeps, no unexpected knightly transfer students, no silly-and-yet-extremely-dramatic invasion by super-intelligent penguins in flying saucers, no nothing. Everything was so peaceful and normal that it was straight-up weird.

But then again, maybe the day was only preparing itself, hiding its reserves of cuckoo-for-Cocoa-Puffs absurdity until the very last moment, only to suddenly strike once we were fully lulled into a false sense of security. As such, we could all agree it was best to be prepared and ever vigilant.

"Oh, man..." my nervously fidgeting friend whispered under his breath, and after giving him a glance, I had to revise my previous statement. Being vigilant was certainly very important, yet everything had to be done in moderation, and Josh was waaaaaay past that point.

"Relax," I said as I fully turned in my chair and faced the guy behind me. All of our classmates have already left the premises, which included the gang, as well, so it was only the two of us waiting for the disciplinary committee to contact us. I thought it would be a nice change of pace, yet Josh looked like he was about to crack under the pressure, so I noted, "You're acting like you're going into a life-and-death battle."

"It might not be life-and-death, but it is a battle... kinda..." he countered between two sneaky glances towards the annoying sliding doors of the classroom.

"You say that as if you've never been in one of those," I pointed out, earning me a scoff from him.

"But this is the first time I'm an aggressor. It's different."

"Is it really that different, though? Is it?" I responded in a contemplative tone.

"It is to me," my friend held defiantly. At the end of the day, I decided it wasn't worth arguing over, so I shrugged my shoulders in acquiescence.

"Fine, then it is. It's still no reason to be this nervous."

"But I don't know what I'm supposed to do," he... well, I don't want to say he whined, per se, because that would've been rude, but he pretty much did, so I'll leave it at that. Josh also looked like he wanted me to say something, but since I steadfastly maintained my silence, he finally blurted out, "Are you sure you can't come along?"

Oh? So that's what this whole agonizing act was for. Unfortunately, as much as I wanted to see the gathering of the placeholder creeps get raided, I had to decline.

"I already told you that I have other things to do. Not to mention, this is your chance to get on the good side of Armband Guy, so you should just stick to him and follow his lead."

"I know, but..." he began, but then his words trailed off into indistinct mumbling, so I decided to throw him a bone.

"How about this: imagine all the up-skirt shots and other voyeur photos they are sharing there. Does it make you annoyed?"

"... Yes," he responded curtly, with just a hint of skepticism in his voice.

"Does it make you angry?"

"... A little."

"If so then take that anger and let it build up. Then, when you arrive there, just let it flow through you with a JOSH SMASH and destroy them all."

"And then?"

Now it was my turn to give a skeptical look.

"And then everything is smashed and everyone lived happily ever after. The end."

"That's it!?" Josh suddenly burst out after, and I shrugged my shoulders once again.

"What were you expecting?"

"Some wise, old, mentor-y advice, for one. Something that would actually help me," my friend grumbled, and this time he earned himself a proper scowl.

"Cut it out with the mentor crap, I don't want to die just yet. Also, I *have* helped you. You aren't nearly as nervous anymore, are you?"

"I'm not?" he blurted out, only to pause right after that and then repeat himself, this time with palpable bemusement. "I'm not. Huh. How does that work?"

"It's just simple, run-of-the-mill psychology, my young friend," I answered just a smidgen smugly.

"Don't you mean my young Padawan?" he shot back with a provocative smirk on his lips, and I was just about to threaten him with filling his piehole with his pencil case for his continued mentorisms when the classroom's door slid open and drew our attention.

We both expected that it would be Armband Guy, yet contrary to our preconceptions, the one stepping into the room was Angie of all people. This time she had her hair in a ponytail, and instead of her uniform, she was dressed in a loose white tank top, a short pleated skirt, sneakers, and a pair of thick, scrunchy pink long socks that reached up to her knees.

She immediately locked onto us the moment she entered, and she jogged to our side with sparkling eyes.

"Thank god, you didn't go home yet!" she exclaimed before she came to a halt and turned a pleading eye to her childhood friend. "Joooooooosh? Could you help me? Pretty pleeeeeease?"

Oh, wow. She even fluttered her eyelashes when she asked. Maybe Judy got the idea from her? Putting that aside, I decided to speak up. If someone had to rain on her parade, I figured I might as well do it myself.

"Sorry, but Josh already has something to do."

"Do you guys have some plans for the afternoon?" the Celestial girl asked as she turned her attention to me, only to turn back when Joshua gave her the answer.

"No. I just have some business with the disciplinary committee."

"Are you in trouble?"

"Nah. Josh just volunteered to help Armband Guy round up some nasty baddies doing secret dealings in the school," I supplied the answer, and it ignited an excited light in her eyes right away.

"Whoa! Is it a sting operation? Like in those police dramas?"

"Nah, I'm not going undercover. I just help the disciplinary committee because... erm... let's just say I have a personal stake in getting rid of some contraband and the like and stuff..."

The tail end of Josh's explanation inexplicably turned into awkward mumbling as he averted his eyes, yet his childhood friend didn't seem to mind.

"So you're just going to help catch them? That's cool, too!" She flashed a toothy grin at us, but then it just as quickly withered as she began to ponder. "So you really can't help me, huh? What about you, Leo? Are you going to strike the criminal element down with the iron fist of justice, too?"

"That's an unnecessarily flowery way to put it, but no, I..." "Have other plans" is what I wanted to say, but before I could do so, she all of a sudden jumped in front of me and gave me the puppiest of all puppy eyes I have ever seen. She even clasped her hands in front of her chest and everything.

"Leeeeeoooo? Could you help me? Pretty pleeeeeease?"

I awarded her repeat performance with a flat look, but she continued to stare me in the eyes all the same, her gaze full to the brim with expectation, so I could only sigh and say, "Depends. What do you need help with?"

"Yesss!" she softly exclaimed with a small fist pump, as if the deal was already in the bag, and then she rapidly explained, "There's going to be a local tournament in two weeks, so the club is having extra practice in the afternoon. We have this really cool pitching machine in the gym storage, but it's kinda heavy..."

"So you need me to haul it to the tennis court," I guessed, and she nodded right away.

"Yes." She paused here for a long moment, then she did that weird gesture where she repeatedly joined and then pulled apart the tips of her index fingers as she meekly added, "Also, we need you to assemble it. Oh, and if you could turn it on and show us how it works, it would be super cool."

"... And pray tell, just how am I supposed to show you how to use your own club's equipment, which, I must point out, I've never even seen?"

"Don't be silly!" Angie replied between giggles as she swiped at me, her earlier display of shyness disappearing as quickly as it came. "You are a boy! Boys know all about technology and stuff!"

I rewarded the enthusiastic Celestial with a look flatter than the salt pans.

"What you just said is no doubt some kind of *ism*. I don't know what kind yet, but the moment I figure it out, I'm going to make a hashtag on the internet out of it, and you're going to feel really stupid."

"Pfff. Hashtags are soooo last year," she dismissed me with an irreverent wave of her hand.

"Don't tell me you didn't know?" Josh barged into the conversation with a voice dripping with fake shock. "I thought everyone knew the internet was just a fad..."

"Yeah!" Angie readily agreed, followed by several quick nods. "Nobody is doing interneting anymore! Everyone moved on to... um... wombat racing! Yes, that's the new hip thing right now!"

"I can't believe you are so behind the times. I feel ashamed for you," Josh mumbled as he dramatically wiped the corners of his eyes.

I waited for them to quiet down, then I asked, "Are you two finished?" The childhood friend duo shared a not-at-all-subtle look between each other, so I hastily raised a palm and added, "Just so you know, depending on your answer, I might have to call Brang and tell him that you can't keep your comic book collection in the secret base after all."

"Hey! That's a blatant abuse of power!" Angie raised her voice in (what I presumed to be mock) horror, and I shook my head with a smirk befitting the situation.

"I'm not abusing anything. I'm just stating the facts. Take it or leave it." I waited for her to respond, but the friendly neighbourhood Celestial only kept glaring at me with her cheeks puffed out like a chipmunk's. I kept up the staring contest for a couple of seconds, but then I noticed that she wasn't breathing and that her face was getting purple, so I decided to be the bigger man and said, "Oh, fine. I'll help you take out the pitching machine, but I make no promises after that. Are you happy now?"

Her expression turned on a dime as usual, and her angry pout was swiftly replaced by a beaming grin.

"Thanks, Leo, you're the best! Or at least you would be if you weren't such a tyrant, so... Second best?"

I gave her a look that unambiguously said "Can it," but it only made her giggle again. Anyhow, since I'd promised already, I stood up and grabbed my bag before I addressed my still-sitting friend.

"I'll go to help the tennis club, then. Break a leg."

Josh frowned at my well-wishes and mumbled, "Thanks, but... why is wishing for someone to break their leg a good thing again?"

"Cuz idioms are weird?" I proposed, and based on the small grunt he gave in response, he apparently agreed.

Anyway, we said our goodbyes, and I followed Angie out of the classroom. She took the lead, since I didn't know where the machine was stored, yet the moment we reached the first floor, she immediately slowed down and sidled up to me. I figured she wanted to talk, so I matched her pace, and the moment I did so, she immediately directed a suspiciously innocent upturned glance at me.

"Sooo... How's it going?"

I wasn't sure what she meant by that, but I decided to answer as well as I could.

"Well, I've mostly recovered from my enchantment fatigue, and preparations for dealing with our recurring bad guy are proceeding relatively smoothly, so I can't really complain."

"That's neat, but to be honest with you, I was more interested in how things are going with your girlfriends."

My eyes narrowed into a small, suspicious frown before I knew it, and I inquired, "Which part are you curious about?"

After our unexpected and slightly baffling discussion yesterday, Judy seemed to be really hell-bent on blowing my middling interest in recreational procreation activities out of proportion, to the point she was having emergency meetings with the princess at every single recess. I'd be lying if I said I wasn't slightly apprehensive about the contents of their discussions, but I figured they would confront me sooner or later, anyway, and there was no point worrying about the inevitable. The real question was whether Angie was sent by them to sneakily test the waters, or she noticed their recent behaviour and she was worried and/or curious on her own.

In the meantime, the Celestial girl thought long and hard about how to answer my question with a finger on her lips, and she ultimately told me, "Please don't take this the wrong way, but... you know that what you guys are doing is weird, right? I mean, if someone told me some guy's openly dating two girls at the same time, I would totally go, 'Pff, that will never work out!'"

"Well, I guess, but—"

"It is, right? And yet here you are, happy as a bunch of peas in a pod! It's crazy weird!"

"Wait, that was the part that you found—"

"Right!" she interrupted me before I could finish my sentence, and she continued with, "Like, before you three started going out, there was always this tension between Judy and Elly, but then it all went poof! They just got along all of a sudden the moment you started dating! It's incredible!"

"I wouldn't really—"

"I still can't believe how you managed to pull it off! I was afraid that it would make things difficult, or there would be fights in the group because of it, but you've been going steady for two weeks already, and instead, the two of them are besties now, and you three look super-adorable together!"

"Um... Thanks, I th—"

"So... What I'm trying to ask is... You know, I'm just kinda curious how you do it. Is there some kind of secret trick to make your relationship work with more than one girlfriend?"

This was the point when I realized that Angie's angle was very different from what I'd originally expected. She apparently wasn't sent by my girlfriends, nor did she notice their conspiratorial huddles, but instead she wanted insider info on how to make a polyamorous relationship work. Considering that she'd already showed interest in the idea in the past, I couldn't help but wonder, could it be that she was sneakily aiming for a harem ending? Considering Josh was favoring Snowy as of late, it wasn't impossible that she also decided to follow Judy's odd take on the prisoner's dilemma.

... But then again, Angie never really struck me as the type who would put that much thought into things, so maybe she just wanted to give it a try because I created a precedent? Not to mention, it wasn't like the option wasn't on the table from the beginning, considering how polygamy-friendly this theoretical battle harem world proved to be.

Anyhow, it was rude to keep her waiting... so I did just that. I mean, she cut me off four times in a row, so it was only fair. I pretended to be deep in thought to allow her to stew in her own juices for a while, and we'd almost reached the gym by the time I decided I should speak up.

"There really isn't a trick to it," I told her, and she immediately frowned at me.

"Come on, Leo! Don't be like that! I swear I won't tell anyone about your secret!"

"But there really is no secret," I doubled down, and I have to admit I was a little taken aback by her insistence.

"I don't believe that. You must do something special to keep a relationship like that afloat."

"I really don't, though. My job is just to spread my affection equally and not play favourites. If anything, it's the girls who are the ones responsible for keeping our relationship working as intended."

"Really?" she suddenly perked up again, but since we just reached the gym storeroom, I waited for her to unlock the door before I answered.

"Yep. I just have to do my best to be a doting boyfriend; they are the ones who have to put up with the inconvenience of sharing my attention between the two of them. After all, if they said no from the beginning, then no matter how hard I would've tried, we couldn't have ever gotten to where we are right now. It's all thanks to them."

"So it's really up to the girls..." Angie whispered under her breath, followed by a determined nod, and the way she was obviously making a mental note of my words immediately confirmed my suspicions.

I secretly wished her luck in her romantic endeavors, but I still added, "To be fair though, the fact that Elly's family is surprisingly supportive also helps a lot."

"What about Judy's parents?" she asked absentmindedly as she scanned the insides of the storeroom for the machine, completely unaware of the fact that her question was the verbal equivalent of dumping a bucket of cold water over my head.

"They don't know yet, I don't think..." She instantly glanced over her shoulder at me, so I hastily added, "I mean, I believe Judy told them we're dating; they just don't know about the whole polyamory thing."

"You really didn't tell them?"

She sounded way more dumbfounded than necessary, to the point I started to feel a little uncomfortable.

"Hey, cut me some slack. Judy's dad is scary."

"How so?"

"He has a gun," I muttered, belatedly realizing that explaining it as simply as that sounded like a poor excuse even to myself.

"Elly's dad is a pure-blooded Draconian," Angie countered, and I could only shake my head. "That's waaaaaay scarier than a gun."

"Yeah, but he's also a friendly goofball. Judy's father is more on the overprotective side. I can deal with supernatural shenanigans, but a normal guy with a gun is a different matter."

"That sounds tough, buddy," the cheerful Celestial told me while mechanically patting my shoulder. "Keep up the good work, and I'm sure things will work out."

"Very amusing." I brushed her off and looked around, as well. "More importantly, where's the machine?"

Angie must have interpreted my attempt to get on with the business we came here to do as my way of closing the previous topic, as she also completely ceased any further attempts at inquiring about my love life. As for said business, we found the pitching machine in its original packaging under a bunch of miscellaneous gym equipment, and it was considerably lighter than I expected.

Once I managed to dig it out, my first question was naturally, "Where's the user's manual?"

"Don't be silly, Leo! Boys don't need manuals! You're just supposed to know how to operate this!"

"That's still not how it works. Also, I still think what you said is some kind of ism," I grumbled as I hefted the box and we headed outside. I still hoped that maybe there was an instruction pamphlet somewhere at the bottom, but since I was going to unpack it once we got outside, anyway, I figured I could leave searching for it until then. With that in mind, I walked outside, followed by a giggling Celestial, only to stop and ask, "What's the time?"

"Huh? I don't have my phone with me, but I don't hear the track club, so it's not four o'clock yet."

"Really? Then I'd better hurry up," I said as I began to walk with some extra spring in my steps.

"Wha—? Hey, slow down! Leo!" Angie tried to follow after me, but in the end, she had no choice but to start jogging to catch up. "Uh! You are cheating! Your legs are too long!"

"Are you sure it's not your legs that are too short?"

Instead of answering, she lightly punched me in the shoulder, and we both stifled a laugh as we scurried along.

As for why I was in a hurry? Well, let's just say that after this detour, I had a very important appointment with a certain school nurse. One that he didn't know about yet...

PART 2

"This is such bullcrap..." I grumbled under my breath as I made my way back to the main building. I was lucky that no one was around at this point, otherwise they might have thought I was some kind of weirdo mumbling to himself... but then again, the fact that I was doing that meant that maybe I *was* one? I left that conundrum to be solved by hindsight, and instead I continued to happily fume without being disturbed by anyone.

The reason behind my foul mood was naturally the tennis club in general and one smug Celestial in particular. I mean, just because the serving machine was really intuitively designed and could be easily put together without the manual, it didn't make her right in any shape or form. They should've been able to do the same without my help, anyway, yet all the placeholder girls were looking at me like I was some kind of knight in shining armour who appeared to help them in their moment of distress, sparkling eyes and all. Except for Angie, of course, because she was just grinning like an absolute wiseacre.

Anyhow, I was about to reach the wing with the nurse's office, so I decided to put my encounter on the tennis court out of mind (though not *too* much; I had to remember it in order to serve my sweet, cold revenge in the future), and focused on step #467 of my implausibly complex plan to help Josh become a real protagonist and finally start carrying his weight, if only so that I could focus on my own endeavors.

Speaking of him, I quickly Far Glanced at him, and it looked like he'd just met up with Armband Guy and they were passive-aggressively quipping at each other. In other words, business as usual.

I contemplated whether I should check the others, as well, but I was in spitting distance of Peabody's little hidey-hole, so I figured I would do it later and get this over with as soon as possible instead. It was like pulling off a mental Band-Aid; it might hurt in the short term, but it's over quicker, as well.

Thinking so, I stopped in front of the familiar door and opened it without even bothering to knock. I'd already checked on him, so I knew the nurse was in, and when I entered, the portly man quickly swiveled around on his chair in surprise, only to ease up once he realized it was just me.

"O-ho-ho! Why, hello, Leonard! It's been a while."

"Yeah, yeah. Good afternoon, et cetera," I gave him something that could be, if you squinted hard enough, considered a greeting, and I closed the door behind me. "I came to talk."

"O-ho-ho? Could it be about your amnesia?" the old guy asked with his eyes open in anticipation.

While at first I wanted to dismiss him out of hand, in the end I had to grudgingly tell him, "No, but now that you reminded me of it, I suppose I should thank you for not telling anyone about my lost memories after all."

"No need to mention it!" he responded unusually boisterously, accompanied by a huge grin. "I believe I've already told you, but I'm as bound by doctor-patient confidentiality as any licensed physician. O-ho-ho! You certainly won't hear me tattling about your condition to your peers, that's for sure!"

"I wasn't really worried about that part," I said a little absentmindedly as another thought took root in the back of my mind. Even though I tried to keep it a secret in fear of affecting the nebulous Narrative in some shape or form, at this point I had more acquaintances who knew about my amnesia than ones who didn't. Since I got to this point, I figured it was about time to let the rest know, as well, so I made a mental note about it before I returned to the conversation at hand and told the nurse, "I was actually more impressed by the fact you didn't tell the arch-mage about it. Very principled of you."

"Thank you for the compliment, but... I can't say I understand what you're—"

"Please stop playing dumb. I'm really not in the mood for it," I cut him off before he could say something silly, like "What is an arch-mage?" "I came here because I wanted you to deliver a message to your nephew."

The moment I said that, the atmosphere in the room went from jovial and easygoing to... well, still fairly easygoing, but with just a teeeeeny bit of tension on the top. Similarly, while Peabody maintained his lukewarm smile, the eyes under his bushy brows opened just a fraction wider, only to then narrow into suspicious slits a mere moment later.

"O-ho-ho? Refreshingly direct, aren't you?"

"As I said, I'm really not in the mood to beat around the bush," I answered with a shrug. "I would also prefer it if you did the same." Peabody only looked at me with a mixture of caginess and expectation, so I told him, "I want you to tell Friedrich that I'm willing to hear him out."

"Is that so?" The nurse's eyes opened wide again at the mention of Lab Coat Guy's name. He obviously didn't expect I would be privy to this detail, and that was the exact reason why I decided to drop his name in the first place.

I naturally pushed ahead to strike while the iron was still hot, so before he could regain his balance, I quickly continued with, "Tell him that I want to meet him in person. I know it's not scheduled, but I want him to arrange one of his little ambushes just after school's out."

"O-ho-ho? Well-informed, aren't you?" Peabody mused as he rubbed his jaw and scrutinized me from head to toe. "Since you told me to keep being direct, let me ask you this: If you want to talk with him, why don't you just go to his workshop?"

I'm not going to lie, the candid way he asked it was really refreshing, even if the question itself was a pain in the neck to answer without giving away too much information. In the end, I settled on, "No offense, but I've heard that your android friend is a little trigger-happy, so I wish to avoid staying in an enclosed space with her for the time being."

"*Very* well-informed indeed," he whispered under his breath.

In the meantime, I pushed him even more by declaring, "This time, I'll be there in person. Unfortunately, I'm being watched as of late, so it would be best if he could make it look like I was caught up in the Purple Zone by chance. That way nobody would suspect we made contact on purpose."

"O-ho-ho? But didn't you just make contact with us?"

"No. I simply visited the school nurse before going home. There's absolutely nothing suspicious about that, especially considering that there's no way for me to suspect that you are related to Friedrich, or the Research Society, or that you're an old friend of the arch-mage, or that you visit the old man using a secret back entrance to the School under this building, or that..."

"I understand! Please say no more!" Peabody suddenly blurted out. Once I fell silent, he let out a tired sigh, reached inside his vest, and then wiped the sweat off his forehead with a yellow handkerchief before he finally told me, "I understand you are *truly, terrifyingly* well-informed. There's no need to highlight it any further."

"If you got the point, then I'll stop," I told him with my patented roguish smirk. "Tell your nephew I'll see him tomorrow."

I wanted to end the discussion on that decisive note, but before I could turn around and reach for the doorknob, I was stopped by a burst of irritating chuckles behind me.

"O-ho-ho! But wait just a moment, Leonard! If you're worried about being watched, wouldn't leaving my office so soon be considered suspicious?"

"Not really," I said as I tried to deflect his words, but he completely ignored me and patted the chair next to his own.

"Don't be in such a hurry! Come and sit. It's been a long time since you last visited here; why not talk a little, if only for the sake of appearances?"

I really wasn't in the mood, and there wasn't anyone tailing me to begin with, but since I wanted to keep up the pretense of this meeting, I had little choice but to go along with his suggestion. I didn't know whether he did it to entrap me on purpose, but looking at the lopsided grin on his face made me doubt he was the mastermind type.

Speaking of which, just what *was* Peabody's type? By that, I didn't mean his preference in women (or men; I don't judge), but as in our own classification. He sure as hell started out as a placeholder; I can still remember when he locked up during our first meeting as if it was yesterday. Yet at the same time, he was the uncle of Lab Coat Guy and an old friend of the arch-mage, two important side characters, to use the terminology of our Narrative hypothesis.

Now, if he was only getting more animated over time, I would have absolutely no problem with his behaviour. It is already well established that when it comes to placeholders, more interaction with them equals more complexity, and with enough attention, they can quickly go from weirdos who would stab themselves with a pencil to quirky girlfriends with minor trust issues (but you didn't hear that last part from me). In Peabody's case the problem was in the fact that, based on his background and importance in the plot, he shouldn't have been a placeholder in the first place.

Let's take someone else for comparison: Melinda. She's by no means a major player in the plot, as far as we're aware of, yet just being Elly's chambermaid, aka being connected to someone important, resulted in her being a relatively normal and animated side character from the very start. In contrast, Peabody was related to not one but two plot-relevant people, yet he was unmistakably a placeholder the first time I met him.

I really didn't like to resort to this, but the most obvious way I could explain this discrepancy was through the application of retroactive continuity (or retcon, for short). This was something that I'd discussed with Judy a number of times: the idea that the universe we lived in would fill in the blanks when we weren't looking, to enforce a sense of coherence. For example, while I can't say for sure either way (as I'd never seen them beforehand), there's a good chance that before my early interactions with Judy, she had no parents. As in, they literally didn't exist until she was deemed important by the Narrative, at which point they poofed into existence to complete her background.

I didn't like this. In fact, I found it about as disturbing as Judy's insistence on the Narrative actively manipulating everything and everyone all the time. That said, it wasn't impossible, and it would've been irresponsible of me to dismiss the idea just because of some instinctual aversion. Sure, Judy and I butted heads over these things a lot, but that was precisely why I hired her in the first place, so that there would be a second opinion I could argue and reason with. If she just blindly agreed with me all the time, then it would just result in complacency. Who knew? Maybe she was correct. I really hoped she wasn't, but ignoring her arguments would've been a folly of epic proportions.

But back to the point: if I presumed that such retcons could take place in this universe, even to already-established people in our social circle, then there was a good chance that Peabody really was a placeholder at the beginning, but due to my unwitting interference, he was recognized as an important character by the world. Following that, he was given a backstory, and said background retroactively linked him to both Lab Coat Guy and Lord Grandpa, all while he remained the same, mostly ineffectual person.

I mean, he was apparently a friend of Amadeus from their school days, yet as far as I knew, he was not a Mage, and he was linked to the Research Society, yet I never saw him doing any magitech tinkering or discussing any technical details with his nephew, either. As a matter of fact, he was so mundane in comparison to his associates it made him stand out like a sore thumb.

But then again, there was at least one alternative explanation I could come up with: maybe he had all of these connections from the beginning, but he used to be a placeholder because, due to the way he had no supernatural abilities, he wasn't really related to the plot, so to speak? In fact, if not for my Far Sight, I doubt anyone would've ever figured out he was related to the important guys.

Anyhow, all of this was food for thought, but for later, and the moment I reached this conclusion, the man in front of me let out another one of his grating chuckles.

"O-ho-ho! So what did you want to talk about?"

I narrowed my eyes at his question and stated, "Nothing. You're the one who told me to stay a little longer, so if anyone wanted to talk, it's you."

"O-ho-ho! Come now, don't be shy," he coaxed me with a disturbingly amicable smile as he leaned forward in his swivel chair. "Boys of your age always have some kind of problem to talk about! Puberty, changes in your body, relationship problems... I'm here to help you with all of those!"

"... What do relationship problems have to do with the school nurse?" I blurted out as my brow climbed my forehead on its own.

"I'm also the school counselor," he declared with an odd sense of pride, after which he let out a small chuckle and asked, "So I gather you do have some kind of relationship problem after all. Why else would you focus on it right away?"

"There could be many, many reasons," I responded a little dourly, but the annoying nurse only continued to chuckle under his breath.

"Now, now. I told you there's no need to be shy! I can listen to all your woes, and none of them will leave these four walls."

My gut reflex wanted to dismiss him right away, but after a moment of consideration, I realized that the man in front of me was the closest thing I had to a normal, responsible adult among my acquaintances, even considering that whole mallet malarkey and the Hippocratic assassins. That... was sad. It also meant that, as absurd as it might've sounded, his was probably the closest to a normal perspective if I wanted to get some normal advice for my current woes.

"Fine. I admit I do have something," I confessed, but before the nurse could break into one of his self-satisfied guffaws, I quickly added, "Let me warn you, though; if you tell anyone about what I'm going to talk about, I will know, and I will make you regret it."

"O-ho-ho? Calm down, Leonard. You should know I'm a professional, and I don't want to get hunted down by the Brotherhood of—"

"Already heard that joke, so stop it," I huffed, but Peabody's smile only widened in response.

"Have you? Oh, what a pity. It is my best one."

"I'm sure about that. So can you listen to me for a moment?"

"O-ho-ho! Certainly! That's what I'm here for!"

"Good. So here goes nothing." I took a deep breath and then began with, "I know that you know that I'm currently dating Eleanor," I started with a half-truth to ease into the conversation.

"O-ho-ho! Of course!" he exclaimed with his usual, grating joviality. "I can remember it like it was yesterday, when you gallantly carried her into this room after school! Believe it or not, I could already see the attraction between the two of you!"

"I'm sure you did," I responded flatly, but then before I could continue, he cut me off with another laugh.

"O-ho-ho! How could I not? Believe it or not, I used to be quite the Casanova in my younger years, and while I might have lost my touch a little over thirty years of marriage, I would've had to been blind not to notice the spark between you two! Oh, the wonders of youth!"

"Yes, yes. Can I actually get to the point?"

"Oh, certainly," he told me while brushing off my scowl directed at him with an affectionate smile.

"So here's my problem: we have been going steady for a while now, and according to my girlfriend, it is about time we take our relationship to the physical level."

"There is nothing wrong with that," he told me almost instantly, his voice sounding suspiciously rehearsed. "You're going through puberty, and the urge to explore your sexuality with your partner is perfectly natural. So long as she consents, go for it!"

That was a significantly more easygoing answer than what I expected. I quickly stifled the groan threatening to escape my throat and told him, "That's nice, but I'm not the one pushing for it. She wants to take things farther, while I'm not really interested at the moment."

"O-ho-ho? Is that so? There is nothing wrong with that, either. Some of us are late bloomers, and you might be one, too! Why, believe it or not, I was a late bloomer, as well! It wasn't until I was twenty when I joined my first swinger party, and I didn't try to use the back door until I was—"

"Too much information! Can we stick to the topic, please?" I interrupted with all my might before the mental image could take root. "So in your expert opinion, not wanting to rush this is not abnormal."

"Not at all! In your place, I would be more alarmed about why your girlfriend wants to take you under the blankets so soon."

"... Should I really?"

"O-ho-ho! Well, *alarmed* might be too harsh of a word. You see, Leonard, she is going through puberty the same way you are, with all its urges and hormone imbalances. It is perfectly reasonable to suggest that she simply has her own needs she wants you to fulfill. Yet, the intricacy of a woman's heart is a twisting road that few of us menfolk dare to tread, and even fewer of us see its end."

"Very poetic, but could you be just a bit more straightforward? Please?"

"Put simply, your girlfriend's desire to have sexual intercourse with you might have less to do with her physical needs than her mental ones. For example, have you considered that she might feel that your reluctance means you find her unattractive? Or that she could feel pressured by the way you act around other girls? If my memory serves right, your little group of friends is full of pretty girls, is it not? Have you considered that maybe she's trying to seal the deal because she is afraid someone else might snatch you away?"

I didn't know what I hated more, the candid way he was talking about these things, or the fact that what he said actually made a lot of sense in context.

"That's a lot of food for thought," I finally stated a little absentmindedly, which earned me another low-key laugh.

"You're welcome. But remember, if all else fails, the two of you should sit down and talk things through. Do not bottle it up, as the longer you leave a problem unaddressed, the harder it is going to be to deal with it once you open that bottle. Why, if only I'd talked to my wife right away after that enema incident back in college, we might—"

"Stop! Too much information! Again!" I exclaimed as I crossed my hands in front of me, but Peabody only continued to grin at me. I rolled my eyes and let my arms down, then I told him, "Thanks for the advice. It was way more reasonable than I expected."

"Oh, and before I forget!" the portly nurse suddenly exclaimed as he reached out and began rummaging through one of the drawers in his desk. "Just in case you experience some performance problems in bed, I have the business card of a great urologist colleague of mine. Where did I...?"

"... I redact my last statement," I grumbled under my breath, but before I could say anything else, there was a series of knocks on the door.

"Come in," Peabody called out right away, probably by reflex, and the door immediately opened wide.

"Sir, I have an injured," an upperclassman announced as he more or less dragged one of the creepy amigos into the infirmary by his shoulder, and he didn't even spare a glance at me. On a closer look, he had an armband on him, meaning he was probably part of the disciplinary committee, and the guy he was pulling along seemed to be a fairly battered Mr. Bedhair.

"O-ho-ho? What happened?" the nurse inquired as he finally stopped searching his drawer, stood up, and gestured towards the nearby bed.

"We conducted a raid against a group of delinquents trading contraband," the upperclassman told him in a flat voice. "He attempted to escape through the first-floor window but slipped and fell. Luckily the hedge by the wall broke his fall, but the captain told me to carry him here for a checkup."

Saying so, he unceremoniously dumped poor (ha!) Mr. Bedhair onto the bed and then immediately turned around and left without even saying goodbye. Placeholders, amirite?

Anyhow, Peabody immediately sprung to action and began to examine the creep. I was wondering whether I should leave or wait for him to finish, but then my dilemma was solved when he looked over his shoulder and told me, "O-ho-ho. It was a pleasure talking with you, Leonard, but I'm afraid this young man needs my full attention."

"I understand," I answered as I stood up. "I'll leave you to your work, then. Just remember to relay my message."

"Worry not, I will."

I gave him a nod in lieu of a goodbye, and I quickly walked over to the still-open door, but just as I was about to cross the threshold, the nurse called out to me.

"O-ho-ho! Just a moment, I almost forgot something!"

I turned around, and found Peabody already standing in front of me with an outstretched hand.

"Good luck," he told me as he pointedly shook his wrist, and after a moment of hesitation, I decided to shake his hand. Unsurprisingly, there was a small, rectangular object in his palm, but before I could refuse it, he'd already pushed it into mine and then followed it up with a playful wink.

That last bit surprised me so much I couldn't react in time, and before I could say a word, he'd already closed the door in front of me. This time I didn't bother to stifle my groans as I shook my head and glanced down at my hand.

"I seriously have no need for an urolo—" I muttered under my breath, only for my voice to halt as I realized that the object in my hand wasn't a business card, but a condom. Correction: a full pack of condoms. The bumpy variety, if the slogan on the front was to be believed. I raised my head to dumbly stare at the door in front of me, then back at the rectangular red packet in my hand, and I couldn't decide whether what I got was better or worse than a business card.

At last, I decided to stop thinking about it and let out a sigh, then I promptly pocketed the pack. I mean, it was technically a gift, so it would've been rude to throw them away. It certainly wasn't because I had a feeling I might have to use them sooner or later. Also, I certainly didn't have a better impression of the nurse after this encounter. Not even a little bit.

PART 3

I checked my phone one more time as I was waiting for Josh by the shoe lockers. It was a little after four, and I'd been standing around while twiddling my thumbs for a little more than fifteen minutes by this point. Last I checked on him, Josh had almost finished his customary verbal sparring session with Armband Guy, so I figured he should be coming my way soon. I wished he'd hurry up a bit, but then again, I was also a bit of an aficionado when it came to the craft of heckling people I didn't like, so I graciously allowed him to take his time.

I was still getting bored, though, so I decided to quickly check on everyone else with Far Sight, partially out of habit, but mostly just to make time go faster. First and foremost, I checked on our resident mad scientist, and I found him in his evil lab, busy building something obviously evil with his evil robotic accomplice. By the looks of it, it was either some kind of infrared death ray super-weapon or a toaster. Based on their discussion, it could've gone either way.

There was nothing else to see there, so I checked Peabody, and he was still taking care of the injured placeholder. Oh, wait. Armband Guy had just arrived to interrogate the guy on the bed. That meant Josh should've been already on his way, or at the very least I sincerely hoped so.

I didn't check on him just yet (where's the fun in that?), but instead I moved on to the members of our little collection of magical misfits first. My first target was Angie, and she was... coming right towards me?

I blinked in a hurry, both due to surprise and as a way to readjust my vision, but by the time I found my bearings she'd already passed by me and stormed out of the school building. She didn't even bother to say hello. Or change her shoes, at that. I wondered what her problem was, but at the end of the day I decided that if it was important, I would learn of it soon enough away, so I moved on with my remote observations.

The class rep was in the School underground doing more paperwork. Go figure. I watched her for a while, but it wasn't exactly what I'd consider riveting, so I quickly moved on. To my momentary surprise, I found the Dracis couple and their butler-cum-secret-ancestor inside a lavish local coffee shop. More baffling still was the fact that they were discussing the details of Abram's and Sebastian's urgent business trip out in the open, and with the enthusiasm (and natural delivery) of a group of community theater actors. It took me a while to figure out what they were doing, but after listening to them a little longer, I had to conclude that they had to be trying to unsubtly spread the info in public, hoping it would reach the Knights' ears.

I had mixed feelings about this kind of approach, and even planned to make a mental note about trying to discuss more effective (and less hammy) methods of spreading disinformation with Abram later. Alas, the idea was soon drowned out by tepid exasperation when I checked on Snowy and found her discussing something with my girlfriends inside my living room. I listened in, and it didn't take long for a groan to escape my lips.

"You can't be serious..." I muttered under my breath without meaning to, not expecting anyone would hear it.

"About what?" A voice from my side jolted me out of my Far Sight session with a perfectly reasonable question that once again reminded me that I should get rid of my bad habit of muttering to myself when I was alone.

I blinked in surprise, and it took my brain a long second to recognize Josh, who for some reason sneaked up to me while I was zoned out. I already had a simple excuse on the tip of my tongue, but then my eyes focused on my friend, and the words immediately dissolved as I noticed that his downcast face had a comically visible hand imprint on it.

"Never mind that. On the other hand, I have a feeling you might have a story to tell me," I told him in place of a greeting, and he immediately rolled his eyes while wincing.

"Yeah, unfortunately, I do. Let me get my stuff first. I'll tell you what happened on the way home," he told me just a touch dourly, so I let him do that.

It took only a minute for him to change his shoes and grab his bag, during which I quickly checked off all the boxes on my people-to-Far-Glance-at list. In short, Rinne was patrolling with a burger in one hand and an extra-large paper cup of Coke in the other, Crowey was sitting at his desk for a change but with the same vacant eyes as usual, and Armband Guy was still interrogating the hapless Mr. Bedhair in the infirmary. In other words, nothing particularly noteworthy.

At long last, Josh got changed, and he walked up to me again, just as I finished my own business. He looked at me as if he was daring me to ask him how he got that handprint. So I did. Because I was a daring kind of fellow.

"So," I spoke up in an upbeat voice that was only a little strained as I gestured for him to follow me. "Correct me if I'm wrong, but I have a sneaking suspicion that the state of your face has something to do with Angie. Am I right, or am I correct?"

Initially Josh only responded with a nod and a grumpy grunt, but once we passed through the front doors and were in the open, he must've noticed I was expecting something slightly more verbose than that, and so he whispered, "Where do I even begin?"

"Try at the start. I've heard that's how most people do it," I advised him, but the look he gave me in return was about as flat as the Dead Sea, so after a small cough I hastily added, "Or wherever else you want. Your call."

My friend took a deep breath, which he immediately exhaled in an exasperated sigh, and then he finally began to recount his no-doubt-very-riveting tale.

"So from the beginning, huh? Okay. In that case, I'll start with what happened after you left the classroom." He paused momentarily as we passed through the school gates, then he told me, "A minute or so later Pascal and four other disciplinary committee members came to pick me up. All of them were from other classes, so it was a little awkward at first, but then he introduced me and I joined the group. He led us to the social sciences classroom on the first floor, and we just walked there without any fanfare. We didn't even bother to be sneaky about it, which was odd, but he told me we were in the right, so there was no reason to hide. Anyway, once we got there, we were joined by two more members keeping an eye on them from the other end of the hallway."

"So there were eight of you in total."

"Yep. Is that important?" he inquired while showing off his eyebrow-raising mastery.

"No. I just said that to show you I'm paying attention," I responded with a small smile, and Josh all but huffed at me in return.

"Whatever, then. Where was I?"

"When you arrived at the The Gathering," I responded as helpfully as ever.

"Right. So once we were there, the committee members started taking up positions around the doors like they were a SWAT team; they even had hand signals and code names and everything."

"That sounds both odd and yet surprisingly fitting for that bunch," I mused as we stopped at a crosswalk for a moment. "So what happened after that? Did they break the door with one of those portable battering rams and throw in a flash-bang grenade?"

"Nah, it wasn't *that* exciting. Pascal just threw the door open, and they rushed in while shouting something about the guys inside being a disgrace to public morals."

"You're right; that's considerably less impressive than I imagined. I also gather you didn't go in with them," I prompted him, and he nodded in the affirmative.

"My job was to stay outside and catch anyone trying to slip out. For a while it looked like I would only keep watch, but then one of the guys inside jumped out the window."

"Yeah, I know." My friend gave me a curious look, so I clarified, "I met the guy in the infirmary."

Josh acknowledged my comment with an absentminded nod and continued with, "So as you can guess, there was total chaos inside, and when Pascal wasn't looking, one of the guys grabbed a small backpack and escaped through the back door."

"Oh, right. These classrooms have two of those dumb sliding doors," I noted with middling interest, hoping we would soon get to the point. "I guess you jumped after him."

"That's why I was there," Josh confirmed with a small shrug. "I guess the guy was on the track team or something because he dashed down the stairs and out through the back entrance of the main building so fast I could barely keep up. I only managed to tackle him in the courtyard." I figured this was the point where the plot would thicken, so after we crossed another crosswalk, I gestured for him to go on, which he did after another sigh. "So I tackled the guy and took the bag from him. Then one of the guys from the disciplinary committee called out to me from one of the first-floor windows, so I raised the bag over my head to show him that I got it... Don't look at me like that! It sounded like a good idea at the time!"

"I'm sure it did," I responded with my most innocentest look that I've ever innocented, but he still seemed less than impressed.

Josh continued to scowl at me, but when I didn't stop beaming innocentism at him, he finally gave up and told me, "Anyway, I didn't notice at the time because I was looking up, but Angie came over at one point. She probably heard the shouting and wanted to see what the commotion was about or something." Here, he paused again as his face twisted like he'd just bitten down on a mouthful of gooseberries. "*Of course* this was the moment that the stupid buckle of the stupid bag decided to fall apart and everything in it spilled over my head! It was full of gym clothes and underwear and all kinds of girly stuff, and it all ended up on me!"

"Odd, but not entirely unexpected," I noted as we came to a stop at the intersection where we usually parted ways after school. "Then what?"

"Then Angie grabbed me by the shoulder, turned me around, called me a pervert, and slapped me before she stormed away," my friend blurted out in a genuinely aggravated voice, following which there was a long beat of silence as I waited for him to continue. To my deepest puzzlement, he only fumed without uttering another word.

"That's it?" I asked with palpable incredulity.

"Yeah."

"... She just slapped you and left?" I asked to be sure, and he nodded. "Didn't she ask or say anything else?" This time he shook his head. "You didn't make any excuses she could misunderstand? Or say something she would get mad about?"

"I didn't even get a chance to get a word in!" Josh exclaimed in frustration as he threw his hands into the air.

I couldn't help but whisper a shocked "Wow..." under my breath. That was... considerably dumber than what I'd expected, and my expectations were already so low they were right next to dinosaur bones.

I mean, silly misunderstandings and being an accidental pervert were the bread and butter of being a dense harem protagonist, but this was just straight-up forced. This situation required not one, not two, but at least five contrived things to happen in rapid succession, from Josh being the one on lookout duty to Angie's completely irrational reaction at the end.

Now, if Judy heard this, I could already picture her giving me a smug smile and declaring "Witness the might of the Narrative, oh ye unbeliever, and despair!" There was just one issue though: if it was indeed a somewhat-conscious effort to enforce this event, then why would the nebulous Narrative make it happen in such an unnatural way? Was it to reach some kind of the-harem-protagonist-must-get-into-a-perverted-misunderstanding-with-a-love-interest quota? Or was it something more insidious, like trying to sneakily sabotage our plans for tomorrow by driving a wedge between Angie and Josh the day before? Or maybe the world was reacting to Angie being interested in the viability of a harem ending on her own, and trying to strain their friendship to push Josh towards a relationship with another member of his entourage?

Or maybe, just maybe, I was getting paranoid. I mean, coincidences are a thing. They happen, and they happen a lot around us anyway, so maybe I'm overthinking this? Maybe there was no malicious intelligence behind this contrivance, just the usual tropes playing off one another and resulting in a mind-boggling result?

Whatever the answer was, one thing was for sure: if this was indeed the result of a conscious Narrative force or entity, then I had no choice but to conclude that it was an absolute hack, as this was some of the worst-written, most blatantly overengineered tripe in existence. Needless to say, I really hoped I was overthinking this. I would've preferred any other alternative, but if Judy was right all along and I had to live in a world governed by a nebulous super-intelligence, I sure as hell hoped it wasn't an incompetent one.

But putting all of that theoretical pondering about the unconfirmed nature of an unconfirmed Narrative overseer aside for a moment, I still couldn't help but roll my eyes at the timing of this event, and I also voiced my exasperation.

"You know that tomorrow is going to be a very important day, right?"

"Yeah," Josh responded a tad late, apparently taken aback by my sudden change of topics.

"Then you know that we can't have you two fighting over a dumb misunderstanding like that."

"I know, but... what am I supposed to do? Apologize again? Like when Lili kissed me?"

"What? No, of course not," I denied his supposition while I opened my bag and reached inside. "That time you were partially at fault for being dense. This time it's entirely on Angie."

"Sooo... No apologies, then? Good. But in that case, what am I supposed to do again?"

"Just give me a minute," I told him just as I finally found my phone.

I fished it out of my bag, unlocked the screen, and immediately tapped on my contact list. The list was in alphabetical order, so I picked the very first entry and raised the phone to my ear.

After a few seconds of ringing, the line connected and I was greeted by a dour, "Yes, Leo?"

I decided to open strong, so I took a deep breath and answered in a low-yet-forceful voice, "Shame on you."

"Um... What?" came a confused mutter from the other side, so I promptly repeated myself.

"I said shame on you. You messed up and caused unnecessary drama. My disappointment is palpable, and my day is ruined. Take responsibility."

"What did I do!?" Angie blurted out in a fit of confusion, and so I went ahead and explained the entire situation to her from the beginning, starting with the purpose of the The Gathering and ending with Josh's heroic actions resulting in the recovering of the artifacts inside the backpack. Once I finished, there was a brief spell of tense silence, and then she meekly asked me, "So... The contraband you guys were talking about was... panties and stuff?"

"Yes," I confirmed in a firm tone.

"And Josh took them from the bad guys."

"That's also correct."

With that came another moment of silence, followed by what sounded like a forehead hitting a desk.

"... Aw maaaan..." Angie exclaimed on the other side, followed by a muffled, "Am I a jerk now?"

"No. You are The Jerk. Capital *T* and *J* and all," I told her, this time in an ever-so-slightly-lighter tone.

"... Aaaawwww maaaaaaan..." she echoed herself, followed by another suspicious thud from her end of the line. "This is soooo awkward! Is Josh there with you?"

"Yes," I responded as I reflexively glanced over to my skeptical friend.

"Could you... maybe tell him I'm sorry?" she asked me with the hopefulness of a drowning man grabbing onto a dangling rope, but I quickly yanked it out of her reach.

"No," I declared in no uncertain terms. "You're going to tell him, in person, and within the day."

"Do I really have to?" the Celestial girl pleaded, and I could totally picture her puppy eyes even without using Far Sight on her.

"Yes, you do."

"Aw, fine," she relented at last, and much faster than I'd expected. "Tell Josh to call me when he gets home, and I'll go over to talk."

"You do that. See you tomorrow."

"Yep. Bye, Leo!"

And with that, I cut the line. The whole conversation took less than five minutes, and all things considered, it went about as smoothly as I could have ever asked for.

I put the phone away and turned to Josh, saying, "She told me that—"

"I heard," he cut me off with a peculiar expression on his face.

"You're welcome," I pointedly told him, and he honest-to-goodness winced in response.

"Errr... Thanks, I guess, but... isn't this totally weird?"

Now it was my turn to give an odd look.

"Weird how?"

"I don't know, man," he mumbled as he scratched the back of his head. "Usually when I have an argument with Angie, we stay mad at each other for a couple of days, then forget about the whole thing afterwards. Doing it this way just feels... I don't even know. Anticlimactic, I guess?"

"What kind of climax were you expecting?" I asked him, single eyebrow raised and completely baffled. "It was a dumb misunderstanding, it got resolved, so there's nothing to be mad about anymore. End of story."

"Yeah, but..."

It was at this point that I let out an unsubtle snort and ever-so-gently whacked my friend on the shoulder.

"Stop asking for more useless drama and go home already. By tomorrow morning I want you two to be ready for action as your usual selves, all childhood-friend-y and swimming in UST, understood?"

"Yeah, yeah," Josh dismissed me with a wave of his hand as he turned around and walked away without saying his goodbyes. I may have heard him mutter something along the lines of "What the hell is UST, anyway?" and I was tempted to yell after him that it was the thing he wouldn't recognize if it hit him in the nose, but I refrained.

But speaking of unresolved sexual tension, it reminded me to check on Judy, and what I saw made my brows furrow without my consent.

"Oh, you've got to be kidding me..." I whispered under my breath, but after another long sigh I resigned myself to my inevitable fate and headed to the closest hidden alleyway I'd scouted out and marked for occasions like this.

Once I arrived, I checked to see if I was followed, then used Far Sight again to see the whereabouts of Mountain Girl, and once I locked onto her, I quickly Phased over. I had to talk with her first because, based on what I'd seen just now, I was pretty sure I was not going to be able to go hunting with her tonight...

CHAPTER 9

PART 1

"So we just patrolled the *entire* university district. Very thoroughly. I'd even go as far as to say we left no stone unturned. Can I go now?"

Even though I'd just addressed her, Rinne paid no attention to me, and instead she continued to sniff the air like a bipedal bloodhound.

At last, she looked at me and declared, "We must go that way. We smell something we have to investigate."

I followed her line of sight, and after a short beat, I glanced back at her without even trying to disguise my trepidation. "You mean, from the direction of the hot dog stand?"

"Yes."

"... You're just hungry again, aren't you?"

Rinne gave me one of her usual "Is this guy dumb, or does he just like stating the obvious?" kind of looks. I was really getting tired of them, but since I'd have to put up with them for only a few more days, I decided to be the bigger man and ignore it.

"It is of vital importance for every hunter to maintain their body in perfect condition, for the calling of the macaroni dance of the hunt may chance upon them at any moment!" she explained to me with a smug expression, which only made me groan harder.

"I think you wanted to say *macabre*," I pointed out, only for her to tilt her head to the side like a confused corgi.

"That is what Rinne said," she insisted with a frown.

"No, I'm fairly sure you said *macaroni*."

"Nonsense." She dismissed me with a sharp wave of her hand. "Your unbalanced ki must have affected your hearing. It must be because of your lack of balanced nourishment affecting your yin." She paused here for a moment, with a distant look in her eyes, then she added, "Onikiri says it's more likely that it corroded the grey matter between your ears." There was another short moment of silence, then she once again continued with, "Do you really have such matter there?"

"Yes. It's called a brain, something your oversized bread knife doesn't have."

"Onikiri says that you should fornicate with a half-breed donkey." After saying that, she had a curious glint in her eyes and asked, "Why does it have to be a half-breed?"

"... How should I know?"

"You don't? We'll ask Onikiri and—"

"Before that, can I ask a quick question?" She sent me an intrigued glance, which I interpreted as agreement, so I inquired, "If I buy you a hot dog, will you stay silent?"

"Since our mouth would be full, we believe we would," she responded with another disparaging look that I didn't even try to interpret, and instead I flashed a relieved smile at her.

"Great. In that case, let's go. You can order whatever you want."

Mountain Girl gave me yet another odd look as she cocked her head to the other side, and I had a sneaking suspicion that she was discussing something with her annoying sword again, but in the end her seemingly bottomless appetite must've overcome her apprehension, as she quickly followed after me.

Once we were at the stand, I bought her a supersized hot dog with all kinds of toppings, and then breathed a sigh of relief as she focused on devouring her food and allowed me to enjoy some precious silence for once.

I felt a little relieved that this was probably the last time I had to accompany her around town; I just wished, in hindsight, that I didn't tell her so the moment we met up. I explained to her that I'd tracked down the Chimera's whereabouts and that we should make our preparations for tomorrow's ambush instead of the usual routine. I figured we'd part ways right away after that, but she insisted that we should still do our usual patrol in the central district as originally planned.

I questioned whether there was any point in looking for nocturnal mini monsters while the sun was still up, but she was really adamant about doing the rounds right away, to the point she was on the verge of throwing a tantrum. At the end of the day, I decided to compromise and agreed to accompany her until around six o'clock in the evening. Speaking of which, I pulled my phone out of my breast pocket and checked the time, and lo and behold, it was just a little after six.

As they say, time flies in good company... which, in retrospect, explained why it felt like we'd been roaming the streets for ages. Oh well, at least I had a lot of time to think about how to deal with the situation developing in my living room in my absence, so... silver linings?

Anyway, I put my phone away and addressed my unwanted companion with, "Hey, Mountain Girl? It's getting late; I think it's about time we call it a day."

Rinne twitched in what I presumed was surprise and glanced up at me with her cheeks full like a hamster. I had a weird feeling as I was looking at this display and couldn't help but wonder, why is it that when Judy did the same chipmunk thing, I found it incredibly cute, but when Rinne did it, it was just so-so? Wait, never mind. That's not the real question.

The important thing to ask was whether this was a coincidence, or was she consciously trying to act cute in front of me? If it was the former, then it was safe to ignore her. If it was the latter... damn, I might have to unironically develop some anti-harem countermeasures, after all. What a scary (and incredibly annoying) thought.

While I was considering this, Rinne swallowed the food in her mouth and whined, "But we haven't finished our patrol! We didn't make a full circle!"

"And whose fault is that?" I asked back with a critically raised brow. "You sampled three fast-food stalls, including this one, we had to go out of our way so you could buy ice cream, and you even stopped by that souvenir shop by the bus station."

"It was very necessary," she countered weakly, almost sulkily, but then she regained some of her vigor as she stuffed the remainder of her hot dog into her mouth, swallowed it with nary any chewing, and then she pointed at me before she announced, "We're finished! Let us continue our pursuit with the haste of hungry wolves! Follow us, and we'll be done soon!"

"No, we're already done for the day," I stated in no uncertain terms. "Listen, Mountain Girl. I told you I have important business, and I'm already a little late because I humoured you."

"What could be more important than the thrill of the hunt and the promise of the crimson lifeblood of the *blah-blah-blah massacre blah-blah blood et cetera...*"

I tuned her out and let her prattle on about her usual nonsense while I seriously considered how I should answer her. I could simply tell her that it was about my girlfriends, but if she really had some kind of bafflingly unwarranted and unwanted interest in me, then doing so could result in all kinds of unpredictable and irrational reactions, such as sulking or throwing another tantrum. Needless to say, I needed her to be in a predictable and at-least-somewhat-rational shape for dealing with the Chimera tomorrow, so I decided that keeping her useful was more important than any anti-harem countermeasures at the moment.

"Blah-blah-blah delight of the... Hello? Are you listening to us, L-Le... L-L-Leeeeo..." Rinne addressed me again, probably because I wasn't really reacting to anything she was saying, but then her words turned into awkward mumbles by the end, only for her to avert her eyes and tack on a quiet, "... nard-san?"

... Okay, it was official now. This was definitely a flag if I've ever seen one. After this whole Chimera business was over, I had to draw the line ASAP before it would lead to some of the dreaded *shenanigans*. In the worst-case scenario, I could accidentally unlock some kind of yandere bad ending route with her. Oh, the (literal) horror.

Trope-y jokes aside, I took a deep breath and told her, "Yes, I'm listening, and no, I still can't stick around. I really have some business to attend to, and I don't think we're going to find any mini Chimeras, anyway." I waited for a second to see if she wanted to say something, and since it looked like she did, I quickly continued before she could. "Anyhow, please don't forget that we have a meeting tomorrow, in the park, just after dark."

"Are you certain the creature of the underworld will be there?"

"Trust me, it will be," I told her in the company of a reassuring smile, my confidence mainly stemming from my trust in Brang's report.

"Very well," she seemingly relented, but then after a moment she looked me in the eyes and leveled the question, "After we've slain the vile creature, may we invite you?" at me.

Her request caught me completely off guard, so before I knew it, I reflexively asked back, "Where?"

"To New Guinea," she replied as easily as if she was talking about some neighbourhood café or something.

"Do you mean the actual country?"

"Is there any other New Guinea?" she responded with something that didn't sound like a rhetoric question at all.

"I don't think so," I told her a little warily, and she immediately nodded with a quiet "I didn't think so, either." Anyhow, I unsubtly rubbed my temple for a moment and said, "Fine, I'll bite. Why do you want me to follow you to New Guinea?"

"To celebrate?" she answered with a question of her own, accompanied by another peculiar expression I once again refrained from translating.

"And we have to go there to celebrate," I stated with my inner Judy channeled to its fullest.

"Yes," Rinne confirmed my supposition with the kind of obliviousness that bordered on innocence. "Where else are we going to find a ropen to slaughter?"

"A what again?"

"A ropen," she repeated with unusual patience.

The word sounded oddly familiar, and after rummaging through the messy filing cabinets of my memory for a few long moments, I managed to put my finger on it. When I looked into the supernatural background of the world for the first time, I checked out a lot of kooky sites in search of clues, which included some about cryptids and other allegedly supernatural creatures.

If my memory served me right, the ropen was some kind of flying pterodactyl thing that glowed in the dark and ate people or something. I didn't really look into it because at a cursory glance it seemed even sillier than the Loch Ness Monster, and considerably less credible (which was saying something).

Because of that, I think no one could blame me for blurting out, "Wait, that's real?"

"Of course," Rinne confirmed, much to my surprise.

"And we celebrate by slaughtering one," I deadpanned at her after I overcame my momentary disbelief, with my inner Judy once again rising to the surface. Her quiet grunt in the affirmative made me feel like I was on the short end of one of those situations where people were discussing an inside joke I couldn't understand. To be fair, though, in this case it was safe to say I didn't really *want* to understand, either, so I settled on telling her, "How about we come back to this tomorrow?"

Rinne looked at me funnily for a moment, but then I recognized that she was once again talking with her sword, and at last her eyes opened wide as if she'd just had a huge revelation.

"You're correct! A true hunter should never drink upon the pelt of the bear ahead of time!" I figured that must've been some kind of esoteric idiom she was brute-force translating as usual, but it didn't stop my face from slackening in perplexity. She completely ignored my reaction, and she added, "Onikiri agrees that we should discuss this once we have already painted the woods in crimson and we know for sure that your tracking of the monstrous creature of the underworld was correct and not just a pathetic attempt you devised to impress Rinne to ensnare us to satisfy your lustful desires."

"... I thought we were over this, but just for the record, I'd like to state that what you said is about as far as it can possibly get from my actual intentions. Also, tell that piece of sharpened scrap metal on your back to take a nice, long bath in nitric acid."

"Onikiri says she doesn't understand, but that you are an anus all the same," Rinne informed me in her usual tone, and I figured this was as good a note as any to end the conversation on. Also, for the record, I was not even a little bit bitter about the fact that my insult, which may or may not have been the result of spending half an hour looking up acids that can dissolve steel at room temperature for a verbal sparring session like this, was completely brushed off. Not at all.

I let out a small, not-at-all-disappointed sigh, and told Mountain Girl, "Whatever. See you tomorrow."

Saying so, I turned on my heel and, after a small wave, I walked away from her with measured steps, forcibly ignoring the longing eyes and the timid way she kept waving towards me right until I was out of sight. Yep, I really needed to ditch her after tomorrow, before she would somehow strong-arm me into raising even more flags and somehow end up in a love trapezohedron.

But putting my potential harem troubles aside, it was time to use my Far Sight to take another glance at my home, and when I did so, I couldn't help but shake my head. At this point I could've Phased over at any moment, but after some consideration, I dismissed the idea and decided to walk instead. I mean, the weather was surprisingly nice today, so there was nothing wrong with enjoying some fresh air. It wasn't like I was delaying the inevitable or anything...

PART 2

"Welcome home, master!"

What can I say? The sight that greeted me when I arrived home was... new. Yes, let's go with that. I'd be lying if I said I wasn't fully expecting this, yet I still had to stop and take a shallow breath to find my proverbial center before I resolved myself to step through the threshold of my own house.

"Hello, girls," I nonchalantly greeted the two French maids giving me deferential bows right in the middle of my entryway. Needless to say, while I was calm on the surface, it was all due to heroic levels of willpower forcing a laid-back, neutral expression onto my face. I had no choice, though; this was but the first grueling battle in a campaign of silent psychological warfare, and I refused to be the first to flinch.

"Let me take your coat!"

Saying so, the strangely energetic blonde maid skipped over to my side and insistently helped me out of my usual long coat. Speaking of which, I wondered if I should buy a duffle coat or something similar for the winter, preferably in a colour other than black. If nothing else, maybe it would finally convince Brang to drop the nickname he'd given me.

While I considered such things, the helpful maid carefully peeled me out of my outerwear and put it onto the hanger by the door. She was wearing what I would've considered a fairly standard maid uniform (and by that I mean a typical maid café type of frilly uniform, not the real Victorian kind), complete with the headpiece and stockings, the latter of which were clear to see due to the somewhat shortish skirt she was wearing. Oh, and on second look, she had a huge bow on the back, which was a nice touch, if a bit impractical.

The brunette maid was dressed in the exact same fashion, except with maybe a bit more frills on the apron and a teensy bit longer skirt. Overall, their uniforms showed some skin, but thankfully they weren't the sexy maid type costumes you could order off some questionable websites. I'm not going to lie, I had no idea how I would've reacted when faced with those. Probably some unique, never-before-seen flavour of horror.

Theoretical skimpy outfits aside, I continued to maintain my nonchalant façade as I slipped out of my outdoor shoes. By the time I put on my slippers, the two maids once again stood right in front of me and bowed more or less in unison.

"What would you like to have first, master?" the deadpan maid asked with the utmost seriousness. "Dinner, a bath, or me?"

It was probably not surprising, but there was an obnoxiously long silence following in the wake of her words, but I managed to somehow preserve my poker face through it all, even though the clichéd line made my blood boil. No, not *that* way. But then, before I could say anything, the blonde maid suddenly cut in, her words tinted with mild panic.

"Tea! She meant tea!"

"Yes, that's most certainly what I meant," the brunette maid conceded the point with just a hint of a pout on her lips. My traitorous hypothalamus immediately made a note of how cute that was, but I successfully maintained my neutral expression all the same because dammit, I was not going to react, no matter how little blood was in my hormone stream! At this point, this was all about the principle!

I softly exhaled and squeezed out a jovial, "It's a little late for that, but sure, I'm not going to turn down a warm cup."

The maid duo shared an awkward glance between the two of them, but they soon resigned themselves to their plans getting derailed right from the get-go. They both gave me another bow, which was followed up by a hand gesture for me to follow them.

"I don't think it's working," the blonde maid whispered in a low voice, which was obviously still perfectly audible to me, as they turned on their heels.

"Just stick to the script," her brunette colleague advised her in an even lower voice. "I get the tea; you get him comfortable."

"On it!" she all but exclaimed, but then she finally noticed that she was too loud. She carefully glanced over her shoulder, and upon noticing that I was looking at her, she let out a small and increasingly rare "Awawa...!" under her breath before hastily adding, "I-I mean, this way, master!"

Steeling my facial muscles was getting harder by the minute, and I rationally knew that I should've cut this whole charade short at the earliest opportunity... but I'd be lying if I said I wasn't curious (and maybe a tiny bit fascinated) about what these two were trying to do, so I wordlessly obliged them and obediently followed after her.

Once we got into the living room, I was faced with another minor shock. In retrospect, I really shouldn't have been so surprised, as I'd seen them preparing something through Far Sight, but the belated realization that they went out of their way to redecorate my whole living room really floored me for a moment. As for what the decor was supposed to invoke, it was hard to tell, with a curious mixture of scented candles and even some rose petals here and there, but if I wanted to sum it up in one word, it would be *tacky*... Nah, I'm kidding! It would be *romantic*. Yes. I'd *never* consider something my girlfriends put so much effort into tacky! Perish the thought!

Seriously though, they might've gone just a liiiiiitle bit overboard. I had no idea where they got them, but they even put a pair of those fancy sterling silver candlesticks onto the coffee table, with matching dinner candles to boot. Not only that, they were surrounded by tall wineglasses and even a prechilled bottle of alcohol-free champagne. Say what you will, that was some serious dedication to the aesthetic. Except for the champagne because it had a cartoon dragon on the side, but still. A- for effort.

The blonde maid once again gestured for me to follow after her, and I did so as soon as I finished drinking in the scenery, after which I got, for lack of a better word, seated in my usual comfy chair. In the meantime the deadpan maid headed for the kitchen, leaving the two of us alone in the living room.

To be honest, I was about 90 percent certain that we would get enveloped by an awkward atmosphere at this point, but my expectations were swiftly betrayed the moment the brunette maid left the premises.

"So? What do you think?" Elly asked in a soft-yet-excited whisper as she pinched the hem of her skirt and twirled around to show off her outfit, followed by a small and perfectly executed curtsy. Just as you would expect from her, really.

I gave my girlfriend a slow once-over, and decided to answer with a flat, "You're breaking character, princess."

"Oh, right! I mean, does the uniform suit me, master?" she inquired in a demure voice, then after a second or two her eyes opened wide as if she'd just recalled something, and she also tried to do that eyelash-fluttering thing that Judy used to terrorize me last night.

As for her question, I had to admit that she looked incredibly cute in that uniform, but saying that out loud would've only exacerbated the misunderstanding about my nonexistent maid fetish, so I decided on the diplomatic answer of, "I don't think there are any clothes out there that wouldn't look great on you, so yes, it does."

The princess quickly digested my words and gave me one of her smug little smirks in return... but then she twitched and quickly assumed a ramrod-straight posture when Judy returned from the kitchen.

"That was quick," I noted, only mildly baffled by the fact that she was carrying the teapot and accessories on a fancy kitchen trolley.

"It's a maid's duty to be prepared to immediately fulfill her master's every desire," she stated in a slightly-more-deadpan-than-usual voice the moment she stopped next to my chair. She picked up the porcelain teapot and gracefully filled up my *I <3 Coffee* mug, which was sticking out of the environment like a sore thumb. Once she did so, she handed it over to me, and when our hands touched, she echoed herself with an emphasized, "*Every* desire," followed by a clumsy wink.

This time it was even harder to keep my poker face from cracking, but I somehow managed it. Oh, the tribulations I had to put up with every day!

"Thank you very much," I responded with a level voice as I took the mug and raised it to my mouth. The tea itself was nothing special, probably because she'd made it in a hurry, but it was nice to have a warm drink after walking outside for a while, so I didn't complain.

In the meantime, Judy and Elly once again took up their spots in front of me and quietly waited for me to finish. Well, mostly quietly.

"Psst! Judy?" Elly whispered after she elbowed my other girlfriend on the side to get her attention. "I really don't think it's working."

"Follow the plan," my dearest assistant responded with a flat look. "We still have seven more scenarios to try."

Well, that sounded about seven scenarios too many, so I hastily gulped down the last of my drink and stated, "How about we skip all that and instead you two sit down so we can talk?"

"A maid must not sit down with the master... I think?" Elly posited a little uncertainly while glancing at Judy again. "Melinda never said it was a rule; she eats with me all the time."

"Neige said it's how it works, so that's how we do it."

"Oh, okay then. In that case, we really can't sit down," my draconic girlfriend reiterated as she clenched her fists with renewed enthusiasm.

Another deep breath later I lightly cleared my throat to maintain my steadily cracking straitlaced façade and stated, "Just sit down, you two. Don't make me stand up and tickle you."

My girlfriends shared another look between each other, resulting in the princess musing, "Maybe it does work after all?"

"No, it doesn't," I finally burst out with a hint of exasperation as I rose from my seat and walked over to them. Elly shuddered for a moment and used her hands to guard her sides, probably worried about any incoming tickling, but I ignored her, and instead I gently grabbed them by the waists and pulled them along on my way towards the couch.

As soon as we were there, I guided them down, with me sitting in the middle, Judy on my left and, by process of elimination, Elly on my right. Once we were comfortable (or at the very least as comfortable as we could be under the circumstances), I once again let out a pointed cough and decided to get rid of the most obvious issue at the moment.

"First off, let's make this clear once and for all: I don't actually have a maid fetish."

"You don't!?" Elly exclaimed in a high-pitched voice, sounding about as shocked as when I'd first told her I had amnesia.

"No, I don't," I repeated while I sent a meaningful glance at my other girlfriend. She averted her gaze, so I soon continued with, "I admit that you put a flattering amount of effort into all of this, but I'm afraid it was more than a little misguided."

"Are you *sure* you don't like maids?" Judy spoke up with a frown, and I shook my head while pulling her a little closer.

"Nope, it's all just a huge, downright aggravating misunderstanding." They appeared to be a little let down by my declaration, so I decided to soften it by adding, "I mean, you two look really cute in these uniforms, but you're like that by default, so it hardly changes anything."

My dear assistant was still giving me suspicious looks, but I couldn't really care much, as the princess quickly grabbed my attention by letting out an enormous defeated sigh.

"So it really didn't work?" she asked with upturned eyes, and I quickly shook my head while I once again beat my hypothalamus into submission.

"Well, not if you wanted to seduce me into doing lewd stuff, no."

"But Judy said you really like maids! And Melinda said it, too! I thought it would really make you happy..."

"Well, I'm definitely not *unhappy*, but you two really didn't have to go to such lengths. You even brought the candlesticks and the trolley and everything."

"Those were all things we found in the house," Judy added a little dourly, and her words immediately put a stop to my previous train of thought.

"Wait, what? Why would I have a kitchen trolley in my house?"

"I don't know. I found these in the pantry and the garage."

I looked my assistant in the eye for a while, but she was entirely serious, so at the end of it I couldn't help but let out a baffled "Huh" under my breath. How come my house was always filled with all kinds of weirdly convenient odds and ends, from food ingredients to food carts? Was it some kind of Narrative tomfoolery? Or could it be that they were left behind by the ever-helpful ninja maids? It was something that certainly required my attention, and I decided to launch a very detailed and meticulous investigation into the issue... later.

For now, I focused my attention on the topic quite literally at hand, as I was still holding my girlfriends by the waists. They didn't seem to mind, so I didn't change my posture, either, and instead I only closed my eyes for a moment to think.

"Okay, let's put all of these things aside for the moment, and let's focus on why you two thought it was a good idea to try to act as fetish fuel for me. I mean, don't get me wrong, the whole play would've been really fun if you'd talked things through with me ahead of time, but you didn't."

I waited for a few seconds, to see if either of them wanted to add something to the discussion, but since they remained silent and only kept fidgeting in my arms, I decided to break the ice myself.

"Listen up, girls. To be frank with you, I simply don't understand why you are so adamant about rushing things like this. Or rather, I have a few ideas, but I don't want to make this conversation heavier than it already is, so let me say this as clearly as I can: I still think it is early for us to jump right into lewding."

"For the record, I still can't help but lament the fact that the word *lewding* became part of our vocabulary," Judy noted on the side, and Elly repeatedly nodded, though I couldn't fail to notice how she was turning red to the tip of her ears just from the mere mention of the term.

"Don't change the subject," I chided my assistant while simultaneously launching a vicious tickle attack on her defenseless waist. Once she stopped squirming, I flashed a refreshed smile in her direction and added, "So let me give you my reasons why I think we should keep things slow, steady, and celibate for the time being. Let me start with the one Judy has already heard: pregnancy. It is more or less the last thing we need in the current situation. Any objections to this point?"

"Oh, I have one!" Elly suddenly raised her hand, only to quickly let it down and mumble, "I mean, it's not that likely for me." She stopped speaking, so I urged her to continue with my eyes, and after taking a shallow breath, she did just that. "When Mom gave me the birds-and-the-bees talk, she told me that we have low fertility. It has something to do with having both human and dragon blood. She said that even when they were, um, trying for me, it took them two years of, uh, t-trying before Mom got pregnant." For some reason, she was extremely embarrassed even though she was using safe-for-work language, and after taking several short breaths she quickly blurted out, "T-that's why it's fine for me! Even if we do l-lewd things, I wouldn't get pregnant right away!"

"But there would still be a chance for it, and Judy is still on the table."

"I already told you, Chief, contraceptives *still* exist," she countered me with a pout. It was probably the aftereffect of my tickling. "I also asked around a little. Amelia said there are artifacts that can completely prevent conception."

"... Did you seriously get the class rep involved in this?"

"She shouldn't know why I asked. I was very discreet," she pointed out. "This means that, if we took all precautions, we could completely negate the chance of pregnancy, and with it, your objection."

"One of my objections, maybe, but I have more! For example, the age difference argument." My girlfriends both gave me an odd look that all but screamed "What age difference?" so I quickly elaborated. "So you know that Leonard Dunning is a fake identity, right?" Elly nodded, while Judy just slightly furrowed her brows, which I decided to interpret as confirmation, as well. "It's blatantly obvious that I'm bigger than the other boys in our grade. Putting genetics aside, I have a suspicion that I might be older than you two, with the date on my fake ID being manipulated so that I could enroll in the school with Josh. It was probably step number eight of some dastardly knightly plan."

"Maybe, but why would that be a problem for us?" came the question from my frowny assistant.

"I looked up some laws last night. If I *am* actually over eighteen, having sex with you would make me a child molester."

"Really?" Elly asked, obviously unconvinced.

"Yes, really. If both parties are under eighteen, it's fine. If both are over eighteen, it's fine. Mix the two, and you can immediately hear the police sirens in the distance."

"Chief, that's just dumb," Judy interrupted me with her deadpanniest expression yet.

"The law?"

"No, your objection," she clarified. "You are seventeen on your ID. End of discussion."

"Yes, but what if I'm really not?" I countered.

"Then the only people who know that would be the Knights, and I'm sure they would've much more obvious objections to our relationship than the age gap."

"Yes! Like me!" Elly agreed and pointed at her inexplicably beaming face.

"And that's why your objection is incredibly silly," Judy concluded, though not to my complete agreement. "Do you have anything else?"

"Yes, as a matter of fact, I do," I grumbled a little before I took a deep breath and began to explain myself. "Putting everything else aside, I simply think it's too early for us. We've only been dating for a short few weeks, and our relationship is pretty unusual to begin with. I still think we need to get closer to one another before we actually jump into the lewdy stuff." I could distinctly hear Judy mutter something along the lines of "You're using that word just to annoy me, aren't you?" but I ignored her and instead told them, "To be honest with you, I have a feeling that getting physical will be the biggest watershed moment in our relationship. You see, this might be obvious, but there is only one of me, and two of you."

"Um... yes..." Elly agreed with a nod, seemingly on autopilot.

"The thing is, while I have some emotional roadblocks I'm steadily chipping away at, I can still say, with perfect certainly, that I love you two, definitions be damned. I want to make this relationship work, and I'm trying to be as fair as possible with you, dividing my time and attention and affection as best as I can. However, when it comes to lewding, I can only do it with one of you at a time, right?"

"That's true," Judy granted me, and so I quickly continued before she could insert a *but* at the end.

"This means that, unless one of you would just sit by the sidelines to watch and twiddle their thumbs while we engage in some good, old-fashioned horizontal gene transfer, it would be something we couldn't do *together*, all three of us at the same time. Well, that is, unless you two want to get it on with each other, but I somehow doubt that."

"Well, I like Judy, but I don't... um... *like* like her..." Elly spoke softly as she did that weird-but-cute thing where she touched her index fingers together.

"Same here. I'm straight," my assistant declared quite firmly, as well.

"You see? That's why, even without any talk about libidos and pregnancy and whatnot, I still think it's not something we should rush until we are close enough where this won't lead to any friction anymore. Are you getting what I'm trying to say?"

"I do, but I also think we are already plenty close," Judy said while gesturing to the three of us huddled together in my embrace.

"I want us to be even closer than this."

"And how do you want to get even closer *without* doing the deed?"

"I have ideas," I responded with a small chuckle. "Spending more time with just the three of us, going on dates, playing games, and just generally talking a lot more about our feelings and problems with one another. Of course, all of this would be for after the current Lab Coat Guy madness dies down. What do you say?"

"So before getting closer physically, you want us to get closer emotionally?" my assistant summed up my argument in a single sentence, and I had no choice but to nod at her. "That's really vague. If we agreed to that, you could use it as an excuse to postpone things until the heat death of the universe."

"Oh please! I wouldn't do that!" Judy was still giving me the skeptical treatment, and it looked like it was about to infect the other girl present, as well, so I blurted out, "Do you want me to set a deadline or something?"

"... That could work," she accepted my not-at-all serious proposal after some thinking, and before I could ask her if she was serious, Elly repeatedly nodded on the other side, cutting off my way of retreat.

"Erm... Okay then? How about Christmas?" I suggested a little half-heartedly.

"Sounds nice," my deadpan assistant responded with a tone of utmost seriousness only slightly marred by her self-satisfied expression.

"So no le-lewding until Christmas, but we get to hang out more until then? That sounds great, too! I'm in!" Elly suddenly declared as she hugged me from the side.

"If you agree, then why are you doing that?" Judy turned a frown at my other girlfriend, or more precisely, her rather sizable breasts pushed flat against my own chest.

"I'm just showing my happiness. That's emotional," she argued back with a grin that would've been right at home on Angie's face, yet suited hers just as well.

"Maybe, but you are doing it in a physical way," my assistant countered her point, then she reached out and poked the grinning Draconian girl's cheek.

"There's nothing wrong with that, though," I pointed out, only for Judy to turn her suspicious eyes at me in turn.

"Is that so?" All of a sudden, she also leaned closer and pressed her slightly more modest (yet just as soft and warm) chest against me, as well. "Normally you'd argue tooth and nail against this kind of thing. Are you one hundred percent sure the maid costumes aren't working?"

"Yes, I am," I replied just a tad dryly as I carefully grabbed hold of the back of their collars (while making sure that I wouldn't damage the uniforms) and gently pulled them off me. "Where did you get these outfits, anyway? They look different from Snowy's."

"I asked Melinda for spares," Elly told me proudly, for some reason.

"Well then, I guess you'd better change out of them before they get dirty. Or do you two want to wear them until it's time to go home?"

"We are sleeping over," the princess caught me off guard by declaring it in a defiant voice. "I already got permission from Mom and Dad!"

"I'm the same," Judy followed it up with a triumphant smirk of her own. "I told Mother that I'd be staying over at Neige's place. That's here."

"Now that you mention it... Where's Snowy?"

"She's staying over in the shelter tonight," my dear assistant explained with her smirk becoming so wide, I could actually imagine that even other people may have realized that she was smiling. Crazy, I know.

Anyway, I quickly used my Far Sight to see if it was true, and lo and behold, I found Snowy surrounded by the Fauns inside the secret base, all right. Furthermore, she was riding on the shoulders of Brang for some unfathomable reason as they were discussing how they should decorate the interiors of the Fauns' living quarters.

I didn't really have the time to observe them for long, considering my situation, so I quickly returned to my body and let out a small sigh.

"So it's just the three of us in the house, and you are staying over, but we are not doing any lewding yet, now what?"

All three of us fell silent for a moment, right until Judy raised her hand and did a twisting motion with her wrist, at which point... we still remained in silence. Once I couldn't bear watching her any longer, I raised my own hand and told her, "I'll provide the sound effect," after which I snapped my fingers.

"Thank you. My finger-snapping app crashed again."

"App?" Elly butted in with a curious look and a bunch of illusory question marks circling around her head.

"It's one of our dumber inside jokes. You're better off not knowing," I remarked before I focused my attention on my assistant again. "So I believe you had an idea."

"Yes, I do. After the disappointment that your movie turned out to be last evening, I tried to find something genuinely terrible to show you what a real bad movie was like. I have the DVD in my bag, so we might as well watch it together."

"... Just when did you have the time to buy a specific DVD like that?"

My question, accentuated by my practiced eyebrow raise, was promptly dismissed on the spot.

"Don't be silly, Chief. I obviously downloaded it from the internet."

"Isn't that illegal?" the princess interjected, her eyes as narrow as they could be.

"Only if someone finds out," Judy told her with a confident smirk. "It's a terrible horror movie about a sentient toaster going on a murder spree in a desert."

"I... I don't really like horror movies," my draconic girlfriend admitted in a mousy voice, her previous suspicion and intensity gone like a candle flame in a hurricane, but my assistant immediately reassured her.

"Don't worry. It's a really bad horror movie, so it's not scary at all."

"That's good, but... if it's bad, then why do you want to watch it?"

"To make fun of it," I supplied the answer. "On my end, I'm fine with it. How about you, princess? I promise it's going to be fun."

"Really? Well... If it's not scary, then I suppose I'm fine, too..."

"Good. I'll go and get the movie," Judy announced, and she immediately jumped to her feet.

"In that case, I'll go make some popcorn and snacks," I proposed as I stood up, and Elly followed right after me.

"I'll go and change into my pajamas then!" she declared in an upbeat voice, and it made Judy and I stop in our tracks.

"Pajamas?" my assistant repeated after her with her brows raised, if not high, but at least noticeably.

"Yes," the princess asserted with a look that obviously found our surprise completely unexpected. "Aren't you supposed to wear your pajamas and hug under the same blanket when the whole family is watching a movie?"

"I suppose you do that at home," I figured, and she nodded again. "Well, we still have the blanket from yesterday over there. As for pajamas, I don't think I have any, but I could check the dressers."

"I don't have any."

We both glanced at Judy upon her statement, and it was Elly who voiced what was on both our minds.

"You knew you would be staying over, and you didn't bring your pajamas?"

"I didn't think I would need them," she admitted. "I didn't have any the last time I slept over, either."

"Wait, then what were you wearing? Did you sleep in your undies?"

"No. I wore one of Leo's shirts."

There was a long beat, but then Elly's eyes suddenly began to sparkle as she exclaimed, "That's such a girlfriend-y thing to do! I want to try it, too!"

"All right, then. Let's go to the Chief's room."

"Hey? Do I get a say in this?" I cut in with a frown, only to immediately get overwhelmed by the princess's enthusiasm when she clasped her hands around mine.

"Of course! Please pick me a shirt, one that you think would look good on me!"

"... If you insist," I yielded almost right away, and I allowed her to pull me towards the stairs.

"If you're picking one for her, do it for me, too," my assistant followed it up with those words, and I couldn't help but sigh.

As cute as my girlfriends were, they could certainly be quite a handful from time to time. Though again, I wouldn't have it any other way.

PART 3

Slowly. Very, very slowly. The trick was to move with deliberate, smooth movements and— Okay, that's one side done. Now, I just had to move this arm to the side a little aaaand...

"Finally..." I whispered under a breath of relief, and then I promptly slipped down the side of the bed. However, the moment my foot touched the floor, my whole body stiffened in alarm.

"Mmm..."

Holding my breath like my life depended on it, I warily glanced over to my left, towards the source of the sleepy mumble that made me halt in my tracks. I stayed perfectly still for what felt like at least two-thirds of an eternity, and only let out a tiny sigh once I was sure the crisis had passed.

It took me a subjectively long time to do it, but I was finally back on my own two feet. I promptly stretched my back, after which I glanced over my shoulder towards my bed, or rather, the two girls on it.

The three of us had stayed up until eleven, watching movies and discussing things, at which point it felt like some kind of switch flipped inside the two of them from energetic to sleepy. Normally I would've found their behaviour really endearing, with all the yawning and eye rubbing, but then came an issue I'd failed to consider ahead of time: they wanted to sleep together. Or rather, Elly wanted to, after Judy told her about how she'd slept on my bed once.

This was, of course, absolutely impossible due to the fact that I didn't sleep. This wasn't exactly a big secret, so I let my draconic girlfriend in on it, yet it did nothing to deter her, so in the end we reached a compromise; I'd stay with them until they fell asleep, and then I'd slip out once they were neck-deep in dreamland. Or, as my assistant had put it, "Once Judybot is dreaming of electric sheep."

Sounded like a nice middle ground, except for one tiny issue: as it turned out, my girlfriends were super-clingy, even in their sleep. No, I should say *especially* in their sleep. As in, imagine a pair of baby koalas, on steroids!

Just thinking back on the hour-long slow and meticulous struggle it took to peel them off me made me want to grumble like an old dwarf fresh out of ale, yet I held the urge back, lest I accidentally wake the girls. I didn't want to go through the whole process all over again... and, on second look, they were all kinds of adorable sleeping together like that, and I really didn't want to ruin that image.

In fact, I may or may not have spent a somewhat unnecessarily long time staring at the two of them under the blanket. And no, I had absolutely no regrets about setting my own deadline, meaning that trying anything physical tonight would've made me an enormous hypocrite, even though they were sprawled out in front of me and unnecessarily willing.

Well, okay, maybe a tiny little bit, but you didn't hear it from me.

Anyhow, once I'd had my fill with the sight, I quickly (and very, very quietly) turned around and tiptoed towards my PC. I brought it out of standby mode with a single click of the mouse, and I was once again grateful for my bank account, as it allowed me to buy a prebuilt machine with a water cooler, so I didn't have to worry about the fans waking anyone. That said, the screen was still pretty bright, and so I quickly turned it down a notch.

I glanced back to check on the girls one last time, and since they were still happily snoring away the night, I let my shoulders relax a bit and lowered myself into my custom swivel chair.

Once I was seated, I made sure to mute the speakers before automatically checking the Hub, mostly out of habit. I skimmed over the new forum threads and browsed the titles of the new reports, but there didn't seem to be anything noteworthy at a single glance. As such, I opened a new tab and clicked on the bookmark of my favourite movie database site, and once it loaded in, I immediately typed the title of the schlock movie we'd just watched.

It didn't take long to find the user reviews section, and after I limbered up my fingers, I quickly typed in my concise review of the film.

"*The Heating Coil of Doom* is the worst thing I've seen since polio. The main character has too much plot armour, the side plots about the lesbian cheerleaders and their pet moose were slow and confusing, and the explicit sex scene between the sentient toaster and the grandmother living in the attic had no buildup or consequence whatsoever. Also, a little gross. The ending also left a lot to be desired, as we never learned if the toaster managed to kill the moose at the end, and the romance subplot between the cheerleaders and the lion tamer from the Danish traveling circus was inconclusive, as well. Overall, it was a bad movie. Two out of ten."

Once I was satisfied with what I wrote, I posted it and moved the cursor over to close the tab, but by doing so my eyes naturally skimmed over the other tabs, and so I inevitably noticed a notification from the Hub. I had a bad feeling about it, but I figured it could also be important, so I closed the review site as originally intended and steeled my nerves before checking the chat logs.

Surprise, surprise; my hunch was on the money.

"W1NG3D N1NJ4: HI BOSS MAN! ARE YOU ONLINE!? (ˉ ▽ ˉ)ﾉ"

"W1NG3D N1NJ4: IF YOU ARE ONLINE, PLZ ANSWER ASAP!!! I NEED SOME ADVICE!!! (˙• ω •˙)"

It was for moments like this that I had stockpiled a lot of exasperated sighs, so I could freely breathe one out whenever I had to. Like just now. Haaaah...

Anyhow, I reached out for the keyboard and began to type my reply.

"Admin: Hello, Ninja. Please tell me you're not looking for relationship advice."

"W1NG3D N1NJ4: HUH!? Σ(ˉ 。 ˉ)"

"W1NG3D N1NJ4: NONONO! THINGS ARE PROGRESSING SUPER-WELL ALREADY! (^▽^)"

Oh, look at that. A classic spit take moment. And here I thought I wouldn't be surprised by anything anymore. Once I got over the first shock, I decided to ask the obvious, just to be on the safe side.

"Admin: With the granddaughter of the arch-mage?"

"W1NG3D N1NJ4: YEP! WE ARE TEXTING EACH OTHER EVERY EVENING, AND SHE IS SUPER-DUPER CUTE!!! EVEN CUTER THAN I ORIGINALLY THOUGHT! LIKE, HYPER-SUPER-UBER-DUPER CUTE!!1! (≧∪≦) ♡"

"W1NG3D N1NJ4: ACTUALLY, I WAS JUST PLANNING TO ASK HER TO HANG OUT!!! WISH ME LUCK!!!1!!ONE! (//>/ ▽ /<//)"

The enthusiasm seeping through the screen was practically palpable, but on my end, questions like "Since when did you even have her number!?" and "When the heck did all of this happen, and why didn't I notice it!?" drowned it all out. Anyhow, I stifled a shallow groan and decided to ask the class rep about it tomorrow. For now, I went ahead and proceeded with the next obvious question.

"Admin: Break a leg."

"Admin: That said, if it wasn't about your love life, then what kind of advice do you need?"

"W1NG3D N1NJ4: RIGHT, RIGHT!!"

"W1NG3D N1NJ4: REMEMBER ALL THE REPORTS I'VE BEEN SENDING YOU? ABOUT ALL THE INFO I GOT OF OFF THE SCARY CHIMERA SLAYER DUDE?! (>﹏<)"

I waited for an embarrassingly long time for him to continue, until it dawned on me that it wasn't a rhetorical question he was asking.

"Admin: Yes, I remember. What of it?"

"W1NG3D N1NJ4: YOU SEE, I RAN INTO A BIT OF A SNAG! (; ̄ Д ̄)"

"W1NG3D N1NJ4: WHO WOULD'VE THOUGHT THAT GETTING UNUSUAL ARTIFACTS WOULD BE SUCH A PAIN IN THE *******?!?!! (#`Д´)"

"W1NG3D N1NJ4: I TRIED TO CALL IN ALL KINDS OF FAVORS, AND EVEN DROPPED MY FATHER'S NAME A FEW TIMES, BUT I STILL COULDN'T FIND ANYONE WITH A NOVEL ARTIFACT FOR THE SLAYERIZER DUDE! (╯_<。)"

"W1NG3D N1NJ4: ALSO, MY FATHER LEARNED ABOUT WHAT I WAS DOING, AND SCOLDED ME OVER THE PHONE... ︵(> <)︵"

"Admin: I see, but could you please get to the point?"

"W1NG3D N1NJ4: SURE BOSS, SORRY BOSS!! (*＿＿)人"

"W1NG3D N1NJ4: THE POINT IS THAT A FRIEND OF A FRIEND HELPED ME CONTACT THIS REALLY SHADY GUY! HE HAS ALL KINDS OF COOL GADGETS, BUT HE IS SUPER-SHADY, AND HE WAS ASKING FOR WEIRD STUFF

IN EXCHANGE FOR HELPING ME OUT! SHOULD I MAKE A DEAL WITH HIM? (¯ _ ¯)· · · ”

"Admin: That depends. Please elaborate on the weird stuff."

"W1NG3D N1NJ4: HE ONLY WANTS ME TO WRITE SOMETHING IN SCRIPT FOR HIM! I THINK HE MIGHT WANT TO FORGE SOME KIND OF DOCUMENT OR WHATNOT, BUT I'M NOT SURE! (¬_¬)"

"Admin: So he's a forger?"

There was a long pause in the textual conversation, so I wrote in another question.

"Admin: Is he one of ours?"

"W1NG3D N1NJ4: I DON'T THINK SO? IF HE WAS, HE WOULDN'T NEED TO ME WRITE FOR HIM!"

"Admin: Fine, then what does he look like?"

"W1NG3D N1NJ4: I DUNNO! I HAVEN'T MET HIM YET! WE ONLY SENT MESSAGES OVER PALINDROME! ┐(¯ ~ ¯)┌"

"W1NG3D N1NJ4: OH, OH! I JUST REMEMBERED! \(★ω★)/"

"W1NG3D N1NJ4: BOSS MAN! DO YOU HAVE A PALINDROME ACCOUNT!? CAN YOU ADD ME AS A PAL!? o(>ω<)o"

For the uninitiated (such as I was until a short while ago), PALindrome was the name of one of the newfangled social media sites that popped into existence with the world's technology doing its damned best to catch up to some arbitrary tech level during the past month or so. I knew because Judy and Elly both wanted me to add them as pals and then set their relationship level to girlfriend, but when it turned out the site only allowed one girlfriend per person (which was a discrimination lawsuit in the making, I tell you), they decided to go back to MateLedger, which was the first site Judy had used to annoy me.

But putting my irritation with the rapidly increasing popularity and influence of these sites aside (which, I would like to add, had nothing to do with the fact that I could've made ten times the money I did with my rudimentary streaming service idea if only I'd realized that making the first social media platform was even an option), I focused on the screen again and gave my answer.

"Admin: I don't think it's wise for an asset to share and discuss information on social media."

"W1NG3D N1NJ4: DON'T WORRY, ADMIN! I WAS SUPER-DISCREET! SO ABOUT ADDING ME AS A PAL...? (^•ω•^)"

"Admin: Let's discuss this again at another time. For now, I'd like you to tell me more about this shady person you want to make a deal with."

"W1NG3D N1NJ4: OKAY! (* ^ ω ^)"

"W1NG3D N1NJ4: I DON'T KNOW MUCH MORE ABOUT HIM, BUT MY FRIEND SAID HE IS NEW TO THE ISLAND, AND HE IS STILL BUILDING UP HIS CONTACTS, AND THAT'S WHY I COULD GET STUFF FROM HIM FOR CHEAP! (¬ω¬)"

"Admin: Do you know where he got his artifacts? Is he connected to the School?"

"W1NG3D N1NJ4: I DON'T THINK SO? HE PROMISED HE COULD GIVE ME ALL KINDS OF WEIRD STUFF I COULDN'T FIND ANYWHERE ELSE ON THE ISLAND! LIKE, HE WROTE HE HAD AN ARTIFACT THAT COULD MAKE TEA TASTE LIKE COFFEE! \(★ω★)/"

I blinked a few times as I reread the last message, and I couldn't help but feel intrigued.

"Admin: Do you mean it turns tea into coffee?"

"W1NG3D N1NJ4: NONONO! ONLY THE TASTE! SOUNDS KIND OF USELESS, BUT IT'S PRETTY WEIRD, SO I'M SURE SLAYER DUDE WOULD LIKE IT! HE'S WEIRD LIKE THAT! (−＿＿−)"

His tone annoyed me a little, but I had to admit that he was right. That most certainly intrigued me. Just how would an artifact change the taste of a liquid without affecting its chemical makeup? Maybe it affected the amino acids that gave tea its flavour? Or it could apply some sort of masking effect on the liquid to deceive the taste buds? Kind of like an illusion for the tongue?

Either way, that sounded really interesting. If it was the former, it might even give me an easy gateway into understanding how the magical substratum manipulated things on a molecular level. I found myself itching to take a look, so after a short minute of consideration, I decided to tell Mike to go for it.

"Admin: He sounds useful. If you think it's safe, try to make contact with him. Be sure you have an escape plan."

"W1NG3D N1NJ4: DON'T WORRY, BOSS! I'M GOING TO HAVE TWO! ε=ε=ε=ε= ┌(; ￣ ▽ ￣)┘"

"Admin: Good. Do you have anything else to report?"

"W1NG3D N1NJ4: NOTHING TO REPORT, BUT... BOSS, DO YOU HAVE EXPERIENCE WITH WOMEN? LIKE, HOW TO MAKE THEM FALL FOR YOU AND STUFF? (^• ω •^)"

The moment I read that, I instinctively glanced back at the two girls peacefully sleeping in my bed, then with mixed feelings I typed:

"Admin: No. Also, I already told you I'm not giving relationship advice."

"W1NG3D N1NJ4: PLEASE, BOSS! I DON'T WANT TO MESS THIS UP! PLEASEEEEEEE!!! (シ＿＿)シ"

Oh, look at that. It was roll-of-eye o'clock before I even knew it. Anyhow, I silently shook my head and responded with a curt:

"Admin: Go ask Moose."

There was a radio silence almost a minute long following my advice...

"W1NG3D N1NJ4: HE'LL MAKE FUN OF ME... (/ω\)"

...followed by another unnecessarily long pause before Mike finally gave up.

"W1NG3D N1NJ4: FINE, I'LL ASK HIM! MAYBE HE'S GOING TO BE IN A GOOD MOOD?! (¬_¬;)"

"Admin: You do that. I have to go now."

"W1NG3D N1NJ4: BYE, ADMIN!!! (•ω•)/"

"Admin: Stay safe."

Following those two words, I quickly closed the chat interface and set my status to offline. I was about to move on with my night, but in the end I couldn't help but feel bothered by this exchange, so I opened the chat log again and sent a PM.

"Admin: Hey, Moose. Ninja is going to annoy you soon. Don't be too mean to him."

"MoroseMoose: Hello, Admin. He is already annoying me."

"MoroseMoose: I'll try not to tease him too much. Not making any promises."

"Admin: Good enough for me. That's all I wanted to say. Bye."

"MoroseMoose: Bye."

With that done, I closed the tab for good and carefully stretched my arms as I thought about what I should do next. It was still the middle of the night, so my options were fairly limited. I couldn't work out, as it would probably wake up the girls. I could go down and make breakfast, but it would get cold by the time they woke up, so it was also off the table. What did that leave me with?

"Well," I whispered under my breath, mostly out of habit. "I suppose I better find out what gives tea its taste. For science."

And with that began yet another long, not particularly eventful, yet strangely relaxing night of research.

PART 4

"Goodbye. Dad! Have a safe... trip!" said one wooden and completely unconvincing voice on my left, its owner continuing to hold on to me as if her life depended on it even while she was bidding a teary farewell to her father. On an unrelated note, I couldn't feel my left arm anymore. Was it a good or a bad thing that I was getting used to that?

"Thank you! My... dear daughter! Daddy is going... to... be back! In a few weeks!" replied a much louder, yet at the same time even less convincing voice from the front. What would you even call that? Woodener? Woodier? Foresty? Let's go with the last one; it sounded about right.

"Oh, Father. I will miss you. So much."

"Don't... cry my! Daughter! I... will only be... gone! For... multiple weeks! Yes! Multiple... weeks!"

While all of this silliness was happening with all the sublime grace of a train crash on a boat, my eyes slowly swept over the whole Dracis household crowding the driveway in front of the gates of the estate. In retrospect, I think it was probably a form of involuntary coping mechanism. Anyhow, the small crowd in front of me included Emese, Sebastian, Melinda, the nameless twins, all the placeholder maids, and even the cooks and the gardeners. All of them were standing at attention, too, and the whole display reminded me of a military parade, except with ladles, feather dusters, and rakes instead of guns.

As I continued to scrutinize the staff, my gaze unexpectedly met with those of the incognito dragon standing by my self-diagnosed father-in-law's side, and the way he immediately rolled his eyes perfectly encapsulated my own sentiment. I gave him a nod of appreciation, and then we both shrugged at once as the father-daughter duo continued their public display of misdirection.

At long last, the excruciatingly arboreal string of goodbyes came to an end, and Abram and Sebastian both got inside the large black limousine waiting nearby, though not before Papa Dracis sent me a meaningful wink. What it actually meant, though, I didn't have the foggiest idea, and they rode away into the sunrise before I could ask.

Then, as if she was waiting for the opportunity, Emese rolled over to us with the help of the braided (and for some reason really grumpy-looking) chambermaid, completely disregarding the way the mansion's staff left the scene in goose steps. For a moment I wondered whether that was because they were placeholders, or whether it was something I should be worried about, but such thoughts were quickly shaken out of my head by the mother of the household directly addressing me.

"Thank you for seeing off my husband, Leonard. Did you three have fun last night?" she asked with the combination of a provocative smirk and a knowing look. It wasn't hard to figure out what she was hinting at, considering Elly was even clingier than usual, while my dear assistant also followed her example for some inexplicable and quite troubling reason.

"You could... certainly say that."

My evasive answer only made her smile widen even further, and she followed it up with a cocky "Is that so? I'm happy to hear that! When can I expect my grandchildren?"

"Well, let's see..." I muttered as I began to count on my fingers. "High school is two more years. College is at least three, five if either of us wants to get a master's degree, plus we should also try to get jobs first, so... about eight or so years?"

My detailed answer obviously caught her off guard, yet by the twinkle in her eyes I could see she already had a snappy comeback on the tip of her tongue, which would've no doubt led to some hilarious skit about baby names and college saving funds, if not for my other girlfriend joining the fray.

"Chief, we should hurry up," Judy remarked, and she showed me the clock on her phone. "We're going to be late for school. You can play with mother-in-law later."

"We are not *that* late..."

My attempted protest fell on deaf ears, as my dear assistant commenced to act like she was dragging me away. Or... was she actually trying to drag me away, but failing? It wouldn't have been the first time she'd done something like this, so it was hard to tell.

Anyhow, since she was about as adamant about her efforts as a Pomeranian puppy trying to take his human for a walk, I decided to humour her and awkwardly waved at the women still in the driveway.

"Bye, mom-in-law."

"Oh well," Emese huffed with a playful bend in her lips, and then she added, "Stay safe, kids. I'll see you at dinner!"

I didn't remember making any dinner plans, but considering the circumstances, I didn't have either the time or the energy to object, especially since Elly decided to join the fun and began to pull on me, as well, and unlike with my assistant, her efforts were significantly harder to resist. As such, I soon found myself walking away from the Dracis mansion, yet I could feel the eyes of the still-crotchety maid and the widely grinning matron of the estate right until we rounded a corner and were finally out of sight.

The moment that happened, I let out a pent-up breath and glanced at my girlfriends in turn. The princess seemed to be in an unusually good mood, while Judy was her usual self, except maybe just a smidge clingier than usual. I wondered if they hadn't given up yet, and this was step four or five in their intricate plans to awaken my libido. I hoped not. They gave me enough trouble yesterday with their cosplay already.

... Actually, now that I think about it, they looked pretty cute in those maid outfits. Borderline adorable. Furthermore, those costumes looked like they were fitted specifically for them to emphasize their charms and what-not. That's not something they could make in an afternoon, so I couldn't help but wonder if the maid cosplay was a premeditated plan instead of something they came up with in a single day. Either way, it certainly brought my girlfriends' sense of priorities into question, but then again, I had my own bugbears to contend with, so I wasn't going to cast the first stone.

In any case, while I was pondering these important matters, all of a sudden someone called out to me.

"Is this what they call having a flower on each arm?"

I turned towards the source of the cheeky comment, and it wasn't exactly surprising that I found Josh there.

"Just where did you even hear that old-school term?" I shot back with a raised brow, and my friend shrugged his shoulders between his greetings to the girls.

"I think it was in one of those god-awful young adult novels Angie made me read a few years ago. Can't recall the title."

"It's probably better that way," I commented, and we shared a sentimental nod between each other. "Speaking of her, where's the childhood friend in question?"

"She should be here soon," Josh said as he fell in line beside us. "She said she forgot her gym clothes and had to go back."

"Should we slow down to let her catch up?" Elly proposed, but Josh ultimately shook his head.

"Nah, she's quick on her feet; she should catch up with us soon. Not to mention, you guys aren't exactly running, either." He paused for a long moment as he looked us over, then he added, "Speaking of which, isn't it uncomfortable to walk like that?"

I figured he was referring to the way my girlfriends arrested my arms, so I replied with, "It's not so bad."

"It also keeps us warm," Judy added somewhat absentmindedly, immediately catching my attention in the process.

"Wait, is that why you are being so close?"

"Among other things," she told me while conspicuously averting her gaze. In fact, I was pretty sure she was doing so on purpose to tease me, so I did the only reasonable thing and ignored her in favor of my other girlfriend.

"Are you also holding on to me for that?"

"I just saw Judy do it, and it looked nice," my draconic girlfriend answered with a dopey smile, after which she honest-to-goodness rubbed her cheek on my shoulder and added, "She's right, though. You're really warm."

"I'm glad to hear that?"

I would be lying if I said I wasn't taken a little aback by that, but then I was taken even abacker when Judy followed her lead and did the same, so I decided not to dwell on it and focus on the conversation with our resident protagonist.

"So I gather you two have buried the hatchet."

"Yeah. Angie even apologized for overacting." Josh fell silent for a moment, his brows slowly scrunching up, and then he added, "It was weird."

"But it worked out, and that's what's important," I noted, followed by the closest approximation of a sage nod I could manage under the continued assault of my girlfriends.

"I suppose." After saying that, Josh's gaze wandered off as if he was lost in thought, but at last he turned back to me and explained, "After she apologized, we played a few rounds of Street Kombat."

"Sounds wholesome," I said half-heartedly, just to keep the conversation rolling.

"Whatever you say," Joshua dismissed my stray comment with a sneaky roll of his eyes, but then he unexpectedly added, "And when it was time for her to go home, she gave me a kiss on my cheek. She said it was an apology kiss. Is that normal? I mean, between friends?"

Wow, look at that. Angie went on the offensive. That was fairly surprising... or maybe not? I mean, she did seem unusually interested in my relationship with the girls and how to make it work; maybe she was actually laying the groundwork? Or maybe it really was just a chaste, friendly peck on the cheek. Who knew?

However, before I could give my tactful and unbiased advice, I was beaten to the punch by Elly of all people saying, "I don't think Leo is a good judge of these things."

Wait, what? This time I was taken the abackest. I never expected Elly to say that, but I couldn't object in time, as my other girlfriend immediately echoed her sentiment.

"True. The Chief is really bad at picking up on these things."

"Hey! I wholeheartedly disagree with that assessment!" I exclaimed as I finally managed to get a word in, and to my most abacktakenest surprise not only Judy, but the princess also gave me a flat look. Luckily the angle from which they were doing so made them look somewhat cute, so it didn't hurt my feelings as hard as it could've, but it was still an unexpected sucker punch.

"Sorry, Chief, but considering how much trouble you caused us by failing to get a clue, I don't think there's any jury in the world that would find you innocent."

"Innocent of what? Also, I once again vehemently disagree. I wasn't unaware; I just decided not to do this whole romance thing yet because of reasons. There's a huge difference there."

"Doesn't that just make it worse?" Elly's innocent-sounding question made us glance at her in unison, so she hastily clarified her point. "I mean, wouldn't willfully ignoring someone when they try to show they like you be worse than just being oblivious?"

"You're right," Judy followed her up with a mighty nod. "What do you say to that, Chief?"

"I have nothing to explain, as I've already told you my reasons when we started dating. Not to mention, things worked out in the end, so all's well that ends well." The two girls clinging to me were still giving me unsatisfied looks, so I decided it was time for a tactical change in topic. "Anyhow, Josh asked a question. Shouldn't we help him out first before we start reminiscing about how our relationship started?"

"I thought we were already doing that," Judy commented while taking a sneaky glance at my friend, who was only looking at us in a mixture of incomprehension and industrial-strength caginess, as if he was afraid our boiling cauldron of a discussion would spill over him, too.

For a short while all three of us were looking at him without a word, and the atmosphere was actually getting a little chilly. Or was it the weather? It was hard to tell sometimes.

"... I don't get it," Josh finally blurted out, which prompted both my girlfriends to let out a sigh in unison.

"Maybe Leo is right." The princess's low-key whisper made me raise a brow in surprise, and so she added, "Maybe the boy being oblivious is more of a hassle in the long run, after all."

"Maybe," Judy echoed the word the third time in a row, yet even though it was supposed to be a form of tacit agreement, she still sounded about as skeptical as an atheist at the midnight mass.

In the meantime, I noticed a ponytail rapidly approaching us from behind, and unsurprisingly enough, it was attached to a heaving Celestial girl. She came to a screeching halt by our side, caught her breath, and then she sent a sharp glance our way.

"You guys are mean! Why didn't you wait for me!?"

"You said you'd catch up soon," Joshua answered his childhood friend's question while he simultaneously stepped up to her and rubbed her back. "Here, here. Any better now?"

"I'm not *that* out of breath," Angie grumbled, but curiously enough she didn't move away or try to stop him. Must've been another one of those childhood friend things.

"I see you two really made up," I noted. "Good."

"I already told you we did," Joshua objected for some bizarre reason.

"Yes, but hearing about it is one thing, and seeing it with my own two eyes is another."

"Yep, we're peas in a pod again. Thanks for the assist." Angie flashed me a toothy grin for a moment, but then she looked us over and took a step back. "Speaking of peas in a pod, is it just me, or do you guys look even cuter than usual? Oh, oh! Can I take a picture?"

"I'd prefer if you didn't." My flat response earned me a stuck-out tongue from the upbeat girl, but I ignored her and instead gestured for the childhood friend duo to get moving because at this rate we would really end up late, even though I could already see the school gates from where we were standing.

Once we started moving again, and there was a distinct lull in the conversation, I decided it was as good a time as any to broach the topic of today's big event.

"So are you guys prepared for the afternoon kerfuffle?"

Both Josh and Angie shared an apprehensive look between the two of them, but then they both nodded in such perfect unison I couldn't help but wonder if they practiced for occasions like this.

"I think we should be fine." Josh's words probably didn't sound too convincing even to his own ears, so he hastily added, "I mean, we reviewed the plan a couple of times, but as Leo would say, those rarely survive contact with the enemy."

"Oh, I've heard that one, too," Angie followed him up right away. "Is it a quote from Rommel? Or Sun Tzu?"

"It's from Helmuth von Moltke the Elder," my dear assistant corrected her, and it took all my willpower not to ask just where the hell she learned that.

"That guy's name doesn't exactly roll off the tongue like the others."

We naturally ignored the Celestial girl's musings, and instead I told them, "The important thing is to be able to adapt to the situation. Your basic plan should be solid, and if there's any trouble, you should be able to improvise with the pieces on the board."

"We'll try, but I'd be lying if I said I wouldn't feel more confident if you were also there," Josh admitted a little sheepishly, which made his childhood friend giggle for some reason.

"Sorry, but I'll have to head over to the park to set the stage for the Chimera hunt so that Mountain Girl will finally be out of my hair." He still looked more than a little conflicted, so I also told him, "Don't worry. As they say, plans are useless, but planning is indispensable, and you have done a lot of it. It will be fine."

"Dwight D. Eisenhower."

"Pardon?" I asked back in reflex as I glanced at the source of the unexpected comment.

"The thing you said about planning is a quote from him," Judy clarified.

I sent a deadpan look at her way, and once I felt it had reached its destination, I also added, "Dormouse, please stop being so smart for just five minutes. You're distracting me."

"Is it because you like smart girls?" she immediately asked back with a cheeky little pseudo-smirk.

"So what if I do? Since when's that a crime?"

"Hey, that would make sense! I'm pretty smart, too!" the princess suddenly injected herself into our skit with her usual tact of a drunken bull in a china shop. "I was always at the top of my grade in my old schools. Aced all my exams, too."

"Now that you mention it, midterm exams are coming up, aren't they?" I mused aloud, yet my absentmindedly spoken words made the childhood friend duo shudder like leaves in a monsoon.

"Aw crap, you are right!" Angie's exclamation coincided with us reaching the school gates, and it earned her a stern look from the disciplinary committee member minding the perimeter.

"We totally forgot to study with everything else going on, didn't we?" Josh commented, and it felt like the words were draining his soul away.

"Mum is going to flay me if my average falls under three-point-five!" the at-the moment-not-at-all-energetic Celestial raised her mournful voice, and her childhood-friend-slash-comrade repeatedly nodded in understanding.

"We're screwed, aren't we?" Josh lamented, his eyes unfocused and looking into an infinite distance only he could see.

Frankly, I felt that they were making a mountain out of a molehill, as I considered supernatural battles of life and death more important than quarterly grades. At the end of the day, though, I just couldn't watch them beating themselves up over their grades, so I proposed, "Do you want to form a study group after things calm down a little?"

"Weren't your grades also pretty bad?" Josh responded with a critically raised brow, but before I could get a word in, Angie cut me off.

"Wait, that's actually not a bad idea! Even if Leo is book dumb, he has Judy and Elly! If we ask Ammy to join, too, we're going to be set!"

"Oh, I like the sound of that!" my friend agreed with a worrying amount of enthusiasm.

And with that, somehow the discussion about dealing with Lab Coat Guy got derailed into forming an impromptu study group for the midterm exams that were still about a month away. I knew I should be happy Josh wasn't too tense about the operation after school, but at least he could stay on topic. Priorities and whatnot.

But I digress. We were already at school, so I supposed we should only discuss the battle plans once we were in a more secluded location, such as on the roof. As such, I decided to drop the whole thing altogether. Except...

"*Book dumb*, huh?" I spoke softly under my breath, then with a not-at-all-sinister smile I added, "Well, that also goes into my book of grudges..."

"Did you say something?" Elly inquired out of the blue, so I faced her and flashed my latest-and-greatest version of my roguish smirk at her.

"Don't worry, I'm just being nefarious."

"Oh, it's okay then," she concluded with a dazed smile on her own, and with that, we headed towards the shoe lockers and began what promised to be quite an eventful day.

CHAPTER 10

PART 1

My arrival at the park was as quiet and unceremonious as usual. Once I found my balance after the long-distance Phasing, I glanced around and quickly found my anchor silently trying to hide his considerable bulk behind two trees. I didn't know why he bothered, considering he was covered in the familiar thin film of magical camouflage, but I figured it might've been a habit. Anyhow, after making sure there was nobody else in the vicinity, I stepped up to him and lightly tapped the cloaked Brang on the shoulder.

The large Faun didn't show any sign of surprise at my sudden appearance; he only turned his head towards me and gave me a smile that was visible even through the distortions created by Snowy's Sigil.

"[Maintain your cloak of transparent shadows, general,]" I warned him in a whisper (or at least the closest thing to a whisper the Faun language could manage) before looking over our vicinity one more time. "[Have your preparations ensued with ease?]"

"[Aye. The young ones have hidden themselves among the trees of this green patch of land, as we have discussed. If the Chimera or thine ireful companion were to arrive, they will keep their distance and observe unless an emergency were to arise.]"

"[Hearing that fills my chest cavity with feelings of reassurance.]" I paused for a moment, then after a few tries I managed to reword that into a slightly less verbose, "[What I meant to convey was that I was glad to hear so.]"

Brang gave me an odd look that was perfectly evident even through his cloaking, but didn't ask. I, on the other hand, let out a relieved breath. My recent efforts to make my Faunish slightly less convoluted were finally bearing fruit. I'd have to thank Karukk and Pip for their help later.

"[Were thine arrangements also in order, Lord Blackcloak?]" It took a single sharp glance from me for Brang to realize that he'd accidentally uttered the two forbidden words in my presence, so he hastily cleared his throat in an attempt to let it slide and pressed on. "[What I meant to say was, you have arrived later than planned. Did thy plans proceed as they were envisioned?]"

"[To a greater or lesser amount.]"

To be honest, things didn't go as smoothly as they could have, but I certainly wasn't lying to Brang. The last-minute planning session with the group started out well, but then Angie had an emergency tennis practice session she had to attend to, and then Ammy awkwardly told me that she actually had plans for the afternoon, though she was very vague on the details.

For the former, I could get her off the hook by talking to the leader of the club (a short-haired, sporty upperclassman placeholder, for your interest), and after leveraging my previous help with the pitching machine, I got her to compromise.

As for the latter, it felt like pulling teeth, but at last I managed to have the class rep confess (in private, of course) that she was meeting up with Mike for an outing. That got resolved by a single phone call, though for some reason she was giving me the evil eye for the rest of the day for meddling in her affairs. To be fair, though, considering how crucial she was in Josh's plan, it was I who should've chewed her out for going on a definitely-not-date smack dab in the middle of a preplanned operation.

Also, a quick mental note: pay more attention to this odd, budding relationship. No, not because it was interesting and juicy gossip, but because it was a completely unexpected development.

To put it bluntly, Ammy was established to be part of Josh's entourage from day one (or three, I can't remember), so the fact that she was suddenly showing even a modicum of interest in another guy, even if he was as smitten and enthusiastic as Mike, felt like a culture shock.

Was Josh's harem protagonist aura fading? Or was it just the class rep realizing that she was losing the race against Snowy and Angie and cautiously testing the waters with others? Or better (or worse) yet, could it be that Mike was scripted to be a love rival for Josh when it came to her attention? I mean, these kinds of love triangles are the bread and butter of any romance story, and harem narratives are no exception.

Let's look at this objectively: Mike was a side character from the start, and a fairly well-established one, at that. Those don't grow on trees. That told me that he was supposed to be important from the get-go, and what could be more important for a male side character than being the protagonist's love rival?

I could already picture the scenario in my mind: If Josh were to pick Ammy to be his love interest, Mike would show up to try to seduce her, making Josh jealous and finally taking the initiative. But then, it would turn out it was just a Celestial ploy to infiltrate the School all along! Oh no, what a twist! Because of that, Josh and the class rep would go through a lot of trials and tribulations, and then it would lead to their relationship rising to the next level, and they would live happily ever after.

This was of course all hypothetical, based on the possible route system on which our world could operate, but if I was a betting man, I'd put good money on it being close to the mark. As such, it was very important for our research to keep a close eye on these two. For research, I stress. Not for gossip. Are we clear on that? Good. Now, where was I before this tangent?

Oh, right, preparing for the counter-ambush. So after all that malarkey with the class rep was resolved, I had to sneakily take Judy home, lest she end up in the middle of the crossfire. Needless to say, that resulted in yet another familiar lecture about safety and contingency plans and how she would flay my ass if I showed up in the living room covered in blood again, yada yada. I, as a good and very safety-minded boyfriend, naturally had to listen to her until the end, and only then did I manage to Phase here. All I'm trying to say is that it was a small miracle I'd arrived as early as I did.

Anyhow, I looked over the area we'd picked for the ambush, and once I was sure there wasn't a single soul around besides us, I extended my hand towards Brang. Without a word, he reached over his shoulder and, after unbuckling the leather holder, handed me the spear on his back. It wasn't his own, but a replica weapon I'd ordered online at the same time I'd purchased our training equipment. It was a simple, undecorated weapon, with a leaf-shaped head that was on the longer side and a smooth, roughly two-meter-long ash wood shaft. It wasn't a fancy weapon, but a well-balanced one, and considering I was planning to leave the lion's share of the fighting to Rinne, it was more than enough for the occasion.

"[I shall lie in wait. Proceed with your duties, general.]"

The mostly invisible Faun slowly nodded in response to my words, followed by a salute. I returned the first gesture, but refrained from the second. He didn't mind; instead he dashed away with surprising speed, at least considering his bulk and his bum leg.

And just like that, I was left alone in the rapidly darkening woods, waiting for a terrifying being of untold bloodlust and wanton cruelty to show itself. Oh, and also a Chimera, I supposed. I exhaled sharply through my nose and glanced up at the cloudy sky above. The weather was perfectly nice until school was out, and then a wave of dark clouds rolled over us like an angry herd of grey sheep. I half wondered if it was just for a dramatic effect. I mean, climactic battles rarely happen in cheerful, sunny weather, now do they? Well, I for one could've done without the trope, as it also made the air cool down even further, and the overcast skies were just a tad too foreboding for my liking. If not for the fact that I was already used to the ambiance, I probably would've been pretty tense by now.

Overall, I was more bored than anything else at the moment, so after a brief consideration I picked a comfortable-looking spot near the base of the same trees the ex-general was hiding behind, and I took a seat on one of the twisting, arched roots sticking out of the ground nearby. I glanced around one last time, but I couldn't see any of the prearranged signals the Fauns were supposed to send up in case the Chimera showed up early.

Next, I Far Glanced in the direction of Mountain Girl, but she was still home, meticulously oiling her infuriating sword using a long stick with a ball of cotton at the end of it. It was a little weird, but not enough to pay any more attention to it.

Now that I'd finished with the obligatory round, I could finally focus on the main dish of the day. With that giddy thought in mind, I switched my perspective over to Josh, and not a moment too soon. He was already well on his way towards the ambush point, and in Armband Guy's company, no less.

The small procession in front of me consisted of the aforementioned pair in the front, with Snowy and the princess following a few paces behind them, and the class rep–Angie duo so far back it was impossible to tell if they were even part of the same group. So far, so good.

"Are you certain?" came the vague question from Armband Guy right around the time I shifted my viewpoint over to him.

"The tip came from Leo, so it must be right."

Josh's answer seemingly placated him for the time being, and my friend let out a relieved breath.

In terms of context, the bait we'd set for Armband Guy went something like this: Using my amazing talent for subterfuge, I infiltrated the group of the local creepy misfits to gather evidence about their misdeeds. During that time, I had also discovered the top-secret location of their secret stash, hidden at an unassuming location in town just in case their little Gathering got raided.

I'd naturally told Josh about the stash, and he informed the disciplinary committee, badgering Armband Guy until he agreed to come with him to oversee the disposal of the contraband. It was a very straightforward cover story made credible by our actions from the day before, combined with just a hint of refuge in audacity. As a matter of fact, Josh was doing really well on the latter front, to the point where even I might've believed him about the existence of the secret stash of underwear if I didn't know better. He was a natural when it came to pretending to be offended and outraged by the state of public morals. I wonder if he ever thought about becoming a politician...

"Speaking of which, where's Dunning?" Pascal inquired in a flat voice and glanced over his shoulder.

The question probably wasn't aimed at her in particular, yet my girl-friend immediately jumped to my defense.

"Leo can't come because of the Chimera!"

"She means Brother is going to come later because he is tracking the Chimera around the city," Snowy interjected in a hurry, keeping my cover story intact.

I was afraid Pascal would try to probe further, but he simply acknowl-edged their words with a blasé "Hm," and faced forward again. I let out a breath of relief I didn't even realize I was holding. I continued to follow him for a while, but even after a few minutes, he was only exchanging a few meaningless words with Josh. It wasn't even the fun, passive-aggressive kind of back-and-forth, just garden-variety boring small talk about school life. I had to wonder, since when were these two getting along? This was the second time I'd missed something like this after Ammy and Mike.

Oh, crap. I hope it's not the same situation! Our lives are complicated enough; we really don't need Josh's harem aura to start affecting guys, too!

Bad jokes aside, since there was nothing particularly interesting to see here at the moment, I quickly shifted my attention over to Lab Coat Guy. He was a whole block away from our guys, and he was standing on top of a... billboard. As in, one of those small, metal-framed billboards businesses put to the side of walkways in intersections.

... Um... What? Why was he doing that? Did I even want to know?

I shook my currently nonexistent head and decided to ignore the guy's peculiar choice of perch, and instead I focused on his immediate environ-ment. I quickly found the trigger-happy android and, let me see... Two, sixteen... thirty-two of those silly *sentai* foot soldier wannabees, plus at least one of those balls that turn into those biomechanical whatchamacallits. In other words, he was fully prepared. Unfortunately for him, we had already prepared for him to be prepared.

He'd also picked a great battleground again. It was the intersection of two of the main, four-lane roads running through the city. The junc-ture itself was already spacious, but then there was an empty supermarket parking lot on one side providing plenty of space for some carnage. On the opposite side, we had an eight-story office building with a number of balconies and fire escapes providing convenient footholds. In other words, whether the battle went horizontal or vertical, the stage was suitable.

However, while I was confident that Joshua could finally leverage his protagonist status to deal with our resident mad scientist, there was still one pivotal detail that could make or break this encounter. While Josh's plan was fine, triggering it required the contribution of Lab Coat Guy, as he had to willingly draw everyone into the Purple Zone on his end. I was a little worried whether he would do so if I wasn't around, so I naturally made contingency plans for this scenario.

I focused my attention to the next red dot on the edge of my vision, and the odd purple hue layered over everything within my sight abruptly disappeared as my point of view moved behind the corner of a nearby boutique. I was relieved to see that Vurrok wasn't held up and arrived at the ambush point on time. I picked him for the job because according to Brang he was the sneakiest of the whole sneaky bunch of them, and I needed him to be on standby near the battle site and act as my anchor, just in case I would need to Phase over to goad Lab Coat Guy into showing his face.

While I could've used Armband Guy or any of the others to do this, and then hand wave my sudden appearance by claiming I was using illusions, I didn't want to overuse that explanation. I was afraid that if I did that, they would sooner or later realize I was pulling the wool over their eyes and would try to come up with ways to counter my ability. As they say, information is power, and misinformation is doubly so.

In the meantime, our totally hapless, not at all prepared, and eager little group came to the intersection where Lab Coat Guy, for some inexplicable reason, was still balancing on top of a billboard. Seriously, why though? Was it a height thing? Maybe he just wanted to make sure he was immediately visible? I mean, if that was the goal, he definitely succeeded, but I wasn't sure it was worth sacrificing his dignity for.

Oh, wait. This is the guy who's doing unabashed *sentai* shenanigans without even a hint of irony or self-awareness. He had no dignity to begin with. Sorry, false alarm.

Anyhow, I held my breath with rapt attention while I waited for Josh and Co. to reach the intersection, ready to move at a moment's notice. And then...

"Kihihi ha ha ha!!!"

... the whole world turned purple again with the sound of manic laughter.

Armband Guy visibly twitched in response to the sudden development, but he kept his cool and only gave the cackling mad scientist wannabe standing arms akimbo on a bloody billboard (no, I'm still not over it) a long, suspicious stare. His reaction was reasonable, as this was an unscheduled attack on my friends, one he evidently didn't expect to happen, let alone get caught up in it.

"What's going on?" he asked my friend at his side, and Josh promptly shrugged his shoulders.

"Exactly what it looks like. An ambush."

"You don't sound surprised," Pascal noted with a frown.

"We've gotten used to it," the princess quipped as she and Snowy both stepped forth, and she even honest-to-goodness cracked her knuckles.

While that was going on, I hurriedly switched my attention over to the class rep. I had to make sure that they were also taken into the Purple Zone, otherwise things would go south really fast, and I was immediately relieved when I found the pair clumsily flying through the air.

"That way," she instructed the Celestial girl, carrying her while pointing at something with one hand, the other one frantically trying to stop the skirt of her magiform from flipping over. I didn't know why she was so embarrassed about it; it wasn't like anyone could see her panties at the moment. Well, except for me, but I didn't count.

Angie nodded, or at least I think she did, as she frantically flapped her transparent wings while holding Ammy under her armpits. While the wobbly way they were flying didn't exactly inspire confidence, I decided to cheer for them all the same and left them to their mission. So far, so good.

Since I'd confirmed that the duo was on track, I moved back to the scene of the real action.

To tell the truth, I was looking forward to the coming battle juuust a little bit, and it wasn't just because I could potentially get to see Lab Coat Guy get his teeth kicked in, but because even after all this time, I'd never had the chance to see a proper supernatural battle from start to finish. I was also really curious about just how much Josh had improved, and getting some data on Armband Guy was also a nice bonus.

As such, I changed my POV again, and when my vision settled, I immediately froze in shock as I laid my eyes on Joshua raising his fist high.

"Today, we'll take you down! Right, Pascal?"

... Josh... Dude. I know that you must be in the moment and all, but why in the name of all that is holy are you posing!? It wasn't part of the plan! Posing should never, ever, be part of any plan!

"R-right! You are going down!" my sister followed him up just a tad awkwardly and... Okay, what the hell!? Snowy, why are you posing, too!? And what's with the way you are holding your hands!? You are not a sailor scout! You can't punish him in the name of the moon!

Okay, calm down, me. Deep breaths, happy thoughts, the works. Now, let's look at this rationally. Maybe they are just really in the mood, and they got carried away in their excitement, and *oh for the love of god, princess, not you too!*

"We are going to make you regret picking a fight with us today!"

Dammit, Elly! If you don't want to be left out, at least stick to the theme! You look like you want to do a crane kick! At least pick a fitting pose! Or better yet, just don't do a pose at all!

I rapidly breathed in and out to calm the fires of my internal rage, but then I realized something. One *sentai* pose could be a mistake. Two, an act of passion. Three? That meant there was predetermination involved. So... maybe this *was* the plan? Was this how they wanted to get Lab Coat Guy's attention? By playing into his theatrics?

If so, then I'll applaud their ingenuity. If not, then I'll give them a stern talk for fraying my nerves like that. In fact, I'll give them a stern talk anyway on principle.

Anyhow, I positioned my point of view at a spot where I could keep my eyes on both them and Lab Coat Guy's little mob of robotic eyesores. I was half afraid that my old nightmare would be realized in front of me and the situation would devolve into a back-and-forth exchange of hackneyed dialogue about justice and whatnot, but thankfully it never came to pass due to Armband Guy raising his voice.

"Are you really going to do this while I'm also present?"

"Kihihi!" The guy still precariously teetering on the billboard continued to let out chuckles that made his weird welding mask rock up and down, and then he declared, "Yes! Your presence is unexpected, but I'm actually glad to see you! With you here, he will have no choice but to show his true colours!"

"Who are you talking about?" Pascal asked back, and my guys also shared an apprehensive look between one another.

"The man who made all the preparations for today's event! I'm sure he arranged for you to be here to test the veracity of my words! Isn't that right..." Speaking slowly, Lab Coat Guy leisurely raised his hand, and then sharply pointed forwards and exclaimed, "Leonard Dunning! Did you think your tricks would work forever!? We already have the means to detect you... with science!"

I could hear Snowy gasp in surprise. I could see Elly blink in confusion. I could also see the nervous sweat drops forming on Josh's brows. But most important, I could see our resident *sentai* enthusiast point... in a completely different direction than where I was right now. Or rather, from where I was looking at the scene at the moment, but let's not get bogged down by semantics.

There was a long, silent beat following his declaration, but since nothing happened, he added on an emphatic "Show yourself!" to little to no avail. Another five seconds of awkward silence later he sheepishly glanced over his shoulder and loudly whispered, "Psst! Galatea!"

"Yes, Master?"

"Are you sure he's over there?"

"Affirmative," the eclectically dressed fembot answered without delay. "The new anti-illusion sensor arrays are detecting an invisible humanoid in that direction. Preliminary biometric scans indicate their height is approximately two meters. The probability of it being Leonard Dunning is ninety-seven percent."

"... I don't think he is that tall."

The funky android gave her master a flat look, then uttered, "Ninety-two percent."

"Whatever!" Lab Coat Guy threw his hands into the air in resignation, almost losing his balance in the process. I really hoped he would fall over and we could get this over with, but unfortunately he quickly steadied himself and pointed in the same direction again. "You hear that, Leonard Dunning?! We can detect you, so come out already!"

Once again, nothing happened, even though everyone was paying close attention to the spot where he was pointing, and they seemed to be expecting that someone would suddenly appear out of thin air to walk around the corner. This, of course, actually included the invisible Faun around said corner. This was one of those moments where words simply failed me, and I had no hands to face-palm, so I had to settle with a long mental groan instead.

This encounter was already off the rails, and I had a premonition we had a train wreck on our hands...

PART 2

So things were getting complicated. That's not new. No need to be flustered just yet. Let's just look at the situation objectively.

First off, it looked like Lab Coat Guy was labouring under some kind of misunderstanding about why we tricked Armband Guy into coming with our group. He didn't run away, though, and he still went through with the ambush, so it's probably not a bad thing.

As for his other misunderstanding, I can't say the same yet. I had momentarily wondered why Vurrok was taken into the Purple Zone along with the rest of the gang, but if he was mistaken for me hiding around the corner, it would all make sense. In fact, in some way this was to our advantage, as this diversion gave Angie and Ammy more time to find the core of the Purple Zone and lock it down. Now, the real question was this: What would Lab Coat Guy do when the Faun didn't come out of hiding?

Or rather, I hoped he wouldn't come out of hiding; otherwise we would have a lot of explaining to do for Pascal and the arch-mage, and it may prove to be a disadvantage during negotiations. Considering that, I actually entertained the idea of waiting until Josh got the bad guys' attention and then sneakily smuggling him out of the battlefield. I just had to wait for the right moment, and...

"Galatea, he's not coming out!" Lab Coat Guy suddenly exploded with anger. "Do something!"

"Understood," she responded in a flat voice, following which she extended her hand towards the corner of the building where Vurrok was hiding, *and oh my bloody god, you have to be kidding me!*

Before I knew it, I'd already initiated a Phase jump and reappeared just behind the confused Faun inside the Purple Zone. The sudden transition, combined with the fact that my body was sitting on rough ground just a moment ago, almost caused me to fall over, but I managed to regain my balance at the very last moment and grab him by the shoulder.

Vurrok let out a high-pitched gasp that would've been hilariously anachronistic under any other circumstances, but at the moment I was so far beyond caring I wasn't even in the same time zone. Instead, I uttered a hasty "[Maintain motionlessness!]" as I wrapped my phantom limb around his waist and picked another red dot to move to before I disappeared, dragging the hapless guy along with me.

"[What manner of ludicrousness is this?]"

I presume that question came from Brang, no doubt really shocked by the two of us appearing right in front of him while he was still on the lookout. As much as I wanted to give him an answer right away, my legs had other plans, and they unceremoniously slipped right out from under me. I stumbled backwards, barely managing to brace myself in time so that I only landed on my butt instead of getting sprawled out on the ground.

It took a few seconds to get my bearings. The rapid Phasing combined with forcefully pulling someone with me did a number on my head. I felt like the whole world was spinning, with my body parts also spinning, but in the opposite direction and at various different speeds. It wasn't particularly pleasant is all I'm trying to say here.

"[Are you all right, my lord?]" Vurrok inquired in a panicked voice as he began to buzz around me.

"[To a degree that is far from satisfactory, yet not one that threatens this life of mine. Now excuse me, for I must reign in the rebellious impulses of my disobedient innards.]"

"[Are you certain thy condition isn't dire?]" came the next inquiry from Brang as he casually leaned on his spear. "[You even forgot to denounce young Vurrok for referring to you by thine title.]"

I gave the easygoing ex-general a critical glance, but he only smiled back like he was oh so clever.

"[All is not lost that is delayed.]" My offhanded response only earned me a subdued chuckle, so I decided even rolling my eyes would've been wasted on him, and instead I focused on somehow standing back up. It was only slightly harder than strictly necessary, but with the help of Vurrok, I managed to stand on my own two feet again.

Brang waited for me to readjust myself, and only then did he ask me, "[Is my presumption correct in that something unexpected happened for you to arrive in thine unsteady state?]"

"[*Unexpected* is a word that places it without due consideration,]" I grumbled before I stretched my back. Then I paused, rewound my words in my head, and after a short yet intense sigh I added, "I wanted to say 'that's putting it lightly.'"

"[We understood thine words.]"

Brang might have said that, but based on Vurrok's expression, no, he didn't. I let it slide for the moment, and I asked the obvious. "Are we still in the park?"

"[Aye.]"

"Which way is the ambush point?" Brang wordlessly pointed to our right. I glanced in the direction, and after rummaging through my memories for a while for familiar landmarks, I finally managed to roughly pinpoint my current location within the park. I wasn't far away, but it would still take a minute or two on foot to get back into position. "Well, I better get back there."

"[Do you require our aid in traversing the grounds?]"

"No, I'll manage. Let's stick to the plan. Maintain your positions for now, and warn me when the Chimera makes its move."

Instead of waiting for the response, I immediately began jogging towards my destination. As expected, it only took about two minutes to get back to the spot where I Phased from, and the moment I arrived, I immediately took a seat on the same root and wiped the sweat from my forehead.

Catching my breath might've been important, but there was something more urgent going on at the moment, so I quickly closed my eyes and picked one of our guys before projecting my point of view over with Far Sight. What welcomed me was utter, unabashed chaos, to the point I couldn't even decide where I should look first.

Okay, let's start with a general overview of the situation. First off, it was hard to see because there was a lot of dust in the air. That should already tell you that there was a lot of collateral damage involved, such as the broken windows on the buildings or the way the utility poles around the intersection were knocked over, but hey, it's the Purple Zone. It conveniently existed so that we wouldn't have to care about wantonly destroying everything at times like this. That said though, the odd mannequins, representing the locations of people on the outside at the moment the zone was opened, getting flattened left and right did feel a little icky, but again, no one got hurt, so it wasn't that big of a deal, either.

One correction though: At the moment, the area could be better described as a Red Zone, with the usual violet hues being replaced by a tense crimson ambiance, with most surfaces also getting veinlike black cracks on them. It was all pretty eerie, even more so than usual, but if I had to guess, I would say it was the result of the class rep working her literal magic on the anchor points to lock down the place. That was reassuring, though I was a little worried, as well, since I couldn't see Ammy or Angie anywhere.

But then again, that wasn't something I couldn't fix in a split second, so I immediately Far Glanced over to their side and sighed in relief when I found the class rep tinkering with a glowing spot on the ground, while Angie had her bow at the ready while sitting on the shoulders of Petra the golem and watching the perimeter. Once I confirmed that they were fine, I quickly shifted my attention back to the battleground.

So back to the overview: Front and center, a transformed Josh and Armband Guy were currently fighting the mad scientist, who was putting up a decent fight, if I do say myself. He was throwing around all kinds of gadgets, and the silly-looking pauldrons he was wearing were, for the lack of a better word, unfolded so that they formed what looked like the torso part of a power armour that also covered his arms with metal plates. This, incidentally, made his legs appear hilariously small in comparison.

That side of the battlefield looked pretty intense, but not nearly as noisy as the others. The parking lot on my left was now in even worse shape than the intersection, with a lot of the cars flattened or lying on their sides as if someone had kicked them over.

"AAAAAARYAAA!!"

Correction: They didn't just look like that, they *were* kicked over, as demonstrated by my lovely, if at the moment absolutely *terrifying*, girlfriend sending a small green sedan tumbling across the lot with a single, draconic-physique-enhanced kick. The poor vehicle didn't get much air-time, but on its last roll it still managed to land squarely on the heads of three of Lab Coat Guy's foot soldiers. It resulted in a metallic-yet-still-painful crunching sound.

It was at this moment that, with the sound of a roaring furnace in an echo chamber, a pair of three-fingered arms reached down and grabbed hold of the already totaled car before sending it careening back towards the princess. Thankfully the Gigant had terrible aim, but she dived to the side, anyway. Elly rolled on the asphalt before she quickly leaped to her feet while delivering an uppercut to the face of one of the nearby Sprockets surrounding her. She had so much momentum that it actually carried her into the air, and then she did a three-point landing and dashed forward to dodge the Gigant's follow up attacks.

If it wasn't completely obvious by the description, my girlfriend was soloing both the mooks and the oversized mini boss, and considering that half of the robots were already in pieces, she was doing really well for herself. Still, I would've preferred if Josh or Snowy was there to back her up, but in the case of my friend, I could at least understand why he was busy, considering he had to keep an eye on and encourage Armband Guy to fight properly.

But speaking of which, where's my sister? I looked for her dot, and to my sincerest surprise, it was pointing upward. I Far Glanced there, and found her flying through the air somewhere halfway between the intersection and where Ammy and Angie were standing. Then, just as my vision cleared up, I almost let out a scream as I found an ice spear flying right at me.

Of course, it passed right through the spot from where I was looking, but damn, it almost gave me a heart attack! I mean, I wasn't easy to rattle, but I have bad memories of those. I let out a small gasp, and once I gathered my wits, I turned around to see where she was aiming, and I found the funky android there. She dodged the incoming projectile with a pirouette and seemed to maneuver through the air using a series of glowing spots on her shoulders, back, soles, and butt. I couldn't tell if they were technolog-ical, magical, or both, but she managed to use them to fly with surprising grace all the same. Well, at least until Snowy used what looked like a blast of snowflakes to stall her, and then delivered a literal flying kick to her back.

In other words, she was also doing well. I had a hard time deciding whom should I watch, but I settled on getting another good look at Josh first, if only so that I could take a better look at Armband Guy's fighting style.

When I returned to them, Josh was in the process of scaling the side of the office building by the intersection; using the superhuman strength given to him by his Abyssal transformation to grab onto ledges and use them to fling himself from one balcony to the next. The way he was doing it struck me as really dangerous, since one wrong move could send him falling tens of meters, but based on his expression, he might've been enjoying this.

"Parkoooour!"

... No, scratch that. He was *definitely* enjoying it. With one last heave, he landed on the rooftop of the building with a heavy thud that made me wince, and he quickly glanced around to find the other two engaged in trading blows smack dab in the middle of the roof. The whole place was flat, save for a few large air conditioners and satellite dishes, so it was a perfect place for a showdown.

Without further ado, Josh rushed towards them in the cover of one of the air conditioners, popping out into the open just as Lab Coat Guy's left shoulder plate opened up and launched a small, round object towards Pascal.

"Duck!" Josh shouted as his hands made a series of subtle motions. There was a flash of light in his palm, followed by a blast of wind aimed at the ball. He didn't manage to hit it head-on, but the wave of air still threw the projectile off its track, and it landed a couple of steps to the left of Armband Guy, where it exploded into a puddle of viscous yellow liquid.

I wondered if it was something like an acid grenade, or maybe some kind of superglue designed to hold someone in place, but my attention was quickly yanked back to the fight when Josh came to a halt beside the bespectacled disciplinary committee member and told him with a grin, "Sorry I'm late. I still have to work on my parkour tricks."

"Your assistance was wholly unnecessary," Armband Guy answered dourly, but then a moment later he added, "Thanks, nonetheless."

"You're welcome. Now, let's take this guy down!"

"Kihihi! Do you think you have what it takes t—!?"

Lab Coat Guy got exactly that far before the whole building shook so violently the three of them could barely keep their footing. I was also startled by the development, so I quickly Far Glanced around to find the cause of the disturbance, and I soon found the culprit on the ground.

Elly was standing on top of the wreckage of a different car, leaning forward and with a series of magical sparkles dancing around her face, her hair cascading behind her like she was in a wind tunnel. I'm not going to lie, she looked outright stunning, but I quickly shut down my lizard brain and its annoying signals, and instead I focused on the direction where she was looking.

Pivoting around, I found myself face-to-face with one of the severed arms of the Gigant, blown right into the middle of the intersection and leaving a nasty indent on the asphalt. More importantly, though, I noticed how there was a huge gash in the side of the office building, almost as if a straight line was gouged out of it with the world's largest ice cream scoop.

Dammit, princess! I know I just mentioned that you don't need to mind the collateral damage in the Purple Zone, but at least pay attention to where you are firing your dragon flame! Friendly fire is still a thing! Also, I'm fairly sure that even if none of the buildings are strictly real, they would kill you if they fell on your head all the same. Be more careful, and... Wait. Could this be how Judy feels when I do something reckless?

Putting any eye-opening revelations aside, I quickly looked around to locate the owner of the large severed arm, not that it was hard to find it, considering it was a honking huge monster thing. The princess's attack only grazed it, as it still had three of its arms remaining. That said, I also noticed a dent on the metal plates centered around its chest region, one that wasn't there the last time I saw the creature, and its shape looked suspiciously like it was left behind by a comparatively tiny fist. Which meant...

Dammit, did I just miss the moment when my girlfriend decked the three-story-tall monster? Why do I keep missing the best parts? Oh, speaking of which, I just realized that there was a series of bright flashes in the direction where I last saw Snowy. I had a feeling something was going on over there, so I moved my point of view, just in time to catch a chase between the android, my sister, and Angie, who must have joined the fray while I was paying attention elsewhere.

The three of them were weaving between buildings and under streetlamps, and while I wouldn't have called it a high-speed chase, per se, they were still moving fast (and frantically) enough to give me motion sickness, so I switched over to Ammy, who was watching the spectacle from the shoulders of her golem. From this vantage point, I could finally see that the flashes of light I was seeing were from Angie firing her bow while flying and the arrows exploding mid-flight as they came into contact with some kind of transparent force field that surrounded the fembot's body.

I kept watching them for a while and cheered them on, though I couldn't see much. I figured I might as well try to follow one of them again once I braced myself for the motion sickness, but before I could get to it, there was an unexpected development in the form of the sound of thunder followed by the office building in the distance beginning to tilt. The moment I realized what was going on, I immediately moved my vision over to Josh, ready to do another Phase-and-grab operation at a moment's notice.

Thankfully my worries were unfounded, as once I arrived, I found them already standing in the middle of the crossroads, right next to an enormous, severed black arm. Before I knew it, Elly also joined the fray, while the Gigant and the remaining silly robots surrounded Lab Coat Guy. Once they squared off, the oversized biomechanical monster thingy casually reached down, picked up the limb that the princess had blasted off with her breath attack, and simply reattached it to the stump on its shoulder.

Wow, that's a handy ability.

I apologize for my terrible pun. I've reflected on my actions, and it won't happen again.

Anyhow, for the moment neither side was willing to make the first move, and I was afraid it would devolve into a stalemate until the Purple Zone got unlocked and allowed the baddies to scurry away, but my reservations were once again overstated, as Lab Coat Guy immediately let out another one of his grating chuckles.

"Kihihihihi! So this is what it came to! This is how it feels to be betrayed!"

"Give up, Robatto! We have you cornered! Surrender now, and I promise we won't hurt you!" Josh exclaimed, his words so protagonist-y it wasn't even funny. But then again, this whole excursion was about forcing him to take up the mantle, partially for my own benefit, so I wasn't exactly in a position to call him out on that.

"You think you've cornered me?! Kihihi! How naive!" All of a sudden, a couple of bright spots, the same kind that I had seen on the android, lit up on the guy's half power armour, and he gradually rose into the air. "No, Joshua Bernstein! The real battle has just begun!"

Ooooh, that was pretty ominous. Also, just a tiny bit cool. Or at least it would've been, if not for the multicoloured pauldrons and the silly welder's mask, but hey, he was still getting better at looking like an actual threat. It was a good start. If he kept it up, at this rate I might even start taking him seriously in a year or two.

More importantly, he was obviously getting ready for some kind of climactic last stand. Or at least I hoped he was, and that this wasn't one of those bad jokes when the villain makes a big show and then turns tail for comedic effect. I mean, not all tropes are bad, but some are, and we certainly didn't need that one in our lives.

I was also itching to finally see a proper battle, so I swore not to get tempted by anything and Far Glance away from the action. So I watched, very closely, as Lab Coat Guy slowly rose into the air, hovered just in front of the chest of the Gigant, and then...!

Someone poked me in the cheek... Wait, what?

I hastily opened my eyes, just in time to get poked again. I followed the long, purple object touching the left side of my face, and found it being held by a certain annoying huntress. She was crouching about two steps away from me, and she was using her wrapped-up sword to prod me.

"Oh, come on! I was just getting to the good part!" I grumbled as I swatted the annoying sword away with my hand. Rinne blinked at me in surprise and turned her head to the side like a doggy.

"You're alive. Good," she stated emphatically before proceeding to turn her head in the other direction. "What were you doing?"

"I was..." I spoke up reflexively, only to catch myself before I would accidentally reveal something to her. After a moment of thinking, I decided to answer with, "I was listening for any signs of the Chimera."

She blinked again, following which her thin brows scrunched up in a frown.

"Onikiri wonders that if you were truly listening, then how come you didn't notice when we sneaked upon your position on our way to the slaughtering grounds?"

I rewarded her oddly sharp question with a critical glance, and then replied with, "You're not a Chimera, are you?"

"No, Rinne is not a vile creature of the despicable underworld," she responded with a huff. "How could you ever mistake Rinne like that?"

"I didn't. That's the point." My level voice even surprised me, as I think no one would fault me for blowing her off. I took a deep breath and carefully stood up while minding my numb legs. Crouching in one place for so long certainly wasn't good for them. "Speaking of which, since you're here, I suppose you're ready for the ambush?"

"The hunt for blood and viscera," she corrected me as if I'd said something silly just now. "Yes, Rinne is ready to slash, maim, mince, and tear apart the abominable creature of darkness tainting the nights of this city."

"Good to hear that," I answered on autopilot as I glanced around to see if any of the Fauns were giving me signals, but as far as I could see, none of them were in the vicinity. That meant that they were probably still on lookout duty. "In that case, let's find a good spot where we can hide."

Mountain Girl nodded, and we began to search for a nice little hidey-hole. At the end of the day we decided on a pair of lush coniferous shrubs that were just thick enough to serve as cover, but we could still see through them enough so that we had a nice view of the nearby footpath.

I took my spot behind the leftmost shrub, and Rinne... also did the same. I wanted to tell her that she could hide behind the other one, but before I could do so, she suddenly asked, "Are you certain our prey will cross paths with us on its own?"

"Yes, it should. Also, you could—"

"Onikiri wonders how you could possibly know that," she casually cut me off and glanced up at me with questioning eyes. "She says you must be a traitorous te... tegriv... ter-giver-sa-tor? Yes, it's tergiversator!" She let out a proud little grunt, but then her eyes clouded over and she followed it up with the question, "What does that mean?"

"... Why do you ask me? You said it."

"No, Onikiri said it, and we don't know what it means." She paused for a long time here, right until her eyes lit up with understanding. "Oh. Onikiri says it means a person who turns coats. ... But you don't have any coats, so Rinne still doesn't understand."

"I think it's better that way. Your sword is a bad influence on you."

"Leonard-san can tell?"

The high-pitched surprise in her words made me raise a brow in turn, but before I could get into what she meant by that, as I was pretty sure we weren't talking about the same thing, I noticed a small, yellowish glow in the distance. I focused my attention over there instead, and I quickly realized that it was a waving Faun. It was either Hrul or Gram. It was hard to tell those two apart even under the best of circumstances, let alone at this distance.

More importantly, the fact that they were giving me a signal meant that the Chimera had started to move. I quickly put a finger on Rinne's mouth to stop her from any further babbling and pointed towards the path where we were expecting the target with my free hand.

"Psst. The Chimera is coming," I spoke in a low voice, and then I slowly removed my finger from her lips.

Mountain Girl gave me a confused look, which then turned into a skeptical one as she whispered back, "How do you know?"

I thought for a moment, and then decided to double down on my previous stray comment and told her, "I can hear it coming."

"Is it how Rinne can smell the vile stench of the underworld?" She suddenly sounded really excited for some reason. "Rinne and Leonard-san may really be compatible after all..."

"No, we're not," I denied her bluntly before I flicked her forehead. Now granted, doing that to an armed person in a decidedly dark park might've been considered a bad idea under any other circumstances, but this time I felt entirely justified in doing so. "Focus on the task at hand."

"Y-yes! Rinne-must-first-spill-the-dark-red-lifeblood-of-the-vile-and-abominable-and-really-really-bad-thing-that-is-coming-our-way-under-the-guise-of-the-night-most-dark-as-if-it-was-made-for-the-sake-of-the-ultimate-hunt-between-the-two-of-us-and-to-paint-the...."

Okay, I'm not going to lie, her motormouth mumbling was once again creeping me out a little, but I decided to ignore her and instead I focused my attention ahead. I really hoped we could get this over with quickly, and then maybe I could catch the tail end of the battle between the others.

Unfortunately, it took nearly five minutes for the first sign of the creature, five minutes which Mountain Girl spent quietly babbling by my side. At last, I could see a large body moving in the dark, so I tapped her on the shoulder and whispered, "It's here."

Rinne immediately fell silent as her body relaxed, and her face was slowly twisted into an impossibly wide slasher grin. Weird as it might sound, I was almost relieved to see that, as it meant she was finally serious. Probably. Hopefully.

Anyhow, it was my turn to get serious as well, so I clenched my hands around my spear and...

Um... Where's my spear? Where the hell is my bloody spear?!

I remember taking it from Brang, and I still had it when I sat down on the roots. Did I leave it there, or... Oh, dammit. I had it in my hands when I Phased over, didn't I?

My eyes opened wider and wider as I rewound my recent memories, aaaand yup. I had the spear with me, and then dropped it in the Purple Zone when I grabbed Vurrok. My feelings at this moment were quite complicated, but I think I managed to sum things up very succinctly as I whispered:

"Well, fuck."

For some moments in life, you need a poet to describe them. This one? Yeah, those two words were more than enough, I'd say.

PART 3

Okay, calm down, me! So I screwed up. Big deal; wouldn't be the first time it happened. I just have to rely on plan B. So what is the first step...? Coming up with a B plan, I suppose.

First things first, let's observe the situation. This might've been wishful thinking, but there was always a chance that things would proceed in an unforeseen direction where I didn't even need to fight the Chimera. Say, it was possible that it wasn't hostile, or that Rinne would take it down in a single strike, or that it would turn out to be a cute little girl who would call me onii-chan. I mean, that last option would've been absolutely terrifying, but it *was* a trope, so it wasn't entirely off the table.

Anyhow, there were a number of scenarios where I could avoid fighting today. Ideally, I would have Mountain Girl do all the heavy lifting, but at this point I felt obligated in a way to put in at least token effort, so... maybe I could act as a distraction? I doubted I could do more than that without a weapon, but considering I'd been serving as bait for so long, I had more than enough experience in the field.

With that line of considerations finished, the next order of business was observing the Chimera. It was a little hard to see due to the moody weather making dusk set in even earlier than usual, so I had to wait for a while before it got close enough for me to be able to take a good look. Once it did, I immediately let out a relieved sigh. Not a little girl. At least the worst-case scenario was avoided.

As for an actual description: this Chimera was considerably smaller than the one I encountered during the school incident, about as tall as I was and a little on the skinnier side, which incidentally still meant it was about as big and well-built as Brang. On the other hand, its shape was almost identical to the first one, or rather, it was the mirror image of the school Chimera's initial appearance when it had showed up in the courtyard.

Its dark-red skin and black fur didn't exactly blend into the background, and its body was an odd mixture of simian and reptilian traits, with a quadrupedal gait that reminded me of a mountain gorilla and an elongated, crocodilian head. It had six glowing eyes, also in the same positions as his predecessor's, but most curiously, its whole head was also giving off a subtle magical glow. Back then I wasn't as experienced with this kind of thing, but I was still about 98.5 percent sure the first creature didn't have a halo like that.

If I had to pinpoint another difference, it would've been the way it was moving. It just wasn't right. The first Chimera might've been an unnatural mishmash of animals, but it still moved just like that: an animal. You could tell that it was prowling, and when it noticed its prey (namely, me), it moved in for the chase like a real predator.

The creature in front of me looked the same, yet moved very differently, sluggishly going through the motions like a tipsy office worker unsteadily hauling himself home after an especially hectic day at work. Not exactly the most flattering of comparisons, but it was quite accurate all the same. Furthermore, looking at it made me wonder just how the heck it managed to avoid being seen for so long. Even the Fauns, who could turn invisible, had slipped up in the past and had public notices about them in the park. This thing didn't even *try* to hide. It boggled the mind.

On another note, I was also surprised that I couldn't see any mini Chimeras around. I told Brang and Co. to try to smack down any they could find so that they wouldn't end up as a distraction at a critical moment, but I was pretty sure at least a few would escape their notice. They were either really good at their job, or one or two of those things were actually present, but lying low just to pop up at the most inopportune moment. I naturally took the second option to be a given, and mentally prepared accordingly.

What I couldn't prepare myself for was that the moment the Chimera got around fifteen or so meters close to us, my hunting partner suddenly let out a shrill cackle and burst through the bushes with her purple shroud trailing behind her like a comet's tail.

"Shinsoku battō-jutsu!"

Before I could even call after her, she'd already made her way next to the Chimera and delivered a diagonal slash aimed at its neck. The brutish creature was apparently so taken aback by the screaming woman that had suddenly popped up in front of its face that it didn't even attempt to dodge, or even block. The ominously glowing blade cut through the air with a sharp sound, followed by a meaty *thunk* as it embedded itself into the creature's collarbone.

Unfortunately for Rinne, it only cut about a finger's width deep into the Chimera's tough hide, and for a second it looked more surprised than in pain. I'm not going to lie, after she hyped her sword and hunting credentials for so long, I expected a little more than a flesh wound from a surprise attack like that. Oh well, such is life.

I also knew that something like that would barely give a Chimera pause, let alone kill it, so I instinctively called out to her.

"Watch out!"

When she heard my voice, Rinne let out another creepy laugh, following which she raised her voice and spoke up, her words eerily articulate and filled with a kind of languid magnetism.

"Hurry up, Leonard! The evanescent dance of life and death waits for no one! Come, and let us caper under the ever-fleeting pale moonlight and taste the sweet nectar of our hunt!"

... Okay, what just happened? Did those words really just come out of Mountain Girl's mouth? Did that mean she just broke character? If she did, then oh crap because that usually meant things were getting serious.

On a related note, I couldn't help but wonder what the Chimera was thinking while it patiently waited for her to finish her piece. I didn't have to speculate for long, though, as just half a moment after the thought crossed my mind, the creature ponderously raised its front leg and tried to hit Rinne with a backhanded swipe.

I instinctively wanted to call out again and warn her, but she was way ahead of me and deftly got out of the way of the attack. In fact, she even had the time to do it by jumping high into the air and doing a backflip and even an axel before landing. Because of this, my original warning turned into a mildly exasperated, "Just dodge out of the way like a normal person, will you?"

She completely ignored my words and lunged forward while shouting something along the lines of *"Sakurabana Ranbu!"* While yelling so, she dashed forth and delivered a shallow, vertical cut onto the Chimera's raised arm, following which she let go of her sword and allowed its momentum to carry it into the air. That was already pretty damn baffling, but then she lowered her stance, turned 360 degrees on her heel, and raised both of her hands to her right ear, and as if it was the most natural thing in the world, her aggravating o-katana (that was the technical term of her sword, by the way) landed in her open palms. Once she grabbed hold of her weapon, she immediately struck forth with a vicious stab that landed on the Chimera's abdomen.

This time it looked like a nice, deep wound, but I knew from experience that it wouldn't give it more than a pause. More importantly, the creature still had its arm raised after the missed backhand slap, and it wasn't hard to figure out what it would do next.

Now then, it was exactly at this moment that I caught up with Rinne, so I did the only sane thing in this situation and grabbed her by the waist. She momentarily stiffened under my touch, but I didn't care, as I immediately heaved hard and flung her to the side, and not a moment too soon, as the aforementioned arm was already in the process of descending upon her head.

She let go of her sword, still embedded in the creature, either by surprise or on purpose for her next move, as the moment we were out of immediate harm's way, she grabbed hold of the billowing shroud attached to the hilt of her weapon and yanked it right out of its belly. It didn't end there, though, as she proceeded to swing the whole sword around in a circle using said shroud.

"Tenka Daiwa Zan!"

I had many questions about that, such as why she was calling her attacks, or how the heck she planned to cut anything like that, without proper edge alignment, but then such thoughts were immediately overwritten by a sudden prickling sensation that told me to dodge right the hell away from where I was standing. My legs moved on their own to comply even before I could give them a conscious order, and before I knew it I was already rolling forward on the hard ground.

That still wasn't enough, so I stumbled even farther forward, and I only stopped when the sense of imminent danger subsided. I hastily rose to my feet and looked back, but couldn't see anything dangerous. On the other hand, I could most certainly hear something dangerous, and when I looked over there, I noticed one of the trees by the footpath begin to tilt and then fall right onto the spot where I'd stood a few seconds ago.

I was startled by the loud cracking noise of the branches breaking, but once I collected my wits, I attempted to put the pieces together and figure out what exactly just happened. It didn't take long to form a hypothesis: Apparently, when Rinne swung her sword around in an orbit, she hit the tree, as professed by the clean horizontal cut on the still-standing stump. Considering we were talking about a tree that was about as thick as my waist, that meant her sword was really freaking sharp, so I had high expectations when I glanced over to the Chimera, only to immediately be let down.

At the moment, Onikiri was embedded about two fingers deep in the creature's shoulder, with Mountain Girl still holding on to the purple cloth on the other end. The same sword, the same strike, two completely different outcomes. Why, though?

I naturally had an idea. If I had to make an educated guess based on the evidence at hand, I'd say that the thing giving the infuriating sword its unnatural sharpness wasn't the actual metal blade, but the ominously glowing magenta mist coming off of it. My gut said that it was probably the result of some kind of enchantment that gave it its terrifying cutting power. However, as the class rep had pointed out on numerous occasions, Chimeras were really scary for all the supernatural folks because they were very resistant to magic. Well, that, plus the fact that they were unrelenting, regenerating murder monsters, but let's not split hairs.

That meant that, with the cutting enchantments nullified, Onikiri was exactly as dangerous to the hulking monstrosity in front of us as an ordinary sword. Some ancient evil-slaying sword, amirite? Now granted, Rinne had still managed to land a couple of really solid wounds already, but I couldn't tell whether that was due to the blade, her fancy techniques, or just the Chimera pretending to be a punching bag.

As if it realized I had just called it that, the eyes of the large creature focused on Rinne, and it opened its mouth to let out a deafening roar. I instinctively braced myself, but to my further confusion, the Chimera only raised its arm again in the exact same motion it did the first time. It didn't try to bite, or to use its claws... Hell, even the way it was moving towards Mountain Girl felt more telegraphed than the bestial pounces the first one did when we fought... or rather when it tried to eat me and I was mostly running away, but again, splitting hairs is bad.

This was weird already, but then Rinne yanked her sword back into her hand and took up a stance, and...

"Sakurabana Ranbu!"

... Yep, it was the exact same move. She did the whole 360 twirl, too, which incidentally took her just under the incoming backhanded slap, and then she once again stabbed forth. This verified two things: Rinne was indeed calling out her attacks, and the Chimera was acting really weird.

I couldn't do much about the former other than shaking my head in disapproval, but the latter was something that deserved closer scrutiny. The creature's movements, while not exactly mechanical, were somewhat stiff and had short delays in them every once in a while, as if it had to think hard before making certain moves.

"Hisho Taikakutachi!"

I ignored the way Rinne attacked by throwing her sword behind her back after a diagonal cut, only to catch it with her other hand, spin around in place, and slash down from the other direction.

On second thought, no. Let's not ignore that. What the actual hell was that!? To be fair, I'm no sword expert (though as far as I know, I might've used to be one, but that's neither here nor there), but even I could tell that randomly spinning around mid-combat, exposing your back to the opponent, and doing all that while also letting go of your weapon in the process was not exactly the most sensible of moves. It looked flashy and a tiny bit cool, but do you know what would've been even cooler? If after all that song-and-dance routine, she'd actually hit the hulking monstrosity in front of her!

I mean, the Chimera was huge and wide-open! How hard could it be to hit it!? Well, by the looks of it, it had either its EVA or its LCK stat maxed because Mountain Girl managed to whiff both the initial and the follow-up stroke! Oh, and now she was extensively flourishing her blade before she tried to parry an incoming fist. It naturally didn't work, as even though the edge bit into the flesh of the incoming arm, it did little to stop its momentum, and Rinne was sent careening into the nearby bushes on the other side of the road.

Now then, since we'd finally gotten a little breather from her oh-so-practical swordsmanship, let's focus on my previous line of thoughts about the Chimera again. In short, it was really peculiar. Just now, it didn't even react to getting cut. In fact, it didn't acknowledge any of its injuries, did it? Sure, you could say that the first Chimera was also prone to under-reaction to, say, getting its arm bitten off, but it was still reacting. This one didn't even flinch from being skewered by a sword. Twice.

Also, while we were still at the differences, there was a startling lack of transformations. By now the Chimera should have shown at least some kind of physical change. Maybe longer limbs, or some kind of carapace on the arms to deflect cuts, or some other kind of adaptation fitting for the situation. For comparison, the first Chimera already had a silly whip arm by this point, but I couldn't see anything even remotely similar to it this time.

Now put all of that together, and consider the fact that the thing's head was still glowing like an off-season Christmas tree, and it didn't take Sherlock Holmes to deduce that something suspicious was afoot. I was just about to formulate a plan for taking a closer look at that magical light show, but then my attention was grabbed by a small movement in the corner of my vision.

I glanced over and saw Rinne jump back out of the shrubbery with a furious glint in her eyes, sword raised high as if she was about to declare that "There could be only one," or some other similarly dramatic line. That wasn't what really drew my attention, though, but the small, indistinct shape following in her wake.

"I knew it!" I exclaimed with a fifty-fifty mixture of exasperation and vindication, my legs automatically taking up the fake Phasing position. I rushed forth, though I technically didn't actually move forward at all, and I reappeared right next to the irate huntress. I caught a glimpse of her shocked expression, but didn't dwell on it, and instead I focused on the small creature leaping through the air behind her.

My right hand extended with a practiced motion, and my fingers unceremoniously grasped onto a thin, lizard-like tail. For a moment I was even surprised how easy this was, but I figured all the Phasing training with Brang paid off. I'm not going to lie, I felt just a little smug at the moment. The Fauns considered my training method of having them toss weapons into the air for me to catch after Phasing across the room to be odd and of little practical use, but look at this! I just caught a... thing.

Speaking of which, it was about time I took a closer look at the tiny creature in my hand. It was about the size of a common house cat, except scaly, with a ratlike head, and instead of front paws, it had something that reminded me of a praying mantis's graspers on steroids. Once its first shock over suddenly being caught and held upside down by its tail passed, it began to struggle and wave its forelegs around with a high-pitched screech.

"Whoa there!" I exclaimed by reflex as I waved the mini Chimera around to keep it from clawing at my arm. I don't know if it was the screech, the words, or just my flailing around, but it made the big Chimera let out an anemic-yet-still-loud roar that startled me for a moment. I glanced at it, and on a whim I swung the creature in my hand towards it.

I'm not going to claim it was thanks to my amazing aiming skills, but I managed to throw the tiny creature right into its gaping jaws. The big guy continued to roar, completely disregarding its flailing spawn in its mouth, and then it closed it without any fanfare, resulting in a crunching noise and a soft "Ouch" from me.

"So that is why you were staying back," Rinne noted beside me as she did that thing where she flicked her sword to get the blood off or something. "We were almost certain your courage must have left you in face of an enduring opponent such as this, yet it appears you have predicted the emergence of threats outside our expectations instead. You have our sincerest gratitude."

"Err... You are welcome," I replied with a good amount of uncertainty. Somehow polite and well-spoken Rinne was even creepier than oddball chuuni Rinne, and the way she talked kept sending shivers down my spine. Because of all this, I weighed my options and decided that it was probably in my best interest to end this battle as soon as possible.

With that in mind, I faced the monster slowly lumbering towards us, with bits and pieces of its unfortunate spawn still hanging from its jaws, and as I did so, something finally clicked with me: I wasn't afraid of this thing. Now granted, I had access to free and unlimited teleportation to get out of harm's way, and the creature wasn't focused on me, either, but the fact that I felt zero apprehension towards it was still odd, so I tried to analyze my feelings. I didn't stand still while doing so, though, as I slowly began to circle the creature from the right. Rinne, as if following my lead, did the same from the other direction, and it took until the three of us formed a more or less straight line for me to finally put my finger on my source of incongruity: my danger sense wasn't giving me any signals.

Granted, it wasn't actually targeting me or attacking in my direction at the moment, but I could still vividly remember the last time I faced off against one of these things, and I had been feeling a constant sense of pressure when I was looking at it. It felt like I had its attention, and it had the potential to hurt and kill me, so my danger sense was constantly warning me to be wary of it. There was none of that this time. Did it mean that I was safe? I wouldn't go that far, but it was certainly a completely different experience.

In the meantime, the Chimera seemingly vacillated about which one of us it should face, and eventually it decided to turn towards Mountain Girl, which incidentally also meant that it completely turned its back on me. This settled it. No creature, no matter how dumb, would obliviously expose its back to an aggressor. The fact that the still-unchanged beast in front of me did so could only mean one of two things: it either completely disregarded my existence, or it didn't possess all of its faculties because of some kind of magical shenanigans. I was inclined towards the latter.

So what would any self-respecting alleged Chimera slayer do in this situation, with their opponent completely open and just asking for a back-stabbing? Well, I wouldn't know because I wasn't one, but I did have a plan in mind, and this guy just made it all the more hassle-free. Step one was to just wait for Rinne to make her move.

"Mumyō kansatsu ken!"

Oh, look. Another new attack with a fancy Japanese name. How very surprising.

This time she flourished her sword, and as she did so, the blade left behind a series of afterimages, following which she delivered a sequence of quick jabs at the Chimera's joints. The wounds were superficial at best, but the pause they gave to the thing was all I could ever ask for. I once again reflexively assumed the sham Phasing stance and then reappeared right on top of it. I raised my arm high, curled my fingers into a fist, and struck down onto the top of its skull.

Needless to say, that was all an act. I didn't want to break my knuckle, so I slowed my descending fist at the very last moment so that I only ended up lightly knocking on its head. There was no reaction whatsoever, but it was no biggie; I more or less expected as much. If it was a complex enchantment, like the curse on Emese, I had a feeling that surface contact wouldn't cut it. I had to go deeper, and thankfully I had the right tool for the job.

With that decided, I immediately brandished my invisible phantom limb and plunged it right into the Chimera's skull. There was no resistance whatsoever, which was just a little surprising. The thing's magic resistance was strong enough to render even a magical sword capable of cutting through a mature tree like it was butter borderline useless, yet my mysterious extra appendage was completely unaffected. It was food for thought, but for later, as I made contact with whatever was giving off the magical halo, and my consciousness was immediately sucked in.

What I found was... odd. Granted, I didn't have a ton of experience with poking around in the metaphysical innards of living things, but after the customary wading through a syrupy river that tasted like turpentine mixed with all the songs of an entire death metal album being played at the same time, I found myself inside of a spacious cavern instead of the core of records I was expecting.

The place itself was perfectly spherical, and there wasn't an opening on it anywhere. This normally would've made me wonder where I'd entered, but I was getting used to the un-intuitiveness of spaces like this, so I didn't let it bother me. Now, back to my environment. I looked around, at least as much as the concept was applicable, and if I had to pinpoint the most striking feature in this cavity, it was definitely the thing in the middle.

Let me try to describe it as best as I can: inside the center of the cavern, there was a comparatively small, white ball of light. It had two long strings connecting it to the opposite ends of the hollow affixing it in place, with countless thin, jointed legs sprouting out of it and touching the walls. All in all, it reminded me of one of those long-legged cellar spiders, except with an absurd amount of limbs. I followed one of them and soon realized that when it touched the wall, it would ever-so-slightly change its shape. Then it would move and tap it elsewhere, which resulted in a different portion of it changing its form or texture.

After some consideration, I also tried to touch the wall of the cavern surrounding me. I gingerly reached out, wary of what might await me, but I made contact all the same. What I found was fairly unexpected. Instead of waves of fragmented images, sounds, and other sensory records, I was hit by a nauseating torrent of nothing. I shut the contact off, and it didn't take me long to realize what had just happened and where I was. This place, this cavern, was where the records of the being were held, right until it died, leaving behind a hollow sphere, the negative imprint of its soul, so to speak.

But then what was the thing in the middle? I cautiously approached it and extended my invisible, intangible hand towards the white ball. What I found was yet another abnormal thing. It was very similar to an enchant-ment I could find on an artifact, but insanely complex, and this time, I didn't mean it in the overengineered way seen on things like the dragon-slaying spear. No, this thing was the real deal.

I didn't know how much time I had to read it, so I tried to skim as much of its functions as I possibly could. From the looks of it, the whole, multilayered enchantment was centered around an extremely extensive and complex series of if/or/then nodes with pathways forming an enormous, tree-like structure, with connections skipping between branches and routinely looping back to the base of the tree. Even as I observed them, I could see small bundles of light traveling down the lanes between the nodes. Some of them seemed to govern basic tasks, such as breathing, while other segments managed complex motor functions and even decision-making based on the state of and feedback from other nodes.

Long story short, the white spider inside the cavern was pretty much a magical artificial intelligence puppeteering the body of the Chimera based on behavioural trees. Of course, this was a gross oversimplification of the simultaneously crude-yet-brilliant piece of magical engineering in front of me, but not an inaccurate one, and if I'd had a mouth, I would've most definitely whistled in approval.

I wondered, could I possibly gain control of the Chimera by taking control of this white spider? I had detected a couple of anti-tampering mechanics, but nothing that would pose an insurmountable obstacle. I just needed some time. Unfortunately, I had less of that than I thought.

Before I knew it, I was abruptly thrown out of the metaphysical space of the hollow cavern, and after blinking a few times, I found myself staring at the sky on my back. It didn't take a genius to figure out that at some point the Chimera must have thrown me off its back, and once I got out of the range of my phantom limb, I was kicked back into boring old reality again. The fact that exiting this way felt pretty much like getting squeezed through the eye of a needle, and its ill effects on my poor brain, went without saying.

I tried to get my bearings first, but then my danger sense abruptly gave me the red alert signal, and so I forced my body to roll to the side, just in time to get out of the way of the enormous clawed fist descending towards the spot I'd occupied just a second ago. I kept rolling and only stopped when I was well out of arm's reach. After a quick shake of my head, I did my best to rise to my feet, made slightly harder by how the world kept spinning even after I stopped.

I was just about to give up on the prospect and instead focus on catching my breath, but I received help from an unexpected source. As I looked up, I just noticed Rinne landing behind the flailing creature after doing another unnecessary axel, and then she dashed over to my side and offered me a hand.

"What have you done to the creature of the underworld?"

"What did it look like?" I asked back as I accepted her help and rose to my feet.

"It stopped moving for approximately four seconds," she answered right away. "After that, it became exceedingly aggressive and threw you off."

I observed the Chimera while listening to her explanation, and seeing how it was randomly roaring and pounding the ground without any rhyme or reason, I couldn't help but wonder if I might've accidentally tripped some kind of anti-tampering fail-safe. Oh well, there was no point in crying over spilled milk; I just had to clean up my mess, and everything would be perfectly fine.

"I think I can end this in one more attack."

My white lie made Mountain Girl nod in approval, and she asked me, "Do you require support?"

I took another look at the flailing creature, and then answered, "I would appreciate it if you could stop its movements for a few seconds."

Rinne gave me another wordless nod, clenched her hand around the hilt of her sword, and she immediately rushed back into the fray. I was honestly a little dumbfounded. Was this the same person I had been forced to hang out with for the past week? Where are the cringy lines? Where are the condescending looks? And when the hell did she become so dependable? I had to wonder, was this the influence of her sword, or the lack thereof? Either way, I had to admit that reasonable Mountain Girl, as much as that sounded like an oxymoron, was pretty useful in this situation.

Anyhow, I let her get the attention of the Chimera again while I found my center, and once I was ready, I broke into a run and circled around the two of them from the left. Once I felt like I was in position, I gave her the signal, and she wordlessly raised her sword over her shoulder in response.

"*Mumyō kansatsu ken!*"

Oh, I think that's the same one she used the last time. Neat. I waited for the target to stagger, and once the path of approach was clear, I once again fake Phased right next to it. This time I decided to add some extra flair to my move, so instead of a fist, I stabbed towards its temple with just two fingers. It was for only show, as it was my phantom limb that did all the heavy lifting, and once it made contact I immediately dived into the space between spaces. This time the process of getting to the cavern was much smoother, and the moment I was back in front of the white spider, I plunged right into it.

I didn't know how much time I would have to do this, so I zeroed in on the more basic metabolic functions. In retrospect, that turned out to be a bad idea, as those nodes were bloody complicated, and I quickly realized that messing with them could easily result in irreparable damage to the body. Since I was running out of time, I decided to go after my second-best bet and scoured the section of the behavioural tree for anything dealing with motor skills. By tracing the branches back as far as possible, I ultimately found the bundle of nodes responsible for communicating between the decision-making nodes, the nodes responsible for interpreting sensory data, and the ones dealing with motor control.

I had no time to mess around, so I swiftly and decisively used my phantom limb to carve the whole section out of the tree. It was unexpected, but throughout the entire process, the knowledgeable corner of my brain remained entirely silent. That meant that none of these nodes were plot relevant in any shape or form. I wasn't entirely sure I liked the sound of that, but it made my life easier, so I decided not to look the gift horse in the mouth, and instead I retracted myself from the cavern.

Upon returning to my body, the first thing I noticed was that I was still standing in the same pose I was when I left, metaphorically speaking. Same for the Chimera, and even Rinne, though she probably did so for different reasons. Anyhow, I took a deep breath, and gently pushed on the head of the creature. The moment pressure was applied, its balance completely crumbled, and it collapsed like a puppet with its strings cut (which was, to be fair, entirely accurate). My companion took a confused step back, but when she realized that the body was not moving, she finally relaxed and let her weapon down.

"Has this creature shuffled off its mortal coil?"

"Erm... Yes, it's very much dead," I stated just a tad forcefully as I assumed a slightly more casual posture, as well.

"What kind of secret technique was that? We have never seen its like," she inquired as she took a step closer to me, and unsubtly observed my right hand.

"It's... a sure-kill move that I developed. It needs a lot of preparation, but if it hits a weak point, it's a one-hit kill," I lied like a champ with all the conviction I could manage at the moment.

"A truly terrifying technique, if there ever was one," Rinne noted with one gloved hand on her chin, and all of a sudden her lips widened into the creepy slasher smile I hoped I would never get to see again. "Let us proceed to spill the vile creature's blood and viscera!"

Aaaand here we go. Bye soft-spoken and reasonable Rinne, hi annoying chuuni Mountain Girl. I was really curious about what *that* was about, but I figured I should try to figure it out on another occasion.

"No. It's already dead."

"But Rinne wants to!" she whined as she waved her sword towards the corpse on the ground. "Onikiri also says that you steal stage lights and that we deserve to see the woods run red with blood!"

"Just leave it alone, will you? We've already killed the Chimera, and that's what's important. Come on, let's go."

"We must dispose of the body," she insisted as she carelessly waved her blade around, forcing me to take a step back. "Let Rinne at least mince it! Just a little bit!"

"You don't have to. It will dissolve like the small ones over time. Let's just leave it here and go." Mountain Girl was giving me a hurt look, and she even puffed out her cheeks in the most overdone display of sulking I have ever seen, so I decided to try to cajole her a little. "Come on, let's celebrate a successful hunt. I know a good gyro place nearby; it's my treat."

As expected, it only took a single mention of food for her to immediately rewrap her sword and state, "Rinne also believes that celebrations are an important part of the hunt. Please lead the way, Leonard-san."

I was tempted to roll my eyes at her transparent gluttony, but I refrained and instead told her, "Let's do that, but first, we should clean ourselves up a little."

I pointed at the leaf stuck in her hair, probably ever since her tumble in the bushes, and then I followed it up by pointing at the restroom by the end of the footpath. That was about all the encouragement she needed.

"Come, Leonard-san!"

"Go ahead. I still have to find something I dropped," I replied, and she did as I told without suspecting a thing. The moment she was out of earshot, I let out a pent-up sigh and said, "[Transport the cadaver to our hidden fort. I shall be with you once I've seen this task to completion.]"

There was no answer, but I knew for sure that the message was received, so after sparing one last glance at the remains of the Chimera, I quietly followed after the gluttonous huntress, my mind already filled to the brim with ideas.

CHAPTER 11

PART 1

"Oh great, and now it's raining, too..." I mumbled under my breath as I held out my hand and felt another small droplet hit my palm. It was barely a drizzle, but considering how dark the clouds were before the sun went down, I had a feeling it was going to get worse, so I hastened my steps on the sidewalk.

I could've certainly Phased over to my destination if the weather truly turned for the worse, but for now, I decided to walk. Mainly because I was already feeling the side effects of manipulating the magical substratum setting in, and I was afraid that taking the shortcut might make them worse, but also because I'd eaten one gyro too many in the company of Mountain Girl, and moving like this helped my digestion. It wasn't like I was late from anywhere, anyway, and the open air never hurt anyone. Well, except those silly aliens from *The War of the Worlds*, but that's beside the point.

It had been just about a quarter of an hour since I'd finally managed to separate myself from my temporary hunting partner, which was unusually tiresome this time around, as she was quite insistent about inviting me to another hunting trip, this time to the Congo to find something called a mokele-mbembe. I naturally declined her offer just as insistently, and she gave up after her second supersized gyro. As for the rest of our time in the restaurant, we'd only talked about small, inconsequential things, like the weather, or the food, or how to clean bloodstains out of fabrics. In the end, we said our farewells on amicable terms, and only then did I realize that I'd completely forgotten to unambiguously tell her about how I was already in a relationship and that she should look for greener pastures.

Oh well. I'd do it next time, I figured. Or better yet, I'd avoid her until she leaves the island, so there won't *be* a next time. That would probably work, too, and it would *definitely* be less awkward. Hurray for procrastination!

While I was considering all that, I continued walking until I unceremoniously arrived back at the spot where I'd left the body of the disabled Chimera. The place was still a mess, with the fallen tree and the bloodstains and everything, but the creature was nowhere to be found. Good. Brang and Co. were really efficient as usual.

"[Did the disposal of the lifeless meat proceed without any unforeseen circumstances?]"

It might have looked like I was only growling to myself, but after a long second the dirt next to me was kicked up by the impact of a heavy body. When I glanced over, I was met with the cloaked, bowing figure of Karukk. I had no idea why he was sitting on a tree branch until I called out to him, but it wasn't exactly important in the grand scheme of things. I waited for him to finish saluting, but when he kept his head down, I prompted him by lightly clearing my throat and uttering a subtle "[so?]"

"[Oh, excuse me, my lord,]" he sputtered in a hurry as he straightened his back. "[Yes, sir. We've taken the carcass of the Chimera to the base, as per your instructions.]"

"[Good man.]"

"[Thank you, my lord. Your kind words are wasted on me.]"

The Faun kept beaming at me even under the scrutiny of my most skeptical look, and in the end I was forced to stifle a groan and turn in place to face him.

"... Okay, time out," I said as I switched to English. "What's the deal?"

"[What could you possibly mean?]"

Karukk's ears swiveled around in the way I'd long since learned to associate with embarrassment. It was an amusing little tic all the Fauns shared, but seeing it in this context only made me even more confused.

"I'm talking about how polite and courteous you're acting right now. It's creeping me out a little."

"[My apologies, my lord. It was not my intention to make you uneasy.]" At this point he finally noticed how I was frowning at him, so he hastily added, "[I-I mean... Seeing your battle with the Chimera finally opened my eyes. I apologize that it took so long.]"

"... Come again?"

"[The way you've slain the Chimera with a single strike, it opened my eyes, and I realized that the general was right about you all along.]" Karukk paused for a long moment, then he lowered his head and added, in a much quieter voice, "[Please forgive the disrespectful ways I've addressed you in the past.]

This was yet another one of those head-scratching moments, where it took me a long time to figure out just what the heck was going on, but then I finally managed to put together a working hypothesis.

It was easy to forget about it, due to how friendly and goofy they'd acted lately, but the Fauns were something of a magically engineered super-soldier race with a warrior culture ethos built into them. They'd been following my lead mostly due to Brang vouching for me and because I was acknowledged as Snowy's brother (and regent, for some reason that was still entirely unclear to me). If my hunch was right, seeing me actually defeat a Chimera might've made Karukk reevaluate me, and then the whole honour-bound retainer thing kicked in, and so he started creeping me out. Quite elementary, and annoying, my dear Watson.

Now, there was only one question remaining: How do I nip this in the bud before it spreads to the others?

"For the record, I didn't actually *slay* the Chimera," I noted as I pointedly faced the bloodstained walkway again.

"[I'm sorry, my lord, but don't understand.]"

I glanced back at him and stated, "I mean that I couldn't slay the Chimera because it was not really alive to begin with. It was just an empty body puppeteered by magic."

"[Are you certain, my lord? I don't think that should be possible.]"

"Well, it is," I grumbled as my brows furrowed once again. "I simply turned off the magic, and the Chimera with it. It wasn't nearly as impressive as it might've looked like from the outside."

Karukk stayed silent for a long while, and for a moment I almost thought I got through to him, but then he shook his head.

"[So you've accurately grasped the weakness of the creature and neutralized it without suffering any injuries in the process. I fail to see how that is any less impressive, my lord.]"

"Oh, come on. Please don't twist things like that."

"[I'm not twisting anything, my lord,]" he answered, accompanied by a genuine smile. "[If anything, your modesty makes me admire you even more.]"

I sent the friendly Faun a flat look, but he was entirely serious, so in the end I let out a sigh and asked, "So for the record, does that mean that you fully acknowledge me right now?"

"[Yes, my lord.]"

"So if I gave you an order right now, you would follow it?"

"[Certainly, my lord.]" He responded without hesitation.

"Without any question?" Karukk gave me a determined nod, so I firmly told him, "In that case, I order you to stop being polite to me. Oh, and also, stop tagging 'my lord' at the end of your sentences. It's annoying."

"[But...]"

Whatever protests he might have had, he immediately swallowed them back after noticing my glare.

"[If that is your wish, then...]" I lowered my brows even further at his words, so he hastily corrected himself. "[I mean, sure, my... um... boss?]"

I kept staring daggers at him for just a little longer, but at last I eased it up and commented, "I give that a passing grade." He was entirely too relieved by my words, so I shook my head and kept the conversation rolling by asking, "When I said that the Chimera was controlled by magic, you said it was impossible. Why do you think so?"

The Faun was seemingly taken aback by my sudden question, and it took him a fairly long time to formulate an answer.

"[Chimeras are very resistant to the mystic arts.]" That was something I already knew, so I gestured for him to elaborate. "[As far as I know, trying to forcefully wrest control away from one's master would be impossible even for a Lord of the Abyss.]"

"What if the thing was already dead, and a complex enchantment was operating the body?"

There was another long beat, and then Karukk told me, in an unsure tone, "[I'm sorry boss, but I'm not an expert when it comes to Chimeras *or* the mystic arts. I have no idea.]"

"Don't worry. I already have a theory about what's going on. I was just curious if you could give me another clue." While we talked, the weather was getting even worse, so I ultimately told him, "I think I should get going soon. Make sure the Chimera arrives at the secret base in one piece. I'll head over later to examine it. Until then, keep an eye on it."

Instead of answering, Karukk only gave me a quick salute, and then he immediately dashed away. He probably found the whole discussion about as awkward as I did, so I didn't blame him. As for the Chimera, I wasn't really worried about it getting up anytime soon the same way I wasn't worried that a car with its ignition cables cut would start up on its own. I also made sure to disable any tracking or surveillance magic I found inside its magical operation system, so I wasn't worried about someone following the Fauns back to the base, either, but taking another look at the enchantment inside it couldn't hurt anyone. Well, except my head, but that was unavoidable.

That said, the drizzle was getting thicker by the minute, so I hastily buttoned up my coat and left the scene of the battle while trying my best to ignore my throbbing head. Because I had to concentrate on that, I walked slower than usual, and it took me a solid twenty minutes to get home. It was already dark outside, and the weather went from *the air is a little wet* to *it's going to start pouring down at any moment so hard that even Noah would be freaked out.* Because of this, and since I could see the light in the living room from the outside, I opened my front door without even bothering with the keys.

"I'm home," I announced my arrival by reflex, only to freeze in my tracks because of the rumbling noise of multiple people rushing towards me. I glanced in the direction of the sound, and I was met with the bewildered faces of the entire gang staring at me from the other side of the door leading into the living room, all of them looking as if they'd just seen a ghost. After a long beat, I closed the door behind me and uttered a supremely confused "What?"

That single word seemed to have drained all the tension out of their air, and my friends let out a collective sigh of relief at my expense, followed by Angie slapping Josh on the shoulder and declaring, "You owe me five Jen now!"

"We didn't actually bet!" my friend objected, only to be literally swept aside as a blonde missile sailed past him, with its targeting reticule firmly set on me.

My otherwise-well-honed girl-catching reflexes may have gotten a little rusty due to the rain, as the princess's charge completely blindsided me.

"You see? I told you he would be all right!" my girlfriend declared as she glomped me, and then followed it up by a rib-cage-creaking hug that pushed all the air right out of my lungs.

"Elly, I just came in from the rain," I tried to warn her, but she completely ignored me and continued to bury her face into my chest with extra vigor.

"I knew you didn't explode!"

"What? Explode? What exactly is—" "Going on?" I wanted to ask, but I swallowed the end of the sentence down as I noticed Judy also coming my way.

Her approach was less bombastic than the princess's, but her expression, which was even harder to read than usual, immediately put me on edge.

"Um... hi, Dormouse? How's it going?"

"Hush, Chief," my deadpan girlfriend chided me while maintaining her inscrutable expression. "I'm currently contemplating whether I should hug you because you're all right, or kick you because you made us worry."

"... Normally I would prefer the former, but as I was just saying—"

I got exactly that far before my dear assistant came to a conclusion, and she stepped forth to embrace me by the waist. Well, so much for my unheeded warning about my coat being drenched to the point I felt like I was wearing a small lake. Oh well, I tried. Let's look on the bright side of things; at least she didn't kick me... though considering her track record, I doubt it would've been more than a tickle, anyway.

While my girlfriends indulged themselves in holding on to me as if they were afraid I'd run away, I turned my attention towards the rest of our group still clustered around the doorway leading into my living room. On a cursory glance, they appeared fine enough. They were still wearing their school uniforms, with only a few small scrapes here and there they probably deemed too minor to bother Angie about. Speaking of our resident Celestial, she was gazing at us with affectionate eyes, but with a smile that told me that if she'd had a bowl of popcorn, she'd be chomping down on it like she was at the cinema.

Aside from her, there was a slightly annoyed Josh shaking his head at the sight (I would've bet my left kidney that he was jealous of my current situation, like the self-awareness-deficient nincompoop he was), a considerably more annoyed class rep (she was even doing her menacing thing with her glasses), and my relieved sister, whose expression told me she'd also wanted to come over and hug me but considered the situation too crowded already. Note to self: give her a suitably brotherly head pat once I was free, for being such a considerate little sister.

Once I'd completed my observations, it was time to address the elephant in the room.

"For the record, I still don't understand what's going on. Could you please tell me why you guys are so worked up right now?"

"We're not *worked up*; we're just relieved because we thought you were dead."

Ammy's answer was surprising enough, but the way the rest of my friends nodded along with her words only made me more apprehensive.

"Why would I be...?" I began, only to stop and then change my original question into, "You know what? How about we discuss this once you let me sit down first? I'm wet, tired, and my head hurts."

"Sure," Josh stepped back and gestured for me to come into my own house, but before I could take the first step, Judy also put some distance between us and began to deftly unbutton my coat. Once she realized what she was doing Elly immediately let go, as well, and stood behind me to help me out of my outerwear. I was thankful for their attentiveness, but the moment my wet coat was off, my dear assistant began to pat me down from head to toe. She completely disregarded my wryest of looks, and once she touched every PG-13 nook and cranny of my body, she stepped back and declared, "He's uninjured."

Elly and Snowy let out a relieved breath in unison, but I ignored them, and instead I deftly slipped by my girlfriends, kicked off my shoes, and entered the living room without any further incidents. I walked over to my usual comfy chair and unceremoniously plopped down onto it. The rest of the group followed my example, though not by literally sitting on my chair. That would've been just plain weird.

"It's a little narrow here..." Elly stated on my left as she tried her best to sit on my armrest.

"It can't be helped," Judy added on my right, almost losing her balance and falling into my lap in the process.

I've spoken too soon, haven't I? Well, at least the rest of the group was slightly more reasonable, as they picked the couch instead. It wasn't designed for four people, so it was a little crowded over there, but they didn't seem to mind it too much.

Once my girlfriends finished their balancing act and everyone settled down, I took a deep breath and decided on a blunt approach.

"Okay, so as far as I can gather, you guys thought I exploded or something. Care to explain what you mean by that?"

"Precisely what it sounds like," Ammy huffed while crossing her arms.

"And I'm asking you to please elaborate a little on that already. I still have no idea what you are talking about."

The peanut gallery shared a look between one another, and at the end of the day, it was Josh who proverbially stepped forth.

"Before the battle with Dr. Robatto, he claimed that you were also with us. He called you out." He paused for a moment, so I gestured for him to proceed, as so far I hadn't heard anything new. "We thought he was bluffing, but then the woman with him pointed her hand at a building, and the whole street corner exploded with a *KABOOM!*"

"Personally I think it was more of a *KRAKADOOM!*" Angie chimed in, only to be summarily ignored.

"Oh, right. That happened," I noted with a belated realization. "But I told you I would be off Chimera hunting, so why did you make such a fuss about it?"

"We didn't at the time," Ammy cut in with a frown. "But then after the battle, we found your spear at the scene."

"Oh, I get it now! Because it was there, you thought I was also at the scene and got vaporized!"

"Don't smile while you say that," Judy chided me while simultaneously pinching my shoulder.

"Right!" my other girlfriend seconded as she pointed a nostalgic accusatory finger at my nose. "We were really scared when we found it in pieces between the rubble, you know!"

"What? It's broken?" I clicked my tongue and whispered, "Damn, it was a perfectly good spear. I didn't even get to properly try it out yet..."

"I'm sorry to hear that, but could we stay on topic?" Ammy interjected again, her fingers already playing with the frame of her glasses. "Were you really in the Restricted Space with us?"

"No, of course not," I replied with the utmost sincerity. I mean, I wasn't lying, as I'd only dropped by for a moment, so statistically speaking, I really wasn't. She was still giving me a critical glare, so I took a deep breath and began to explain myself.

"I had one of the Fauns act as a lookout in the area. Lab Coat Guy thinks that I can use illusions, so when they detected someone there with Snowy's Sigil hiding them, they thought it was me."

"And why was he holding your spear?" came the next logical question from the class rep.

"Due to a long string of inexplicable coincidences," I vaguely told her with a toothy grin, much to her frustration.

"Is he all right?" Snowy inquired in a low voice while Ammy was busy silently glaring at me, so I sent her a considerably more natural smile and nodded.

"Yeah, Vurrok's fine. Don't worry."

My sister let out a relieved breath, but before she could add anything else to the conversation, Ammy cut in with the words, "And how exactly do you know all that?" I sent her a small smirk in return, telling her to figure it out on her own, and then a second later I could see the proverbial light bulb light up over her head. "Oh, right. That was a silly question."

I wanted to tell her that it indeed was, using my most mysterious and inscrutable voice, but I was beaten to the punch by Angie suddenly raising a hand high. I turned my attention to her, but she kept trying to raise it even higher. I figured she was waiting for me to give her the green light, which I did with a small gesture, earning me an impish grin in return.

"Question: Does that mean that you went Chimera hunting without a weapon?"

I let out a small groan and responded in a flat voice.

"Yes, Angie. It means I did just that."

"And? How did it go?" the Celestial girl pressed on with sparkling eyes, and while the others were less blatant about it, they also seemed just as curious.

"Fairly well. The Chimera showed up on schedule, and it went down with only minor collateral damage. A tree got cut down by accident, but hopefully it won't make the news."

"Collateral damage?" Josh asked while demonstrating his mastery of single-eyebrow-raise-fu. "Didn't you fight it in a Restricted Space?"

"Things kind of developed too quickly for that..." I answered just a touch sheepishly, yet it was enough to satisfy his curiosity.

"What about the hunter woman?" Judy inquired as she clumsily entwined her arm around mine, probably to stabilize herself on the armrest. When Elly realized this was an option, she hurriedly followed suit, as well, so I waited for them to finish fidgeting before I gave them my answer.

"Well, there's nothing to hunt here anymore, so with some luck, she should be leaving soon to the Congo."

"Good. That means no more moonlit dates with her, I presume."

"They weren't dates to begin with, but yes, you are correct."

My ever-so-slightly-exasperated tone fell on deaf ears, as Judy and Elly glanced at each other with a knowing look. I had a feeling I was left out of some kind of inside joke, but before I could ask, my attention was drawn to my dour best friend crossing his arms on the couch.

"So at least you managed to achieve your goals, huh? I suppose that means this day wasn't a complete bust after all."

Josh's grumbles made me raise a confused brow, but then a realization suddenly hit me like a runaway bullet train. The gang was a little down, even after they'd learned that I was fine (except for Angie, but she was Angie, so it meant nothing), but I wrote that off as just combat fatigue. However, if I had interpreted his words right...

"Please don't tell me Lab Coat Guy got away."

The frustrated groan escaping Josh's mouth was answer enough, but I still waited for him to spell it out.

"He did." There was a long beat of downcast silence after his declaration, and only then did he explain what exactly happened. "Pascal and I got him cornered for most of the battle."

I already knew that, but I figured it would've been rude (and suspicious) to tell them that, so I waited for Josh to continue. Unexpectedly enough, it was Elly who chimed in instead.

"I took care of the big one and the small ones."

Based on the combination of the proud grin and the expectant eyes, I figured she was fishing for compliments, so I didn't let her wait for long.

"That sounds amazing. You did well."

Her proud smile immediately turned into a smug one (it was a small yet very profound difference), and she snuggled even closer to me. Well, at least no one could say she was hard to please.

"I took care of the anchor point as planned," Ammy cut in with a tired voice, and when I faced her, the Celestial girl by her side also spoke up.

"I was there, too! And Lili also helped when that Galatea woman showed up! We flew all around the buildings and stuff!"

"I... I did my best," Snowy concurred, so I had no choice but to praise them, too.

"So it was a team effort. Good job."

"So, as I was saying..." This time it was Josh who raised his voice to get the reins of the conversation back in his hands, and once everyone calmed down, he continued with, "We had him on the ropes for a while. We climbed to the top of this nearby building, and then..."

Josh continued to explain what I'd already seen with my own ethereal eyes, and a few small details notwithstanding, he did a pretty good job. The only thing that made me raise a brow was when he described the top half of the office building crumbling down as "We also had some minor collateral damage," but I didn't call him out on it.

"... and then, when it looked like we finally got him for good, he fused with the big thing."

"The Biomechanical Gigant," Judy noted on the side.

"Yes, that," Josh acknowledged with a nod.

"Please elaborate," I requested, as this was the part where I wasn't present anymore.

"Right. What happened was that he flew into the air, and then he merged into the big thing's chest."

"Wait, that's not right," Elly cut in with a frown. "He didn't *merge*; the chest part opened up, and he just flew in."

"Yes, but the inside was filled with this transparent goo or what have you," Josh countered.

"I thought that was just a force field and the inside was empty," my sister added her five cents, and Josh immediately snapped his head to her.

"Was it?"

"I think so, too," Angie further agreed. "At least that's what it looked like from the air."

"Well, maybe, but..."

"Can we get to the important bits?" I asked in a low voice, and they all seemed to agree.

"You're right. Either way, Dr. Robatto entered into the thing—" Josh began to explain, only to get cut off by my assistant pointedly clearing her throat, so he quickly corrected himself. "The Gigant. He flew into the Gigant, and then it transformed."

"... I'm afraid to ask, but what exactly did it transform into?"

"It was weird!" Angie cut in again as she began to wildly gesticulate while trying to illustrate her description. "It grew even bigger, and it somehow grew a lot of these blocky metal plates all around!"

"Those looked kind of like Robatto's armour, didn't they?" Josh spoke up again, and his childhood friend readily nodded.

"They sure did! And then the arms grew together, and even those got a lot of blocky plating!"

"It looked like if a giant was wearing a costume made of cardboard boxes," Ammy noted, only to get literally booed by the enthusiastic Celestial.

"Boo! It didn't look like that at all! It was much cooler!"

"To be fair, it looked and moved like it was too bulky," my sister supplemented the description next, much to Angie's shock and horror.

"You, too, Lili!? I thought we agreed that it looked really neat!"

"I-it looked neat, but... Maybe not *really* neat?" Snowy floundered for a moment, so I decided it was a good moment to cut in myself.

"So the biomechanical whatchamacallit turned into a blocky metal monster, and it was medium-level neat. Got it. What happened after that?"

"After that, the robot woman with the big breasts came flying back." That comment made his entire entourage send him some pointed glances, so he immediately went on the defensive and added, "What? That's what she is! She is a robot, a woman, and she has big—"

"So before you dig yourself even deeper," I interrupted with a sigh, "What did she do?"

"She flew to the top of the blocky Gigant," Snowy answered in a hurry, trying her best to move the conversation away from the previous tangent.

"You know how those things don't have heads?" came the entirely rhetorical question from Angie, and I promptly nodded in the affirmative. "So she flew to where the head was supposed to be, and then a bunch of metal plates grew around her, and then there was suddenly a head! A robot head, with a big helmet! With a huge gem in the middle, and horns!"

"Wait, hold on for a moment," I requested as something finally dawned on me. A huge, blocky robot, with bulky limbs and an inexplicable horned helmet. That... sounded entirely too familiar. "I know this might sound dumb, but did any of you take a picture?"

The whole group shook their heads, but then Snowy weakly raised her hand and proposed, "I could try drawing it for you."

"You could?"

"Didn't you know?" Josh gave me an odd look and explained, "Lili's drawing skills are amazing. Her sketches alone are ten times better than the best thing I can make."

"First time I've heard about it," I admitted without any reservations and sent a questioning look at my sister in turn.

"I-I'm not that amazing. I've just... had a lot of practice because of my Sigils."

"Come on, Lili, don't sell yourself short!" Angie encouraged her even further, and I couldn't help but notice the way she was addressing her. Calling her Lili once could be a fluke, twice a mistake, but three times in a row?

Anyhow, while I pondered whether or not this was significant, the childhood friend duo successfully convinced my sister, and she left the room to get a pencil and some paper. My girlfriends also let go of me and headed for the kitchen (which they already treated as their own territory) to get some drinks, while Ammy left for the toilet, and the childhood friends began bickering about whether the colour scheme of the big robot was lame or not.

Using this impromptu break in the conversation, I decided to collect myself a little. First and foremost, I closed my eyes as I leaned back in my chair and began to gently massage my temples. The headache from before was still getting worse, but for the moment it was still manageable. It wasn't like I could do much about it, so I moved on to the next point on the agenda: Lab Coat Guy.

Considering that I'd just gotten the opportunity handed to me on a silver platter, I decided to capitalize on it by using Far Sight on him, knowing full well that doing so in my current state would only make the pounding in my head even worse. I took a deep breath, and a moment later the darkness of my closed eyelids disappeared as I found myself staring at the familiar ceiling of the common room inside Lab Coat Guy's secret headquarters.

"... and we have to do it now!"

If I could, I would've blinked in surprise at the sudden outburst near me, and so I quickly reoriented my field of view and found the three people I was expecting. The escapee of the day was in the process of power pacing up and down in front of the large aquarium, while Peabody and the at-the-moment-casually-dressed fembot were both sitting on the large beanbag chairs nearby.

"Please calm down, Friedrich. You shouldn't jump to conclusions like that," the portly nurse attempted to chide his nephew, but his words fell on deaf ears.

"I'm perfectly calm!" he exclaimed at the top of his lungs before coming to a halt and stomping his feet. "I tell you, we were deceived by the arch-mage! They set a trap for us!"

"I still think it was a great big misunderstanding..." Peabody whispered, prompting Lab Coat Guy to shake his head.

"Impossible! Think about it, Uncle! Leonard Dunning knew about things only the arch-mage could've told him about, and Pascal was there, too! They must have conspired to entrap us!"

"The probability of that is less than twenty percent," the android spoke up, only to be dismissed right away.

"I don't want to hear any more probabilities from you after what happened today, Galatea!" The fembot averted her gaze with a very human "Hmpf," following which Lab Coat Guy began pacing again.

"I tell you, we have to cut our losses and leave while we still can! They already know about this place, so first we have to move to the backup workshop at the docks!"

"If you think it's necessary..." Peabody mumbled in a disheartened tone that didn't escape the mad scientist's notice.

"Yes, I think so, and we have to do it ASAP!" he snapped, and then pointed a finger at the fembot and ordered, "Galatea, go and have the MkIII Sprockets pack everything that can be moved! Also..." At this point he paused for a while as he deeply considered something, then he concluded with, "Make sure our *guest* is also ready for transport."

Now, I didn't need to be a genius to figure out the implications of *that* line, but before I could further look into it, my break time was cut short by someone grabbing my arm again. I opened my eyes, which also cut off my Far Sight, and looked at the princess awkwardly trying to sit on the armrest again, an endeavor made considerably more difficult by the fact that she was holding on to a steaming mug with one hand while doing so.

Without further ado, I reached out to take it from her before she would accidentally scald both of us, and only then did I realize that it was my mug. I directed a questioning glance at my blissfully grinning girlfriend, and she readily told me, "It was my turn to make your tea. Go ahead, give it a try!"

She didn't need to say it twice, as I was just starting to get a little parched, anyway, and I took a sip. It was slightly different from the tea I would make, and slightly subpar compared to Judy's Annoying Butler™ blend, but it wasn't bad by any means of the imagination. I sincerely thanked her and took another gulp, only to pause when my eyes swept over the table and noticed the sketch Snowy was making under the questionably constructive oversight of the childhood friend duo.

I blinked once, just to make sure my eyes weren't playing tricks on me, then I calmly swallowed the warm drink in my mouth because I would sooner die than to do something as clichéd as a spit-take. Then, and only then, I let out a long sigh and calmly noted, "Goddammit, it really *was* a Megazord after all, wasn't it...?"

PART 2

"Take care, Chief. Be sure to rest well."

While saying so, Judy straightened my collar. It was already about as dark as it gets outside, and we both stood under the eaves of my house while she kept fiddling with my clothes, obviously reluctant to leave.

"Don't worry, Dormouse; I'll be fine," I told her as I cupped her outstretched hand in mine and gently squeezed it. "I already took some painkillers, and I don't have a fever yet, so I'll probably live."

"Nevertheless, make sure you take a hot shower once everyone leaves. Also, no more playing with enchantments for the day."

"Yes, yes. I promise."

My other girlfriend looked just a tad impatient behind her, probably because her limo was already parked in front of my driveway, so I told the both of them, "Take care on your way home, and please tell Emese I'm sorry I couldn't join her for dinner." My dear assistant only clicked her tongue in response, so I also added, "Speaking of which, have a fun evening."

"It's not going to be that," Judy grumbled under her breath, earning her a curious glance from the princess.

"Why? I thought you got along with Mom."

"It's not that," she denied with a shake of her head. "Because the Chief isn't going to be there with us, she's going to ask all kinds of *mom* questions. It's going to be embarrassing."

When I heard that, I unconsciously raised a brow as high as those things could go. Unfortunately my assistant didn't get the message, so I had to grudgingly speak up, anyway.

"Okay, I bite. What are these *mom* questions you are talking about?"

She responded with a long stare that said she wasn't entirely sure if I was serious, but then she ultimately explained herself all the same.

"Questions about how far our relationship has progressed." She paused for another long moment, and then used her chin to point at the blonde girl at her side and added, "With her."

"Oooooh, now I get it," I noted with a knowing smile, only to get gently kicked in the shin for my trouble.

"Don't laugh. It's your fault," my sulky assistant declared between two small kicks.

"What's my fault?"

"This whole misunderstanding about how our relationship works," she clarified as she finally ceased her futile, if somewhat adorable, attempts at inflicting physical violence on my poor legs. "That's why Elly's mother believes we are also going out with each other."

"We aren't?" Elly cut in with a baffled expression, so I explained:

"What Judy means is that while we are all going out, you two, in particular, are not romantically involved."

"Oooooh, I see."

The princess nodded to herself with an enlightened expression, which made my other girlfriend direct an annoyed frown at me.

"Why can't you explain things to Emese like that?"

"You could do it, too," I proposed, only to be dismissed by a shake of her head.

"I tried, but ever since you healed her injury, she's become much harder to handle. I believe she thinks I'm just shy, and she dismisses all my objections because of that."

"Wait... are you trying to tell me that Emese thinks that you're a tsundere?"

My dear assistant's eyes opened ever-so-slightly wider, only to then go to the other extreme and narrow into dangerous squints. By Judy standards, I mean.

"Chief, this isn't funny."

"I know. Do I look like I'm laughing to you?"

"Not on the surface, but I know that you do it on the inside."

"Since when can you read my mind?"

"I could always do that." After that flat response, her face finally slackened a little, and she tagged on an uncertain "What?"

"Nothing. I was just kind of expecting a Judybot gag right around now."

"Please, Chief. We must avoid overusing the same skit, or it will become stale."

"True, I suppose. By the way, what were we talking about? Before we established that I don't find this incredibly amusing in any shape or form, I mean."

"Something about Mom thinking that Judy is something called a tsun-something or something," my other girlfriend provided the answer, and my assistant responded with an appreciative grunt.

"That was one *something* too many, but you're right. The point is, we really need you to be there to clear this up; being blunt and impudent with your elders is your specialty."

"How unusually cheeky of you to say that." I punctuated my words with an irreverent shrug and then added, "Either way, you know I can't go with you guys today. I'm terribly sorry."

"No, you are not," Judy noted with a voice about as dry as the salt flats.

"... Yeah, you are right. I'm not." The roguish smile accompanying that admission only made both of my girlfriends flare up with mild disapproval, so I hastily switched over to my Charming Boyfriend Smile™ version 0.12.1, and added, "Anyhow, I wish you the best of luck, and if things really get out of hand, you can always just call me, and I'll try to smooth things over through the phone."

"That would presume you'd pick it up in the first place," came the next verbal jab my way, and I couldn't help but shake my head.

"I told you already; I didn't pick up my phone because I put it on mute, and I did that because the last time I forgot to do it before fighting a Chimera, it nearly got me killed. Multiple times, if I may add."

"I know," Judy admitted, albeit grudgingly and with another love tap on my shin.

She was obviously on the threshold to enter into a full-blown sulking mode. As a responsible boyfriend, it was my duty to prevent that from coming to pass, which I did by swiftly putting my arms around her and pulling her into a good, old-fashioned bear hug.

"Hey! No fair!" my other girlfriend called foul right away, so I opened one arm to make space for her, which she immediately took with her usual gusto. We stayed like this for a few seconds, but then I remembered something.

"Hey, princess?"

"Yes?" she responded by glancing up at me from my chest.

"Don't forget about the charm."

For a moment her brows twisted into a confused frown, but then her expression lit up as she finally realized what I was talking about, and she gave me a confident nod and an enthusiastic, "Sure!" Said nod of course ended up with her headbutting my ribs, but I was getting used to that by this point.

With that done, I said my goodbyes to my girlfriends, including multiple farewell kisses, another hug or five, and a grudging promise about talking to Emese at the earliest convenient occasion, and only then did they finally get into the limo and leave. I stayed outside and waved after them until they rounded the corner, and waited till they were completely out of sight before I headed back into the house.

"What took you this long?" came the immediate, and palpably prickly, question from the girl with the glasses still sitting on my couch. Snowy was already upstairs, based on the sound of the hair dryer coming from there, and the childhood friend duo left a while ago, so it was only the two of us left in the living room.

I gave the impatient class rep a subtle smile and told her, "Sorry, but my girlfriends can be a little high-maintenance from time to time. It's what makes them fun to be around."

"How gratuitously wholesome," was what she said, with an implied eye roll in tow. It was completely uncalled for, as I wasn't even bragging, but she moved on before I could call her out on it. "Now then, could you please tell me why you asked me to stay behind?"

"I'm fairly certain that I already did that."

"No," she rebuffed me with a temperamental huff. "You only told me you were going to show me something neat, and then winked at me."

"Did I?" I mused aloud while absently stroking my nonexistent nefarious goatee. "Oh well, it's easier to show you than to explain. But before that, give me a minute." Saying so, I walked over to the stairs, and called out, "Sis!"

After a moment I could hear a door opening on the first floor, and soon Snowy's platinum head came to view. She had her hair down, and by the looks of it, she'd recently had a quick shower.

"Yes? Is there a problem?" she inquired as she quickly made her way down the stairs and stood in front of me.

"Nah, I just wanted to tell you that Ammy and I are going over to the secret base. That said, since you already came over to my side..."

She stiffened for a moment as I raised a hand, and she let out a baffled "Hup?" sound as I placed it on the top of her head and began to vigorously rub it. Also, for the record, her hair was indeed a little damp.

"Uh... Why are you petting me?"

"Just for being a good girl in general," I told her as I continued ruffling her hair.

"Thank you?" Her response was a tad uncertain, but she didn't shy away from my touch, so I continued to spoil her right until her eyes suddenly lit up with realization and she asked, "You said you're going to the hideout, right?"

"Yes."

"Can you take a package with you?"

"So long as it's not too big, I suppose I could."

My tentative confirmation made her flash a delighted smile at me, and she ducked out from under my palm and rushed into the kitchen.

"I'll be right back; give me a minute."

I couldn't help but smile at her as she disappeared from sight, but my expression soon turned upside down when I noted the weird look the class rep was giving me.

"What? Is there something on my face?"

She looked me over, and then one dramatic glasses tweak later she told me, with the utmost seriousness, "Seeing you two acting like that, I can't help but wonder if you really have no intention of adding Neige to your harem."

"No, and I don't have a harem," I responded just a touch indignantly. "It's a semi-platonic subtype of the polyamorous Type 8 triangular relationship."

"Don't play with semantics," Ammy told me, this time changing things up a little by pushing up her glasses on the bridge of her nose instead of fiddling with the temples. "If it walks like a duck, floats like a duck, and quacks like a duck, then—"

"It must be a mallard," I cut in with my sagest of nods.

"That's also a kind of duck," she responded with her Judyest of looks in return.

I shrugged my shoulders and told her, "Now look who's playing with semantics."

"It's not semantics; it's literally the same thing."

"Yeah, right. Next time you're going to tell me witches are also literally ducks because they weigh the same."

My verbal sparring partner gave me a long, critical look, and then stated, "I get the reference, but that was still silly."

"Maybe, but not as silly as calling my relationship a duck," I countered, but before she could counter-counter my counter, Snowy came back with a small package wrapped in napkins in her hands.

"Here," she handed me the package, and only then did she realize the lingering tension in the air and murmured, "D-did I miss something?"

"Nah, just a couple of confusing, waterfowl-based analogies," I answered offhandedly as I hefted the small pack in my hand. "On a different note, what's this?"

"Spices," she answered matter-of-factly. I wiggled my eyebrows at her to urge her to elaborate, and she did so with surprising zest. "Uncle Brang asked me to bring him some seasonings because the last time I stayed over, they couldn't make anything special for me, and I had to eat the same thing they had for dinner."

"I should've known it was something like that," I muttered under my breath before I used my free hand to ruffle her hair one more time and told her, "I'll deliver this. We won't be over for long, but just in case: don't open the door to strangers, don't forget to do your homework, and be in bed before ten."

"Understood!" Snowy actively rubbed her head against my palm for a moment, and then she turned on her heels and walked up the stairs again, only stopping once she reached the first floor, at which point she gave us a small wave. I returned the gesture, which made her giggle, and only then did she head back to her room.

With that sidetrack over, I gestured for Ammy to follow me (all the while pointedly ignoring the persistent suspicious looks she was giving me), and we headed to my one and only secret teleportation closet. The gently glowing runic circle on the inside was the same as usual, and after making some space, I stood in the middle and called my passenger over to me.

This wasn't her first rodeo, so she took up her position in front of me with practiced steps, and before you could say *Llanfair-pwllgwyngyll-gogery-chwyrn-drobwll-llan-tysilio-gogo-goch*, we quickly Phased over to our destination without any complications. When we arrived, I knocked on the metal door and Rabom, serving as my anchor on the other side, quickly opened it up.

"I still can't get used to this," Ammy noted as she followed after me, no doubt referring to our reception. I didn't pay her much heed, as I was focused on the saluting Faun by the door, and after a few grunts, I managed to pawn my delivery off on him and handed over the package in my hands. The class rep waited for me to finish, and when she saw that my attention was back on her, she immediately added, "Also, on a second look, I'm now absolutely positive that your magic circle is complete gibberish."

"Yeah, sure, whatever," I grumbled just a touch half-heartedly while massaging my aching temple, and then I turned around and gestured for her to follow me.

I'd braced myself for it ahead of time, and it wasn't the first occasion I'd had to transfer with someone while already suffering from enchantment backlash, but the combination of the pounding headache and the violent nausea wasn't something one could simply get used to. I also had a feeling I was going to get a nasty fever sooner rather than later, but at the moment I was still reasonably fine on that front, so I reckoned I should get everything done before my condition inevitably turned for the worse.

While I was considering all that, we exited the reception room of the base, and upon coming into the main hall, we were greeted by a line of stiffly saluting Fauns, with a grinning Brang at the head.

"Erm? Leo? What's going on with your Fauns?" Ammy inquired in a reserved voice reminiscent of the way she used to talk all the time when I first met her. Those were the times! No monsters, no battles, no menacing tweaking of one's glasses... It all felt like it was such a long time ago.

Anyhow, I glanced at the Faunish parade line with undisguised disapproval and uttered, "Just follow my lead, and ignore them with extreme prejudice."

Subsequently, I walked past the whole group, and I made sure to extra-ignore the frantic Rabom trying to sneakily circle around us to get in line. The class rep followed after me, and it didn't take long to find our ultimate target. It wasn't a particularly hard feat, though, considering it was limply sprawled out in the middle of the training field, right where I'd last saw it when I checked on the Fauns.

"Is that what I think it is?" came the tentative question from Ammy the moment she laid her eyes on the body, and I couldn't help but direct a toothy grin at her.

"Only if you think it's a Chimera."

She didn't acknowledge my answer; instead she moved over and began to cautiously examine the beast, her eyes burning with unabashed curiosity, no doubt thrilled by the novelty of the situation. She wasn't alone in this regard, as the sight was new even for me. After all, this was the first time I'd gotten to see a Chimera under proper lighting conditions, and let's just say that the better visibility didn't do it any favors.

The motionless creature was about as ugly as I remembered, but with several nasty cuts and gashes on its body adding a gory edge to its already overwhelming natural charms. None of them were bleeding at the moment, but they weren't healing, either, which was probably a side effect of my meddling with its operating system or what have you. Bearing those wounds in mind, combined with the way it was sprawled across the floor and had its long tongue lolling out of its mouth, even I would've thought that it was deader than Hitler's painting career.

"Was it this corpse that you wanted to show me?" the class rep inquired a little uncertainly as she crouched down to gingerly poke the hairy shoulder of the creature.

"Among other things," I confirmed with a nod. "Oh, and for the record, it's not actually dead."

Ammy's hand, which was just about to touch one of the fangs of the Chimera, froze mid-motion as she slowly, borderline mechanically, turned her head to look at me over her shoulder.

"That's not funny."

"Of course it's not because I'm serious. I only immobilized it."

There was one hell of a tense beat hanging in the air for several seconds as her eyes opened wider than I thought was humanly possible, but then she abruptly jumped to her feet with an unexpectedly girlish "Eeep!" and she frantically scampered over and hid behind my back.

"Leo! What were you thinking!?"

"What? It's just a mostly dead Chimera," I teased her a little, just on principle.

"Only mostly!? That's the problem!"

Her high-pitched voice didn't quite echo in the hall, but it was still loud enough to make the Faun honour guard wordlessly following behind us flinch, so I decided to tone things back a little.

"Easy there, class rep. Easy. Listen, this Chimera is one hundred percent dead. It's not going to get up. Well, technically it could because it's something like a zombie, but it won't, because it can't. Do you get what I'm trying to say?"

"Zombie?" she repeated after me with a forty-sixty mix of incredulity and apprehension.

"Yep," I reaffirmed with an assertive smile. "Now then, since this is a perfect segue, I might as well ask this now: Do we have necromancy?"

The sudden ninety-degree turn in the conversation obviously threw Ammy on a loop, as for a while she could only blink at me while her brows had a hard time deciding whether they want to go up or down.

"You mean... right now?"

"No, just in general," I clarified while making sure I was keeping up my confident smile to reassure her. "Is necromancy a thing among the magical folk?"

"Yes..." she answered a little uncertainly while still making sure that I was standing between her and the body on the ground.

"Would you care to elaborate?" I innocently asked back while making sure that keeping me between her and the Chimera was as hard as possible. Ammy glared at me, but it didn't interfere with her ability to explain things, so I let her.

"Necromancy is the mystic art of binding souls, ghosts, and wraiths."

"Aren't those three the same thing?"

"No, of course not."

"Then please define your terms," I requested, and she gave me a "What are you, my teacher?" kind of look, but at the end of the day she diligently did so, anyway.

"Souls are the thing every living being has, and it disappears when you die. Ghosts are the negative imprints left on the world after a traumatic death, retaining some of the deceased's memories and personality, but they do not know they are dead. Ghosts can't retain any new memories and would fade away with time. Wraiths are powerful ghosts that actually understand that they are dead, shed the identity of the deceased, and steal mana from living beings to keep themselves alive, in a sense."

"Oh, I see," I nodded along. Halfway through I realized I'd already read most of this in one of Judy's reports, but since I'd already asked, cutting her explanation short would've been just rude. "So necromancers use those to take people and make them into the undead?"

"No, of course not," Ammy scoffed as if I'd just said something stupid. "If you're dead, then you're dead. End of story. It's one of the core tenets of magic."

"Ooookay, then what do they actually *do*?"

"Magically binding contracts, most of the time. They can also heal the damage done to the soul, or they can bind ghosts and wraiths so that they don't cause any havoc."

"That's... considerably more anticlimactic than I expected," I grumbled, though I was secretly a little bit relieved that I wouldn't have to worry about a crazy necromancer starting a genre shift into a stereotypical zombie apocalypse scenario.

"It's a respectable job," the class rep responded to my comment, completely unaware of my inner turmoil. But then again, by this point I was already thinking about something else.

"So, for the record, necromancers cannot take a dead body and make it into a semi-independent puppet?"

"I don't think so, no," Ammy answered a little warily.

"In that case, who could do that?"

She thought for a few long seconds, and I patiently waited for her to collect her thoughts.

"It could be done. The efficiency would be really bad, as a dead body without a soul in it couldn't heal and would slowly decompose over time without constant maintenance, but a good conjurer could certainly do it."

"I presume that would involve putting some kind of complex enchantment into the corpse to emulate the soul," I continued to lead her on, and she nodded in confirmation, none the wiser.

"Yes. It would be something like a golem core, like the one I have in Petra."

"I figured as much. Now, here comes the million-dollar question: Could anyone install such a core into the body of a dead Chimera?"

For a moment or five Ammy obviously couldn't fathom my question, but then she glanced over to the body behind me and a shocked gasp escaped her mouth.

"Wait a moment! So when you said the Chimera was mostly dead...?"

"I meant that it was a dead body controlled by magic," I completed her revelation. "Since it was technically an enchantment, I used my trick to disable a few crucial parts, and the Chimera with it. Well, that, and all the tracking and surveillance markers, but that goes without saying."

"But... But I thought this would be impossible." While murmuring so, Ammy finally overcame her fear of the not-quite-dead beast and once again walked up to it. "A Chimera is naturally resistant to the mystic arts of all but the Abyssals."

"But not immune," I noted on the side as I followed after her. "So just to reiterate: Since we already know it can be done, just who would be capable of performing such a feat on this island? He must be some kind of expert conjurer, maybe even a master of it! And he would have to have the tools and resources required to reconstruct the body and install the fake core into it. Just who could it be...?"

"I get it," Ammy griped and sent me an irritated glance over her shoulder. "You think it was my grandfather."

"Yep," I nodded without a hint of reservation. "The real question is whether we can prove it. What do you think?"

"I... honestly don't know. I might be able to find something, but not without any tools." She fell silent for a while as she observed the creature's head, and then she finally stated, "I could try to borrow some from the Artificer's Lodge. There is going to be a symposium soon, so there should be a lot of spares lying around in preparation."

"Good. Until then, what should we do with the body? Do you think we should refrigerate it?"

"I don't think that's necessary." She shook her head and gingerly placed her hand onto the Chimera's forehead. "It has no heartbeat, but it's still warm. That means it must already be in some form of stasis. Maybe a form of temporal lock, or maybe an engraved restoration circuit set on a stable loop within the core?"

"That's something I'll let you figure out." I took a step back and was about to leave her to her examination, but then I had a sudden idea and asked her, "Once you borrow those tools, do you need a separate space to do your tests? I'm asking because we still have a couple of empty nooks and crannies in the base."

"It certainly wouldn't hurt," Ammy responded without looking up.

"In that case, how about you take Brang with you, pick a room, and tell him how you want it to be furnished?"

"I don't know. It doesn't sound like a bad idea, but..." She stood up and stepped away from the body, and then she finally whispered. "No offense, but I would prefer if you were there, too."

"Why? He doesn't bite."

"Because they acknowledge you as the one in charge," she countered. "For anyone else, they are still really scary."

"Oh, please! You guys are just prejudiced. Brang is like a giant teddy bear."

"A muscular teddy bear armed to the teeth."

The subject of our conversation let out an embarrassed cough, which I still ignored with extreme prejudice, but when all was said and done, I had no choice but to relent.

"Fine, whatever. I'll go with you."

With that, I gestured for her to follow, and the Faun fell in line behind us without any further ado. This of course meant that playing around with the enchanted core of the not-quite-undead Chimera had to wait till another day, but considering how my forehead was getting a little too warm for my liking, maybe that was for the best. After all, I still had to take the class rep back, and then... well, let's just say I also had other places to visit today.

PART 3

Stone walls and eerie blue lights set in fancy wrought iron torch sconces. As far as ambience was concerned, the School's private back entrance had the whole medieval dungeon aesthetic down pat. Well, except for the glowing green *Emergency Exit* sign on the ceiling, but few things in this world are perfect.

All of a sudden, there was a soft sound in the dark as a door opened up to the outside. There was no light coming in, which wasn't surprising, considering it was well after ten at night.

"Galatea. Time."

"It's ten hundred and eleven hours, master."

Correction: it was *only* eleven minutes after ten. The creeping duo of the mad scientist cosplayer and his ever-faithful android companion gingerly closed the door behind themselves in order to make as little noise as possible. Their cautious glances and the furtive way they moved were so obviously sneaky even a blind man could tell they weren't supposed to be here.

"Status report," Lab Coat Guy whispered under his breath after setting his back against the wall. Unlike his usual appearance, this time he was wearing a pristine black lab coat, with matching trousers, sneakers, and a similarly coloured beanie keeping his hair in check. By the looks of it, it must have been his stealthy attire.

"The alarm wards have been successfully circumvented," the fembot declared, after which she dramatically raised the high-tech night-vision goggles covering her eyes. "We are in the clear, Master."

Speaking of goggles, her outfit was considerably more professional than Lab Coat Guy's. In particular, her getup looked like it was modeled after police riot gear, except trimmed down to show off her curves, and with a window in the middle of her vest to allow a peek at her generous cleavage. Honestly speaking, the fact that this could still be considered more sensible as far as stealth was concerned said more about Lab Coat Guy's outfit than hers.

"Kihihi! Good. Very good indeed!"

Once he learned that it was safe to move around, the man in the beanie detached himself from the wall and strode in the middle of the hallway with all the undue confidence that characterized the kind of fools who would willingly go into the lion's den. Luckily for him, this time the world must have been too busy to punish his conduct right away. However, all is not lost that is delayed.

The android woman seemed just a bit more cautious, and she continued to monitor the perimeter through her night-vision gear, occasionally pausing and pointing a finger at one glowing spot on the floor or the walls or another. Whatever she was doing, it worked, as the two of them successfully reached the stairwells leading to the bowels of the complex, and after descending three flights, they reached a large, riveted steel door set into the stone wall and secured by multiple enormous, old-timey padlocks with distinct keyholes on them.

This time it was Lab Coat Guy's turn to shine. After a couple dozen military-style finger gestures, he managed to communicate the incredibly complex notion of "Grab this door, dammit!" to his companion. Once she got into position and clamped her fingers onto the door, he proceeded to take out a pair of sophisticated entry tools from his breast pocket. In technical terms, one was an omnidirectional percussive force applicator, while the other was an elongated, acicular mechanical force transmitter made of a ferrum-oxide alloy. In layman's terms, it was a hammer and a rusty nail.

Instead of the padlocks, his target was the hinges, where he promptly knocked the pins out of each one of them, and then the fembot anticlimactically lifted the door out of the casing and pulled it aside just enough for someone to slip through the gap.

There was a small lull in the operation while she collected the discarded pins and Lab Coat Guy took a sip from the energy drink he had in his other breast pocket for some inexplicable reason. After they finished their intermezzo, the android carefully stuck her head through the opening, and after a few short seconds, she turned back and told her creator, "I have successfully accessed the observer orbs, Master. Do you want me to proceed with the looping?"

"Kihihi! Of course!" There was a long beat of silence after even the echoes of his request had died down, but then she nodded with an implied

"Done and done." Lab Coat Guy let out another shrill chuckle and exclaimed, "Great! Let's go!"

With that, he slipped through the door, and it only now became apparent that it led to the familiar, if currently dark, hallway where the arch-mage's office was situated. The androidess followed after him and reset the door behind herself, after which they hurriedly made their way over to the fanciest door in the vicinity.

"It's your turn again, Galatea," Lab Coat Guy urged her forward, and so the fembot took a small, rectangular box out of her cleavage... somehow. Said box had a series of dials on its sides, with the only free part completely covered in minuscule magical script and circles gently glowing in the dark. She attached it to the office's door, and the gadget made a series of whirring noises reminiscent of a cappuccino vending machine trying its best to function without water.

She let out a small grunt, and then proceeded to twist a few of the knobs, which resulted in a different series of noises, followed by more twisting and turning. The process repeated itself a couple dozen more times, and Lab Coat Guy seemed just impatient enough to start complaining when the door let out an unexpected clicking noise, and she declared, "We are in, Master."

"Kihihi! Marvelous! Quick, let's move!"

Under his urging, the android woman pushed the door open, and they both quickly entered the familiar office of the island's supernatural de facto oligarch. The place was unusually untidy, with even more documents scattered around than usual, and a half-empty open bottle of rum was still sitting on the desk in the middle. The duo scanned the perimeter, and once he concluded that they were in the clear, the resident mad scientist whispered, "Make sure you don't touch anything."

"Understood, Master," the fembot nodded with a serious expression, and they immediately took a beeline towards the unassuming door in the back. So far, things were proceeding unexpectedly smoothly for the infiltrator duo, but they were about to meet a challenge that they simply could not have ever anticipated.

For you see, the door to the archives was protected by a technique that denied one's ability to unlock it on a conceptual level, something that no lockpick, magical or mundane, could overcome. It was such an ingenious defense line that it took the two of their combined intellects over ten minutes to surmount this devious defense mechanism operating on the ingenious principle of you cannot lockpick a door that's already open.

"Argh! I can't believe this!" Lab Coat Guy grunted aloud as he finally realized what was going on and threw the door open. "We wasted so much time on this!"

"Aggravating. The chances of the door being left open were under zero point zero three percent."

"I know, right?" he continued to grumble, but not for long, as he soon entered the archives and quickly pinpointed their main target. He gestured for his accomplice to follow after him, and this time they were prudent enough to actually check the door of the safe before they broke out the stethoscopes. It was, naturally, open. The two shared a completely understandable incredulous look between each other, but didn't dwell on it for long before they proceeded to rummage through the documents inside. Then, as he reached the bottom of the pile, Lab Coat Guy's eyes lit up with excitement. "Kihihi! Jackpot!"

"Scanning. Processing..." After a few moments, the robotic woman nodded towards her master and declared, "One hundred percent match. It's the original of the binding contract."

"Goooooood!" Lab Coat Guy had a frankly creepy grin on his face, as if he'd just found some kind of treasure, but he quickly wiped it off and turned to his companion again. "Galatea, the misdirection, please."

She nodded and wordlessly reached into her cleavage again (or, in retrospect, maybe an inner pocket accessible through the cleavage window on her vest, but it was functionally the same) and successfully retrieved a folded-up piece of paper.

The black-clad scientist let out a subdued cackle and placed the handwritten page inside the safe, and then immediately closed it with an expression hovering on the border between relief and excitement.

"Kihihi! Mission accomplished. Let's get out of here!"

Without any further ado, the two of them tiptoed out of the archives, and did the same to the office as well, making very sure not to touch even a single fallen piece of office paper on the floor. They proceeded to open the door again, and then the fembot put the magic gadget onto the door and did the entire knob-turning song-and-dance routine backwards.

And then, just as they were about to leave, confident in their flawless success, a tall, smart, handsome, and criminally humble devil appeared on the other side of the door, with them none the wiser!

Jokes aside, my arrival was subtle and unceremonious as usual. I readjusted the balaclava on my head with my gloved hands, as I had to put it on in a hurry when I realized where our genre-shift agents were heading. I didn't have time to put on a jumpsuit this time, but based on my previous experience with infiltrating this room, even the headgear was a bit of an overkill. Still, it never hurt to be cautious, so I made sure I had it on properly before I did anything else.

I'm not proud to admit it, but the fact that I'd managed to catch these two red-handed was entirely due to blind luck. I'd just Phased back from the base, and I was sick as a dog after the multiple transfers and being unable to stop myself from messing with the disabled Chimera, anyway (I'm starting to think I might have impulse-control issues), but I still forced myself to do a roll call on the usual suspects. As they say, the rest is history.

Now then, first I should find out what this misdirection was supposed to be. I made my way into the archives, without bothering with leaving the scene intact, and I soon stood in front of the safe. Thankfully they were considerate enough to leave the new piece of paper on the top of the pile, so I didn't even have to look for it.

"Let's see..." I whispered under my breath, and my eyes skimmed over the content. "Blah-blah-blah, your fort's defenses are lacking, wingless one, yada yada, we now hold your secret in our hands, something-something glory to Deus. Huh."

So, on the first read, this page was supposed to make it look like the Celestials infiltrated the school, stole the contract binding Lab Coat Guy, and were planning to use it to blackmail Lord Grandpa into doing some entirely vague stuff or else they'd reveal it to the Assembly, and that's apparently going to make him embarrassed or something. Needless to say, the whole thing was written in Celestial Script, which also meant...

"Goddammit, Ninja..." I grumbled aloud before quickly Far Glancing in his direction, and... yep. Mike was currently enjoying the hospitality of an honest-to-goodness giant metal cage inside a certain mad scientist's backup lair. How come I wasn't even surprised?

My first instinct was to just Phase over, grab him by the scruff of his neck, and deposit him somewhere else, but I quickly reined back the impulse. Not only because I was feeling queasy enough without another forced transfer like that, but because then I would have to somehow explain how I could actually do it to him, and considering that he was still mainly loyal to the Celestial Intelligence Network, I doubted he would keep it a secret just because I'd asked nicely.

The more I thought about it, the more annoying the situation felt, so I ended up letting out a groan and throwing the whole kerfuffle with Mike to the back of my mind in favor of focusing on the kerfuffle in front of me.

In short, I felt irritated over other people making my life complicated, so I did the most natural thing that came to mind under the circumstances and decided to vent by making those people's lives extra complicated in return. With that determination in mind, I casually crumbled up the piece of paper in my hand, and whispered, "As they say, revenge is a dish best served complicated."

That sounded much better in my head.

"Oh well, you can't win them all," I muttered, and then promptly headed back into the office. I still had the whole night ahead of me, but that didn't mean I shouldn't start cooking my complicated dish as soon as possible.

CHAPTER 12

PART 1

I threw my curtains open to be greeted by the light of the morning sun... except not really, because the sky was still completely overcast. I opened the window, as well, and stuck a hand outside.

"Oh great, it's still raining," I grumbled to myself before closing the window and wiping the drizzle off my hands onto the back of my pants. It was such a nice morning, too. Why couldn't the weather match my mood for once?

I shook my head and put such irrational thoughts aside for the moment in favor of continuing my morning routine. PC turned off? Check. Schoolbag packed for the day? Check. Mysteriously well-ironed school uniform? Check. My umbrella? Now we had a problem.

After rummaging through my room for a while, I still couldn't find one, so I did the logical thing and checked the entryway. On my way there, I ran into Snowy preparing her lunch box, and after the customary head pat, I finally reached my destination and searched every nook and cranny in the room.

My efforts bore fruit, as I soon found an umbrella. On the other hand, it was only a single one, which posed a different kind of problem, namely that there were two of us in the house.

"Hey, sis?" I called out as I walked back into the living room. In the meantime I also absently inspected the thing in my hand. It was huge, black, and with a hooked handle, the kind that Mary Poppins would hold on to as she flew off into the sunset. It was also heavy enough where I figured it could serve as an impromptu self-defense weapon. Seriously though, this thing was so solidly built I imagined it could stand in for a parachute if push came to shove.

Meanwhile, my sister stuck her head through the kitchen door with a curious look on her face, so I asked her, "Do you have an umbrella of your own?"

Her brows furrowed at my question before she completely entered the living room and shook her head.

"No, I don't think so. I've never needed one until now."

"Well, that's a pickle because this is the only one we have, and the rain doesn't look like it will let up anytime soon."

She glanced between me and then the umbrella in my hand, and at the end of the day she timidly proposed, "We could share that one. It looks big enough."

"Sure, but it's a trope I don't really want to deal with," I replied, earning me a funny look in return, so I hastily shook my head and told her, "That said, it's not like we have much of a choice in the matter."

With that sorted out, she went back into the kitchen to finish packing her snacks. Once she was out of sight, I stretched my back a little and then glanced at the clock. We were still quite early, but considering that I still had to pick up Judy, and then Elly after that, it never hurt to get moving soon-ish.

With that in mind, I put on my outerwear, put my phone away, and put up with waiting for Snowy to do the same (I kid, she was done quite fast), and once the morning routine was well and truly over, we closed the door behind us and headed out. My sister, naturally, took shelter under my enormous umbrella, its big, black bulk sheltering us both from the outside world. I think there was a metaphor hidden in that somewhere, but I was still a little brain-dead after the previous day's overexertions, so I didn't even try to unravel it.

On our way to Judy's place, I couldn't help but let my mind wander and make small, inconsequential observations left and right. For starters, even after two months, the streets were still impeccable as ever. Scratch litter or dust; not even any puddles were left behind by the rain. In retrospect, that wasn't too surprising, considering that those generally formed in indentations or potholes on the road, but since everything was still brand-sparkling-new, there obviously weren't such imperfections present. Well, either that, or the invisible ninja maids not only swept but also mopped the road whenever nobody was looking. One or the other.

Aside from that, we also had a lot more placeholders on the street, especially considering the weather. The variety of them had also increased a lot; we had everything from elementary schoolers in bright yellow raincoats and office workers in business casual, to housewives carrying bags with obligatory baguettes and celery sticking out of them and even the occasional high schoolers with matching uniforms and colourful umbrellas over them. All in all, the streets finally felt completely natural... save for the uncanny cleanness, but hey, it was still progress.

While I mused about these things, we unceremoniously reached our first stop on our daily commute. We came to a halt in front of the picket fence in front of Judy's house, and a couple of seconds later, the front door opened to reveal my girlfriend's absurdly youthful mother.

"Good morning, cubbies! Judy will be here in a second!" She greeted us with an energetic wave of her hand holding a pair of wooden-handled metal grill tongs. No, I don't know why this was her *thing*, but I have long since accepted it. Also, for the record, cubbies are supposed to be us. Don't ask why; she just started calling me cubby one day (it had something to do with my name having to do with lions, and lions having cubs or something), and since Snowy was my sister, we both turned into cubbies. Some say I have an odd naming sense, but that was still a stretch even by my standards.

Anyhow, I thanked her, and we waited for my dear assistant to arrive. It really didn't take long, as she soon burst through the door holding a small, foldable white umbrella featuring some kind of brand logo: a big-eyed cartoonish teddy bear, with a snazzy green bowler hat. It looked vaguely familiar, and it took until Judy walked over to us for me to finally remember where I'd seen it.

"Did you get that umbrella from the amusement park?" I inquired, and my girlfriend gave me a curt nod.

"It was one of the consolation prizes during the shooting game," she told me as she opened it up, and now that I could take a better look, it was indeed one of the park's many mascots.

"Oh, so I was the one who actually won that? Sorry, after the tenth or so attempt to get your owl plushie, I completely ignored the other prizes and—"

"Never mind that," Judy cut me off as she stood in front of us and made a vague gesture in our direction. "What's this?"

"What's what?" I asked back reflexively, head tilted juuust a smidgen to the side and one brow raised high.

"You're sharing an umbrella," my assistant pointed out in a flat voice that still sounded more than a tad sulky to me.

"Is there a problem with that?"

"Of course there is," Judy declared with one hand on her hip. "That's something you do with your love interest. That's me."

"I'm fairly sure you are way beyond that category, but putting semantics aside... do you seriously want to invoke that tired old trope on purpose?"

My incredulous rhetorical question was met by a completely serious nod.

"Not all tropes are bad, Chief," she reproached me with a huff, and then explained, "Walking under the same umbrella became a trope because it's inherently a very heartfelt and romantic situation. Just because it's overused, it doesn't mean it's bad and shouldn't ever be invoked."

"That's true, I suppose, but that doesn't mean you *have* to invoke it," I countered, only to be dismissed out of hand.

"No, Chief, we must. I believe the most surefire way to solidify our relationship against outside threats is by purposefully engaging in wholesome romantic tropes."

"Do we really have to though? Do we *really*?"

"Yes," she replied in no uncertain terms. "It's about time we start exploiting some of the more benign tropes by manually enforcing them."

I was under the impression that I had been doing that for a while now, but my protests fell on deaf ears as Judy unceremoniously wedged herself between Snowy and me. It was getting a little crowded, but then she turned to my sister and presented her umbrella to her.

"Here, Neige. You can have this."

"Hey!" I immediately protested. "Dormouse, you are being really, really rude right now."

"I detest your accusation, and I will see you in civil court over defamation charges," she responded offhandedly, but then she finally noticed my less-than-amicable expression, and she hurriedly continued with, "Excuse me. What I meant to say was, 'Neige, I wish to trade your place by the Chief's side for this limited edition Bonta Jr. umbrella.'"

"Come again? What the heck is a Bonta?" I complained, but I was immediately overruled.

"Hush, Chief. I'm negotiating." After proclaiming so, she turned back to my sister and added, after reaching into her pocket, "I'm also willing to throw in this limited edition Kowalski Jr. key chain."

She dangled the small plastic figurine of a penguin wearing a top hat and monocle in front of my hapless sister, and to my sincerest bafflement, her eyes instantly lit up with greed.

"Can... can I really keep both?"

"Yes," Judy confirmed with a big nod.

"For good?"

"For good," my assistant nodded again.

After only half a second of hesitation, my sister snatched the items out of her hands and took a step to the side, allowing Judy to immediately move up to me and link her arm around mine on my free side.

"Was... I just traded for an umbrella and a key chain?"

"Don't sweat the small details, Chief," my girlfriend told me and then rested her head against my upper arm.

I wanted to complain, but both of the girls seemed very satisfied with their deal, with Snowy already in the process of hanging her new acquisition onto the side of her bag. Maybe it was a new fad I didn't know about? Or was it just Snowy who was really easy to please with cute things? Looking at the giddy expression on her face when twirling her new Bounty Sr. or whatever umbrella made me lean towards the latter, but one could never know.

"Let's go. We're running a little late," I prompted the girls, and they followed my lead in silence... for exactly ten seconds before Snowy threw us on a loop with a simple question.

"Leo? What's a trope?"

"Pardon?" I asked back reflexively, and she might have thought I couldn't hear her, for she immediately repeated her question.

"What's a trope? You two talked about it just now."

Judy and I shared a distressed glance for a moment, and it turned out she was quicker on the uptake this time around, as she quickly explained, "A trope is a common element in a story."

"Precisely," I followed up with an authoritative nod. "Like... Do you remember that bad movie we watched the other day? Where the hero points his mecha's gun at the bridge of the big bad's skull-shaped ship and says, 'Alas, poor Yorickus. I hardly knew ye' before he pulls the trigger? That's a trope called a premortem one-liner."

"It was also an overwritten, badly justified reference," Judy added after a click of her tongue.

"True, but that's kind of beside the point," I chided her, and she accepted it with a shrug.

"I see," Snowy mused aloud as she absentmindedly twirled her new mascot umbrella left and right, but then she point-blank asked us, "But why were you talking about these tropes just now?"

The question was innocent, but it caused us no little headache to explain it to her without revealing too much, and it took us until we arrived at Elly's place to make her come to the conclusion that "Oh, so it is like... an inside joke?"

"Exactly," Judy agreed on the spot, and that was the end of the discussion for the time being, as even though we'd barely stepped in front of the gate, Elly was already running towards us. That wasn't surprising, but the fact that she was wearing a dark-green camo-patterned raincoat was.

"I'm ready; we can go!" she declared as she slipped through the wrought iron gates and closed them behind her, but then she looked at me and Judy and added, "Is it just me, or are you two even closer than usual?"

"They are doing a trope," my sister helpfully informed her, but it only made the invisible question marks over her head multiply faster than rabbits in Australia.

"I don't get it," she finally admitted, only for my sister to shrug her shoulders, as well.

"Me neither, but it looks nice."

"Your turn is tomorrow," Judy suddenly cut in, warning my other girl-friend before she could say anything, and I once again couldn't help but feel left out of the loop, especially when the princess subtly rolled her eyes with an expression that said, "Isn't that obvious?"

Anyhow, once the customary morning greetings were over (read: one kiss for Elly, and then an extra kiss for Judy because I'd forgotten to give her one before), we continued our merry commute towards the one-and-only Blue Cherry High. Most of the way was spent on small talk about the weather, which then led to Elly noticing my sister's new umbrella and fawning over that Bojack Jr. or whatever mascot, after which the conversation progressed into the topic of mascot key chains. Apparently it really was a fad, and the three most important girls in my life were all inexplicably neck-deep into it.

I, being a manly man, full of manliness and testosterone and all that good stuff, naturally only scoffed at their cutesy girly stuff with prejudice of the most extreme variety. It was due to that that I only sporadically engaged in their discussion, mostly just to explain to them in rational terms and in very meticulous detail why, in fact, the baby panda with the fedora and handlebar mustache was *definitely* the best because mustaches are manly and stuff. Though again, the puzzlingly Irish baby seal key chain Elly had got sideburns under its green, buckled top hat, so that also got a few points in my book.

Like that, we swiftly arrived at the school, and to my surprise, the childhood friend duo was already waiting for us in front of the closed gates. Angie was wearing a white plastic raincoat, but she had the hood down and stood under my friend's multicoloured umbrella.

"Hi guys!" the Celestial girl greeted us while we were quite a distance away, and she even waved at us with a happy-go-lucky grin on her face.

"Good morning," my sister greeted them back properly, but then after she looked them over, she turned to me and asked, "Are they doing the trope, too?"

"I actually think they are."

My response earned me a couple of puzzled blinks from the duo, and Josh ultimately asked me, "What are you guys talking about?"

"Nothing. It would take too long to explain," I told them before point-edly glancing at the closed gates. "So what's up with that?"

"Oh, that? You're not gonna believe this," Josh answered while his childhood friend repeatedly nodded. "The school is closed for the day. Do you know what that means?"

Before I could say anything, Angie threw her fist high into the air, almost knocking the umbrella out of Joshua's hand, and exclaimed, "It's a long weekend!"

"Errr... Cool, but why?" I inquired after I overcame my first surprise at her display of unbridled enthusiasm.

"Something about a gas leak," my friend told me while checking his umbrella for damage, and once he made sure none of the spokes were bent, he added, "Ammy was also called inside, so I think things are more complicated than that."

"You think so?" I prodded him to continue with a knowing smile that didn't escape my assistant's notice, but she didn't point it out for the time being.

"Well, yeah? I mean, if they only let Ammy in, it means it has something to do with the magical School. Maybe there was an accident there?"

"Or it could be because of what happened yesterday," Elly supplied the next guess with a finger on her lips.

"Or that," Josh granted her that, and there was a short lull in the conversation as everyone considered this new bit of information. On my end, though, I was more curious about something else entirely.

"For the record, since when did you know there wouldn't be school today?"

"Oh, that?" Josh responded a little late, and then after some thinking he told me, "Since we came here, so about fifteen minutes?"

"And couldn't you call me to tell us about this?" I posed my next question, and my friend flashed an impish grin at me.

"I figured we shouldn't be the only ones who had to walk here in the rain." I rewarded his honesty with a flat and in-no-way-or-shape-threatening look, so there was no reason why he would hurriedly add, "A-also, I figured that once we meet up here, we could go to my place together. You know? To talk, and plan, and have that Street Kombat tournament we've wanted to do for ages?"

In the end, I couldn't help but let my shoulders drop in resignation, and I ultimately told him, "Fine, we might as well do that. I suppose we should wait for the class rep first."

"I'm here," came the sudden declaration from our left, and we all glanced there in unison.

"Uuum... Hi, Amelia," Snowy greeted her first, if a little uncertainly.

"When did you even get here?" I mumbled as I looked her over. She was also part of the raincoat club, and hers was a blindingly bright orange one with reflective stripes. How we'd all managed to miss her was a complete mystery. My working theory still involved ninjutsu.

"I've been here for a while," Ammy huffed, but then she abruptly shook her head and stated, "It doesn't matter. Listen, there's pandemonium down in the School; everything's on lockdown until further notice."

"What exactly happened?"

The class rep glanced at Judy, then at me, and after a short sigh she explained, in a low voice barely audible over the sound of the rain.

"Someone broke into Grandfather's office last night."

Shocked gasps! Wide-open eyes! Mouths hanging open in disbelief! Bizarre *dun-dun-dun!* sounds in the distance! All of those... were things that obviously didn't happen.

"So that's why school's out!" Angie exclaimed with a toothy grin, completely unfazed by the dramatic revelation.

"This is no joking matter!" Ammy reprimanded her on the spot, and then for some reason she turned to me next. "Leo?"

"Yes?"

"By any chance, do you know anything about what happened?"

"Nope," I denied it on the spot with my patented I'm-as-innocent-as-a-newborn-lamb-in-the-virgin-snow expression.

"Why, what happened?" Judy gave me a saving throw with impeccable timing, forcing the class rep to explain herself.

"Last night, someone circumvented the wards protecting Grandfather's office," she repeated what we already knew, and then after a deep breath she expounded, "They took several important files from the archives, and at least one very, *very* valuable item." She paused here, probably looking for a reaction, but I was giving her only the same innocent smile, so she soon gave up and continued with, "They also stacked up all the paperwork in the office, threw away all the trash into the bin, and they took all of Grandfather's liquor."

"You mean... all of it?" Judy muttered, half astounded and half impressed.

"Yes," Ammy nodded, and then after a second added, "Including the cabinet in which it was stored."

"... Are you serious?" came the next question from Josh, resulting in another nod. "How did they even move that out from underground without anyone noticing a thing?"

"We don't know yet," the class rep admitted, but then she ominously declared, "However, we're soon going to find out. Whoever the thief was, they left a message on Grandfather's desk."

"Really?" Angie burst out as she leaned forward, her eyes sparkling with excitement. "Was it a calling card?! Is it a phantom thief?! Is it?!"

"N-no, probably not," Ammy replied with a stutter, obviously taken more than a little aback, but then she quickly collected herself and clarified things. "It was a letter written in Celestial Script."

"Oh, oh! Do you need me to help?" Angie jumped to the opportunity with her hand raised high, and this time Josh was fast enough to get the umbrella out of the way. She didn't even notice.

"No. We have experts for things like this."

After saying so, Ammy fell silent for a long while, all the while drilling a hole into my forehead with her gaze.

"Why are you looking at me like that?"

"It's because I'm sure you know something about what happened," she told me frankly. "Any time something really weird or seemingly impossible has happened in the past couple of weeks, you were always related to it."

"Well, I can't deny that..." I muttered under my breath, but before I could get to the actual denial part, Ammy cut me off.

"Leo. Look me in the eye, and tell me the truth."

Well, that was an easy request, so after a momentary consideration, I did just so.

"Oh, fine. I swear that I didn't *break* into your grandpa's study, I didn't take anything valuable *yesterday*, nor did I *carry* an entire liquor cabinet anywhere at any point in time."

"Why did you emphasize things like that?"

That calamitous question came from Elly of all people, so I did my best to keep up my smile, and I told her, "It's important to be specific when you are testifying, to avoid being too vague. Isn't that right, Ammy?"

The class rep gave me a noncommittal noise in place of an answer, but for the time being, it seemed I had successfully allayed her suspicions. All hail the power of half-truths.

"So now that we're over that sidetrack, where does all of this leave us? Can we do anything?" I spoke up mostly just to move the conversation forward, but for the moment nobody gave me an answer. "In that case... Josh?"

"Mm? Yes?"

I sent my friend my brightest grin, and asked him, "What suits an impromptu fighting game tournament better: pizza or Chinese food?"

"I dunno... Pizza, I suppose?" he responded a bit uncertainly, only to immediately get overruled by his childhood friend crossing her arms in front of her.

"Hold it right there! This is a serious issue! I propose we should put it to a vote!"

"Can we do that while we walk?" I proposed, feeling a little chilly despite Judy's best efforts to warm my side.

"We might as well." Josh shrugged, and we all began walking, even the slightly confused class rep, who apparently wasn't around when we'd discussed this bit, after all.

"So, Elly? What do you vote for?" the Celestial girl interviewed her first subject, even going as far as to pretend she was holding out an invisible microphone to her.

"I... don't really know," my girlfriend answered, her face already scrunched up in a complex expression. "I've never eaten pizza or take-out food before."

"Did you seriously pick this of all moments to play the ojou archetype?" my other girlfriend grumbled under her breath, but the princess still over-heard her.

"Excuse me? What is a... what was that word again?"

"It's a trope!" my sister suddenly declared on our right, and then after a beat, she tentatively followed it up with a subdued "Right?"

I gave her a small nod, and while the relieved smile she flashed me tickled my big-brotherly instincts, I couldn't help but feel that we might have accidentally let a genie out of the lamp without realizing it...

PART 2

It had been a while since I'd last visited Josh's place. To be precise, it was just before he was kidnapped and the whole school incident with Crowey. It felt like it had happened ages ago because of all the crap we'd had to deal with recently, but it'd only been a little more than two weeks since that fateful night. I couldn't help but wonder, was my sense of time out of whack due to my lack of need for sleep? Or was this a normal reaction to shit hitting the fan over and over again? Maybe a combination of the two?

I would've probably kept pondering this for a while longer, but I was knocked out of my train of thought by my sister offering me some cola. I thanked her and took a leisurely sip as I looked over my surroundings. We were inside Josh's living room. His parents were nowhere to be seen, just as you would expect from a protagonist type. Reasonable and responsible parents are the kryptonite of exciting, wacky, and occasionally dangerous adventures. Also, for the record, my parents didn't count for the trope, as they didn't even exist. Probably.

But back to the scenery: the short, black wooden coffee table in the middle was buried under a small mountain of pizza boxes, their previous contents already safely stored away in our bellies. Behind those,

Joshua and Elly were sitting on a pair of cushions and were having a heated battle of epic proportions on the screen of the Bernstein family's old-school-yet-fairly-big CRT television. The princess was a newbie, but she took to the game really quickly, and she was putting up a good fight against Josh's cheap zoning efforts.

On my left, Judy and Ammy were having a soft-spoken-yet-still-oddly-animated discussion about how to use communication artifacts. On my right, Angie made some space for Snowy to put down her tray of drinks onto the table, and then they both sat down by the two contestants in front of the TV and silently watched the beginning of the third round.

All things considered, things were obnoxiously peaceful, especially considering everything that had happened yesterday. Or could it be that everyone was relaxed like this specifically because of what had happened? I mean, for the longest time I'd advocated enjoying ourselves to the fullest between the occasional episodes of supernatural peril, so it could be that everyone had simply adopted my philosophy over time. Anyhow, this kind of atmosphere wasn't bad at all; too bad it didn't last long.

Everyone raised their brows in unison, save for myself, when a not particularly loud, yet very insistent, whirring sound rung out in the living room.

"That's the doorbell," Josh noted without bothering to look away from the screen.

"Aren't you going to let the guest in?" I asked after finishing up my drink, but my friend only shook his head.

"I'm busy at the moment," he insisted while hammering on the controller with his thumbs in a frantic effort to dodge the super-move my girlfriend had just pulled off by good, old-fashioned button mashing.

"I'll get it," Angie proposed after rolling her eyes at our host, and then she jumped to her feet and casually strode out of the room. For the next couple of seconds there was curious silence hanging in the air, but at last she returned with an entirely unexpected person in tow. Well, for the others, at least. I'd cheated with Far Sight, as usual.

"Hello, Pascal," Ammy immediately greeted the guy walking behind Angie, even before she'd gotten a chance to introduce him.

Armband Guy stopped just past the threshold of the room and looked over each one of us in turn with barely disguised discontent. The rain had actually gotten worse sometime after noon, and even though he was mostly dry, his pants under his knees and his socks were still drenched. More importantly, he had not one, not two, but a grand total of three flying, glowing eyeball things circling around him. Speaking of eyes, his gaze ended up landing on Josh at last, and it was at the precise moment when he let out a vigorous, "Hell, yeah! That was close!" followed by a fist pump.

"Don't worry, Elly. You'll get him next time," I told my momentarily disheartened girlfriend and gestured for her to come over to my side for her consolation prize in the form of a head pat. She, naturally, complied right away.

In the meantime, our host finally noticed the newcomer and turned 180 degrees in place while still sitting on his cushion and raised his hand in a lazy wave. "Hey." Armband Guy returned the greeting in the form of a small nod, after which my friend scratched his chin and asked, "I don't think I've ever invited you over before. How did you know where I lived?"

"I knew your address from your school records," Armband Guy answered with a tone that clearly wondered if that was really the most important question at the moment. I found myself unexpectedly agreeing with him, but then I was immediately startled when he reached out to his face and dramatically readjusted his glasses in an eerily familiar fashion. I couldn't help but wonder if the class rep had learned this habit from him, or if it was the other way around. Either way, after a similarly dramatic pause, he stated, "All of you are here. Good. That makes things considerably easier for me. That said, I would be lying if I said I was not surprised to find you so unperturbed, considering the severity of the current situation."

"What situation?" I blurted out without missing a beat, mostly to hasten the conversation a little.

"Have you not heard about what happened last night?"

"Not in detail, no," Judy noted while she indiscreetly took out her phone to make notes.

"If it was important enough to barge in on us uninvited, you might as well tell us yourself," I proposed, only to realize I might be rushing things a little, so I subsequently added, "But before that, how about you sit down first?"

Armband Guy sent me a sharp glance but only said, "Please do not mind if I do," and then he promptly took a seat at the only free seat, which happened to be right next to me. Just as planned.

Josh's living room had one large and one smaller couch, which meant that with his addition, all the seats were taken up, forcing Josh, Angie, and Snowy to bring over a few wooden chairs from the kitchen. The rest of us patiently waited for them (except for me, since I was busy swatting down the observer orbs with my phantom limb), and at the end of the day we successfully formed a circle around the coffee table in the middle. The whole thing almost felt formal, if not for the pizza boxes and the TV playing a demo match of Street Kombat in the background.

Anyhow, once everyone had settled down, our unexpected guest pushed his glasses up the bridge of his nose and turned to Ammy.

"How much have you told them?"

"Everything, though in broad terms only," she responded a little sourly, something which Armband Guy either didn't notice or just didn't care about.

"I see," he nodded and, after a long moment of consideration, he began his explanation. "Last night, approximately just before twenty-three hundred, someone infiltrated the School complex through presently unknown methods."

The guy's direct, almost militaristic way of reporting momentarily raised the tension in the room, so I subtly redoubled my head patting efforts, and once Elly let out a blissful "Nyu" sound, things went back to normal. Well, except that now Armband Guy was glaring at us, but hey, sometimes sacrifices had to be made for the greater good.

"The identity of the infiltrators is unknown," Ammy cut in, most likely in order to keep the conversation on track, but then our guest immediately shook his head.

"That is no longer the case," he stated, then after a dramatic pause (he apparently had an affinity to those) he continued with, "But I am getting ahead of myself. Let us establish the circumstances of the crime first." When he said that, his eyes blatantly skimmed over us in general, and me in particular, obviously looking for a reaction. Maybe he expected that we would know something? Or maybe even that we were involved in some way? Well, I was, but it would take more than a few pointed looks to break my well-practiced poker face, so when his gaze lingered on me for too long, I simply raised my brows to urge him to go on.

"After checking the inventory, it became evident that the only three things they took were the liquor cabinet, a valuable heirloom of the previous arch-mages, and a certain document." He once again paused while looking for a reaction, but since nobody knew anything, and I was still holding up my nonchalant façade with the help of my overly affectionate girlfriend, he once again came away empty-handed. "More importantly, the perpetrators left behind a single written note in Celestial Script."

The moment that was mentioned, Angie immediately perked up. I figured she still hoped that it was a calling card, the kind that stereotypical phantom thieves in kids' shows left behind at the scene of the crime after they'd successfully taken something really valuable without anyone being the wiser, only to taunt the authorities and... oh crap. It *was* a calling card, wasn't it? Dammit, does that make me a phantom thief?

Questions for later. For now, my attention was drawn to Josh, who asked the obvious question that was on everyone's mind.

"What did it say?"

"Celestial Script is notoriously hard to translate, but allow me to paraphrase the content based on the reading of our expert." After saying so, he took a big breath and then cleared his throat. "It said, 'Dear Old Fart! You stabbed me in the back, so I took your fancy box in return! See you never! PS I took your booze, too, because screw you!'"

"That... wasn't very eloquent," Angie noted with palpable disappointment in her voice.

I inwardly apologized to her; if I knew things would turn out like this, I would've made the note more playfully flamboyant, but at the time, my main goal was to piss off Lord Grandpa. Also, it wasn't surprising, but Armband Guy purposefully left out the segment about the contract. That told me they were still trying to cover up their connection with Lab Coat Guy. How cute.

In the meantime, Ammy visibly paled, and she addressed Armband Guy in a low voice.

"By fancy box, does it actually mean...?" He raised a finger to his mouth, but nodded, confirming that it was just as she thought, which made her eyes open even wider with military-grade bewilderment, and she mumbled something along the lines of "What kind of lunatic would dare...?" I gracefully decided not to hold it against her, as she obviously didn't know she was talking about me.

"So," I spoke up, to keep things rolling. "Thanks for telling us this, but I can't help but wonder if you barged in here just to do so."

I intended that as a somewhat-confrontational jab, but Pascal gave me an appreciative look instead, as if I'd just helped him broach a subject he didn't know how to handle.

"The lord told me to come and tell you about the contents of the letter for a very simple reason. I must ask you this: Based on what I told you, who do you think the perpetrator could be?"

There were several seconds of tense silence following that question. I was ready to step up if things went awry and to guide them towards my preferred (and only slightly misleading) deduction, but thankfully Josh had enough brain cells to rub together to come to the obvious conclusion on his own.

"It might be Robatto," he stated with a thoughtful expression, and Elly immediately agreed with him.

"Right! Didn't he talk about being betrayed during the battle? That really sounds like him!"

Since things were proceeding in the right direction, now my role went from gentle conversation guide to the devil's advocate, just to make things sound more natural.

"I don't know," I commented with intentional nonchalance while rubbing my chin. "If it was really Lab Coat Guy, where are all the *kihihi*s?"

"Chief, people don't write those into letters," my dear assistant rebuked me right away.

"Well, I do," I doubled down, throwing the ball back into her court.

"Yes, but that's because you're weird," she told me with the utmost seriousness.

I wanted to give a snappy reply, but then my other girlfriend gently grabbed hold of my free hand and told me, "But that's why we love you," and then she rested her head against my shoulder with a giggle, making me unable to say anything in return. Well played, my dears. Well played.

"As much as I would like to deny that, I can't," Judy piled on with a coy smile only I could see, while Armband Guy was giving me a decidedly skeptical look. I couldn't blame him, as while our poly relationship wasn't exactly a secret, we didn't announce it outright, either, and since Elly was the more visible out of my two girlfriends, Lord Grandpa and his posse thought I was only dating her. Well, that would probably change now, I surmised.

That said, this was all a tangent we didn't really need right now, so once my mischievous girls calmed down a little, I turned my attention to Armband Guy again.

"So back to the point; do you also think that it was Lab Coat Guy?"

"It is one of the possibilities," Pascal answered in a neutral tone that neither confirmed nor denied our slight suspicion. I waited to see if anyone wanted to pick up the ball, and after some thinking, it was actually Ammy who leveled the next question at him.

"But if that's the case, then what reason would he have to write the letter in Celestial Script? And more importantly, how?"

"That we cannot say for sure yet," Armband Guy freely admitted, so I decided to adapt my most thoughtful expression ever and once again nudge him in a direction that wasn't necessarily the right one, but the most advantageous at the moment.

"Could it be a distraction?" I proposed with a conflicted frown hiding just how much I was enjoying leading the whole conversation by the nose. This was rapidly becoming a guilty pleasure of mine.

"Possible," he granted me. "However, if he attempted to shift the blame towards the Celestial Intelligence Network, then it was a sloppy job."

Pascal ended up responding quite negatively this time around, but I didn't let the topic go just yet.

"Not necessarily. After all, you had to spend a lot of time and effort on translating and double-checking the contents, time that our perps could use to get a head start on their escape."

"That... is a distinct possibility," he granted me again, if a little tentatively, but then he followed up with, "Nevertheless, it is an awful lot of effort to go through, using Celestial Script of all things, just for gaining a few hours of headway."

"Is that Script that special?" Josh interjected, and I was tempted to give him a subtle thumbs-up for steering the conversation in the right direction, even if by accident.

"Yes," Armband Guy declared, but when Joshua kept giving him an expectant gaze, he soon let out a small breath and he elaborated. "Celestial Script is more than a simple writing system. It not only conveys words, but complex thoughts and emotional states, as well, leading to multiple possible, often radically different readings of the same sentences. It is not only exceedingly hard to translate, but due to the way it is structured, only the Celestials themselves can write it. Artificial Script is easily distinguishable from the genuine article, and this note is genuine without a doubt."

"Does that mean it was written by a Celestial?" came the next reasonable question from Snowy, and everyone involuntarily glanced at Angie.

"It wasn't me!" she instantly denied the unspoken accusation while frantically waving her hands, which earned an almost-amused-sounding scoff from our guest.

"We never even entertained the thought. The Script used on the note was a complex yet archaic dialect with at least three meaning layers beneath the surface text. It is not something someone your age could produce."

"That's... both reassuring, and a little irritating," our resident Celestial grumbled under her breath, but it only lasted for a second before she bounced back with a question. "You said there were under-Scripts, right? What did they say?"

"That's right! Maybe there's a clue there!" Josh backed her up right away, and everyone turned their rapt attention at the upperclassman in our midst.

Instead of answering right away, Pascal's brows slowly knitted into a deep frown, to the point even his nose was scrunched up, and then, after no doubt thoroughly considering how much he should share with us, he finally opened his mouth again.

"As I said, Script is notoriously hard to translate, and the difficulty rises exponentially the deeper one tries to interpret it." He paused here one last time, probably further considering how much he would say, and after glancing at Ammy for a moment, he seemingly found his resolve and explained, "The second interpretation was along the lines of 'I'm an assassin with extended buildings, a captive of science. A microphone.'"

"A... microphone?" the class rep echoed him, and Pascal slowly nodded.

"As I said, deeper translations get increasingly more unreliable." At this point he let out a small snort, and amended, "Case in point, every translation attempt of the third layer resulted in unintelligible gibberish about fried cheese."

There was a long moment of baffled silence hanging in the air, during which my assistant was sending me an insistent, prickly stare. Armband Guy, fortunately, didn't notice it, and before I could tell her to cut it out, she actually spoke up first.

"I believe that settles it. I don't believe we know anyone else nonsensical enough to write something like that down other than Dr. Robatto."

"I agree!" Elly, well, agreed on the spot. "It sounds like something only someone crazy like him would do!"

"I think that we are all in agreement now," Joshua spoke up, suddenly adopting the role of a mediator. "The one who left the message, and therefore the one who broke into Ammy's grandpa's office, was almost certainly Robatto."

I'm not going to lie, this development left me more than a little dissatisfied, not just because of my girlfriends' jabs at me (be they intentional or inadvertent), but because while Josh's assertion was technically correct, the way he came to his conclusion was completely illogical and even ignored the bread-crumb trail I'd left for them to follow. It was ever-so-slightly absolutely aggravating. But then again, there was no point crying over spilled clues, so I let the whole thing go with a small, dejected sigh that nobody noticed.

"I see," Armband Guy spoke softly, and after taking a long breath, he suddenly raised his voice. "This was our suspicion, as well. Since you have come to this conclusion independently, I believe I can explain to you part of the reason behind my arrival. For you see, out of everyone on the island, you are the ones who have interacted the most with the aforementioned Dr. Robatto, so the lord felt it was prudent to ask about your opinion before we jumped to conclusions. Thank you for your cooperation."

"You're welcome," Josh responded just a little flippantly, but before he could add anything else, his spotlight was taken by his childhood friend again, as she leaned forward and did her whole investigative journalist routine, invisible mic and all.

"You said that was *part* of the reason. Is there something else you are not telling us?"

"As a matter of fact, no, since I am going to tell you right now."

"Oh..." Angie was taken aback for a moment, but then her enthusiasm flared up again like a propane torch in a storm. "Out with it then!"

"I am here to deliver a warning," Pascal proclaimed with tremendous gravitas, made only slightly comical by the fighting game music still blaring from the TV in the background. "Due to this incident, the Assembly has decided to lock down the island. No one may leave without our knowledge and permission. We are afraid that the Research Society, once they discover they are trapped on the island, might grow desperate and target you again."

"How is that different from everything being the same as usual?" I blurted out without too much thinking, but Armband Guy only shook his head without taking offense.

"Trust me, it is. I recommend requesting asylum in the School until the agents of the Assembly arrive and capture the perpetrators."

"Oh?" This time I outright scoffed as I raised a brow. "So when we were constantly being targeted by ambushes, you couldn't spare the manpower, but the moment someone stole Lord Grandpa's liquor cabinet, you guys immediately swing into action and offer us shelter. Doesn't that strike you as inconsistent?"

"The circumstances are wildly different," Armband Guy rebuked me with a sour bend in his lips, then after a moment of thinking he quickly added, "Also, this has nothing to do with the liquor."

"If you say so," I responded with an irreverent shrug before swinging back into the offensive again. "More importantly, though, considering our track record of keeping that dastardly Lab Coat Guy and his rascally robots at bay, especially compared to yours, I honestly don't see any merit in asking for your protection."

"The School possesses the most powerful wards and the tightest security system on the entire island."

"I'm sure it must be super-impressive! I mean, it's not like a certain Abyssal Lord and his mistreated sister managed to successfully lock down the school grounds and summon a gate to the Abyss. Or that a ridiculous-looking mad scientist could break into the heart of your compound and waltz away with the prized liquor collection of the freaking arch-mage of the island."

"... Why are you so fixated on the liquor cabinet?" the class rep abruptly interjected, and I gave her the flattest look I have ever flatted.

"Because the fact that someone could steal an entire cabinet full of booze from under the nose of the 'tightest security system on the entire island' is absolutely hilarious," I responded with just a hint of pride in my voice, but only Judy was aware of it, at least if the way she immediately rolled her eyes was any indication.

"Sorry, Ammy, he got you there," Josh came to my support like a good friend should, and he raised his hand to his face and held his thumb and index finger a coin's width apart. "It's a liiiitle hilarious."

For a change, the target of the class rep's menacing glasses tweaking wasn't me, but Josh either didn't understand the meaning behind the gesture, or he'd gotten used to it over the years, as he immediately laughed it off. In the meantime, Armband Guy slowly shook his head and addressed me again.

"The lord told me you would most likely react like that."

"Did he now?" I raised a single brow on incredulity, and Pascal gave me a stiff nod right away.

"Indeed. It was because of this that he ordered me to guard you until the current crisis was resolved."

"Guard us?"

The incredulous question came from the class rep of all people, and for once, I had to completely agree with her.

"So just to make sure I get this right," I spoke up with a raised voice. "When we were definitely under attack by a bunch of mechanical misfits, you couldn't spare the manpower to look after us, but now that we *might* be targeted by that scaaary scientific simpleton and his gaggle of goofball goons, *now* we must have a bodyguard."

"... Yes. That is precisely what I am telling you."

"Oh... Okay, just checking."

After that, there was a long moment of awkward silence in the room while no one knew what to say. It was situations like these where an overly enthusiastic genki girl was useful to lighten the mood, so I signaled at Angie with my eyes, and she got the message right away.

"Hey! Hey! So what are you planning to do? Are you going to just stand on the side with a stoic expression? Like those agents in the movies? You know, the ones that protect the president and stuff?"

"That was the plan..." Pascal confirmed just a tad awkwardly, and my friend immediately shook his head.

"No way. Having someone looking after us like that sounds awkward as hell."

"It's not that bad," Elly commented with a thoughtful expression, and when she noticed the others were giving her doubtful looks, she hastily clarified herself. "Our family often hires bodyguards, so I'm already used to people like them. They are just part of the scenery."

"Maybe for you, princess, but none of us have had bodyguards to get used to them like that," I gently explained to her, but she immediately retaliated with a smug little smirk.

"All the better! You should consider this part of your groom training!" She let out a triumphant chuckle, but then she gasped and pointed at my other girlfriend in turn. "The same goes for Judy, too!"

"I'm not your groom," my dear assistant deadpanned back at her, but it wasn't enough to break her moment.

"I fail to follow this conversation," Pascal stated with an odd expression.

"You'll get used to that if you hang out around us long enough," Ammy told him with a self-deprecating smile, which only made the guy even more confused.

"Never mind that," Josh suddenly cut in with a smile that said he just had a great idea. "So since we can't have you just standing around, there is only one thing left to ask!"

"Which is?" Armband Guy asked back with a guarded frown.

"How good are you at Street Kombat?"

"... The game?"

"What else?"

Our guest-slash-self-appointed-bodyguard fell silent for a moment, but then he stated, "I used to play the original in the arcade a lot back in middle school."

"Were you good at it?"

"It has been a while, but I reckon I could beat you guys with one hand behind my back."

"Oooo! Oooo hooo hooo!" Josh's lips parted in a wolfish grin at the guy's flippant answer, and he raised his hand and pointed a controller at him like a famous defense attorney before declaring, "Those are fighting words, pal! Come over here, and I'll have you eat them!"

"It is your funeral," Pascal shrugged in the company of a rare smile and promptly got up and walked over to the TV. He grabbed hold of the offered controller and sat down onto one of the cushions followed by my unusually fired-up friend, and a moment later, they were already on the character select screen.

"... The heck just happened?" I asked no one in particular, but my assistant, who exploited the fact that the space beside me got vacated and moved over, answered it all the same.

"I believe it's the beginning of a hot-blooded manly friendship."

Hearing her idea, my eyes involuntarily narrowed into a squint, and after a moment of thinking, I whispered back.

"Are you sure it's not just Josh's aura?"

"Not entirely impossible. We need to gather more data on the subject," she whispered back, only to then loudly clear her throat and grab hold of my sleeve. "Sorry, Elly, but I have to borrow the Chief for a moment. It's important."

"Oh... okay then," my other girlfriend reluctantly untangled our fingers, and before I knew it, I was already being dragged out of the living room and into the kitchen (though again, gently being led while Judy acted like she was hauling a mountain was more accurate, but I digress).

Once we arrived, my assistant went as far as to close the door behind us, and once she was sure nobody could see or hear us, she looked me in the eyes and let out a tired sigh.

"Chief. Please tell me what you did last night?"

"Do you really want to know?"

She lowered her voice even further, and whispered, "No matter what you say, I promise I won't kick you."

"... That was *very* specific."

"Chief..." she stressed the word, further emphasized by an unholy mixture of a threatening frown over a pair of puppy-eyes.

"Oh, fine," I finally relented and told her all about my misadventures in Lord Grandpa's office.

Needless to say, I got kicked anyway.

CHAPTER 13

PART 1

"... and that concludes my explanation of the current situation."

The moment Judy declared so, my living room burst into a mixture of surprised, excited, and occasionally indignant murmurs. On one side, Ammy and Angie were aghast. On the other side, Elly and Snowy were mildly perturbed by the news. Josh was... well, he was zoned out at the moment. Couldn't blame him; even I was a little exhausted after Judy's info dump, to the point I pretty much melted into my comfy chair like a deflated balloon. As for why we were in my house again, that is a tale for... well, I wanted to say another time, but really, why delay the inevitable exposition, amirite?

Seriously though, it all started a long, long few hours ago, in a Josh's house far, far away, and as with all great epics, it began with a tale of conflict as old as time: a powerful man defeating and humiliating a less powerful individual... in a sixteen-bit video game. This momentous and highly dramatic event of mythic proportions naturally resulted in a declaration of an eternal rivalry of the hot-blooded variety that would echo down the ages, or some such. I'm not entirely clear on the details, as I was being interrogated in my very own Spanish Inquisition at the time, but the way Josh recounted the event, it might as well have been one of those ancient Greek classics.

Anyhow, back to the inquisition part: Once she made me confess all my sins, Judy decided that we needed to have an emergency meeting to discuss what to do with, among other things, the resident mad scientist, the captive Celestial, and the missing liquor cabinet, not necessarily in that order of importance. Of course we couldn't exactly do that with Armband Guy loitering around us, so after some leading questions, we (read: me alone, because the others couldn't read the mood if it was written in seventy-two-point Arial Black) successfully convinced him that if he was worried about a surprise attack on our group, my house with Snowy's warding around it was by far the safest place for us to stay.

The thing is, I'd completely underestimated just how seriously he took his bodyguarding duties, as he acted so much like a professional that even Elly was impressed. He planned out the safest route to my place, gave instructions about how we should line up based on whether we were more offensive- or defensive-oriented, and the way he was constantly scanning our vicinity for threats on the way was the spitting image of an especially skittish meerkat.

Oh, and before I forget it: I finally discovered his power set! Apparently, Armband Guy specialized in the Negation branch of Abjuration, which in layman's terms meant he used a whole lot of barriers and force fields, mostly the semitransparent-bubble variety, though he also showed off a few fancy hexagonal shields, as well. It was slightly unexpected, but when I mentioned to Judy that this was usually the playing field of a trope-y archetype called the barrier maiden, she only rolled her eyes and told me to stop tempting fate. I was more than a little baffled by her reaction, as even if her interpretation of the Narrative could be influenced by somehow tempting fate like this, I doubt it would lead to Pascal suddenly changing his gender overnight to match the trope. That said, she didn't elaborate, so I didn't dwell on it for too long, either.

Where was I? Oh, right, our trek to my house. So after frequent stops and a whole lot of obnoxious safety measures forced on us, we successfully arrived at my place, just in time for the rain to finally stop. Then came the next problem: How do we get rid of Armband Guy without raising suspicion? No, wait. Let me rephrase that: How do *I* get rid of him without giving a single damn about suspiciousness? As it turned out, very easily.

As such, after treating him to a customary cup of hot drink, I promptly kicked him out by invoking the my-house-is-my-castle rule, meaning I could expel whomever I wanted, whenever I wanted. He took it surprisingly well, and based on later Far Sight observations, he kept patrolling around the neighbourhood with unwavering determination. I'm not going to lie, I found his dedication a tiny bit commendable. Not enough to substantially raise my opinion of him, but enough to feel a little sorry for him being ordered to go on a wild goose chase like that. I wondered if maybe I should Phase over after the meeting and give him another warm drink. Or make some "Kihihi!" noises to liven up his uneventful afternoon. One or the other.

But speaking of the meeting, let's return to the present, where the initial commotion over my assistant airing some of my dirty laundry finally settled down into an apprehensive and just mildly judgmental silence. That last part was mostly due to the class rep. Shocking, I know.

"So you've been busy," Josh spoke up in a jovial voice in an obvious attempt to ease the mood. It didn't really work.

"This is *not* the time to joke around!" The vehement rebuttal naturally came from Ammy, and she immediately proceeded to send me the mother of all menacing glasses tweaks. "If this is all true, we have to do something about Robatto!"

"Do we?"

My sister's innocent question was met with a frown so fierce it made her shrink back right away. Not that it took much to make her do so, so the class rep's expression was definitely overkill.

"Of course we have to!" she declared, her voice all but dripping with indignation.

"I don't know," Josh raised his voice at once as he unsubtly came to my sister's defense, his arms already crossed in front of his chest and one brow raised high. "We did our best yesterday, but we couldn't catch the guy. Now we don't even know where he is."

"We actually do." Upon her interruption, Josh's curious brow was immediately aimed at my assistant, and after a long beat, she amended, "And by that, I mean that the Chief knows where he is."

"Of course he does," Ammy grumbled under her breath, but before she could question me, Josh spoke up again.

"Even so, I don't see why we can't just leave it to your people." That comment earned him the dreaded Class Rep Glare™, so he hastily added, "I mean, we could just tell your grandfather where Robatto's hiding, and then have him take care of them."

"Weren't you listening!?" Ammy's voice actually broke for a moment, so a quick clearing of the throat was necessary before she could continue with an equally heated, "They have Michael, and since *someone* decided to somehow fake a note in Celestial Script at the scene of the biggest heist in the history of the Assembly, he's going to be arrested on the spot!"

"So?" Josh blurted out quite bluntly, much to my surprise.

"He's innocent. We can't let him get caught up in this," Ammy stressed while subtly averting her eyes, something that didn't escape our notice.

"Right! We have to save him!"

The in-retrospect-not-too-unexpected call of support came from Angie. She clenched both her fists in front of her, and her face was overflowing with determination to the point it formed a small, illusory puddle under her. Josh still looked skeptical of the prospect, so she faced him right away.

"Mike is my dad's second cousin's stepson! He's practically family!"

"How many times removed is that?" I wondered, only to be dismissed out of hand by her.

"He's family all the same! We *have* to rescue him!"

"Fine, whatever. He's your relative, then," Josh finally relented with the grudging grousing of an ornery mule, and then after a short while he turned to Ammy again. "Is his situation really that bad? Can't you just ask your grandfather to let him go after he was captured, or recaptured, or whatever?"

"It's not that simple," she responded in a dour voice and sent a sharp glance my way. "A *certain someone* stole one of the most important relics of the Magi from grandfather's office. He's keeping the scope of the incident under wraps for the moment, but the rest of the Assembly is already preparing to send specialists to look into the situation. If they learn that one of the Grimoire Keys was taken from under Grandfather's watch, it will greatly affect his standing; he might even lose his position in the Assembly. Now consider that our School is mainly a research institute, with the only two combat-ready members being Grandfather and Pascal, which means they would have to be the ones to assault Robatto's hideout. Considering all that, do you really think he's going to be in the mood to negotiate the release of a Celestial captive involved in the incident?"

"If you put it like that..." Josh mumbled under his breath as the last of his resistance crumbled.

"I think we should help him, too," came the next unexpected comment from my sister of all people.

"You do?" I blurted out in surprise while unconsciously mimicking Josh's expert eyebrow technique, and she immediately nodded in the affirmative. Her answer, on the other hand, was slightly less confident.

"I-I mean... They are the bad guys, right?" The rest of us shared an odd look between one another at this point, but for the time being, I gave her the benefit of the doubt in that she was getting to a point, so I gestured for her to continue. "If they are the baddies, and if we fight against them, that makes us the good guys, right?"

That was a slightly dubious conclusion, but I figured this wasn't the time or place to discuss the nuances of moral relativism, so I gave her a small nod. Snowy let out a pent-up breath, as if she'd just overcome a serious hurdle.

"Then, if we are the good guys, isn't it our job to defeat the bad guys and rescue the people caught up in the conflict?"

Her rhetorical question was met with a long beat of silence, followed by a still-grumpy Josh muttering, "Well, I can't really argue with *that*."

Once again, I felt like there were plenty of good arguments to be made here, but I decided to stay silent and let the others work this out among themselves.

"Let's put it to the vote!" my draconic girlfriend proposed at once, with a serious face that said this was the most logical idea in the world and she wouldn't hear anything to the contrary.

"Sure," Ammy agreed before I could even react and raised her hand. "All in favor of capturing Robatto and rescuing Michael, raise your hand."

"I'm for!" Angie came forth at once, raising both arms and waving them with enough enthusiasm for three people.

"I suppose I'm in, too."

Josh's half-hearted reply and equally limp raised hand was still met with a high five from his childhood friend. The next member of our group raising her hand was naturally Snowy, and while she didn't get a palm slap of her own, Angie was about as happy about her decision as when Josh had entered the fold.

That left only my girlfriends and me. The way the two of them looked at me said they could go either way depending on my decision, and the trust they placed in me would've been fairly heartwarming if not for the fact that we were at three against four, so the vote was already decided.

"Sure, let's do it."

My agreement was met with exhalations so relieved they were honestly a little off-putting. I mean, what difference would it make if I said no? While I tried to logic out the reason for my friends' reaction, Elly also raised her hand high.

"If Leo's in, then I'll help, too!"

"I can't do much, but for the sake of completion, let me also throw a yes onto the ballot," Judy proclaimed, thus closing the vote.

"Great." Ammy's single word had a surprising amount of gravitas behind it, and for a moment it seemed like things would calm down a little. Then she dropped a bombshell. "When are we setting out? Do we wait until dusk?"

"Wait! Hold your horses for just a minute!" She fell silent the moment I raised my voice, and her hand was already in the process of reaching for her glasses when I continued with, "You seriously want to do it today? Without any plans?"

"We have to," she argued back at me in the company of a displeased frown.

"But why though?" I challenged her right back, and she rolled her eyes as if I'd just asked an oblivious question.

"The agents of the Assembly could arrive at any moment. We have to resolve this on our own, and as soon as possible."

"I agree with Ammy." I glanced at the source of the class rep's unlikely supporter, and when he noticed my gaze, Josh simply shrugged his shoulders. "I mean, if we decided to do it, we might as well do it ASAP and put his whole Robatto and Michael business behind us."

"I wholeheartedly agree with the previous speaker," Angie exclaimed with her usual brand of enthusiasm, and she raised her hand high. For a moment I thought she was fishing for another high five, but then she proclaimed, "All who are in favor, raise your hand!"

"Hold on... We didn't put this up to vote," I protested, only to get summarily disregarded when Ammy added to the momentum by raising her hand.

"Now it is. Who else is with us?"

"As I said, I'm still in," Josh joined the fray with one palm held high.

"Oh, come on! At least try to pretend you have a plan before you jump in!"

"We had a plan the last time, and Robatto still got away," Josh noted without letting his hand down.

"Right, which means we would have even less of a chance to catch him if we try it without any preparations. For example, I doubt you could convince Pascal to join us out of the blue. In the worst-case scenario, he might even get in the way, or report it to Lord Grandpa."

"And that's why we can't tell him," Ammy told me, and this time it was my turn to send a frown her way. "Even if he wouldn't tell Grandfather right away, Pascal would not let Michael go. If that happened, we'd be back to square one."

"Then what? Just do this on our own without any backup?"

"I could ask Uncle Brang for support?" Snowy suggested in an uncertain voice, but the class rep quickly dismissed her idea with a shake of her head.

"No, they are too conspicuous. If Robatto saw them during the assault, he would certainly talk about them during the interrogation."

"You're right. That would be hard to explain," my sister granted her without any resistance. I, on the other hand, couldn't help but exhale a short-yet-decidedly-lung-rattling groan.

"So let me see if I've got this straight," I said in a low voice as my hand unconsciously rose to my head to massage my temple. "You want to rush in and assault Lab Coat Guy's hidey-hole without any plan, without help from Armband Guy, and without involving the Fauns in any shape or form. What exactly makes you think things are going to turn out better than the last time like that?"

"You would be there?" Josh answered with an honest grin that gave me pause for a moment.

"I don't think that would make as much of a difference as you think," I answered just a tad dourly, but it didn't stop my friends to keep looking at me with expectant eyes.

"I think it would, actually," Ammy noted on the side, drawing my attention.

"And in that case, you would be wrong," I told her flatly, but the atmosphere refused to change. I glanced over everyone present one at a time, and at last my eyes landed on Judy. I closed my eyes for a second, then after a long breath I rose to my feet and pointed at her. "Okay, I need some time out to think this through. Dormouse, please come along."

"Sure," Judy responded without missing a beat and slipped her phone into her pocket.

"Just the two of you?" Elly asked with puppy eyes, but unfortunately this wasn't something where I could compromise, so I planted an apologetic peck on her forehead. It wasn't a perfect solution, but for the time being it calmed her down enough.

"Sorry, but this is a tactical discussion."

"Didn't you already have one at my place?" Josh mused, and before I could answer, Ammy also joined the fray.

"Right. Also, if it's tactical, isn't it all the more reason why you should do it where we can also contribute?"

"No," I told her, and when she looked like she was getting ready to argue back, I added a stern, "And that's final."

In the meantime Judy got ready, so I gestured for her to follow after me, and we walked over to my teleportation closet while staunchly ignoring the scrutinizing eyes following us. I opened the door, and my dear assistant walked right in. Once we were inside, she turned on her heels and gave me a questioning glance, but I shook my head and wrapped my phantom limb around her.

A few moments later we both walked out into the reception room of the secret base, and after a few steps, Judy repeated the whole turning-on-her-heels thing, but this time she straight-up asked me.

"What's the problem?"

"You mean besides the way things are developing at the speed of a runaway freight train?" She didn't appreciate my snappy answer, so I took a deep breath and reiterated. "What I was trying to say was, I'd like to ask your opinion on the situation."

"Narrative implications included?"

"Naturally. Why else would I take you over here?"

"Noted," she responded with a nod, and then she casually took her phone out again. While she did that, we walked over to one of the padded benches and sat down.

"First and foremost, I wanted to hear what you think about the whole impromptu operation. Do you think we should go through with it the way Ammy wants to?"

"Since when did you ask for my permission to jump headfirst into risky affairs?"

"Come on, Dormouse. Not now," I chided her, but she seemed entirely serious, so after a short while I gave up and told her, "Listen, I admit that I might've taken a few slightly dangerous options in the past couple of days, but this situation is on a different level entirely. We are no longer dealing with *sentai* shenanigans. There's no longer a contract holding Lab Coat Guy and his posse back, and Ammy in her hurry to rescue Mike has already cut off most of our safety nets. If we do this, the guys might get hurt, or worse."

"I think I'm starting to see where you are coming from," Judy noted, and then fell silent for a long while. "Before we discuss anything else, do you have an alternative way of dealing with the situation?"

"Honestly, I was planning on framing Lab Coat Guy and then letting him and Lord Grandpa duke it out between each other, and then deal with the fallout of Mike later. What I didn't expect was that taking the Grimoire Key would escalate things so much."

"You should have."

"Hey, give me some slack. Hindsight is always twenty-twenty." My protests fell on deaf ears, so I decided to move the conversation along by saying, "Anyhow, while my original plan could still be executed, I would have to smuggle Mike out before the confrontation between the two, and I can't do it without revealing my Phasing ability."

"You shouldn't do that in front of a Celestial agent."

"I know, that's why I haven't done it. It's still my emergency plan in case the guy is in danger, but for the time being, he is safe, if confined."

"So in the end rescuing him the old-fashioned way is the only reasonable option?"

"Yeah, I just don't know why it has to be us," I paused here for a moment as a new idea sprouted in the back of my mind, and asked, "Do you think it's a bad idea to leak his capture to the Celestials?"

"Depends. Is causing a scandal between the supernatural superpowers and a possible three-way battle a bad idea?"

"... In that case, scratch that. What other options do we have?"

"Chief, I'm sorry to say this, but this is a bed you made. You must lie in it."

"Can't you say anything reassuring today?"

"I would love to, but no, I can't."

"Well... darn."

After that exchange, we both fell silent for a subjectively long time. I was just about to consider my options for the third time when Judy poked me in the elbow to draw my attention.

"Why don't you just go along with the others?" My expression was probably pretty odd at this moment, as she also added, "It seems like the Narrative really wants you to do this. They, too."

"Yeah, and it's creeping me out. I mean, the latter, not the possibility of things escalating because the Narrative is on the verge of having a blue screen of death. Have you seen how they were looking at my reactions? It's almost as if they thought suddenly everything would work out if they got me involved."

"That's not *almost*; it's literally what they think."

"Yes, and th—" I began, only to stop with my mouth halfway open. "Excuse me, but could you repeat that?"

"They really think that if you are with them, things will go smoothly."

"... And how do you know that, if I may ask?"

"Amelia said so, and Angeline also agreed. They also think that the reason why they couldn't catch Robatto the first time around was because *you* weren't around."

"That's just silly."

My dear assistant looked me in the eye for a moment, and then she declared, "Chief, please stop avoiding your responsibility. You've acted as the group's leader from the beginning, and there is nothing silly about their trying to rely on you."

"Yeah, but I never really tried to be the leader on purpose. I'd prefer if Josh, or even Ammy, would step up to the plate instead."

"Well, I never wanted to live in an artificial world and would've preferred if I could have you for myself in a monogamous relationship, but sometimes you just have to work with the hand that life deals you."

We kept looking eye to eye for a while longer, but at last I had to give up, and after looking up at the ceiling I muttered, "To quote a famous harem protagonist, I really can't argue with *that*."

"You better not. Otherwise, I would have to kick you."

"Oh, the horror," I responded in a dull voice and then exhaled sharply through my nose to clear my thoughts. "Fine, I'll pretend to be a responsible leader type for the time being. Now let's move on to the second part of our discussion: How would you describe the current situation on trope-y terms, and how did we end up with it?"

"I have a hypothesis," Judy declared with a new sense of vigor in her voice. "I think the current arc is being aborted."

"Ooookay. Please elaborate."

"We've already discussed this in the past, but in my opinion, the Narrative operates on the basis of plot arcs. I believe that with your latest stunt, you messed up the current arc centered around Friedrich Günther Wissenschaftler and Lord Amadeus Endymonion past the point of recovery, so the Narrative is cutting its losses before it would start affecting future arcs."

"In other words, the thing we joked about the last time kind of came true... Does that count as tempting fate?"

"Probably, but stay focused," Judy reproached me with a huff. "If the current situation really is the result of an arc being aborted, then there are a few things we should look out for."

"Such as extensive info dumps about the antagonist's tragic backstory and revealing all the special abilities and power ups they were supposed to unveil over the arc all at once?"

"Precisely," she stated with a nod, and for a moment I was lost for words.

"I... was actually half joking about that."

"It doesn't make what you said any less accurate. It is likely that in this confrontation, the Research Society is going to reveal all of their hidden cards and go out with a blaze of glory."

What she'd said made a certain kind of sense, at least as far as fiction was concerned. When a story gets axed for one reason or the other, authors often try to condense as much of the original story they dreamed up into the premature finale as they could. If Judy's idea was even in the ballpark of the truth, then it wasn't unreasonable to expect that Lab Coat Guy would pull out all the stops and reveal all the hidden aces up his sleeve he was supposed to use one at a time over his time in the limelight. But then again, this was hardly any different from simply being cornered and being forced to use everything at his disposal, but that was probably only my inner Watsonian argumentator speaking.

While I was considering all that, the door leading into the main hall of the secret base opened to a crack, and one of the Fauns cautiously poked his head through. He glanced around and straight-up froze the moment he noticed us. After a long moment of silence, he hastily threw the door open and walked over with rushed steps, only to come to a screeching halt in front of us and give us a salute. Now that he was closer, I finally recognized that it was Vurrok, but before I could greet him, he lowered his head to the point I thought he was about to get down on all fours.

"[Please forgive me, my lord. I did not expect your arrival.]"

I gave him a wry look, and told him, "Don't apologize; you were on anchor duty like you were supposed to be."

He let out a relieved grunt in response and finally straightened his back. Seriously though, will I have to order each one of them to stop calling me *my lord* individually? Well, that was a concern for another time, and since he was already here, I decided to put the Faun to good use.

"On a separate note, could you get me a spear?"

"[You mean... *that* spear?]" he asked back, a little uncertainly, and I immediately shook my head.

"No, of course not. I'm talking about the backup spear in the armoury. Please bring it to me; I'm going to need it later today."

"[Your wish is my command, my lord!]" he exclaimed, and he immediately turned in place and practically jogged out of the room.

Once he was outside, Judy finally stopped trying to hide behind me while I was still sitting on the bench, and after she fixed up her skirt, she asked me in a voice so artificially nonchalant it almost hurt my ears.

"If you're asking for a weapon, I suppose you decided to go along with the Narrative."

After a moment of thinking, I slowly shook my head, and with my mouth already set in a sly smile I told her, "Do you really take me for someone who would just let some trope-y crap dictate my life?"

"I was under the impression that you also wanted to get rid of Friedrich Günther Wissenschaftler and any chance of a genre shift."

"Yes," I confirmed, with my smile growing even wider (and maybe just a tad sinister) as I appended, "But on my terms."

PART 2

"{Testing, testing. Can you hear me?}"

"Clear, though not particularly loudly," I responded to the voice of Judy that felt like it was coming from right inside my head.

"{How about now?}"

"Much better."

My girlfriend let out an affirmative grunt and moved on to check the connection with the others. In the meantime, I checked the time, followed by a brief Far Glance at Armband Guy. It was already past seven in the evening, but he still didn't notice that we'd sneaked out of the house. Well, on second thought, saying *sneaked out* was slightly inaccurate, as I'd actually Phased everyone over to the secret base, and we set out onto our impromptu operation from there. It was this late because my plans to order a couple of cabs to take us to the docks was vetoed by Ammy (apparently it would have been too suspicious), so we trekked over to the closest bus stop, and then we took the island's reliable mass transit system to the outskirts of the dock district.

Explaining why I had a spear with me to the driver was a little tricky, but I managed by claiming that we were a LARPing group scouting out the nearby woods in advance of a session, and then I overwhelmed the poor placeholder with so much useless detail, he completely locked up and we used the opportunity to slip by him.

Anyhow, putting my transportation tribulations aside, we arrived in the vicinity of our destination a little after six, and then came the somewhat-arduous task of actually locating Lab Coat Guy. It was a little tricky due to a quirk of my Far Sight: while I could instinctively identify his dot, and I knew of its general whereabouts, it didn't exactly give me the GPS coordinates to pinpoint the precise location. Because of this, I had to get creative by using a primitive form of triangulation, telling Snowy and Angie to both walk twenty steps away from me in different directions, and then using their relative distances from me to get a more accurate grasp on Lab Coat Guy's position.

Once we got into the neighbourhood, it didn't take a genius to figure out where to look for him. I mean, picture this: One long street parallel to the waterfront. From left to right, we had a boat lender, a commercial dock with a ton of containers, a tariff office, a mermaid-themed Hello Kitty souvenir shop, then a huge-ass, completely abandoned, and somewhat-crumbling military warehouse with an open courtyard and signs of recent movement around the enormous metal doors leading into the building, and then finally, a sailor pub called Davy Jones's Liquor. I mean wasn't it just blatantly obvious that the secret base would be none other than the souvenir shop?

... Nah, I'm kidding. It was the warehouse, or to be more specific, the extensive basement hidden underneath the already-imposing concrete complex, but let's not split hairs about it.

"{I'm done. Everyone can hear me.}"

"Roger," I muttered in response to Judy's declaration, and I looked over the rest of our group, all of whom were already in their Magiforms. Anyhow, it took some phantom limb elbow grease, but I managed to finish the communication artifact I'd promised for Judy a while back, and it allowed her to talk to us regardless of distance or if we were inside a Purple Zone, and with it, she could serve as our remote mission control. Said artifact incidentally looked like a pair of incredibly gaudy, star-shaped sunglasses (originally supplied by Mike), but it was the only thing that already had the required visual enchantment in place, so I had to build on that to finish things on time.

It looked hideous, something on which we both agreed, but she was staying in the base at the moment, so it wasn't like anyone was going to laugh at her appearance. Especially after I prohibited the Fauns from doing so, under the threat of a court-martial.

But I digress. Now, as for the thing's actual functionality: by reactivating and tweaking the original surveillance enchantments on the Magiformers, it allowed her to see and hear everything the currently observed user could, with a few extra helpful metrics on top. No, I'm not talking about health and mana gauges, but technical stuff, like atmospheric mana density, or various overlays that let her see heat signatures and the like. In short, it was a bootleg version of the vision enhancements a tribal hunter space alien with dreadlocks and a really horrid mouth would use.

There was only one slight issue with it (aside from the way it looked), namely the fact that I'd made it to be compatible with the Magiforms, and I didn't have one myself. Nor could I use one even if I had, due to a lack of magical mojo. Well, *technically* I could have, if I'd really wanted to, by using the same kind of mana battery that allowed Judy to use her mission-control glasses without being able to use magic on her own, but I never got around to making one, mainly because doing so would've been not only a long-term job, but a huge pain in the neck to boot. Redesigning a specialized suit that was intended to run on esoteric energies of the mystical variety drawn directly from the user and not from an outside source, was... well, I wanted to say "Beyond my expertise," but it was honestly more of a beyond-my-headache-tolerance situation.

The point is, for the time being, I had to do with a simple silver ear wrap, which aside from making me look fabulous (in Angie's words, not mine, and she received her well-deserved forehead flick for her trouble), provided me with an alternative as far as communication was concerned, at least for the time being. It wasn't exactly my size, so I had to bend it a little to comfortably fit me, but beggars can't be choosers. It only allowed verbal communication (so Judy couldn't peep on me), and the line could only be opened or closed from her side, but it was better than nothing.

Speaking of better than nothing, while I couldn't wear a magical school uniform, that still didn't mean I'd resigned myself to be completely defenseless. For a start, under my usual long coat I was wearing a ballistic vest I'd ordered online. It wasn't exactly military grade, but it would protect from shrapnel, and it even had a few ceramic plates to protect my squishier bits just a little better. I also put on a pair of heavy, steel-toed work boots, as well as padded airsoft pants. Of course none of those would help me against, say, a direct hit by a magitech plasma cannon, but they didn't interfere with my movement, and if they deflected just a single stray projectile in the thick of it, they would already earn back their price.

But back to the situation at hand: I was currently standing behind the corner of a nearby building with a good view of the warehouse. Josh and the princess were on lookout duty, while our two magical experts were out to set up an anchor point for a Purple Zone, with Angie ostensibly serving as their sentry while they worked. According to the class rep, it was a necessity due to the area being warded by our antagonists, which made calling down an anchorless Purple Zone on it an exercise in futility. Her explanation was a lot more technical, but that was the gist of it.

"It's quiet. Too quiet," Josh noted on the side quite ominously, which naturally earned him a very pointed eye roll.

"Please stop tempting fate."

"{That's funny when it's coming from you,}" my dear assistant chimed in completely unannounced or unneeded, resulting in an eye roll in the other direction.

"Dormouse, I know that you enjoy having a direct line to my head, but please don't open communications just for idle chatter."

"{I'm combining work with pleasure,}" she responded in a slightly more animated voice than in face-to-face conversations, but I was already used to that. It was a bit of a culture shock for the others, but that's a story for another time. "{Amelia and Neige completed their objective, and they are on their way back to the rendezvous location. ETA is twenty-five seconds.}"

"... You really enjoy your mission-control roleplay, don't you?"

"{I'm just happy to be helpful,}" she responded, but then a moment later she yanked the steering wheel of the conversation to a ninety-degree angle by unexpectedly asking, "{How's your head?}"

"Manageable," I replied under my breath. In fact, I'd almost managed to successfully ignore the drum solo of stings going on in my head until she reminded me of it, but I wasn't going to tell her that.

It wasn't an unexpected development by any stretch of the imagination. While the backlash was considerably less severe than what I expected, I still hadn't fully recovered from my jaunt with the Chimera the day before, and then I further overexerted my phantom limb with all of this last-minute enchantment tweaking today. While my headache was little more than a throbbing buzz at the moment, I had a feeling I was running on borrowed time, so I wanted to get things over with before I would crash. With my luck, I didn't have any illusions about everything going smoothly, but I hoped I could set things into motion and then sit back while Josh and Co. picked up the pieces.

I mean, that's what leader types do, isn't it? Pretend to know what's going on, act stoic in the face of all the weird and unexpected stuff inevitably happening around them, and then when the dust settles, they flash a nefarious smile and declare that everything went according to keikaku (*keikaku* means "Shit conveniently happened in a way so that it looked like I was on top of things"). Or was that the strategist archetype? Either way, I planned to act my part while trying to spare myself as much as possible.

Anyhow, while I pondered about the finer points of leadership, the three girls on anchor duty finally arrived back at our vantage point.

"Private Angie, reporting for duty, sir!" the upbeat Celestial declared the moment I laid my eyes on her, and since I'd already rolled them a lot recently, this time I settled on a mildly disparaging sigh to express my feelings.

"Judy acting as mission control is having a bad influence on you guys," I murmured as I stopped leaning against a wall, only to receive an instant rebuttal.

"{Your baseless accusation hurts Officer Judy's feelings.}"

I naturally completely ignored the girl having way too much fun with her new role and focused my attention on the girl with the glasses at the back.

"How did it go?"

"We set down two anchor points near the outskirts," Ammy answered while she passed by the still-saluting Angie. "Any more than that would've made them aware of our presence."

"The buildings are more heavily warded than we first thought," Snowy added as she passed by the Celestial from the other side. She was still standing at attention while giving me an expectant look, so I whispered a grudging "At ease" in her general direction, if only to keep things moving. She stopped saluting, but instead she was now grinning with even her molars showing.

"How long will it last?" I asked once I had my focus back on the returnees.

"About forty minutes, an hour at most," Snowy noted, only for the class rep to immediately follow up with her much-less-generous prediction.

"The School is on high alert at the moment, so the Diviners should be on the lookout for any Restricted Spaces being erected on the island. I'd say we'll have about half an hour at best before Grandfather will dispatch someone to the docks. Ideally, we should already be gone by then."

"Thirty minutes should be enough," I told her before addressing the whole group. "Gather up, guys. It's homework time."

"What now?" Josh grumbled as he came closer, and I waited for everyone to gather up before I continued.

"Let's make sure we are on the same page: Our primary goal today is not to capture Lab Coat Guy or his accomplices, but to rescue our distant Celestial acquaintance before the local Magi raid this place, Mike gets recaptured by Ammy's grandpa, and he gets vivisected or something."

"Hey! Don't slander our School! We no longer do that!"

That was a rather disturbing bit of implication I could definitely live without ever knowing about, but for the time being I decided to staunchly ignore the class rep's objection, and instead I focused on the briefing at hand.

"Theoretical dissections aside, I want *you* to recite the plan we agreed upon, just to make sure you remember it."

"Er... Sure, I suppose?" Josh responded a little uncertainly, and after glancing at each of the girls in turn, it finally dawned on him that by speaking up first, he more or less nominated himself to start the explanation. "So, um... First, we turn on the Restricted Space, and drag in everyone except that Celestial guy inside the building over there."

"Everyone but him and the big biomechanical things," Angie corrected her friend while sticking her head over his shoulder, and Josh gave an appreciative grunt in return.

"Right, the Gigants stay so that they can't transform into the large horny robot."

"So far so good," I told them with a nod. "Then what?"

"Then we make a huge ruckus to draw them out," Elly said, and the rest of the group nodded in agreement.

"You also said you would take care of this part," Ammy elaborated while pointing at me, and I confirmed her words with a smile.

"Yeah, you can leave that to me."

"{It is only logical, as you're an expert at getting under dangerous people's skin,}" Judy commented on the side, and by the way Angie and Josh suddenly started snickering, I probably wasn't the only one who'd heard it.

"Hush, Dormouse. Let's focus on the next step of the plan. Anyone?"

"We hold their attention?" Snowy answered a tad timidly, so I flashed her a brotherly smile to ease her nerves.

"We should also prioritize our safety and only prevent Robatto from escaping for as long as possible," Ammy added right away, followed by, "In the meantime, you leave the Restricted Space and get Michael out of captivity."

"And because all the baddies are going to be in the Zone, you can just walk in and out without a single obstacle!" Angie concluded with an excited grin, and while I wanted to argue that it wasn't quite that simple, I decided to hold my objections in for the time being.

"After that, you will give us the signal to retreat," the princess remarked, then after a short pause she added, "And then we all sit back and watch the mayhem when the arch-mage arrives. I think."

"That's what Leo said," the hyperactive Celestial noted, and they shared a glance of mutual understanding.

Their explanation was accurate on all the broad strokes, so I let out a quiet hum of approval and said, "Yes, that's the gist of it. Any questions before we begin?"

"How are you going to leave the Restricted Space?" Ammy leveled one at me right away, which wasn't much of a surprise.

"I have my ways," I answered mysteriously, only to get undermined by my dear assistant.

"{The Chief is a man of many talents, but giving smooth elusive answers is unfortunately not one of them.}"

"Dormouse, please stop being sarcastic; you're distracting Angie," I chided my girlfriend while pointing at the still snickering Celestial, and then I told our group, "If there's nothing else, we might as well get on with it."

"Just like that?" Josh blurted out with a raised brow, and I reaffirmed my previous statement.

"Yes. We don't need to overcomplicate this." Saying so, I undid the safety cloth wrapped around the head of my spear and set its butt against the ground with a satisfying thud, then after some deliberation, I decided it was time for a leaderly display of raising the morale before the battle. "Let's just get in there, draw the guy's attention, and then get out with everyone in one piece. I'll try to be quick, so you'll only have to bog them down for a few minutes, and before you know it, we are already going to be back home watching the next season of *Trucy the Werewolf Huntress*."

"Sure, just give me a minute," Josh mumbled a smidgen absentmindedly while rummaging in his pockets for one of the small containers holding Snowy's and the princess's blood samples. We'd prepared them just before we left the base, and they were kept fresh and liquefied in the tiny medical capsules I custom ordered for this purpose. Using these to transform Josh didn't last as long as directly taking it from the source, and the blood held in the containers spoiled after about a day, but they were still a hell of a lot more convenient than having to prick the girls on-site every time Josh needed to fight.

In the meantime, he finally found one of the capsules, and then he noted, still absently, "By the way, are we up to the sixth season already?"

"Aw... that season sucks," his Celestial pal responded with overexaggerated trepidation. "Now I don't feel like doing anything anymore..." I sent the girl a critical glance, and when I raised a hand and bent my fingers a little, she immediately hid behind Josh while guarding her forehead and hastily declared, "I'm kidding! Just kidding! I'm totally pumped and everything!"

One disappointed sigh later I gestured for the group to follow me, and our small procession walked over to a fairly unassuming corner of the warehouse in question.

"Okay, we're in position," I told them, prompting a number of confused glances towards the perimeter.

"Here?" came the incredulous question from Ammy, and so I pointed at one certain part of the wall. They couldn't see it, but there was a small, glowing magical something there, which reminded me of a steampunk version of an artificial eye, with a lot of random gears and metal tubes sticking out of a blinking orb in the middle. Needless to say, it was Lab Coat Guy's own brand of magical surveillance, so after giving it a small wave, I turned back to the class rep.

"Please open the Purple Zone. No need to be ceremonious about it, either."

She grumbled something under her breath which I couldn't quite catch, but whatever it was, she still faithfully followed my request, closed her eyes, and a few long seconds later the world went negative, and then all purple.

Looking around, I was once again reminded of the fact that humans were really adaptive creatures. The first time I was taken into this convenient battleground space, I was quite freaked out, but by now, it was nothing special. Hell, even Josh, who was newer to the whole supernatural shebang than me, was too busy discussing which was the worst episode of the werewolf huntress show to even care about his surroundings turning the colour of eggplants. On a side note, I was getting a little annoyed by how laid-back they were acting, so I gently poked his feet with the blunt end of my spear.

Once my friend stopped hopping on one leg while sending a death glare my way, I let out a pent-up sigh and looked right into the magical camera. There was a long beat while I Far Glanced over, and once I was sure I had their attention, I took a breath so deep the air needed spelunking equipment.

"Hey, Friedrich!" My bellow may or may not have scared my friends, but I was in the zone at the moment, so I didn't care. Instead, I continued with, "We're here to have a talk! Or a fight! Whichever one you prefer!" There was another long pause I spent using my Far Sight on them, then I added, "No, this is not a joke! Please come out at your earliest convenience, or we might have to invite ourselves in!"

"What exactly are you doing?" Ammy abruptly interrupted me while tugging at my elbow. I glanced over my shoulder, and then simply shrugged them.

"Psychological warfare?" I proposed, but then my Far Sight caught something else, so I turned back to the steampunk orb and yelled, "No, your boots are under the table, in the big duffel bag! You don't need them, though; just come out already!"

The class rep looked like she wanted to say more, but at the end of the day she slowly slouched her shoulders and walked back to the rest while shaking her head. In the meantime, I continued my verbal assault without missing a beat.

"Stop wasting time looking for your biomechanical whatchamacallits! They are not in the warehouse! No, not even the small one! Also, tell the fembot her voice is also annoying, and she doesn't see me call her out on it! Yes, I've heard that, too! ... No, I don't know where your master is hiding his secret stash of porn magazines, and I don't really care, either! ... Stop bickering and just come out already, will you?! We don't have all day!"

My one-sided conversation continued for about a minute longer like this, but at last I could let out a breath of relief. It was about time, too; my throat was about to get sore from all the yelling. Turning around, I saw that Josh was already in his Magiform, Angie had her bow out, and the class rep had summoned her golem, as well. Elly and Snowy were the same as usual, but even so, our group was decidedly combat ready.

"They are coming. Get into position," I instructed my friends, and while they looked skeptical and maybe even a little appalled (even the princess, which hurt me a little), they followed after me all the same, and we took up our spots in front of the enormous sliding metal doors of the warehouse.

A minute or so of tense waiting later, said door began to open up with the pained creaks of rusty metal, and just like that, Lab Coat Guy and his company came into sight. The man himself was still wearing his costume, including the custom welder's mask and the magitech shoulder pads, except instead of boots, he had a pair of bright plastic clogs on his feet. I was the one who'd told him not to waste time searching for his usual footwear, so it might've been hypocritical of me to say this, but I could barely stop myself from laughing out loud the moment I noticed that. The others probably skimmed over this detail, as they finally acted with the seriousness befitting of the situation, and I decided it was for the best that I didn't draw attention to it, either.

Beside the aforementioned fashionably challenged mad scientist stood his personal android. She wasn't wearing a costume, opting for a way more reasonable woolen sweater and thick cargo pants, plus a grey scarf around her neck. Her attractive figure, combined with her casual-yet-somehow-still-oddly-stylish apparel, only made the contrast with Lab Coat Guy even more glaring. Also, apparently fembots could also get chilly. Who would've thought?

Finally, behind these two stood several rows of silly *sentai* foot-soldier robots. They all looked entirely identical save for the five bots right behind the two ringleaders. Each one of those had different body types; one was a bit more buff than average, another had extra spikes on its shoulders and slightly longer arms, and so on and so forth. They were also coloured differently, as while the rest were uniform yellow, these ones were all covered in different primary colours. In other words...

"Oh look, we have elite mooks now. Lovely," I grumbled under my breath to no one in particular, yet I was still heard.

"{It was inevitable, just like death, taxes, and you having to explain our relationship to Elly's mother from the ground up.}"

"... Dormouse, if you keep using this line just to throw jabs at me, I'll revoke your mission-control privileges."

My dear (if sometimes just a liiiiiitle bit trying) girlfriend stayed wisely silent, so I left it at that. In the meantime, our antagonists for the evening came to a halt about ten meters away from us, and as such we suddenly had a classic standoff on our hands in the middle of the tarmac-covered front yard. Like in the movies, but without tense music and no flock of easily startled white doves in sight.

"Kihihi!" Our conversation was started with Lab Coat Guy's familiar-yet-no-less-irritating laughter. "If it isn't Leonard Dunning himself!"

"Yup. Good evening," I greeted him with a lazy wave, but he didn't appreciate the courtesy.

"Are you here to finish the job you started?" he leveled the odd question at me, and before I could respond, he raised his voice both in volume and pitch as he added, "Did you come to deliver us to that traitorous old man?!"

"Well, no, not really," I responded reflexively, but then I remembered that this time I was actually looking for a fight, so de-escalating was not a good idea. "I mean, yeah, sure. We are totally here to do that. Very treacherously and stuff."

My disinterested act was not convincing at all, but by this point Lab Coat Guy was already so worked up he didn't care.

"I knew it!" he declared, but then his android companion unsubtly poked his side with her elbow.

"Master, I'm eighty-seven-point-seven percent certain he was being sarcastic."

"Is he?"

"Oh, not at all. I'm completely sincere and about as serious as an *Onion* article on politics," I told them, only for the fembot to send me a glare for my trouble.

"Master, now I'm one hundred percent sure he's making fun of you."

"Kihihi! So what if he does? I don't care!" he declared, followed by another bout of hysterical chuckles. "He already saved us a lot of trouble by delivered himself to our doorstep, so he can have whatever final words he wants!"

The android turned her disapproving gaze at her master this time, and after a very human sigh she proposed, "I request permission to shoot him with my plasma disintegrator and then go back and watch TV."

"No! I told you that you're not allowed to fire that thing off anymore! We are going to kick his ass *manually*!"

I had no idea what he meant by that, but we were slowly steering off topic, so I raised my voice to get his attention again.

"Um... For the record, you can see that I'm not alone, right?"

"Kihihi! Of course!" Lab Coat Guy exclaimed while excitedly rubbing his palms together, and then he yelled out, "Numbers one through five! Go to the front!"

Following his words, the five elite mooks took a few steps forth in unison. Their movements were slightly less mechanical than their common brethren's, yet still overexaggerated enough where it was hard to take them seriously.

"Kihihihihi!!! Look upon my works and despair!" Lab Coat Guy exclaimed with undue glee as he dramatically extended his arm towards us, his palm pointing at me and his fingers spread. "The Sprocket MkIVs are the final amalgamation of science and the mystic arts, and they owe their existence to you! Yes, you! It was your combat data that allowed me to perfect them! They know all of your strengths and weaknesses! They are—"

"Wait, time out!" I called out while making an awkward *T* with my hands. "By any chance, did you build these robots specifically to counter each one of us?"

"Yes!" he declared quite proudly.

"Does that mean each one of them is specialized to counter *one* member of our group in particular?"

"Erm... Yes. Obviously," the mad scientist told me, this time a bit less enthusiastically.

"You heard that, Dormouse?" I whispered very softly, and I got an immediate answer.

"{I did. Do you want me to take care of the obvious instructions?}"

"Only if the guys are too slow to do the obvious by themselves," I responded, earning me a curious and slightly confused look from the android. I made sure to talk really quietly, but she may have still heard me with her super-scientific sci-fi sensor arrays... or just read my lips. Either way, my short conversation with Judy was already over, so I glanced behind me over my shoulder and told the guys, "You've heard the guy. Have fun trashing these mooks. As for me..."

I was about turn back, but then my danger sense suddenly flared up, so I hastily twisted my torso to the side, and not a moment too soon, as the space that my chest had occupied just a moment ago now had a hand sticking through it. I looked at the surprised android, but before she could collect herself, my body was already moving by reflex as I swung my spear at her legs. She turned out to be faster than me just by a hair, as she deftly backed out of the way of the shaft. I kept up the momentum by immediately reversing the direction of the strike, and this time I aimed a diagonal strike at her upper body.

Instead of dodging, this time she opted for a block, and she extended a hand and grabbed onto the spear just under the head. Since I was swinging from an awkward position, my attack didn't have enough momentum behind it, and so she managed to stop it in its tracks. The moment she did that, I pulled the spear back without hesitation while also taking a large step back, both as a way to put some distance between us and to regain my stance, and since her hand would've been cut by the blade if it slid any farther down towards the point, she immediately let go of my weapon and also took a step back.

This short exchange lasted for only about two seconds, and it was over before any of my friends could get over their first surprise and move in to support me, but it was still enough to tell me that my opponent was a highly trained (or programmed, or whatever) combatant with excellent senses. By my rough estimate, she was better than the average Faun, but slightly slower and considerably weaker than Brang, and now that we had some distance between us where I could leverage my weapon's reach, it didn't feel like she'd pose a lethal danger to me anymore. Well, unless she started firing off her destructo-beams, or break out some other sci-fi weapons, but that was neither here nor there.

By this point Lab Coat Guy also overcame his first shock, and he called out to his partner with a mixture of anger and concern.

"Galatea! Just what the hell are you doing!"

"I'm kicking his ass manually, Master," she answered completely nonplussed, though it was hard to call it anything but a bluff at this point.

"Well, that was surprising," I commented with a sigh before shaking my head. "Anyhow, while I'd obviously love to have a terrifying battle of life and death with you, I'm afraid I'm needed elsewhere."

"... What does that mean?" the fembot inquired with a deadpan yet decidedly annoyed gaze.

"In short... bye!"

"Wha—?"

And just like that, I was suddenly inside an abandoned storeroom. I let out a small sigh as I relaxed my body and suppressed the sudden spike of headache assaulting my brain. Once that was over, and my eyes adjusted to the darkness of the room, my gaze was met with an honest-to-goodness rectangular metal cage with thick, iron bars in the corner. Ever since I first saw this thing through Far Sight, I couldn't help but wonder just how the heck they managed to get it inside the chamber, but I decided that it was a question for later as I walked over to the enclosure and tapped on the metal bars with the butt of my spear.

The occupant of the cage, who used to be lying in the middle on an inflatable mattress and under a pile of blankets, jumped up like he was hit by a cattle prod. And then he fell off his bed. And then he rolled on the floor while making weird noises. And *then* he got tangled in the sheets and blankets and looked like an oversized caterpillar.

"... Dude, are you for real?"

The question escaping my mouth made him stop struggling for a second, and then, after clumsily wiggling for a while to face me, he exclaimed, "L-Leonard!? Is that you?"

"Who else?" I grumbled while inspecting the padlock holding the cage's only door shut and pointedly not looking at the guy inside.

"What are you doing here?"

While asking so, he finally managed to peel himself out of his blankets. He had bags under his eyes, and his hair could give a pile of hay a run for its money, but overall he didn't seem worse for wear. I was still disappointed by his conduct, so I grumpily told him, "You missed your last delivery, so I looked into your whereabouts. When I learned you were held hostage, I figured I might as well help you out." My small lie made the guy's eyes sparkle, so I amended a jab to the end of it. "Just what kind of secret agent gets captured on the job by a group of nerds, anyway?"

"Erm... Sorry. In my defense, I'm not a full operative," he excused himself. "Also, I was caught off guard."

"How so?" I inquired on autopilot as I looked around the room in search of a key matching the padlock.

"Well... Um... First they distracted me," Mike explained, and even in the dark room, I could somehow still tell his face was getting red. "When I arrived, I was greeted by this woman wearing this really revealing costume."

"The one with the neckline plunging down to her navel?" I ventured a guess, and he nodded repeatedly.

"Yes, that's the one! So, you see, she wasn't my type. I like more modest girls, the kind who are maybe a little shy but easy to talk to, kind of like..." He must have realized he was blabbering, as he awkwardly cleared his throat and told me, "I mean, *they* were right there! In the open! I'm a guy, so of course I'd pay attention to *them*!"

"Uh-huh," I grunted a tad non-committally, followed by a shallow sigh. I was just about to give up on finding the keys. I mean, in retrospect it made sense that they wouldn't keep them in the same room as someone who could use magic. As in, imagine that they just put the key onto a huge keyring, and then hung it on the wall. Mike could just use some basic telekinetic magic to levitate it to himself and then open the lock. Now granted, he still couldn't just walk out, but it would've still been a grievous and unprofessional oversight on the side of Lab Coat Guy, so... maybe that was the reason I was half expecting it?

"So... Um? Leonard?" the captive Celestial addressed me as he grabbed hold of the bars holding him. "Are you really here to get me out?"

"That's the plan," I responded while checking the padlock one more time. Unfortunately, it was still entirely mundane, with no easy-to-break enchantments to make my life easier.

"Really?" The guy's face lit up for a moment, but once the first rush of relief receded from his eyes, his brows knit into a confused frown, and he asked, "But... how are we going to leave? And how did you even get in here? No, wait... how did you even find me?"

"How about you ask all of these things *after* we leave?"

"Ah, right. Sorry, sorry. I'm just... I don't know what to say right now..."

"How about you say nothing and let me work?" I proposed, and the guy immediately fell silent with his hands on his mouth.

Anyhow, now that I had the opportunity to consider my options in silence, and even my headache was slowly receding, I narrowed them down to three. One: I go out and search for the key. The pro was that it was the most convenient solution; the cons were that it might take too long, or I might not even find the key. Two: Use Phasing to take Mike out of the cage. The pro was that it was the quickest way to do it, but the con was that then I would have to explain what had just happened to the guy, and keeping my abilities from inadvertently ending up on the Celestial Hub was the main reason why I didn't just Phase in and spirit him away ages ago. Three: Just break the lock with some good old-fashioned elbow grease. On the pro side, it was a fairly simple solution, but on the con side, I didn't have any tools at hand, and I doubted I could do it with my spear.

... But then again, the padlock looked pretty cheap, and the hoop was wide enough so that I could probably wedge the shaft of my spear in and then apply enough pressure on it to snap it.

"Let's give it a try," I whispered as I set the back of my spear against the lock. "I'll try to force this open. Please step back and—"

I got exactly this far. I didn't even have the time to stick it through the hoop when I was startled by a borderline panicked voice echoing inside my head.

"{Chief, we need you here right now. The base is under attack.}"

I froze mid-motion and muttered a slack-jawed "What?" under my breath, but once the words finally sank in, a rush of adrenaline cleared my head, and I called out, "Sorry, I really have to go now. I'll be back."

And with that, I immediately disappeared from the room, leaving the poor guy in the cage quite shocked and alarmed. To be fair, I had a feeling my current state of mind beat him in both regards. A moment later, I appeared beside Judy, and even before the Phasing completely finished, I could already hear angry shouting coming from the other side of the door leading into the main hall of the secret base.

Judy was momentarily startled by my sudden appearance, so to jolt her out of it, I emphatically told her to hide, before I turned on my heel and rushed towards the sounds of battle without even bothering to ask for an explanation of what happened. I threw the door open, and then immediately stopped in my tracks the moment my eyes skimmed over the scene.

There was the body of the Chimera in the middle. There were all the Fauns scattered in the hall, some of them obviously injured. And in the middle, there was Brang, currently silently squaring off against a short person with a billowing purple shroud flapping behind her.

"Oh..." I muttered as cold sweat ran down my back and my fingers tightened around the weapon in my hand. "This is gonna suck."

CHAPTER 14

PART 1

Okay, Leo, deep breaths. Things are chaotic at the moment, but not unsalvageable. No need to panic. Panic is for horror movie heroines with obnoxiously high-pitched voices, and I sure as hell wasn't one. Let's just observe the situation for a moment before jumping in. As they say, look twice, act once, live considerably longer.

So let's start with observation number one: Rinne somehow found the secret base, and she was currently wreaking merry havoc in the middle of it. Observation number two: the Fauns were trying, and apparently failing, to restrain her, with Hrul and Pip bleeding on the side. Fortunately, their wounds didn't seem to be life-threatening, so how's that for a silver lining? As for observation three: some of the metal scaffolding by the sparring arena was cut into pieces, which meant that Mountain Girl was rampaging around without any care about collateral damage once again. I couldn't help but wonder just how long it took her to cause this much mayhem.

As if reading my mind, my slightly rattled girlfriend immediately supplied the answer.

"{The Faun didn't say anything until she was already inside. I called you the moment I heard them fighting.}"

So she did all of this damage in well under a minute. How come I wasn't even surprised? For a split second I almost wondered if the shop warranty would cover this, but I quickly shook the idea out of my mind. This wasn't the time for idle thoughts.

"Tell the others I'll need some time to resolve this," I said so fast I almost bit my tongue, and after one last breath of determination, I dashed forward with all my might.

Rinne and Brang looked like they would be at each other's throats at any moment now, so before anything else, I had to defuse this situation. Once I was close enough, I took a deep breath, and then shouted, "What the hell are you doing?!" from the top of my lungs.

Both combatants froze up for a second, but contrary to my hopes and expectations, the unreasonable huntress took this as an opportunity to lunge forth with her sword raised instead of standing down, right towards the momentarily distracted Faun. It was a quick attack, but not unreasonably so, and I thought Brang would at least try to parry her strike, but instead he belatedly tried to dodge out of the way, and his bad leg nearly buckled under the stress of the sudden movement. Rinne seemed ready to capitalize on his loss of balance, so I had no choice but to directly involve myself in their duel, even at the risk of further escalating things. Since I was out of time and reach, I did it the only way I could: by Phasing over to the Faun's side and parrying her stab myself.

Or rather, that *was* the plan, but when I did so, I belatedly realized why Brang decided to back away instead of blocking her initial sword strike. The idea was to start the windup motion of my parry before Phasing over, thus allowing me to give my swing a longer arc to collect momentum for batting her weapon away, but when the two met, Onikiri's edge bit into the hardwood shaft and cleaved a solid twenty centimeters off the butt end of my spear with minimal resistance.

On the bright side, my sudden appearance and unexpected attempt at getting in her way also startled her into withdrawing, and she took two hasty steps back before assuming a defensive posture, with her sword held diagonally in front of her. This momentary lull allowed my poor brain some breathing room, and so it immediately noted that goddammit, this was the second perfectly good spear that got broken in two days! Well, at least it got cut close to the butt end, so I could still use it as a short spear. That was also a silver lining, I supposed.

But putting my brain's odd priorities aside, I decided it was in my best interest to lead the conversation, so I raised my voice and repeated my previous question, this time even more forcefully and filled with as much righteous indignation as I could manage at the moment.

"As I was *saying*, what the *hell* do you think you are doing!?"

There was a long beat following my exclamation, but my words seemed to have fallen on deaf ears, as the currently guarded monster slayer's eyes only kept jumping between Brang and me without her saying a thing or even moving a muscle. After a while, I decided it was probably more productive to address the person behind me rather than the one in the front.

"[Regroup and tend to the wound bearers. I shall attempt to quench the flammable cord of the circumstances,]" I grunted in Faunish while making sure I didn't take my eyes off Rinne even for a split second.

Brang didn't argue, but instead he warned me, "[Understood, my lord. I wish you the best of luck, though I'm afraid thine fellow's grasp of her sanity has already slipped well out of reach.]"

I could tell that much without his input, but I let out an appreciative noise all the same. A moment later, I could already hear him backing away, his direction made evident by Mountain Girl's eyes following him for a while before suddenly snapping back to me, her expression constantly vacillating between a confused deer-in-the-headlights stare and her patented brand of slasher grin. To my dismay, she ultimately settled on the latter.

"Leonard-san saved the creature of the underworld... Was Onikiri right all along?"

Her ominous whisper made a cold shiver run down my back, and so I hurriedly raised my hand and told her, "Wait, don't jump to conclusions just yet. Put down your sword for a moment, and we can talk."

"Rinne doesn't believe you," she responded with a sense of finality that was somewhere between a death knell and the second end credits of a superhero movie. Be that as it may, I had no choice but to press on, anyway, as the clock was already ticking. I still needed to get Mike out of his cage, notify the others so that they could retreat in time, and on top of all that, now I also had to deal with this mess.

I had many questions, such as how she managed to find this place, or how she got inside, or why all of this had to happen now of all times, but I put all such quandaries aside for the moment and forced a harmless smile onto my face. Before I could worry about anything else, I first had to try to negotiate myself out of this situation.

"Come on, Mountain Girl, don't be like that! Just hear me out, okay?"

My attempt to cajole her fell on deaf ears once again as she slowly shifted her center of gravity into a more threatening stance. My instincts told me to raise my weapon in turn, but doing so would have escalated things right away, so I restrained myself.

"No. The time for honeyed words of deception is over," she declared, making me barely able to hold myself back from burying my face in my hand.

"No, it's not! I mean, not the deception part, but this is *definitely* the time for words!"

"Onikiri was right all along," she muttered as her slasher smile widened even further, with the corners of her mouth practically on the verge of creeping off her face. Also, was it just me, or was there an ominous purple aura coming off her? That couldn't be good. "You are a scion of a female dog indeed."

"No, I'm not, and... are you even listening to what I'm telling you?"

"Onikiri wonders what the colour of your blood is."

Well, that more or less answered my question, didn't it? Her threatening question was then followed by the odd purple aura surrounding her becoming even thicker to the point it resembled some kind of mist. Also, her eyes were now shining in a yellowish hue. I was about 97 percent sure they weren't doing that second ago, but I tried not to let it bother me as I did my best to remain as nonthreatening as possible.

"If you really want to know, it's red. Mystery solved. Now, could you please—?"

Suddenly, the purple mist dissipated, as if it was blown away by a sudden gust of wind, and it took the violent tension weighing on my shoulders with it... but then why was my back crawling with all kinds cold sweat?

"You have betrayed the trust Rinne invested in your personage," she stated out of the blue, and now I knew.

"Oh crap, did you just—" "Go soft-spoken on me?" I wanted to ask, but then I was rudely cut short by a blade aiming right at my neck. Thankfully it was only metaphorical this time, as my head remained perfectly attached to my everything else thanks to my ever-helpful danger sense, and I managed to duck out of the way just in time, if not particularly gracefully.

Rinne didn't dally around in the meantime, and she drew back her sword into a stance as she whispered, "You must suffer the consequences of your betrayal," followed by a considerably louder, *"Mumyō kansatsu ken!"*

Normally I would've shouted something along the lines of "Since when's that a capital offense?!" but this really wasn't the time to trade witty quips and banter, as her sword already began drawing a series of afterimages in the air in preparation for some kind of fancy and no-doubt-quite-lethal technique aimed at my squishy bits. Needless to say, I did the only reasonable thing in this situation and immediately got out of sword's reach by Phasing over to Brang's side.

The currently-quite-murderous huntress was startled by my disappearance, but even after her eyes found me, at least some parts of her brain had to be working properly, as she didn't blindly rush into our group. At least not yet. Speaking of which, Brang, and consequently I, was currently standing near the edge of the training grounds and surrounded by the other Fauns, with the two injured members in the back row. I glanced over to the largest guy by my side, and then curtly stated, "[Negotiations have broken down.]"

He grunted with an implied "I told you it would turn out like this" hidden somewhere in it, but by the time he'd let out a proper Faunish growl, his sentiment turned into, "[How shall we proceed? Do you wish to eliminate her?]"

"[Most certainly not. We must subdue her and then make her see reason.]"

"[Doing so would be an ordeal several magnitudes more perilous than simply overwhelming her,]" Brang responded in a skeptical tone without taking his eyes off the huntress eyeing us. "[Her weapon is dangerous, and our arms and armour offer little protection against her strikes. My experience tells me that if you desire us to fight her while attempting to preserve her life, one or more of our kin might lose theirs in her stead.]"

"[Cease your pessimism,]" I grumbled in his general direction before taking a deep breath and considering our options.

In short, the biggest problem when facing her right now was the fact that she was wielding a Japanese bootleg lightsaber that cut through everything like it was made of alpine butter. On top of that, she was fast, vicious, and didn't pull her punches, so trying to wrestle her sword away from her was guaranteed to end up with a couple of missing limbs.

In that case, let's rephrase the question: What options did we have to subdue her? Getting her away from her sword was a perilous proposition, so how about disabling her movements? It could've been a feasible idea if we had a pair of bolas or a net, but we didn't, not to mention they probably wouldn't have held her for long, anyway.

How about knocking her out, then? Well, I didn't have a tranquilizer rifle in my back pocket (not that it would've helped, as delivering the right dosage was a bit more complicated than what the movies would have you believe), so that was out. A hit to the head was also an option, but that was just as likely to give her a serious concussion or even brain hemorrhage, and while she wasn't exactly the apple of my eye, I still didn't want to cripple her. A more reasonable option was a choke hold, but that was also harder to do than it appeared, not to mention, without taking her weapon away first, it was just asking for a blade to the head.

No matter how I looked at it, the first step had to be getting her unreasonably dangerous weapon away from her, but it was easier said than done when we had nothing that could even block her long enough to attempt a disarming maneuver. That was a bit of a pickle, but then as I considered the possible tools we had at hand in the secret base, I had a sudden and, if I do say so myself, somewhat brilliant idea.

"[General, follow my lead. We shall steal sand from the hourglass and treat her like a child's paper toy in the wind.]" I said so, but then I paused as I rewound what I just said, and then silently cursed the obtuseness of the Faun language under my breath. Brang seemed to have understood my meaning well enough, though, so I decided to roll with it and followed things up by addressing the rest of the group. "[Karukk, I strongly request that you retrieve the emphasized pole arm from its storage. The rest, attend the wound bearers, and then join us as distractors of the mind.]"

The younger Faun had considerably more trouble understanding what I meant, but once he did, he tentatively asked, "Do you mean *that* spear?"

"Of course I mean that one!" I barked back and then immediately followed after the already-dashing Brang. By the looks of it, Mountain Girl got tired of waiting for us and decided to assault everyone at once, so the ex-general broke away from us to meet her halfway. She wasn't fazed by the huge body charging towards her and leveled her sword right at her opponent's neck. Going for the vitals right away meant she was aiming for a fatal wound, but such single-mindedness also made her easy enough to read so that Brang could change his trajectory and get out of the way of the incoming blade. There was a momentary standoff between the two, which I quickly joined by taking a position near her blind spot. Because of this, she had no choice but to break her engagement with Brang and share her attention between the two of us.

That was more or less my intention, as currently my main objective was to tie her down and slowly chip away at her endurance until we could safely capture her, if only so that we could have a proper discussion without the danger of getting my head separated from the rest of my body in the process. In some ways, our positions at the moment were reminiscent of how we'd two-teamed the Chimera, except this time Rinne was on the receiving end. She wasn't mindless enough to completely ignore one of us, but at the same time she also wasn't reasonable enough for us to maintain the balance of the stalemate just by moving in and out of her zone of control.

As such, the momentary lull in the combat only lasted for a few seconds before she decided to break through by attacking Brang first. As for why, I imagined she either wanted to get rid of the bigger target first, or more likely, she might've considered him easier prey at the moment. The ex-general, most likely due to being afraid of losing his spear and symbol of office to a single unlucky swing of the infuriating katana, opted to use a short sword instead. It was actually a replica Roman gladius that I mail ordered the same time I got the spears and the rest of the weaponry for the Fauns. It was standard size, but in his hands, the short thrusting sword looked more like a dagger, especially after he put it in a reverse grip and held it up in a defensive position as if wielding a combat knife. Furthermore, he was wielding it while still buckled into its scabbard, making it an improvised blunt weapon to comply with my plan to catch Mountain Girl alive.

"*Sakurabana Ranbu!*"

Rinne called out the name of her attack as she made a diagonal cut from the bottom right side. Brang managed to avoid the telegraphed first strike, and it seemed like he would go in for a grapple. It was fortunate that this particular attack of the creepy huntress was one that I had seen her use multiple times against the Chimera, so I knew that even though the way she let go of her blade for a moment and she was spinning around might have looked like an opening the size of a skyscraper, she would be inexplicably able to stab forth in a split second, anyway.

"[General, waterfowl to the sinister side!]" I called out in a hurry, and although this time even I couldn't readily untangle just what the hell I meant by that (thanks, Faun language), he still pulled back from his planned grab and swerved to the side, just in time to avoid the straight trust of the o-katana whistling thought the air.

I wasn't resting on my laurels, though, as I swiftly closed in the distance and swung my spear. Stabbing with the pointy end was naturally out of the question, and while normally I would've poked her in the back with the butt end of my weapon, she'd cut it off at such a sharp angle that I was afraid that if I did so, I would still end up wounding her, anyway. Despite my best efforts, I inflicted practically zero damage on her with my strike. I not only lacked the familiar leverage due to my shortened weapon, but she also seemed to instinctively roll with the incoming force, as I barely felt any resistance when the shaft of the spear met with her shoulder.

Rinne tumbled on the ground without making a single sound, only to almost immediately spring to her feet while shouting yet another string of Japanese syllables and raising her sword high as she leaped at me. My trusty danger sense caught her abrupt attack well ahead of time, and I Phased right out of the way, reappearing by Brang's side with a small gasp. While such short-range teleports normally weren't that taxing, this time each one of them was making my headache ever-so-slightly worse. It was still bearable at the moment, but I was afraid it wouldn't stay that way for long.

"[I shall be her opponent. General, use the art of illusions bestowed upon you by your liege and limit yourself to harassing the interloper while I narrow her view of the world only to my person.]"

"[Understood,]" he grunted back right away, and he began to radiate magic, only to add, "[Are thine orders to spare her life still in effect?]"

"[Naturally.]" After saying so, I considered things one more time, and in the end I added, "[Restrain yourself for the time being, but once her inner reserves appear spent, use your natural bulk to subdue her when the opportunity presents itself.]"

He nodded in acknowledgment, and a split second later his whole body was enveloped in the orangish rippling shine I'd long since associated with the cloaking Sigil activating. From Rinne's point of view, it probably looked like he'd just vanished into thin air, so she immediately went on guard. That gave me a second or five to catch my breath, so I did just that and awkwardly put the lopsided end of my shortened spear against the ground to lean on it.

"Come on, Mountain Girl. Do we really have to do this?"

Instead of answering right away, she warily glanced around the area, probably thinking that I was trying to distract her while Brang got into position to ambush her (on which point she wasn't entirely wrong, per se, but I digress), but at last she looked me in the eye and stated, "You are a lackey of the powers of the underworld."

"Well, no, not really." My response drew a curious look from her, so I explained, "Technically, they are the ones who work for me."

"{Chief, I can't believe you thought that was going to convince her of your innocence.}"

I ignored my assistant's biting comment and instead whispered a deadpan, "Status report?"

"{I told the others about the situation at the base. Joshua said they are going to buy you as much time as they can, but asked you to hurry up.}"

"As if it was that simple," I murmured under my breath before focusing on Rinne again. "So are you one hundred percent certain we cannot stand down and talk this through?"

"Yes," she nodded without any hesitation.

"Are you *really* sure? We could do it while we eat. I'll throw in a full meal, too; you can even pick the restaurant."

For a moment her eyes actually wavered, even though I was half joking, but she ultimately overcame her weakness and firmly declared, "You are Rinne's enemy. Rinne must fight you."

"But wh—" was as far as I got before I was once again interrupted by my danger sense insistently telling me that moving was in my best interest, and so I graciously obliged by leaping backwards with all my might. While I was doing that, my opponent dashed forward as if she was shot from a bow and swung her blade horizontally while yelling something about iaijutsu or something. Her strike still wasn't anywhere close to hitting me, but it didn't deter her from trying again, and again, and again. The series of strikes she threw at me was as simple as a floorboard, but their speed (plus being unblockable, of course) still made them really threatening.

We exchanged several blows under these circumstances, though more realistically speaking, it was mainly just me dodging out of the way of her sword while occasionally throwing a few feints at her to break her rhythm. For the moment, I decided to devote all my mental faculties to upholding the status quo until Karukk could come back with the thing I requested, and so I continued eluding her strikes like it was going out of style. That said, even though my situation wasn't exactly peachy, I still had some breathing room to think, and so I used the opportunity to further analyze my opponent.

By my subjective judgment, facing Rinne gave me about as much pressure as when I was fighting Brang in a Dominance duel; each of their attacks felt really dangerous and potentially fatal, but as long as I kept my cool, I could sidestep them with relative ease. As far as actual physical combat prowess was concerned, she had a noticeably shorter reach than my usual Faunish sparring partner, as well as much more limited threat projection, mainly since she lacked the intimidating bulk and weight of a Faun.

Based on her performance against the Chimera, as well as her current attempts at cutting me into ribbons, she had slightly worse control over the spacing and rhythm of the battle than the big Faun. She wasn't an amateur by any stretch of the imagination, but when I sparred with Brang, I always had to be on the lookout for feints and be wary of being drawn into his pace, and I often had to rely on my inexplicable sixth sense of mortal danger to get me out of the way of an unexpected jab. Compared to that, Rinne's fighting style was much more straightforward, to the point where I felt that once I got used to her moves, I could probably run circles around her.

There were only two problems that made this fight into an enormous pain in the neck: The first was the fact that I couldn't block or parry her strikes. That was a big deal, as it left me with no other choice but to avoid all of her attacks, which forced me to move my whole body a lot more than usual, and that meant that I was most likely burning through my stamina faster than her. The second issue was...

"Kenzen Ichinyo!"

"Son of a..." I muttered as I immediately Phased a few steps back to avoid her strike. Whenever she called out one of her attacks, it played havoc with my danger senses, and triggering my fight-or-flight reflexes made me teleport out of the way before even considering any other options. That, naturally, wasn't good for my migraine, and I was starting to be afraid that my head would give out sooner than her fatigue.

Anyhow, while I was forced back, Brang immediately picked up the pace and tackled Rinne from her blind spot. She might have had some kind of sixth sense of her own, as she managed to roll out of the way, but by the time she jumped back to her feet he'd already retriggered his cloak and allowed me to take his place again. This kind of strike-and-fade tactic wasn't the most honourable in the world, but he didn't complain, and it worked wonders for keeping Mountain Girl off-balance.

After that, things returned to the status quo by my rushing in and keeping her occupied right until she would use another one of her fancy named attacks, then Brang would pick up the pace while I retreated, rinse and repeat. Not exactly the most dynamic, pulse-pounding battle in the history of supernatural combat, but in my defense, I didn't really have much of a reason to change things up. Keeping Rinne localized like this prevented more collateral damage from her swinging her exasperating blade through our furniture, and on top of that, it also kept everyone relatively safe until Karukk could finally show up with his delivery.

"[My lo... I mean, boss! Over here!]"

Oh, speak of the devil. The friendly Faun called out to me just after he returned from one of the as-of-yet-unfurnished side chambers of the base, and he waved a long, thin object wrapped in a thick layer of protective canvas that helped to keep it from getting dirty, kept moisture away from the sensitive metal edges, and most importantly, blocked any eyesore magical glows it might have radiated from giving me pink eye.

But putting such things aside, I held back from letting out a frustrated "Finally!" and instead I distanced myself from the berserk huntress and waved for Karukk to bring it over. I thought that was the obvious thing to do, but for some reason he remained in place and only gave me a dumb look while alternating between looking at me and the object in his hands. Then, after an objectively-short-yet-subjectively-torturously-long moment later it seemed like something finally clicked with him as he raised it over his head and...

"Wait, don't throw it over to—!"

I was too late. He threw it. Maybe he thought I wanted to have it right away, but for god's sake, man! If I was in such a hurry, I would've Phased over to your side already! You could've at least taken off the covering! How was I supposed to use it like that?

But alas, there was no point crying over spilled milk, so I swiftly moved in to intercept it... except I nearly stumbled when my danger sense began to blare at me like a World War II bomber alarm. It wasn't hard to figure out why, either; I was moving to catch a spear with a fixed trajectory. That meant that my own movement became predictable, which in turn led to Mountain Girl instantly moving in to intercept me.

So there I was. On my right a crazed woman with her sword raised over her head, ready to swing it down upon me. On my left, a spear thrown towards me on a flat flight curve designed to be easy to catch. In between the two, a choice: Do I catch the weapon and risk getting cut, or do I avoid the incoming slash and then run around like a headless chicken trying to recover the weapon? After a short but intense internal debate, I decided on a third option, and with a low grunt, I threw the spear already in my hands into the face of the incoming huntress.

She was more startled than anything by my actions, and she brought down her blade in a swift, vertical cut, neatly bisecting the shaft in the middle and pushing the pieces aside in her continued rush towards me. Still, it gave her a pause, and that was all I needed.

Goodbye cheap, nameless spear. We hardly knew ye, but your heroic sacrifice shall not be forgotten. Anyhow, while Rinne was momentarily distracted, Brang also revealed himself for a moment and let out a threatening roar that made even me twitch, even though I was already used to the guy. For our home invader, the sudden appearance of the blaring Faun must've been even more surprising, as even though he didn't do anything afterwards, his T-rex impression still provided me with ample distraction time to display my trained weapon-catching skill.

Ooooh, so that's why Karukk threw the spear at me! It had to be muscle memory from the times we trained my post-Phasing weapon-catching technique together. With that mystery solved, I reached out and elegantly snatched the unusual projectile out of the air, and then I brandished it in a slightly less graceful manner. I blame the damn canvas for the last bit.

I still did a small flourish with it, unwieldiness be damned, and took up an offensive stance, with my legs spread wide to provide a solid foundation and the spear in my hands held at shoulder height with the point angled slightly down.

Once I was in position, I sent a provocative smirk my opponent's way, and her reaction was quite predictable. She instantly resumed her rush towards me, her torso slightly bent to the side and away from Brang, and blade held in both hands and angled for a diagonal slice from bottom right to top left. I, in turn, shifted into a more defensive posture, and eagerly waited to see whether my gambit would pay off.

Blocking a sword strike with a spear was a tricky one. In the movies, you often see one actor hold their pole arm horizontally to stop a vertical slash, only to get locked in a contest of strength as they both push against each other's weapons. This is all very dramatic, as it allows for a moment of pause in the combat where they can trade angry quips with each other while the camera zooms in on their faces. It makes for an intense scene, so long as nobody starts wondering why the swordsman doesn't just slide his blade down the shaft and cut off his opponent's fingers. But then again, this is the kind of thing where a little willing suspension of disbelief (and the general populace's lack of need for armed combat knowledge) always pays dividends.

Needless to say, I didn't even try to do any of that. Instead I opted to take half a step back with one leg to brace myself while simultaneously swinging my weapon around to gather momentum, meeting my opponent's strike on a deflective angle. And that, ladies and gentlemen, is where the magic happened. As in, literally.

The moment our weapons met, there was a blindingly bright flash of light reminiscent of a welding arc followed by a numbing electric jolt running up from my palms all the way to my shoulders. All of these distractions nearly blotted out the sound and impact of enchanted wood meeting enchanted metal, but at the end of the day my hunch was proven correct, and the dragon-slaying spear successfully deflected the aggravating sword. That's a plot device for you, I supposed.

Well, to be fair, I would've been satisfied with either outcome; if it blocked Onikiri, neat. If not, at least this damn thing would be out of my hair. It would've been tricky to explain it to Sebastian, but I was prepared to do so from the beginning.

As for why I even had this spear in the secret base at the moment, simply put, I set Elly up to be my anchor, and I sneakily spirited it away before it could inevitably serve as a rogue element during the upcoming attack by the Knights. But putting all that aside, the collision between the two enchanted weapons had caused something of a magical shock wave that undid the knot fastening the cloth onto the spear, so after pushing Rinne back a step, I did another small flourish and used the opportunity to discard the canvas and reveal my weapon in all of its glowy glory.

Once she overcame the first shock, Mountain Girl swiftly reasserted herself by raising her sword up to the level of her face, signifying that she was about to go on the offensive again. This time, however, I had no reason to shrink back, and I met her assault with an aggressive posture of my own, and when she was about to rush forwards, I abruptly shifted my hands down the shaft and positioned the tip right in the way of her predicted lunge.

She was already moving by the time she realized what I'd done, so she had no choice but to awkwardly twist her body while simultaneously attempting to sweep the spearhead in the other direction. I didn't allow her to do so, as I quickly yanked the spear back, causing her to ineffectually wave at thin air instead. Doing so disturbed her stance even further, so I quickly struck at her sword in the back draw, causing her to completely lose her balance and letting me strafe to the side to keep an optimum distance.

This small exchange was the textbook example of the very basics of armed combat. First, establish favorable spacing, then read your opponent, bait them into making a mistake, and then punish them for it. It wasn't as flashy as throwing sword beams at each other or as visually stunning as repeatedly bashing our blades against each other until sparks started flying, but damn me if it wasn't effective.

By having a weapon with a longer reach, I naturally opted for a wider spacing, used my range advantage to disturb her attack, baited her into a miss to further unbalance her, then I used the opportunity to reestablish my preferred distance. As for punishing, if I really wanted to, I could've probably stabbed her upper arm or shoulder, but for now I opted for keeping the fight bloodless and aiming to disarm her instead.

Honestly, I didn't think that having a weapon capable of parrying her would make such a difference, but with this small change, the battle went from *this is dangerous, and a single mistake could result in serious injury or worse* to *this is not that hard, but the constant flashing magical lights are making my eyes hurt.* By the way, yes, that was still a thing; every time our weapons met, there was a bright light that gave the sun a run for its money, and by the looks of it, only I could see it. Also, if we're talking about nuisances, the spear itself felt a tad unwieldy in my hands, no small part thanks to its still giving me small electric shocks every once in a while.

The other big factor that turned the situation around was even more surprising. Rinne, the self-proclaimed hunter of supernatural nasties and highly visible ninja, was apparently entirely inexperienced when it came to fighting someone who had a weapon. Or rather, she seemed completely bewildered by the idea of her opponent being able to block and counter her, and once I broke her momentum with that and didn't let her slip close enough to get into her preferred spacing range, she became surprisingly easy to handle.

"*Sakuraba*—! Ouch!"

Just like that. Whenever she was about to try one of her unreasonable moves, I immediately punished her by extending my weapon and slapping her shoulder or thigh with the flat of the blade, or occasionally interrupting her by targeting her weapon before it could gather momentum. It still resulted in a few shallow cuts every here and there, but I kept telling myself that once she was tied up, Angie would take care of them, so it wasn't that big of a deal. That said, even I was astonished by how easy it became to suppress her. Was she really this bad? Or maybe Judy was right all along, and I really did have a knack for armed combat?

"Stop it!" she suddenly burst out, and on a closer look, I could see tears of frustration in the corners of her eyes. "Fight properly!"

"I'm fighting properly," I answered while swatting away a surprise thrust and countering by whacking her on the wrist before retreating by two paces. "You're the one who is flailing around."

She yelled something at me that sounded like gibberish mixed with random Japanese swear words, so I shut her up by feinting a thrust towards her head, and then immediately pulling back and smacking her hastily raised sword again, eliciting a pained hiss in the process. Odd as the turnaround was, I definitely wasn't going to complain, as by the looks of it I was going to be able to either wear her down or disarm her before long. Now I only had to pace myself and make sure she wouldn't run away before we could—

"{Chief, we have a situation.}"

My thoughts were abruptly interrupted by Judy's voice, and she somehow sounded even more worried than the last time she'd called me.

"I noticed. I'm dealing with it right now," I whispered curtly, much to Mountain Girl's confusion. "I have it more or less under control."

"{No, we have a new situation.}"

"What? Did something happen with the others?" I asked back while parrying another strike and feinting a thrust towards Rinne's abdomen to force her back before adding, "Please don't tell me it's another giant robot..."

"{No, Chief, we have a *brand-new* situation,}" she told me impatiently, and this time she didn't wait for me to react before throwing a bombshell. "{Mother-in-law is in trouble.}"

"Emese is in trou— Wait, come again?" Judy didn't say anything, so I presumed I'd heard it right. "Dormouse... For the love of god, please, *please* tell me it's not the Knights..."

"{Sorry, Chief, but it's the Knights,}" she responded in a voice that managed to be both apologetic and flat at the same time.

"... What the bloody hell on earth is going on with this godforsaken..." For the sake of brevity, let's just say that what followed after this point was a solid fifteen-second-long litany of curses, courtesy of yours truly, which put an unexpected and quite awkward end to the hostilities while it lasted. "... goddamn son of a goat merchant!"

I finished in the company of a ginormous groan. Letting off some steam like that helped a bit, and one sharp breath later I glanced at the still-cloaked Brang waiting for an opening on the side. I had to move fast, and considering how much trouble I'd gone through to get it out of the mansion ahead of time, I wasn't going to take the dragon-slaying spear back there, so once I was sure I had Brang's attention, I unceremoniously tossed my weapon over to him.

The Faun general almost fumbled, but ultimately managed to catch the spear with a confused look on his face.

"[I request that you hold the line. My presence is required elsewhere.]"

Brang was nothing if not adaptable, and once he'd digested my words, he undid his cloaking and took a threatening stance to draw Rinne's attention away from me. With that, I felt confident that the situation should be under control here, so I closed my eyes and quickly Phased away with a looming sense of trepidation about what other kinds of fresh hells this day would still have in store for me...

PART 2

When I arrived at the Dracis mansion, I was immediately thrown off-balance by a cacophony of voices. Also, it was pitch-black all around me, though my eyes adapted to that one far quicker than my ears did to the noise. I'd come over in a hurry and didn't really have the spare time to observe the situation before jumping into the middle of it, but I seriously didn't expect to see all of the household's maids, cooks, and other assorted personnel stuffed into a single room like sardines. They all looked... well, not exactly frightened, but at the very least tense. On the bright side, I couldn't see any injured among them. There was also a low, arrhythmic thumping noise in the air, and everyone in the room was so focused on its source that only a few of them even noticed my arrival.

"I said no!" I was startled by Emese's sharp voice, and following it led my eyes to the only entrance of what I belatedly realized to be the poker room on the first floor.

"Ma'am, with all due respect..." the large, well-built man she'd just yelled at tried to speak up, but he was cut short by an angry scoff and what I presumed to be a commanding glare. I could only guess, since she was facing away from me. There were also a couple of other similarly built men behind the speaker, all dressed in black suits and wearing sunglasses indoors, even though it was dark and two of them were even holding flashlights, and my honed trope senses told me they were probably security.

Meanwhile, the draconic woman still pretending to be wheelchair bound pointed a finger at the large, antique wardrobe still being held by two of the man's colleagues and told them, "That is an heirloom from my great-grandmother's time! You're explicitly forbidden to use it to build the barricade!"

Speaking of which, it finally registered with me that the thumping sound was coming from behind the group, or to be more precise, the heavy wooden doors currently held shut by the sheer bulk of three security guys.

"Then what can we use?" the man in the middle asked, and I decided this was as good a moment as any to make my presence known.

"Try the couch; it's pretty heavy," I advised, making everyone freeze up for a moment before Mama Dracis whipped her head around to look at me over her shoulder with astonished eyes.

"Leo!" Her excited exclamation was accompanied by a surprised look that quickly morphed into an uncomprehending one. "Why are you here?"

"I was told there's trouble," I answered while walking over and carefully leaning onto one of the handles of her wheelchair. "Weren't you the one who called Judy?"

"No, that would be me," came the answer from a new voice, and its owner promptly made her way out of the throng of servants and stood next to us.

The look Melinda was giving me was slightly suspicious, but I was more surprised that I saw no magical glow, and consequently no communication artifact on her, meaning the way she'd contacted my girlfriend almost certainly had to do with the ye olde brick phone in her hand. Just how exactly Judy got a mobile signal in a bomb shelter inside a mountain while I often had signal issues even in the middle of the city was one of the more mundane-yet-nonetheless-mind-boggling mysteries of our existence.

Anyhow, I was quickly jolted out of my train of thought by another thud coming from the direction of the door, so I cleared my aching head with a shake and addressed the room in general.

"So could any of you brief me on the situation?" After saying so, I paused for a few seconds, and then also added, "Moreover, while you're telling me, somebody should really start moving the couch already. I don't like the sounds the hinges are making."

"You heard him," Emese prompted the reserved security guys, and after they began to move, she turned in place to face me. "Did you know the accursed Knights would be attacking today?"

"No, I just learned about it, too," I answered a little absentmindedly while looking for something else to lean on, and I ultimately settled on a nearby chair.

"Then how come you're here?" Melinda leveled the question at me, which naturally earned her a please-read-the-situation-and-shut-up glare before I turned a considerably more amicable look at my self-appointed mother-in-law.

"It's a long and complicated story, and not exactly relevant at the moment. On the other hand, I'd really appreciate it if one of you could please start the explanation I asked for."

My words were further emphasized by yet another impeccably timed thud coming from the door, so the two draconian women shared a meaningful glance between each other, and ultimately decided to drop the issue of my sudden appearance.

"The assault started about half an hour ago," Mama Dracis explained in a tone that didn't seem all that concerned with the circumstances. "It was ahead of schedule, but we'd already discussed what to do with the staff, so no one panicked. We couldn't erect a Restricted Space over the mansion because of their interference, and we couldn't evacuate, either, so once the alarm sounded, we all headed to the safe room under the mansion."

"... I can't help but notice that we are not there," I noted, and Melinda quickly stepped forth to explain the discrepancy.

"Milady was on this floor when the accursed knights rammed through the front gates with their vehicle, so while the mansion's security held them back, we decided to move to her side instead."

"They cut the power cables before the attack, and without the elevator, carrying me down to the safe room on the stairs would've taken too long. These wheels are really inconvenient, aren't they?" Emese added in a light tone that didn't fit the severity of the situation at hand, but I decided to let it slide. Also, this finally explained why we were currently sitting in the dark. One mystery solved.

"So you came to this room instead and barricaded the entrance? Not a terrible idea, I suppose. It's a smaller room with only a single entrance and one window, so it's reasonably easy to mount a defense here. I have just one question though: Why did you hole up here instead of fighting back?"

"I was under the impression the plan was that we lure the accursed Knights in, and then hubby and Sebastian would hit them from the back," Emese explained. "I was also afraid that if we fought them head-on, we would cause a lot of damage to the building. It's better to wait for them, and then catch the enemy in a pincer maneuver and quickly overwhelm them, right?"

I looked the woman seeking validation in the eye and replied with, "I don't want to burst your bubble, but I doubt they are going to make it. In fact, let me check."

"Check what?" Melinda inquired with narrowed eyes, but I ignored her for the time being, and instead I focused on my Far Sight and glanced over to Abram's location.

"... Yeah, just as I expected," I murmured under my breath once I ascertained their situation. "Unfortunately, they are currently being held up by the Magi. They probably didn't know that the island is under lockdown and got caught when they tried to sneak back. It must've happened pretty recently, too."

Emese looked like she wanted to know how I knew that, but then it was a different question that escaped her lips.

"Since when is the island under lockdown?"

"Long story." My answer made both the lady of the house and the chambermaid narrow their eyes with a frown, so I ultimately decided to elaborate a little. "Fine, here's the footnotes version: we tried to catch the guy who was ambushing us, he got away, he stole something from Lord Grandpa, and now the Magi are running around like headless chickens and won't let anyone off the island."

"That's... a problem," Melinda stated the obvious, but I didn't hold it against her.

"Yep. In short, instead of waiting for dad-in-law and Sebastian to come home anytime soon, I think we have two options: you could either transform and fight back, or you could continue to stay on the defense, and instead we could call the police." Mama Dracis was giving me an unusually baffled look, so I clarified, "We aren't in a Purple Zone, so the Knights actually broke into your real, realspace house. The police can't exactly ignore that, and since the Knights cannot harm innocents, they would be forced to retreat so that they wouldn't get into conflict with the law."

"No," my self-imposed mother-in-law abruptly declared in no uncertain terms. "If law enforcement gets involved, it will leave a permanent record that could lead to us even after we move again, and removing that would require the help of the Magi. Our relationship with the arch-mage might be cordial, but I don't want to be in his debt."

"Really? I thought it would be a rather elegant solution."

My stray comment was met with a frown, so I raised my hands in surrender.

"Fine, fine. When in Rome, do as the Romans do. This is your home, so if you want to deal with them without involving the authorities, then be my guest."

"That's right. This is our house, and we would be a laughingstock if we couldn't protect it ourselves," Emese declared while beaming with dignity, which was only slightly marred by the clumsy way she tried to dramatically rise from her wheelchair.

"Fine then," I ended that part of the discussion, only to take a deep breath and reluctantly raise my voice again. "I have about three other places to be already, but I think I can spare a few minutes to help you out. First off, how many bad guys are we dealing with?"

"At least twelve squires," came the answer from an unexpected source as the main security guy walked up to us. Apparently, they had finished building their barricade, which looked a tad flimsy, yet it was holding out well enough, so I probably shouldn't complain. Once he was sure everyone's attention was on him, he continued in a grave voice. "We've also confirmed the presence of no less than two Entitled Knights."

I almost asked what he meant by that, but I managed to swallow the words back as the hamster wheel operated gears and pulleys I jokingly call a brain managed to drag the term out of the bottom of my memory. According to one of Judy's reports I'd read not too long ago, the Knights with the Long Ass Name didn't have centralized leadership; in its stead, certain members held specific titles in the organization, usually passed down in the family or to apprentices. Normally each of these Entitled Knights operated their own little clandestine circle of operatives, and whenever an important issue came up that required the whole organization to act, they would come together and vote on the issue, probably while standing around a round table inside an old European castle or something.

I could also recall that they actually used to have a proper leader who was supposed to hold the whole organization together, but he passed away a few hundred years ago and left their super-special-awesome sword embedded in a suitably stereotypical magical rock. Insert typical Arthurian tropes about pulling out said sword here. More importantly though, the Entitled Knights were more or less the equivalent of mini bosses, with specialized magical gear and unique skill sets, so fighting them face-to-face was just a tad too dangerous. There was also something else I remembered finding odd about them, but I couldn't recall what it was at the moment. I blamed the headache.

"Which named ones are here?"

My absentminded inquiry was answered by Melinda.

"I've seen one of them from a distance, and based on the armour he was wearing, he was most likely the Griffon Knight."

"Oh," I exhaled in surprise as her words further jogged my memory.

The last important thing about the Entitled Knights was that they were each named after some animal, either mythical or real, and their namesake was part of their insignia. It was kind of a cringy thing if you asked me. I mean, Blackcloak was bad enough, but I'd probably drop dead from embarrassment if someone called me Sir Leonard Dunning, the Hippopotamus Knight or some such.

Emese most likely mistook my momentary silence for requesting more details, as she told me, "We more or less expected him, but nobody could take a good look at the other accursed Knight. He was a man, so he couldn't be the Unicorn Knight, and the Eagle Knight was recently injured, so he's probably off the list. That leaves either the Minotaur Knight or the Kraken Knight."

"There is also the Lion Knight," the security guy noted, and Mama Dracis gave him an appreciative glance.

"True, although he's been inactive for the past couple of years. Hubby even speculated that he probably died and no one inherited the position yet, but it's not out of the question. But then again, the Raven Knight has been missing for years, as well..."

"Okay, time out," I raised my voice to make them stop before those names made me die of secondhand embarrassment. I mean, Unicorn

Knight? Really? Sheesh. "So we have two dangerous people and a bunch of goons. What are they armed with?"

Everyone in the room was looking at me like I'd just asked something really dumb, but then the security guy cautiously answered, "Erm... Swords and spears, as usual?"

"Only melee weapons?" He nodded to my question. "No guns?" This time, he shook his head.

On the second look, I only just realized that none of the security guys had any firearms on them, either. In retrospect, I shouldn't have been so surprised, as I had already been made aware of the insanely strict gun laws of the island when I tried to buy a pistol, just in case, and was stonewalled so hard I couldn't even find a black market vendor who would deal in them. In fact, the unavailability of handguns was so absolute that Judy even had a theory about the Narrative artificially restricting them because supernatural battles and guns rarely mix well.

Anyhow, if not even the cutthroat cavaliers of the supernatural world used firearms, I figured no one else would, either. I wasn't going to complain, though, as it made the situation slightly less dangerous from my point of view. I mean, I put a lot of trust in my inexplicable-yet-incredibly-reliable danger sense, but I doubted that I could dodge a bullet even if I was forewarned about it. Now, there was only one question remaining.

"You said you couldn't erect a Purple Zone. Is that normal?"

"If you mean a Restricted Space, then no. The Knights brought an artifact with them that made it harder to invoke the Restricted Space, so we decided to forgo it for the time being." Mama Dracis paused for a moment, as if just realizing how weird it was, and then she asked me, "Do you have any idea why they would do that?"

"Oh, I have an idea all right," I grumbled as I stopped leaning on the backrest of the chair beside me and took a deep breath. "All right, here's the plan: First and foremost, lay the groundwork for a Purple Zone. I'll go and scout around a little, and if I can, I'll try to snatch or disable their jamming artifact. Once that happens..." I looked at Emese, who actually perked up for some reason. "By that time, you should get ready to cause some havoc, mom-in-law."

"You can leave that to me!" she immediately declared with a vicious grin that somehow still reminded me of Elly. Speaking of which, I really hoped things were going all right on their end. I really didn't expect that things were going to turn out like this, so I wanted to wrap everything up over here as fast as I could. Brang could probably handle Rinne on his own, now that he had a proper weapon to use, but originally Josh and the others had had to hold up Lab Coat Guy for only a few minutes while I freed Mike, and I figured they were getting a little worn out by now.

"Do you plan to use the window?" Emese asked while pointing at the only window in the room, which currently had the poker table covering it.

"No, I plan to use this wall," I answered while pointing in the other direction. "It would take too long to explain. Let's just say it's a thing I do."

After saying so, I walked over to the wall in question, bent my knees for a sprinter's start, and told them, "I'll be right back," before bursting forward and then simultaneously Phasing to the room on the other side. My body came to a lurching halt, and it took a couple of short breaths to steady myself before I could stop leaning on the nearby table.

After glancing around a bit, I soon realized that I was inside Abram's trophy room. That was a pleasant surprise, as I could've sworn that it wasn't right next to the poker room. But then again, I didn't exactly have the full map of the mansion in my head, so I didn't dwell on it. The stuffed animal heads on the walls were even eerier than usual in the dark, but more importantly, I could remember a couple of other odds and ends in the room. For example, there were all those stereotypical African tribal spears and javelins in the corner. I was almost tempted to pick one up, but after some consideration, I decided against it. I didn't plan to fight the Knights in the open, and even if I did, after my recent experience with Rinne, I doubted that some mundane spears were going to make a huge difference. Ideally, I would quickly find the magical jamming whatchamacallit, break it, and then once the Purple Zone was up, I'd let Mama Dracis clean up the rest while I focused my attention elsewhere. Easy peasy.

As to how I was supposed to find said jammer thingy, that was another matter entirely, but I figured that if it was a powerful magical tool, it would be lit up like a Christmas tree; if I found the most glaringly eye-watering object in the invaders' possession, I was probably on the right track. As such, instead of a weapon, I decided to look for another item that I'd noted when I visited the room the last time, though it was pretty hard to find anything in the place considering most of the little illumination the streetlights outside provided was blocked by the curtains. It also didn't help that just as I was about to reach for said curtains, I was startled by a voice echoing right inside my head.

"{Chief, more trouble.}"

"Oh for the love of..." I reflexively cursed under my breath, but I quickly reined in the impulse and once I felt collected enough, I asked, "New trouble?"

"{In a way. Amelia was taken hostage by Dr. Robatto.}"

The news made me pause in my tracks, and instead of asking for more information, I decided it was more efficient to just Far Glance over there. It took me a few seconds to digest the situation, and once I did that, I let out an exasperated sigh and addressed my girlfriend again.

"Judy, please remind the class rep that I put an anti-grappling function onto the Magiforms for a reason."

"{Roger.}"

"Also, tell her that it's two for two. If she gets captured by the next bad guy, too, I'm going to bench her."

"{Noted.}"

After Judy's s response I also used my Far Sight to observe the events on that side of this evening's multifront flustercuck. I made a quick tally, and at a glance, it seemed that one of the special robots and about a third of the normal ones were turned into ugly-coloured scrap metal scattered around the place. In the middle of all the expected collateral damage, Lab Coat Guy was currently holding the class rep in a clumsy choke hold while rattling off his demands to the rest of the group. Or rather, the rest except for Josh because for some reason he was having an epic duel with the android woman on the rooftop of the warehouse. I wasn't even surprised anymore.

Anyhow, it looked like Judy had just finished relaying my message to our hostage, for her eyes abruptly lit up with belated realization behind her glasses, and not a moment later, there was a sharp banging sound that reminded me of the last dying gasp of an industrial jackhammer. What followed was both comical and yet immensely satisfying, as the guy in the clogs was sent flying as if he was punted by a giant, invisible leg. That was nice, but Newton's third law also reared its ugly head at this moment, the killjoy, and while magic allowed quite a bit of leeway when it came to creatively reinterpreting classical mechanics, it was practically impossible to stop a small amount of counterforce elbowing its way into the equation. This naturally resulted in Ammy getting ever-so-lightly shoved in the opposite direction of where our resident mad scientist was currently soaring, falling forward and right onto her chest. Insert amusing witticism about how she had a cushioned landing here.

Crude jokes aside, things quickly returned to their previous chaotic state, so I stopped paying attention there, and I decided to redouble my searching efforts, and they were soon rewarded when I found the oval object I was looking for. Regrettably, it was inside a locked glass vitrine, and I didn't have the time to mess around, so after whispering a quick and absolutely-100-percent-sincere apology to Abram, I picked up a nearby musket from one of the weapon stands and shattered the display case with one firm strike of its butt. It made quite a bit of noise, but I figured that with all the commotion outside, no one would really care.

I reached inside the vitrine while making sure I wouldn't cut myself on the broken glass and managed to fish out my target with relative ease. As for what it actually was, the best way I could describe it would be a jester's mask, the kind that one would find in the Carnival of Venice but without the cockscomb crest on the top, leaving an oval, dominantly black porcelain mask with silver highlights around the eyes, depicting an ominously grinning man. It wasn't exactly perfect, but it was the best disguise I could procure under the circumstances. I mean, it was either this or one of those traditional African tribal masks on the wall, and if I had to decide which one looked less jarring with my usual black long coat, there wasn't really a competition. It was a little tricky to put it on in the dark, but once I secured it onto my face, it fit surprisingly snugly, and it didn't even restrict my vision as badly as I'd feared.

Thusly disguised, I felt that my identity was, if not completely hidden, at least harder to tell at a glance, which was all I was hoping for. After all, the only reason why I even bothered was so that I could maintain plausible deniability if the Knights came knocking on my door. It was never a good idea to cut off a potential mark that could be squeezed for possibly lifesaving information. With all that in mind, I was just about to Phase to the next room and start looking for the Purple Zone jammer when I was once again interrupted in my tracks.

"{Chief.}"

I suppressed the indignant "What now?" bubbling out from the bottom of my gut, and after a shallow breath I whispered a considerably more polite, "Yes, Dormouse?"

"{I need some help. Josh isn't listening to me.}"

Did... Did she just sulk? That was mildly unexpected, and once I shook off the initial surprise, I quickly asked her to clarify what she meant.

"Did you lose the connection?"

"{No. He's just not listening to what I'm telling him.}"

"Is he still dueling the fembot on the roof?"

"{No. He's currently flirting with her.}"

My hand that was just about to put the unloaded display musket away came to a surprised halt with a quiet, "Pardon?"

I mean, Judy had a very broad definition of flirting, and I've been on the short end of that stick a couple of times, but I couldn't really imagine how or why Josh would try to make a move on the fembot in the middle of a battle. But then again, he was a harem protagonist, and this kind of thing wasn't exactly unheard of, so I quite eagerly waited for Judy's explanation.

"{Amelia is still unsteady on her feet, and the girls need his support, but he's too busy giving a sentimental motivational speech to his opponent, and I'm not getting through to him. Please do something.}"

"Okay, so I heard it right the first time..." I muttered before raising my voice and asking, "But how exactly am I supposed to do anything about it? I'm kind of in the middle of something here."

"{Chief, you can teleport,}" she told me as if it was something I forgot I could do. "{Please go over to him in person and tell him to regroup with the others. Apparently, it's not good enough if only the mission control says it.}"

Yep, she was definitely sulking. Wonderful. Now I'll also have to console her, too, when this is all over. More importantly, though, what she said just now made me raise a single incredulous brow.

"Need I remind you that we want to keep my ability to teleport around without any support infrastructure a secret?"

"{I thought the cat was already out of the bag,}" she responded a smidgen impatiently. "{You're already present at two different locations, with multiple witnesses. Three, if we count your monster hunter frenemy.}"

"Yeah, but I can probably explain my way out of this once things calm down," I retorted, only to immediately get shot down.

"{Then there is even less of a reason to hold back.}" I stayed silent for maybe a bit too long, as she soon added, "{Just go to Josh's side already. He's killing me with his speech.}"

"Fine," I grumbled, and once I'd made sure that I could still Phase in and out of this room later, I let out a long breath and muttered, "Oh well, this is still only the second-worst day I've ever had. At least no one stabbed me today... yet."

And with those words, I promptly disappeared from the room.

PART 3

"... and that's why it doesn't matter if you are flesh and blood or not; what really matters is th— Ouch!"

Whatever impassioned speech Josh was delivering came to a screeching halt after I, without sparing a single second for whys and wherefores, immediately slapped him on the back of his head the moment I arrived at the tattered warehouse roof inside the Purple Zone.

"We don't have time for this," I grumbled while gesturing towards the fembot down on one knee not far away from us, her hair and clothes visibly disheveled after a no-doubt-astonishingly-epic battle of might, magic, and magitech. "Since she's already down, how about you capture her first and *then* discuss the philosophical implications of androids dreaming with electric sheep after that?"

My currently very Abyssal-ish friend, still holding the back of his horned head, turned an indignant look in my direction, only to instantly freeze up on the spot when our eyes met. For several seconds there was silence on the battlefield (or at least on our side of it; by the sounds coming from downstairs, Elly and the girls were still busy with breaking Lab Coat Guy's mooks into chunks of recyclable size), culminating in Josh muttering a wide-eyed and somewhat uncertain "Leo?" towards me.

"Yes, what is it?" I responded maybe just a tad snappily, but he was still looking at me weird, and it took me an embarrassingly long time to realize why he appeared so dumbfounded. "You're wondering about the mask, aren't you?"

"Among other things," he confirmed with a nod. "Like... why do you have a hunting rifle?"

Now it was my time to be surprised, as I didn't even realize I'd accidentally taken something else with me when I Phased over.

"It's actually a musket, and it's a long story" was my reply, a phrase I'd repeated so many times as of late I was afraid it was going to become my catchphrase.

In the meantime, the kneeling fembot unsteadily rose to her feet and was intently staring at me.

"Reappearance of the primary target is confirmed. Anti-illusion sensors appear to be ineffective." She fell silent for a beat, and then she abruptly raised her hands towards me. "Commencing the firing sequence for plasma disintegrators at thirty perce—"

"Oh no, you don't!" I exclaimed in a mild panic and reflexively flung the unloaded firearm in my hand at her.

Galatea's eyes opened a fraction wider in response and tried to raise her arms to defend herself, but by then the stock had already whacked her in the forehead with an unexpectedly meaty *thunk* noise followed by an uncharacteristically girlish "Eep!" After finding its mark, the musket spun away and out of sight, presumably landing somewhere on the ground below, while the trigger-happy android fell backwards while discharging a pair of tear-shaped, gut-shaking blasts into the sky from the middles of her palms. Odd. I could distinctly remember her firing from a barrel inside her forearm the last time around. Maybe she got an upgrade when I wasn't looking?

While I mused so, there was another long moment of awkward silence hanging in the air as we both stared at the android woman splayed out on the rooftop. At first I thought she was just shocked by the events, but on closer look, it turned out she was knocked out cold. That was... mildly unexpected, to say the least. Then, at last, the momentary lull was broken by Joshua letting out an indignant groan by my side.

"Dude! Why did you do that!?"

I spared him a skeptical glance, then flatly told him, "In case you're wondering, this is called self-defense. When someone tries to vaporize you with a plasma whatchamacallit, you're entirely justified for knocking them down."

"No, I don't mean that!" came his animated retort, but then he froze up for a moment and then amended, "I mean, if you didn't suddenly appear, then she wouldn't have tried to attack you in the first place... but I suppose that's beside the point. More importantly," he began to wind up again, raising his voice in the process, "More importantly, who the hell throws a rifle?!"

"... I do?" I replied, suddenly feeling like we weren't exactly on the same wavelength. "Seriously though, is that really your biggest concern at the moment?"

"Ah, you're right! I should check to see if she's all right," Josh suddenly declared and leaped over to the fallen android's side. "Maybe she got a concussion."

"No, that's not what I..." I began, but then the end of my words trailed into a sigh. Can androids even get a concussion in the first place? Anyhow, at the end of the day I let it go with a soft-spoken "Never mind."

Considering the situation, I decided it wasn't really the time to argue about small details like that, so I simply followed after my friend, only to catch the tail end of the seemingly unconscious fembot muttering something while her face subtly twitched every once in a while.

"What is she saying?"

"Something about rebooting," Josh replied off the cuff while observing her forehead where my improvised projectile hit her.

"Error," Galatea began to murmur again without opening her eyes, and this time I listened closely to her exaggeratedly robotic voice. "Probability of primary target using Object: Archaic Firearm as projectile: zero point zero two percent. Beep. Error. File corrupted. Beep. Rebooting is required after rebuilding the probability calculation engine: seven percent. ... eight percent..."

Also, yes, she actually said *beep*. Not an actual sound, but the onomatopoeia. What is this I don't even.

"You see?" Josh addressed me with a triumphant smirk in the meantime while pointing at the unconscious Galatea. "Even she agrees with me."

I would've face-palmed if not for the mask already covering my face, so I decided that an unsubtle eye roll had to do for now, and I instructed my friend, with my best leader impression, "Josh, I'm way too tired for this right now. Stop messing around and grab her."

"By grabbing her, you mean...?"

"Throw her over your shoulder or something," I told him ever-so-slightly impatiently. "After that, regroup with the others on the ground. I'll see you there."

"Erm... Okay," he responded a bit uncertainly, but I didn't have the time to argue with him, so I turned my back on him and Phased over to the rest of the group. Normally I wouldn't have been so flamboyant with my teleporting ability, but considering the circumstances, I was ultimately of the same mind as Judy and decided to worry about explaining things after the situation got un-buggered.

Anyhow, after arriving at my destination, I spent a few seconds observing the situation, which also served as a brief respite to collect myself a little after rapidly Phasing all over the place. In short, the front of the warehouse was currently covered in a layer of white ice, no doubt the handiwork of my sister. On my left, Elly was fighting two of the elite mooks (the neon green and the blue one, to be precise) on her own while holding one of the run-of-the-mill mooks by its ankles and using it as an improvised blunt weapon. In other words, pretty much what I expected from her.

Meanwhile, on my right, Snowy was floating about a hand's width above the ground with her wings spread wide-open and three long ice spears hovering above her raised right hand. She was currently keeping Lab Coat Guy at bay; his upper body was covered in the now-familiar magitech power armour, and he was hunkered down with his arms crossed in front of his chest while a couple of glowing spots on his shoulder pads were projecting some kind of barrier in front of him.

Finally, right next to me, Ammy was sitting on the ground, her glasses missing and with one hand clamped on her bleeding nose while Angie and the golem were holding back the red and the purple elite mooks from closing the distance. I observed all of this in great detail, yet it took my poor, overexerted brain several long seconds to realize I could do so because everyone on the battlefield went stock-still the moment I arrived. Even Elly, who was just about to beat a mook into a pulp with another mook.

Speaking of which, I turned towards my girlfriend and told her, "Don't mind me, just carry on as you were."

The princess once again proved to be really adaptable (or she'd just stopped thinking and decided to go with the flow, one or the other), as by the time I finished my sentence, she'd already swung the unlucky Sprocket and sent both of the elite mooks flying. Attagirl.

"Leo?" came the incredulous question from my side. I glanced over, and once I met the class rep's confused eyes with my own, I couldn't help but groan in exasperation.

"Don't ask about the mask; it would take too long to explain," I told her right off the bat before addressing the others. "Snowy, keep him occupied for a bit longer. Angie, focus on crippling the big guys. Princess..." I paused for a second as I looked over my girlfriend still holding the broken, severed leg of a goon-bot, and in the end I settled on, "You're doing great; keep it up."

"What about me?" Ammy asked, seemingly out of reflex, only to immediately come to her senses and follow it up with an indignant, "Wait, no! First, explain where...!"

I figured she either wanted to ask where I'd disappeared to, or where I'd come from, but I didn't have the patience to answer either of those questions, so I extended a finger towards her lips to silence her before replying with, "I'm going to need your golem in a moment. Please stand by until Josh arrives."

Needless to say, she was quite dissatisfied with my interruption, but before she could voice her complaints, we were all startled by a loud cry coming from the roof of the warehouse.

"Parkoooooouuuuuuur!!!"

I'm not going to lie, for a moment I couldn't decide whether I was more impressed by the way my friend jumped off the roof and managed to land without breaking his legs, while carrying someone on his shoulders no less, or annoyed by his weird battle cry. After some consideration, I decided it was the latter. Unfortunately Josh was completely unaware of my frame of mind, and once he got his bearings, he casually jogged over to my side with a grin on his face.

"Did you see that? I didn't even need to bring the wings out!"

I sent the guy riding on an adrenaline high a wry look and told him, "Josh, you're completely wrecking the tone of the situation. Stop it."

"Yeah, whatever," he responded with a shrug that rattled the still-unconscious android woman on his shoulder, but then he finally noticed the glare I was sending his way and clumsily cleared his throat. "So I brought her over, but what am I supposed to do with her? I think she just reached seventy percent..."

"Put her down over there," I instructed him before turning to the still-wobbly Amelia. "Class rep, call your golem over."

"Why?" she asked, though by the time the words left her mouth, the aforementioned golem already began to retreat from the front lines and headed in our direction.

"Have it stand over there," I directed her without bothering to answer her question, and pointed to the spot right next to the unmoving fembot. I was just about to tell her what to do next, but my words were cut short by a magical projectile sailing way over my head. It wasn't picked up by my danger sense, probably because it was way off the mark, but it still drew my attention to the man who launched it.

"What are you doing!? Let her go!"

Lab Coat Guy was obviously more than furious at the moment, but he was kept at bay by Snowy sending wave after wave of icicles flying towards him. Ugh. That brought back some bad memories, so I decided to ignore that corner of the battleground for the time being; instead, I turned my attention back to the golem and pointed at the android on the ground.

"Sit."

"What?" Ammy blurted out in surprise, so I repeated myself.

"Make it sit on her, or lie on her, or whatever you want, so long as it stops her from moving."

"Wait, wouldn't that crush her?" Josh objected right away, so I overruled him with a shrug.

"I'm fairly sure that she's tougher than that, but even so, I'm not *that* invested in the well-being of someone who tried to disintegrate me multiple times."

"Fair enough, I suppose," Josh grumbled, though obviously not convinced.

"Reboot compl— Ouf!"

Credit where credit's due, unlike our resident harem protagonist, the class rep had no problem with following my orders, nor did she have any qualms about her golem pushing the breath out of the fembot... Speaking of which, that pained "Ouf" sounded really authentic. Did she actually have lungs? What kind of android has lungs? Wait, now that I think about it, I've seen her eat with Lab Coat Guy and the nurse, too. Was she really an android?

"Questions for later," I muttered under my breath before turning to the class rep again. "Nice work. Now come here."

Ammy only took a wobbly and decidedly hesitant step towards me, so I exhaled with all the enervation of the world and unceremoniously grabbed her by the waist.

"{Chief? What are you doing?}"

"Not now, Dormouse," I whispered under my breath before turning to the others. "Things are being a little chaotic right now back at the base and at Elly's place, so I'm taking the class rep with me. You guys keep stalling, listen to Judy's instructions, and make sure you stay close and cover one another. Got that, Josh?"

Instead of my friend, it was the princess who raised her voice in alarm.

"Something is wrong at home?"

"I'm already dealing with it. Don't worry, and just focus on scrapping these guys."

"Um... Okay," she responded with a carefree voice that said "If Leo's on the case, everything will be fine," which would have been flattering under normal circumstances, but this time it only gave me unnecessary pressure, so I quickly nodded in her direction and before anyone else could say anything, I wrapped my phantom limb around the flustered class rep.

Not half a second later, we both reappeared inside the sparsely lit impromptu prison room in realspace.

"Uwah!"

Yep, we'd barely arrived, and I was already getting irritated. I let go of the class rep and took a step away from her and towards the large cage in the corner and the hapless Celestial in it.

"Holy crap! You almost gave me a heart attack!" Mike exclaimed while dramatically clutching at his chest, only to freeze up a moment later and immediately stand ramrod straight. "Amelia! Hi! What are you doing here?"

"That's a good question," she responded while aiming a glare at me, and she even raised her hand to her temples, no doubt reflexively trying to tweak her missing glasses. "What am I doing here? And how? We were outside and in a Restricted Zone just a few moments ago!"

"Do you really think this is the best time to ask this?" I asked back while unsubtly glancing towards the captive sleeper agent, but she didn't get the memo, so I resolved myself to give her a quick explanation.

"Ancient super-powerful artifact that can warp time and space," I declared as I unabashedly pointed at the mask on my face. "Hard to control, dangerous, might cause all the atoms in my body to explode at the speed of light if I'm not careful, but we are in a tight spot at the moment, so I had to use it, anyway. There. Now can we actually move on?"

Ammy gave me an uncharacteristically doe-eyed stare for a second or five, after which she hastily took a step back and mumbled something along the lines of, "Y-yes, sorry. I shouldn't have asked."

I was tempted to immediately retort with a miffed "Yeah, you shouldn't have," but I managed to hold myself back and a deep breath later I softened it into a more moderate, "Good. Now, I have to go because I still have two more situations to deal with. Since you're injured, I figured you wouldn't be able to contribute much to the battle, so please help this guy get out of that cage in my stead, and then escape before your grandpa shows up."

"... Okay," she agreed in an unusually weak voice and took a step towards the cage, only to recoil when Mike rushed up to the bars with thundering eyes.

"You're injured?! What happened? Who hurt you?"

The class rep glanced over to me for some reason, then back at the guy, and finally told him in a meek voice, "We were distracting Dr. Robatto, and in the process I fell down and hit my face. I don't think it's broken, but..."

"Come closer; let me see! Ah, your nose is bleeding! Quick, I'll heal you!"

In the meantime, Ammy got into arm's reach of the cage, so Mike extended his hand and put it over her bruised nose. I didn't feel like watching the scene unfolding in front of me, so I bid a quiet farewell and Phased away, barely catching the end of the Celestial mumbling something along the lines of, "Oh, I forgot I can't. The cage is—"

Well, whatever that was, I decided to put it out of my mind and trust the class rep. She would hopefully get him out of there in a jiffy, so that was one issue out of my hair. I would've told Judy about this, but I couldn't open a communication line on my end, so I only made a mental note about instructing her to keep an eye on Ammy and tell the others to retreat the moment she and Mike were out of the area.

More importantly, I was finally back in the pitch-black trophy room inside the Dracis mansion. Based on the thumping noise coming from outside, the Knights were still trying to break down the barricade from the outside. That meant I still had time to find the jamming artifact. Or wait, should I Phase over to the other side of the wall and tell Emese to hold tight a little longer first?

It was at this point, while I was vacillating between the two options, that the door of the trophy room was kicked in with a deafening bang that cut my thoughts and filled my aching head with white noise.

"Captain, wait! Sir Roland said...!"

"Ah ken whit he said!" the huge man thundered back to his subordinate in an accent as thick as tar. He was decked out in full plate armour, capped by a great helm adorned with a pair of stubby horns at the top, and all of his equipment was giving off a faint magical glow that ironically made things even harder to see in the dark. He was also freaking huge, easily the size of one of the Fauns, though still just slightly less massive than Brang. He walked into the room with a confident stride, and he was followed by a couple of smaller, yet similarly dressed men clutching shields and short swords in their hands.

"Th' wyrmblood is richt oan th' ither side o' this dyke! Ah will sooner be damned than let th' chance gang juist sae that he cuid...!" he yelled at one of the men beside him, but then a moment later he came to a screeching halt and grabbed the hilt of the heavy executioner's blade hanging from his waist, and his helmeted head faced my general direction. "Thare's someain hidin' haer!! Shaw yersel', knave!"

I... had a lot of different things to say. Things such as "I wasn't even hiding, idiot," or "Knave? Really?" or even the incredibly obvious, "What kind of accent is that? You sound like a Russian mobster trying to speak ye olde English with a Scotsman trapped in your throat!" but at the end of the day, I decided that none of those were right for the situation.

Instead I took a step forth so that my silhouette would be outlined by the light coming from the outside, and with a deepened voice I greeted the flabbergasted group of Knights with the most ominous, malicious, and downright gleeful "Good evening, gentlemen" the world has ever heard.

And why? Because I might not have a weapon, and I might not have any fancy spells and superpowers, but as long as I had my refuge in audacity, I was confident I was still going to make these guys regret they ever set foot inside this mansion.

CHAPTER 15

PART 1

There was an odd, tense silence in the dark trophy chamber, which lasted exactly until the Knights outside rammed the barricaded door of the neighbouring room for the umpteenth time. The dull sound of the impact made the large man in the middle twitch as if he'd just woken up, and he hastily raised his heavy blade to assume a defensive stance. The squires, as the security guy called them, also overcame their momentary stupor at the same time and bunched together in the doorway. They all raised their kite shields and blocked the exit with something that, if you squinted hard enough, might be possibly considered the twice-removed stepcousin of a proper shield wall.

Once everyone was in place, the big guy in the middle took an almost comically heavy step forward and pointed his blade at me with one hand. It was all veeeeeery dramatic, and not at all silly, I swear.

"Wha urr ye? Eydentify yersel' a' wance!"

I inhaled a sharp breath and was about to give a suitably snarky reply, but as I opened my mouth I stiffened for a second and then snapped it shut with a slightly painful clank of my teeth.

"That's... actually a very good question," I mused aloud, much to the belligerent men-at-arms' bafflement.

I mean, really, who *was* I? And no, I didn't mean that as some kind of profound question of Jungian psychology or the like, but as an entirely practical matter. As in, I sure as hell *wasn't* Leonard Dunning at the moment, especially after the trouble I went through to disguise myself. That naturally meant that I wasn't Blackcloak or the resident Chimera slayer, either. What other options did I have?

Admin? The guy was supposed to be on the other side of the globe, so if it got out that he was here, it would undoubtedly raise a few Celestial brows, which was bad for my sustained espionage efforts. If not him, then who else could I be? I needed a context-appropriate, nonconflicting, and at least reasonably cool fake name.

The Jester? Nah, too on the nose. Persona? Too Jungian. Bel of the Tenebrous Flames? Too chuuni. Nyarlathotep? Too eldritch. The Kingpin? Too copyrighted. Shadow, the True Self? Heck, that's both Jungian and chuuni!

Okay, screw it, my brain was obviously too much of a mush at the moment to come up with something fitting, so...

"Give me a second. I'll be right back."

My words caused no small amount of confusion among the men in front of me, but I reckon not nearly as much as my subsequent disappearance from the room.

"Hey, Dormouse," I greeted my ever-so-slightly-surprised girlfriend, but to her credit, she looked stupefied for only a moment before she directed a welcoming poker face at me, which was made only slightly ridiculous by her party-glasses-shaped communication artifact. I also noted that, judging by the faint light of the magic circle under our feet, we were inside the fake teleportation closet for some reason, but that was beside the point.

"Hi, Chief. What are you doing here?" I was about to formulate an answer, but then her expression subtly darkened, and she added, "Why are you swaying like that? Are you injured?"

"Nah, I'm just a little light-headed," I told her while indiscreetly leaning against the nearby wall. "Too much teleporting around in a short time. I'll live. More importantly, I need your brain."

This time my girlfriend's face was the spitting image of the anthropomorphic personification of skepticism.

"You look bad, but I don't think you're a zombie just yet, so please elaborate in a way I can actually understand."

I took a deep breath, and once I felt steady enough, I quickly explained myself.

"I'm currently planning to verbally engage some dastardly Knights and tease some info out of them before the inevitable hostilities, but I need a fake identity for the charade. I want to pretend to be a mysterious, powerful, and knowledgeable villain of indefinite origins."

"So the same thing you used to do in the past, just with a mask on your face."

"And ambiguously evil."

"So an outside-context villain?"

"More or less. Do you have any ideas?"

Judy's brows once again furrowed ever so imperceptibly, and after a few seconds of consideration, she ultimately proposed, "How about masquerading as an Abyssal, like when you got Neige's ID forged?"

"That's... something I totally should've thought of myself," I muttered, after which I flashed an appreciative smile at her. She didn't react, and it was only then that I belatedly remembered that I was still wearing the carnival mask, so I voiced my sentiment as well. "Thanks, Dormouse. You're the best."

"You're welcome."

I was about to leave so that I wouldn't let the gaggle of swordsman wait for long, but before that, I quickly added, "Also, could you support me? I'm a little slow right now, so I think I might have further need for your grey matter."

"Sure. I can multitask," she responded with just the barest tinge of smugness in her voice. Or was it just run-of-the-mill confidence that only sounded weird when it came from her? While I pondered on where the line was between the two, I gave her a small nod, and promptly reappeared inside the trophy room again, eliciting a series of shocked gasps from the agitated antagonist populating the premises.

"Whit manner o' foul sorcery...!?"

"Please do forgive my tardiness. I had urgent matters to attend to, but now you may enjoy my undivided attention," I cut him off with my best sleazy villain impression. I'm not going to lie, it came out way easier than I expected.

"Ye! Wha th' hell's bells urr ye!?"

To further emphasize his question, the big man vigorously waved his weapon in my general direction, but I didn't feel any threat from him, so I casually ignored his attempts at intimidation with a shrug.

"You may call me..." I began in a casual tone, only to pause as I realized that I'd forgotten to actually come up with a proper cover name. Worse yet, now that I began to give my answer, I couldn't backpedal out of it without ruining the image I was building right now, so after another moment of hesitation, I blurted out. "Bel."

"Bel?" came the befuddled whisper from one of the squires in the pseudo–shield wall.

"{Bel?}" echoed the voice of my girlfriend, her tone a curious mixture of puzzlement and skepticism. Normally I would've made an excuse to the effect of "Hey, they put me on the spot! At least I didn't accidentally add 'of the Tenebrous Flames' to it!" but considering the circumstances, I concluded that directly communicating with Judy would've only made things even more confusing.

"Bel of the Abyss," I stated offhandedly, and a second of hesitancy later I also added a scraping bow for the sake of showmanship. "Pleased to make your acquaintance."

What followed was exactly half a second of silence before the big guy in the middle let out a stifled battle cry and lunged towards me with his weapon held high. Oddly enough, my danger sense still didn't warn me about any incoming grievous bodily harm, but it was better to be safe than sorry, so I immediately Phased two meters to my right and well out of his immediate range. Oh, and I did that while still maintaining my bow, not on purpose, but because that's how Phasing worked.

In retrospect I probably shouldn't have bothered with it at all, as the big guy stopped his vertical swing midway, and based on his posture, he would've most likely done so whether I tried to get out of the way of the strike or not. The sudden attack also awakened my adrenal glands, as I was feeling a sudden rush that finally dispersed some of the fog dulling my thoughts, and I soon came up with a working hypothesis for his odd behaviour.

"Now, now, Sir Minotaur; do be careful." Saying so, I straightened myself and controlled my body language to appear as laidback and nonthreatening as possible. "You almost broke one of your oaths there. Hurting poor, innocent me would've been quite a blunder, I say."

"If yer innocent, then a'm th' queen o Sassenach land!" the horny knight scoffed, his odd dialect still as hard to decipher as ever, but at the very least it didn't seem like he would try to turn me into mincemeat again. For the moment, at least.

"Really?" I responded with a sneering grin that wasn't visible, yet it was important all the same. It's a lesser-known fact, but even when people's faces are hidden, their expressions subtly change their voices, just enough so that the perceptive listener could pick up on it. "My apologies, your majesty. I didn't recognize it was you under all of that metal, and... oh my, did you put on some weight?"

"Ye think yer funny?"

"No, I know I am," I answered without a shred of shame before unceremoniously Phasing to the other side of the room, startling everyone and pushing them even further off balance. For a short while the big guy was looking left and right in mild alarm, and for some reason he failed to notice me twice, so I let a resigned sigh slip out between my teeth and walked forward until he finally managed to see me in the dark. At this point, he took up another aggressive stance with his weapon held high, but he didn't seem to be about to take another swing at me just yet.

For the time being, I decided to stay silent and used this lull in the hostilities to draft out my priorities. First off, I had to find the magic jammer. It apparently wasn't on Mister Minotaur, but then again, he was shining from head to toe, so it was still possible that the glowing tree was just hidden in the eyesore forest. Secondly, I needed to mark at least one of the Knights here, a prospect made quite tricky by the fact that they were wearing full plate armour with gambeson under it and full helmets, leaving little to no skin exposed. Thirdly, I wanted to squeeze some info out of these guys, and there was no better way to make them talk than to have them think we were already on the same page and they weren't actually telling me anything I didn't already know. In other words, my old and trusty fallback plan for teasing information out of others.

Now then, with my priorities set, I decided to get the ball rolling by some small talk.

"Jokes aside, you're quite rude, Sir Knight," I addressed the guy in the middle as I began to slowly circle around him. He constantly turned in place to face me as I did so, and I couldn't help but notice that the eyes glaring at me through the slits of his horned helmet were of an unusually piercing, icy-blue colour, a bit of data that I immediately filed in the back of my brain before I continued with, "To think that you wouldn't even introduce yourself even after I did so! How unchivalrous!"

"{The name of the current Minotaur Knight is unknown,}" Judy chimed in, immediately picking up on my subtle request for support. "{However, according to records on the Celestial Information Network, the mantle is passed down in the MacCumhail family.}"

At first I could only blink in surprise when I heard Judy's info, but even though what she'd said sounded incredibly silly, the way she said it was anything but, so I had no choice but to trust her. That said, it meant that the Minotaur Knight was a Scottish man with an Irish name. At this rate, I wouldn't have been surprised if it turned out he was an Asian man with blue eyes and red hair who grew up in Australia and was raised by Polish immigrants. But putting my confusion over the man's ethnicity aside, I raised my hand to my temple, and after feigning concentration for a moment, I snapped my finger as if I just recalled something.

"Ah, don't tell me! You must be the descendant of old MacCumhail, aren't you?"

The moment the word left my mouth, there was a series of shocked gasps coming from the sideline, with one of the bricks in the faux shield wall even muttering an almost pitiful, "He just pushed the Cumhail button..." which incidentally caused Mister Minotaur to start literally shaking with what I presumed was bottled-up fury.

"I's pronoonc'd MacCool, you feckin' bampot!"

"Really?"

"{Really?}"

Judy and I quite literally echoed the same sentiment, but I didn't have the time to dwell on how you could possibly read it like that, as following his exclamation my opponent immediately rushed forward to swing his blade at me, and this time my danger sense told me it wasn't a feint. I quickly Phased out of the way of the incoming strike and reappeared behind him, but before I could get a word in, the armour-clad man turned on his heel and swung his sword in an almost-360-degree arc.

"I'll kill ye!" he shouted, his voice barely stifled by his helm, but he naturally only cut the air.

"{For your interest, the Minotaur Knights of the past were infamous for their short tempers.}

"Oh really? I wouldn't have noticed if you didn't say so!"... was what I would've said if I wasn't too busy getting out of the way of the next diagonal slash coming my way.

"Now, now. Calm d—"

I tried to speak up, only to get interrupted by a low slash aimed at my legs, so I immediately Phased out of the way.

"Listen to—"

This time it was a half-swording stab targeting my neck, forcing me to Phase back to my previous location.

"I..."

And now he was using the same half-swording grip to spin his weapon around and try to clobber me with the pommel. As for my reaction, it could be best summed up as "Oh, come on! Could you let me finish just one nefarious sentence? Pretty please?" Oh, and also Phasing out of the way, but at this point I believe that was a given.

My unspoken pleas naturally fell on similarly deaf ears, so for the time being I kept Phasing out of the way of the egregious equestrian hell-bent on inflicting grievous harm on poor old me. To be fair, I was fairly certain that if push came to shove, I could probably avoid his graciously well-telegraphed strikes without relying on Phasing, but at the moment I was pretending to be a mysterious and powerful Abyssal of unknown affiliations, so abusing my short-range teleportation ability felt more fitting for the role. Thankfully doing so within the bounds of just one room didn't strain my already-battered brain that much, and the adrenaline rush of the bulky Knight repeatedly screaming and swinging at me kept the vertigo at bay, as well. On the other hand, the same yelling was also giving me a headache, so I couldn't say everything was just peachy, either.

However, just as I was about to get into the rhythm of the battle, my danger sense suddenly threw up a warning sign right after I Phased out of the way of yet another unnecessarily elaborate twirly slash, and I instinctively twisted my upper body just enough to avoid an armoured fist sailing past my torso. My opponent spun around, apparently still carried by the momentum of his swing, before he came to a halt by stomping his feet hard and turning his weapon towards me.

"Surprised, aren't ye?" he sneered at me, and even though I obviously couldn't see it, I had a distinct feeling that the burly man of indecipherable ethnicity had his mouth set in a wolfish grin behind his faceplate. "A've git yer wee trick figured oot awready!"

"You do?" I blurted out in a mixture of surprise and apprehension, only to remember that I was supposed to be a mysterious trickster type at the moment and hastily added, "I mean, please go ahead, do tell."

"Ah admit yer trick wis gey unexpected, fiend, bit ye hae tae git up earlier tae deceive me!"

"Did Sir Duncan already figure out his opponent?" came another stray comment from the peanut gallery, followed up by an enthusiastic, "Of course! Sir Duncan is the second-best duelist of the Brotherhood! There's no way someone shady like that could match him!" from another amateur battle commentator.

The big guy let out a grunt in response and used his sword to confidently point at three spots on the ground.

"A dinnae ken wha yer, bit tis ah kent that awreedy yer 'ere tae buy time fur th' dragons!" For a moment I honestly wanted to point out that if anyone was wasting time here, it was him, but I never got the chance to voice my opinion. "Ye aimed tae deceive me, bit ye hae chosen th' wrong opponent tae speil yer petty trickeries upon! Fur a'm th' Knight o' th' Minotaur!" By this point even I was a little curious about where he was going with this, so I decided to ignore the impressed gasps and stray comments coming from the direction of the shield palisade in the entrance and subtly gestured for the big guy to continue, and he did so with a confident grunt.

"Ah bear th' marc o' th' Minotaur," he repeated, for some odd reason, only to then immediately expound, "Ah possess th' Authority o' th' Maze!"

"Uh-huh, neat," I muttered with a nod while waiting for the rest of the strangely smug explanation.

"Ever sin oor brave squires o' th' Knightly Brotherhood o' th' Maist Heroic Bloo'lines barred th' doorway, this room became mah domain, 'n' by spreading mah aura oan th' flair, ah hae discovered that ye ainlie shaw yersel' oan them three plooks!"

I glanced around for a moment, figuring that he was talking about the three places where he was pointing at not long ago, and I could already feel my head getting filled up by question marks. I mean, yes, that's where I'd appeared when Phasing around because those were the only free spots in the room not taken up by chairs or coat hangers or what have you near the Knight guy. There wasn't anything special about them.

"Ye wanted tae mak' me think that yer fleet, bit in fact, ah kin tell that yer feet ne'er touched th' ground anywhere else ither than they three places! Ye ne'er moved!"

There was an incoherent noise already trapped in my throat at this point, and I nearly let it out of form an uncertain "Eh?" or a stupefied "Uuurm?" but neither was destined to be, as I was interrupted by Judy's voice, forcing me to swallow my reaction noises back down.

"{Chief, what are you doing?}"

"You mean, right now?" I asked back in a whisper, my voice hidden by the continued and boisterous explanation coming from the armour-clad man and his eagerly cheering audience by the door. "I'm listening to the big bad Knight explaining his ability and how it allegedly counters mine."

"{So you're having an Explaining Your Power to the Enemy moment.}"

"Yes, it's a... Wait, that's a trope?"

"{Of course it is,}" my assistant replied with just a hint of disapproval. "{Did you really never hear about this? It's very common in Japanese battle manga and—}"

"No, I know that the trope exists," I cut her off just a tad indignantly. "I just didn't know it was called that. Don't tropes usually have snappier names than that?"

"{Not every trope can be Aluminum Christmas Trees,}" she stated with undue solemnity. "{On a separate note, can you actually understand what he is saying?}"

"More or less."

"{Odd. I can only recognize about half of the words. Maybe he is half Faun?}"

I almost told her that, considering this guy's size, he might as well be, but Mister Minotaur didn't give me the chance to do so.

"Awright! Urr ye listening tae me, fiend?!"

I exhaled a long sigh and responded with, "You made this place into your territory by spreading your aura or whatever, which created a bounded field upon which you could enforce your authority, whatever that is, and so now you oh-so-inescapably cornered me with your super-special-awesome Cretan Labyrinth Magic or what have you. I've heard everything loud and clear."

"{Chief, you are breaking character,}" my dear assistant warned me, but I couldn't help but roll my eyes in return.

"Well, I can't very well break something this guy never let me establish in the first place," I answered in an angry whisper, following which I cleared my throat and turned to address the man in the horny helmet again. Or, at the very least, I wanted to, if not for...

"WHA URR YE CAWIN A CRETIN YE RADGE WEE SHITE?!"

... that. Also, to punctuate his very eloquent response, the Knight immediately raised his weapon over his head and lunged at me, his whole armour suddenly shining even harder than it already did. That looked mildly fatal, an assessment that my danger sense wholeheartedly agreed upon, so I quickly Phased to the right... only for my sixth sense to add a PS to its previous warning and force me to Phase again to avoid a follow-up kick. Since I wasn't really keen on the current situation, I decided to put a bit more of a distance between us this time around.

"Yer trick is auld!" the big man bellowed in a triumphant voice even before I'd fully reappeared and reoriented myself in the corner. "Noo ah ken whaur yer true body hides!"

I would've asked just what the hell he meant by that, but then my attention was once again occupied by my sixth sense screaming at me, accompanied by the sound of something cutting through the air.

Now, here's the thing: There is this common idea that when someone is in mortal danger, time comes to a crawl. This was, unfortunately, something that I'd already experienced once, courtesy of my little sister. What I'm trying to say is that I should've been, if not used to, then at the very least familiar with the phenomenon. However, familiar or not, nothing in this world could possibly prepare me for the sight of a heavy war sword very, veeeeeeery slooooowly hurtling towards me in the air while spinning like the world's least practical boomerang.

Now, I think we can all agree that being caught flat-footed by a flying sword of all things was a pretty dangerous situation. Also, very novel. I mean, just how many people can claim that someone threw a sword at them? That's a conversation starter, that's for sure.

However, my rambling aside, my brain currently felt like one of those spinning loading icons stuck at 89 percent, *this* close to finishing processing just what kind of fresh hell was careening towards me, yet seemingly in perpetual limbo. Then, just like that... my weapon-catching training got validated! Again!

My right hand, with little conscious input from my frontal lobe, reflexively reached out towards the weapon sailing through the air with a distinctly dangerous-sounding whistling noise, and before I knew it, my fingers were unceremoniously grasped around the grip of the sword with my mouth involuntarily uttering an elated "Zoink!"

Now, I don't toot my own horn often, but I have to say that this was, without a doubt, a perfect ten-out-of-ten catch. Go, me. After dispersing its remaining momentum with a small flourish, I held the softly glowing blade vertically in front of me, and couldn't help but grin in satisfaction.

And then the grin slowly withered from my face as I realized what I'd just done.

What the bloody hell was I thinking?! That was insanely dangerous! If my timing was off by just half a second, I could've lost a finger or four! Thank god or Buddha or whoever that Judy currently didn't have a visual feed, or she would've killed me!

"{Is everything all right?}"

Oh, look. Speak of the devil. How utterly unexpected.

"Yes, everything is perfectly and one hundred percent fine and absolutely safe. There is no reason for you to worry, none at all," I spluttered in a hurry, and this time my ever-so-slightly-panicked words must have been heard by the Knights around me, in no small part due to the fact that the silence in the room was downright deafening at the moment.

"{Good,}" Judy responded, sounding a little absentminded, before quickly adding, "{There's still a lot of noise coming from the main hall over here. Could you tell me what's happening? I'm getting a little worried.}"

"Can't you check?"

"{You told me to hide,}" she huffed. "{I'm still in the closet, and I'm not coming out until everything is over.}"

"Fine, I'll check," I relented before once again clearing my throat and sending a carefree (if mostly hidden) look at the Knights still rooted in place, including the big one who still didn't completely come out of his throwing posture. First things first, I theatrically hefted the weapon in my hand and made a show about inspecting it before nodding to myself. "A gift? Oh, you shouldn't have! Still, I must sincerely thank you for your generosity. This is a fine blade, indeed."

"Wha…?"

Based on his dazed voice, the burly Knight still hadn't completely digested the situation, so before he could do so, I flourished the blade one more time. Strangely enough, even though it was a heavy sword with a high point of balance, it was deceptively easy to handle, and unlike the temperamental dragon-slaying spear, this one not only didn't give me any nasty shocks, but it felt outright comfortable in my hands. Anyhow, after I was done with that, I pointedly tapped the rounded tip of the blade against the floor and subsequently leaned onto the pommel like it was a walking cane.

"Whit dae ye think yer daein'!?" came a sudden bellow from the armoured man in the middle of the room, apparently finally nudged out of his momentary stupor by the sharp sound of metal meeting the ground.

"As a matter of fact, I'm thinking about adding this outstanding gift to my collection," I told him with as much forced schadenfreude as I could muster at the moment, and then I gleefully added, "In fact, I can't wait to do so! I will be back shortly!"

Needless to say, I didn't wait for the owner of the sword to make a complaint, and instead I immediately Phased over to the secret base. It was also at this point that it became obvious that I didn't pretend to use the sword as a cane only for show, as it actually served me in that purpose at this moment. I felt, for lack of better terms, supernaturally exhausted. Each long-distance teleport felt harder than the last, kind of like when I was working out and my muscles started getting tired; I felt like I still had a couple of push-ups in me, but I could also distinctly tell that I was slowly but surely reaching my limit.

Anyway, once I caught my breath, I finally looked around and... what the hell?

"[Blackcloak!]"

Brang called my name the moment he laid his eyes on me, but he might as well have screamed for help by the looks of it. Somehow the training area was in even worse shape than when I'd left, and there were even cut marks on the concrete floor around the area where the lion's share of the battle between Brang and Rinne must have taken place. Speaking of which, the general was currently in a sorry state. His beard and his clothes were caked in blood, and while he was standing firmly, a single glance was enough to tell that he'd suffered several small wounds since the last time I'd seen him, and at least one deeper cut on his right forearm, which was dripping blood even at this moment. Not only that, but the rest of the Fauns were more or less down for the count, with only Pip and Karukk trying their best to support the old Faun.

More surprisingly, while Rinne's usual pantsuit was torn at a few places, she didn't seem to be worse of wear, and based on the enormous (and equally creepy) grin on her face, she was having the time of her life. When she heard him call out to me, she glanced over, and when she realized I wasn't right next to her, she apparently decided to use the unexpected distraction I provided to lunge at the wounded Faun.

"Oh no, you don't!" I whispered through gritted teeth as I forced my body to move and Phased next to Brang, just in time so that my rising blade could parry her descending one. When metal met metal, there was a familiar outburst of magical sparks, but my borrowed weapon held out and deflected Onikiri with little trouble, forcing Mountain Girl to retreat a few steps in order to regain her balance.

In the meantime, I glanced at the ex-general by my side, and while a certain, indignant part of me wanted to yell 'You had one job! One! Job!' my more reasonable side tempered my reaction into a more appropriate, "[Is the condition of your earthly coil severe?]"

"[Nay, only wounds of the skin,]" he responded with what I was sure he thought was a reassuring smile.

"[Please clarify the nature of the events that transpired in our abode. I myself was labouring under the notion that by the means of the succor of the endowment I provided to you, the aggravation of facing the leering hunter would be momentously diminished,]" I told him, and even though I tried to be extra concise, somehow I ended up even more long-winded than usual. Faunish, amirite?

"[Facing thine wayward companion is... difficult,]" the old Faun told me, followed by a pained sigh. "[Standing by her side makes us dull. It's akin to facing a warrior of the merfolk in their element.]"

Okay, so I learned two things from this: being in Rinne's presence somehow weakened the Fauns, and mermaids were real. I didn't remember Judy ever talking about the latter, so it was quite a shocker, but for now, let's focus on the first issue: even if he'd had a proper weapon to use, apparently Brang and his merry band were still at a disadvantage against her. I had no idea of the mechanics of that, but for now, the important thing was that I needed a way to keep her busy without putting my self-appointed minions at risk.

"Leonard-san."

"Hm?"

The way Rinne suddenly addressed me threw me for a loop for a moment.

"Have you left the premises of this blood-drenched field of battle to properly arm yourself? Good. Rinne was afraid that Rinne would have to search for you after Rinne dispatched these brutes of the netherworld. Facing your demise in the company of your underlings is commendable."

"Thanks, I suppose," I responded on autopilot while the gears in my head slowly began to spin until they came up with an idea that seemed really dumb on the surface, and it was probably pretty dumb even under the surface, but with today's track record, I had a distinct premonition that it would 100 percent certainly work out *precisely* because it was so. With that in mind, I unsubtly cleared my throat, pushed the mask up to the top of my head, and raised my voice as I addressed the creepy huntress. "Say, Mountain Girl? Since I'm already going to be demised with extreme prejudice and everything, could you maybe tell me, in excruciating detail, how and why you can weaken these guys? It must be some kind of amazing secret technique, right?"

Rinne was just about to take up a stance, but my words made her hesitate, and at the end of the day she let her sword down and declared, "You're correct, Leonard-san! The weakening of the foul spawn of the netherworld is due to the ancient technique of yada yada inherited in the third century blah-blah-blah and my ancestor of something something clan of..."

Okay, first and foremost... wow. Just wow. I didn't think that would work right away, let alone that well. I was honestly a little floored at the moment, and I wasn't the only one utterly baffled by the ease of this development, either.

"{Did you just get her to monologue?}"

"More or less," I whispered back to my assistant before hastily adding, "More importantly, please pay attention for me and give me the abridged version after all of this is over."

"{Roger.}"

With that settled, I only had to come up with a plan before Mountain Girl reached the end of her explanation about something called a Night Parade Suppressing Divine Aura of Amaterasu. I had no idea what it was, but I was sure Judy would write a neat report on it. Anyhow, the first and arguably most obvious option was to just sneakily grab her from behind and Phase her out of the secret base. While simple and sound in theory, there were only two practical problems with it: I didn't have any anchors I was comfortable dropping an angry, psychotic swordswoman upon, and more importantly, doing so would've not only been a temporary resolution, but it would also reveal one of my hidden trump cards to an enemy.

In the end, I discarded the idea and looked for an alternative. Actually beating her was also an option, and now that I'd borrowed an enchanted sword as well, Brang and I could theoretically tag team her into oblivion, or at the very least submission. However, after thinking it through, I also dismissed this idea. The general was already injured, even if he was enduring it with a stiff upper lip and pretending to be fine, and I really couldn't waste time with dueling her when the Knights were still running loose in the Dracis mansion.

In short, I needed something to, at least temporarily, hold her attention. Something other than the Fauns. Something that she would focus on, but wouldn't get cut after a single swing of Onikiri. Something that was already here...

"Crap, I have to use that thing, don't I?"

"{What thing?}"

"Nothing, never mind," I answered by reflex, but then amended to, "For the record, things are probably going to get extra noisy out here. Don't come out of the closet."

She didn't respond, which I interpreted as agreement. Now then, first off, I needed to warn Brang while pretending to be listening to Rinne's history lesson about the joining of this demon hunter clan and that orthodox sect or whatever, so I tried to aim my voice at him while remaining still.

"[General, I shall attempt to create a sustained diversion until my ability to deal with her shall no longer be obstructed. I request that you retain your pelt in a single piece in the interim.]"

"[I will strive to adhere to thy order,]" he told me right away, though I could tell he didn't have his heart in the answer. I didn't let it bother me, as I was pretty sure that if he knew my plan, he wouldn't have had any other body part in his answer, either.

I took a long, deep breath, and prepared myself for something that I felt would make me really, really hate myself this time tomorrow, granted I was alive and/or conscious to do so. Once I felt mentally ready, I sharply inhaled through my nose before growling out a decisive "[Scatter!]" interrupting Rinne's diatribe in the process.

When they heard the word, the Fauns immediately followed suit, much to Mountain Girl's initial bafflement. I, on the other hand, simply disappeared out of her field of view and Phased over to the middle of the training grounds, and without any further ado, plunged my phantom limb into the limp body lying on the ground there. The process was subjectively long, confusing, and tasted like the sound of an electric guitar underwater... in short, it was the same as usual, so instead of mincing my words, let's cut to the chase, shall we?

Once I was out, the previously limp body of the Chimera twitched and shook from head to toes as if it was being tased by an entire police squad, but at last it opened its many redundant eyes and ponderously rose to its four feet. Once it found its bearings, it quickly locked onto its target, and a moment later the injured-yet-far-from-harmless semi-dead beast broke into a limping dash towards the apparently very confused huntress. Needless to say, I was nowhere near the creature by the time it got up, and I observed all of this from the safe sidelines on the other end of the main hall, right next to Brang and Karukk.

The younger Faun was just about to unroll a pack of bandages to treat the ex-general, but he paused mid-motion to send a skeptical look at the rapidly unfolding rematch by the training grounds.

"[My… um… boss? Are you sure this was a good idea?]"

"Not at all," I replied between suppressing two dry heaves, and once I was sure I was going to be able to keep my lunch down, I carefully pulled the mask back onto my face and continued with, "In any case, the Chimera was programmed to consider her its main target. She also can't cut it all willy-nilly, so it should keep her busy for a while. For now, just keep an eye on them and hold the line."

"[As you command,]" Brang noted, and he would have probably given me a salute if the other Faun wasn't in the process of bandaging his arm.

I waited for Karukk to finish patching the old Faun up before I gestured for him to pay attention to me, and after a brief moment of hesitation, I ultimately handed my newly acquired weapon over to him. It was a shame, as I actually really liked this sword, but it was best to keep the Knights as far from their weapons as possible, and considering that I was just about to go back to the Dracis mansion, I figured it was the prudent thing to do.

"If the need arises, you can use this to defend yourself."

The friendly Faun first only blinked at me, his eyes repeatedly moving between the sword and my face and ultimately settling on the former as he gingerly, almost reverently took it from my hands. I had a feeling that there was another misunderstanding in the making there, but I have run out of damns to give to such a degree that my damnlessness was about to reach the level of the national damn deficit, so I ignored him and simply turned on my heel.

"Stay safe."

Since I felt that things were… well, I wanted to say less chaotic, but that would've been a lie. Let's go with in state of directed chaos. Anyhow, I didn't dare to dawdle for too long, so after I made sure that the Chimera was still resistant to Onikiri, I took a deep breath to steel my nerves and Phased over to the Dracis mansion.

Upon my arrival, I had to blink a few times to make sure I was at the right place, but on closer inspection, it was definitely the trophy room, though it had definitely seen better days. I wasn't away for too long, yet it looked like an entire season's worth of hurricanes had passed through here in the meantime. Mister Minotaur and his flunkies were nowhere to be seen, either, so I figured that he was the most likely cause of the mayhem in front of me. Even the poor gnu head on the wall couldn't escape the havoc and was currently sitting upside-down on the antique (and slightly broken) chair on which Abram sat the first time I'd met him.

Speaking of which, I quickly Far Glanced in his direction, and to my relief, it seemed like he was already in a car and heading back to the mansion in the company of Sebastian, and based on the urgency of their expressions, they probably already knew about the attack. Good; that should be a nice bargaining chip... so long as I could meet a Knight I could properly talk with.

Anyhow, there was nothing to see in the room, and I couldn't hear the battering coming from outside, either, so I cautiously stuck my head through the door. I couldn't see anyone in either direction, but I could hear something that sounded like muffled speech in the distance. To be perfectly honest, with Papa Dracis and the annoying butler on the way, I felt that things were much less perilous than before, and I even entertained the thought of leaving the mop-up to them, but then I remembered that I technically hadn't achieved any of my stated goals. I hesitated for only a moment, and then ultimately disappeared from the doorway.

I repeatedly Phased through the mansion, following the sounds of someone talking (or rather, yelling), and I soon arrived at the foyer of the mansion. Upon my arrival, I immediately hid behind the stairs leading to the first floor and observed the situation. At a single glance, it seemed like all of the Knights were gathered inside, forming a semicircle and keeping watch around a pair of men in the middle. One of them was the familiar robust Knight with the horned bucket on his head, and he was animatedly yelling at his colleague while wildly gesturing with his hands.

As for the other man, I figured he was the Entitled Knight that Melinda had seen during the evacuation. He was almost a head shorter than the big guy, yet he somehow had an even more imposing presence. If I had to say why, it was probably due to his bearing; his back was ramrod straight, and he had one hand on the hilt of the cavalry saber hanging from his waist while his other hand was raised with his palm pointing at the enraged Mister Minotaur. He was also wearing a lighter set of armour, with the light blue of his gambeson being clearly visible through the gaps in the shiny metal plates. Most strikingly, he had a golden-plated, large winged helmet on his head with a beaked face guard that completely hid his face.

"Calm down, MacCool," he chided the large man with the air of a teacher scolding a student, his deep, rich voice simultaneously authoritative and yet reassuring.

"Howfur cuid ah calm doon!? That bas teuk mah sword!"

"All the more reason you should keep your head cool. Shouting won't make him appear."

Now, *that* was an invitation if I'd ever heard one, so I figured I should oblige before the conversation moved along.

"Once again, good evening, gentlemen," I greeted the group after Phasing into the ring of Knights, and after the first moment of shock passed, the squires immediately closed the circle around the three of us.

"Ye! Gimme back mah sword ya hackit bawbag, or ah—!"

"Duncan!" the second Knight sharply raised his voice, silencing his comrade before turning a pair of sharp green eyes hidden under his helmet towards me, and after a long and tense beat, he returned my greeting in a composed, borderline-courteous voice. "Good evening to you, as well, stranger. I don't believe we are familiar yet."

Oh? Ooooh!? Did I hear that right? An actual level response? Finally!

I forced my body language to stay calm and not betray my excitement as I repeated the same scraping bow I did when I'd introduced myself the first time.

"You may call me Bel, Sir Griffon Knight," I told him with a smirk hidden by my mask.

Refuge in Audacity Two: Electric Boogaloo was about to start. Let's hope this time would be smoother than the first...

PART 2

All right, Leo, this is it. Time for a new set of priorities.

Priority number one: find the Purple Zone–restricting MacGuffin.

Priority number two: mark one of the baddies for future use.

Priority number three: try to learn about their goals and operations.

Priority number four: buy some time for Papa Dracis and the butler to arrive, because pincer maneuvers are fun.

Priority number five: actually establish my nefarious villain character.

That's about it, I supposed. Easy peasy.

"{Is everything all right? You've been silent for a while.}"

"Just thinking," I whispered under my breath, and my girlfriend let out an ambivalent noise at my expense.

"{You just met the Griffon Knight, am I right?} She didn't wait for me to respond before she continued with, "{Unlike the Minotaur Knights, the title of the Griffon Knight is not passed down in the family. Because of this, the name of the current Griffon Knight is unknown. According to the Dracis records, one of them was called Boreas. Whether that is a given name or a surname wasn't indicated, nor when the record was originally penned down, but it was in the section that predates the time Sebastian's daughter married into the family, so at least one hundred years ago.}"

Well, that wasn't much to go on, but more than enough for my purposes, so I whispered a muffled thanks under my breath and focused my attention on the expectant Knights still waiting for my next words. I straightened my back and looked the more reasonable one in the eye before saying, "It's such a pleasant surprise to see you here. Tell me, how is good old Sir Boreas doing these days?"

The man with the winged helmet momentarily froze up while he processed my question.

"If you mean my teacher's teacher, I'm afraid he has already passed away," Mr. Griffon stated in a voice that said he didn't know what to make of me, which was exactly the reaction I was fishing for.

"Really?" After uttering that word, I theatrically shook my head, raised my hands with the palms up, and then shrugged in the classic oh-well gesture. "Please excuse my tactless question, Sir Knight. At my age, it feels like I met him yesterday."

"Ye age? Ah knew it; yer a wyrm, aren't ye!?"

I sent an annoyed glance at the horned Knight and shook my head again.

"I believe I've already introduced myself to you, Sir Duncan, but just to reiterate: no, I'm obviously not. Now, I'd like to ask you to stay quiet while the adults are talking."

"Bite ma bawsack ya mangled fud!"

"Oh, how rude," I responded with flamboyant swoon, only to then add, in a flat voice, "Or at least, I presume. It is sometimes hard to tell with your slight accent."

The big guy was about to share further insights into his linguistics, but he was stopped by the other named Knight tapping on his breastplate with the back of his hand, and Mister Minotaur immediately sucked down whatever cute insult was about to leave his mouth. This, incidentally, also shed some light on the pecking order of the people present, as Mister Griffon appeared to be in charge, even though the Entitled Knights were all supposed to be peers with no hierarchy. Apparently all Knights were equal, but some were more equal than others. Go figure.

Anyhow, once the griffon guy got his colleague under control, he turned a pair of narrowed eyes, barely visible behind the slits of his helmet, in my direction.

"So if I understand this correctly, Mister Bel is not related to the wyrm-bloods living in this mansion?"

I mulled over the question for a moment, and ultimately I decided to go with an ambivalent shrug and continued to flesh out my character by telling them, "Who knows? After a few millennia, it's hard to keep track of one's ancestors and who else they might've sired over time. It's a problem your organization probably has more experience with than I do."

I must have touched a nerve, as for a second I could sense an almost palpable sense of tension emanating from Mister Griffon, but at last he let out a shallow breath and muttered, "I see," before raising his voice back into its previous polite-yet-not-deferential form. "I can't help but ask, if Mister Bel is not related to this family, then why are you here?"

"That's a good question, one that applies just as well to you, gentlemen, wouldn't you say?" I waited for a second to see if he wanted to respond, but since they stayed silent, I soon continued with, "With your well-known disposition in mind, I presumed that you're here to terminally pester the descendants of some old flying lizard or the other, but then why did you decide to do so right now, instead of when all of them are present? Most curious."

"Oor reasons ur oor ain 'n' hae hee-haw tae dae wi' ye, fien'!"

I tilted my head to the side while sending a dismissive grunt towards the aggressively Scottish man, following which I directed a slightly more amicable look at his colleague.

"On second thought, don't tell me just yet! I love riddles like this!" Saying so, I began to nonchalantly walk in a circle around the two named Knights inside the wider circle formed by the squires, but it still wasn't blasé enough, so I also raised my hands and made various gestures with them to further elucidate my words and baffle my audience. "The only person with non-negligible dragon blood in them is upstairs, yet instead of attacking her with all you've got, you were content with only sending half of your numbers to harass them. A most curious choice, if your goal was to deliver harm of the most grievous variety unto her, as you tend to do." I paused for a beat, then Phased over to the opposing side of the circle, eliciting a series of surprised gasps in the process before raising my voice into a considerably loud "However!"

"Fockin' 'ell, he is daein' it again!"

I ignored the exclamation coming from Mister Minotaur and began walking in the opposite direction as before while expounding my marvelous time-wasting tirade.

"However, you didn't break down their door, even though the good Sir MacChill could've probably put those oversized shoulders of his to good use. But no! Instead, half of you were content with banging on the door with the menacing flair of a Visigoth horde. One could even imagine you didn't want to actually fight the dragoness upstairs, only keep her at bay."

At this point the two Knights shared a subtle look between each other that naturally didn't escape my notice, so I let out a mirthful little chuckle befitting the situation.

"But if so, what other goals might you have to keep you from your knightly duty of slaying dragons, rescuing princesses, and then celebrating by repeatedly ramming your thick, hard rods into one another?" I let a meaningful silence hang in the air for a moment, only to innocently ask, "Or do you maybe no longer do that? Please forgive me, I've yet to catch up on modern times; is jousting no longer considered a prime form of entertainment?"

I got no answer, so I shrugged and Phased to the other side of the actually important men once again.

"Och fur fock's sake! Stoap that!"

I waited for the squires to stop running around as they tried to reform the encirclement around us, and while doing so, I placed my chin on the back of my hand as if I was deep in thought, only to promptly shake my head.

"Never mind that. We were at your unwillingness to attack the owner of this fine abode here. I can only think of two possible reasons: you were either restricted by one of your many oaths, or more likely, you had a different goal in mind when coming here. Could it be you were looking for someone else? Or rather... *something* else?"

Oh, look at that! They actually both twitched at the same time. How delightfully transparent. This time I didn't speak up, and instead I gestured for the more reasonable Knight to pick up the rein of the conversation, and he did so, though not before considering his words for ample time.

"Correct me if I'm wrong, Mister Bel, but I believe Sir MacCool mentioned something about your being a collector, if I'm not mistaken."

"In a way, I indeed am," I responded with the voice of a fisherman whose hook had just caught onto a prized catch. "It is but a small hobby of mine, a trait I inherited from the scalier side of my family. The number of curios I've accumulated over the centuries could barely fill this room."

"Thon's... quite a lot," Mister Minotaur mumbled under his breath, and his colleague agreed with a nod.

"Oh please, do not patronize me," I responded with a dismissive wave of my hand. "I could hardly call that much; it's only a minor collection."

"In any case," Mr. Griffon began to speak, his voice dropping half an octave as it gained a suspicious undertone, "Have you come here to add something to your collection?"

"I may have." After responding so, I added a nefarious little chuckle for dramatic effect, though my audience didn't seem to appreciate it. "Could it be that you were also looking for something here?"

The soft-spoken Knight only hesitated for a moment, but then he took a deep breath and bit on the bait with the abandon of a starving shark.

"Please forgive me for being blunt, but are you perchance in possession of an old spear that used to be inside one of the smaller rooms on the ground floor of this mansion?"

Ho? Hohohooo! Now would you look at that! I totall—

"{Called it,}" Judy cut off my thought, and I couldn't help but huff back at her.

"No, you didn't," I grumbled in a low voice while inconspicuously turning to the side, hoping that the men around me wouldn't hear it. "I called it; you just agreed with my hunch."

"{You're just splitting hairs,}" my girlfriend told me in a sulky voice, and one eye roll later I decided to ignore her chatter and turn back to Mister Griffon. A long beat later I let out a noise of recognition, as if I'd just recalled some minor piece of trivia, and snapped my finger for extra emphasis.

"Oh, you mean *that* spear! Why didn't you say so in the first place? It caught my eye while I was passing through the neighbourhood, so I took it. Is there a problem with that?"

"It is a precious... *heirloom* of ours," the Knight with the winged helmet explained, though I couldn't help but silently snicker at his very peculiar word choice. "Our brotherhood would be indebted if Mister Bel could return it to us."

"Hmmm... I don't know," I mused as I dramatically touched the chin of my mask. "I'm afraid I can't just do that. *Finders keepers* is the phrase for this situation, I believe? And what a wonderful phrase it is!"

I let out another low chuckle, but no one laughed along with me. Oh well, sometimes you get a tough crowd. That said, playing the nefarious villain like this every once in a while felt strangely liberating. Therapeutic, even. However, while pushing on with the act was unexpectedly amusing, I quickly reminded myself that I wasn't supposed to completely antagonize the Knights before I'd accomplished all my prestated goals, so I toned things back with a shallow sigh.

"That said," I spoke up, my words accompanied by a mischievously raised finger. "Your eloquent friend over there already gave me a nice gift, so I'm actually in a good mood right now."

"Get tae fock ya fart box! Ah didnae gie ye mah sword!"

I smoothly ignored the yelling Scottish-Irish-Russian-Greek man and continued.

"You see, I'm not *completely* unreasonable. If you can provide me with something interesting in exchange, I might consider a fair trade." There was a meaningful silence left in the wake of my words, which I let linger for a while for dramatic effect, and I was about to press on when I remembered that I still had a connection to my very own all-encompassing magical encyclopedia, so instead I whispered, "Psst, Dormouse? How rare do you think an anti–Purple Zone artifact would be?"

"{I don't know. I'll ask Amelia.}"

Well, okay, maybe she wasn't quite all-encompassing, after all, but I wasn't going to hold it against her. Anyhow, that meant I had to buy some time for her, so I promptly focused my attention on my current company.

"I would of course require something of comparable value, and by the looks of it, you value this spear very highly!"

"What makes you think so?"

"Oh, but it's obvious, isn't it? You've gone through quite the trouble to try to steal... I mean, recover this heirloom of yours, and you did so under some very unusual conditions. Invading someone's home while they are away is very unsportsmanlike. In fact, it is, dare I say, quite unchivalrous of you."

"... Maybe," Mister Griffon agreed, much to my surprise, and a second or so later he even let out a sigh that sounded oddly self-deprecating. "The times are changing. So must we."

"Such a delightfully unexpected response."

I would've continued with the small talk after that, but Judy connected to me before I could.

"{Amelia says that artifacts that can affect a large area are very rare, and one that could interfere with the opening of a Restricted Space should be even rarer. It would also require a strong, magically conductive base material suited for the purpose, such as a wraith skull or a unicorn's horn.}"

Now, there were many ways I could've reacted to her explanation, such as being surprised that unicorns were also real, or asking, "Since when do wraiths have bones?" but my attention was currently preoccupied with a small revelation, and I couldn't spare the brainpower for quips. As for the nature of said revelation, let's start by restating the fact that the men around me were all glowing, or rather, most of their equipment was doing so. The swords, shields, and other assorted enchanted gear of the squires were one thing, but the items on the two important guys were shining from head to toe. Besides being an eyesore, this meant that even if I'd tried, I couldn't immediately recognize the magic jammer they had... However, I'd actually made note of the odd, elongated cloth bag hanging from Mister Griffon's belt. It looked a little like one of those recorder flute cases I'd seen around the school, probably on members of the music club, and for the life of me I couldn't figure out what it held. Now, I had a strong gut feeling about it, and I was willing to bet on it.

"{On a related note,}" Judy continued speaking before I could get a word in, "{she sounded really angry, and she told me to tell you that she can't get Michael out of the cage, and she needs help.}"

"Seriously? Can't anyone do anything on their own today?" She didn't respond to my perfectly reasonable inquiry, so after a while I added, "Tell her to keep trying. If she can't get him out by the time I'm done here, I'll bring some tools over or something."

"{Roger.}"

Okay, so where was I again? Oh, right, the Knights in front of me. It was kind of a silly thing to forget about, but in my defense, I felt like I was at four different places at once.

"So, since Sir Knight is so flexible, I presume you wouldn't have any quandaries about making a deal with me. All you need is something of comparable value."

"Do you have something in mind?" he asked back, just a tad tentatively.

"Oh, let me see... How about some precious raw materials? Your little club has been around for a while, so I'm fairly sure you must have some rare articles in your possession. How about some orichalcum? Oh, I'm also fresh out of unobtanium, so I could really use a bar or two! No, wait!" Falling silent for a moment, I used both my hands to point a pair of finger guns at Mister Griffon. "I'm fairly sure some of your ancestors used to have a unicorn horn or two."

The moment I uttered the words, the slightly shorter Knight's free hand immediately moved to cover up the long bag on his belt. In other words, I hit the bull's-eye. That was more or less the final piece of the puzzle I needed to be done here.

"Mister Bel, I'm afraid—"

While the Griffon Knight prepared to make his excuse, I checked on Papa Dracis, and I was delighted to learn that he was only a couple of blocks away from the neighbourhood. It was perfect timing, and also my cue to move on, so I raised my left hand to shoulder level, with two fingers pointing forwards, and at the same time let my right hand down and opened it with the palm facing outward.

Before anyone could react, I immediately Phased over to the side of a nearby squire, and then jabbed forward with my left hand, aiming at the small gap between the man's helmet and his spaulders. I didn't pick him at random, either, as he was one of the only three guys in the circle who wasn't wearing a gorget to protect his neck, allowing me relatively quick access to his skin. I mean, no one said I had to mark one of the considerably more dangerous Entitled Knights to keep track of them, right?

Oh, but speaking of those guys, the moment Sir Squire McNotproperlyarmoured let out a panicked shout, Mister Griffon immediately grabbed onto the grip of his saber... leaving him wide-open for my next maneuver as I unceremoniously Phased right in front of him, and before he could properly reach, I clasped my open right hand around my actual target, and then a forceful tug later I Phased away, leaving behind a satisfied "Zoink!" in my wake.

"Eeeep!"

"Hi mom-in-law," I greeted the currently uncharacteristically flustered Emese the moment I arrived.

"Future young master?" Melinda muttered in a bit of a daze on the side, so I lifted the mask off my face and gave her a reassuring smile that might've looked less heartening than I'd intended, as she somehow turned even paler. At the end of the day I decided to ignore her and turned my attention back to Mama Dracis.

"Long story short: I've got the magic jammer thingy." I paused for a second as I plunged my phantom limb into the item inside the bag, and a moment later added, "And now it's off. Dad-in-law and Sebastian are on the way, so if you want to have a piece of the action, now's the time to go out. That said, you might want to lay low instead; the Knights weren't actually here for you, and they should be leaving soon. I leave it up to your discretion. Oh, also." I threw the package over to Melinda, and she almost managed to drop it. I didn't call her out on it, and instead I told her, "Please hold on to that. I have to go now."

"Oh... Okay. Bye?"

I almost chuckled at Emese's odd response, but at the end of the day I settled on flashing a smile at her before lowering the mask again, and a deep breath later, I Phased over to my next destination. A short, increasingly nauseating blink of an eye later I was inside a similarly dark room, right behind a certain Mage girl currently ineffectually hammering on the padlock with something that looked like a comically oversized Allen wrench.

"Hi, class rep."

"Eeeep!"

This time the surprised squeak came from the guy behind the bars, while Ammy only froze up for a moment before turning on her heel and directing a pair of thundering eyes at me.

"Leo, what exactly were you...!?" she started, only for her words to quickly trail into silence, followed by a flat-yet-distinctly-alarmed, "You're bleeding."

Now it was my turn to be alarmed as I uttered a short "I am?" and looked over myself. It was hard to see at first, probably because my eyes were still adapted to the magical light show at the mansion, but on closer look, there really was a long, vertical cut on my abdomen. Odd. I wasn't feeling any pain, yet by the looks of it, I was most certainly cut.

I reached down and used two fingers to feel around the area. It went through my coat and then sliced across the ballistic vest I was wearing under it, leaving a long, thin cut on my stomach, yet even when I touched it, it didn't really hurt, nor did it actually bleed much. Wait, on second touch, I couldn't feel the area around it, either. How about other parts of my body?

Nope, pinching my forearm didn't really hurt, either. That... probably wasn't good. Oh well, let's look on the bright side: at least my slightly disconcerting numbness allowed me to inspect my wound without any hassle.

"Don't spread it!" Mike called out to me, but I only shook my head.

"Don't worry, it's literally just a scratch. I probably got it when the Griffon Knight drew his sword, but it barely broke the skin."

"Griffon Knight?" Ammy repeated after me, but I quickly shook my head, lest I would accidentally reveal even more incriminating evidence.

"Never mind that. I'm just rambling. More importantly, what's the problem here? Why is he still in the cage?"

"It's because of you," the class rep burst out, and once she realized I had no idea about what she meant by that, she followed it up with, "You just left me here without any way to open this lock!"

"Why don't you use your magic?" I asked what felt like the obvious, and Ammy almost stomped her feet in reaction.

"Because the room is warded from the outside! It interferes with any low-tier spells!"

"That's why I couldn't escape on my own," Michael informed me a little sheepishly, though his comment was mostly beside the point.

"You said low-tier spells, right? Why didn't you just summon your golem?"

"Because if I summon Petra, then who is going to sit on Galatea?"

"Ah, right," I admitted with a tinge of embarrassment in my voice. "I didn't think of that. Ah, but you could've summoned your staff."

Ammy's expression was practically seething at this point, and she unceremoniously pointed to our left. I followed it, and there I found a familiar staff on the ground... in two pieces.

"Um... My condolences?" She was still less than amicable, so I raised my hands to pacify her and uttered, "I'll help you make a new one later; how about I go and get some proper tools for the job first?"

"You better," she grunted, but then her expression eased up, and she wondered, "But... how did you even come in here? The door is locked, and..."

"Oh, look at the time, I better get going, bye."

"Wait…"

I didn't, and before long, I was inside the secret base. I looked around, and the first thing I naturally noted was that the Chimera was pretty much down for the count, suffering a death of a thousand cuts under the continuous assault of the creepy huntress. Another thing that didn't escape my notice was that, at the moment, I felt quite fine. I was light-headed, and I was feeling a bit odd, but my previous nausea had almost entirely subsided, and my head no longer hurt. Or maybe I just couldn't feel it anymore? The thought was a little disconcerting, but not enough to sidetrack me from my next objective.

"[General, I request that you brief me on the present condition of affairs.]"

"[Ah, Blackcloak, welcome back,"] the old Faun greeted me as he finally noticed my presence, only to tense up as he looked over me. Following his gaze, the rest of them also glanced my way and showed a similar reaction. "[You are injured.]"

"So are you, and you won't see me gawking," I snapped at them, and the small gaggle of Fauns immediately (and quite conspicuously) averted their eyes. Speaking of which, our group was currently crouching in a small huddle behind the counter in the recreational area of the main hall, and for a change, someone finally showed a bit of competence, as they were all cloaked at the moment and let Rinne and the Chimera duke it out between each other.

The awkward silence lasted for only a few short moments before Brang forcefully cleared his throat and addressed me.

"[We have regrouped and tended our wounds, as per thine orders. Thine associate remains belligerent, and thus we stayed out of her way till thine return.]"

"The Chimera's in bad shape," I noted, and Gram (or Rabom; it was hard to tell under the bandages) let out a grunt in agreement.

"[I'd say it would go down in a few minutes.]"

"[I give it less than five,]" Pip noted, only for the rest of the group to nod in agreement.

"[What do we do then?]" came the next, entirely reasonable question from Karukk, and the others also seemed to share his interest based on the way they were looking at me.

"I kind of have to go and help free a wayward Celestial, but I suppose I can't really leave her alone any longer, can I?"

That was an entirely rhetorical question, yet for some reason the seven Fauns all shook their heads in unison. That was mildly aggravating, but I let it slide for now, and instead I thought long and hard for a few seconds before coming to a resolution.

"I have a plan, but I will need your help. Who is the least injured among you?"

There was a long moment of silence, but when Brang sent a glance at him, Karukk awkwardly raised a hand, his ears drooping so low they almost disappeared under his hairy head fur hair thing. Let's not get into the semantics of that.

"You still have the sword, so it should work," I told him before taking a deep breath to collect my thoughts. "Listen up; first, I need you to sneak up on her and wait until the Chimera goes down and can no longer move."

"[You want me to hit her in the back?]"

"Actually, no. I want you to appear nearby, preferably so that when she faces you, she would have to turn her back this way. Draw her attention, and then challenge her to a duel."

"[Um... Boss, no offense, but this sounds like a terrible plan so far.]"

"Less back talking and more listening," I chided him, and then once he fell silent, I followed it up with, "I don't need you to *fight* her, per se. Your job is to draw one of her silly named sword moves out of her."

"[So you want me to get hit by a sword art?]"

"No, you're not going to get hit by anything. Listen, you just have to make sure you are not too close to her; about two paces should do the trick. I'll take care of the rest."

"[Okay,]" he agreed, if a tad apprehensively, and I gestured for him to get going, as the Chimera was on its last legs (literally, as it had lost one front and one hind paw), but after half a step he turned back and whispered, "[How should I get her attention?]"

"Taunt her or something. Be creative."

"[I'll try...]" he muttered with a distinct lack of confidence, but after some more silent spurring he finally got going.

For the time being, the rest of us watched over him while he edged closer to the brutal battle of attrition in front of us, and not a moment too soon, as with one solid lunge, Rinne stabbed forth and impaled the battered creature through the neck. The Chimera let out a low, guttural whine, and once she retrieved her sword, it collapsed onto the bloodied concrete floor with a thud, immobile, though not unmoving, as even then its paws kept ineffectually clawing at the ground.

Mountain Girl also looked pretty out of it; her hair was a mess, and her usually impeccable outfit had several tears in it, though she had nothing worse than the scratches I'd originally inflicted on her. She was also breathing hard, though I figured after being engaged in melee for this long, it wasn't entirely unexpected. Her stance, on the other hand, was as stable as ever, and once she made sure the Chimera wasn't going to get up anytime soon, she raised her blade and scanned the perimeter. She was just about to look our way, but Karukk, either by design or by pure chance, decided to reveal himself just before she could have noticed me.

"You!" he exclaimed in a rumbling voice while pointing his borrowed blade at her, startling Rinne into taking a defensive posture. There was a short beat of awkward silence, then he declared, "Your mother! A hamster!"

Really, Karukk? Really? I'd just spent a bunch of time maneuvering around a pack of Knights, and it's *you* who makes a Holy Grail reference? Since when did you guys even watch British comedies? What's next; are you going to tell me you had cable TV in the Abyss? That's just *silly*!

Note to self: next time I meet that MacCumhail fellow, I absolutely have to tell him that his father smelled of elderberries because dammit, I refuse to be outdone in combat banter by Karukk of all people.

More importantly, though, after such a grievous insult, Mountain Girl naturally couldn't hold herself back and immediately lunged at Karukk. He followed my advice and retreated while doing his best to parry any incoming strikes, and even by a cursory look, I could tell that he was indeed affected by some kind of external, suppressive force, as his moves were positively sloppy. He still held his own fairly well, though it was probably more due to Rinne being tired than his own skills, but that's beside the point.

While all that was going on, I also took up a stance in preparation, bending my knees for a runner's start and getting ready for an explosive dash at a moment's notice. The rest was all down to timing, so I held my breath and focused all my attention on the two of them, or rather, the sword in the huntress's hand. I didn't even dare to blink, which was ever-so-slightly uncomfortable, but thankfully I didn't have to wait too long, as...

"Sakurabana Ranbu!"

That! That was exactly what I wanted to hear! Honing my focus to a single point, I watched her wind up to an upward slash that managed to knock Karukk off-balance even though he successfully deflected it. Now came the crucial part; it was all about timing. I waited, and waited, and then...

"ZOINK!"

In the literal blink of an eye, I let loose all the potential energy in my legs and let them propel me forward, while at the same time I also Phased right behind Mountain Girl just as she crouched down and was about to do her 360 spin. Our eyes met for a moment, and I doubt she could even register what was going on as I leaped over her, using one hand to boost myself by pushing down on her shoulder while my other reached out and expertly grasped the hilt of the sword flying through the air. However, even after I caught it, I still had to disperse my momentum, so I did a not-particularly-graceful-yet-effective tumble upon landing.

The lesson of the day: letting go of your sword for some fancy-pants special moves is a bad idea. The more you know, amirite? Once I stopped rolling, I immediately jumped to my feet, wary of how Rinne would react to this development, but unexpectedly enough she was simply sprawled out on the ground with a vacant expression on her face. I was just about to call out to her, but then she abruptly sat up as if she was poked by a needle and looked around in mild panic, and once her eyes met mine, she practically screamed out to me.

"Leonard-san, no! Let go of Onikiri! Quickly, before she—!"

I'm not going to lie, I was slightly taken aback by her reaction, but not as much as when I glanced down at the sword in my hand. I was holding it in a reverse grip at the moment, and... wait, when did the shroud get wrapped around my wrist?

I had a couple of other questions, as well, but then they were all drowned out by a strange, ethereal sound. It took me some time to realize that it was a voice, or rather a set of voices. One was silky and sensual, another was low and growling, and yet another was like the screech of nails upon a chalkboard. They were all strangely feminine, and even though the words were unfamiliar, somehow I still understood their meaning.

"<What a surprise. We might be actually compatible,>" the voice declared, and I could feel the shroud around my wrist tightened even further. There was also a creepy, crawling sensation slowly making its way up my arm that became even worse as it added, in a tone that was both alluring and terrifying, "<Let me in.>"

Oh, great. And now the stupid sword wanted to possess me or something. Lovely. Because apparently my day just wasn't crazy enough yet...

CHAPTER 16

PART 1

How should I describe the peculiar sensation that was currently crawling up my arm? Uncomfortably warm would be a good one. It was also, for lack of a better word, crawly; it was as if the legs of several large centipedes were tapping at my skin as they moved around, but from the inside. Overall, it wasn't exactly painful, but still thoroughly unpleasant. Even so, my trusty sixth sense wasn't telling me I was in immediate danger, so for the time being I forcefully suppressed the anxiety slowly welling up from the pit of my stomach and faced the distressed huntress still sitting on the ground.

"Your sword is asking me to *let her in*. Is that normal?" I asked with as level a voice as I could manage at the moment.

"What? No!" she shouted back to me, which I acknowledged with an absentminded nod.

She apparently wanted to say something else, as well, but before she could, I let out a long grumble in Faunish.

"[I can't help but discern that our disarmed interloper has yet to be apprehended.]"

As if woken from a daze, Karukk and the other Fauns who came into the open once I took Rinne's sword sprung to action, practically tripping over one another in their hurry to be the first to subdue her, and in about a second she'd completely disappeared under a mountain of bodies. I'm not going to lie, the sight was a tad unnerving, but I had more pressing matters at the moment, therefore I smoothly ignored the ruckus in front of me and focused on the blade in my hand.

"<Come, boy! You have so much power sleeping in you! Let me show you the limits of your potential! Together, we can achieve great things, *kill* great things, you and I!>"

"{Chief, I'm hearing some kind of static noise. Is everything all right out there?}"

"Sorry, Dormouse, I'm kind of busy right now; I'm being tempted to join the dark side at the moment."

"{By that Rinne woman?}"

"No, her annoying sword." I realized that what I said must have sounded quite silly, so I quickly added, "It's a long story."

"<Who are you talking to, boy?>"

I naturally ignored the creepy voice demanding my attention, and focused on the much more soothing, if currently equally ethereal, voice of my girlfriend instead.

"{I imagine,}" she responded, her tone telling me that she was expecting a proper explanation once things settled down a little. "{If you have the leeway to talk like this, I suppose it's not a serious situation.}"

"It's hard to say. We're not at the body-snatching battle-of-the-wills part yet." I didn't get any reaction to that, and maybe for the better. "Jokes aside, the battle is over out here, so you can come out of the closet if you want to."

"{I'm fine here; don't worry about me. Rather, did you just say body-snatching?}"

"I'm just exaggerating... I think."

While I was chatting with Judy, the Fauns successfully subdued the huntress, and even tied her up with some kind of thin, bright-orange rope. They also looked really proud of their handiwork, which I didn't mind, though there was one small question that still bothered me about the situation.

"Where did you get that?"

My inquiry made the guys glance at one another, as if to decide who should answer me, right until Hrul raised his hand.

"[It's an extension cord. Milord said he wanted to capture her alive, so I grabbed it when I brought the bandages.]"

"[Wise,]" Brang noted with a satisfied grin.

"Yeah, good thinking," I agreed without any reservations. "Remind me to give you a performance bonus once I get around to giving you your first paycheck."

In the meantime, the currently kneeling Rinne, flanked by one Faun on each side, appeared to be utterly bamboozled by the situation, which probably wasn't helped by her understanding only one side of the conversation. After taking off the mask and sparing one last glance at the annoying sword still clinging to my hand, I turned to her for some answers.

"So now that things have calmed down a bit and nobody is trying to kill anyone, can you please explain what the hell is going on with this stupid sword?"

"<Stop being obstinate, boy! Stop denying your own dest—>" It was at this point that I started running out of patience, so I gestured for Brang to raise the spear I'd loaned to him, and the moment he did so, I unceremoniously whacked the flat of the blade against it. "<Hey! Ow! Stop it!>"

"Quiet, you dumb, oversized bread knife."

"<How dare you treat me like this! I'm the blah-blah-blah, and my body was forged by yada yada yada, and...>"

"{I'm hearing some static again,}" Judy noted, barely audible under the background noise.

"Just ignore it; that's what I'm doing." Saying so, I completely disregarded the raving katana and focused my attention on Mountain Girl again. "So just to reiterate: Why is your sword trying to crawl up my arm?"

Rinne continued to blink at me in utter incomprehension for several seconds, but at last there was a glint of resignation in her eyes, and she began to speak in a level, somewhat-lethargic voice.

"Rinne... I... got upset when I saw you here, and so Onikiri also became agitated. Normally Onikiri chooses a new wielder only once in every generation, but in her current state, she might be trying to forcefully make you accept her." She paused her unusually cogent explanation for a second and looked me in the eye before stating, "You mustn't. Please return her to me. She's my burden."

The Fauns shared an uncertain look between one another, apparently just as taken aback by the change in her demeanor as I was. Or was I? Honestly, I was getting a little light-headed again, and my headache had also started to act up, so I couldn't really tell how I felt about her behaviour at the moment.

"Well, excuse me, but I'm afraid I have to refuse," I responded flatly.

"<Yes. Yeees! I knew you would come around, boy! Now come, and embrace my power! Let us baptize this land in blood, together as— Ouch!>"

After another quick, sparking whack on the blade, I instructed Brang to keep the dragon-slaying spear close by in case I'd need it again in the near future and turned back to the downed huntress.

"As I was saying, I went through a lot of trouble to get this damned thing away from you, so I'm not going to hand it back."

"Why?" she blurted out, her brows instantly rising like toilet paper stocks in a pandemic.

"Because then you would probably try to kill us again, duh."

"Oh, right... Rinne probably..." She abruptly cut herself short, and then restated, with added emphasis, "I mean, *I* probably would."

"I'm glad we are on the same page," I noted with an only-slightly-strained smile before amending, "Seriously, though, if it wasn't blindingly obvious yet, your stupid sword doesn't want to let me go."

To emphasized the point, I raised my arm to show off the shroud wrapped around my hand, and as I looked at it, I noticed something quite alarming. I reached out with my other hand and pulled the sleeve of my coat up a little, only for my brows to immediately knot into a baffled frown.

"Oh, great. And now my veins are glowing on my forearm," I muttered under my breath, which naturally didn't escape Judy's notice.

"{You have Volcanic Veins?}"

I observed the sickly green, pulsing light emanating from under my skin for a short while, and ultimately told her, "First off, that's a nice trope name. Secondly, yeah, I pretty much have that."

"{That could be either good or bad. What's the colour?}"

"A kind of ugly neon green," I stated while twisting my arm left and right to get a full look.

"{That's not good. According to traditional colour coding, glowing green means evil.}"

"Leonard-san!" Before I could answer my girlfriend, Rinne demanded my attention with a panicked yell.

"What?"

"You must cut it off!" she continued to yell while frantically struggling against her bindings, forcing one of the Fauns to hold on to her shoulders lest she would fall forward and face-plant onto the concrete floor.

"The cloth?" I asked back, though a hunch told me that wasn't what she meant.

"No, your arm! You must cut off your arm before the corruption spreads any farther!"

"Oh well, that's a great idea, but you know what, I have a better one. How about... no?"

"This is no time to joke around!" Rinne retorted with a scorching scowl. "If you don't, you're going to be crippled!"

"I don't see how cutting off a hand would make me less so, but for a start, I would like to know more about this corruption you are talking about."

She stared daggers at me for a while, but it didn't take her long to relent.

"Onikiri is the holy sword of our clan, bestowed upon us by the great—"

"Wait, hold on," I cut her short with both hands raised. "Could we skip the exposition and just explain it in simple, relevant terms?"

The disapproval on her face was practically palpable by this point, but once she collected her thoughts, she rapidly explained herself in a wooden, matter-of-fact tone.

"Onikiri was corrupted by the miasma and bloodlust of the creatures she has slain. If you harmonize with her to become her wielder, then two become one, and you remain unaffected, but if you fail, the miasma will corrode your body. If you resist..." she paused for a beat, and then used her chin to point at my hand. "... that's what happens."

"Thank you, that was very succinct," I responded while raising the hand with the sword to eye level. "So if I get this straight, if I don't let her in, she will corrode me from the inside, but if I do, she gets into my head?" Rinne mulled over my words, and at last gave me a nod. "Well, neither of those are viable options."

While muttering so, I confirmed that the glowy veins had reached just above my elbow, and even though I still wasn't feeling any pain, my arm was getting more numb by the second, to the point it became hard to keep it raised to eye level. I tried to consider all of my options. First, cutting the shroud. I extended my hand and tapped the wrapped-up part against the spearhead still held steady by Brang, but I only got an eyeful of magical welding light for my trouble. I'd already noticed it during the duel with Rinne, so this just confirmed that the cloth was as impervious to damage as the blade itself (probably a perk of being an enchanted weapon), but hey, it was worth a try.

The second option was... well, I wasn't cutting my hand off, so no, that actually wasn't an option. Then I could always allow Onikiri to possess me, and then we could engage in silly body-sharing shenanigans, and... nah, that wasn't even good for a joke. Which meant I only really had one option.

"Judy, are you listening?" My dear assistant let out a grunt in the affirmative, so I continued with, "This might either take a while or no time at all, depending on how subjective timey-wimey tomfooleries would work out in this case, so don't be alarmed if I don't respond for a while."

"{Noted. Also, for the record, if you end up body-snatched, I'll be really angry and will possibly hate you for real.}"

"Well, then I'd better avoid that, I suppose."

"{You better.}"

I couldn't help but chuckle at her response before I let out a sharp breath and prepared myself for what I expected to be something that I was going to regret soon, and I would probably doubly regret it in a few days if I was still alive. Bad jokes aside, I reached out with my phantom limb, and without any further ado, I plunged it inside the sword.

First off, the obvious question: Can I break the enchantment on the sword? It was quickly answered when I tried to cut it with my ethereal appendage, only for a disobedient part of my brain to start yelling at me while waving at least ten red flags at once, telling me that this was, in fact, another plot device I wasn't supposed to touch. Great, there goes my quick and easy solution. Not that I was too surprised, to be honest; after today's track record, I would've been incredibly suspicious if something actually worked out for me on the first try.

In other words, it was time for a deep dive, which was something that I really wanted to avoid, considering I had a sneaking suspicion the only reason my head was no longer hurting at this point was that I'd already run out of pain receptors. Not that I had much of a choice in the matter, so I steeled my nerves and headed even deeper.

Reaching the core of the enchantment was considerably less of a chore than the usual fare, and after only a subjective few minutes of what felt like jogging through a sewage treatment plant during a hurricane, I successfully arrived at... something. Let me try to paint a mental picture: First off, I was inside space with no clear beginning or end. Inside that space, there was an absolutely enormous black thing with glowy green highlights that kind of looked like some sort of malformed, constantly shifting sea urchin. On closer look, the whole thing seemed to be made of, or at the very least covered by, a thick, viscous substance.

Now, I didn't need to be a genius to figure out that an ugly sludge that smelled like puppies crying and was fluorescing in a mixture of death black and uranium green might have been, just maybe, a representation of the corruption that Mountain Girl had alluded to. Call it a hunch.

Seriously, though, as much as I was annoyed by the clichéd appearance of this thing, at least it was easy to recognize, so I obviously avoided it and looked for something else. Unfortunately though, there didn't seem to be anything else in this non-Euclidian space, not even any sign of the actual enchantment I was looking for. I had my own suspicions about that, but for the time being I decided to first check the spines of the sea urchin thingy.

Each of the long, needlelike protrusions on the dark blob in the middle started out the same dark colour, and as they stretched towards the infinite distance, they grew thinner and changed from an oily black to smoldering neon green. Not only that, but these needles were constantly moving, at times retracting, only to be replaced by new ones. Sometimes they merged, while at other times one could divide into two or more new needles, constantly moving around in a frankly-disturbing-and-yet-somewhat-familiar display. Not only that, looking into these spines revealed that each had a practically infinitely thin, colourless string inside of it, and when I tried to follow them back to the source, I could finally discern a comparatively small, softly glowing sphere in the middle of the sludge urchin.

For a while I tried to take a better look at the thing from the outside, but the constantly shifting surface of the blob made it nigh impossible to see any small details, so after a long minute of hesitation, I decided to try my luck and get closer. First, though, I had to figure out whether it was even safe to touch this nasty muck, so I proceeded to very gently poke it with the tip of my phantom limb. To my pleasant surprise, the black, gooey substance not only didn't cause any obvious ill effects, but under the gentlest touch of my ethereal limb, it parted like the skin of an overripe tomato cut by a freshly sharpened knife. I waited for just a little longer, to see if there were any delayed effects, and then I carefully shifted my disembodied point of view towards the gash on the surface.

"Ugh."

While I didn't actually feel anything wrong when I finally crossed into the sludge, I still couldn't help but let out a disgusted grunt. There were no good ways to describe the tactile sensations surrounding me, but none of them were particularly pleasant. Still, I soldiered on and quickly made my way over to the glowy bit in the middle. Once I was within phantom limb's reach, I could finally see it for what it was, and my initial suspicion was ultimately confirmed by the sight.

First off, there was a semitransparent outer layer made of two halves, kind of like one of those balls in those vending machines where you have to crank a lever for a random toy to pop out. I think they were called gacha balls? Anyhow, it was actually roughly the size of a small house, which I was no longer surprised about; sizes and distances were screwy enough in this place so that I kind of got used to this sort of thing. On an even closer look, the two halves of the hollow ball turned out to be a single interlocking and stupendously complex enchantment array housing a familiar-looking sphere of multilayered, transparent yarn. It was slightly smaller than the one I'd seen when I fixed Emese's injury, but it looked practically the same, even down to the filaments that reached out through the enchantment case and towards infinity. It was precisely these threads that, after passing through the muck, formed the countless spines of the sludge urchin visible from the outside.

This... actually put the situation into a new perspective. If my interpretation of the ball of yarn being the core of a character in this world, a kind of soul, if you will, was correct, then it meant that Onikiri wasn't just a sentient weapon, but one housing an actual person. It was both intriguing and somewhat annoying at the same time. I mean, if it was a malfunctioning virtual intelligence of some sort, I wouldn't have minded fixing it, in my own way, but if it was really a person locked up in that semitransparent ball (or a loose definition of person, at the very least), it complicated things a bit.

But speaking of the enchantment ball, I decided to focus my attention on it and try to touch it with my phantom limb, parting the greasy substance surrounding me in the process, aaaaand... yep, red flags. By the looks of it, it was definitely something I shouldn't carelessly manipulate, so I proceeded to observe and lightly poke it instead to look for clues, just like how I'd dealt with Emese's curse. I mean, that was a perfect example of why, just because it was something a slightly-more-knowledgeable-yet-infinitely-more-unsociable part of my brain recognized as a thing that should not be tweaked under any circumstances, it didn't mean I couldn't manipulate its environment and effects to get the same result. It might have sounded like a semantic difference, but it was the same kind of difference as between dropping a brick on someone, or just putting a brick on a ledge so that someone could accidentally nudge it and drop it on their own head. One was murder; the other was just *unfortunate* and had nothing to do with you.

Now, back to the observations: the shell was quite intricate, and while on the surface it appeared to be written in a different enchantment language, so to speak, than anything I'd seen so far, its underlying principles when viewed from the supernatural stratum were exactly the same as any other enchantment I had experimented with. It was also incredibly high-quality stuff, easily on the level of the spider controlling the Chimera from the inside, and upon further inspection, I came to the conclusion that it served three purposes: it protected the yarn ball inside, it was responsible for the sword's attributes in the outside world, and unexpectedly enough, it was also responsible for the sludge accumulating around it.

To put it into layman's terms, the enchantment was designed to take samples from anything the sword had slain. Using that sample, it would proceed to adapt and strengthen itself so that it would be more effective against the same kind of opponent the next time. However, each time it did so, it was during a situation when the opponent died, so they were naturally in a heightened state of emotions, which then piled up over time to form this nauseating muck. Whether that was working as intended or a design flaw, I didn't know.

That said, if I dedicated enough time to it, I was fairly sure I could find the answer to that question, but I figured it was about time I stopped dallying around and took a look at the inside. Piercing right through the outer shell was something I could've probably done... if not for the insistent nagging of the enchantment-savvy part of my brain whenever I even considered the idea. Since the forceful approach was apparently ill-advised, I started looking for alternatives, quickly arriving at a certain function of the array. It was what allowed for the threads from the inside to reach out while also making sure the sludge and everything else remained on the outside. By doing a bit of reverse engineering that I didn't 100 percent understand, but looked intuitive enough, I figured that if I pretended to be one of those threads, I could theoretically slip right through with the seal being unaffected. My plan went through a few boring reiterations and some trial and error I shall omit for the time being, but once I got a hang of it, I was fairly confident it should work.

"Here goes nothing," I whispered, my words sending visible ripples through the oily sludge around me. I decided to ignore the sight, as well as the question of how I could even talk without a mouth, and instead I focused my attention on the task at hand. I twisted, and contorted, and almost became one-dimensional for a second or two. At last, I managed to find the sweet spot, and my point of view simply slipped through all the seals of the external shell with absolutely zero resistance, so that I was right in front of the ball of yarn... except when I wasn't, and before I knew it, I suddenly landed on my feet.

Wait a moment. That felt subtly wrong. Since when did I have feet at times like this?

I glanced down, and to my further bewilderment, I could see my whole body, except it wasn't really my body. For a start, I was pretty sure I wasn't completely smooth between my legs, and on second look, my abs and biceps were just a tad more defined than in what I jokingly called my reality. That was... *mildly* odd.

It was also a conundrum for later, as it was much more important to figure out my current situation, and to do so I first had to know where the hell I was. At a quick glance, I actually had to consider hell as an actual option. I was on a hilltop that was made entirely out of blood, including the grass under my feet that melted back into fluid at a simple touch. Oddly macabre, but that would've been fine on its own. Then I noticed that on my left, there was something that looked like a ruined Japanese shrine, with broken sculptures, a small building with a caved-in roof, and even one of those characteristic gates with the crescent top. Oh, and it was all on fire. Blue fire, to be exact, which didn't really help the eerie atmosphere one bit.

"Is this some kind of artificial environment, or..." I mumbled aloud without even realizing it, only to almost fall over when the ground under my feet shook with a deep, groaning sound. I turned towards the source of the impact, and I didn't even realize what I was looking at until I raised my head so much my neck started to hurt. I was facing, for lack of better words, a black giant made out of indistinct, roiling fog that still appeared to be perfectly solid. The leisurely sitting creature in front of me had a vaguely feminine shape, with long, thin limbs. On its ankles and wrists it had four sets of large prayer beads, its only article of clothing, so to speak. Most of its body was covered by her thick, ankle-long, and rather unruly hair that waved and undulated as if it was on fire.

"<What is THIS?>" In response to the giant's voice, the whole world around us trembled. It leaned forward with slow, leisurely movements that reminded me of a well-fed cat, right until it was practically on its knees, and it slowly closed the distance until its enormous head was right above me. "<Is that you, BOY?>"

The creature's featureless face hung over me, completely motionless. It had no nose or mouth, only two perfect, glowing circles where the eyes were supposed to be. It was quite unnerving, to say the least.

"<This has NEVER happened before,>" the giant noted with a voice that felt like Onikiri's already uncanny voice was cranked up to eleven, and then some. "<My wielder WASN'T supposed to enter MY sanctum. EVER. Are you DEAD? ARE you a GHOST?>"

"No, and neither am I your wielder," I answered with a frown that quickly turned into an expression of alarm when the giant Onikiri thing extended a hand towards me.

"<Let me TAKE a better LOOK at you.>"

The request might not have sounded threatening on its own, but the fingers ending in curved talons heading my way sure as hell were.

"Back off!" I yelled out as I took a step back and instinctively swung my phantom limb at the incoming palm.

"<Hu—!?>"

To my sincerest shock, my extra limb not only came out on top in the clash, but when it met the hand of the giant, she was outright thrown back. After the first surprise, the enormous body let out a terrifying (or maybe terrified, though the two weren't mutually exclusive) roar as it lost its balance and rolled down the hill. For several seconds I could only blink in surprise, though not because of the improbable outcome I'd just experienced.

When I struck the creature, it didn't feel like I hit an object. In fact, it was exactly the same as when I interacted with an enchantment. Following that logic, I tried to touch the ground with it, and then my own body, and the results were the same. Apparently, my first hunch was correct: this place was indeed fake, or rather, a sort of illusion created by the enchantment. In short, the shell surrounding the soul ball in the middle had two layers: the outside, which was supposed to protect it from external effects, while the inside had a separate array that created this rudimentary illusion. Well, rudimentary compared to the simulation outside, but I digress. No time for existential musings right now.

That said, now that I was aware of this fact, I could not only clearly perceive the workings of the enchantment array through the supernatural stratum, but I could also see that the yarn ball was still in front of me under the layers of the illusion.

I was just about to try to decipher this new discovery, but my time to do so was cut short by the ground trembling under my feet once again.

"<How DARE you!!!>" the giant Onikiri demon thing roared with indignation practically dripping from its wounded pride as it ran up the hill, each hard step giving a small earthquake a run for its money and its hair flailing in the wind, making it look even larger in the process.

"Okay, calm down for a mo—" "Ment!" I would've said, if I was given the chance, as the giant didn't stop when it reached the top of the hill, and instead it swung its leg and tried to punt me like a soccer ball. My whole body tensed up for a moment, and even though I knew I wasn't in real danger, the giant, incoming feet still scared me for a moment.

Then it met with my phantom limb again and instantly stopped as if it had hit a stone wall. There was a moment of silence, and then the creature let out another terrifying roar, made more impressive by the fact it did so without having an actual mouth, before it fell down on its butt and grabbed hold of its big toe.

"<AAAARGH!! HOW!>" It bellowed between pained hisses before it focused all of its attention on me again. "<HOW is this POSSIBLE! This is MY sanctum! MY world!>" While it boomed so, the blue flames around began to burn brighter and brighter, until it felt like we were standing (or sitting) in the middle of a roaring inferno. "<I can DO or CREATE anything I WANT in HERE! HOW could you DO this to ME!?>"

"First off, stop shouting," I told it with a sigh while using my hand to wave away some of the sparks landing on my shoulders. "If it makes you feel better, I'm just your natural nemesis. You manifest and control a world created by a complex enchantment. I'm someone who can dismantle and modify most enchantments as I want. We are simply on a different level."

"<That's not FAIR!>" the unstable (in more ways than one) giant screamed as it once more tried to reach out towards me, only to be rebuked by another slap from my phantom limb.

I waited for it to finish having its outburst, and a couple of minutes plus a few more slaps later it finally calmed down a little.

"So now that we've established the pecking order," I noted while dividing my attention between it and analyzing the inner workings of the inner layer of the shell around the yarn ball, "How about you stop being obstinate and let me go? In reality, I mean."

"<NO!>" she roared, yet instead of being scary, she simply sounded petulant. "<I WANT you to BE my WIELDER!>"

"But why? Don't you already have Rinne?" I tried to reason with it, but the giant had none of it.

"<I DON'T want HER anymore! YOU are STRONGER! I EXIST to KILL! I NEED a strong wielder to KILL strong APPARITIONS!>"

"Okay, I get that, but..."

"<I want YOU! I WANT YOU, I WANT YOU, I WANT YOU!!!>"

Well, great. And now the giant, scary demon thing was throwing a literal tantrum like a kid, complete with repeatedly banging its fists against the ground. I could still try to talk, but I had a distinct feeling that it was pretty much impossible to argue with the unreasonable creature in front of me. I was just about to entertain the idea of doing something slightly unsavory, like hacking the enchantment to turn her into a chicken and threaten to eat her for dinner if she didn't behave, but then I stumbled onto something during my exploration of the array.

So just to reiterate: even though that miasma or corruption or what have you completely covered the shell housing Onikiri's soul, it couldn't actually get in. However, while it couldn't touch the yarn ball itself, the strings that reached out and through the shell were also all part of what made up the entity called Onikiri. This meant that it was likely affected by at least some of that, which would explain why it was so uncooperative and moody. However, if we turned it around, would that mean that if I got rid of the stuff outside, I could theoretically make her see reason?

It was worth a shot, especially considering that even if it didn't work out, if I could get rid of this corruption thing, I would stop the whole Volcanic Vein business from getting worse, and at the very least buy myself some time to deal with everything else on my plate. As for how I could do that... well, the sludge was easily cut by my phantom limb, so that was a start, and I could probably improvise the rest.

"Okay, that's it," I raised my voice with exaggerated indignation. "If you're refusing to cooperate, I'll just go out and do it my way."

The giant looked at me with a befuddled expression, or at least as befuddled as something can look without actual facial features, but I didn't wait for it to form any response and instead I quickly wiggled out of the shell around the soul ball the way I came. Truth to be told, folding my illusionary body into a one-dimensional dot was way weirder than when I only did it to my disembodied point of view, but it wasn't the time to dwell on that.

Once outside, I first tested if I could even properly cut the sludge, and to my immediate relief, the whole process turned out to be really easy, if time-consuming, though it didn't take long for me to discover that even if I managed to detach a piece of muck from the central blob, I had nowhere to put it, and it would gravitate back towards the rest of it. This almost made me reconsider the notion, but then I suddenly had an ingenious idea, if I may say so myself.

I dived back to the middle and accessed the shell again. I leafed through the functions of the external array, and I quickly found the part that I was looking for. It was the bit responsible for giving the blade an edge that could cut through most things with ease. I ran into another issue at this point, though, namely the fact that I couldn't actually change the function to suit my purposes because of the whole *Plot Device: Do Not Touch!* thing. It was such an elegant idea, though, and I wasn't willing to give up on it just yet, so after some further consideration I folded myself up one more time and entered into the shell.

"Hey, Onikiri?"

When I called out to it, the giant practically jumped to her feet in surprise, only to stop and tilt its head in puzzlement.

"<YOU look DIFFERENT,>" it stated, and I shrugged.

"Don't mind the clothes; they're only here for my peace of mind," I told her while pointedly straightening the coat I'd manifested on my way in because Barbie doll anatomy or not, modesty was important. "Listen, I need you to do something."

"<WHAT?>" it bellowed, and I quickly and concisely explained that I wanted it to channel mana into the edge of the blade for me, though with considerably more specific terminology, but who has time for that? Anyhow, once I finished my explanation, it asked, "<WHY would I DO that? YOU still refuse ME!>"

"Easy, easy," I soothed it with my hands raised, and once it calmed down, I took a deep breath and told it, "Let's say I want to cut something, and so I—"

"<WHY didn't you SAY so!>" the giant abruptly exclaimed, making me wonder if it was pulling my leg or was really this easy to convince. "<I'll SHOW you how AMAZING I am, and once you get a TASTE, you'll BEG to ME to let me IN!>"

"Yeah, sure, that's exactly what's going to happen," I spoke using my best Judy impression, but it didn't catch up to it and instead let out a satisfied laugh that made me wonder if it was an idiot.

Either way, once it agreed, I headed outside again, and by the time I arrived, there was already a steady stream of something that I presumed to be mana flowing towards the nebulous outside. My plan was fairly simple in theory, though for some reason I had a feeling if I wanted to explain it to the class rep, she would probably blow a fuse halfway through. Anyhow, here's what I did: First I went a layer deeper, and entered the supernatural strata of the world. There, I found the mana stream, and with a bit of elbow grease, I tied the miasma directly surrounding me to it, so that when it was channeled, it sort of pulled the muck with it. As for what happened afterwards... well, imagine one of those enormous mobile pump trucks they bring out during floods. Got that? Now imagine one of those things being used to empty a kiddie pool. There was no contest whatsoever.

The whole process took about three minutes from my own perspective, plus another ten or so that I spent scraping the remainder of it off the bases of the spines in a bit of metaphysical labour, but once I was done, there was not a speck of the nasty black sludge remaining in sight. I let out a sigh in appreciation of work well done, yet couldn't help but notice that even after I was done, the mana stream heading towards the real world was still going at full force. Shouldn't Onikiri have already noticed what was going on by this point? Well, there was no sense in asking a question that I could answer with minimal effort, so after preparing myself for a few seconds, I once again slipped into the inside of the sphere and...

"... What the hell?"

The question slipped through my lips before I even knew it, but I doubt anyone could blame me. The blood hill was replaced by a perfectly nice knoll. The burning shrine gate was replaced by a new one that was about twice as big. The shrine building itself was not only no longer in shambles, it was both taller and more lavish than the original. And as for the giant creature...

"O-kami-samaaaaa!"

I could practically taste the cold shiver running down my back the moment I heard a young voice calling out to me, followed by the equally foreboding sound of small feet running towards me. As I turned around, I was met with a pair of large golden eyes staring right back at me, their owner coming to a screeching halt just a step away from me. A short-yet-infinitely-long beat later the young preteen girl in front of me let out a small gasp and bowed at a ninety-degree angle, her long, straight black hair almost reaching the ground as it hung from her head.

"Please accept my sincerest apologies for my previous conduct, O Kami-sama!"

Her voice, oddly low-pitched yet still girly, was filled with palpable shame as she maintained her posture, and if the prayer beads around her wrists and ankles weren't enough to spoil her identity, her words made it an absolute no-brainer.

I stared at the top of her head for an embarrassingly long time, then I closed my eyes, counted to five, and then opened them up in the company of a long, drawn-out sigh.

"Three things," I began while raising my right hand with the same number of fingers extended. "First off, I'm not an o-kami. Secondly, stop bowing." At this point I waited for her to stop doing so, and only then did I add, "Thirdly, you said this is your world where you can create and do whatever you want, right?"

The girl looked me in the eye, and then her lips slowly bent into a demure smile before she nodded, so I, naturally, straightened my fingers and whacked her right over the top of her head with the edge of my palm before exclaiming, "Then put on some damn clothes already!"

PART 2

"So in short," I mused aloud while standing under the eaves of the traditional Japanese shrine, my arms crossed and my brows refusing to unfurrow, "You originally weren't a sword, but since you were about to die due to an *accident*, a legendary sword smith and a legendary priest, both of whom you just *happened* to know and who just *happened* to be in the area at the time, put you in the sword. Did I get that right?"

The young girl sitting on her knees in front of me immediately nodded with a bright expression. She was thankfully wearing clothes by now, which included a loose, bright-red skirt and a white upper garment with red trimming around the baggy sleeves, and her long hair was tied back, using a pair of borderline-comically-large red ribbons, into a pair of tidy twin tails flowing down her back. It didn't take a genius to deduce that she was supposed to be wearing a shrine maiden outfit, just with a couple of added frills (though, at the very least, it wasn't one of those miniskirt versions popular in certain genres). Also, if everything else didn't make it blindingly obvious yet, the hairdo made it 101 percent clear that she sure as hell wasn't a placeholder, either the run-of-the-mill or the unique variety.

While I pondered on this, she unexpectedly leaned forward into a deferential bow and told me, "In my previous life, I used to be called Azusa Ichiko. I would be honoured if Tsukuyomi-okami-sama would call me by my given name."

I was about to roll my eyes, but then I stopped midway. Wait, which one was her first name again...? Ugh, Japanese name ordering always gave me a headache, especially at times like this, where I was pretty sure neither of us was speaking English, and the enchantment just auto-translated our thoughts on the spot. Where the occasional gratuitous Japanese came from, I had absolutely no idea. Maybe the enchantment was a weaboo? Bad jokes aside, we were at addressing her by her name, weren't we? Well, I had a fifty-fifty chance to get it right, so I figured I might as well give it a shot.

"So... Ichiko?" I guessed, and the way her lips twisted in delight when she looked back up at me told me I got the coin toss right, so I allowed myself a relieved smirk in return before adding, in my flattest voice, "Also, I'm not a Tsukuyomi-okami-sama."

That comment immediately made her smile wither as she sat up straight and let out a disappointed sigh.

"Truly? I was sure I would get it right this time..." Her words were followed by a defeated shrug, and then she told me, "Tsukuyomi-sama was always a mysterious one, so I believed that if there was a great god hiding among the masses, it would be him, and... Ue-sama? Why are you holding your head like that? Are you hurt?"

"No, this is called a facepalm," I told her through clenched teeth. "Also, I think I already told you that I'm not a great god. Could you please stop casually calling me one?"

"But, my ue-sama..."

"Yeah, and that, too," I cut in again while redoubling my face-palming efforts. "I'm not that, either, whatever that means."

"Then how shall I address you?"

Her completely earnest question only made my headache worse, so I might have responded a smidgen impatiently.

"You already know my name. Just call me Leonard or something."

"I understand, Leonard-ue!"

Her reply came packaged with a beaming smile that would have been right at home on Angie's face, but I couldn't muster anything more than a deadpan reaction.

"My name has no *-ue* in it."

"Then... Leonard-dono?"

"Just Leonard will do."

"I wouldn't dare to be so disrespectful to a great—" She might have noticed the glare I was sending her way, for at this point she immediately let out an unsubtle cough and said, "I mean, my *benefactor*."

"I don't mind at all." With that, I cut the name discussion short and aimed to move things along by asking, "You said you wanted to talk to me before I leave, didn't you?"

"Ah, right! I beg your pardon for taking up your precious time." After apologizing, she bowed her head one more time and proclaimed, "Please wield me!"

"Denied," I replied right away, followed by the tactical nuke equivalent of a forehead flick that sent her reeling back.

"Ow-ow-ow!" She held her forehead with both hands and directed a wounded, teary-eyed stare at me. "Why did you hit me?"

"Because we've already been over this," I told her in the company of a groan.

"But... you're not supposed to hit girls!" she protested in a whining voice that only made me shake my head.

"You're a sword," I corrected her, before adding, "Also, while you look like a girl right now, it's just a proxy body created by the enchantment housing you. There's nothing stopping you from becoming that giant flame-y thing again, is there?"

"I wouldn't do that!" the little girl in front of me protested with a puffed-out cheek, and if she wasn't kneeling, I was pretty sure she would've stomped her feet. "I only looked like that because I was overwhelmed by the corruption!"

"Then why didn't you get rid of it yourself? I think I just demonstrated that it wasn't that hard," I countered, though after but a moment, I realized that I was probably being a little unfair. After all, she didn't exactly have access to the same tools I did.

I was just about to grudgingly correct myself, but she let her hands down from her forehead and sent me a pitiful look while grumbling something along the lines of, "I never knew it could be done. I was always bad when it came to formations and arrays; my mother always said I just wasn't smart enough for it." She paused here, and I almost managed to get a word in when her eyes suddenly lit up as she looked up at me again. "I get it! You must be Toko-yo-no-Omoikane-no-kami-sama! I should've realized right away when you said you could manipulate arrays at will!"

She was giving me a bright, almost triumphant look, so I promptly swallowed back whatever verbal olive branch I'd originally wanted to offer her and instead proceeded to flick her forehead one more time.

"Ow-owwww! It was the same spot again! It hurts!" I allowed her to roll on the ground a few times, hoping she would learn her lesson, and then used my phantom limb to interface with the internal enchantment that materialized everything around us and simply turned off the injury I'd caused to her.

It was actually way easier than one would think. I mean, removing an injury out of existence like it never happened sounds like it's some kind of amazing magical feat, but due to this enchantment creating only a surface-level illusion, without bothering to simulate pesky things like internal organs or skeletons, let alone cells or atoms, I literally just disabled the pain like you would change a variable in a spreadsheet. Of course, the comparison wasn't entirely on the nose, as even with the simple materialization, the underlying enchantment was way more complex and occasionally more counterintuitive than any other enchantment I'd ever seen.

To put it into perspective, simple enchantments were like looking at a page full of programming script: complex, but once you understood the language and the internal logic of it all, it was fairly intuitive. Complex enchantments, like the one on the dragon-slaying spear, were more like someone who either didn't know how to code, or knew how to do it but couldn't be bothered to do it well, slapped something together that technically worked as intended, but had a lot of superfluous lines and spaghetti code. This one right here was something that was made by someone who not only had the know-how but also spent the time to debug their script and sprinkle in a lot of annotations to explain what the heck each of the myriad of interlocking bits were supposed to be doing. It was mind-numbingly complex all the same, but still the second-best thing after a straight-up graphic user interface... though I didn't even know if one could be made for the *thing* I was inside of at the moment, as it seemed to be using colours and flavours instead of numbers, but I digress.

Anyhow, once she stopped flailing, the obnoxiously cutesy girl finally sprung to her feet again and showed a look so pitiful I was momentarily tempted to pat her on the head, but then I remembered that she was pretty annoying, so I stayed my hand.

She was about to say something, which would have no doubt led to further hijinks, but then we were interrupted by the world around us quaking, and by that, I don't mean the ground trembling like when she used to be bigger and slightly more unreasonable (with *slightly* being the keyword here), but the artificial space itself. That was ever-so-slightly alarming, so I raised a finger to make her stay silent and quickly checked the enchantment, but at a cursory glance, I couldn't see anything unusual. I was just about to write it up to some freak happenstance, but then the space around us quaked and twisted once again, this time even harder, momentarily stretching and deforming everything in sight.

"Okay, I don't know *what* that was, but I didn't like it one bit," I muttered, but since even a second glance didn't show any anomalies, I looked my host in the eye and told her, "I'll go out for a moment and see what's going on. I'll be back soon."

I didn't wait for her answer, and more or less faded out of the area by detaching myself from the artificial world... only to come back about ten seconds later, much to her apparent shock.

"Did... Ue-sama find the problem?"

"In a manner of speaking," I answered with some hesitancy. I graciously ignored the way she addressed me again and stated, "I have some bad news, so you might want to sit down first."

I didn't mean that literally, yet she immediately sat onto her knees again and turned a pair of attentive, if currently somewhat distressed, eyes at me. I waited for yet another small space-quake to pass, and only then did I give my explanation.

"So in a nutshell, the issue is that you're currently breaking apart the enchantment that's housing you."

"I am?" she blurted out, incredulity written all over her face, and I nodded in the affirmative.

"Yeah. Not on purpose, I believe, but... how should I say this... Have you ever seen a blobfish?" She tilted her head to the side and gave me an odd look that was only missing a small question mark floating over her. If she'd done this just a few minutes ago, I might have flexed my newfound comprehension about our surroundings to conjure up one myself, but it really wasn't the time for horsing around, so instead I collected my thoughts and tried my best to explain what was going on. "You see, a couple of thousand meters under the sea, there is a ton of water pressure weighing down on everything, including the fish living there, so they have adapted to it and look perfectly normal at that depth. However, take one of these blobfish up to the surface, and without the external pressure keeping them in check, they swell several times in size and become this amorphous blob. Are you following me so far?"

My audience blinked at me a few times, and at the end of the day she timidly told me, "No offense, Ue-sama, but has anyone ever told you that your analogies are hard to understand?"

"Yes, but you're not allowed to do it."

"I-in that case... no?"

One sigh later I faced her again and explained, "You're the blobfish. In a manner of speaking, the sludge outside used to put pressure on you, so your soul or whatever you want to call it got compressed. The protective array on the outside also shrunk to fit around you. However, now that the sludge is gone, your soul suddenly began to expand to its original size, and the enchantment cannot keep up, and it's getting pushed apart by you."

"That... that's really, really bad!"

"To put it mildly," I commented a little half-heartedly, but then was shocked when she grabbed onto the hem of my coat with a pleading expression.

"Ue-sama!"

"W-what?"

The girl kept clinging to me even as I tried to back away and gave me the puppiest puppy eyes ever.

"What's going to happen to me if it breaks?"

"I don't think it will break. I mean, it was designed to accommodate you, and it can—"

"But what if it does?!" she cut me off while turning the pleading look up to eleven. "I just got better! I don't want to die!"

As if to punctuate her words, there was another quake that shook the land and air around us, and I couldn't help but bury my face in my hand again.

"Listen, as I was trying to say, there's a good seventy percent chance that the enchantment will hold out just fine, and then the inner enchantment will stop glitching out as well."

"Would you bet your life on those odds?"

The biting question made me stop in my tracks right away, and after trying to come up with a fitting counterargument, I ultimately had to go with, "Fine, you got me there, but what exactly do you want me to do about it?"

"I don't know! Ue-sama is the genius master of arrays! If anyone knows how to resolve this, it's you!"

I gave her a glare for several seconds just to see if she was taking the piss out of me, but she only gazed at me with sparkly, expectant eyes, so I was forced to just let out a low groan and tell her, "Listen, it's really not that simple. For a start, I can't even really touch the outer layer, let alone manipulate it."

"Is it truly so fragile right now?"

"Erm... Sure, let's go with that," I agreed with a tired shrug. "The point is, I can't make it expand faster, and as for reducing your size... I suppose we could do that by shoveling all the muck back to compress you again, but that would be both counterintuitive and obviously take a while."

"No, not that!" she exclaimed while shaking her head so hard I was pretty sure she was— Oh, wait, she *did* get dizzy. How did she even do that? I was pretty sure her inner ears weren't even simulated, but I was too lazy to check at the moment, so instead I grabbed her wobbling head like a coconut and held her steady.

"I wasn't serious. I couldn't do that even if I wanted to; we expelled it all into the outside, remember?"

"Did we? I didn't really understand what happened back then, but after Ue-sama told me what to do, I was too relieved by the miasma disappearing, and then I was too busy tidying up this pocket space for Ue-sama's return, so I forgot to pay attention."

I once again couldn't help but frown in incredulity, but she seemed entirely genuine, so I decided to file her under the cutesy, clumsy moe-blob archetype and move on.

"So, as I was saying, we don't really have a lot of options here. Since I cannot tweak the outer shell, and I obviously cannot tweak you, I suppose the only other option would be to move you somewhere else before things irreversibly break down."

"That! I like that idea!" she exclaimed while pointing a finger at my face, which was made even sillier by the fact that I was still holding on to her head. Not that she seemed to mind, as she tried to repeatedly nod even though I kept her still. "Please do that, Ue-sama!"

"That was just a hypothetical," I blurted out a tad helplessly in the face of her relentless assault of confidence in me. "It's not like we have anything ready to house a soul just lying aro... und..."

"What? What?"

As my words trailed off, she began spamming beams of hope in my direction, and as much as I was trying to ignore them, they were somehow still getting to me. In the end, I closed my eyes (though it was only a token gesture, as it wasn't like I was seeing the enchantment simulation through them in the first place), and after mulling over the feasibility of the sudden idea I'd just gotten, I began to measure its pros and cons.

On one hand, it should theoretically work, and if my understanding was correct, it would have a fairly high chance of success. On the other, I wasn't even sure I *could* do it, as I had never tried something like this before, and even if it worked, there was no guarantee there wouldn't be any further complications. After pondering for a couple more seconds, I realized it was probably simpler if I just asked the girl clinging to me for her opinion, as it was ultimately up to her.

"So, Ichiko?" I began, and she immediately perked up. "I think I actually have a feasible plan to get you out of this sticky situation, but I'm not sure you are going to like it..."

PART 3

When Leonard Dunning exited the transplanar space, his eyes were still focused on the blade held in front of his face by a slightly trembling arm. The once-black sword was now pure, matte white, as if covered by a fine layer of frost. The familiar purple shroud still grasped his hand like a vise, but it was of little concern at the moment.

After observing the weapon for three more seconds, Leonard Dunning's face clouded. There was a pervasive, acrid odor that stung his nostrils with every breath. It was the combination of the bloodied stench of the writhing Chimera and the black bile covering the ground around his feet. Leonard Dunning stepped away from the puddle of black, bubbling tar slowly eating into the concrete floor and focused his gaze upon the fallen life-form.

His advance was momentarily stalled by a body blocking his path. He glanced at the being in front of him; Brang Shadowfeet of the Faun Inanna-Dunning. He attempted to communicate, but Leonard Dunning simply walked around him and stopped next to the Chimera. He lowered himself to one knee and momentarily observed the weakly flailing creature, and he ultimately utilized his ******** to completely disable the artificial intelligence governing its actions.

The creature's body became completely limp and lifeless in short order. Leonard Dunning's expression didn't show any change as he patiently waited for its heart to finish its last beat, and then he carefully placed the tip of the blade against an already-present wound on its torso and inserted it into the chest cavity of the Chimera. Karukk Thunderer of the Faun Inanna-Dunning uttered an inconsequential comment, which he completely ignored while focusing on the task at hand. From the outside, it appeared he was only staring at the motionless body in front of him, which lasted for several long minutes before he exhaled a long breath, retrieved the blade from the insides of the Chimera and—

"Chief?"

I blinked once. Then two more times for good measure while I tried to stop the world from spinning in front of my eyes. Finally, after I no longer felt like I was sitting on a carousel, I glanced up at the girl nervously tugging at the collar of my coat.

"Hi, Dormouse. I thought you weren't going to come out of the closet until things calmed down."

My girlfriend let out a subtly relieved breath in response to my words and let go of my coat, only to immediately grab onto me again when I tried to stand up and almost face-planted when my internal merry-go-round suddenly went in reverse.

"He told me you were acting strange," she explained to me while clumsily trying to use the hand holding on to mine to point at Karukk.

I sent the Faun a questioning glance, but since the only reaction I got out of him was a sheepishly averted face, I decided to ignore him and focus on the girl holding on to me.

"You're not possessed, right?" she asked, her eyes suspiciously measuring me from head to toe.

"Nah, I was just..." I wanted to say "Spaced out," but the expression didn't feel exactly right, so after some consideration, I settled on, "I was kind of *detached* for a moment."

"Are you better now?"

"*Better* is a relative term, but at least my head is comparatively clear."

"How's your headache?"

"It's... actually not that bad. That said, my entire body is pretty numb right now, so that doesn't mean much."

Now, truth be told, I wasn't entirely truthful with Judy at the moment, as while my head was indeed tolerable (or at the very least it only felt like I was standing by the speakers at a death metal concert with earplugs that could fall out at any second), my right forearm was stinging pretty badly, which considering my current state probably wasn't a good sign. Speaking of which, the shroud was still wrapped around my hand, so I shook it to loosen the fabric up, and after a couple additional tries, I successfully managed to get it off. The skin under it was unnaturally red, but after wiggling my fingers a little to confirm they still functioned, I decided to disregard the problem for the time being and have Angie take a look at it once the universe finished using me as its chew toy.

In the meantime I also couldn't help but notice that the Chimera next to us had started breathing again, so to avoid any future misunderstandings, I loudly cleared my throat to get everyone's attention.

"Listen up, everyone! If the Chimera starts moving again, don't be alarmed. She's probably going to start transforming soon. I think she's not a bad kid, but keep an eye on her, anyway."

"She?" Judy leveled the question at me with a sharp look, earning her an especially tired eye roll for her trouble.

"It's a long story. I'll explain the nitty-gritty details once things have calmed down. If you still feel insecure even after you see her, feel free to apply some countermeasures at your convenience."

"I'm not insecure. I'm just not sitting on my laurels," my assistant responded with a microscopic pout, but a blink of an eye later her expression abruptly changed, and without any warning, she began dragging me along. Normally this would be the point where I would make an affectionate joke about how she looked like some kind of traditionally adorable small animal while she was ineffectually tugging at me, but it probably spoke volumes about my current state that it *actually worked*.

"Hey, easy there," I grumbled, barely managing to stop myself from stumbling. She helped me keep my balance, but was just as insistent as before, so it didn't take long for me to just go with the flow and ask, "Where exactly are we going?"

"You reminded me of something, so we're going to do it now, before you find a convenient excuse to avoid it and then tell me that you couldn't do it because of the circumstances."

I wanted to argue at first, but after considering my options, I ultimately folded and obediently let her lead me along. Seeing us walking, Brang and Karukk immediately fell in line behind us doing their best honour guard impression, and on our way to our destination, we passed by a couple of other, currently-hard-to-identify Fauns, as they were doing their best mummy impressions. Speaking of which, the injured seemed to have been fully bandaged (maybe even excessively so, if you ask me), so I couldn't help but wonder how much time had passed outside while I was fiddling with Onikiri and the little miko inside it.

"Hey, Dormouse? How long was I in this time?"

Judy fumbled for a second as she used her free hand to fish her phone out of her breast pocket, and to my surprise, she actually had a timer running on it, which she immediately stopped.

"A little over fifteen minutes," she stated after a glance, then hurriedly pocketed the device again so that she could use both hands to support me. It wasn't exactly necessary anymore, but I appreciated the gesture.

"Really? Everyone got their wounds treated in just fifteen minutes?" I spared one more glance at the Fauns standing at attendance, and noted, "You guys are really efficient, as usual."

My words made all the Fauns present subtly puff up their chests with more than a hint of pride, so much so that my hard-to-restrain teasing instincts wanted me to add a line about how I wished they were half as useful in combat, but my grumpy comment never managed to leave my mouth once we arrived at our destination. In front of us, Rinne was sitting on one of the benches around the training area, her arms still tied behind her back with the extension cord, and she was flanked by a grim-looking Pip, who was apparently on guard duty.

"Chief, please introduce us," Judy much less asked than demanded, and to further set the scene, she clamped her arms around mine and snuggled even closer than before.

"Wait, are we really going to be doing what I think we're doing right now?"

"If you mean implementing countermeasures, then yes," Judy noted with an expression that said she would hear no objection to this. I tried, anyway.

"We're still in the middle of something. Is this really necessary?"

"Yes, because if we don't do it now, then you're just going to say, 'It's a long story, I'll explain later,' but then you never do it, so that it will lead to a series of increasingly ludicrous misunderstandings. I'm not having any of that."

"... Well, if you put it like that, I can't really argue," I griped while observing the far corner of the hall because it was really interesting, and nothing else. It had nothing to do with what Judy had said, and even if it did, I could absolutely look her in the eye with confidence any time I wanted; I just found that corner really thought-provoking at the moment and decided not to do so right now. Scout's honour.

"You better not," Judy commented following a triumphant little "Hmpf!" noise, and she tugged on my arm again. "So what are you waiting for? Introduce us."

One short-yet-infinitely-exhausted sigh later I turned to the woman on the bench, and I was about to just get it over with a few words when I noticed that she was staring at me with eyes like saucers.

"Um... Hey, Mountain Girl. I see you've calmed down a little." I opened with a bit of small talk, which, based on how Judy's elbow poked my side, my girlfriend didn't really appreciate. The abnormally overwhelmed huntress didn't say anything, but I decided to interpret the way she slightly lowered her head as a nod, so I swiftly continued with, "Neat. Anyhow, this is Judy Sennoma."

"And I'm your...?" my dear assistant prompted me, followed by another unsubtle prodding with her elbow.

"And she's my girlfriend," I uttered a tad wearily, and then we both waited for her to respond.

For the next two seconds, she kept staring at me without as much as blinking, but at last she looked me directly in the eye.

"Leonard-san... have you... purified Onikiri?"

Now it was my turn to stare at her in puzzlement for a long while, but before I could answer her, Judy cut in with an indignant look in her eyes.

"Don't change the subject. Did you hear what the Chief said? Did you actually understand it? Have you properly internalized it?"

"Wow, easy there, Dormouse," I chided her while simultaneously rubbing the hand that was holding on to mine. "You're coming on a bit too strong, don't you think?"

"No, Chief, this is important. I don't want to run into a situation where she could claim, 'Oh, I, like, totally spaced out or whatever, and I, like, seriously don't remember like anything you said.'"

"I don't think that would happen. Also, why do you make her sound like a Valley girl? She's Japanese."

"It's because I can't do a Japanese accent," she retorted as if the answer was blatantly obvious.

"I'm sorry that you had to learn it like this, but you can't do Valley speak, either," I shot back, only to get my foot stomped for my trouble.

"Chief, stop being a contrarian. You're already on my bad side for making me worried. Now, let's stop this sidetrack and focus on explaining to her how you only have space for one relationship in your life."

"Um... You mean two, right? There is also E—mfff..."

She... actually covered my mouth. As in, she literally put her hand over it. What the heck?

"Chief, *she* doesn't need to know that," Judy all but hissed at me, only to glance over to the still strangely unresponsive huntress and hastily add, "So as we were saying, we are in a steady relationship, and there is absolutely no space for someone else between us. Zero. Nil. Nada. Are we clear?"

This time Rinne actually gave us a proper, if still absolutely befuddled nod, and at last my girlfriend removed her hand from my face as well while muttering, "How come you're so smart, yet you make the dumbest mistakes from time to time?"

"Hey, I take umbrage to that accusation, young lady!" I raised my voice with an exaggeratedly wronged frown on my face, culminating in, "I'm most definitely *not* smart."

"It takes a smart person to claim to be dumb to avoid being accused of making a mistake they shouldn't have made," my dearest assistant countered with an indignant huff, practically forcing me to roll my eyes.

"Oh please, stop that! Catch-22's are unbecoming of you!"

"A not-smart person wouldn't even know what that is. I'm sorry that you had to learn it like this, but I'm afraid you suck at being dumb."

We would've continued that for a while longer, but I was starting to feel sorry for Mountain Girl, who looked positively lost at the moment, so I decided to graciously let Judy win our nonargument (which meant that technically I didn't lose because I did it on purpose; elementary logic, my dear).

"So you were asking something, weren't you?"

The de-creepyfied huntress blinked in surprise when she realized I was talking to her, and she nodded no less than three times in rapid succession.

"Yes, Leonard-san. Ri— *I* asked if you purified Onikiri."

Since she couldn't use her hands at the moment, she used her chin to gesture towards the white blade in my hand. I glanced down at it, too, and after a short beat I let my fatigued shoulders droop a little before facing her again.

"Well, let's just say it's a long..." I couldn't finish my sentence, as my side abruptly got reacquainted with Judy's elbow again. "Oh, right. I wasn't supposed to say that anymore." My whispered words were then further punctuated by lightly bumping my unusually poke-y girlfriend with my hip, following which I turned back to my conversational partner and ultimately told her, "In a manner of speaking, yes, I've purified the sword. You can get the details from her later."

She gave me an ambivalent grunt instead of an answer, which I interpreted as some form of acknowledgment. With that settled, I turned back to Judy again, and while ignoring her repeated efforts at trying to hip check me back, I squeezed her hand to get her attention.

"Say, Dormouse? Now that we're done with the countermeasures, can I get going?"

"Depends," she replied after one last, hopping hip bump that still bounced off me like a tennis ball. "Do you feel better?"

"Well, my headache is still there, if kind of fuzzy, and my body is numb from head to toe, and I kind of feel like I'm floating about two centimeters off the ground, and for some inexplicable reason the inside of my mouth tastes like turpentine, but otherwise I'm perfectly fine."

"Chief, be serious."

"I am. I doubt I'm going to get any better from just standing around, so I might as well get things done while I *can* stand."

Judy stared daggers at me for a second or five, but at the end of the day she grudgingly surrendered with a click of her tongue and separated from me.

"Fine, but let me check the situation first."

Saying so, she reached into one of her pockets, and with one smooth motion, she put on her magical party glasses as if she was the main lead in a crime scene investigation show. After drinking in the sight for a moment, I glanced around, and immediately noticed the weird looks the Fauns were directing our way.

"[The injunction on merriment at the expense of my other half is still in effect.]"

Karukk and the others immediately averted their eyes, while Brang was still giving us an affectionate and disturbingly grandfatherly look, which I decided to simply ignore. That left only one person, so I turned to Rinne and added, "That applies to you, too. No laughing."

"... Okay?"

Her response was a tad uncertain, but good enough. Once that was done, I quickly turned on my Far Sight. Out of courtesy, I didn't use it to look at anyone Judy could, and instead I focused on the Dracises first. For a second I couldn't decide whether I should focus on Emese or Abram, but it ended up completely moot, as they were both at the same place.

Once my point of view stabilized, I found myself in a currently very purple rendition of the Dracis mansion's courtyard, where the draconic couple was currently clashing with the two Entitled Knights. I observed things for a while to see if they needed any help, but by the looks of it, the Knights were already in retreat. On a closer look, the squires were in the process of setting up some kind of magical emergency exit out of the Purple Zone using a bunch of glowing metal rods, while the two important guys kept the owners of the estate at bay. They also didn't suffer any casualties, which was something I was of two minds about. On one hand, reducing the number of dangerous aggressors aiming for the lives of my girlfriend and in-laws wasn't exactly a bad thing, but on the other hand, people dying was not only always a tragedy, but something I considered to be best avoided just in case it would escalate things and shift the world into a more grimdark direction, with considerably less plot armour to go around.

Anyhow, since they seemed to have everything handled over there, I moved my perspective over to Armband Guy... and found him in another Purple Zone. More alarmingly, he wasn't only inside the same one as Josh and the others, but he had Lord Grandpa right next to him.

"Chief, we have trouble," Judy called out to me, and I immediately snapped out of my Far Sight. While I was about 95 percent sure about what she wanted to tell me, I still waited for her to say it. "Lord Endymonion arrived at the scene and captured Robatto and Galatea. Elly said he is currently arguing with Josh about the nature of justice. Neige thinks that once they're done, the Magi are likely to take them into custody, as well."

"Well, crap," I muttered, my words laced with industrial-strength exasperation, following which I rubbed my deeply prickling temples and asked, "Did they find the class rep and Winged Ninja?"

"Give me a moment," Judy responded while tweaking the hinges of her glasses, which was how she could cycle between targets linked to her artifacts, and after a few long seconds of silence, she shook her head. "They're still locked up in the basement. I think the arch-mage focused on subduing Robatto first, so they haven't searched the building yet."

"Good, then I still have some wiggle room."

With that said, I pulled down the mask onto my face again, and I was about to give my girlfriend a suitably cool exit line when I was suddenly hit in the back hard enough that I almost tumbled forward.

"Ue-sama!"

The moment the tinkling voice resounded in my ears, my whole body froze up, only to then straighten itself with sheer force of annoyance. I glanced over my shoulder and found a completely naked little girl clinging to my back, with her arms linked around my neck. It might've been because the mask was hiding my currently quite irate expression, but she immediately flashed an ear-to-ear grin the moment our eyes met.

"Ichiko, let go of my neck."

She immediately followed my order and landed on the ground with the characteristic sound of bare feet meeting the floor.

"Look, Ue-sama, look! I did it! I already got a human fo— Owie!"

One well-placed forehead flick later the tiny troublemaker hunched over and used both of her hands to protect her forehead.

"Don't you *ue-sama* me! Why the hell are you naked again!? No, wait, I have a better question! Didn't I expressly tell you *not* to turn into a human yet?"

"But... I couldn't help it!" she retorted against my indignant words with a pitiful voice and a pair of large, tear-filled eyes. "I haven't had a real body for so long! How can you expect me to turn into something else for the first time?! That's just cruel!"

I was about to reward her back talk with yet another flick of the finger, but then my attention was grabbed by a single, positively chilling presence locking its attention onto me.

"Chief?" my dear assistant inquired with an innocent voice underlined by a pair of ice-cold eyes partially hidden behind her star-shaped glasses, and she pointed an accusative finger right out of the princess' repertoire at the still-very-naked little girl cowering in front of me. "Would you care to explain what's going on?"

First I glanced at her finger, then at the teary-eyed-yet-still-strangely-energetic girl, then at the Fauns standing a couple of steps behind her. I used my eyes to direct the unspoken question of "I told you idiots to keep an eye on the Chimera! What the hell were you doing!?" which they answered with shamefully averting their gazes, which pretty much meant, "W-we looked...." Feeling completely browbeaten by the situation, I finally returned my attention to my expectant girlfriend, and after carefully considering my options...

"It's a long story. I will explain later."

And just like that, I esca—, I mean I retre—, *cough*. What I'm trying to say, is that *I Phased away in a hurry to help poor class rep and Mike as soon as possible*. I mean, I had no choice in the matter; as a leader, it was my duty to do it right away, without wasting time on explaining unimportant things. Yes, it was perfectly reasonable.

God, I'm so dead...

CHAPTER 17

PART 1

"He's back!"

To my sincerest surprise, my arrival at the makeshift prison cell under the warehouse was met with excitement, of all things. Well, at least from Mike. Ammy was considerably less enthusiastic. I was about to greet them, but before I could do so, I was hit by a tremendous wave of... lack of vertigo. That was weird. Normally the more I teleported in a row, the worse it got, but this time there were absolutely no ill side effects present. I couldn't help but wonder, was that a good thing, such as a sign of my getting used to Phasing, or was it just a symptom of a kind of supernatural runner's high, and I would get completely plastered once I crashed?

I pondered this question longer than strictly necessary, as the class rep soon turned a disapproving frown at me, followed by an inquisitive, "I guess you're not going to explain how you can teleport in and out of this locked room at will."

I could have sworn that I had already done so (or rather, I'd already given an excuse), but since she asked, I figured I might as well be straightforward for once and shake my head.

"How come I'm not surprised?" she grumbled while idly sweeping aside a stray lock of hair hanging in front of her eyes. "Can you at least tell me where you got that sword? I don't think I've seen it before."

I was just about to dismiss her, but a short-yet-intense moment of consideration later I decided to keep being slightly more forthright and told her, "Long story short, the crazy huntress attacked me, so I took her sword, and now she's sitting in the base, tied up like a Christmas present. There's also some malarkey going on with the Chimera and the sword and Judy probably killing me once this is all over, but that's beside the point."

"{I beg to differ,}" came a series of deadpan-and-yet-quite-chilling words from the communicator, but for the time being I chose not to respond to her.

"Anyhow, I brought this to get him out of there, so I'd appreciate it if you took a step back."

That comment was aimed at the guy in the cage, yet Ammy also scampered behind me at the same time. I sent her an ever-so-slightly-dubious glance, and she gestured towards the padlock in return.

"Hurry up, Leo! Grandfather could get here any minute now!"

"Oh, that? Didn't Judy tell you?" I inquired as I raised the sword over my head and swung it at the bars in front of me, only for the blade to be nearly torn out of my numb grasp when it bounced off the metal. I couldn't help but blink in incomprehension and mutter, "That wasn't supposed to happen. Give me a minute."

Having said that, I immediately entered the weapon one more time using my phantom limb, and it didn't take long to figure out what the problem was. Just for context: the outer layer of the enchantment ball was responsible for the real-world effects of the weapon, including the whole cuts-everything-like-it's-made-of-lukewarm-butter thing. Normally that kind of stuff would be pretty impractical because it puts a lot of strain on the weapon, so to make it work, Ichiko would be turning the effect on and off in short bursts from the inside just before the edge would make contact for maximum efficiency. While the enchantment was still working as intended, with the tiny miko gone, there was no conductor present to operate it, and because the whole thing was designed with the idea of an annoying little girl calling the shots in it, there were no external ways to turn it on by design, ergo there was no iron bar slicing, either.

It was a bit of an issue, but not an insurmountable one, and I managed to jury-rig a temporary solution by emulating a command from the inside that would permanently put the sword at about 40 percent output. It had to be manually disabled after I was done using it, but hey, at least it worked. I also had a vague idea about reproducing and repurposing the complex behavioural-tree-type enchantment that used to be in the dead Chimera to emulate an automated switch, but it was a project for later.

I exited the extra-nonsensical space between spaces and shook my buzzing head to clear it a bit, and once I confirmed that the magic glow around the blade grew in intensity, I unceremoniously swung it again. This time the effect was much more satisfying, as while there was some resistance, I managed to cut cleanly through the iron bars with a series of high-pitched tinkling sounds reminiscent of tiny little cymbals. Once I confirmed that the enchantment was working, I repeated the cut from the other direction, and this time each *clink* was followed by a much louder *clank* filling the room as the bars fell to the wayside one by one.

I let my weapon down and observed my handiwork, which resulted in a large hole right next to the only door of the cage, big enough so that even Mister Minotaur could jump through it, let alone our captive.

"That... was awesome," said Celestial noted with eyes as wide as saucers, so I gave him a light wave that could be translated to a casual "All in a day's work" before I faced the class rep again.

"So as I tried to tell you before the technical difficulties: your gramps is already here."

"What?!"

Ammy's sudden exclamation (besides being so sudden it nearly made Mike fall on his butt mid-step as he was trying to get out of a cage) was so loud it made my ears ring. Or were they ringing to begin with? It was honestly hard to tell.

"It's exactly as I said," I reiterated while massaging my temple with my free hand. "He's already upstairs and put Lab Coat Guy in custody. Josh and the others, too, but that's beside the point."

"Then... what do we do now?" came the very, very insecure question from Mike, and I gave him an obligatory nod he might have misunderstood, based on the way he twitched when I looked at him.

"A good question, and the answer depends on a few variables. First off..." I paused as I faced away from him and followed it up with, "Dormouse, are you still listening?"

A long and decidedly petulant moment of silence later...

"{Yes, I'm here.}"

"Great. Are Lord Grandpa and Co. still in the Purple Zone?"

"{... Yes.}"

"Can you tell Josh and the others to stall them as long as they can?"

"{Can I? Wouldn't that involve explaining things to them? I was under the impression we no longer did that around here.}"

I closed my eyes for a moment, and then told her, "I promise once we are done here, we'll sit down, and I'll tell you everything about the sword and the kid, but we really don't have time for that now. Would you please do as I asked?"

There was another long beat of silence on the line, but at last my girlfriend relented with a still audibly sulky, "{You're lucky I'm a professional.}"

"I sure am." After responding so, I gestured for my increasingly-more-confused companions to follow after me, only to stop and point at the broken staff by the cage. "Don't forget that."

Ammy seemed affronted by the very idea that she would do so, yet she didn't utter a single word and simply hurried over to pick up the pieces. In the meantime I walked up to the door and, with three quick slashes, I cut a triangular hole around the doorknob, and then rammed the door itself with my shoulder. It flew right open with a loud bang, leading us into another slightly larger, yet just as poorly lit room. It was likely used for temporary storage by the looks of it, as it had a bunch of large plastic boxes filled with various raw materials and components, including one particularly eye-catching container full of porcelain doll heads. I... honestly didn't even want to know.

Mike meekly followed after me like a lost duckling, and we were soon joined by the class rep clutching the remains of her destroyed weapon.

"This way."

Following my lead, we passed through the room and out into a long corridor filled with air that was somehow staler than the rooms themselves. At one end of it, we could see some light seeping in through the half-open doors at the end of a short metal staircase, and it didn't take a genius to logic out that it was the way to the ground floor of the warehouse. We, naturally, went in the opposite direction.

"So, errm... What's the plan?" Mike asked in a voice tense as an over-tuned guitar.

"For now, just follow my lead."

My answer didn't exactly reassure him, but I didn't really care at the moment, as we'd just reached an unassuming door near the other end of the corridor. I was vaguely familiar with this place due to all the time I spent observing Lab Coat Guy, and this time I didn't need to cut my way in, as the door was left unlocked. As I opened it, we were hit by a gust of extra-stale, musty air, but I walked in all the same, and after a moment of fiddling I found the light switch. The small room, now lit by a single light bulb hanging from a plain wire nailed to the ceiling, wasn't much larger than my bathroom, and it had unplastered walls with the red bricks clearly visible.

"What are we doing here? Shouldn't we be escaping?" came the next question from an increasingly impatient class rep, and if she still had her glasses, I was sure she would have pushed them up the bridge of her nose about five times by now.

"That's what we're doing right now," I answered a tad absentmindedly as I was counting the bricks from the light switch. "According to what I've heard, every self-respecting mad scientist must have an emergency escape route in their lair. As it happens, Lab Coat Guy's is here."

"Seriously?"

She was understandably skeptical, but in my defense, I literally parroted the resident mad scientist's words when he described this room to his fembot assistant. More importantly, though, after a couple of tries, I finally managed to find the right brick, and after pressing down on it, the wall in front of us let out a series of clicking noises before a whole segment of it detached from the rest. I grabbed the edges of the secret door and slid it aside, revealing a long, narrow tunnel; its completely smooth walls were unexpectedly well lit by evenly placed red emergency lights. After making sure there was nothing dangerous inside, I turned around and knocked on the displaced panel.

"Fully mechanical fake wall. Makes it harder for Magi to detect it, if they can do so at all. It should lead to the basement of an apartment building a couple of blocks away from here."

"Wait, stop! Hold on for a moment!" I raised a brow at Ammy's abrupt outburst, and it went even higher when she actually reflexively tried to tweak her still-missing glasses. Once she realized there was nothing on her face, she forcefully waved her hand and continued with, "How did you even know about this?"

"Need I remind you that I'm an information trader? It's my job to know these things."

"Okay, wait! I just remembered your *thing*; that was the wrong question. Let me try this again." She paused here to take a long breath, and then asked, "Since *when* did you know about this escape route?"

"I learned about it when Lab Coat Guy moved in," I told her the truth, but it only seemed to make her angrier.

"Then why didn't we use this route to get Michael out?"

"{Good question,}" my dear assistant agreed, much to my chagrin.

"We really don't have the time for this, but for your interest, here are but a few of the reasons: Number one, I don't know the exact end point of this tunnel, only that it's at an apartment complex. Number two, even if I knew the precise location, the door at the other end only opens from the inside. Number three, even if I knew where to go and figured out a way to open the door from the outside, I couldn't do it because we had to mount this rescue operation ASAP before the Assembly's investigators arrived. Is that explanation good enough for you?"

The last question was aimed at both the girl in front of me and the one on the other end of the telepathic communicator, yet neither of them said a thing, which I interpreted as agreement.

"Good, now get in there. I'll close the door on this side. Once you reach the other end of the tunnel, go into the basement, close the door behind you, and lay low for about half an hour. After that..." At this stage of the instructions, I took out my wallet and pointed at the hapless Celestial. "You'll be leaving first. Even if Lab Coat Guy talks, his interrogation is going to take a while, so even if you happen to run into some Magi on the street, they shouldn't be looking for you yet. Here's some spare change; take a cab to the station and then ride a train home. Try not to draw attention to yourself in the process." I paused for a second to let them digest this, and then I turned to the class rep and took out another bill from my wallet, "You should come outside about an hour or so after this guy's gone. Call a cab and have it take you to the School. With some luck, I should be able to resolve the whole situation by the time you get there. Are we clear?"

The two of them nodded with different levels of enthusiasm (or the lack thereof), so I shooed them into the tunnel, though not before taking the two halves of her staff from Ammy.

"This would draw too much attention. I'll take it back to the base with me and will hand it back to you later."

She agreed without any back talk, and after one last warning, I watched them walk down the narrow tunnel one after the other before I unceremoniously slid the fake wall back to its original location and locked it into place with a satisfying click. With this, our original objective from before this incident ballooned out was accomplished, though the day was far from over. Thinking so, I turned on my heel, left the small, moldy room behind, and headed towards the other end of the corridor and the door leading to the warehouse, determined to use the little time I had before the Purple Zone got dispelled and Lord Grandpa or his goons barged in here to its fullest.

PART 2

There was a loud thump on the door leading into the secluded office in the corner of the building, followed by stifled cursing. For now, the good old chair-under-the-doorknob trick was holding, but I didn't know for how long, and I really needed more time, because goddammit, Lab Coat Guy was criminally disorganized. I'd been searching for minutes, but I couldn't find what I was looking for in the mess of random papers in the old, rickety filing cabinet in front of me. I had, however, found the guy's childhood photo album. Why anyone would store that next to important documents was entirely beyond me.

"The door is locked," announced a voice on the other side, followed by another impact that made the entire doorframe creak.

"Wait, look. There's a shadow. Someone's inside," said another oddly wooden voice, no doubt a placeholder Magi dispatched to secure the premises.

"Stand back. I'll blast it open," declared a third voice, and that was my cue to leave.

Since I still couldn't find what I wanted, I decided to screw it all, and while making sure that I was still holding on to all the other miscellaneous-yet-possibly-useful junk I'd collected on the way, I extended my phantom limb and Phased away without any further ado. A short-yet-long moment later, I arrived within the familiar confines of the main hall inside the secret base. My arrival was then announced by a loud bang, following which the piece of furniture I'd carried with me began to teeter on its edge before abruptly falling over with a deafening impact that echoed for several seconds in the open space.

After getting over my first surprise, I looked around, and my eyes immediately met with about a dozen completely baffled stares directed at me.

"What? Have you guys never seen a filing cabinet before?"

My jest to ease the mood fell on deaf ears, so I opted to stop caring and simply walked over to the nearest Faun and dumped everything in my hands save for Onikiri onto him.

"Take these to the recreational area. I'll sort through them later."

"Was that Amelia's staff?" Judy asked as she walked over, still wearing the communicator glasses.

"Yeah, I'm holding on to it for the time being."

"It's broken," she noted with a disinterested voice while still edging towards me.

"Stuff happened. I already promised her that I'll help her fix it."

"Very gallant of you," came the next comment, but then she suddenly pounced forward and grabbed hold of my free hand with a triumphant "Caught you!"

"Um... Yeah, you did. It wasn't very hard," I noted with just a hint of bewilderment. "For the record, I wasn't planning on going anywhere for the time being."

"Better be safe than sorry," she declared with an unnecessary amount of conviction, and then she dramatically took off her glasses and pocketed them before she reaffirmed her grip on my sleeve and began to pull me towards the benches. "Now come quietly and explain the situation."

"Sure, sure."

My compliance apparently didn't reassure her one bit, as she kept an iron grip on my arm until we arrived at the aforementioned benches. There, Rinne was still sitting ramrod straight with her arms tied behind her back, and Pip was still trying to do his grimmest guard impression behind her, but now we also had an extra addition in the form of a small girl sitting with her legs crossed. At first she seemed to be immersed in a conversation with Mountain Girl, but when our eyes met, she immediately perked up and began waving at me with a beaming expression. Thankfully she was actually wearing clothes this time around, namely one of my backup tracksuits I kept around as a makeshift disguise in case I needed to infiltrate somewhere in a hurry. This one was coloured light blue, and it was a few sizes bigger than my normal clothes so that it could be worn over another outfit if necessary. Needless to say, it was so oversized on her that I was fairly sure she was only wearing the jacket, and yet it completely covered her.

Once we got closer, the overly friendly sword spirit gave me a small bow while still sitting and addressed me directly.

"Welcome back, Ue-sama!"

"Uh... yes. Welcome back?" Rinne followed suit, though her greeting was about as natural as a PVC pipe.

"Here we go, Chief, round two," my dear assistant prompted me with a tug on my hand. "Introduce us."

I glanced at her, then at the still-grinning little girl, and in the end I couldn't help but let a groan escape my throat.

"Are you serious, Dormouse? You're aware that she is a hundreds-of-years-old sword piloting a Chimera who looks like a nine-year-old kid?"

"Yes, and you should be aware of what kind of world we're living in and what tropes apply to her. Now, stop stalling and introduce us as you did with her."

I was really way too tired for this, but if it would give her some peace of mind, I figured I might as well comply. That didn't mean I would do it happily, though.

"Oh, fine. So Dormouse, this is Azusa Ichiko, the ex–sword spirit of Onikiri."

"It's a pleasure to meet you, Dormouse-san!" the tiny girl in the oversized jacket cut in with another shining smile, much to my assistant's annoyance.

"You see, she is my girlfriend," I told her, at which point her smile immediately disappeared and she gave us another small bow.

"Please forgive me, Dormouse-sama. I was unaware of your affiliation with Ue-sama."

"Hold your horses for a moment," I called out with a steadily rising sense of exasperation, and waited for her to stop bowing before telling her, "Her actual name is Judy Sennoma; only I'm calling her Dormouse."

"Ah, I see. So it's Judy-sama's true name! Please forgive my carelessness." She gave another small bow, this time aimed at my girlfriend in particular, but when she noticed that she was giving her a harsh look, she quickly muttered, "Is... Is my address still wrong? Would you prefer Sennoma-sama? Or maybe Sennoma-ue?"

Judy kept staring at the clueless Ichiko for a few more seconds before her expression softened and she glanced up at me with a defeated look in her eyes.

"Is she always like that?"

"She's been like that since I first met her. Or rather, the third time I met her. It's complicated." That explanation obviously didn't satisfy her, so I added, "She's something of a moe archetype, and while slightly annoying, she's mostly harmless."

"If you say so."

I figured we were more or less done with the basic anti-harem counter-measures, so I lightly cleared my throat as a way to signal that we were moving on.

"Say, how about you two figure out the proper way to address you while I put this away?"

Saying so, I lightly waved the wrapped-up sword in my hand around to indicate what I was talking about, but instead of letting me go, Judy only clamped down on me harder.

"Before you do that, why don't you first explain the sequence of events that resulted in a sentient sword becoming a young girl?"

"Rinne would also like to know," Mountain Girl commented on the side, and she was so focused on the blade in my hand she even forgot to correct herself. My girlfriend didn't let up, either, and for some odd reason even the tiny miko was looking at me with expectant eyes (even though she was, you know, *there when it happened*), so I figured I might as well get it over with.

"Fine. In short, Ichiko here originally wasn't a sword, but was put into Onikiri as a last resort. When she tried to merge with me, I in turn interfaced with the enchantment housing her; we expelled the sludge surrounding her from the outside."

"Sludge?" Rinne muttered, and the little girl immediately provided an explanation.

"It was the miasma!"

"Yeah, and once it was removed, she stopped burning and became human-sized again."

"Wait, what was that about burning?" came the next question from Judy, who at this point was unreservedly taking notes on her phone.

"Right, I kind of skimmed over this part, but the first time we met, so to speak, she was this enormous, burning demon thing only wearing a bunch of—"

"Kyaaa! Please don't reveal my shameful past!" Ichiko interrupted me with quite a panicked expression, but I could only shake my head in disbelief.

"You act like you have a shred of shame, you unrepentant exhibitionist."

For a moment it seemed like she wanted to object, but then she stopped mid-breath, and instead she leaned over to the tied-up woman sitting beside her.

"Psst, Rinne-san? What is an *exhibitionist*?"

"Rinne isn't entirely sure," she replied a little absentmindedly before proposing, "Isn't it the person who manages an art gallery?"

"It could be..." the smaller girl concluded with a thoughtful hum before turning back and pointing a hand at me, with about half of the jacket's sleeve limply dangling at the end, and declared, "I'm not a manager of art galleries!"

During the ensuing beat of silence, I seriously contemplated whether I should correct her or not, and in the end decided that it was simply too much of a hassle, so instead I just continued with my explanation of the events.

"So as I was saying," I began, completely ignoring the tiny miko's still-outstretched hand, "Getting rid of the sludge had some unforeseen effects, so she couldn't stay in the sword. Since the only other place I could put her was the body of the Chimera, I transferred her there. Then, contrary to my explicit instructions, she turned into a girl. End of story."

"I see," Judy whispered under her breath while typing, only to look up and say, "I have two questions."

"Only two?"

"For now."

"Go figure," I whispered under my breath, sighed, and told her, "Ask away then."

She lightly nodded, and after another glance at her phone, she began with, "You said that she turned into a girl 'against your instructions.' Does that mean she can turn into something else?"

"Why don't you ask her?"

Following my advice, my assistant turned a pair of questioning eyes at the small girl, and the moment she realized the attention was on her, she instantly brightened up.

"Ah, you see, Sennoma-ue..."

"Just Judy will do."

"Oh, then Judy-ue, you see, my maternal grandmother was a pure-blooded kitsune, and even though I wasn't able to do it when I was alive..." At this point she abruptly paused and began to wave her hands around while spluttering something among the lines of, "I mean, before I was Onikiri! I don't mean I'm dead now! At least I don't think I am... But anyway, this body is much more suited for the transformation arts that Grandma taught me when I was alive, or not dead, or... not not alive?"

To her credit, my girlfriend's deadpan expression didn't waver for even a second, and once Ichiko fell silent, she only glanced up at me with the word, "Kitsune?"

"Japanese fox girls," I replied off the cuff, but it only made her imperceptibly furrow her brows.

"Japanese? As opposed to what?"

"Chinese fox girls?" I proposed, only to then roll my eyes when she continued to give me a skeptical stare down. "Don't look at me like that; it's a thing. I think they are different subspecies of the same phantasmal species."

"So it's like the difference between Western dragons and Eastern dragons."

"Yeah, sure," I agreed, though for the love of me I couldn't recall what she was talking about.

"Noted," she, well, noted before continuing with, "And how exactly did this whole 'I moved her from the sword to this dead monster' process work?"

"It's, uh... kind of complicated. It had to do with the supernatural stratum and the customizing of the controller enchantment in the Chimera and then Phasing her from one body to the next and then jiggling her back and forth on the q-axis until she stuck, and a whole lot of other unintuitive crap. I'll tell you the process in detail after today's madness is over."

"Fine," she relented, if a bit grudgingly, and once she finished typing on her phone, she put it away and turned her attention to the two in front of us. "What are we going to do about these two?"

"Honestly, it depends. First, I have a few questions for them." When they heard that, both Rinne and Ichika gave me expectant-and-yet-simultaneously-worried looks. I inhaled a deep breath, and by the time I let it out, I felt clear on what I wanted to ask. "All right. So just to make sure we're on the same page, I want you to remember this: you guys broke into our base, injured my sister's retainers, and caused a lot of collateral damage. I think just the fact that you were only disarmed and captured is lenient enough, let alone all the trouble I went through to help you out."

That last comment was obviously aimed at the ex-sword, and she repeatedly nodded her head in acknowledgment. Mountain Girl also followed her example, but that was neither here nor there.

"In short, if you want to stay in my good graces, I ask, and you answer with perfect sincerity. Are we clear on that?" They agreed in unison, so I immediately posed my first question. "First off, you're now aware that attacking us was wrong, right?"

The two briefly glanced at each other and soon mumbled a disheartened yes, more or less at the same time.

"I can't hear it."

"It was wrong," Rinne stated in a low voice, following which Ichiko added a similarly disheartened, "Sorry."

"Good. Next, I want to know just how much each of you was responsible for that." I paused for effect here and focused on Mountain Girl. "If I recall correctly, you mentioned something about 'becoming one,' but I can distinctly remember the two of you talking to each other when she was still inside the sword."

"Oh, that's easy!" the physically-and-mentally-younger-yet-objectively-way-older girl exclaimed after a giggle. "It's like... uh..." I waited for her to actually explain herself, but she just crossed her arms and no matter how long I waited, she didn't speak up.

"Let Rinne try." This time we focused on the other captive, and after a moment of thinking she told us, "It's like taking two eggs, and breaking them into the same bowl. The whites become one big pool, but the two yolks remain separate."

"Yes, that's it! See, I told you it's easy!" the mini miko exclaimed with so much enthusiasm one would think it was her who came up with that. "Rinne-san's analogies are much easier to understand than Ue-sama's."

"Hush, you." After chiding her, the overly friendly little girl fell silent, and I considered their words for a while. "So does that mean that while you retained your sense of self, you also partially merged together?" The two of them mulled over my words and then nodded more or less at the same time. "Okay, so which one of you was responsible for all the raving about killing and blood?"

There was a very, very long moment of silence hanging in the air until Ichiko meekly raised her hand.

"That... was mostly me," she confessed in a meek voice, but a second later she forcefully added, "But it was the miasma's fault!"

"The miasma, huh? Okay, then who was responsible for all of those rude comments?"

"That... that was also me," came the next disheartened answer from the smaller girl. "But, but the...!"

"Yes, yes, it was the miasma, I get it," I cut in with a sigh. "Final question: Who was responsible for being a glutton?"

"Oh, oh! That was *definitely* Rinne-san!" Ichiko declared in high spirits, much to her previous wielder's chagrin.

"No, Rinne wasn't!"

"N-nonsense! How could I be responsible when I couldn't even eat? I was a sword, baka! Swords don't eat!"

While the two argued, Judy subtly tugged on my sleeve to get my attention.

"Chief, shouldn't you be asking another question of them?"

"... Sorry, but I don't know what you mean."

My dear girlfriend gave me her deadpan 2.0 look, which was at least 20 percent deadpanner than its predecessor, and after sending one last glance at the commotion by our side, she stood on tiptoes and whispered, "*Ouyay ouldshay askyay ichwhay oneyay asway interestedyay inyay ouyay.*"

"Wait, what are you...?" I blurted out by reflex, only for things to finally click together a second later, "Oh, right. Pig Latin. It's been a while." After muttering so, I spent a few seconds untangling her words, which resulted in a tired sigh on my end. "Do I really have to? You've already set the basic anti-harem countermeasures, and considering all that happened today, I don't think pushing it even harder would be effective. Please let it go for the time being."

It was also around this time that I was starting to get fed up with the argument unfolding in front of us, so I pointedly cleared my throat, and when that didn't work, let out a not particularly loud yet quite forceful "Cut it out, you two!"

Half a second later, our one-and-a-half captives were both sitting ramrod straight and looking forward, with an innocent expression that would've given newborn pandas a run for their money. I considered my options for a while longer, and in the end decided that even if she was no longer super-creepy, letting Mountain Girl loose was not a good idea, and as for Ichiko... well, she might've looked cute as a button at the moment, but let's not forget that she was technically a Chimera, or rather, about a third of one, as bits and pieces of the other half were still lying on the ground near the training area. Either way, letting her go was not a good idea.

"I've decided what to do with you two. Mountain Girl?" The currently somewhat lethargic huntress slightly perked up when she heard me calling her nickname, and I looked her straight in the eye before telling her, "I'm sorry to say, but until things calm down a little, I'm afraid I have to insist that you remain our guest for the time being."

"I understand."

The way she immediately conceded took me aback for a second, but I was already on a roll, so I acknowledged her with a curt nod and turned to the mini miko, who for some odd reason was looking at me with positively sparkling eyes.

"What about me, Ue-sama?"

I opened my mouth, only to close it again, and then some more mulling over later I decided on telling her, "For a start, I believe you still owe me for putting up with all your nonsense and even helping you out in the end, so—"

"Do I have to work? I'm fine with that! I'm good at cleaning, and small tasks, and cooking, and... uh... maybe not cooking after all, but anything that requires attention! Mother always said I had a great eye for details!"

For a second or five I didn't know how to react to her interruption, but at the end of the day I decided to just shrug a tad indifferently.

"You know what? Sure. Do you want to pay back the favor? Start by helping me find the incriminating evidence in that filing cabinet."

"Understood, Ue-sama!"

She jumped to her feet without any further ado. Even though she was still only wearing the tracksuit jacket, it actually reached down to her ankles, so there was no danger of another flashing incident. She did look gosh darn comical, though, but it didn't stop her from nimbly skipping past us and rushing towards the cabinet I'd surreptitiously appropriated without even waiting for me to explain what she should be looking for. I let my shoulders droop in resignation and gestured for Pip to listen up and then pointed at the still-seated Rinne.

"Take her to one of the smaller rooms for the time being. You can unbind her, but make sure she's still under strict surveillance." I paused here while looking for another Faun, and eventually I settled on Vurrok. "As for you, please take this sword off my hands and store it somewhere else."

I held out the hand holding the wrapped-up Onikiri, and I don't want to sound too dramatic or anything, but it took way more effort than expected to peel my fingers off the grip. They were throbbing like hell, as well, so that probably wasn't good. I bore it with a stiff upper lip so that I wouldn't worry Judy, and once the Faun received it with almost reverent motions, I gently pulled Judy along and headed towards the filing cabinet and the little girl currently spelunking in it. We got about halfway there when she suddenly jumped to her bare feet with a comically overexaggerated look of awe on her face, and she immediately dashed over to our side.

"Look, Ue-sama! Look! I found this evidence! I'm sure it's incredibly incriminating!"

Proclaiming so, she pushed the thick rectangular book in her hands towards us and opened it wide so that we could take a good look. Judy, after overcoming her first surprise, leaned forward to scrutinize the contents for a short while before she looked back at me.

"Who's that?"

"Lab Coat Guy, I presume," I answered off the cuff, following which my girlfriend resumed her scrutiny of the Polaroid photos in the album.

"He looked surprisingly cute as a kid," she mused, but I let her comment go in one ear and out the other as I tapped on the enthusiastic little girl's head with a single finger.

"This wasn't what I was looking for. There should be a magically enchanted piece of paper in a manila folder in there. It's hard to miss; it has a big, red thumbprint on the first page."

"Oh, I see!" she muttered while rubbing the spot where I'd poked her, even though this time I was fairly gentle. "I'll go find it!"

Just like that, she snapped the photo album shut and skipped back from whence she came, and clumsily dragged one of the drawers open, which was actually pretty difficult considering that the cabinet was still sitting on its side.

"She's certainly enthusiastic," my dearest assistant noted in a tone that was just a touch disgruntled. "One would almost think she's trying to get into your good graces."

"Well, she probably is," I answered, only to finally notice the way she was looking at me, and subtly roll my eyes. "It's not for the reason you think, though."

"Really? So you can tell me what I think?"

"I can only guess, but I'd bet it's something harem-related again."

All of a sudden she squeezed my arm and exclaimed (or at the very least raised her volume a teensy bit), "Impressive. Keep this up, and soon you may not only attract a lot of women but actually understand them."

"Oh, ha ha. Very funny."

"Thank you, I practice a lot," Judy quipped back without a shred of shame. "But if it's not related to your harem protagonist aura, then why else would she be this eager?"

I instinctively wanted to point out that, unlike Josh, I didn't actually have any such aura, but getting bogged down in another silly argument about that wouldn't have been particularly productive, so I swallowed my indignation.

"Probably because she wants to prove herself useful so that I won't turn her off."

"Does that mean you already turn her on?"

I let the silence linger in the air for a moment, and then I turned a pair of stern brows towards my girlfriend and firmly warned her, "Dormouse, please stop doing that, or I swear to god I'll flick your forehead so hard even our theoretical future kids will feel it." I kept up the pressure until she finally averted her eyes with a click of her tongue, at which point I clarified, "Before I put her in the empty Chimera, we made a deal, and I jury-rigged an off switch onto the enchantment so that I can put her into suspended animation if she doesn't behave herself."

"So you have a form of control over her? That sounds somewhat like a familiar," Judy pondered aloud, followed up by an especially deadpan, "You're not allowed to have her call you master."

"I never planned to do that to begin with," I protested, and it was around this point when our slow, meandering, hand-in-hand walk reached its destination.

In front of us, Ichiko had already taken out all the documents from the already-half-open drawer, and at the moment she was trying, and failing, to pull out another one. She struggled with it for a while more before she let out an angry huff and looked around. When our eyes met, she perked up for a moment, but then she hesitated, and she conspicuously looked away and continued her search. In the end her eyes settled on Karukk, who was still keeping an eye on her, as per my instructions. Once their gazes met, it immediately made the proverbial light bulb light up over her head with an idea (whether good or bad, only time would tell), and she pointed a flappy-sleeved hand towards the Faun.

"You there! Evil minion of the underworld!"

The hapless evil minion could only blink in surprise at first, after which he glanced my way. I lightly shrugged my shoulders as a way to tell him to react however he wanted, and so after a bit of hesitation, he looked back at her and pointed a finger at his own chest.

"The little one talks to me?"

"Yes!" the little girl exclaimed in apparent delight as she put her hands on her nonexistent hips. "Come, minion! O-kami-sama tasked me with a mission of the utmost importance, and your brutish muscles are in need! Hurry and help me raise this cabinet!"

At this point Karukk sent me a more overt glance, and after some consideration, I gave him a nod. The guy let out a tired sigh, but otherwise didn't complain, and obediently walked over to the filing cabinet and easily upended it so that she would have easy access to the drawers. Ichiko flashed me a triumphant smile, followed by a quick bow at the still slightly confused Faun, and then she immediately resumed her search.

It was only when she was once again completely absorbed in her job that Judy tugged on my hand to get my attention.

"Did Dr. Robatto really put the contract he made with Lord Endymonion into a shabby place like that?"

"I figure he was going for a hide-a-forest-in-the-tree kind of approach."

"Chief, I'm fairly sure that's the other way around."

"Whatever, I'm tired. Cut me some slack."

"Fine, but just this once," she responded, her previous cheekiness back in full force again. "What are you planning to do with the contract if it's really there?"

"I plan to engage in some aggressive negotiations with Lord Grandpa and Lab Coat Guy, and I need the leverage."

"With both of them?"

"At the same time," I answered, and after closing my eyes for a second for a quick Far Glance, I added, "The latter is already being escorted to the School, so I'll wait until he's there."

That said, since I was already using Far Sight, I figured I might as well take a quick peek at the others, too. Mike was... in a taxi. Does that mean that more than half an hour had passed already? Either way, he wasn't followed, so that's good. The class rep was still holed up at the bottom of a stairwell, presumably near the exit of the emergency escape tunnel, and she was furiously texting someone. One blur of the scenery later I was looking at Josh and the others, who were all out of their Magiforms and were sitting in a black minivan along with Pascal. They all seemed thoroughly uncomfortable, but on the other hand, they weren't cuffed or otherwise bound.

The same could not be said about Lab Coat Guy, who was in something that looked like a modern version of a yoke, while his fembot companion had it even worse, with her legs chained, arms tied back in an honest-to-goodness armbinder, and a thick, magically glowing metal collar around her neck. Not only that, but they were each surrounded by two men in black, complete with old-school sunglasses and those earpieces with the coiled wires.

Overall, while the situation wasn't ideal, at least it was no longer wildly out of control. That was progress, I supposed.

"So what's the plan?" Judy's question made me raise a brow, so she clarified, "I meant to ask, are you going to use your new identity to strike up a deal with them?"

"Nah, that's not going to work," I told her with a sigh. "It might still work on the Knights in the future, and I can probably make it work with the Celestials as long as I can make sure Mike doesn't report anything incriminating, but Lab Coat Guy already saw me before and after I put the mask on. If I show up wearing that, he would immediately spill the beans."

"That means you are going there to negotiate as yourself?"

"Well, kind of." She looked unexpectedly curious, so after a few short seconds I gave in and told her, "Lord Grandpa was the one who pushed the title onto me, so let's see how he likes when Leonard Blackcloak the Chimera Slayer pays him a visit..."

If we were at a sitcom's set, this would have been the ominous moment when the *dun-dun-duuuun!* music played. Instead of that, there was a loud metallic crashing noise ringing out not a moment after I finished speaking, as the little girl in front of us accidentally toppled the cabinet. Then, it was followed by a flustered "Aaaah! Evil minion, help! It fell over again!"

So much for setting the right mood, I supposed. Oh well, at least I tried.

PART 3

"Quick, clear the way! Put those away already!"

"Yes, sir!"

Following the bellows of the senior Mage, a dozen or so men and women of various ages immediately redoubled their efforts to move the various odds and ends out of the room. The School under Blue Cherry High was as busy as an anthill, and while the middle-aged man giving instructions was dressed from head to toe like a ye olde wizard (sans the pointy hat, of course), the younger generation doing the busywork around him were mostly wearing business casual, no doubt due to being called in due to the emergency.

The School, chiefly a research institute, was apparently not only suffering from a distinct lack of combat-capable magic users, but also of spaces for holding involuntary guests for an indefinite period of time, and by the looks of it, they were currently busy freeing up one of the lesser-used storage rooms for that purpose. As for its prospective inhabitants, they were already on their way, just exiting the main elevator.

The small procession was headed by Lord Amadeus himself, flanked by two of his generic men-in-black agent types. His left eye was no longer bloodshot, but instead he had enormous dark bags under his eyes, which slightly spoiled the dapper-elderly-gentleman look he was going for with his khaki suit and panama hat. Behind those three walked Lab Coat Guy and Galatea, with two more men built like wardrobes in black keeping an eye on them from behind. The harbinger of *sentai* shenanigans was still dressed in the same outfit he'd worn during the fight in front of the warehouse, including the plastic clogs, but with a magically glowing yoke around his neck, his hair even more frizzled than usual, yet his eyes still boring holes in the back of the arch-mage walking in front of him. Besides him, his android assistant had an indifferent expression on her face, apparently only mildly inconvenienced by the bondage gear restraining her.

Finally, a couple of steps behind the first group, there was Josh, Snowy, Angie, and the princess, with Armband Guy closing the procession. Unlike the people at the front, the second group appeared considerably more relaxed, even if they were just as silent. It was also worth noting that, although they no longer wore their protective gear, their Magiformers weren't confiscated. But then again, considering everyone present could transform and use their abilities without one, their captors might simply not have cared much about them.

As Lord Grandpa entered the room, one of the junior Magi, a young woman wearing a knit sweater, almost bumped into him while carrying some kind of metallic instrument with a couple of glowing runes on it. One quick apology later she scampered away like a mouse that had just run into a cat, allowing the elderly Mage to walk in and direct a critical look at his surroundings.

"Paul?" he called out in a raspy, tired voice, and the moment he did so, the middle-aged Mage immediately rushed to his side.

"Please excuse us, milord. We tried our best, but there just wasn't enough time. I've already asked for help from the maintenance division, and Mikhail said they would bring over some furniture from the second-floor lounge, but they haven't arrived yet."

By the looks of it, the head of the School already expected that something like this would happen, and after a few short seconds, he pointed towards the corner of the room and said," For the time being, I reckon you should leave those boxes behind. Our guests must be tired; we should at least provide some amenities so they may not be forced to sit on the ground."

"Yes, milord." The Magi equivalent of a middle manager nodded at once and began barking new orders to his hapless subordinates.

In the meantime, Lord Grandpa turned around with a weary expression and observed the guests behind him.

"Please do excuse the spartan conditions, but as you could already hear, this is the best our School could provide on such short notice. I am afraid I must insist that you stay in this room for the time being."

"How long are we talking about?" Josh asked back without reservations, probably still too high on adrenaline from the battle and his prior argument with the man to care much about etiquette.

"Until the investigation concludes," the old man responded with a thin smile that didn't touch his eyes. "It should not take more than a few days."

"Are... Are we in trouble?" came the next, unusually timid question from Angie, partially hidden behind Joshua's back.

"It all depends on the results of our investigation," Lord Grandpa responded in a diplomatic tone, but a few moments later he casually added,

"Take solace in the fact that no matter what, you are in nowhere near as much trouble as the young man over there."

Sensing that the comment was aimed at him, Lab Coat Guy let out an angry huff, but otherwise didn't say anything in his own defense. After that, the arch-mage turned to Armband Guy.

"Pascal, please look after the needs of our guests. That, of course, includes her, as well." He indicated the silently glaring fembot, and then looked at the resident mad scientist in turn. "As for you, I am afraid we need to have a serious talk. In private."

Lab Coat Guy didn't object (not that he had much of a choice in the matter), and after a few more short instructions, Josh and Co., along with Armband Guy, the fembot, and two burly guys in black got settled down in the room while Lord Grandpa and the rest left in a hurry. Lab Coat Guy was escorted to the elevator, and they rode it to the bottom level of the underground complex. Then, once the automatic doors opened, the rebellious *sentai* scientist spoke up for the first time.

"Uncle?"

On the other side of the doors, the portly old man let out a familiar yet still just as annoying "O-ho-ho." By the looks of it, he was completely unfettered, let alone yoked like his nephew.

"Hello, Friedrich. I'm happy to see that you're relatively unharmed considering the..." Peabody paused at this point to direct a conspicuous glance at the arch-mage and finished with a heavy, "... circumstances."

"What are you doing here?"

The words leaving Lab Coat Guy's mouth were much less spoken than hissed out, and the implicit sense of betrayal made the old man's customary smile falter for a second.

"My old friend came to me to advocate in your stead, young man," Lord Grandpa noted on the side with a voice so dry it would make most deserts hang their heads in shame.

"O-ho-ho, that's right," the nurse responded with a jovial, if slightly stiff, chuckle, but then he heaved a shallow sigh and continued in a somber voice. "Friedrich, you know that I'll support you no matter what, but there are some lines that should never, ever be crossed. Once you do that... the best I can do is to try to mitigate some of the damage."

The yoked man looked upon his uncle with an odd mixture of defiance and trepidation, but ultimately remained silent. Sensing the mood, the arch-mage shook his head and strode forward with heavy steps.

"Come, gentlemen. Let us continue our discussion in private; such things should not be uttered in the open, for there may be privy eyes even within these walls."

Peabody nodded in agreement and fell in line with him, while Lab Coat Guy followed along, lacking any choice in the matter. They all made their way into the heavily warded office of the head of the School, leaving the pair of sunglasses-wearing agent types outside. Oddly enough, the entire room was completely cleaned out, save for the large mahogany desk, the padded chair behind it, and a couple of cabinets on the side. It was most likely the result of the internal investigation conducted during the day. Either way, this meant that the two guests had nowhere to sit once Lord Grandpa planted his butt onto the only available seat. As such, Lab Coat Guy stood in front of the desk, while Peabody came to a stop by the side of the same desk, slightly closer to the seated old man than his nephew, a clear reflection of the current dynamic between the three if there ever was one.

"I have to confess, this was arguably one of the longest days of my life," the arch-mage broke the developing silence with a casual comment that still managed to raise the tension in the room. "As such, I will refrain from mincing my words. Friedrich. Did you break into this office last night?"

The man in the middle stared at the elder behind the desk in disbelief for a moment before his face twisted into an expression of disgust, followed by a barely stifled, derisive chuckle.

"Kihihi... You say you won't pussyfoot around, yet you still ask something you already know. Hypocrite."

"A simple yes or no would have sufficed," the old Mage noted with a disapproving scowl. "Considering your words were an indirect admission of guilt, I have only one question left for you: Where are the contents of my safe?"

"Kihihi. Well, wouldn't you like to know?"

The provocative reply very nearly blew Lord Grandpa's fuse, but then the school nurse quickly inserted himself into the conversation.

"This isn't a joking matter, Friedrich. I know that there was some friction between you and Amadeus, but going as far as taking his Grimoire Key? What on earth were you thinking?"

The youngest man in the room was just about to give another flippant response, but then he finally registered his uncle's question, and his words immediately got trapped in his throat.

"Wait, hold on! Hold on for a moment!" he exclaimed while waving his yoked hands in a desperate (and simultaneously a little comical) display. "I don't know anything about that!"

Lord Grandpa raised a critical brow at the flailing man's expense and reiterated in a low, level voice.

"You broke into my office."

"Yes, I did, but I don't know anything about the key! I wouldn't even know where to look for it!"

"It was in the safe," the arch-mage stated dryly. "The safe that you incidentally emptied."

"I didn't! I only came for the contract! I didn't take anything else, let alone one of the freaking Grimoire Keys! Do I look suicidal to you!? I'm not insane!"

"Let me be honest with you, young Friedrich; breaking in here is already something I would hardly consider sane," the old Mage noted with some exasperation, following it up with, "I still cannot understand why. Why would you go so far to annul our contract? What was your plan?"

"Me!? You were the one who broke the terms first! If there's anyone here who'd have some kind of plan, it's you!" Lab Coat Guy shouted back, his normally pale face red with rage.

"What are you talking about, young man? I have held myself to both the letter and the spirit of our contract."

"Bullshit!" the yoked man spat back with his arms straining against his bindings. "You set me up from the very beginning! You...!" All of a sudden, his face slackened, only for his expression to morph into a chilling death glare a moment later. "I get it now. This is still part of your setup! You must have lost the Grimoire Key, and you're using me as a scapegoat!"

"I have absolutely no idea what you are talking about," the arch-mage responded while his fingers drummed on the desk. "Your baseless accusations are both ungainly and becoming quite aggravating."

"Baseless, huh?" Lab Coat Guy scoffed back, his glare just as severe as before.

"Precisely," the old man stated with emphasis before subtly glancing at the school nurse silently standing nearby. "I have contacted you for the task as a favor for an old friend. I had no ulterior motives, let alone anything regarding the Grimoire Key."

"And you really expect me to believe that just because you say so?"

"Allow me to pose the same question to you, as well," Amadeus responded as his fingers began to drum on the wooden desktop again. "You have admittedly broken into my office, entered my archives, pilfered the contents of my strongbox, and yet you expect me to believe that you have not taken the key that had gone missing at the same time, all based on your word alone?"

"But I didn't take it!" came the indignant answer, and if he hadn't had his hands restrained, Lab Coat Guy would have probably slammed his palm on the desk in fury. "I broke in to get the goddamn contract so that I could get away from you and whatever twisted scheme you had for us! Do you seriously think I would take the Grimoire Key with me when my whole goal was to have nothing to do with you anymore?!"

"If so, then can you explain where one of our most valuable artifacts, one that I was entrusted with, disappeared into thin air?" Lord Grandpa asked back, his polite veneer slowly peeling off to reveal the rising impatience beneath it.

"How should I know?! I didn't even know it was in that damned safe! I thought it would be kept in a more secure location!"

"I assure you, until your break-in, the archives were definitely the most secure chamber on this entire island."

"Secure my ass! You didn't even lock the door!"

"Friedrich," Peabody spoke up, his bushy brows already in a disapproving frown. "Please keep things civil. If you really don't have the Grimoire Key, there is no need to antagonize Amadeus."

"If you truly do not have it in your possession," the man behind the desk stressed, though for the first time he sounded a little doubtful.

"I tell you, I never even saw it!"

"But then if you do not possess it, can you explain how it could disappear on the very same day you one-sidedly broke our contract and retrieved its proof?"

"How should I know? Maybe someone else took it," Lab Coat Guy responded with a shrug, much to the old Mage's annoyance.

"Young man, I am aware that you might not think highly of the enchantments guarding this room after your successful foray, but the main archives of the School is not a place where someone could enter at their own leisure."

To accentuate the point, Lord Grandpa vaguely gestured towards the direction of the door leading to said archives, which was a beautiful example of tempting fate and asking the world to prove you wrong in dramatic irony. That said, even if the rules of narrative timing weren't paying attention, there was at least one dashing rogue element ready to pick up their slack, as before the old man could let his hand down to resume his incessant tapping on the desk, the indicated door casually opened up.

The silence in the room was deafening as the three men present all turned disbelieving looks towards the entrance, which turned into alarmed ones when they noticed there was someone standing under the frame.

"Good evening, gentlemen," the newcomer, namely I, greeted the shocked trio with a harmless smile, before adding, "Do you mind if I join in? I believe we need to talk..."

PART 4

This was one of those you-could-hear-a-pin-being-dropped situations, and even after I politely announced my intentions, things refused to improve. As a matter of fact, the men in the room were staring at me with such aghast expressions I was starting to feel a little uncomfortable. Was it my outfit? I unconsciously glanced down, but I couldn't see anything wrong. Since all the hostilities were more or less resolved, I'd taken off the sliced-up ballistic vest and the padding I wore under my coat and slipped into a spare set of jeans and shirt I had at the base. Sure, the black overcoat had a small gash on it, but since the front was open when Mister Griffon grazed me, it wasn't exactly ruined, either. Judy had even combed my hair while I got the shallow cut on my abdomen dressed, so all things considered, I should've looked at least presentable at the moment.

Yet, the trio inside was still looking at me like I was the most terrifying thing in existence. I mean, okay, I'd waited until a suitably dramatic moment to make my appearance, and showing up out of the blue had to be pretty shocking, but their treatment was still a tad harsh if you asked me. As such, since they didn't welcome me in, I decided to forego the formalities, as well, and simply walked up to the desk.

"What is he doing here?" Lab Coat Guy blurted out the moment I stopped, and his voice finally seemed to jolt the other two out of their stupor.

"I assure you, that is something I would very much like to know, as well," Lord Grandpa commented with an air of intimidation rising around him, though to be frank, at this moment I was so far beyond caring that I couldn't even be bothered to feel irritated about him. There was also a small flash of ethereal light around his head that passed through his hat unhindered, so I subtly rolled my eyes at his expense.

"Don't bother. I've already blocked all outgoing communications through the wards," I told him, but he tried it, anyway. Honestly, after all the abuse I'd already put my poor brain through today, manipulating the interlocking wards surrounding the room wasn't the wisest of ideas, but I figured that avoiding any interruptions at this point was worth the head-ache. Not to mention, unlike with the irritating spear or Ichiko's previous housing, the spatially locked enchantments weren't actually plot devices, to use my colloquial terminology, so manipulating them was slightly less taxing than expected.

Anyhow, once the arch-mage realized that I was serious and that he was locked out of the wards with the supernatural equivalent of a parental control password, his already-narrowed eyes slowly gained a tinge of hostility.

"What exactly is the meaning of this?"

"Long story short, I'm here to hear you talk," I told him as I met his glare with a frown of my own. "You've caused me quite a lot of headache, both figuratively and literally, and so I'm here to hear your explanation."

"Explanation?" the elderly Mage repeated after me, so I simply nodded in the affirmative. "Considering you have entered here uninvited, I cannot help but wonder why I should be the one to explain myself in this situation."

"Cut the crap, old man. I've already had a tiresome day. I had to corner that idiot over there, save some hostages, deal with the Knights with the stupidly long name invading the home of my potential in-laws, as well as have a fight to the death against a possessed, unreasonable monster huntress, and that's not even counting all the other things that happened in the past couple of hours. In other words, I've long since run out of damns to give, so I would appreciate it if you started your confession."

"So now you are looking for a confession instead of just an explanation? You are quite bold to make demands, young man, considering you are currently inside *my* School. How does this sound instead: Can you give me a reason why I should refrain from single-handedly capturing you for the crime of breaking and entering?"

When I didn't answer right away, the irritating old man's lips parted in a grin that revealed all of his teeth, earning him another exasperated look for his trouble.

"So we are already at the threatening stage? Fine, have it your way." Saying so, I reached into the breast pocket of my coat and retrieved a small box. "For a start, I believe you are quite desperately—"

I got exactly that far when the air around the arch-mage began to boil with magic, and he was apparently about to unleash some kind of spell based on the unintelligible chant he was speed-muttering under his breath. Whatever it was, I had a feeling it probably wouldn't be great for my well-being, so the moment the magic began to coalesce into a multilayered ball of some sort, I immediately lashed out with my phantom limb and bisected it without any fanfare. The two pieces hung in the air for a second before dissipating into nothing, and to his credit, Lord Grandpa's expression barely twitched when he realized that his spell was mysteriously countered.

"So as I was saying, you really want this thing, don't you?" I asked with just a hint of provocation, and after a short yet intense staring contest, the old man gave me a nod.

"So it was you!" Lab Coat Guy exclaimed with an expression that told me he would have strangled me if his hands weren't bound. "You followed us when we entered last night!"

"Without your notice?" Peabody mused aloud while casually wiping his forehead with a handkerchief, and his nephew immediately nodded, at least as much as the yoke allowed.

"He must have hidden himself with an illusion spell. In fact..." He slowly narrowed his eyes, and after observing me for a while, he declared, "I bet you're not even here right now, are you?"

The look I gave him in return for his guess was flatter than a pancake, but he didn't get the message, so I told him, "Maybe. Or maybe it could be that you aren't here at all. Maybe you're all still standing in front of that warehouse at the docks and blankly staring into thin air while under a complex illusion."

"I wasn't at the docks," the school nurse blurted out, so I gave him a shrug.

"Then that means that you're not real but just an elaborate illusion to deceive these two." Both Peabody and his nephew looked downright horrified by the idea, so I stopped playing around and told them, "Or maybe I'm just messing with you. Who knows?"

I let them mull over that and returned my attention to the owner of the room, who by this point had seemingly digested the situation.

"In retrospect, I should have known you would not have revealed you are in possession of the Grimoire Key unless you were confident you could hold on to it even in my presence," he noted in a low, almost dejected voice, and at last he retracted whatever caused the air around him to roil. It incidentally also made him appear slightly less irritating, but it was to such a minuscule degree that the difference was purely academic. At last, he exhaled a long sigh and stated, "It appears I am at a disadvantage in these negotiations."

"These are not negotiations," I told him frankly. "Those only happen when both parties have a leg to stand on. Right now, I'm holding all the cards. I'm not here to negotiate. I'm here to deliver my demands." I waited for him to respond, but since he only continued to frown at me, I ultimately proclaimed, "First off, I've already asked for you to explain your actions regarding this enormous chain of marinated bollocks you caused. I'm still waiting."

Lord Grandpa continued to look me in the eye, but at the end of the day he came to a decision, and his shoulders imperceptibly slouched.

"What do you want to know?"

"For a start, explain to me why you hired this clown to harass my friends."

Lord Grandpa glanced over at the indignantly-huffing-yet-conspicuously-silent Lab Coat Guy, and after crossing his fingers on the desk, he stated,

"I have a long history with my good friend Archibald, and when I became aware of the fact that his nephew required..."

"Stop, my bad," I hastily interrupted him with a raised hand. Now, ignoring the fact that the name Archibald was completely wasted on the portly nurse, I apparently wasn't clear enough when asking my original question. "I'm not really interested why you chose this guy *in particular*, but why you conspired to set up all those fake attacks against us in the first place."

By the looks of it, my inquiry gave the old man some headache, but after mulling things over for a second, he continued his explanation.

"Your group is... highly unusual. An unmasked Celestial agent, the heiress of the de facto ruling family of the western Draconians, the blood sister of one of the Abyssal Lords, my very own granddaughter, a young man with mundane circumstances and yet unusual powers, and last but not least you yourself. While you might be relatively safe right now, whether one or all of you would be targeted by outside forces is not a question of if, but when. I simply hoped to provide some practical experience and instill a sense of caution into your group while also repaying some personal debts and forging a connection with the famously talented yet fickle black sheep of the Research Society."

"That would be him," I guessed while pointing with my thumb, and the old Mage let out a grunt in confirmation. "Quick question: Are the Assembly and the Research Society on good enough terms that you could do that without any pushback?"

"O-ho-ho, the Non-causative Science Research Society was originally a School of Magi," Peabody answered in the arch-mage's stead. "The occasional heated academic debate notwithstanding, relations are relatively amicable, so even if it was revealed that Friedrich and Amadeus worked together, it would not affect their reputations."

I sent a glance at the still-profusely-sweating school nurse and acknowledged his comment with a nod. He most likely spoke up to dissuade me from trying to use their contract as another bargaining chip, but to be honest, it didn't matter to me either way. Not to mention, I had a sneaking suspicion that he was purposefully underplaying the rivalry going on between the established supernatural power bloc and the uppity newcomer, but I didn't press the issue and faced Lord Grandpa again instead.

"So you're telling me that you orchestrated all of these attacks on us out of the kindness of your heart, to prepare us for the unforgiving power plays of the supernatural world or some similar slop? Do you seriously think I'd buy that?"

"No, I did not," he answered a tad indignantly. "I do not deny that I had my own considerations and personal gain in mind, as well, but I swear upon my name as an arch-mage of the Assembly that I never intended to cause you or your friends any harm, whether directly or indirectly."

"No harm, huh? Then please explain the dead Chimera puppet next."

The look he gave me at this point told me he wasn't expecting that question. Or was it one of the particular adjectives in the question? Either way, he closed his eyes and let out a long breath before he gave his answer.

"The Chimeric beast was... a whim, but at the same time, a necessity." He soon noticed my dubiously raised brow, so he hastily clarified that incredibly vague statement. "After news spread about your achievement of slaying the creature in question, I had considered its ramifications. Chimeric beasts are a rare breed, and I can guarantee that the Winged Lords of the Abyss would not allow someone capable of hunting one to walk the earth in peace. As such, I have looked into many an option and ultimately decided on one that would not only benefit you, but also allow us to potentially forge a connection with the elusive phantasmal hunters of the Kage clan. As much as I loathe to admit it, even the words of an arch-mage like myself mean little to their ilk, so I was forced to employ a more... *creative* solution."

"You've made the Chimera into a bait," I guessed, and he immediately confirmed it. Not only that, but based on the reaction of the uncle-nephew duo on the side, they weren't aware of these details until now, either.

"It was something proposed by the head of our artificer department. A dead Chimeric beast, while rare, holds little practical value, but by inscribing a newly developed, experimental Sun-grade enchantment onto the body, it could be put to use before it completely decayed."

"So just to see if I've got this right," I spoke up while casually using the edge of the box in my hand to scratch my chin. "You reanimated a Chimera, let it loose on the island to lure in Rinne, gave her information on me, and then told me to look into both the Chimera and her so that we could... do what exactly? What was the end goal of this convoluted scheme of yours?"

"I would hardly call it convoluted," the old man objected with a slight grimace. "As far as I was concerned, it was one of the safer plans I have ever put into motion. Even if you never met her, or never collaborated, so long as the experiment was a success and the body could be moved, our Artificers' Lodge would have benefited. As for its ultimate goal..." He fell silent for a beat, probably considering how much he should say, but when I pointedly shook the box in my hand, he immediately continued. "I hoped that you would develop a bond with the elusive holder of the Kage clan's sacred blade, and she could act as your mentor."

"... You're actually serious," I muttered in shock, much to my conversational partner's confusion.

"I... Yes. That was my hope, yet even if you could not build familiarity upon your shared experiences of fighting monstrous creatures, I believed that bringing her to the island had many benefits. In the worst-case scenario, where she would leave after tracking down her prey, I believed that by carefully manipulating the rumors, we could at the very least convince the Abyssal Lords into believing that she was responsible for the slaying of the original creature to draw attention away from you and, by consequence, my island. In the best-case scenario, I hoped she would take an interest in you and by staying on the island could help bolster our defenses."

"So it was a win-win situation for you that you completely screwed up by not doing any research on her personality."

"Is that so?" The arch-mage absentmindedly stroked his short beard and added, "If my sources are to be believed, she is a dutiful, soft-spoken young woman, and surprisingly easy on the eyes, as well."

"I have no idea what that last part has to do with anything, but no, she was more of creepy, psychotic, gluttonous woman-child with a split-personality disorder," I complained, but then I realized that I'd said too much, so I quickly amended, "Or at the very least she used to be, before I beat her and took her sword away. Now she's mainly just dejected and suspiciously amenable."

"That is right. I was meaning to ask," Lord Grandpa spoke up with a troubled expression. "You have mentioned something about a fight to the death, I believe?"

I knew that he was only fishing for information, but it wasn't like this was a secret, so I told him, "In short, I took the double-dead Chimera home for investigation, she misunderstood and went on a rampage, I had to beat her up and disarm her, then I had to purify her annoying sword and turn her into a little girl, but then stuff happened, and now she's locked up at a secure location." By the looks of it, my explanation caused more confusion than what it clarified, so just for the heck of it I also added, "Oh, and by the way, now her sacred sword is in the body of the Chimera, so I can't give it back to you. Don't even ask."

"I... was not planning, but... Did you say little girl just now?"

"That's beside the point." I dismissed him with a wave of my free hand and concluded, "So in short, you had *the best intentions*, but your overengineered failure of a plan went off the rails and caused this whole mess."

"I would not necessarily call it a complete failure," the old man objected.

"You would think that, but you would be wrong. Anyhow, here's what's going to happen now." While saying so, I raised a hand and presented the box I was holding through all of this discussion. "You want this back before the investigators from the Assembly arrive so that you can save your position in the organization and at least a shred of your dignity. I'm not against returning it to you, but I have a couple of demands."

When I said that, the atmosphere in the room immediately tensed up again, and after a long moment of consideration, the arch-made quietly uttered, "I'm listening."

"First off, I want you to let my friends go."

I might have started a little weak, as the old man nodded right away.

"Naturally, though, I believe it would be best if they spent the night in our custody, for appearances' sake."

"I can compromise that much," I responded after but a moment of thinking. "However, at the very least provide them with proper food, beds, and a board game or something to pass the time."

"I... do not believe we have any such games in the School, but I will see what I can do," Lord Grandpa noted with a hint of amusement in his voice. "Anything else?"

"Just have them taken to my place by tomorrow morning, without any guards or those annoying surveillance spells attached to them. Next, I want official access to your archives, without any supervision."

"I believe we can arrange that," he agreed, though this time he was slightly more reserved.

"Thirdly, I want him," I declared and once again used my thumb to gesture towards the yoked guy nearby.

"W-what? Me?" he yelped out while pointing at himself.

"Precisely," I responded as I turned to face him.

I wasn't kidding, either. Letting this guy loose was a really bad idea, as I couldn't know when he would turn up again to bring back his *sentai* nonsense. While Crowey, Lord Grandpa, and the Knights in general were more dangerous opponents, they would still operate within the framework of the current setting, so to speak, while he was easily the most troublesome rogue element as far as the narrative structure and tone of the world were concerned.

"You're too dangerous to be left to your own devices, so I'm going to keep you on a short leash, where I can keep an eye on you." I paused here to let my words sink in, and then continued in a slow, level tone. "No more giant robots. No more disposable goons. No more silly costumes. Finally, and maybe most importantly, no more plasma disintegrators. Screw up on any of those points, and I'll give you a fashionable pair of concrete shoes and kick you out into the middle of the Atlantic Ocean. Are we clear on that?"

Lab Coat Guy and the nurse both repeatedly nodded in unison, so I turned back to the man behind the desk.

"Oh, and by the way, while he'll work for me, you're still going to be footing his bills. We'll work out the contract later, but I wanted to be clear on that."

Lord Grandpa looked at the yoked mad scientist, and before I knew it, the corners of his lips were bent upwards into something resembling a delighted smile.

"To be perfectly honest with you, young man, that sounds like a fantastic idea to me."

"Hey! Don't I have any say in this matter!?"

"No," I responded to Lab Coat Guy's desperate objection and addressed the old man again, "Aside from that, all I ask for is some courtesy. Don't make any more convoluted schemes, don't cause me or my friends any trouble *for our own good*, and if some unsavory types arrive on the island, like, say, a bunch of grown men with buckets on their heads known for attacking relatively innocent dragons, notify me instead of allowing them to operate on your bloody island."

"Buckets...? Do you perchance mean the Knights?"

"Of course I mean the Knights!" I exclaimed in exasperation. "Don't tell me you couldn't at least tell my self-appointed mother-in-law that they were already on the island! Do you have any idea how much headache that would've saved me today?"

"I only learned of their presence recently, and in my defense, I was already engaged in a different incident."

"Which was the result of the aforementioned convoluted scheming," I remarked before placing the box onto the desk. "So do we have a deal here or not?" The arch-mage was eyeing me even more suspiciously than before, so I felt obligated to add, "For the record, don't even think about double-crossing me. I took your artifact once, I can take it again, and even if you teleport it to the moon or something so that I can't use it as leverage, with the contents of your safe in my hands, I still have enough dirt on you to have you kicked out of the Assembly so hard you might even achieve a stable orbit."

"I understand," he uttered just a tad begrudgingly, and he reached out towards the box. Before he could touch it, though, I stopped him by offering a hand.

"Deal?" I asked with my most harmless of smiles, and after staring at my outstretched palm for a second or five, the head of the School ultimately grabbed it, and we shook hands.

"I accept your generous conditions," he stated flatly, and oddly enough, his expression told me that he considered the act of the handshake a bigger deal than our agreement itself. I didn't really care, though, as I was simply delighted that I could finally mark him for Far Sight.

I removed my hand from the box, and surprisingly enough Lord Grandpa didn't immediately snatch it up. If nothing else, I had to commend his willpower. Once he let go of my hand, I immediately turned around and stepped up to Lab Coat Guy.

"Once you let my friends go, have them escort him, as well. I'll deal with the rest." Saying so, I decided to make one last show of having the upper hand, and firmly poked the yoke around the man's neck with two fingers. It let out a buzzing sound and opened with a soft click, much to the mad scientist's befuddlement. I ignored him and instead used the opportunity to extend my phantom limb and interface with the wards of the office, and once I turned off the restrictions I'd put on Lord Grandpa, I turned on my heel and walked towards the open entrance of the archives.

"Now then, it was a pleasure, gentlemen, but I'm afraid I have to go. You still have a lot of this mess to clean up, and I have to make sure the Celestial Intelligence Network will stay in the dark about what went down tonight. See you all tomorrow."

Just as I finished, I closed the door behind me, and before Lord Grandpa could collect himself and try to follow after me, I immediately Phased back home.

"Welcome back, Chief," my dear girlfriend greeted me the moment I arrived, but before I replied, I immediately fell into my comfy chair with a relieved sigh. Judy gave me an odd look as she sidled closer to me and asked, "How did the negotiations go?"

"Fairly smoothly, I'm just tired as a... fox?" I uttered in surprise as I noticed the thing in Judy's arms. In short, it was the biggest, fattest, fluffiest red fox I'd ever seen in my life. I was just about to ask what that was, but then the fox opened its mouth, and to my further bafflement, spoke up in a familiar voice.

"Look, Ue-sama! I could really do it!"

"Ah... I should have known," I muttered under my breath. Using one of the neighbours as an anchor, I Phased Judy and the tiny (and currently quite foxy) miko home, so that my girlfriend could put some proper clothes on her. Needless to say, even though she insisted that she could transform using some ancient fox girl art of illusionary whatever, I never expected her to do it while I was away.

"Chief, can we keep her?" Judy suddenly asked with a tone so serious I was completely sure it was a joke for a moment.

"Are you serious? What about your countermeasures?"

"I'm not insecure enough to be jealous of foxes," my girlfriend stated a tad indignantly before grabbing Ichiko under her front legs and presenting her to me. "Also, she's really fluffy."

"... I never figured you were the type who would get swayed by cute animals," I whispered too quietly for her to hear, and I concluded the conversation with an ambivalent, "Let's discuss this in detail later."

The fox in her hands let out a series of delighted yipping sounds, which honestly didn't help my slowly-but-surely rising headache, so I poked her stomach. It only made her laugh out louder (she was possibly ticklish), and I had no choice but to agree with Judy on one point: she was indeed incredibly fluffy, especially for a sword-Chimera-miko-loli-fox.

Damn, that's a lot of traits right there. If she was a little older, that would probably make her a prime love interest material in a harem narrative. But then again, considering the conventions of some of the visual novels I'd run into during my research, her appearance might actually be a selling point for a certain demographic.

"Make sure you keep her away from Josh and his harem protagonist aura. The last thing we need right now is the local version of FBI showing up looking for him," I jested half-heartedly, yet my girlfriend nodded with the utmost seriousness. Anyhow, I'd never really realized how comfortable my favourite chair was. Or maybe it was just the fatigue speaking? Either way, I glanced over at Judy and told her, "Let me rest for a moment, then we can discuss what happened today in detail."

"Okay. I'll go brew some tea."

"Oh, oh! Judy-ue, I can help! I can show you my family's traditional green tea recipe!" the fluffy ball exclaimed as she wagged her bushy tail in my girlfriend's hands.

"I don't think we have any green tea, but let me check," she responded on her way to the kitchen, and the way she casually ignored the tail repeatedly stroking her on the neck drew a small chuckle out of me.

I felt really tired, though, so after a while, I leaned my head onto the backrest of my chair, closed my eyes, and let my mind rest for a few minutes. After a day like this, I think I deserved this much.

GESTURES OF FRIENDSHIP

"My lord, there really isn't anything wrong with the wards."

"I implore that you inspect them again, just for the sake of certainty."

The middle-aged artificer, dressed in his usual garb consisting of a brown apron worn over a business casual suit and an adjustable loupe strapped to his forehead, gave the owner of the room a dejected look, but at the end of the day, he returned to his task.

Needless to say, the inside of Lord Endymonion's office was filled to the brim with tension, which not even the presence of the school nurse elegantly slurping his tea from a large porcelain cup could ease. At the moment, there were exactly three people inside: the aforementioned portly old man, currently leisurely drinking while sitting on an armchair that certainly hadn't been there half an hour ago, the arch-mage himself behind his desk with a face sourer than a vat of undiluted vinegar, and the artificer, who was busily reinspecting the walls of the room with a flat handheld device seemingly made out of glowing blue crystals.

The silence in the room didn't last long, as after pinching the bridge of his nose for a moment, Lord Grandpa let out a groan conveying about 60 percent exhaustion and 40 percent frustration.

"I cannot help but conclude that I have severely misread the current situation," he noted, and in response, Peabody put his beverage down with a nonchalant shrug.

"O-ho-ho, it happens even to the best of us." His encouragement obviously didn't work as well as he'd hoped, as the man behind the desk lethargically took off his hat, if only so that it wouldn't get in the way when he buried his face in his hands for a second. "Now, now, Amadeus. Don't be so hard on yourself. Why, even *I* thought it was Friedrich who took the key!"

The moment he heard that, the arch-mage immediately looked up to send a glance at the artificer still immersed in inspecting the wall, and once he was sure he didn't react, turned to the school nurse again.

"That is still confidential information," he hissed between clenched teeth before tapping on the bulge on his chest, no doubt the current resting place of the aforementioned Grimoire Key, and when he was sure it was still there, he let out a curt sigh. "More importantly, I am not speaking about your nephew."

"Oh? In that case, you must mean the young mister Dunning," Peabody noted with a flat smile, much to the other man's barely hidden chagrin.

"Yes. I have obviously misjudged his capabilities, not to mention his audacity."

"O-ho-ho. Reminds you of someone, doesn't he?" the portly man commented between two chuckles, and this time Lord Endymonion didn't even bother to hide his distaste and promptly rolled his eyes.

"Spare me your witticisms, Archie. I am really not in the mood right now."

"Cheer up, cheer up. Things might not have turned out how you originally wanted, but the situation is not that bad, is it?"

"No, but it is also considerably far from ideal, as well," the arch-mage jabbed back before letting out a huge breath and slouching back in his chair. "That said, you are certainly correct in a sense of the word. While things might not have proceeded along the path I have envisioned, the ultimate result is still something I can utilize. If only he had not taken the..." He abruptly paused here, and after sending a glance at the still-working man with the glowing crystal slate, he finished in a low voice. "I only wish we could have reached this point without the confidential item ever being taken. It created an unforeseen opening, and I am afraid the Conservative faction is going to try to use this incident against me."

"O-ho-ho? Are things getting heated up between the Conservative and the Reformist parties?"

"In a manner of speaking, but in this case, I am almost certain that it is arch-mage Saahira pulling the strings. She had been trying to gain a senior seat for close to a decade, and utilizing the inner conflicts of the Assembly to her advantage is certainly not something below her."

"Saahira? The tall girl with chestnut skin and braided hair?" Peabody inquired absentmindedly while reaching for his tea again, and the arch-mage all but snorted in response.

"She is hardly a girl anymore. As a matter of fact, I believe she has just stepped into her fifth decade a few months ago."

"O-ho-ho? Has it really been that long since I last saw her? Oh, how time flies by."

"It indeed does." There was a long beat of silence while the school nurse continued to sip his tea, and once he finished, Lord Amadeus quietly added, "She had been a thorn in my side for more than half of those decades, though I believe it is to be expected, considering we are competitors in the same field."

"Is she also researching artificial life?" Peabody inquired with a curiously raised brow, apparently hearing about this conflict for the first time.

"In a manner of speaking. My School is aiming to create homunculi with artificial souls yet capable of utilizing the mystic arts. As you are already aware, we already had a few minor successes in the endeavor a decade and a half ago, but ever since then our research efforts have been stagnating."

"If you put it like that, I'm sure she must have had a breakthrough in the meantime."

"Multiple, even," Lord Grandpa uttered with a complicated expression. "If her research were to bear fruit, it would allow one to transfer their soul to a new artificial body. Understandably, many of the other seniors in the assembly have a vested interest in her research."

"Justifiably so," Peabody nodded with an expression that said he'd just realized something.

"Certainly. She had been using her research to leverage the support of the Reformist faction of the Assembly, and since we could not stop the rumors regarding the break-in, it is only a matter of time before a nominally unbiased group of investigators will arrive on the island. I am almost one hundred percent certain that she and the other members of the Reformist faction will attempt to use this opportunity to drag me down."

"You don't seem too worried about the prospect," the nurse noted, and the arch-mage let out a small chuckle in response.

"I cannot say I am. After all, I know them, and I know their methods. Let them try; I have been playing this game far longer than Saahira or her ilk."

"O-ho-ho? Now that is the confident Amadeus I know!"

The lord of the School politely waited for his friend to finish chuckling, and only then did he heave a tired sigh.

"Nevertheless, I must be vigilant in the future; I cannot afford any further unforeseen interference from Leonard Dunning. I must make sure he will not sabotage another crucial plan in the time to come."

"Speaking of which," Peabody mused while slowly refilling his cup from the teapot on the arch-mage's desk in a sophisticated manner that could be best described as aggressively British. "What exactly was that original plan of yours? I gather you really wanted Friedrich involved because he made Galatea, but I am quite foggy on the rest."

"You knew I had plans for him, and you still acted as a bridge between us?"

"O-ho-ho! Of course! I know that you take care of your people, so there was no harm done."

"True enough, I suppose," the old man shrugged and once again slouched back in his seat before explaining himself. "There is no point lying about it at this point; our School is really desperate for a breakthrough. I'd hoped that the expertise of your nephew would grant us the push we need to further our craft, but I naturally also put a number of other plans into motion, most important of which was enticing the Kage clan and their sacred sword to come to the island. Did you know, old friend, that if rumors are to be believed, their sacred blade houses the soul of an Eastern saintess?"

"Is that so?" the nurse asked back, most likely just to keep the conversation flowing.

"Indeed! If that is true, it means that sword must hold the secrets for preserving a soul for centuries! Possibly indefinitely!" Lord Grandpa explained with unusual zeal. "If we could get our hands on it, or even just examine it, it might not only provide a vital clue to our own research and allow our homunculi to function without the looming menace of an unexpected breakdown, but it might also serve as a crucial bargaining chip that would allow me to gain the upper hand against Saahira!" He paused here for a second, and once his head had cooled down a bit, he continued in a considerably more subdued voice. "But alas, enticing the free-spirited folk of the Kage clan was no easy task, and even after I managed to lure the wielder of the sacred blade to the island, it was imperative to provide her a good reason to stay, so that we might observe her or even establish a bargain once sufficient familiarity was reached."

"O-ho-ho? That's an unusually timid approach for you," Peabody noted between two sips. "If it was so important, I'd have thought you'd take the sword by any means necessary."

"Please, Archibald! Do you think me a brute?" the old man scoffed, yet a moment later he added, "Yes, I have indeed had a contingency plan ready in case she was about to leave the island ahead of time, yet it was definitely a last resort. The wielder of the sacred blade is known to hunt all manner of phantasmal beasts, and her prowess with the blade is quite notorious; facing her in direct confrontation, even if it was within a trap I arranged ahead of time, would have most likely involved casualties we could scarcely afford." There was a beat of silence here as he recalled something, and his white brows immediately furrowed. "But then again, such theoretical speculations have already become completely moot thanks to the interference of a certain Leonard Dunning."

"Quite a troublemaker, that young man!" the portly nurse exclaimed, followed by a hearty chuckle. The other old man naturally didn't find it half as funny.

"Troublemaker is putting it quite lightly," Lord Amadeus noted with a grimace. "The most dangerous thing about him is his unpredictability. I also cannot, even after meticulous research, discern his origins or affiliations. At first, I was fairly certain he was related to the Brotherhood in some shape or form, but then he entwined himself with the young heiress of the Dracises. Considering how pedantic they are in regards to their bloodline, it also meant it was all but certain that he was not related to any of the Winged Ones by blood. That, and his considerable expertise concerning countermeasures against the mystic arts, artifacts, and illusionary arts made me contemplate the possibility that he was sent by one of the rival Schools to infiltrate us, but then he would not have readily returned the item that shall not be named to me in return for a few minor concessions."

"That's quite a pickle," Peabody noted, which earned him a skeptical look from the arch-mage.

"Archie, do you actually know something about his background?"

"O-ho-ho? What makes you ask so?"

"I know you. You always look away when you are hiding something."

"Oh, am I?" The school nurse made a conscious effort to look the man behind the desk in the eye, and told him, "Even if I knew, I'm afraid I can't say. You see, I really can't afford to anger the Brotherhood of Hippocrates. They have eyes and ears everywhere."

Lord Grandpa gave the comically serious old man a long, flat look, and ultimately let out a lung-rattling groan that made even the artificer working in the background shudder.

"Archie, that joke was already old when we first met more than half a century ago."

"O-ho-ho! It's not old; it's vintage," Peabody responded with a wink, earning him another small groan.

"Let us ignore this tangent and continue the previous conversation," Amadeus proposed, and his partner agreed with a nod. "For the time being, I believe Leonard Dunning and his group of eccentrics can be considered a neutral party as far as our future plans are concerned. He currently possesses two things we need: your nephew's talents, and access to the holy sword of the Kage clan. While our relationship is far from harmonious, I believe it can be gradually improved over time."

After saying that, the arch-mage took a piece of paper out of his drawer and began drawing on it with a focused expression.

"First and foremost, while he demanded custody of Friedrich, he also requested that we fund his expenses. This tells us two things: instead of keeping him in captivity, he wishes to utilize your nephew's talents for himself, and he does not have the resources to do so by himself. This gives us an opportunity to steadily build a dependent relationship that would enable future cooperation and eventual co-option."

"Sounds reasonable," the nurse noted as he leaned forward to take a better look at the flowchart the old Mage was drawing.

"Next, we must ease the tensions. Amelia might have picked their side already, but she is still my scion, so if I ask, I am certain she would advocate for our cause. By his accord, Pascal has also been on good terms with the Bernstein boy. I shall ask him to deepen their bonds and enter their circle, so that we will have another voice speaking for us. Finally, I am thankfully in a cordial association with the Dracis patriarch. By exchanging a few favors, I might be able to have him subtly influence the young mister Dunning." After drawing another circle and a few more arrows, Lord Grandpa paused for several seconds before stating, "If all else fails, creating a crisis might also force them to consider creating closer ties with the School."

"A crisis? What kind of crisis?"

"I am considering a kidnapping scenario, or possibly arson," the arch-mage noted with an almost-disinterested voice, as if he was only talking about the weather. "Ideally it should be combined with framing one or more of our adversaries. The Winged Lords of the Abyss seem to be the obvious choice, though revealing a hint of the inner conflicts within the Assembly and turning their animosity towards the Reformers would naturally also have a certain allure. Once they face this unfortunate crisis, we would naturally offer our full support as a gesture of friendship. As for the exact details of such a ploy, I shall consider the finer points at a later time."

After declaring so, the old Mage continued to tap his pen against the paper in front of him, deep in thought, occasionally adding a few words here and there. This continued for about a minute before he finally noticed that the artificer had stopped poking at the walls and was silently waiting by his desk.

"Yes? Did you find anything unusual?"

"No, my lord," the man shook his head with an exhausted face. "I've checked every single anchor point and the integrity of every minor ward one by one. There was absolutely nothing wrong with any of them whatsoever."

"Preposterous," the arch-mage huffed a tad indignantly as he put the pen aside and began to drum on the desk with his fingers. "I was denied access to my own wards. There is absolutely no plausible way such a thing would leave no evidence."

"With all due respect, my lord, there's really nothing here. Maybe it wasn't your access that was denied, but the connection itself? As in, could it be that there was a faux ward set up to intercept your command and make you think you were cut off?"

"I have made these wards. I know them like the back of my hand. I tell you, there is no way I would be mistaken about this."

The two men locked eyes for a few seconds, and it was naturally the middle-aged one who averted his gaze first.

"I have no reason to doubt you, my lord, but there is simply no way that—"

It was at this point that everyone in the room was startled by the sound of a heavy impact, followed by the tinkling of shaking glass. The three men in the room instinctively turned their heads towards the source of the noise, only for their eyes to land on a tall (if presently slightly hunched), dashing (if currently just a teeny-weeny bit haggard) guy in black.

"Oh, sorry for intruding," I called out to the group with forced cheerfulness. "I realized I had forgotten something the last time, and as they say, there is no better time than today, so I figured I might as well get it over with ASAP."

To punctuate my point, I forcefully tapped the side of the wooden cabinet by my side, which incidentally made all the liquor bottles inside shake once again.

"Ah... um... Leonard?" Peabody addressed me while once again wiping his forehead with a hankie that I was about 300 percent sure he didn't have just a moment ago, so I gave him a nod in place of a greeting. He only began to sweat even harder. "When, exactly did you get here?"

I almost reflexively told him that I'd obviously come in just now, but then I remembered that currently I was still in the process of confusing them about what my powers were, so instead I said, "Who knows, maybe I never left? Maybe even this liquor cabinet was here all along, but you just never noticed it? Eyes are such fallible little organs, don't you agree?"

"... I'm fairly sure I walked over there," the artificer noted a little absent-mindedly, obviously confused by the situation.

"Oh, but did you really? Or do you just think that? It can be hard to tell sometimes," I replied with a grin, only to then suddenly remember something and add, "By the way, Gowan?"

"Yes?" the man answered reflexively.

"Good, I really hoped I didn't misremember you. I'm bad with names, you see. Anyhow, I just wanted to tell you that, considering the circumstances, I'm afraid I can't attend the symposium tomorrow."

"Ah? I see, but... it has been postponed because of the break-in," the vaguely Scottish artificer noted, apparently still more than a little baffled by this entire situation. Not that I could blame him.

"Really? That's a shame. Oh well, if you have a new date, please inform me." I didn't wait for him to respond, and instead, I turned to the owner of the room still sitting behind his desk and conspicuously concealing a piece of paper with his arms. How cute. "Anyway, as I was saying, *while our relationship is far from harmonious at the moment*, I figured I would be the bigger man and give you an olive branch. Unfortunately, I'm fresh out of those, so for the time being, please make do with this cabinet here. Consider it a *gesture of friendship*, if you will."

I gave the arch-mage a supremely ominous wink and waited for a short while to see if he would react, but to his credit, the dapper Mage maintained a perfect poker face, while the other two remained befuddled as ever. That was kind of boring, but in retrospect, I don't know what I was expecting.

"I see that you are busy with something, so I better get going," I stated with mock reluctance. "I will see you around. Bye, and remember: no double-crossing."

And with that, I left Lord Grandpa to stew in his own juices, and I Phased home, where I would no doubt have to listen to an earful from Judy for disappearing in a hurry. Oh well. The sun rises in the east, the river runs to the ocean, the lion eats the zebra, and the Judy gets mad at the Leo when he disappears in the middle of a conversation. Such is life.

This was totally worth it, though.

KNIGHTS OF THE SQUARE TABLE

The island of Critias had, for the longest time, been a literal gold mine. For decades, the land has been explored and exploited for valuable metals, rare earth minerals, and the occasional diamonds here and there. However, nothing lasts forever (no, not even diamond deposits), and while the central areas around the caldera still saw continued mining efforts, over time the island's businesses began to focus more on the blossoming tourism industry. Some of the old mining settlements managed to move on with the times, and became the hosts of wellness resorts, some even exploiting the local geothermal spring waters to create honest-to-goodness hot springs, bringing wealth to few and continued middle-class existence to others.

However, not all the small settlements peppering the land were suitable for these endeavors, and once the local ore veins ran dry, the mine workers and their families either moved to other, as-of-yet-not-fully-tapped sites, or to one of the few larger cities on the island, leaving slowly decaying, abandoned houses behind. Well, at least they would have if everything didn't look brand-new and completely spotless, anyway, but that's beside the point.

In one of these small hamlets a couple of kilometers southwest of Timaeus, consisting of maybe a couple dozen mostly vacant houses, a group of stern people were seated around a standard-sized family dining table. It was already dark outside, though it was impossible to tell due to all of the roller shutters on the windows being completely down. The inside wasn't much brighter, either, as the house where the men took shelter apparently didn't have electricity, and thus they had to rely on a couple of old copper kerosene lamps for illumination. They gave the otherwise simple, if somewhat bare, living room a decidedly spooky atmosphere.

Currently, there were six people inside the room. Around the table in the center sat three of them on robust wooden chairs, all wearing plate armour from head to toe, and for some unfathomable reason, they were still wearing their helmets, as well, even inside their impromptu safe house like it was completely natural. Aside from the men in the middle, there was one squire, also still fully dressed in metal, keeping a lookout by peering through a gap in the blinds, while two others were stationed at the two exits of the room. The rest of the squires were also in the building, either dressing their wounds in the bedrooms or consuming the canned food stockpiled in the kitchen. Needless to say, they were all wearing their helmets, too. Yes, even the ones eating. The Knights were apparently *very* fastidious about their headgear.

"So in conclusion," one of the men by the table broke the silence, his unfamiliar pointed helmet contrasting his familiar deep, gravelly voice, and he simultaneously placed his hands clad in red gauntlets onto the table. In fact, his entire armour was a deep shade of red, with copious amounts of silver filigree in the shape of feathers. Since the spot of the Griffon Knight was already taken by the man sitting by the other end of the table, it meant he was either the Eagle Knight or the Raven Knight, not counting any as-of-yet-unrevealed avian-themed chevaliers. Anyhow, after a long beat, he continued with, "Today's attack on the abominable wyrmbloods was an abject failure."

"More or less," Mister Griffon noted with a nod that made his armour clank quite audibly, though nobody seemed to mind.

"A' leest we didnae lose a'body," the burliest of the three steel-clad men noted while crossing his arms, and Mister Red and Feathery immediately sent him a skeptical glance visible through the visor of his helmet.

"True, everyone survived, but I would hardly say you didn't lose anything. Such as your sword," he stated while using a finger to point at the conspicuously empty scabbard hanging from Mister Minotaur's waist.

"Och shut yer gob! Ah coudnae dae anythin' aboot it! If ainlie ah hud mah axe..."

"Then it would have been your axe that the mysterious mister Bel took instead," Mister Griffon interjected in a flat tone, immediately arousing the ire of his companion.

"Big gab frae someain fa git 'is pooch pick'd in th' open!"

"Sir Duncan is right," the third Knight agreed with a solemn voice. "Don't cast the first stone when you yourself lost the Talisman of Purity to the enemy."

"Yea, at leest ah only tint mah ain sword! Ye tint Penny-gurl's a'tifact! She's gonnae be pished!" Mister Minotaur piled on with a triumphant nod, only to reel back when Mister Red smacked his hand against the table.

"It might have been just your sidearm, but you still lost an heirloom of our order, brother! You have no reason to sound so full of yourself."

"Ah ken, ah juist..." the big guy mumbled in response, but he didn't manage to give a proper answer.

There was a long moment of silence, which lasted until the Knight in the red armour raised his hand to his helm in a gesture that might have looked like a facepalm if not for the, well, helmet. So... helmet-palm? Either way, after taking a deep breath, he finally let his hand down and spoke again.

"I should have gone with you two, after all."

"I fail to see how it would have improved the situation," Mister Griffon spoke up with a voice that said he was already tired of this conversation. "You are still recovering. Getting out without any casualties was already a small miracle; the last thing we needed was you in the field."

"Roland!" Mister Minotaur exclaimed in outrage, but quickly fell silent after receiving a glare from the man with the winged helmet.

"You know that I'm right. There is a reason why we left Sir Arnwald behind; until he can properly walk again, let alone run, he would be a liability on the battlefield."

There was another long moment of tense silence hanging in the air, once again broken by the man in red.

"You are right. Bringing the entire operation ahead without waiting for sister Penelope to arrive was already a mistake. Whether I was with you or not wouldn't have made things any better." As if he'd just recalled something, Mister Red clicked his tongue and added, "Brother Leonard might have helped, though, but I couldn't reach him."

"Aye, wasn't he suppose tae be oan th' island awready?"

"He is, but I couldn't contact him in time." The red Knight let out a regretful sigh at this point and continued with, "He is deep undercover, and the one time we talked, the reception was so bad we could barely hear each other. I should have asked him about the situation back then; even if he couldn't join us, he might have learned about the miraculous recovery of the wyrmblood in the mansion."

"Speaking of him, are we sure his cover is still intact?" the Griffon Knight inquired out of the blue, apparently surprising his comrades quite a bit. "No matter how I think about it, the wyrmbloods reacted too quickly. Our invasion of their territory was only finalized the day before to capitalize on the absence of their eldest, yet even if they were informed the moment we broke down the gates, they arrived back too soon."

"Whit urr ye getting' at?"

"I think there is a chance that he was discovered," Mister Griffon responded ponderously before scratching the chin of his helmet in a thoughtful (and also kind of comical) fashion. "If they knew he was on the island, they might have deduced that we would attack them soon. It's not implausible that they have purposefully baited us into revealing ourselves, only to strike us in the back."

"Juist th' craven schemes ye wid expect fae thair kind," Mr. I'm a Kettle Calling the Pot Black noted with a sage nod, and he was summarily ignored by the other two senior Knights.

"That would explain how they could arrive at the scene so fast, but there is still one very important element of today's disaster that is left unanswered."

"Th' mask'd arsepiece."

"Precisely," the Knight in red nodded without batting an eye at the big man's choice of words. He was apparently already used to it.

"He called himself Bel of the Abyss," Mister Griffon commented with an audible frown. "I've never heard of anyone by that name. What about you?"

"Neither have I. Based on the name alone, I would think he was from the netherworld, but that sounds too obvious."

"Agreed. He managed to outwit us, so I doubt he would announce his affiliations so openly. Not to mention, the way he could move through space as he willed was truly peculiar."

"Aye. Ah tried tae keep track o' him wi' mah territory, bit ah it pure wis as if he telepo'ted. A dinnae ken whit kind o' witchery that wis, bit 'twas truly wyrd."

"Not just that," Mister Griffon said solemnly, "But I couldn't see him chant, or move his hands in the odd gestures of the prisoners of the Abyss. Whoever he was, he used techniques I've never heard of."

"Maybe it was some kind of illusion or a space-warping spell used through a preset formation," Mister Red mused before ultimately shaking his head. "We should ask brother Agravain. If anyone has heard of this Bel fellow or his unique mystic arts, it would be him."

"I thought Sir Agravain was also undercover," Mister Griffon cut in at this point, and he pointedly tapped the table with his finger. "I was under the impression he was still working on dismantling the local wyrmbloods' enterprise."

"I contacted him before the attack, and he said he'd already completed his plans in Indonesia, and he would come here as soon as possible. He hoped he would be able to inspect and take care of Ascalon after we recovered it."

"E'cept tis in th' hauns o' that radge wee shite," the big man grumbled, and the other senior Knights all but rolled their eyes at his expense.

"At least it's no longer in the hands of the wyrms," Mister Red noted in a voice that said he was trying to find a silver lining, yet couldn't. "However, I'm afraid we will only be able to communicate on the phone, as I doubt he would be able to come to the island anytime soon."

"Why's that? Did something unexpected happen over there?"

"Not there, but over here. You probably haven't heard because you were holed up in the safe house before the attack, but someone broke into the local School. The Mages are in a complete uproar and locked down the entire island. Brother Agravain already made deals with the arch-mage of this island, and if he came here under these circumstances, he would be recognized and possibly detained right away. I sent him a message saying it would be better if he waited until things calmed down a little, but he hasn't responded yet."

"Hold on, the island is under lockdown?" Mister Griffon spoke up with a hint of alarm in his voice. "Does that mean we can't leave, either?"

"I wouldn't risk it. The arch-mage here has a finger in many pots. If he decides that he needs to buy the support of the wyrmbloods, and we get caught trying to leave with our equipment, we might get sold out."

"Whit aboot Penny-girl? Is she aff tae be safe?"

"Her gear is already here, so it shouldn't get her caught during inspections," Mister Griffon mused aloud. "She is also of the same generation as Leonard, so if he could operate on the island until now, she should be able to do so, as well, without anyone recognizing her."

"True 'at. Ah juist fash yerse abit 'er, fur she's sae paukit," Mister Minotaur mumbled while awkwardly scratching the back of his neck.

"Compared to brother Duncan, all of us are tiny," Mister Red jested, and the other Knight also played along by patting him on the shoulder. "That said, we should be prepared to hunker down on this island for the time being."

"It seems we have no other choice," the Knight with the winged helmet noted a little reluctantly. "Do you have any plans for the time being?"

"Ah wull collect speirins by blending in wi' th' locals," the big Knight proposed, and after a long beat the three grown men began to snicker like kids.

"Yes, great joke, brother Duncan. Seriously speaking, though, we absolutely should attempt to gather information about the current state of the island."

"I will do it," Mister Griffon proposed. "I have a few Mage contacts in Timaeus; I'll ask them about the internal situation of the School."

"I will try to establish phone contact with brother Leonard and Agravain. With some luck, we might learn something about this elusive Bal individual," Mister Red added after some consideration.

"Then ah suppose ah wull set up a freish base o' operations in th' toon. Dinnae tak' me wrong, this hoose is cozy 'n' a', bit thare insae a sinlge howf the lenth o' th' yak kin see, 'n' that juist wull nae dae."

"The lack of pubs aside, there's also no internet, cable TV, electricity…" Mister Griffon stopped counting on his gloved fingers for a moment and asked, "Do we have tap water?"

"A dinnae ken, bit if we dinnae, th' cludgie is aff tae stink tae heich heavens."

"Yes, a new base is imperative," Mister Red concluded with a nod before adding, "Also, since we don't know how long we will need to stay on the island, we should adopt new identities. Do any of you know a good document forger?"

"I know one, but he is in Berlin."

"That's not exactly viable right now. In that case, I believe we should be fine so long as we improvise."

"Hoo come dinnae we ask Leonard?"

"We can't," came the answer from Mister Griffon. "If his cover is compromised, showing up on his doorstep might blow ours, and even if his cover is fine, our appearance might raise suspicion. In some ways, the fact that Arnwald couldn't get Leonard involved in the raid might be a blessing in disguise."

"That's right. It's best we refrain from contacting brother Leonard until it is absolutely necessary. His mission is not related to the wyrmbloods, so if his identity is still secure, it would be best if we allowed him to continue avoiding their notice."

"Agreed. Do we have anything else to discuss?"

"Ah dinnae think we dae," Mister Minotaur responded a little sluggishly, and Mister Griffon promptly stood up from his seat.

"In that case, I believe we should all rest. This was a long day, and we need to prepare for the troubles to come."

"I'm in agreement," Mister Red and Feathery approved as he also stood up, and so did Mister Minotaur after a moment of hesitation. "Let us sleep, brothers. We should stay here until Monday, and then put our plans into action with rested minds."

The three Entitled Knights nodded in unison, and left the bare living room in a single line, leaving behind the two guards and the one conspicuously vacuous sentry who continued to peer through the blinds without reacting to any of their conversations.

In fact, the gorget-less squire seemed to be so immersed in his duty, he didn't even bat an eye when in the next room a certain oversized Knight exclaimed, "Och fannybaws! We re'lly dinnae hae runnin' water! Dae we seriously hae tae jobby in th' woods?!"

CHAPTER 18

PART 1

"Chief, you're burning up," my girlfriend told me with one hand on my forehead.

"I've already noticed, thank you," I answered with a tired grumble, though she didn't seem to mind and simply retracted her hand.

"I'll go get a cold towel, then," she proposed and waited to hear my response.

"It didn't help much the last time, but I would still appreciate it."

My reply apparently pleased her, as she gave me a determined nod before she swiftly turned on her heel and walked out of my room, leaving me alone in front of my PC. Well, okay, not entirely alone, as the tiny miko, still in her fluffy fox form, was currently curled up in my lap and watching the monitor in front of us with sparkling eyes.

"Ue-sama! Ue-sama! Click on that!"

"On what?" I griped under my breath, and she raised one stubby paw to gesture towards the corner of the screen.

"They have hakamas! And kosodes, too!"

It took me a couple of seconds to figure out just what she was talking about, but then I finally noticed an animated advertisement banner near the bottom. It was... certainly a miko outfit, except less of an authentic traditional-style one, but more of a... Oh, fine, let's not beat around the bush: it was an ad for a web shop selling fetish costumes for frisky couples who wanted to spice up their sex lives. If the see-through nature of the upper wear didn't make that perfectly obvious, the various latex tools showing up as the banner kept scrolling made things blindingly obvious. Thankfully the fox girl on my lap didn't know how they were supposed to be used (even I was a little baffled by a few of them), so before she could ask, I quickly right-clicked on the banner and added it to my ad blocker's blacklist.

"Sorry, but I doubt they would have it in your size," I told her flatly, but then after a moment of consideration I added, "If you behave yourself, I'll get you one from a cosplay maker or something."

"Really? Thank you, Ue-sama!"

I ignored her wagging tail, and after placing my orders on the currently open site's shop for the various materials required for making a holding cell or two, I closed the window. Under that, there was the utilitarian interface of the Celestial Hub. I'd originally internally debated whether or not I should even show this to Ichiko, but considering I still had my off switch for her, I didn't think letting her catch a glimpse of the Hub would make a difference.

More importantly, though, a quick glance at the recent uploads section told me that there were already a couple of reports coming in regarding today's events. I quickly skimmed them, but there was nothing in them I already didn't know about. In fact, there was actually quite a bit of misinformation, which was nice. That meant even they weren't sure what was going on, so I could probably completely lead them astray by a few well-placed reports with validated information telling them that, say, it was all Lord Grandpa's fault and the teens involved in the incidents were totally unimportant. Speaking of which, a quick glance at the forums also showed that the regulars were all busy speculating about what had happened, and the prevailing theory was that everything surrounding the break-in at the School was just an elaborate ruse by the Assembly to try to get a reaction out of Celestial Information Network, and advised the local agents to stay low. That also sounded like a nice lead I should encourage.

But now that the resident assets came up, it reminded me of a certain Celestial, so I went back to the repository, yet couldn't find any reports or posts made by Mike. That was a little odd, considering how deeply involved he was this time around. On a whim, I decided to Far Glance at the guy, and I found him in his apartment, seemingly safe and sound. He was sitting in a well-lit room, he was hunched over his computer, and coincidentally, he was staring at the very same interface that I was. That was odd, considering that the last time I checked his status it showed that he was offline, but then I came out of Far Sight and used my administrator privileges to check his profile directly, and it showed that he was actually just hidden.

This all felt slightly suspicious, so after thinking things through, I decided to send a PM to him and see how he would react.

"Admin: Ninja, are you online?"

I waited for over a minute for him to react, and I was even considering another Far Glance when he finally wrote back.

"W1NG3D N1NJ4: HELLO ADMIN! THANK DEUS YOU CALLED, I'M IN SOME DEEP POO RIGHT NOW!!! ︶(> <)︶"

"Admin: I see there was an incident on Critias. Were you involved?"

I'd just finished typing that when Judy came back with a familiar ice bag wrapped in a white towel. She wanted to apply it to my forehead right away, but when she noticed I was busy, she put it on the back of my neck instead.

"What are you doing?"

"I'm probing Mike," I told her while readjusting the towel.

"I see," she whispered, and then a short beat later she pointed at my left hand. "Why are you only typing with one hand?"

"My right hand is still a little numb," I lied to her without batting an eye. In fact, I literally couldn't move my fingers at all, and even raising my arm hurt like hell, but she didn't need to know that.

In the meantime, the Celestial on the other side of the screen finally finished typing.

"W1NG3D N1NJ4: I WAS KINDA INVOLVED BUT KINDA NOT. IT'S COMPLICATED......... (″ > _ <;″)"

"W1NG3D N1NJ4: MORE IMPORTANTLY, PLEASE HELP ME OUT!!! (シ_ _)シ"

"W1NG3D N1NJ4: I'M ASKING THIS FOR A FRIEND: LET'S SAY MY FRIEND HAS A FRIEND WHO IS NOT REALLY A FRIEND AND IS ACTUALLY A LITTLE SCARY! THIS FRIEND OF A FRIEND HELPED OUT MY FRIEND, AND NOW MY FRIEND KNOWS ABOUT HIS SECRET! (‾ ω ‾ ;)"

"W1NG3D N1NJ4: I MEAN I THINK IT'S A SECRET, BUT I'M NOT SURE, BUT IT'S A BIG DEAL, AND OTHER PEOPLE WOULD PROBABLY LIKE TO KNOW THIS SECRET, BUT MY FRIEND OWES HIM ONE AND DOESN'T KNOW WHAT TO DO!!! (O_O;)"

"W1NG3D N1NJ4: ADMIIIIIN! PLEASE HEEEEEELP MEEEEE!!! (シ_ _)シ"

"W1NG3D N1NJ4: I MEAN, PLEASE HEEEEEELP MY FRIEEEEEND!1!!!! (シ_ _)シ (シ_ _)シ"

I pondered how I should respond for a few seconds, and in the end I decided on a slightly forceful approach.

"Admin: When you said 'helped out,' do you mean a small favor, or something more significant?"

"W1NG3D N1NJ4: VEEEEERY SIGNIFICANT! LIFESAVING AND STUFF!!! (//•ω•//)"

"Admin: I see. And is this friend of a friend a threat to our cause?"

This time there was a longer pause before the answer.

"W1NG3D N1NJ4: I DON'T THINK SO. HE IS REALLY COOPERATIVE AND HELPFUL. (≧ω≦)"

"W1NG3D N1NJ4: AND SCARY... {{ (>_<) }}"

"W1NG3D N1NJ4: BUT NOT A BAD GUY! DEFINITELY NOT! (>﹏<)"

"Admin: So he is helpful to us, not a threat, and saved your life."

"W1NG3D N1NJ4: YES!"

"W1NG3D N1NJ4: I MEAN NO! HE SAVED MY FRIEND, REMEMBER!!!!1!!!one!!! (//•ω•//)"

"Admin: Yeah, sure."

"Admin: Anyhow, this friend of a friend sounds like a useful asset. Unless his secret is directly threatening our continued operations, I'd personally prioritize maintaining a productive relationship with them."

"Admin: If sharing certain information about them would jeopardize that, I'd recommend keeping it a secret for the time being."

"W1NG3D N1NJ4: YESSS!!! THANK YOU ADMIN, YOU ARE THE BEST!!! \\(≧▽≦)/"

"Admin: You're welcome."

After I finished typing, Judy took the opportunity to shift the ice pack over to my forehead while simultaneously sticking a thermometer into my mouth.

"He's quite gullible," my girlfriend noted after a single glance at the screen, and if it wouldn't have disturbed the pack on my head, I would've probably shrugged in agreement.

"That's a mean way to put it, but not inaccurate. That said, I'm actually glad he isn't particularly competent; this way I don't have to worry too much about him secretly subverting us."

"He could be playing a role to lower your guard," she moved the conversation along while wiping the sweat off my neck, and I could instantly tell that she didn't actually mean it.

"I keep him under surveillance, so unless he plays the fool even when he's all alone on the toilet, I'm fairly sure I would have noticed any nefarious scheming by now."

"You like to peep on people on the toilet? Chief, I never figured you would have such a fetish."

"You're not funny," I grumbled, but instead of responding, Judy took the thermometer from my mouth and raised it to her eye level.

"Thirty-nine point seven degrees Celsius." She noted before pocketing the device and adding, "That's almost forty. If it doesn't go down soon, you're taking a cold shower."

"That sounded more like an order than an advice..."

"Because it was. If this continues, we might have to go to the hospital."

"Or we could just ask Angie to heal me?" I proposed, only to be immediately shot down.

"It didn't help the last time you had a fever from overworking."

She locked eyes with me, and after enduring the mounting pressure for a few seconds, I let out a sigh and told her, "Fine, cold shower it is; a visit to the doctor's if it doesn't work."

"Good. Now behave yourself, and no more random teleporting today."

"... Are you still mad about that?"

"I'm not mad. I'm just concerned," she replied a tad unenthusiastically while removing the wet towel, airing it a bit, and then rewrapping the ice pack before placing it on me again.

"Ue-sama and Judy-ue have such a beautiful relationship," the little fox commented on the side between stifled giggles, and for the love of me, I couldn't see what she meant.

Judy was about to say something else, but then we were all slightly startled by the sound of a car horn coming from the outside. My dearest assistant swiftly moved over to the window, and after a single glance outside, she turned back to me.

"Father's here. I'll be right back."

"Wait, hold on for a moment," I stopped her in her tracks before she could leave the room. "I think I'm missing something. Why is your father here again?"

"When I phoned home and told my parents that I'm staying over, I also took the opportunity to ask them to bring over some of my old clothes that no longer fit me." I probably made quite a befuddled face because she quickly added, "I told Mom that one of your distant relatives is staying with you, but her luggage got lost, and she needs a change of clothes."

"Clever."

"Thank you," she responded with a thin-yet-obviously-delighted smile. I was a little taken aback by that. I mean, it wasn't like I didn't praise her when she deserved it (which was quite often), so her reaction felt a little too much... but then again, most people probably couldn't even notice her smile, so maybe I was getting oversensitive?

"Judy-ue brought me clothes!" the chunky fox on my lap exclaimed with obvious mirth and jumped off me with a happy *yip!* noise, instantly cutting my train of thought short in the process. "Can I come along? Can I see them?"

Judy glanced at the fluff ball on the floor, then back at me, and when I didn't voice any objections, she ultimately told her, "Yes, but no talking in front of my dad."

Ichiko nodded over and over again in response and scurried next to Judy's feet, but before they left, my girlfriend sent me one last sharp look.

"No Phasing while I'm away," she warned me, and I couldn't decide whether I wanted to laugh or cry.

"Dormouse, I'm having a forty-degree fever and can barely stand on my legs, let alone teleport around."

"It didn't stop you an hour ago," she countered.

"Yes because back then I only had a *thirty-eight*-degree fever. Big difference." She apparently didn't find my objection amusing, so I heaved a sigh and told her, "Fine, I promise I won't disappear anywhere. Just go; don't keep your father waiting."

She looked me in the eye for a while with an expression that could be easily translated to "You better be here when I come back, or I will kick your butt!" and considering how weak I was feeling at a moment, she actually had a good chance of keeping her end of the threat. That would have been pretty embarrassing, so I put on my trustworthiest visage and flashed a hopefully-not-too-strained smile in her general direction. At last, she left in the company of the foxy miko, and the moment she closed the door behind her, I couldn't help but let a long groan escape through my clenched teeth.

I really was feeling pretty terrible at the moment. The headache was back, with a vengeance, and more troublingly, it was still getting worse over time. My right hand also hurt like crazy, though if I didn't try to move it, it was still bearable. All my other joints were sensitive, as well, but that was probably because of the fever. Oh, and I could barely feel my legs, but that was mainly due to Ichiko sitting on them until now, so it didn't count.

In conclusion, I was in pretty bad shape right now. That was nothing new, though, so once I collected myself a bit, I turned to the PC again so that, if nothing else, it would at least divert my attention a little. I refreshed the Hub, and to my momentary surprise, I actually found a new report signed by Mike.

"That was quick," I whispered under my breath while I waited for the file to open.

After skimming it, I was relieved to see that, while he broadly detailed his perspective on today's events, the method of his escape was left fairly vague. Also, if what he wrote was to be believed, he interacted with Lab Coat Guy using a fake identity, so even if he'd spilled the beans while in Lord Grandpa's custody, at most he could give only a general description of Mike's appearance. Even if the arch-mage decided to look into him, there was a good chance he wouldn't be found... but then again, the guy was quite enamored with his granddaughter, so that might complicate things.

I was just about to Far Glance at Lab Coat Guy to see if he was being interrogated, but then Judy suddenly burst into the room, startling me for a moment.

"... What?" I blurted out with a no-doubt-quite-befuddled grimace spreading over my face.

"Nothing," my assistant stated with an even pokerier face than usual as she gently closed the door behind her. "I'm just glad to see that you really didn't go anywhere."

"I told you I wouldn't...!" I objected, only to swallow the rest of my complaints and instead tell her, "Never mind. In case I forget, please remind me to ask Lab Coat Guy about how much he told the Magi about Mike."

"Will do," she answered while walking up to me and putting a hand on my cheek. "You're still burning up."

"Yeah, and I have a feeling it's not going to get better anytime soon." It was around this time that my brain finally registered the conspicuous absence of a certain red fur ball. "Where's Ichiko?"

"In the guest room. She said she wanted to see if any of the clothes that Dad brought fit her. Also, speaking of my father, he told me to remind you that he still has a shotgun."

"Your dad is as charming as ever," I griped in a voice flatter than the salt pans, and Judy simply shrugged my complaints away.

"He's just protective."

That line of conversation fizzled out right there, so after a long-but-not-necessarily-uncomfortable beat later, I gestured for Judy to sit on my bed, and I also rolled closer in my chair.

"So since hopefully the day is over, how about we discuss this epic mess we just weathered?"

"I concur. The sooner, the better," she agreed right away and took out her phone with practiced motions.

"Good. So let's start by summarizing the current situation." I paused to take a deep breath, then began. "First off, Lab Coat Guy is neutralized, and I convinced Lord Grandpa to put him in our custody. With some luck, that should put an end to the genre shift, and we could prevent any future resurgence of *sentai* shenanigans."

"You say *custody*, but what exactly are we going to do with him?"

"Good question. I haven't thought much about it yet, but for the time being I think I'll lock him up in the secret base and have the Fauns keep him under surveillance. As for later, I think we might be able to use him. So long as we provide him the means and the incentive, I think he could be useful for probing the supernatural substrate and the limits and exact mechanisms of the world. He could also aid us in performing some of the experiments we couldn't do because of lack of equipment and resources."

"Sounds feasible. He's a scientist, even if a mad one," Judy commented while speed-tapping on her phone, and I nodded while waiting for her to finish.

"That's right. As for the fembot, we might be able to put her to use after her weaponry is removed."

"Are you planning on turning her into a maid, too?"

"Oh, ha ha," I said, rolling my eyes in the process. "That's a really original joke that I've never heard before. How utterly amusing."

"I was serious, though."

I sent my assistant a flat look in return for her honestly and told her, "For the umpteenth time, I don't have a maid fetish."

"We did get a reaction out of you when we dressed up, though," she noted without even a hint of shyness, prompting me to roll my eyes again.

"Yes, but it was just a tiiiiiiiiiny reaction, and only because it was you two. I don't want to just arbitrarily put everyone into maid costumes."

"So if I understand this right," Judy began, only to dramatically pause and lower her phone before finishing with, "You don't like maids, but you like it when Elly and I dress as maids."

"... In a manner of speaking," I admitted a tad begrudgingly.

"So it's all right if we dress as maids."

"Maybe every once in a while," I finally relented, at which point my girlfriend directed a downright triumphant smirk at me, annoying me to no end. "We're veering way off topic. How about we discuss your fetish for dressing up as maids later and return to the previous conversation?"

"Chief, don't just insinuate something like that and then change the subject," my dearest assistant protested, only to be summarily ignored by yours truly.

"Too late, I already did," I declared with a grin before adopting a more serious expression and saying, "Next, the Knights attacked sooner than expected. Thankfully there were no casualties on either side, and we even got a new sword and a rare artifact out of the deal."

"We also learned that they were specifically looking for the dragon-slaying spear," Judy noted, though the way her brows were ever-so-slightly angled told me she was still sore about my previous comment.

"Yeah. Good thing I figured something like this would happen and took it ahead of time. It will be a little tricky to explain it to Sebastian, though, but I'll cross that bridge when I get there."

"You marked one of them, didn't you?"

"Yeah, I did. They are going to be staying on the island because of the lockdown, and there are more of them coming, but for the time being they should be laying low. I'll try to keep an eye on them, but I only managed to mark one of the grunts, so I won't be able to see all of their movements."

"That still leaves us with more information than what we had yesterday," Judy remarked, and a few taps later she also added a question. "Let me address the elephant in the room: What are we going to do with Rinne and Ichiko?"

"You mean the fox not in the room?" I jested, but then exhaled a short breath and told her, in a more serious tone, "The two of them weren't exactly in their right minds when they attacked us, but they still tried to kill me. Rinne is a little tricky to place. Her temper seemingly calmed down quite a bit after she was separated from her sword, but I think we're probably best off keeping her in custody for a while. If she behaves herself, we can probably let her go."

"You don't want to recruit her?" she asked, though I couldn't help but feel that there was the tiniest of edges in her words. "You have a habit of doing that to people that tried to kill you."

I wanted to protest, but then I thought about it for a moment. Brang, Snowy, Lab Coat Guy and his fembot, the fox girl in the next room... Okay, maybe she did have a point, but not in this case in particular.

"Not if I can help it, though I admit she would be a nice hidden card in case things go south like today. Unfortunately, I don't really have a way to ensure her loyalty, and considering she's a wandering monster slayer, she probably wouldn't stay here for long, anyway. Not to mention, if we detain her for too long, her as-of-yet-only-mentioned-but-never-seen clan of ninjas might come and pick a fight with us, and I really want to avoid that."

"Reasonable. What about Ichiko?"

"That's... a trickier question," I mused aloud, and after fixing my posture and readjusting my ice pack, I came to the following conclusion. "Unlike Rinne, she both owes me a big favor, and I have a direct means of control over her. Not to mention, she seems to be quite attached to me already."

"That's one way to put it," my girlfriend whispered under her breath, but did so loud enough for me to hear her. Probably on purpose. "So you plan to keep her?"

"That's also one way to put it," I confirmed her suspicion with a small nod. "I mean, she's technically a sentient, shape-shifting Chimera under my control. No matter how you look at it, that could come in handy in a number of scenarios."

"Such as?"

"Such as being your bodyguard," I dropped the bombshell I was preparing ever since I first thought of putting the tiny miko into the Chimera's body and learned that she could transform into other shapes, and based on how Judy immediately froze up, it actually rattled her a bit.

"Come again?"

"All right, just keep an open mind and hear me out: I told you I plan to outfit you with some defensive artifacts, but those are hard to make and require regular refilling because you can't use magic. The thing is, as long as you're around Elly and me, which I presume is going to be for quite a long while, it's only a question of time before someone gets the bright idea to target you, as well. So since I can't hover around you twenty-four/seven, the next-best option is to have a bodyguard. Someone who can stay with you in your house, doesn't draw attention, and yet powerful enough to deter most kidnappers, assassins, and other assorted bad guys. If you think about it, I think a tiny Chimera disguised as a fox would be perfect for the job."

Judy gave me a very long, very deadpan stare down, put her phone away, looked me in the eye, and calmly stated, "Chief, is it just me, or does that sound like yet another major case of post hoc rationalization to you, as well?"

"Oh please, Dormouse! Give me some credit! There's nothing post hoc about it; I thought this up at least five minutes before I put her into that body!"

"Your defense of your actions makes paper seem like battle-tank plating," she jabbed back at me, but at last she sighed and told me, "I'll consider the idea, but I don't know if my parents would agree to let me adopt a fox."

"Tell them it's just a rare dog breed. Also, you can have her act cute in front of them; that should convince them."

There was a long pause in the conversation as my girlfriend's guard slowly but steadily crumbled, and at last she asked, "If, theoretically, I would take her home, what should I tell Mom and Dad?"

"Well... how about this: Say that she belongs to the distant relative that came to my place, but she cannot be kept at my place because Snowy is allergic to dogs, so I asked you to take care of her for a few days. Then a couple of days later we tell them that there were some complications, and she'll have to stay over a bit longer, and then make that *a bit longer* into *indefinitely*, and then she can stay over at your house forever."

"Not forever, only until after we finish high school and I move in with you," she corrected me, and I couldn't help but smile at her.

"You're thinking way ahead, as usual. Anyhow, I think that takes care of the fox issue, so let's move on. Next, there is Lord Grandpa. I have finally marked him, so now I can keep a direct eye on him. More importantly, while I managed to keep him in check for now, he strikes me as the type who will try to scheme anyway just for the heck of it, so even though we aren't exactly enemies, we aren't going to be friends, either."

"I remember you saying you wanted to gain access to the archives in the School. Did you manage that?"

"Yeah, though I have a feeling they are going to scrub them before they'll let us in. Still, access to the papers on magical theory and more cross-reference materials for the Hub and the Dracis library could be invaluable in the long run."

"I see. Anything else?"

"Not much. We had some collateral damage in the secret base, some minor injuries, and Rinne's clan and the Knights are currently rogue elements, but otherwise things are under control."

"I mostly agree." Saying so, Judy theatrically swiped her finger across the screen of her phone, probably to switch to another file in the note app, and proclaimed, "Since the in-universe issues are clarified, I believe this is the point where we discuss the narrative ramifications of today's events."

"And you'd be correct," I answered, "Though I'm not fond of the term *in-universe*."

"Mundane?"

"That just sounds weird when all we are talking about are supernatural things."

"Then how about profane, then?"

"Sounds a bit too religious."

"Intradiegetic?"

"... And to think there was a time when I had to explain to you what an otaku was..." I uttered in mild amazement before stifling a chuckle and telling her, "Sure, let's go with that."

"Noted," she answered as she did just that on her phone, and then she waited for me to speak my mind.

"First and foremost, we can more or less conclude that we put a forceful end to the potential *sentai* genre shift. That part went as planned, in a manner of speaking. However, the way the rest of the events happened is very suspicious."

"Should we go with the usual Doylist and Watsonian explanations?"

"Yeah. I'll start with the Watsonian one this time," I answered, and once I collected my thoughts a little, I began with, "The attack on Lab Coat Guy was, while rushed, technically under our control, and we had good reasons for it, as we needed to rescue Mike. We needed to rescue him because we needed to get him out of the cross fire before Lord

Grandpa captured him along with Lab Coat Guy, and he would do that because I *borrowed* his Grimoire Key without telling him ahead of time." I waited here for Judy to finish taking notes, then added, "Rinne attacked the base because she followed the trail of the Chimera left behind by the Fauns transporting it. The Knights attacked the mansion with the intent to smash and grab the dragon-slaying spear while Abram and Sebastian were away. Each of their actions makes internal sense, and none of them were aware of the others."

"Yet the timing was way too much to be a coincidence," Judy added with just a hint of skepticism in her voice.

"Not necessarily," I posited, as my role as the devil's advocate demanded from me. "Our own operation was done on short notice because of time constraints, but Rinne showing up at the base a day after the apparent defeat of the Chimera was entirely reasonable. I mean, if she did it out of the blue, that would've been pretty contrived, but since the trail was still fresh, her being able to follow her nose to the base still makes a modicum of sense."

"But if she could follow the trails of Abyssals so well, how come she never found the base by following the Fauns?"

"That's... a very good question. She also couldn't recognize Snowy being an Abyssal, so maybe there are some conditions? I don't know; we should ask her about it later."

"Among other things. We still haven't properly interrogated her."

"True, but it's not like we're in a hurry; I doubt she could escape anytime soon while being hog-tied and guarded all the time. Putting her appearance aside, let's move on while my brain's still operational." Judy nodded along, so after another deep breath, I moved on to the third party of today's incident. "Explaining the timing of the Knights is a bit trickier, but still possible. Let's presume that their main goal was the spear and nothing else. Abram and Sebastian leaving ahead of time was something they couldn't have foreseen, but if their goal wasn't assassination, then two being absent actually provided a great opportunity for them. As for why they chose the exact moment when we attacked Lab Coat Guy and Rinne showed up... I can only chalk that up to freak coincidence."

"So that was the Watsonian version. Do you want me to do the Doylist?" Judy asked, and I quickly shook my head.

"Wait, I'm not finished yet," I replied, and once I heaved the mother of all sighs, I began in earnest. "So while the perfect timing of the events is still up in the air, I think the reason why everything crescendoed today is not. Simply put, it's because of my actions. For one, if I hadn't told Brang to bring the Chimera to the base, Rinne could've never found it in the first place. In fact, if I hadn't tried to keep it but disposed of it on the spot, she would have had no trail to follow to begin with."

I paused here for a moment to let Judy digest and note down my explanation, and I only continued after she finally looked up from her phone.

"As for Mike, he got captured because I asked him to gather artifacts. If he hadn't contacted Lab Coat Guy and gotten captured by him, and he'd used some generic placeholder Celestial to construct his frame-up job instead, we would've had no reason to rush in to rescue him. Not only that, but the only reason we needed to rescue him today was because I took the MacGuffin from the School, Lord Grandpa went on the warpath against Lab Coat Guy, and we needed to get to Mike before he did." I punctuated my reasoning with a short pause here, and then concluded with, "Finally, for the Knights, they attacked ahead of time because I told Elly's family about myself and the original date of the attack, and because of that, they set a trap that inadvertently prompted the Knights to strike earlier than planned. In short, by going against the grain, I messed up the original order of events, and thus I'm indirectly responsible for what happened today."

I fell silent after my monologue and waited for Judy's response, and soon she put her phone aside and told me, "A valiant effort, Chief, but you didn't go far enough."

"Oh? All right, I'm listening," I prompted her, and she gave me a curt nod in return.

"The attack by the huntress and the Knights could certainly be chalked up to one-off coincidence, but it is also entirely possible that they were influenced by the Narrative. Rinne's supposed role was to hunt down the Chimera on the island. There's a possibility that, due to your interference, she didn't technically fulfill this role, and thus the Narrative led her to the base to finish the job, with her supernatural olfaction serving as means to explain how she could find it."

"Maybe, but whether it was because of the trail or because of Narrative influence, it still leads to the same conclusion, and while we still don't know enough about the way the world enforces certain events, it was already established that she's a hunter and tracker, and that she can smell supernatural nasties like a hound. In short, I find the presence of Narrative influence in this explanation to be superfluous."

"So you are invoking Occam's razor?"

"More or less," I supposed with a shrug.

"Fair enough. However, the other two events coinciding is still too conspicuous, and I believe it's because the Narrative was trying its best to course correct."

"Please do elaborate," I asked, and she immediately complied.

"By stealing the Grimoire Key, you caused a serious disturbance in the original plot. For the sake of the thought experiment, let's presume that the original involved Robatto butting heads with Lord Endymonion, and Josh and the others helping to defeat and capture him in the following days, and then when it looked like things would return to the status quo, the Knightly Brotherhood of the Most Heroic Bloodlines would stage their attack, raising the stakes and paving the way for the next arc. Are you following me so far?"

"Yeah, of course. I might look bad because of the fever, but my brain still works. Mostly."

"I'm glad to hear that," she said, though she still looked more than a little skeptical. Or worried. Or both. It was hard to tell, but in my defense, my brain was only mostly working at the moment. Anyhow, she soon continued her theorizing. "With the previous hypothetical scenario in mind, here's what I think happened: by stealing the Grimoire Key while framing Robatto, you did two things that unintentionally messed up the Narrative: You completely changed Lord Endymonion's priorities regarding Dr. Robatto, and you caused the island to be locked down. The first was an issue because it would logically force the arch-mage and the School to strike down Robatto on their own, thus robbing Joshua and the others of their final confrontation with the antagonist."

"So you think the Narrative manipulated us to take down Lab Coat Guy before Lord Grandpa could do it?" She nodded in confirmation, and I couldn't help but frown in return. "I... honestly don't think I felt manipulated or sidetracked, though. Sure, I wasn't really happy about how much we had to rush it, but the whole idea felt logical at the time, and it still makes internal sense to me."

"I don't think we were all influenced by the Narrative, only Amelia," Judy proposed in a solemn voice.

"Now that you mention it, she really was the one who pushed the hardest for Mike's immediate rescue," I concurred while crossing my fingers in my lap. "Not to mention, her rapidly developing a fondness for the guy is also a little suspect."

"Precisely my point. In my opinion, to preserve the final confrontation without breaking the internal consistency of the world, the Narrative rushed the scenario and had Amelia be there to justify it to the rest of us. I also think that the way we all agreed was a little too easy, but as you said, I didn't feel anything out of place at the time."

"So the first point is that to preserve the action climax against Lab Coat Guy, the Narrative twisted itself into a pretzel to justify a rushed resolution, and Ammy was manipulated, either directly or indirectly, into pushing us all in that direction. Okay, I can grant you that as a hypothesis for the time being. What about the second point?"

"The School locking down the island and the coming of the Assembly investigators," Judy reiterated. "I believe it was the cause behind the Knights' abrupt attack. I doubt the lockdown will be lifted for a while, even after you gave the Grimoire Key back to the arch-mage, because they have to keep up appearances in front of the rest of the Assembly. That means the Knights currently on the island cannot leave, and their reinforcements will have a harder time infiltrating, limiting their numbers to just the small group already on the island."

"There's going to be one more Knight on the island," I noted, and since Judy gave me a curious look, I explained, "I used Far Sight on them, and overheard that one more Entitled One was already on the way to the island. She's probably the Unicorn Knight, and if these guys are to be trusted, she should be able to join them without triggering any alarms."

"Good to know," she responded half-heartedly, and after jotting the new info down into her notes, she continued with, "Either way, their numbers on the island were limited at the time, and since Abram and Sebastian were already back, the Narrative likely pushed the attack forward in the small gap where they would still have the opportunity to take the spear without the interference of the men of the family or the Assembly."

"Except I'd already taken the spear."

"Yes, but by that point things were already in motion, and I think the important part was the confrontation itself, not the spear. You also further interfered with them, effectively neutering them as a potential threat. This might have some serious consequences in the next arc."

"In case we really are operating in arcs, you mean. Anyhow, let me try to sum up your argument: by taking the MacGuffin, I accidentally caused a situation that would've sabotaged the original climax of the theoretical arc if it had played out as theoretically planned, so the Narrative tried to course correct by rushing the Lab Coat Guy and the Knight plots to a conclusion, while Rinne was just..."

"A spanner in the works," my assistant stated. "Either that, or she was always meant to go crazy and attack us, and since the Chimera subplot was already resolved, the Narrative arranged things so that she could do it, anyway."

"Considering how unstable she used to be, that's not entirely off the table," I whispered in response, but I wasn't exactly convinced, either.

Her interpretation of the events sounded plausible, and this time I was almost tempted to believe her hypothesis, if for nothing else than because it meant that this nebulous Narrative of ours was not infallible. After all, if she was right, then everything happened today because I accidentally derailed the original plans, but instead of forcefully course correcting us, it resulted in a patchwork mess where events were pushed around and a couple of plot devices, such as Emese's wound or the taking of the spear, ended up completely subverted. We still had a scary entity that may or may not be consciously orchestrating our lives, but at the same time, it wasn't omnipotent or omniscient enough to keep things sticking to the rails. Judy got her Narrative pet theory seemingly validated, and I got my reassurance that hard work and some arguably less-than-reasonable stunts could still provide us a way out of possible predetermination. It felt like having my cake and eating it, too. In a way, it was almost too good to be true.

Maybe that was why I had a hard time accepting it. As far as hypotheses were concerned, it was an okay one, but it all hinged on her hypothetical original scenario without my interference being on the mark, something we simply couldn't confirm. In fact, while exploring the supernatural limits of the world provided us with something to work on, and we could still perform certain simple experiments, the original roadblock we'd run into a while back was still present: without actually being able to see what the original plot was supposed to be like, it was impossible to tell what effect, if any, our actions had on it. Case in point, while we'd spent all this time discussing how my actions may or may not have affected the Narrative, and how it may or may not have pushed back by influencing Ammy, the Knights, and possibly Rinne, there was no guarantee that today's events weren't how things were supposed to happen from the very get-go, and we were still solidly on the rails. Until we could find a way to somehow overcome this hurdle, I was afraid most of our theory crafting would stay just that.

Anyhow, all of this was something that definitely required more mental elbow grease, and preferably when my head wasn't feeling like it had a red-hot woodsman's axe embedded in it.

"I still think we're missing a few steps, and coming up with a few alternative explanations wouldn't hurt, but considering how fresh the events are, I don't think we can analyze them any further right now. Also, I'm feeling really damn battered at the moment, so should we stop now, or do we have something else to discuss?"

"We have a lot of things to discuss," Judy answered a bit peevishly, probably unhappy about how I still wasn't in complete agreement with her, "But considering how sick you are, I'll let you rest after one last thing."

"How gracious of you," I replied with a grin that made her look a tad worried, so I quickly wiped the expression off my face and said, "I'm listening."

"What happened after you came out of the sword?"

"Oh, that?" I collected my thoughts for a second and told her, "Well, since Ichiko was in trouble, I decided to move her into the body of the Chimera. It wasn't exactly simple, but since it didn't have a soul but an already-installed control enchantment, I managed to do it anyway, aaaaaaaand that's not what you wanted to know, is it?"

Judy immediately shook her head with a minuscule frown.

"No, I meant while you were acting weird. The Fauns said you completely ignored them, and you didn't answer to me when I called out to you, either."

To my surprise, and concern, she seemed almost rattled for a moment, so I quickly told her, "I honestly don't know. I can remember what happened, but everything is a little fuzzy. I felt... kind of detached for a moment. Like I was not completely back in my body after I finished tinkering with Onikiri."

"So it was caused by the sword?"

"Not necessarily. My two cents are on simply overworking myself, or some kind of interplay between spending so much time inside the supernatural stratum while already being sick from Phasing too much. We probably won't know until I try overexerting myself again under controlled circumstances."

"Not now," Judy warned me, and if I wasn't afraid the ice pack would fall off my head, I would have rolled my eyes harder than eyes have ever been rolled in the history of mankind.

"Obviously. Still, it was... How should I put it? Back then, I think I was hyperaware, or knew things. Important things that I can't remember right now, but they felt really important. It was... kind of like when you are in a dream, and inside the dream everything makes sense, but when you wake up, you don't remember any of it."

My girlfriend sent me a wry look and immediately reached out to touch my forehead.

"Chief, I think you're starting to get delirious. How would you know what it feels to dream when you never sleep?"

"I'm talking in general, not from personal experience."

"Either way, you're getting that cold shower, and then we will discuss this again."

I was just about to protest, but the words could never leave my mouth, as our alone time was interrupted by a new voice entering the fray.

"Ue-sama! Judy-ue!"

We both looked towards the slowly opening door, and from the other side came a little girl wearing a light-green summer dress that reached down to her knees. She wasn't wearing anything other than that, not even socks, but hey, it was still better than running around naked. Though again, she was doing that as a fox, anyway, but that's beside the point.

"How do I look?" Asking so, Ichiko did a small pirouette, her long hair and the long skirt both billowing around her before she came to a stop.

"Decently cute," I noted, only to receive a sharp look from my girl-friend. "What?"

"You're only allowed to call her cute when she's a fox," Judy declared with the kind of finality usually reserved for supreme judges.

"Well, whether I'm allowed or not, she is. Anyone would be cute in those clothes. In fact, I bet that you would look downright adorable in that kind of outfit."

For a moment Judy didn't seem to be able to decide how to react to that, but in the end she chose to take it as a compliment. Or at least I think so because she didn't bother me about it any longer. In the meantime, the tiny miko started squirming, and after a short while, she turned to my assistant.

"Judy-ue? Where's the toilet?"

She gave her a skeptical look, but since she looked entirely serious, Judy stood up and took her by the hand.

"This way. I told you not to drink so much tea."

"But it was sweet..." the little girl whined, and before I knew it, I was once again alone in my room.

Well, at least they got along. That was a positive.

Thinking so, I rolled back to my PC, opened up the browser again, and once I saw that there was nothing noteworthy happening on the Hub, I opened a new tab and typed *summer dress, light green* into the search bar while wondering how I could find out Judy's size without her being the wiser...

PART 2

The morning of the first day of November was mild for the season yet other-wise fairly unremarkable, especially considering it marked the beginning of the third month I'd lived in this weird world of ours. This kind of occasion normally warranted standing by a window and looking at the dawning sun with a forlorn expression, with either a warm cup or a cuddly cat to com-plete the picture, but considering that I was feeling like ten pounds of agony packed into a five-pound bag, I graciously refrained from doing so. I was, however, standing near a window, if only so that I would have a good view of the street outside. It was exactly at nine in the morning, not a minute later, when a black passenger van with tinted windows leisurely rolled onto our street and came to a halt in front of my driveway.

"Chief, I think they are here," my dear assistant called out to me as she walked down the stairs, wearing a set of backup clothes she stored in my guest room in case she stayed over, and her hair was still slightly damp after taking a shower not too long ago.

"Yeah, but not all of them," I answered as I absently observed the generic-looking-yet-impeccably-dressed men-in-black letting our friends out of the car one at a time.

"I'll let them in."

I wanted to quip something about how it was obvious she would, as I probably couldn't drag myself to the door even if I tried, but by the time I formulated something suitably snappy, she was already out of the room. I didn't dwell on the missed opportunity for... doing something unnecessary? Why did I want to do that again? Man, my brain was a mess.

Anyhow, since there was no reason for me to stay by the window any longer, I hauled myself over to my traditional sitting spot, dropped my posterior onto my trusty comfy chair, and waited for our group to arrive. Oh, and incidentally, Ichiko was also in the room, and once I moved, she also scurried next to my seat with a guarded expression. She was also in her human form at the moment because after we discussed things with Judy, we decided it was best to quickly come clean about her so that everyone would be aware of her and her abilities.

Speaking of abilities, it turned out that the way she shifted between her fox and her little girl forms was not at all like how Chimeras transformed. If anything, it was closer to Elly's way of changing into her draconic form, but with some extra magical lights thrown into the mix to hide the process. Oh, and not only that, but she didn't adhere to the laws of conservation of mass, either, which wouldn't have been all that weird, except both the Chimera and Elly did! Or rather, I can only speculate regarding the Chimera, based on what I saw when I encountered it, but for the princess, I actually asked her to tell me her weight before and after transformation... and she didn't because apparently that was something I shouldn't ask from a girl. Go figure. In the end Judy did the experiment in my stead using our bathroom scale, and she assured me that her mass remained the same. The little miko, on the other hand, weighed less than half as much as a fox as she did as a human.

That was fairly interesting thing to think about... or maybe not, and I was just zoning out again. Either way, I rubbed the bridge of my nose to compose myself, and in the meantime the new arrivals entered the living room. There were only four of them present, with Snowy at the front, followed by Angie and Elly, and finally Josh closing the procession, though I could barely see him because he was all but completely hidden under a pile of colourful boxes.

"Wow, Leo! You look terrible!" Angie declared the moment she laid her eyes on me, much to my chagrin. I mean, she wasn't wrong; I was currently in my casual clothes, wrapped in a blanket around my shoulders, and a wet towel on my head, but the upbeat way she made the remark was still annoying.

"Yeah, I second that," Josh agreed after placing the boxes onto the table. "You look like you didn't get a wink of sleep last night, and you weren't even the one who got imprisoned in a room underground until morning!"

"Hey! Leo was working the hardest out of all of us yesterday!" the princess sprung to my defense right away, and both Snowy and Angie were in wholehearted agreement with her.

"Hey, I never questioned that! I just find it peculiar, that's all," my friend defended himself, and to be fair, he had a point.

For one, they were wearing their Magiforms while they were fighting, so even though they went through quite a scuffle, their actual school uniforms were perfectly clean. Not only that, but even though they were officially in custody, they were given the opportunity to clean themselves up, so unlike me, they looked like perfectly healthy and lively high schoolers ready to go to school.

"Where's Amelia?" Judy cut in between the three frowning girls and the rapidly backpedaling Josh, and he immediately took the opportunity to change the subject.

"Ammy and Pascal are coming with the next car. She said they have something to take care of first, and then they will be joining us later."

"So Pascal's coming, too. That means I need to prepare eleven drinks," Judy murmured and, after sending one last glance at me (probably to see if I was still all right), she headed towards the kitchen.

"Wait, I'll help!" Snowy proposed right away, and she dashed after my girlfriend.

"Eleven? That doesn't add up," Josh whispered while obviously counting in his head, but no one paid him any notice at the time.

In the meantime, the princess made her way over to my side and leaned closer to take a better look at me.

"You really look sick," she noted before gingerly extending her fingers towards my forehead, and her eyes opened wide as saucers the moment she made contact. "Wait, you don't just look bad; you have a fever!"

"Well, yeah. I overworked myself a little. Again." I was only very slightly downplaying my current condition, but my draconic girlfriend refused to have any of it.

"Angie, come over here! Leo needs healing!"

"I can check!" the upbeat Celestial proposed right away and bounced over to my side, much to my momentary annoyance. I mean, being worried about me was sweet and all, but we had more important things to discuss, and I could ask Angie myself later.

"Don't look at me like that, Leo!" Elly protested in a low voice, followed up by her trademark pout. "Your health comes first; we can talk later."

"... Princess, did you just read my mind?"

"I don't need to! I just know how you think," she stated with just a hint of that subliminal smugness that I found so adorable, so before I knew it, I gestured for her to come closer.

She didn't understand at first, but then she must've figured out what I wanted, as she carefully put her arms around my shoulders and leaned in for a kiss, which would've probably landed right on the intended target if not for a sudden squeal coming from behind the backrest of my favourite chair.

"U-U-Ue-samaaa! What are you doing!?"

After the expected moment of complete bafflement passed, I heaved an exasperated sigh befitting the situation and gently pushed Elly back, if only so that I could lean to the side and take a look at the little girl hiding behind the chair.

"The better question is, why are you curled up behind me like that?" I asked the first thing that came to mind, and the tiny fox girl immediately stiffened in response.

"I-it's because he is scary!" she declared in a heated-yet-at-the-same-time-mousy voice while pointing in the general direction of Josh, though even if she wasn't, considering that he was the only other he in the room besides me, it wasn't hard to figure out whom she was talking about. However, before I could ask just why exactly she was wary of him, she collected herself and let her hand down, facing me again. "More importantly, why is Ue-sama cheating on Judy-ue in front of everyone?"

"I'm not cheating. She's also my girlfriend."

"Really?" Her eyes opened wide for a second as she digested the new information, but then she finally registered that she was in the cross fire of everyone's attention. A blink of an eye later she blushed crimson in embarrassment and exclaimed, "I will ask Judy-ue!"

And just like that, the little miko dashed out of the living room and into the kitchen, leaving an odd silence in her wake.

"Soooo... Who was that?" Josh voiced the question on everyone's minds while trying to peep into the kitchen, but when he couldn't catch a glimpse of her, he turned back to me and reinforced his question by directing one of his world-class single raised eyebrows at me.

"Her name is Ichiko," I told them, my voice feeling a little weary even to myself, so I quickly cleared my throat and continued in a more normal tone. "She used to be a shrine maiden who then turned into a sword, but now she is a Chimera that turned into a girl. Also a fox, but not right now."

The people in the room shared an incredulous glance between one another, and it once again fell on Joshua's shoulders to ask, "Which part of that was the punch line?"

"None of it. I'm entirely serious," I responded, but since they still seemed skeptical, I decided to move things along. "I'll explain in detail when they are back."

After saying so, I gestured for my draconic girlfriend to come closer again, so that she could receive the welcome kiss she'd missed because of the interruption, while Angie took the situation in stride and began to hum some kind of song, no doubt as part of either her diagnosis or treatment of me. I wasn't holding my breath, since she couldn't do much about my fever the last two times I'd overworked myself, but considering I had a couple of other injuries, I wasn't going to turn her down.

"So I counted again with the kid included, but we are still short of eleven people," came the unexpected comment from Josh, and after some consideration, I decided to straight out tell him what was going on.

"It's because Lab Coat Guy and his android are also coming."

"Wait, what? Why?"

This time the question came from Elly, and she seemed baffled and outraged by the prospect in equal measure.

"I've made a deal with the arch-mage. They are not going to be prosecuted for the mess they caused, but instead they are going to be in our custody, and I'm planning to put them to work in the secret base."

"Custody? Since when are we allowed to do that?" Josh followed up with yet another skeptically raised eyebrow.

"It's not really a question of being allowed or not, but necessity. For now, I plan to stick them into one of the unused rooms in the base."

"And who's going to guard them?"

"These guys," I answered while pointing with my left thumb, and it took an embarrassingly long time for the two Fauns in the corner to realize I was talking about them and remove their cloaking.

"Ack!" Josh of all people reeled in surprise, but once he regained his wits, he let out an embarrassed groan followed by a peevish, "I hate it when they do that!"

"Apologies," Karukk said in the characteristic, rumbling voice of the Fauns, while Vurrok beside him averted his eyes and pretended this situation had nothing to do with him.

"Hold on! Why are they like that?" Elly spoke up again as the obvious white bandages failed to avoid her eagle eyes.

"We had a bit of a battle in the secret base, there was some collateral damage, the perpetrator was detained, and her sword is now the little girl you just saw." I noticed that Josh was giving me another "Is this guy pulling my leg?" look, but before I could clarify myself, Angie called out to me for a change.

"Collateral damage? Is the air hockey table safe?"

Now it was my turn to give someone a doubtful look.

"I'm glad to see that your priorities are the same as usual," I jested. "And yes, it's fine."

"That's good. I still need to have my rematch with Elly," the Celestial girl noted while moving her hand in a circular motion in front of me, only to then pause and ask, "You have a small cut on your stomach. Do you want me to treat it?"

"While you're at it, might as well," I shrugged, and she gave me a happy-go-lucky "Yessir" before resuming her humming. "So air hockey tables aside, I'll explain everything in detail once everyone arrives. Now, here's a question from me for a change: What's with those boxes?"

"Oh, you mean these?" my friend asked back as he raised the topmost one to show its front to me. "I have no idea why, but Ammy's grandpa gave all of these board games to us last night. We didn't even have time to try them out yet, but then when we wanted to give them back in the morning, he told us we can keep them."

"They look pretty sweet!" Angie chimed again. "I really wanted to try the one where one player has a castle and the other has an army, and you have to shoot each other with catapults and cannons!"

"Of course you'd want to play the one game where your goal is to break stuff," Josh scoffed on the side, earning him a not-at-all-unexpected glare from his childhood friend.

"Says the guy who only wanted to play the game where you crush clay figures with a Rube Goldberg machine!"

It looked like the two of them were just about to descend into yet another one of their usual childhood friend spats, but then it was cut mercifully short by the reappearance of Judy and the two youngest girls following behind her, all carrying trays with either soft drinks or snacks. For some inexplicable reason, my kitchen had those stocked all the time, but it was a mystery I was already used to.

Judy and Snowy looked the same as usual, but Ichiko in particular was unusually twitchy, and while on her way to the table to place her tray, she kept sending sneaky glances at me, Elly, and Josh, in that order. Then, the moment her hands were free, she dashed away from the others and came to a screeching halt in front of me before melodramatically falling to her knees and doing that weird bowing thing when her forehead touched the ground.

"I'm sorry, Ue-sama, for lacking faith in you! I couldn't know that Princess-ue is also your lover! I brought shame upon myself!"

"Please get up and stop being so overdramatic. You're embarrassing me." The moment I said that she immediately jumped to her feet, but didn't quit bowing her head. "Stop that, too. Also, only I'm calling her princess; her name is Eleanor."

"We call her Elly," Josh commented on the side, pretending to organize the boxes while obviously paying full attention to our conversation.

"So it is like with Judy-ue and her second name! I should have known!" Saying so, she immediately bowed to Elly in turn. "Please excuse my lack of etiquette, Elly-ue!"

My draconic girlfriend looked at the newcomer with considerable confusion, and after some consideration she eventually concluded, "She's weird."

"Yep, she is," I agreed before pointedly clearing my throat. "So I think it's about time I properly introduced her. Everyone, this is Ichiko. As I said, she used to be a sword, but due to some circumstances, right now she is inhabiting the empty body of the Chimera that we encountered during the incident with Crowey. Oh, and as I said, she can also turn into a fox."

"Seriously?" Elly suddenly asked with a surprised look on her face.

"A fluffy one," Judy added with a solemn nod that was way too serious considering the situation.

"Can I see it?" came the next interjection from the Celestial girl by my side, and I shook my head.

"I know you guys like cute things, but this is really not the time. Also, let me introduce you guys, too." I waited for the little miko to pay attention to me, and then I began our roll call by pointing at the people present one at a time. "You already know Judy and the big guys in the corner, so let's skip them. This lovely girl is Elly, my other girlfriend, and she is Draconian. This silly girl over here is Angie, and she is Celestial. That scary guy over there is Josh, and he is weird, so you better not get too close to him."

"Hey," Josh protested, but I summarily ignored him.

"Finally, that cute girl is Snowy, currently my little sister, and she's from the Abyss. We are also soon going to get more company, but I'll introduce them when they get here."

"I see, I see..." Ichiko nodded a couple of times. "So it's Elly-ue, Angie-san, Josh-san, and..." Suddenly she paused when she got to Snowy, and after wracking her brain for a second, she sends a pitiful glance at Judy, and somehow my girlfriend could read her intention right away.

"Snowy is what the Chief calls her. Her real name is Neige."

"So it's Neige-ue!" she beamed like a well-fed cat or, well, fox, and once again nodded to herself in satisfaction.

"So first Lili, and now her... Are you going to adopt her, too?" Josh teased me with a smirk, but I kept my cool and shook my head.

"Nah, I'm perfectly satisfied with one little sister, thank you very much."

"In other words, she's going to be your daughter. Ichiko S. Dunning, huh?" Josh remarked with absolute seriousness, and if I'd had any suitable projectiles in arm's reach, I swear I would've totally thrown something at him. Oh, wait. I did.

"Blegh!" my friend yelped out as I flung the towel from the top of my head at him, which earned me a scolding from Judy and a few stray giggles from the rest of the girls, so it was a net positive.

Things quickly calmed down afterwards, allowing the little fox miko to personally introduce herself to each member of our group in turn while we waited for Ammy and Co. to arrive. As luck would have it, we didn't have to wait long, and we still had more than half of the snacks left when another black van pulled up to my house.

"Leo, they are here!" Snowy reported from the window, and I gave her a thumbs-up with my left hand before reaching behind me and pulling the blanket off my back and handing it over to Judy.

"Please put this away. Also, am I in a presentable condition?"

"More or less," she told me in a deadpan tone, but knowing her, she would've at least combed my hair if I wasn't, so I straightened my back in my seat and assumed the closest thing I could manage to a self-assured, complacent posture.

I didn't mind the class rep seeing me under the weather, but in front of Armband Guy and our two new recruits, I had to pretend that I had no chinks in my armour. Once I felt suitably poised, I gestured for the Fauns using one of the hand signals that Brang had taught me, and they grudgingly put down the cheese scones they were eating and silently walked upstairs with their cloaking Sigils turned on. I already knew that the fembot could see through their invisibility, so I had to send them away, lest she draw attention to them while Armband Guy was still around. With that done, I glanced down at the girl on my right, but she was too engrossed with her work to notice, so I had to let out a small cough to get her attention.

"Angie?"

"Hm? Yes?" The Celestial girl glanced up at me with a distracted look in her eyes, and after finally realizing what I was getting at, she shook her head. "No, I'm still not done."

"Then how about we continue later?" I proposed, only to be immediately shot down.

"No, I'm at an important part. Just stay still."

We locked eyes for a second, but considering how unusually serious she was, I figured it was better not to get into an argument right now. I mean, everyone knows that if you know what's best for you, you never mess with the party's white Mage.

As such, I had to let Angie continue her work, and in the meantime the new guests finally arrived at the front door, and my sister and the princess both rushed out to let them in. A short time later, Ammy finally entered the room. Unlike the rest of the group, she was no longer wearing her school uniform, but a thick orange turtleneck sweater with matching skirt instead. She'd also procured a spare set of glasses, and since the ones she was wearing right now had thicker rims, the combination with the rest of her ensemble made me think she was about to jump into a garish van and start solving monster mysteries with a talking dog at any moment.

Jokes notwithstanding, the look fit her surprisingly well. On the other hand, Armband Guy behind her stuck out of the environment like a sore thumb, as for some reason he was dressed in a khaki business suit with a blue tie and a matching hat. On second look, I figured he was trying to emulate the style of Lord Grandpa, but he simply wasn't pulling it off at all.

Finally, behind these two stood the pair of Lab Coat Guy and Galatea. The fembot being tied up no longer surprised me anymore, though at least they had the courtesy to put a loose grey trench coat on her so that it wouldn't be obvious at first glance, but Lab Coat Guy was another matter entirely. Gone were the yoke, the frayed lab coat, and the silly clogs. No, he was actually wearing a perfectly sensible pair of washed jeans, sneakers, a plaid flannel shirt, and most importantly, he had his semi-long hair properly combed and parted in the middle. In fact, if I didn't know him already, I would've thought he was one of those stereotypical otaku types from certain shows, only missing the big swirly glasses and the headband. I was so surprised by his appearance that it took me several seconds to collect myself and greet the newcomers.

"Um... Hi, class rep. You guys, too. Come in; we still have some snacks."

Armband Guy ever-so-slightly narrowed his eyes, but otherwise didn't react, and instead he walked over to me. It was at this point that I noticed that he had a briefcase in his hands, and the moment I laid my eyes on it, he instantly offered it to me.

"The lord told me to give this to you. It contains the inventory of all the items confiscated at his hideout, which will be delivered to a location of your choosing by the end of the week. You can also find the necessary forms to requisition further resources, presigned documents you may use to employ specialists contracted to the School, as well as the required forms to file for tax exemption on the island."

"I'm happy to see that bureaucracy is alive and well even in the supernatural underbelly of the world." I followed my words up with a sigh and gestured towards the spot next to my chair. "Just put them over there. I'll give them a look later."

Armband Guy immediately followed my instructions and placed the briefcase next to me, after which he added, "The lord also instructed me to give you all courtesies, and to forward the following message: in the future, his doors will be always open for you, but he would kindly ask you to announce your intent to parley in the future."

"Of course. So long as he keeps his side of the bargain, I'm happy to be the very model of courtesy," I told him with a smile, and that seemed to be enough for him, as he gave me a nod and immediately turned on his heel.

"Please excuse me, but I'm afraid I cannot stay. The delegation from the Assembly will arrive soon, and the lord requested my presence by his side."

"No problem, have fun."

He completely let the words in through one ear and out the other, and after giving a meaningful glance at Ammy, he bid his farewell to the rest of the group, including the slightly baffled Ichiko, and left the house as quickly as he came.

"Well, that was unexpected," I whispered with a wry bend in my lips, but before I could say anything else, I was suddenly assaulted by the class rep breaking right into my personal space and glaring at me from a hand's width away.

"Leo. What exactly did you do to Grandfather?" she hissed through her teeth, and after overcoming my first surprise, I gave her a flat look, put my index finger on her forehead, and gently but firmly pushed her away.

"I made a deal with him. For now, please be satisfied with that explanation. We have to take care of a few other things first."

"Such as?" she asked back, so I pointed at the two captives silently glaring at us on the side.

"Those guys, among other things. But even before that..." I put my fingers in my mouth and let out a loud whistle, and a few seconds later, the Fauns dashed back down the stairs. "Take those two. Also those boxes and this briefcase. You know the rest."

The two invisible Fauns nodded in unison, gave me a salute, and then immediately jumped into action.

"Wait, Leo?! What's going on?!" The class rep raised her voice in protest, so I raised a hand to calm her down while Karukk picked up the flabbergasted fembot (which incidentally turned her invisible in the process) and headed towards the back kitchen door leading to the garage.

"Don't worry; it's something I've already planned for," I told her while gesturing for the panicked Lab Coat Guy, who also disappeared a moment later when he got picked up. "Since your grandpa learned that I can detect his surveillance balls, I figured he, or someone else, might try something more mundane to spy on us, so I bought an anti-surveillance kit online and taught the Fauns how to use it. We're first going to check those two and everything else we received from him for bugs, and only then will we take them to the secret base."

Ammy gave me a withering look, and ultimately uttered, "There's no way Grandfather would do something like that."

"You can never know. After what happened last night, I wouldn't be surprised if he went even farther than just a few listening devices. Oh, speaking of which," I gestured for the Faun who was just about to pick up the briefcase, and told him, "Just to be on the safe side, first take that outside and open it from a distance with a rake or something, just in case there's a bomb in it."

"Leo!" Ammy cried out in pure, undiluted outrage, apparently completely revolted by the mere idea I was suggesting.

"It's better to be safe than sorry," I told her without any room for disagreement.

"Chief, that's not really convincing when it's coming from you of all people..."

"Hush, Dormouse. I'm trying to be a responsible leader type here. Please don't undermine me."

I took my girlfriend's subtly rolled eyes as a sign of agreement, and soon things calmed down after the helpful Fauns left the room. In fact, things might have been a little too quiet, as everyone was giving me odd looks. As such, since we were all present, and there were no further hindrances in the way, I decided to stop delaying the inevitable.

"All right. I believe I promised that I would explain things in detail once we were all here."

"Yep," Josh nodded.

"You said that," Elly agreed with an even bigger nod, for some reason.

"Yes! I also remember that Ue-sama said that!" came the third, and this time wholly unnecessary agreement from the little girl in green.

"... Who's she?" Ammy broke the chain with a small frown and a habitually menacing tweaking of her glasses.

"Well, I suppose I might as well start there..."

And with that, I began my long, detailed, and mostly-white-lie-free description of the last day's events.

PART 3

"So she's like a familiar," Ammy concluded after hearing my explanation regarding how Ichiko ended up in our group, and at the end of the day I resorted to an ambivalent shrug to convey my answer.

"Something like that, I suppose."

"Interesting," she whispered, and then picked up another tea biscuit to nibble on. Incidentally, by this point it was almost noon, and everyone was sitting in a close circle around me made possible by taking all the dining chairs from the kitchen. I'd spent most of the morning explaining the previous day's events, and due to a quick agreement we made before I started, they listened to me without interruptions. That was a nice change of pace, but talking for so long made my throat a tad sore, so I didn't mind the slight lull in the conversation.

But then again, while I make it sound like the last few hours were just me dryly describing the events of the past evening, there were plenty of breaks in there. Such as when the girls convinced Ichiko to transform, and then...

"Yip!"

"Haha! She's so cute!"

... Yeah, that. She was currently in her fox form, lying on her back, and enjoying the attention of Judy, Snowy, and Elly. Not only that, but even the ever-serious class rep and the currently preoccupied Angie couldn't help but occasionally glance at the furry little menace with longing eyes. In the end, I had to conclude that women really were remarkably weak against cute, fluffy animals. This was, of course, terribly clichéd, so to save them from becoming so stereotypical, I had no choice but to keep her in my lap, and yet even so, she still commanded all the girls' attention. As such, I was forced to scratch her behind the ears because... um... Wait, why was I doing this again? Damn, my brain must be malfunctioning. That was the only reasonable explanation.

Okay, let's put silly stuff like that aside for a moment, and let's be serious. Like Joshua, who actually listened to my explanation from beginning to end without ever letting himself be distracted by the fox's perky ears or her fluffy tail. Truly a man of principles. Or he was just afraid of her because she bit him. One or the other.

Anyhow, after doing his best to absorb everything I had said, Josh crossed his arms in front of his chest and said, "All right, I suppose I'll break the ice and ask the obvious, though I would bet my left kidney you won't give me a straight answer."

"Give it a go; you might be surprised," I replied with some forced playfulness in my voice, and my friend gave me a mirthless smile in return.

"Fine. If I get this right, we attacked Robatto, the hunter woman attacked the base, and the the Knightly Brotherhood of the Most Heroic Bloodlines attacked Elly's house all at the same time."

"Yes, but don't say *the the* like that. It's giving me the The Gathering flashbacks."

"What's that?" Elly asked while she sneakily leaned over to pat the little fox's snout, and I immediately shook my head.

"You're better off not knowing, right, Josh?"

"Yeah, we can agree on that," he concurred with a troubled nod, but then he quickly refocused himself and said, "But that's not important. What I want to know is how you could be at all three places at once."

"Four," Ammy corrected him and adjusted her glasses. "He also was there with me in the room where they locked up Mike."

"That's even more confusing, then!" Josh exclaimed with smoldering indignation, as if somehow being at three places at once was *less* impossible than being at four places. "Don't tell me it was an illusion or something like that; I saw you throw a rifle at someone, and it hit her squarely in the head. Illusions don't cause concussions."

"Some can," Snowy added, but then didn't elaborate, so the class rep took the stand in her place.

"She's right. Some very high-level illusions can not only fool your eyes and ears, but all of your body, and they can cause actual harm that way. That said..." She paused here to tweak her glasses again and ominously added, "I doubt even the world's most powerful illusionist could make steel bars believe they were cut."

Figures. I hoped I might've been able to use the master illusionist misunderstanding to my advantage, but they'd seen too much for that to work anymore. The cat was well and truly out of the bag. As such, I had no other choice but to take a bigger bag made out of subtle misdirections and stuff the cat into that instead.

But first, I needed to set the scene. Step one, I had to act like I was really reluctant, so I spent a couple of seconds glancing around the room with my best I'm-totally-conflicted-and-stuff expression. Then, once they were getting suitably impatient, I let out a long, lung-rattling sigh and hunched my shoulders in an obvious, if maybe slightly overdone, show of resignation.

"Listen up, guys; what I'm going to tell you now cannot leave these four walls. Am I clear?" They obviously expected that I would say that, as everyone nodded right away, including not only the fox in my lap, but even Judy and Showy, who were already aware of my Phasing ability. "Fine, then, let's not beat around the bush. I'm sure you already figured it out on your own, but I can, with some restrictions, teleport on my own."

"I knew it!" the class rep yelled out with unusual intensity and leaned closer, as if afraid that she would somehow miss some small detail of my clarification if she was a few centimeters farther from me.

"Simply put," I began with an expression of utmost sincerity plastered on my face, "I can create anchor points, and with some effort, I can move between those points instantaneously."

"So that thing in your closet really isn't a proper magic circle after all, right?"

"No, it's not," I admitted, much to Ammy's triumphant delight. "It's just the point from where I teleport people between here and the secret base."

"So the circle is your anchor," Josh mused as he rubbed his chin, then he slightly tilted his head and asked, "But then how did you teleport around in the middle of the battle? There were no circles there."

"Oh, I get it!" Elly suddenly exclaimed with an enlightened look on her face. "Leo made the Magiformers, so they must double as his anchors."

"That makes sense," Ammy agreed, and I patiently waited for them to figure out the rest.

"Hold on. None of us were at Elly's house, so how could Leo teleport there?"

"I think I already know," the princess declared a tad smugly. "Leo gave me a charm to put on the doorknob of Sebastian's study! It was an anchor, too, wasn't it?"

"Yes, I used that bracelet as a way to get into his room and take the spear before the Knights could show up and take it," I told them in my most truthfulliest voice, which wasn't hard considering I technically hadn't told a single actual lie so far.

"You could've told me," Elly stated with a frown, so I mouthed a silent "Sorry" in her direction, but by then the conversation had already moved along.

"So you could move between these anchors, even when they were inside a Restricted Space?" Ammy pondered aloud while sizing me up. "But how? Teleporting to a designated target without a proper receiver array is theoretically possible, but incredibly risky and wasteful. Just doing it once could sap a lesser ley line dry for days, but you did it repeatedly. How did you...?" It was at this point she recalled a crucial detail, and she pointed at my face. "That mask. The one you were wearing back then! You said something about it being a unique artifact that could affect space-time."

"Yes, that's what I said," I agreed with a small smile, playing into her preconceived notions.

"That was something like that?" Elly spoke up on the side, and for a while she was deep in thought. "I could swear I've seen that mask somewhere..."

"It looked like one of those jester masks," Josh contributed, and the others nodded at once.

"Where is it now, anyway? Can I take a look at it?" Ammy inquired, and I shook my head with a pained grimace.

"The mask is powerless at the moment, and it needs a lot of work if I want it to do more than just hide my face. You see, I kind of overexerted my powers while wearing it," I said two truths, which added up to one lie, so to speak.

"Did it fizzle out from overuse?" The class rep was suddenly crestfallen upon hearing the news, but then she suddenly perked up as another question came to her mind. "Does that mean that you cannot freely use your power anymore?"

"To put it mildly, currently I can't even teleport between here and the secret base. That's why I had the Fauns take our two guests there on foot."

"Speaking of which, do you think they arrived there in one piece?" came the next question from Josh, who still seemed to have some reservations towards Fauns, especially when they had tied-up people draped over their shoulders. It probably gave him some unpleasant flashbacks.

"More importantly, how are we going to move there in the future?" came the next perfectly reasonable question from Amelia.

"Don't worry; I'll figure something out," I told so to reassure her, and she apparently took my words at face value, but only to pause when she noticed that Snowy was still busy playing with Ichiko, and her eyes soon narrowed into apprehensive slits.

"You three are suspiciously silent," she addressed Judy, Snowy, and Angie at once.

"Hm? What?" the Celestial mumbled as she looked up in mild confusion.

"Did you know that Leo can teleport?" Josh reiterated the question, and his childhood friend's eyes opened wide in surprise as she looked at me.

"You can?"

"Yep. With some limitations," I stressed, but she was strangely impressed all the same.

"Weren't you paying attention?"

"Sorry, I was kind of busy," she answered Josh a smidgen half-heartedly, yet he didn't press the issue, and instead he turned to the others.

"What about you two?" he inquired in a polite-yet-somewhat-critical tone, and after a moment of hesitation, Snowy raised her hand.

"I... I knew about it," she admitted as she awkwardly averted her eyes.

"I also obviously did," Judy added while she patted my sister's head. "I'm his girlfriend."

"What do you mean *obviously*?" the princess suddenly burst out in protest. "I'm also his girlfriend; why didn't I know about this?"

"Because you are terrible at keeping secrets," Judy told her with the bluntness of a boxing glove, and even though at first she wanted to object, at the end of the day the princess closed her half-open mouth, crossed her arms, and began to sulk with the power of a thousand suns.

"Come here, princess," I waved for her, and although she was still pouting, she stood up and walked over to me nevertheless, so that I could hold her in a one-handed hug. After I pulled her close enough, I directly whispered into her ear. "I'll tell you some other stuff Judy already knows later, so don't sulk."

"I'm not sulking," she muttered, but then instead of returning to her seat, she sat down onto the armrest of my chair and stuck close to me. I didn't mind that in the slightest, though the fact that she used the opportunity to monopolize the attention of Ichiko in the process had drawn the ire of the other girls in the room. Maybe keeping her was a bad idea after all...?

"So we've finally learned another of Leo's secrets," the class rep mused on the side, apparently feeling quite satisfied with the truth they had uncovered, only to then abruptly raise her hand to her glasses. "But you still haven't told *all* your secrets to *everyone*."

"We talked about this before; secrets are a resource like any other, and it's best not to waste them."

My answer obviously didn't satisfy her, but Josh came to my rescue.

"Considering how sick Leo gets every time he uses his powers, I suppose it makes sense he keeps them a secret." Ammy now directed her oh-so-intimidating glasses at him, so my friend hastily added, "I mean, knowing about this would've made some things easier, but if we took it for granted that he could swoop in at any moment to bail us out of a sticky situation, it would put a lot of pressure on him."

"I suppose you're not wrong," the class rep conceded, if begrudgingly, and Josh took this opportunity to move things along.

"So Robatto is now going to work for Leo, and the Chimera is a fluffy fox. Does that mean things are going to calm down a little?"

"Hopefully," I said, though I had a feeling it was just wishful thinking. "There's still some fallout after yesterday's kerfuffle that we have to clean up, and I still have to explain to a certain butler why I borrowed the spear from his collection..."

"Sebastian's going to be maaaaaaad," the princess said something really scary with a cheery smile, which felt really foreboding, but for the time being I put it out of my mind and focused on Josh's original question.

"We still have a couple of loose ends. The Knights are still on the island, and while I have a deal with Lord Grandpa, it might actually draw us into Assembly politics in the long run, and then there's always the possibility of an outside-context problem rearing its ugly head... but for the short term, yes, things should settle down a bit."

"Good," Josh sighed in relief. "I was getting really tired of all the ambushes and fighting."

"Tell me about it," I concurred. "I think we all need some downtime."

"Mainly you, Chief," Judy interjected with her eyes locked on my face. "Somehow you're looking even worse than you did this morning."

"Should we continue this conversation later?" Josh proposed on the spot. "Leo needs rest, and Angie's dad already called me because they were worried about where we'd disappeared to."

"Why did he call you instead of her?" came the entirely logical question from my draconic girlfriend, prompting Josh to let out a tired groan.

"It's because she is a total scatterbrain who left her phone at home."

"Hey!" the subject of our conversation protested with palpable indigna-tion. "Don't blame this on me! I wouldn't have left it behind if I didn't have to kick you out of your bed yesterday morning, you freaking opossum!"

"Wha...? Why *opossum* of all things!?" Josh objected to the weirdest thing, as usual when it came to these two's arguments, so I decided to summarily disregard them and rest my eyes for a moment. My eyelids felt unusually heavy, and if I didn't know I didn't need it, I would've thought I was being sleep-deprived.

Anyhow, the spat between the childhood friends didn't last long, and once it was concluded that if anything, Josh was a marmot, everyone decided to head home for the day and continue this conversation at a time when I no longer looked like a zombie. I appreciated the gesture, and in the following minutes, one car after the other pulled up to my driveway to ferry my friends and one significant other home. Speaking of which, Sebastian personally came to pick her up, but once he saw my condition, he graciously agreed to strangle me another day. How nice of him.

Anyhow, even though they were the ones who prompted the exodus from my house, somehow Angie and Josh ended up staying the longest. Even Judy left before them, though only after she once again hammered into me that I should rest up and not do any Phasing shenanigans, no matter the circumstances. That was more or less what I expected, but the way Angie subtly nudged her to go almost made me suspicious of her.

"Hey, Josh? Dad is about to arrive; why don't you wait for him outside?"

"Because it's cold out there?" my friend responded with reasonable bafflement, but then his childhood friend all but pushed him out of the room.

"Don't be such a baby! Just go. I'll follow after you in a minute."

My friend didn't even have time to protest before he was mercilessly kicked out of the house, and soon Angie came back while dusting her hands. Okay, scratch that, I was no longer almost suspicious of her.

"Time out," I called out, making her stop in her tracks. "What exactly are you doing?"

"Making sure the others won't overhear what I'm about to tell you," she answered with an unexpectedly serious voice, but just after that she conspicuously glanced around. "Are your sis and the fox still upstairs?"

"Yeah," I said, slightly weirded out by the girl, and she didn't make me feel any better by the way she sidled up to me.

"Good. Listen up; there is something I really need to tell you, but I didn't want to freak everyone else out."

"Is it Celestial related?" I guessed, but she immediately shook her head.

"No, of course not. It's about your hand," she told me while simultaneously pointing at the offending appendage. A moment later her brows knit in frustration, and she continued in angry whispers. "Just what the heck did you do to it?"

"I... think I already explained that it happened when I grabbed Onikiri, and Ichiko tried to make me her wielder or some such. Weren't you listening?"

"No, of course I wasn't!" she exclaimed, only to tone her voice back down right away. "I was way too busy trying to save your hand, you dunderhead!"

"... Was it that bad?"

"It still is. It's like you lit up a separate blowtorch in every single bone in your hand!"

"That... sounds pretty bad," I uttered in mild alarm and glanced down at the offending limb. "I mean... it hurts, but not *that* much..."

"It's because you also frayed most of your nerves there!" Angie huffed before poking the back of my hand with her index finger. "I did the best that I could, but you really need to have a professional look at it."

"I guess you don't mean a physician."

"No, I'm talking about a magical expert who can heal nerve damage. The longer you wait, the higher the chance that it may never heal properly."

"Oh, great. Another thing to worry about," I grumbled, and my Celestial friend must have taken pity on me, as she stopped scowling and instead put her hands on her hips with an expression that would have been right at home on the face of a put-upon mother scolding a rambunctious child.

"For now, don't worry about anything. Just go and have a good rest; it's very important for recovery. I can help you look for someone qualified once you no longer look like you're about to fall asleep at any moment."

"Trust me, I won't," I told her, but she only smiled at me in return. Maybe she thought I was acting tough in front of her? I really wasn't, though, and before I could get another word in, Josh yelled in through the door.

"Angie! Your dad says that if you don't hurry up, you won't get any dessert at dinner."

"Aaaaand that is my cue to leave!" she declared with a toothy grin, her previous intensity all but gone, and she pointed a pair of finger guns at me, saying, "See you later, cowboy! And make sure you get your eight hours of beauty sleep!"

"Yeah, sure, whatever," I dismissed her with a wave of my good hand, and a short giggle later she dashed out of the room to join her childhood friend waiting outside.

The moment I heard the front door close, somehow all the tension escaped from my shoulders in the form of an exhausted breath. Maybe Angie was right. Maybe I should really try to rest a bit. With such thoughts in mind, I forced myself off the chair and dragged my legs up the stairs one step at a time. As I passed by her room, I could hear Snowy and Ichiko animatedly discussing something. I could only hear a few snippets through the closed door, but by the sound of it, they were getting along. That was nice.

Once I passed by them, I momentarily vacillated about whether I should first wash my face with some cold water, but after a short-but-kind-of-blurry amount of time later I simply entered my room and immediately fell onto my bed. I lay on my back while staring at the ceiling for a few minutes, my brain slowly turning into one of those grainy snowstorms you see on TV when there's no broadcast. This was weird, as I actually had a lot of things to think about, including what to do with Lab Coat Guy, how to proceed with Lord Grandpa, whether or not I should feel just a tiny bit guilty about misleading my friends today (for the record, I shouldn't because I technically didn't tell even a single lie), or the apparent fact that my hand needed professional healing. All of these things kind of slipped through the cracks, like dry sand through my fingers, and my eyelids were starting to feel really heavy again.

My eyes must be tired, I concluded, and I saw no reason why I shouldn't close them. Just for a minute, to let them rest. Then I would get up and load the Hub to see what's going on there. Or at least that was the plan until, against predictions and prior precedent... I fell asleep.

The fact that I was still aware and looking at myself lying on the bed probably wasn't a good sign, was it?

Well, under normal circumstances this would've been the point where I felt it was entirely reasonable to contemplate whether I should start panicking or not, but then as time went on, my consciousness slowly dulled, as well, and before I knew it, I was... somewhere. It was a... kind of room, except not really? It was also pitch-black, yet lit by a distant-yet-ever-present warm light at the same time. It felt *weird*, but also strangely safe and comfortable, and before I knew it, I slowly drifted into a state that was both sleeping, and yet not. And that was how *I*, for the first time since I could remember, dreamed under the light of a red sun.

EPILOGUE

"So he is not outside, but he's not inside, either," mumbled a familiar-yet-heavily-distorted voice a couple of parsecs past the edge of my hearing. Maybe it was precisely because he sounded like he was auto-tuned by a walrus, but it piqued my interest enough to wake me up, in a manner of speaking. I focused my attention on the source of the voice, and my consciousness slowly reached out towards it until I was all of a sudden inside an alien-yet-very-familiar not-dark not-room, just in time to experience the full brunt of The Man abruptly exclaiming, "Then where is he!?"

"We don't know. That's the problem," came the chiding answer in the voice of The Woman, currently nothing more than a distant twinkle of crimson waters barely beyond my sight, and if she had eyes, I was sure she would've rolled them *very* derisively.

"Maybe it's another one of his pranks," The Boy proposed, though his own tone made it sound like even he thought it was unlikely.

"And he completely disappeared for that?" The Man argued back, his words all but dripping with incredulity. "I couldn't do that even if I tried, let alone do it for a prank!"

"Yes, but that's you," The Girl chimed in with a disinterested voice while masquerading as a glowing dune of sand (or was it the other way around?), and The Woman... nodded? Undulated? Gestured, let's go with gestured. In an up-and-down motion that was like nodding, except completely different.

"He was always an odd one, but also quite ingenious when it came to causing trouble," she noted with a tinge of nostalgia colouring her words. It was purple. I don't know how, I don't know why, but apparently nostalgia was purple. Or maybe a bit closer to violet, now that I think about it.

I would've probably spent about half an eternity pondering what colour emotions were, but I was cut short by The Boy timidly raising his voice.

"But... Isn't that bad?"

"What are you talking about?" The Man growled, and for a moment I could clearly see the face of a mustachioed middle-aged man's frowning overlapping with a bolt of thunder illuminating the pitch-blackness of the night on the dark side of a barren moon. It only lasted for a split second, and then both melted away until I was once again only vaguely aware of the direction the voices were coming from.

"I mean... If he isn't in here, but not out there, either, doesn't that mean he's *missing*?"

The word *missing* immediately made the tension in the room freeze over by about four octaves.

"No way. He must be just hiding," The Man said a tad nervously, as if he was trying to convince himself, but The Boy pressed on.

"But what if he's not? What if the ********* look into his disappearance and..."

Whoa there! Slow down! What was that again? **********? I repeated the... well, it wasn't really a word, per se, but I repeated it in my head again a few times to get a feel for it, anyway. It was something like a concept that had another concept in it like a giant, metaphysical matryoshka doll, and if I had to transliterate it, it was something along the lines of "A/the thing/things that have emerged from/in the process of emerging from the state of not emerging/vacuum." It also had an extra qualifier attached to it, so after some more finagling, I decided on the rough term of Venerated Emergents. It wasn't entirely accurate, but at least it was classy.

So with that new bit of revelation in mind, let's listen to The Boy's words again.

"But what if he's not? What if the Venerated Emergents look into his disappearance, and it turns out we were the last ones to see him?"

"Oh, don't be such a worrywart," The Girl spoke up with a fittingly girlish giggle reminiscent of underwater birdsong. "Even if the Venerated Ones send someone to inquire about his whereabouts, we honestly don't know where he is, and we don't know anything about his disappearance. We'll be fine."

"But we do know something about his disappearance," The Boy pointed out a tad impatiently. "He disappeared after he hit the trap we set up. If they look into it, they might think we are responsible! No, I'll go even farther! They might think we *made him disappear...*"

There was a very long, thin, and slightly elastic silence in the not-dark not-room, ultimately broken by The Woman breaking out into barely stifled laughter.

"You cannot be serious! Us? Accidentally killing him? *That* guy!?"

"Yeah," The Man jumped on the bandwagon with some gusto. "He's four generations ahead of us! Five, for you! Sure, he might not be a Venerated One yet, but even if we ganged up on him at once, I would be surprised if we could even inconvenience him!"

"Yes! That's why we set a trap for him, remember?" The Girl followed it up with an indignant huff, as if the mere mention of the idea was absurd.

"I know, but... I'm just worried," The Boy relented after being thoroughly browbeaten by his companions.

"There's no need to even think about something as impossible as that. How about we just focus on what's right in front of us instead, and just keep a lookout for any traces of him?" The Woman proposed, and the rest agreed in silence. "So did we have any further anomalies?"

"Nothing major," The Man responded just a touch dourly. "Things are proceeding in an unexpected direction, but nothing the Simulacrum can't handle."

"It's the second Free Actor, isn't it?" came the obviously rhetorical question from The Woman, and The Man grunted in confirmation.

"He's been causing a lot of deviations," The Boy noted while doing something that caused the lack of air in the not-dark not-room to oscillate. "He caused divergences in most main scenarios, some of which made no sense at all at first glance. At first I thought it was caused by *him*, but when I looked into his attributes, it turns out he has three times as many traits and conditional triggers as any other Main Actor."

"Well, it couldn't be helped," The Man scoffed. "He was supposed to be a fixed point present in all the main scenarios, and he was only supposed to have access to the abilities and traits that were relevant to the scenario in question. He wasn't ever meant to be a Free Actor, so I never put any restraints on him. Hell, he isn't even a ********** ************!"

Okay, time out again. That was another weird four-dimensional thought rendered in two-and-a-quarter dimensions, so let me try to unpack it. The first half of it was about being under something, but not literally. Kind of like being below the surface? I don't know *what* kind of surface, but that was the best I could figure out. As for the second half, it had something to do with cradles, or pens, or at least some kind of enclosed space where small, fragile beings were held safe. So if I put them together, it was something like "The one/many that are submerged outside a curvature tensor of—"

Wait, where did that bit about tensors or whatnot come from? That wasn't in my original interpretation. Dammit, this is confusing, so let's just go with Submerged Ones for the time being.

"For reference, how powerful is he?" The Woman inquired, and The Man did the closest thing a moon circling around a gas giant could do to a shrug.

"I have no idea. I'm fairly sure he wasn't supposed to be able to teleport the way he does, but with the number of different abilities he has, even I can't say for sure some weird combination of traits couldn't have resulted in that."

"Are you sure you didn't also make him a Free Actor?" The Girl teased him with an irreverent tinkle in her voice. "You put a lot of effort into him, so maybe you accidentally did that, too!"

"I don't do anything by accident," The Man retorted with an angry snort.

"No, I have a feeling it was *his* doing, after all," The Woman noted with a smiling voice. "While his approach is less overt than usual, picking an already-overloaded Actor with a preset role and letting them loose to mess with us still bears his signature."

"But... we didn't detect any tampering..." The Boy muttered, only to be dismissed offhand.

"It just means he covered his tracks well."

"Not to mention, even if he tampered with the second Free Actor, it's hard to investigate it until the Simulacrum runs its course," The Girl added with a know-it-all nod and... wait, since when did she have a head again? Oh, and now she is gone, replaced by a vortex of ominously glowing winds ceaselessly blowing over endless deserts. Damn, this conversation was getting harder to follow by the second. Not that it lasted much longer...

"Indeed. Until then, we have to ensure that everything works as intended, so how about we get back to work?"

"But we just finished a routine check..." The Boy, suddenly filling my entire vision with rainbow-coloured orbital rings peeking through thick red clouds, whined, only to be grabbed, in a certain sense of the word, by The Woman.

"Don't slack off; we can rest all we want once this is done."

And with that, the pair of them slowly sublimated out of my plane of existence, soon followed by the other two, leaving me all alone. Since I had no reason to linger, I also slowly retracted my consciousness. Somewhere, deep down, I was aware that once I woke up, I would not remember much of what I'd just witnessed. It couldn't be helped, considering the circumstances, but I figured I might as well try to etch something into my mind. There was nothing to lose, so as soon as I returned to the place I never left, I once again folded in on myself and repeated a single word in my mind, hoping that it would stick.

"Simulacrum."

And with that, I had slowly fallen into an even deeper dream, one that lasted longer than the last, yet at the same time not even for a second. I only hoped that when *I* woke up, this time things would be slightly less hectic. Somehow I doubted it, but whether I was right or wrong was a story for another time.

ABOUT THE AUTHOR

Gábor Horváth is a Hungarian social worker employed in a nursery home for the elderly. He studied archaeology but, due to a financial crisis in the family, was obliged to withdraw from university and enter the workforce. Also known as Egathentale, Horváth has been writing for his own amusement ever since high school and started publishing his work online at the encouragement of friends.

www.ingramcontent.com/pod-product-compliance
Lightning Source LLC
Chambersburg PA
CBHW031925110726
47902CB00001B/42